The Storm
Beneath the Glass

WYATT LARSEN

ROBERT WYATT   TODD LARSEN

THE STORM BENEATH THE GLASS

THE ULTIDEIC PROPHECIES

GATESTONE PUBLISHING

THE STORM BENEATH THE GLASS

Book 1 of The Ultideic Prophecies

Copyright © 2024 Robert Wyatt & Todd Larsen

Cover Copyright © 2024 Robert Wyatt & Todd Larsen

Editing and Publishing Services Provided by Edits By Stacey

Maps Created by Robert Wyatt

Cover design and illustration by Jeff Brown Graphics

Published by Gatestone Publishing LLC, Idaho USA

theultideicprophecies@gmail.com

Library of Congress Control Number: 2024914379
Paperback ISBN: 978-1-964192-00-0
Hardcover ISBN: 978-1-964192-02-4
Digital Book ISBN: 978-1-964192-01-7

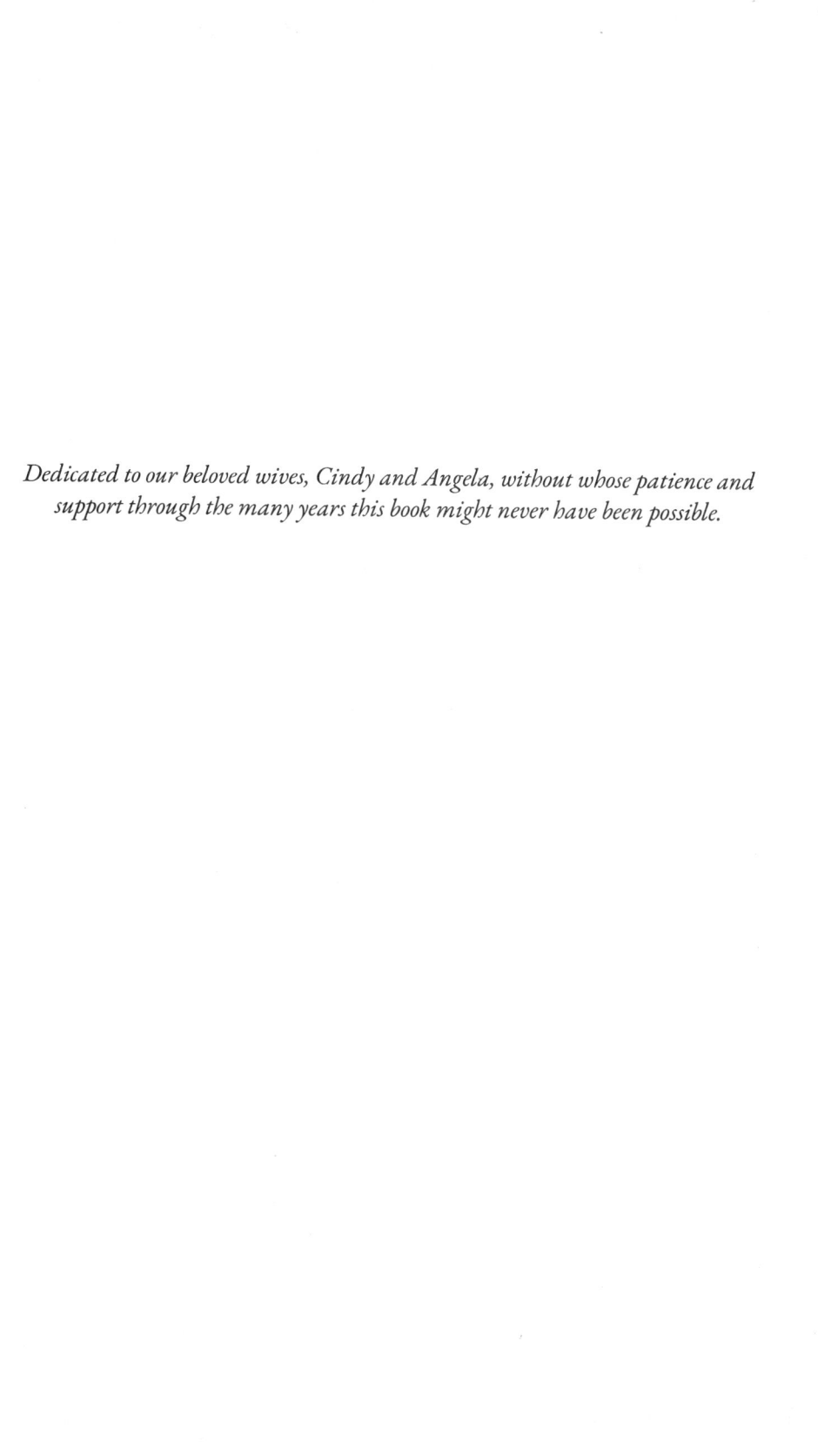

Dedicated to our beloved wives, Cindy and Angela, without whose patience and support through the many years this book might never have been possible.

The Continent of

VESTURA

Distance in Kilometers

| 200 | 400 | 600 | 800 | 1000 | 1200 | 1400 |

| 125 | 250 | 375 | 500 | 625 | 750 | 875 |

Distance in Miles

Zordgardz

Jorvik

Lingon Shu

Djuzhen

Tsegannur

Sarrsfjord

Campertia

Nowsli Hordes

Washi Dawa

Khar

Maltagena

Habenstock

Wakaru

Candin

Calavia

Vartosa

Calavia

Ibaru

Shunikawa

Inland Sea

Renstadt

Gulf of Inchari

Gilterrada

Tennury

Steadleigh

Banbridge

Remalia

Deock

Bright

Teris

Kiruvesi

Velspar Mountains

Jhari

Kollathi Wilds

Sunapra

Luresh

Kushaan

Warariki

Bangarh

Kochwari

Sarakesh

Dipoor

Rajpura

Kashpur

Rishakesh

Emerald Sea

Sanupalava

AURORIC OCEAN

UMBRIC OCEAN

THE CONTINENT OF

IUVENTIA

Distance in Kilometers

200   400   600   800   1000   1200   1400

125   250   375   500   625   750   875

Distance in Miles

Kushaan Campaign

Explore the World
through the interactive maps and wiki

Visit
TheUltideicProphecies.com

BOOK OF HEZEF

THE OLDEST AND MOST COMPLETE
OF THE LITURGIES CONTAINING

THE ULTIDEIC PROPHECY

ORIGINAL AUTHOR UNKNOWN

1. I heard a voice calling me by name. And I looked heavenward, and behold, a window into the heavens was opened unto me, and a voice as of a chorus of eight trumpets—for the ninth remained silent—spake unto me, and I was sore afraid.

2. I beheld a being clothed in robes that surpassed the brightness of the noonday sun. The countenance of the being was of such glory that I could scarce look upon it, and my hands were for naught to shield my eyes from the radiance thereof. And the being had eight faces—for the ninth was apart from the others, whose face was without form, and void—and the brightness thereof was so great that I could scarce make out one from another.

3. And the voice was as of thunder, and spake unto me, saying, "Come hither, Prophet, and I shall shew unto thee the Will which shall henceforth come to pass."

4. And immediately I was brought as it were by my spirit through the window of heaven, even unto a sea of glass, spread out before me both to the right and to the left and before me, beyond sight.

5. Behind me was a throne room set in heaven, with eight thrones—for the ninth was apart from the others—of purest gold which shone above the brightness of the sun.

6. One was of the finest workmanship, inlaid with bdellium and lapis and jasper, and all manner of fine carving. Another was of the straightest of lines, perfect in its exactness. And each throne was of a peculiar workmanship in its own right so as to denote which was the work of each.

7. The voice said unto me, "Look." And I looked and beheld the sea of glass. And beneath the glass stretched the tapestry of Creation, upon which all nations and peoples, all mountains and deserts and waters known to men were sewn.

8. And I beheld that the tapestry was of wondrous workmanship, so fine that I could not see the end of it. So great was it that its threads numbered more than the sands of the deserts and the stars in the heavens.

9. I looked at the nations thereupon, and lo, the skies gathered a storm to unleash upon the nations of the earth. And the Eight rode upon the storm—for the Ninth stood apart from the others—crowned in the glory of lightning, armed with great bows and arrows.

10. And the thunder and the howling thereof began as a distant whisper and grew in might until it filled the measure of its coming.

11. The storm was born in the East, but it was the Center before it was the East. And such was the force of the storm that it covered all the tapestry. Mighty were the works of the storm.

12. And I beheld the storm beneath the glass as it billowed forth across the tapestry. And the winds thereof held exceeding fury.

13. Fierce thunderings shook the land. And the people upon the tapestry quaked in fear and ran before the noise thereof, some here and some there. But the nations recognized it not.

14. And behold, the Nine were the storm, and the storm was the Nine.

15. And the nations were consumed thereby, and bewailed the storm-shattered peace, and there was nowhere to hide from the storm.

16. Lightnings flashed, and voices sounded, even to shake the people.

17. A rain fell upon the tapestry in a great torrent, and where the rain covered the people, contention was sown, and a great clamor grew. Wars and rumors of wars spread throughout the land upon the winds of the storm and everywhere the rain fell.

18. And the seeds of the tempest were sown, and great was the contention thereof. Neighbor turned against neighbor, friend against friend, fathers turned against their sons, and mothers against their daughters.

19. And I saw a great serpent was born of the tempest.

20. And the serpent began to writhe about on the winds of the storm. Great was the destruction that came thereof. And the shadow of the serpent spanned the tapestry, covering all the threads thereof in a brume of darkness.

21. The serpent was held aloft by the winds of the storm, and the storm was sustained by the fury of the serpent. And the serpent had legs in number of nine. His head was wreathed in fire and lightning.

22. And the serpent roared with the thunder of a thousand thousand trumpets. And the golden thrones shook where they stood above the glass.

23. The mouth of the serpent was lined with teeth like spears, countless as the stars, and poison fell from its teeth like rain. And a hail of blood fell across all the face of the tapestry, and upon all the inhabitants thereof.

24. And the serpent hungered and gorged itself upon the peoples of Creation, but its hunger could not be satisfied.

25. And the fangs of the serpent fell upon the people, and there was death. And great were the lamentations of the people. The cries of those who mourned exceeded even the mighty trumpets of the storm. And I tried to stop my ears, but my hands were of naught, and I could scarce bear the sound of it.

26. I cried for the being with the eight faces to end my suffering, but my voice was lost in the tumult and lamentations beneath the glass.

27. The Eight began to see—for the Ninth remained apart—

that the serpent and the storm would not carry them all. And great were the trumpets they carried. Mighty were the thunderings that blasted forth as they blew upon the trumpets. Fearsome were their bows and their arrows.

28. And the people of the tapestry heard the voices of the Nine, and their lamentations became the songs of praise and the prayers of the faithful. And a lull in the storm fell upon Creation for a season.

29. After a season, the songs of praise became the horns of war. And the tumult across the tapestry was great. And the nations were shaken and began to fall.

30. And I beheld a great commotion issued forth from among the people, some crying here, and others crying there. And the nations began to assemble with the Nine, some here, and some there—though the Ninth stood apart and scorned them.

31. And a door like unto a tomb was opened in the tapestry, among the threads of the mountains, and a great multitude was called to join the nations.

32. And the voice from the stones issued forth across the tapestry, calling anew. And the people began to hear and give heed. The voice spake as one of old, though it were new. And it came forth out of the stones to lead the people.

33. The voice from the stones was not a voice of thunder, neither a voice of trumpets, but a voice that did pierce to the quick.

34. And I looked, and behold the Eight on the storm contended one with another—for the Ninth stood apart. And as it was in heaven, so it was across the face of the tapestry.

35. Nevertheless, the voice came forth as a stone rolling forth from the mountains, gathering power and might as it fell. And none there were who could stop it.

36. And lo, there was a banner to the nations erected, and on the banner a sword of flame and a crown of light. And lo, the banner rent in twain, and all the people were divided to one side or another.

37. And a third part of the hosts of the tapestry aligned them-

selves with the banner of the crown. And a third of the nations did likewise.

38. Yet a third part of the hosts of the tapestry followed after the banner of the flaming sword, with their spears and their javelins and their swords and their arrows. And a third of the nations did likewise.

39. And a third part fell by the wayside, joining themselves not to one part or another, and having no power to act, but only to be acted upon. And they fell beneath the banners and were trampled.

40. And behold, the land divided in two. And the Eight contended among the nations. And some there were that sought after the Ninth, and contended against the Eight.

41. And the armies of crown and sword filled the tapestry. So great was the contention thereof that the heavens shook.

42. And I heard a multitude of voices in the heavens, crying out as it were from beyond the stars to the armies upon the tapestry beneath the glass, some shouting for triumph, others pleading for peace. But the armies heard them not.

43. And the nations gathered for a mighty battle. The dust from their feet rose up, even till it blotted out the sun. And the sun became as dark as soot. And the moons became as ash. And the gloaming of the gods commenced.

44. And one by one the golden thrones began to fall from their place, even as the pillars before Vayen-elan in her fury, burning as it were a lamp whose oil is spent until only two thrones remained.

45. And the Eight that were Two rode forth at the head of their armies, one against the other.

46. And the great serpent went before them. Behind them followed a hail of brimstone and fire. And a third part of the nations were consumed. And a third part of the trees were burned and a third of the ships were lost to the waves of the sea.

47. And the Two strove against one another as their armies did battle. And great was the destruction thereof.

48. And the threads of the oceans became as blood. And the

threads of mountains, also. Yea, the threads of the whole tapestry ran crimson.

50. And so great were the strivings and the contentions and the warfare of the nations and the Two that the tapestry should be torn asunder.

51. But behold, and lo, the armies of One bowed the knee. And the Nine became One. And the Will was made manifest.

52. And the winds of the tempest did cease, and the serpent fell from the sky, and great was the fall thereof.

53. And the One returned to the heavens to rest for a season. And there was a silence across the land.

54. And the people of the tapestry knew peace.

55. And I was left alone in darkness till the sea of glass faded from sight.

56. And I remembered no more.

57. Thus it finished.

CHAPTER I
ANDRIC

"Duke Garamond is the one I'm worried about." King Jevorak leaned back in his armchair, concern written in his steel-blue eyes. The hint of a frown tugged at the corners of his mouth that was framed by a carefully groomed, graying beard. A fire blazed in a large fireplace, warming the king's private study. Spring had come late to Teris, and mornings still felt the chill of winter's grasp. "I need his troops in the field, as much for the extra lances when we march against Kushaan as to keep him from causing mischief at home while we're away. If we don't find some way to bring him around, we will have to leave a much larger contingent behind to secure the region."

Prince Andric reached for a stray lock of his sandy-brown hair as he tried to think of something useful to say, but stopped himself, not wanting to draw a rebuke from his father. He had no idea what the king could do to convince the stubborn Duke of Massonly to commit more than the token force he had already offered, and the prince found it difficult to muster more than a passing concern for the matter at all. Today was the beginning of the annual Charge Days celebrations, and all Andric wanted was to be out of the palace. The festivities didn't begin until tomorrow, but anything had to be better than sitting in these interminable discussions with his father and the king's advisers.

The holiday was officially called the Days of Hamoth's Charge. It was a celebration and commemoration of the famed battle centuries past when King Hamoth had rallied his people and led a great charge of thousands of cavalry to face the overwhelming barbarian hordes, to stave off certain destruction and carve out a united Kingdom of Remalia. The festivities covered three days that included a day of fasting and religious devotions, a day of contests, tournaments, and martial displays—including a retelling of Hamoth's victory—ending with a day of grand celebrations and feasting.

Today was Preparations Day, the first of the three-day celebration. Breakfast was the only meal of the day, followed by a day-long fast until breakfast the next morning. Evening devotions would be held at the temples. The day commemorated the deprivations and sacrifices made by their forefathers in the days of great strife and the blessings of the gods in saving the people from destruction and granting them victory over their enemies.

"My lord," Crown Prince Stephir said cautiously, his green eyes fixed on the king. "Perhaps it would be wise to wait one more year. Even without Garamond's additional troops, the losses to our food stores in the Vastan Province this winter make it difficult to see how we can sustain a campaign of more than a few months."

Andric knew his older brother had more fundamental objections to the proposed war than just logistics, but he hadn't voiced them to their father in several weeks. This was no doubt Stephir's last attempt to speak his mind before they held the war council this evening and their path forward became set in stone.

Before the king replied, High General Kuymon shook his balding head in disagreement. "The Curritan and Kesh Provinces will have plenty of food to augment our supplies once we take them. You've done an admirable job of establishing our supply lines, Your Highness, and I'm sure we will have what we need to sustain—" Kuymon stopped as the door to the King's study opened and a guard stepped into the room.

Light glinted off the guard's polished armor and the steel head of his halberd. It was unusual for the Divinarim, the holy knights that guarded the royal family and the palace, to interrupt these sessions. "Forgive the intrusion, Your Majesty. Minister Turtan says he has an urgent matter to report."

"Very well, send him in," the king said heavily, clearly not happy to have any more to worry about.

Andric guessed his father was relieved to not address Stephir's concerns again. The prince gazed through the large windows that faced the soaring, snowcapped peaks of the Velspar Mountains to the south. If all went according to the king's plans, they would be on the other side of those mountains, fighting the Kushaani within a month's time. The prospect of finally seeing his first battle thrilled him. He would fight in the Charge Days tournament tomorrow as he had the previous two years, but no tourney bout could compare to real battle.

"Your Majesty, my lords and lady," Minister Turtan said, bowing with the formality and flourish characteristic of the clerics of the goddess Sharin Dara. "I apologize for interrupting, but I just received word of another incident at a temple in the city. I thought you should be informed immediately."

Andric recognized the sudden anger written in the hard set of his father's face. "Go on," the king instructed.

"Of course, my lord. It was the Temple of Venerate Alscome, the Teraithian temple in the Oettan District. Several clergy and temple guards were killed or injured, and the building was badly damaged. They're claiming..." Minister Turtan paused, pursing his lips, and took a deep breath before continuing, "...claiming that they were attacked by a celestial creature."

"Someone summoned a daemon to attack a Teraithian temple?" Stephir asked in disbelief. "It seems more likely it was one of their own that got out of control."

Temples were permitted to summon creatures from the realms of their respective deities for use inside the temples, but otherwise summoning was forbidden in the Kingdom of Remalia. Temples of the goddess Teraithia were known to sometimes summon ferocious daemons to guard their brimming treasure vaults.

"The Teraithians are claiming it was a creature from the realm of the Holy Couple."

"Of course they would say that," Stephir said dismissively. "We all know the Teraithians have been getting more aggressive in their efforts to undermine the other faiths. I wouldn't put it past them to orchestrate this attack so they can blame a rival church."

Remalia had no official state religion, but it was generally known that the royal family favored Yonvaar and Kerail, the Holy Couple, largely due to the late queen's influence. Although she had died when the princes were young, King Jevorak had allowed them to follow in their mother's footsteps. Perhaps because Stephir remembered more of their mother than Andric did, his brother remained singularly devout to the Holy Couple, though he eschewed the title Servari, the name given to those who worshipped the god and goddess who espoused love and service to others as the highest virtue. Andric instead chose to see the best in the worship of each of the nine deities.

"I wouldn't be too quick to rule this out as a retaliatory move by one of the other churches," Andric said, tactfully disagreeing with his older brother.

High Consul Penrossart, the presiding high priestess of the Sharinist faith in Remalia and one of King Jevorak's closest advisors, finally spoke. "Unfortunately, I believe you may be right, Your Highness. There is certainly plenty of blame to be leveled on all sides. I fear the religious strife is getting worse, and if not abated soon, it may reach a tipping point. With so many pilgrims in the city for Charge Days, we could be facing riots if we don't respond swiftly."

"Then let me go as a representative of the crown and assess the situation," Andric urged his father. "I can ensure there is security in the area and ensure that further violence will not be tolerated from any quarter."

"If I didn't know better, I might suspect you were trying to escape this session," the high consul said with a slight smirk, a rare moment of her mild playfulness coming through. Turning to the king, she continued. "Prince Andric's suggestion does have merit, Your Majesty. A personal response from a member of the royal family would likely help mollify the Teraithians and reinforce that ending the violence is a priority for the crown."

"Very well," the king said. "But I insist you take a double contingent of Divinarim. And tell the city guard I want increased patrols in the Oettan District. And I want daily reports about their investigation into the attack until the perpetrators are arrested."

"Of course, Father." Andric shot Stephir a subtle, gloating glance as he quickly rose from his seat before anyone could change their mind.

"And make sure you're back in time for the evening devotions. We need all the divine support we can get before the war council," the king added.

Andric gave a perfunctory bow. "Will you be needing anything else from Minister Turtan? If not, I could use his assistance."

"You may go," Jevorak said to the priest, who bowed much more elegantly than Andric had then followed the prince out of the room.

Andric stopped to speak to the knights that stood guard outside the king's study. "I am going into the city. Please arrange to have guards join me at the White Gate."

"A double contingent of guards," Minister Turtan clarified as Andric moved on with the priest at his side and two Divinarim trailing them.

"Yes, thank you," Andric replied flatly. Six knights to escort him through the city seemed completely unnecessary, but he let it go. It was a small price to pay to get out of the palace. He needed to dress the part if he was going to be on official business, so he headed for his room to change, questioning Turtan as they walked along the sunlit corridor.

"What do you think is really going on with the attack?" Andric asked.

The minister had a network of eyes and ears throughout the kingdom, especially here in the capital city of Teris. The man seemed to always know more about what was happening than he let on. Andric knew of a handful of plots Turtan had quashed before they were carried out and was sure there were many more he never heard about. He was tempted to take the minister into the city with him, but he already knew the priest would politely decline.

"I hear many rumors of these kinds of actions being contemplated, Your Highness, but this one, I am troubled to say, came as a complete surprise."

"So you have no idea what happened?" Andric asked dubiously.

"Well, I wouldn't quite say that. The Teraithians appear to be behind many of the misfortunes suffered by other churches in recent months, but it has proved difficult to find sufficient evidence to charge them with. Frustration is mounting among certain factions over the perceived lack of justice, so I am inclined to agree with your assessment that this is probably a retaliatory strike. The Dorothi would normally be my first guess, but this business with the summoning does not fit their usual patterns. This may simply be what it appears to be—an attack by the Servari."

They arrived at Andric's quarters, and he didn't bother to wait for a servant to come assist with changing. He quickly worked on the ties and buttons of the quilted wool doublet as Minister Turtan continued.

"This probably has nothing to do with the attacks, but it could prove useful in your questioning of the temple's seraph. My sources indicate that the man frequents the Sykorian temples and has been using his temple's funds to pay for his indecorous habits."

The Sykorians were known to offer patrons indulgences in keeping with their goddess's hedonistic doctrines.

"You want me to blackmail the seraph?" Andric asked, curling his lip in disgust.

"No, nothing so uncouth as that. It's just a piece of information to keep tucked away until it might prove useful to clear an obstacle or loosen his tongue."

Andric only half-listened as Turtan continued offering advice on how to conduct the royal inquiry. He enjoyed being warmed by the bright morning sunlight streaming through the large windows. His room commanded a breathtaking view that extended from the Trilumen Lakes northward to the snowcapped peaks of the Lithowen Range in the east, providing a majestic backdrop to the awe-inspiring temples and other structures that shared prominence with the royal palace atop the Mount of the Gods, the broad hill that rose up in the midst of Teris against the imposing backdrop of the Velspar Mountains.

The vast city proper stretched out below the Mount in a sweeping arc. Unlike the grand buildings crowning the Mount, which were made of the most exotic and rare materials from around the world, much of the city was constructed of ordinary stone and wood with slate or gray tiled roofs, slanted to keep the occasional snowfall from building up during harsher winters. The occasional copper roofs dotting the cityscape, green with age, stood out from the rest of the charcoal-colored rooftops.

The pristine blocks of the rare white granite brought from the Tybalan Hills far to the north were visible at the edges of the huge Celendrian rug covering the floor. The sunlight sparkled brilliantly off the reflective flecks in the stone, giving them an unexpected splash of color and setting a dazzling background for the vibrant curtains and tapestries that adorned the walls.

He opened a pair of large armoires and selected a pair of dark blue trousers, high black leather boots, a long-sleeved white blouse, and a black vest with gold embroidery. The vest and loose blouse were more in the fashion of Calavia, but they happened to be in vogue within the higher social circles in Remalia, which suited Andric nicely. From a polished brass stand, he lifted his royal sash made of elegant blue and heavy white velvet, embroidered with the thread-of-gold rearing stallion of his family crest. He fastened it about his waist and over his shoulder in a practiced manner.

It was becoming increasingly popular for noblemen to wear swords outside, but Andric usually chafed at the discomfort. Only the royal family and the Divinarim were permitted to carry weapons in the palace, so going without one was not at all conspicuous. However, during the Charge Days, he was expected to wear one. He buckled his gilded longsword as he faced the armoires. He considered a heavy cloak to protect against any chill, but instead chose a light gray riding cloak and quickly fastened it on his shoulders. The cloak hung awkwardly, being hampered by the sword, but there wasn't much to do about it.

"Thank you for your assistance, Minister Turtan," Andric said, checking the mirror to ensure his wavy, sandy-brown hair and clothes were presentable before hurrying out of his chambers. "I will have a report sent to you later."

The priest bowed as Andric strode out of the room, followed by his two Divinarim protectors. Andric nodded politely to those he passed as he made his way through the palace's sunlit corridors.

Once outside, he crossed the sprawling palace grounds toward the royal stables. The night's frost quickly turned into morning dew wherever the sun found it, the shadows the last fading refuge of the lingering cold. Andric did his best to stay in the warm sunlight and wished he had chosen his winter cloak when he passed through the cold shadows.

He had sensed for weeks, with unsuppressable anticipation, the life force finally seeping out of the depths of the world to the surface as the overdue sun burned away the blanket of frost and snow under which the world slept. Andric had been fooled in past years when a week or two of warm weather seemed to hail the arrival of spring, only to have his hopes dashed when winter roared back in with a mocking vengeance. This year, with the slush and mud accompanying the thawing season finally behind them, Andric felt life finally flowing back into him as well.

Teris was not a place known for harsh winters (at least according to others), but neither could they be called mild. It was not uncommon for the snow to arrive and stay for several months, especially in the eastern foothills of the Velspar Mountains where the city of Teris stood. Teris was one of the mightiest cities on Baon and the capital city of the Kingdom of Remalia.

Andric spent all winter dreaming of the warmer days of summer. That was still a few months away, but today he was in high spirits and grateful to have escaped the confines of the palace. Although the clear skies the night before had meant a cold morning, it boded well for a beautiful day ahead.

Arriving at last at one of the stable gates with his Divinarim in tow, Andric entered the central stableyard and scanned the grounds for the stable-master. The stables, while magnificently constructed, only housed the score of horses that belonged to the royal family. Most visitors to the palace were required to leave their horses at one of the larger stables outside the wall that ringed the Mount of the Gods. The king had a much larger stable in the countryside where his horses were bred, trained, and housed when not residing in the palace stables. Andric rarely visited those anymore, though he had enjoyed spending time there as a boy.

The palace stables were built over a hundred years ago by Andric's third great-grandfather. According to the histories that Andric had been required to study growing up, Hovac Laconeus was an eccentric but visionary man who wanted to bring pieces of the wide world to Teris. Remalians didn't take easily to change, and many of Hovac's projects had not endured down through the years to Andric's day. The palace stables were the most notable exception.

Built in the style of Byanthine, a powerful empire that existed halfway around the world in the days of Hovac, Andric felt they were a spectacular contrast to traditional Terisian architecture. Forged from centuries of war, the Kingdom of Remalia was built first and foremost with utility and endurance in mind, and the palace was no exception. Although beautifully adorned with masterpiece paintings, tapestries, and sculptures, the massive and austere structure was built with the finest materials, constructed to endure to the end of time.

In contrast, the royal stables were a breathtaking masterpiece of impossibly delicate and ornately sculpted stone and wood meshed into lifelike scenes of the military exploits of Hovac and his forefathers, wild herds of horses on the plains of Remalia, and forests, mountains, and seas. Hovac had enlisted master craftsmen from Byanthine who used *met'elan* to imbue their otherwise fragile work with the strength to withstand the ravages of nature and time. While not every king since Hovac appreciated his contribution to the palace complex, none of them could bring themselves to destroy or even alter the magnificent structure. Andric often found it amusingly ironic that their horses, admittedly some of the finest in the world, lived in more opulence than the king.

Andric continued into the courtyard toward the smallest of the three corrals and called to a lean woman with steel-colored hair who was giving attention to a young filly and a stable hand. The woman wore a simple white sash over a red vest, the sign of her station as stablemaster. Upon seeing the prince, she quickly finished her instructions to the young man, then briefly whispered to the filly, gently stroking her neck as she handed the horse's tether to the stable hand. After a moment she turned and made her way toward the prince.

"Milord, how can I be of service?" she asked, bowing with her hand over her heart. Her voice bespoke respect. The woman's weather-worn and tanned skin was edged with a few age lines, and her manner was infused with kindness and patience.

"Good morning to you, Mistress Teer. And good Charge Days. Will you ready Wind and six more for me?" Andric asked warmly. He liked the stablemaster. She had held her position for many years before Andric was even born. It was Mistress Teer who had taught Andric to ride. Her exceptional affinity for training and caring for animals was unparalleled in the kingdom. Andric grew up hearing rumors that although she was no elantir, Mistress Teer used the arcane powers of met'elan to bewitch the animals. Andric had outgrown such superstition, but he did not doubt the stablemaster connected with her animals in a way that bordered on the mystical.

"Certainly, Your Highness." Mistress Teer shouted the order toward the stables, and three nearby stable hands immediately leaped into action. "Milord is in unusually high spirits today," she observed.

The prince had always been impressed by Mistress Teer's sense of empathy, not only with animals but with all those around her. Andric had asked her about it once. She had smiled patiently and explained that it wasn't a thing she had learned, like training animals, but rather a gift from the gods she had been blessed with since her youth. She then imparted a bit of wisdom.

'We all have special gifts, milord Andric, but we must guard how we use them. With them, we may improve life or degrade it.'

With youthful fervor, Andric had asked how to know the difference, and Mistress Teer's eyes had seemed to sparkle as she chuckled.

'If you ever figure it out, you must share the secret with me. See that you always do your best to improve life for yourself and especially for those around you.'

Though the words could have been easily dismissed by the young prince, they had made an impact and kept him often turning to the stablemaster for advice on more than just horses. Whether it had been a touch of prophecy or just a profound insight on Mistress Teer's part, the stablemaster had touched on Andric's deepest longing—to truly make a difference in the world. He had not yet discovered any gifts that seemed particularly beneficial to anyone.

Stephir, on the other hand, had been abundantly endowed with gifts. He was the ideal charismatic, decisive, and astute prince that any kingdom could hope for. He had become their father's right hand. Andric was not jealous of his brother's skills or even of his position. On the contrary, Stephir had ensured they developed a close relationship despite the ten-year difference between them. Together with their middle sister Hellen, his siblings had practically helped raise Andric. But Stephir had married when Andric was just six, and Hellen had married a few years later and left to live in Tennury with her husband's family.

Even though Stephir now had two children of his own, he still connected with his younger brother and helped him feel they were on even footing. At times, Andric was grateful for having a lighter load of responsibility; it freed him to pursue more entertaining activities. Besides, Andric was not sure if he could ever live up to the expectations placed on Stephir. However, the older Andric got, the more he found it frustrating and disappointing that his father never entrusted him with any real responsibility. Perhaps one day that would change.

None of that was allowed to stay on the prince's mind today. Andric inhaled deeply and smiled at the stablemaster. "High spirits indeed. Not even the morning cold can keep me shackled today," he boasted, stretching his arms wide in a gesture of freedom. Unfortunately, his cloak flew open, and a sudden chill ran down his spine and he shivered violently, his skin turning to goose flesh.

"It seems it would rather shake Milord to death," Mistress Teer chuckled.

They spoke casually for a few minutes until the stable hands approached, leading a beautiful dappled white mare and six heavy destriers Remalia was so well known for. Andric walked around his horse, nodding in approval at the obvious care she had received from the skilled stablemaster and her staff. He patted the mare gently on her neck. The coat's glossy sheen and softness belied the hard muscles that tensed under his touch. She seemed as eager as he was to enjoy the sun that the day promised. Taking the reins, Andric mounted Wind and bid Mistress Teer a good day.

Two additional Divinarim joined the prince's party, one on each side and two behind. Only the royal family was permitted to ride while on the Mount of the Gods, so the Divinarim escorted the prince on foot. Andric usually didn't mind the slow pace, but today it bothered him. He trotted slowly out of the stable yard gate and wound his way through the broad, tree-lined paths of the palace gardens, recently reawakened from their winter slumber. Within minutes, he made his way onto the Grand Avenue.

The Grand Avenue was eight times as broad as any other road in the city and cut a straight course from the front steps of the palace, north across the Mount of the Gods, down through the city to Hightowers' Gate, and into the countryside. The palace, which stood at the southern end of the Mount facing north, shared its vantage with seven other edifices: six temples, one to each of the gods with the exceptions of Sykoria and Akraharr, (and the Holy Couple, Yonvaar and Kerail, who required only one place of worship), and the House of Falan, headquarters of Remalia's military. The eight buildings faced the Grand Avenue running down the center of the Mount, all bound together and separated from the rest of the city by the inner wall set like a gleaming white granite crown upon the head of the Kingdom of Remalia.

Wind's iron-shod hooves clicked loudly on the cold, close-fitting cobblestones. As Andric approached the White Gate leading from the Mount out to the city proper, he heard a busy workday well underway. There had been an unusually high level of activity in Teris leading to the Charge Days' celebrations. What most people didn't know was that the heightened activity was not a coincidence. The king was using this year's Charge Days to mask preparations for a possible war with Kushaan.

Two more Divinarim awaited the prince at the White Gate, halberds gleaming in the morning sun. In addition to guarding the royal family, the Teraithian holy knights in the Order of the Divine Flame were also given the sacred duty of guarding the Mount of the Gods, the most sacred site in all of Remalia, perhaps even the whole of Baon. Today there was a larger-than-normal contingent of the Divinarim guarding the White Gate. Outside, the city guard and several soldiers from the army worked together to manage the crowd that was already gathering.

Each year, on Preparations Day, all Remalians were invited to the Mount of the Gods to attend the temple of their choice for the evening devotion. Many already lined the Grand Avenue outside the White Gates, waiting for their chance to enter. For many who lived in the city, this was an annual tradition. For most in the kingdom, it was a once-in-a-lifetime pilgrimage to the grand temple of their chosen god. By sundown, the crowd would stretch down the Grand Avenue and along many of the side streets.

"Good morning, Your Highness," a knight greeted the prince as both men saluted sharply, right arms across their chests and fingertips touching the pole of their halberds. Andric nodded his acceptance of the courtesy. "I understand we are headed to the Temple of Venerate Alscome in the Oettan District."

"We'll be stopping by the Library of Selmarine first," Andric answered.

"Of course, my lord."

All six Divinarim stepped on the mounting blocks, attended by squires in white and blue livery to help the armored knights onto their mounts. The guards knew well where the obscure Viancian temple was located. It was one of the few places Andric regularly visited in the city. Today was not just a casual social call to see his friend though. He wanted Barak's help investigating the attack on the Teraithian temple. Not that Barak had any particular expertise in the matter, but the young scholar was one of the most brilliant minds Andric had ever known, and often saw connections that others missed.

Andric nudged Wind forward, and the guards moved into place, forming a protective ring. They sauntered through the White Gate and into the city amidst myriad voices in the waiting crowd who pointed to the prince as he passed. Ropes had been set up to keep the crowd cordoned off, allowing Andric to casually make his way down toward the largest of the open-market districts, no doubt already teeming with activity.

Everywhere Andric went people recognized him, bowing respectfully or offering wishes for good Charge Days. He smiled back warmly, nodding now and then in acknowledgment. Everything looked bright and cheerful. Poverty was not readily seen in these prosperous times. Andric knew it existed, but it was tucked away in the far corners of the city, far from the places where decent people congregated.

As the prince approached the edges of the market, the heavier traffic prompted Andric to tuck his small leather purse into the inner pocket of his vest, though he doubted it was all that necessary. Thievery was usually kept to a minimum by the city guards, at least in the inner city, especially around the market. Stealing from a member of the royal family on horseback and surrounded by six Divinarim was almost laughable.

People crowded around the small food stands and carts that lined the street entrances to the market. Shoppers and merchants mingled, enjoying a taste of the morning meals. A familiar din filled the air as hawkers shouted their wares to all within earshot. A chaotic blend of smells wafted through the air; the smell of freshly baked bread merged with a potpourri of exotic spices, both sweet and acrid. One moment he wished he had not already begun the Preparations Day fast, the next he was glad he had a settled stomach and hoped it would stay that way.

A tall woman in a costly dress and fur cloak stood on a bench beneath a few trees, the first leaf buds of spring forming on the branches, shouting at passers-by.

"Kerail loves you! Come to her arms and accept her divine embrace! She will protect you in these troubled times! She will give succor to your wounded soul. How long will you wander as children, straying from the path of peace?"

Religious street criers had become increasingly common of late. Andric tried not to pay them much heed.

"Shut up and go back to your tea parties!" another woman, attire and olive complexion indicating Calavian origin, yelled back.

The woman on the bench opened her mouth to reply but paused as Andric drew near. She curtsied gracefully to the prince, even while standing on the bench. Gesturing toward Andric, she raised her voice for the crowd.

"There is a true son of the Holy Couple! House Laconeus has ever been recorded among the names of the faithful."

Andric felt uncomfortable with the unwanted attention as some in the crowd, most of whom seemed to have been largely ignoring the woman, looked up to notice the prince. He gave a curt nod and turned to look at something else—anything else.

A little further up the road, the atmosphere was lightened by an old folk tune performed by a small group of musicians. A couple of city guards saluted Andric as he passed—the younger one smartly, his senior a little less so. A group of young women, none of them particularly attractive he thought, pointed and giggled together as he approached. It wouldn't be proper to more than casually acknowledge them, he told himself. He casually directed Wind to the right, but he could not help glancing back to see if the maidens were still looking at him. Only one was, to whom Andric threw a charming smile and a wink. The others would never believe her.

He chuckled to himself as he continued to ride through the now-packed streets of the marketplace. Colors danced as people waved a variety of fabrics and clothing. Aided by his guards, Andric pushed Wind slowly through the river of bodies.

Once free of the crowd, he felt a slight tug at his boot. He glanced down at a filthy Cannessi girl. He could not tell how much of her dark skin was dirt or her natural coloring, and her ratty hair probably hadn't been washed since the last rainfall. Her tattered, and in some past age vermilion, dress hung loosely on her frail frame. Andric guessed she was probably only five or six. He looked around to see if he could spot the child's mother or older sibling but saw no one. Her size had probably allowed her to slip past his guards. Suddenly, a Divinar cut his horse in close to the prince and reached out with his heavy booted foot to shoo her away, but Andric stopped him.

"It's all right," Andric said, waving the man off. "What's your name, little one?" He kept his tone friendly, though he noticed, with some distaste, that the fingerprints on his boots matched the grime on her hands. He was often less patient than he should be with subjects such as this girl—certainly less than Stephir usually seemed—but he knew what was expected of him as a prince and a Laconeus.

The little girl simply looked back at him with huge, round eyes. The sun shone down upon her face, penetrating the long lashes that arced over the deep pools of green that were her eyes. With a quick move she held up a dried wildflower she must have gathered from the summer before.

"How much?" Andric's smile was glued on his face in what he hoped was a reassuring and empathetic manner. He knew there would be many in the crowd watching him. The sprite lifted her other hand, all five fingers splayed wide. The prince offered a silver coin in exchange for the flower. She probably had no concept of its worth, which gave him some genuine satisfaction. A beaming smile split her dirt-stained face and her eyes widened in delight at the sight of the shining coin in her hand. He waved to her as she turned and darted into the crowd.

He knew as soon as word got out that he had given the little girl the coin, he would be surrounded by other children wanting to sell him their goods. Deciding Barak had probably finished his morning routine by now, he headed out of the market in the direction of the temple where his friend resided.

Andric's invigorated mind took note of some of the sights that, on most days, he passed without noticing. There was one sight he was unfortunately already familiar with. Scaffolding ran like latticework up the blackened face of the burned-out husk of a vaisoht, a place of worship for followers of the god Vai Doroth. Workers moved on the scaffolding with cleaning equipment and tools restoring the building. It had only been two weeks since that fire had been set to the vaisoht in the middle of the night. From the accounts Andric had heard, the attackers had been dressed in the black robes worn by the clerics of Vai Doroth, but they had also donned black hoods to hide their identity.

There was conflicting speculation about the identity of the vandals. Some named them as a rival faction of Dorothi clerics who were outraged by a proclamation from vaisoht's chief cleric that Vai Doroth would soon abandon this world because of the pervasive unbelief and chaos so abhorrent to the god who espoused order, justice, and above all, self-discipline. Others said the arsonists were radical Teraithians or Sykorians. Whoever they were, it was the third such attack this year before the attack last night, and none of the criminals had been caught.

These hostilities had been going on for years in Kushaan, Jankar, Celendria, and other parts of the world. Even some of the less civilized regions in Remalia suffered the same turmoil. But to have it here in the capital city, his home, was beyond troubling. And it was not just the violence. People had abandoned their homes to move to the wilderness and establish religious settlements, while others had become no better than bandits, attacking people in the name of one god or another.

Andric could almost appreciate Vai Doroth wanting to abandon the world.

CHAPTER II
ANDRIC

The Library of Selmarine was a small temple of the goddess Viance located in the shadow of the towering city walls. Today, Andric didn't wish, as he had a hundred times before, that Barak would move to the Great Library of Viance on the Mount of the Gods.

Andric had tried to convince Barak that if he moved to the mount, he could have unfettered access to vastly more research material, including some of the greatest scholars in Baon, a prince of Remalia, and by association, all of the most important people in the kingdom. While these may have been good reasons, Andric knew his friend could see through them. The real reason Andric wanted Barak to move was for the prince's own convenience.

Selmarine had an in-depth library devoted to the theories of the arcane power of elan. The elantir guilds may have had other works not found in the library, but the guilds forbade everyone but their members from having access to their knowledge. There was no such concept to the Viancians as forbidden knowledge. The central tenet of the goddess's teachings was that all knowledge was of worth, and striving for knowledge was the greatest good to which a person could dedicate their life. Of course, knowledge could be used for good or ill, but Viance's doctrine did not concern itself with those matters—that was left to the province of the other gods to work out with their followers.

Viance's doctrine fit Barak perfectly. His friend was happy to live at the small temple, nestled in the eastern quarters of the city, away from the bustle of the political center and the distractions that usually went with it. The treasured books were enough to keep him occupied for now. Besides, Barak reasoned, he still had access to any of the works in the larger collection at the Great Library whenever he desired.

Andric dismounted and handed Wind's reins to a Divinar, ordering the guard to wait at the outer temple gate. He knew they didn't like leaving the prince alone, but they didn't argue. With religious tensions high throughout Teris, having the distinctly Teraithian knights in the Viancian temple might not be helpful despite their charge to protect him.

He passed through a low arched passageway into the inner courtyard. No one was there to greet him, but this was typical of his visits to his friend. The priests of Viance were far more concerned with their studies than they were with proper formality and courtesy for their visitors, even if that visitor was someone from the ruling family. It used to bother him, but he had learned long ago not to take offense at it.

The sounds of the city outside were impotent to penetrate the divinely produced peace found within the temple walls. Andric walked casually along the stone walkway. Some of the faces he passed were familiar, although he knew few of them by name. Barak, of course, knew all their names. Not by any particular effort, Barak simply remembered things easily. It was usually not something that played in Andric's favor, and he had learned not to argue with his friend about details from the past. Indeed, he did not argue with Barak about much of anything if he wished to keep his pride intact. He would only engage the Cannessi's sharp mind for practice in keeping his own wits honed.

The two friends had met under unusual circumstances. Andric had many tutors growing up, each an expert in their field. Master Scholar Encavath, High Priestess of Viance at the Great Library on the Mount, was tasked with selecting his courses of study and his teachers. When Andric was thirteen, the master scholar determined he should have a deeper understanding of met'e-lan, the ability to manipulate elan, the life force throughout all creation.

Andric later learned his father had initially refused, not wanting his son to waste his time delving into impractical subjects. But Encavath had persisted. Was met'elan not simply another form of power, used for good or ill as directed by those who wielded it? Would it not be better for Jevorak's son to understand such power's proper place in the world? Should he not be prepared to take informed action if he ever was forced to deal with the abuse of that power? Their father relented, and Master Bellubont became his tutor. Much to Andric's delight, Stephir decided he could benefit from the same education and often joined the tutoring sessions.

Master Bellubont was a priest of Viance who served at the Great Library, and he was also an elantir. Andric believed the man harbored some undisclosed resentment toward the princes (or perhaps all the nobility), and he took every opportunity to include his "assistant", a brilliant young Cannessi refugee a couple of years older than Andric, in the princes' tutoring sessions. Andric was convinced Bellubont just wanted to show how dim they were by comparison. It had irked Andric at first, but Stephir told him to appreciate the fact that there would probably always be someone better in some given skill, and his job was to harness those abilities in the service of Remalia. The young prince just wanted to be the best at something—anything.

He decided to take Stephir's advice and tried to see what he could do to use Barak's talents "for the good of Remalia," which in his mind translated to "for the good of Andric." Despite Master Bellubont's intentions (and perhaps in no small measure due to Andric's changed mindset), Barak's unassuming manner and unabashed honesty were endearing and left Andric in awe of the quirky Cannessi who seemed to know something about everything and a lot about many things.

One day, Andric mentioned Barak's uncanny abilities to Stephir, who laughed. "You realize he's just making educated guesses about most of it, don't you? Do you think he has any actual knowledge about military strategy, economics, foreign policy, swordsmanship, horseback riding, or Calavian cuisine?" Andric tried to catch Barak at his guessing, but it never paid off. Barak readily admitted when he was just making a guess, and he was more than happy to explain the logic behind his guesses, which made him seem all the more brilliant.

Andric pushed himself harder when Barak was around, in part trying to avoid giving Master Bellubont the satisfaction of so much of a gap between the young men. But his progress came in fits and starts. Some days he was able to focus his mind and soul to channel elan with an ease that left the priest begrudgingly impressed. On other days, he could barely get his thoughts to slow down enough to measure his breathing, let alone feel the currents of the life force within himself and the world around him.

Stephir did well enough, managing to light a candle within only a few months of study. Andric had melted the whole candle in a burst of flame that splashed hot wax everywhere, which no one found nearly as funny as he did.

Barak, for all his brilliance, simply could not perform even the simplest elant. When Andric had pressed him about it, Barak claimed it was an inherited trait; not for all Cannessi, just those that came from the western Velspars. Barak claimed he was one of the rare Cannessi who could even sense elan, but still could not touch it or use it—as if it were always just out of reach. He tried to feign indifference, but Andric could tell the young scholar was frustrated and at times seemed depressed about it. At first, Andric held his successes with met'elan with great pride over Barak, but he grew uncomfortable with his own pettiness and learned to keep his pride to himself.

The high priestess finally called an end to that course of study, but had noticed the change in Andric and asked if he would like to have Barak join in some of his other subjects. Andric had considered the pros and cons. On the one hand, Barak would always outshine Andric (at least in scholastic subjects), and he imagined what the other nobles might say about a refugee being a study companion to the prince. Of course, Andric took some pleasure in turning the situation into a case for his magnanimity, showing his great charity for the poor Cannessi refugee boy. If it started going wrong, Andric could always change his mind.

It had actually taken some convincing to get Barak to accept! He only wanted to focus on learning all he could about met'elan. Eventually Andric prevailed, but Barak insisted he would only attend the lessons on the condition that he could continue to live at the Great Library. Andric just assumed that was a foregone conclusion and didn't consider or mind that Barak had no qualms about putting conditions on a royal's request to join in their tutoring. It would have been beyond impertinent from anyone else, but it never came across that way from Barak.

Andric learned to accept his friend's astute mind for what it was, and he used it for his own benefit. Occasionally he would argue something he had heard from nobles and courtiers to see how Barak would respond. More than once, Andric took Barak's words back to court, engaging in a vicarious debate between his scholarly friend and those at the palace. He was proud of his friend when he heard those same words later plagiarized by others. It was too bad Barak had neither the pedigree nor the desire to run in the same circles as the nobles. Andric knew Barak would surely keep them in their place better than anyone, or would so offend the lot of them that they would seek to take his life.

Being friends with Barak had proved beneficial in another unanticipated aspect. Andric continued developing his skill with met'elan even after Master Bellubont's tutoring had ceased. However, without formal instruction, it had proved difficult. Andric turned to Barak for help. Even without the ability to perform met'elan himself, Barak was an apt teacher, guiding Andric through the theories and exploring unorthodox ideas Andric otherwise would never have encountered.

It had been nearly a year since Barak left the Great Library to live at the Library of Selmarine. Although his friend still focused heavily on his study of met'elan, his hunger for obtaining knowledge in many disciplines made him a natural fit for the Viancian faith, and the priests allowed Barak to live as one of them even though he quietly declined to take the oaths of the priesthood. As much as Andric wished Barak would move back to the Mount, ever since his father had made it clear he didn't consider met'elan a worthy pursuit for a prince of Remalia, it had proved useful to have a place away from the immediate orbit of the palace to study and practice without feeling the weight of the king's scrutiny. Fortunately, Jevorak was too preoccupied with preparations for war to focus his attention on Andric's visits to Selmarine.

Andric walked along the halls of the dimly lit temple, knowing where he would find his friend. The priests and priestesses of Viance usually kept to a strict routine of disciplined study interspersed with necessary practical tasks. While he had no desire to emulate their spartan existence, Andric could not help but have a degree of admiration for their simple and focused lifestyle.

He arrived at the library wing of the temple, sure to find the Cannessi lost in some tome or another. Two priestesses sat on a bench near the doors, lost in a discussion he vaguely recognized as elantic theory, neither paying him any attention.

"Similarly, as one can control the amount of refraction by altering the angle or the medium, couldn't one change the harmonic resonance of a met'elantic conversion by transmission through various intermediate corpuses?" the younger one asked.

"In certain circumstances, yes, but that won't always balance with the sub-integer frequency synthesis in the Hygrerian theorem. You could lose too much..."

He walked past them and pulled on one of the heavy double wooden doors but was surprised to find it locked. He tried the other one and found it locked as well. In fact, they were more than locked. They didn't even rattle when he pulled on them. It was as if they were a solid part of the wall rather than the dark, iron-bound doors he had opened many times before. After giving them a few firm yanks, he was convinced it was a useless exercise.

"May we help you, my lord?" the senior priestess asked, pausing her conversation with the other priestess.

Andric turned to face her, attempting to keep the confusion from his face. "The doors to the library appear to be locked. I don't suppose you have a key?"

"May I inquire as to the nature of your visit to the Library of Selmarine?"

Andric was again surprised. The library had never been closed before, let alone had anyone questioned him about why he was there. "I am here to see Barak Ve'Aurben." Whether they knew who Andric was or not, he could not be certain, but the woman inclined her head, apparently satisfied with his answer.

"Now, as I showed you..." the woman said to the young priestess seated next to her.

The cleric bowed her head and Andric guessed she was preparing to perform some elant. He was curious to see if he could sense what she was doing, so he opened his center, the place in his chest where his perception of elan was principally located. After a moment, Andric felt a shift in the elantic field as a thin stream of elan modulated to volkh, one of the seven elantic modalities (or nine, if one counted the two forbidden ones), flowed from the cleric toward the doors. The volkh modality was commonly employed when hardening or softening material, so that made some sense, but it didn't fully explain why the doors did not move at all.

He was surprised when he also sensed the subtle pull on his consciousness that told him someone nearby was attuning to one of the deities' divinessence. He couldn't discern which divinessence it was unless he was also attuned to the same divinessence, but in most cases, it was easy enough to deduce. The ability to attune to a deity's divinessence did not come from his elantic center but from being sufficiently aligned with the deity's mind and will.

Andric was not singly devoted to Viance, but he had a deep respect and love of her doctrine and will. Especially in this moment, desiring to learn what the priestess was doing, it wasn't difficult for the prince to deepen his alignment with the goddess. His craving for knowledge intensified as he oriented himself with Viance's will that all should seek deeper understanding of the world and the mysteries of life. His sense of her divinessence coalesced until it felt like a gossamer aura surrounding him. He extended his consciousness to meld with the divine.

The wonder and awe already swirling through him surged, imposing on his mind a second orientation, as if he was simultaneously existing in two different worlds. It had been overwhelming the first time he had attuned, but his recent practice with Barak helped him maintain his balance. In the fabric of Viance's divinessence permeating the area, he could sense the attuned priestesses, attracting him like a moth to a flame.

The older priestess shot a glance at Andric, no doubt sensing his attunement, before admonishing the younger one. "Don't let yourself be distracted.

You must maintain a tighter link with the divinessence. It shouldn't waiver so much."

It was good advice for Andric too, as he strained to hold on to both the elan and his attunement to the divinessence. He had some vague guesses of what the priestess was about to do. There were certain applications where elan and divinessence could be combined, but it was dangerous and great care had to be taken. To do so for the mundane purpose of locking doors seemed reckless. The familiar discomfort of the elantic vibrations resonating through his center suddenly amplified as the woman's elantic flow was infused with divinessence. He braced himself against the painful intensity, channeling his own elan and modulating it in counterpoint to volkh to dampen the effects.

By the time Andric refocused on the priestess's elant, it was already done. The senior priestess nodded in satisfaction and gestured for him to proceed into the library. He felt inclined to admonish the clerics about the dangers of what they were doing, but he knew it was pointless. They were just following the orders of their superiors. Besides, if anyone understood the dangers of what they were doing it was the Viancian scholars themselves. Andric bowed and went through the doors that now opened without a hint of resistance. The two companions immediately resumed their discussion without another word to the prince.

The doors silently closed behind him, unnaturally cutting off the words from the priestesses' conversation. Andric was a bit disconcerted that he could no longer hear any hint of sound from outside the doors. He nodded in polite greeting to the elderly priest sitting next to the entrance, presumably there to unlock the doors for those wishing to leave. The prince was tempted to continue puzzling through the unlocking elant, but he thought his experimentations might not be appreciated and headed off to find Barak.

He passed row after row of tightly packed shelves that left barely enough space for a person to fit between. The aisles were as dimly lit as the rest of the building, something Andric always found odd, but here and there, pools of light from alchemical lamps fell on desks where members of the order studied or transcribed various books or scrolls. Glancing down the far end of the wide center aisle filled with tables, Andric discovered Barak was not at his favorite spot.

After a quick check along the far wall of the library, Andric found him in another of his usual spots on the east wall. His diminutive friend looked like a child as he sat perched on a stool in front of a greatly oversized book that rested on a highly polished oak bookstand. Andric smiled to himself. Barak was a creature of habit if ever he had known one. He wondered if that was a result of living among the clerics of Viance, or if Barak had chosen this life because it was a natural fit to his own nature.

Andric tiptoed up behind his friend, who likely would not have heard a legion of mail-clad warriors running at him in a passionate battle cry. The prince felt like a great fellcat, ready to pounce on an unsuspecting deer. With a sudden swoop, Andric grabbed Barak's hunched shoulders and gave a simultaneous roar. It had the desired effect. The small scholar nearly jumped out of his skin, producing more of a yelp than a roar himself. Andric made sure to keep a steady grip on his friend to keep him from falling off his seat but leaped backward at the first sign Barak had his balance, narrowly avoiding the quick jab of a sharp elbow that was unwittingly aimed at his manhood.

"Careful Barak. Many a maiden would be most displeased should your elbow ever find its mark," he joked.

"Or rather they might thank me," Barak retorted coolly, having regained his composure. His friend had always appeared young, due in no small measure to his short stature and slight build characteristic of the Cannessi. His ashen-gray skin was like aged and weathered wood, though lighter than some of his nationality, no doubt due to a lack of time spent out of doors. In keeping with the tradition of his adopted home in Teris, Barak usually kept his coal-black hair trimmed short. During the winter he had let it grow longer than usual, and the slightly wavy locks brushed the low collar of the loose-hanging brown robes worn by priests.

Barak did not wear the sash reserved for ordained members of the order, which was draped from one shoulder to the opposite hip. The robes were remarkably simple compared to the vestments worn by priests and priestesses of most of the other gods. That was typical of Viance though. The goddess's disciples had no use for pomp or material beauty, although most of the art Andric had seen depicting the goddess represented her as indeed beautiful with some ineffable quality of sublime refinement and fairness.

"What brings you to assault me so early in the day, Andric?"

The prince put on an injured face and started to protest but was cut off as a priestess marched around the corner of a nearby bookcase.

"Young man," she began sternly, but seeing it was the prince, quickly stiffened her posture and appeared to reconsider her words. "This is a place of study and worship, Your Highness. If you would please keep quiet and allow the others their thoughts, it would be greatly appreciated."

Andric was surprised at being addressed so, but glancing around at the other tables he saw other priests bathed in the light of their lamps casting disapproving looks in his direction. Slightly embarrassed at the commotion he had caused, he chose to overlook the slight to his station. "My apologies, Scholar..." he hesitated before conjuring her name, "Mella. I will keep that in mind and help preserve the honored reverence here." Andric was proud of the formality of his words but surprised that the priestess stiffened further. She opened her mouth slightly but quickly closed it with a frown and a curt nod before turning on her heels to stonily return the way she had come. Andric waited until she was out of earshot before looking at his friend and shrugging with a sheepish expression.

Barak shook his head and smiled ruefully. "It probably would have gone better for you if her name was actually *Mella*."

Andric winced at his mistake.

"What time is it?" Barak asked, straightening his back with a stretch.

"A few hours past sunrise," Andric answered.

His friend shook his head as he glanced at the ceiling. "You know something? As somewhat of a historian, I must make a special note of this singular occasion. Let us mark it with a celebration." Barak's voice took on a deeper, if hushed, tone and, with one hand raised above his head as if holding a goblet in a toast, slipped into an archaic speech as Andric looked on, a bit bewildered.

"Henceforth shall this day be had in remembrance from generation to generation, down through the endless corridors of time, as the Day of the Awakening. The day when the good Prince Andric of Remalia, son of Jevorak Laconeus, was raised as if from the dead by some miraculous power at an hour not looked nor hoped for by any who knew the sad curse that ever held the young lord in unnatural slumber long after the rest of the kingdom had risen to greet the day."

Andric rolled his eyes and groaned but could not completely suppress a smile.

"Henceforth shall it ever be a day to be celebrated by all good citizens of Creation rising at daybreak, to behold and pay homage to the majesty of the rising Morning Star—"

Andric jumped in. "A celebration indeed." Playing along was usually less injurious to his pride than trying to come up with some witty retort. And who knew how long Barak would go on if given the chance? "For 'tis the strength of the sun's warmth which raises the dead earlier than due course." Andric was not as adept as Barak at the old style of speech but knew his childhood tutors would be pleased with his attempt. "Thus, if thou shalt accompany—"

"Wilt," Barak corrected offhandedly.

"If thou *wilt*," Andric repeated in a tone of insincere annoyance, "accompany me on a ride of Mother Baon," he was pleased with himself for using a more unusual name for their world, "we shall revel in the day!" he finished triumphantly.

Barak smiled and clapped quietly. "Well spoken, Your Highness."

Andric bowed at the applause but gave a sour look at the honorific. He expected it from most people and even enjoyed hearing it from the pompous courtiers. But he never liked hearing it from Barak, who considered the whole affair of titles a bit childish. Andric let it pass, refusing to have his spirits dampened.

"I'm glad you're here," Barak continued. "I thought of some things we could try to make the heat conservation more efficient in your auxonic elants. You see, I—" Barak's words quickened, as they often did when he was excited about an idea and was about to launch into a lengthy explanation.

Andric cut him off before he could get too far. "Actually, I need your help with something else today."

Barak looked a bit disappointed but nodded. "All right, if I can."

"There has been an attack on a Teraithian temple in the Oettan District. I am making an official inquiry for the crown, and I would like you to go with me."

"Another one? Maybe she was right," Barak mumbled to himself.

Andric waited a moment to see if Barak was going to clarify what he meant, but his eyes were fixed on the floor, a sure sign he was getting lost in his own thoughts. "Who was right about what?" Andric prodded.

"What? Oh, Scholar Idduak. She was giving a discourse on the Ultideic Prophecies. Her thesis was that we are in the time of their fulfillment. It was a well-reasoned lecture, but I haven't had the time to delve into the matter. With all of these religious attacks though... neighbor turning against neighbor, strife, and animosity growing everywhere, the contest of the gods does seem like a storm roiling across the world."

"And I suppose she argued that Viance was going to be the victor."

"Actually, no. She said there is no way of knowing how it will end, just that the signs point to the end being near."

"I hope she's wrong. I like the balance between the gods. I can't imagine the world with only one god remaining. Except maybe Sykoria," Andric joked, putting a look on his face as if he was considering the hedonistic possibilities.

Barak's expression turned disapproving. "That's a world I would prefer not to see." Barak had such a sense of moral purity that if Andric didn't know any better, he might suspect Barak was a Servari instead.

"I wouldn't worry about it too much," Andric said dismissively.

"The prophecies or her thesis?"

"Either of them. I suppose the prophecies have some truth to them, but like all prophecies, they're too vague to be of any use. People see what they want to see, and there are those in every generation who believe the prophecies will be fulfilled in their lifetime."

"Well, eventually someone will be correct. What if it's Scholar Idduak?"

"Sounds like a good reason to come with me to visit the Teraithian temple that was attacked."

"How did you make that grand leap in logic?" Barak asked, his voice laced with heavy skepticism.

"You'll get to examine a piece of the evidence firsthand," Andric offered.

"No, thank you. Perhaps Scholar Idduak would like to go. I would be happy to make an introduction."

"I could really use your help, Barak. It isn't clear who's responsible, but they're claiming it was servants of the Holy Couple. It certainly seems plausible that it could be a retaliatory strike by one of the other churches. I will be occupied with the politics of the situation, and I want you to be another set of eyes and ears that can pick up what I might miss."

Barak slowly shook his head, but Andric could tell he was considering it.

"Reportedly, the attack was carried out by summoning a daemon," Andric added almost as an afterthought.

Barak's eyes snapped to Andric's face. "Really? What did it look like? Are there any traces left?"

"I don't have many details, but apparently it caused quite a bit of damage and killed several people. Come with me and see for yourself."

Barak heaved an exaggerated sigh. "Oh, very well. I'm too distracted now to concentrate on my studies anyway." Andric knew that was not true; Barak could always fall into his studies, but the prince was not about to argue.

Barak glanced at the scholars at other tables and smiled, leaning closer to Andric and lowering his voice. "Besides, I think they'd all like to see me leave for a while after our disturbance."

Andric followed his friend as he returned the large book to its place on a shelf, and the two of them made their way out of the library.

"I'll go get Steed and meet you at the front gate," Barak offered. It still amused Andric that Barak had named his horse Steed. Barak had brushed aside any suggestion that he needed to pick a better name.

"By the way, what's the story with the library doors?" Andric asked, following the Cannessi scholar.

"I consider myself a decent historian, Andric, but I'm afraid I don't have any idea about the origins of the doors. I would be happy to research the matter if it's important to you."

"Yes, please do." Andric was kidding, but there was a decent chance Barak would do it. "But I was more interested in current events. Why couldn't I open the doors?"

"In order to keep you out, I imagine."

"Stop being obtuse. They're more like solid stone than doors," Andric retorted.

"They wouldn't be very effective at keeping people out if they weren't."

Andric had been more curious about *how* the doors were secured, but now his interest was piqued by a different question. "Why are you trying to keep people out? The library has always been open to anyone."

"Not anymore."

"Why do you need to keep people out of the library?"

Barak stopped and looked directly into Andric's eyes in that unnervingly sincere way he sometimes did. "After the attack on the vaisoht near the Gazana Market, and now this attack on the Teraithian temple, do you really need to ask?"

Andric understood. "Has anyone attacked Selmarine?"

"Some books on met'elan were destroyed and the shreds were left in the library. We suspect it was members of one of the guilds. They've become increasingly..." Barak paused, probably searching for a particular word "... *intolerant* of anyone having elantic knowledge that they don't control or condone."

"I could have guards posted outside the temple."

Barak shook his head. "That would simply call us out for more unwanted attention. The library is safe for now."

As they approached the sealed library doors, Andric asked, "Would it offend anyone if I tried opening the doors myself?"

"You don't intend to blast your way out of here, do you?" Andric was fairly sure Barak was joking, though there was no hint of it in his voice.

"I got a sense for how they did it when I came in. I just want to see if I can replicate it."

Barak shrugged and approached the elderly priest sitting near the doors. "Scribe Yponnil, Prince Andric would like to try his hand at opening the doors. Would that be all right with you?"

"As His Majesty wishes," the man replied indifferently. *Majesty* was an honorific reserved for the king, but it was such a frequent mistake made by the common subjects that Andric hardly gave it a second thought as he carefully considered what he needed to do.

He had only recently begun training with Barak on how to infuse divinessence into an elant. Barak helped Andric learn the theory, but after some painful first attempts, they resorted to asking for assistance from Master Tuuthard, one of the master scholars at the temple who specialized in the subject. She had resisted at first, but a handsome donation to the library helped convince her otherwise. She was a harsh teacher, but Andric had come to appreciate that about her as he learned the dangers this exercise posed. He was lucky he hadn't been killed in his first unguided attempts.

The safest approach was to begin the elant and then infuse it with the divinessence, but it was challenging for Andric to bring himself into sufficient alignment to attune to the divinessence if he was already focused on channeling elant. Andric primed himself by reciting in his mind the practiced words of a sacred Viancian devotional.

Flame of knowledge, illuminate my path. Guide my feet, that I may find the light. Open my eyes, that I may see the light. Quicken my mind, that I may comprehend the light. Loosen my tongue, that I may share the light.

Andric's heart resonated with sincere desire for the spirit and promise of those words to be true in his life. He would never be the scholar Barak was, but he had always found joy and exhilaration in discovery and finding new treasures of knowledge. Like laying beneath the warm sun with his eyes closed but still perceiving its golden light, Andric sensed Viance's divine power around him, flowing into and through him. He attuned his mind to the divinessence and felt the disorienting surge of divine connection.

With a sliver of his consciousness, he opened his center. He needed only a small amount of elan, so he could afford to draw it from his body instead of siphoning it from the world around him. He willed a small void to open in his center and felt the elan flow into it, sharp and alive. He modulated it to volkh and sent it out like a thin tendril snaking toward the doors, seeking to connect with the trace amounts of elan in the wood, iron, and stone.

Nothing.

He probed with the thread of his elan, looking for an anchor point or node of some kind, like a blind man sliding a key across a lock searching for the keyhole. *Perhaps that's what the divinessence is for*, Andric thought.

The most difficult part of learning to combine divinessence and elan was training himself not to think of it as difficult. The two energies did not naturally interact with each other, at least not in any way mortals understood, but a conscious mind could coax the elan to connect with divinessence and take on a part of its quality.

Andric relaxed his senses, letting them float in the font of divinessence within him. He pictured the divinessence forming itself to the shape of his body, filling every part of him. Then he imagined his physical body fading away, leaving behind his consciousness to occupy the divinessence-self.

He was still aware of the elan flowing through his center, but it was separate from the new divinessence-self. He dampened the vibrations of the elan in his center to protect himself from the intensity that was about to come through. Slowly he merged his elantic center into the imagined ethereal body. The elan jumped ecstatically, threatening to break out of its modulation to volkh. Andric avoided his novice mistakes of trying to control the divinessence-infused elan. Instead, he allowed it to race along the flow of his elan that was already connected to the doors. He single-mindedly focused on volkh, felt its rhythm throughout his divinessence-self, and the elan followed suit, almost as if it now had a volition of its own.

This time, his elan connected to the divinessence-imbued elan in the doors, but something was different. The doors were not hardened, as he had expected. He didn't fully understand how it was done, but it was as if some of the nature of the stone in the floor and doorframe was infused into the doors, blending and binding them together. In some way he could not quite define, they were one.

"I don't see…" Andric had learned a long time ago not to say *can't* around the Viancians, "…what to do with the thread. I have searched for an anchor point or node of some kind, but there doesn't appear to be any."

He was hoping for some suggestion from Barak, but the priest spoke first. "You're trying to connect your elant to the physical. But that's not what holds the door fixed."

Andric tried to puzzle out what the old man meant. *What* is *holding the doors shut?* There was not enough elan present to…. He lost concentration on dampening the elantic thread in his center and the frenzied energy sent a painful jolt through his core. He winced but carefully coaxed the vibrations back into a tight rein.

"Try introducing a seam between the door and the stone," Barak offered.

Andric was grateful he didn't have to try to solve the problem himself. His mind was already tiring from keeping so many pieces in his thoughts at the same time and would have to give up soon. He slid his elan into the space between the doors and the stone doorframe. *A seam*? He pictured the elan already there as if it were a single piece of cloth running through the wood and stone. *How do I make a seam?* He had been thinking of volkh as hardening the doors, but maybe if he inverted the modulation and applied it to the elan he could weaken it enough to fold it.

Inverting a modality was fairly easy once one developed a sense for it, like singing the octave of a note. Andric hadn't worked much with volkh, but he had always had a talent for modulating the modalities. The elantic flow shifted, and it felt like a key finally slipping into place. He rolled his elan to fold the doors' elan on itself and sent that fold running around the perimeter of the doors. When the fold completed its loop around the doors, the connection with the stone evaporated. They were just doors again.

"Impressive for your first try, Your Majesty," the priest said, nodding approvingly. Andric released his elant, then the divinessence. A headache pounded behind his eyes, but he was pleased with himself.

Barak shook his head slightly. Andric smiled. Barak only did that when he was impressed, which was no easy feat.

"Thank you for your help, Scribe," Andric bowed slightly to the old cleric. Turning to Barak, he added, "We really should be going." Andric tried to sound casual, but some amused gloating crept into his voice as he pulled one of the doors open and held it for his friend.

"You really have no idea how blessed you are," Barak said, shaking his head again as they walked along the colonnaded path toward the dormitories.

"I know. You *are* a pretty good friend, but don't go getting a big head about it," Andric joked. "I'll meet you out front."

Their paths diverged and Andric made his way out of the temple. He mounted Wind and waited with his guards in front of the temple for his friend, who soon appeared on a beautiful and slender chestnut horse perfectly suited for his small stature. It was much to Andric's credit that Barak would mount a horse at all. He had a phobia of them when they first met, but Andric had insisted. Now Barak could hold his own and proved it as they trotted toward the Oettan District.

CHAPTER III
BARAK

Barak rarely found a need to leave the library, particularly during the winter when Andric had little interest in taking rides outside the city. He tried to remember the last time he had been outside Selmarine's walls; sometime around last Harvestcrest if he remembered correctly. *Has it really been almost three months?* Perhaps he was overdue for a change of scenery after all.

He had never liked spending time out in the streets of the city. Being Cannessi had always made him a target for suspicion and mistreatment, and the growing tensions made everything worse. It certainly was never safe to go out alone, especially dressed as a priest. Today though, the streets were unusually crowded for Charge Days, which was even more reason to stay within the safety of his temple.

It was reassuring to be protected by several of the most well-trained knights in the kingdom, even if they were Teraithian. Barak enjoyed watching the churning stream of bodies part to open a clear path before them, hardly hindering their progress at all. He reflected on what a fitting metaphor that was for Andric's life in general, and how little his friend truly appreciated how much he benefited from the ready assistance and constant deference.

"Why is it called the Oettan District?" Barak asked Andric as they skirted one of the open street markets. He was uncomfortable confronting an unfamiliar situation, and he managed his anxiety the way he usually did, by gathering information.

"If I remember correctly, Oettan was the name of the architect or chief builder of some of the estate houses and other buildings in the district. His designs were distinctive, so the area picked up his name."

"And the temple that was attacked, is there anything noteworthy about it?"

Andric squinted slightly in the way they did when he was trying to work things out in his mind. "Not that I'm aware of," he finally said.

Barak suspected there was something, but decided it was best not to push.

"By the way, you're coming out to Hamoth's Field tomorrow, right?"

Barak sighed. "We'll see," he said noncommittally.

"I would hate to be forced to have a word with Headmaster Gowend about how disappointed I would be if my good friend Master Ve'Aurben couldn't attend the tourney."

Barak was not entirely certain it was an empty threat. He didn't give much credence to positions of authority, but the headmaster was one of the few that could make Barak uncomfortable. He sometimes suspected the woman used the divine benefaction of dispositioning on him whenever they spoke, though if she did, she was very subtle about it. Thinking of benefactions brought him back to the task at hand.

"Who will be investigating the summoning? I would assume attacks of this kind would normally be investigated by the city guard, but are they capable of dealing with something like this?"

"The city guard will technically be responsible for investigating, but I suspect the Teraithians will make their job difficult, preferring to handle things themselves. Unfortunately, they have far greater resources than the guard does, so they can probably do a better job of it. But that won't likely lead to any justice. Not legal justice at any rate."

"And how are you going to keep the Teraithians from retaliating again? Because you know they will do everything they can to come out on top." Barak felt a little awkward speaking disparagingly about the Teraithians in front of the Divinarim, but not enough to curb his tongue.

"By making it clear that we will bring the harshest penalties against whoever is involved in these religious attacks on either side."

"But if this attack was just a retaliation for a previous attack by the Teraithians, shouldn't that mitigate their punishment?"

"No. It just means more necks for the headsman's axe."

Barak grimaced to show his distaste for the brutality of the suggestion. "You know, there are much cleaner ways to punish high criminals. In Celendria, for example, they have a priest disposition them into a quieted state, then elantir simply stop the heart. It takes longer, but it's supposedly painless."

"We'll have to save the discussion of the merits of execution techniques for another time," Andric retorted.

In the street ahead, a large crowd had gathered in front of imposing wrought iron gates that closed off the grounds of a large structure that resembled a small castle more than a temple. Whisps of smoke drifted into the morning air from open windows in the central tower; not enough to make Barak think the building was currently burning, but still a clear indication of a recent fire where none should have been. His stomach knotted at the thought of a fire burning through the Library of Selmarine.

A row of heavily armored Teraithian knights barred the path to the gates, long polearms at the ready to keep anyone unwelcome from getting too close. Barak noticed additional guards patrolling the immaculate grounds of the temple behind the wrought iron fence. Golden images of Teraithia's holy symbol, two overlapping angles, one pointed to heaven and the other pointed to the earth, capped the larger iron posts spaced along the black fence, providing a touch of ostentatious beauty.

"Those are the archseraph's guards," Andric said, squinting again.

Now that Andric had named them, Barak noticed the torso-length wing made of black leather feathers hanging from the back of each knight's left pauldron, marking them as members of the elite Seraphic Guard.

"What's he doing here?" Andric wondered aloud.

One of the Divinarim addressed the prince firmly. "Your Highness, might I suggest we take you around to a side entrance."

"No, it's important that I am seen here."

"Very well, m'lord. Master Ve'Aurben, please move behind the prince."

Barak had been with Andric and his guards enough to know these kinds of instructions were always for their safety, so he did as he was told. All six guards drew in tighter as he maneuvered Steed behind Andric. They adjusted their grips on their halberds and lowered their polished heads to just above the people standing in the street, which proved an unnecessary precaution.

The crowd quickly parted, opening a path to the gate. Most people bowed their heads and placed their hands over their hearts. Barak wondered if it bothered Andric, or if he even noticed, when some did not offer obeisance. Voices whispered recognition of the prince, and though they generally sounded pleased, there was something else he could not quite identify. Frustration perhaps?

City guardsmen stood in the street keeping the crowd at bay. The temple guards drew up to attention and saluted, left arms across their chests, finger-tips at the hafts of the tall weapons they held in their right hands, as the Divinarim opened ranks to let the prince move to the front. Barak noticed the heads of the temple guards' polearms were a different design than the halberds carried by the Divinarim, and wondered if the differences were practical or purely aesthetic. He detested being ignorant of so many things.

"Prince Andric," one of the knights greeted them loudly enough to be heard by the crowd. "To what do we owe the pleasure of your visit to the Temple of Venerate Alscome?"

"I am here at the direction of His Majesty the King to ensure the tranquility and safety of his people." Andric's voice was likewise raised to be heard by the crowd. Murmuring ran through the onlookers, and Barak scanned their faces to gauge their mood. Some nodded, others slowly shook their heads, and many spoke under their breath, too quiet for Barak to hear.

Then someone shouted, "Akraharr take your tranquility. We want justice!" More than a few voices shouted their agreement.

An angry voice from elsewhere in the crowd retorted, "They got justice last night for once!" Approbation for those words was more subdued but seemed to register on more faces. Even surrounded by heavily armed knights, Barak felt exposed and vulnerable.

"Justice belongs to the crown alone," Andric said firmly, trying to sound as if his words were definitive on the matter.

Barak sensed that many of those gathered didn't see things quite the same way.

"I am certain Archseraph Charin will be most pleased to have your assistance, Your Highness." The knight gave a firm wave of his gauntleted hand and the others moved quickly to open the black gates. They saluted sharply again as Andric rode onto the immaculate temple grounds.

Barak glanced back as the gate clanged shut behind them. He felt safer, but also trapped. *Why did I agree to come? I have no business being here.*

There were more temple guards posted along the wide cobblestone path that ran from the gates to the marble steps of the temple where a handful of priests and priestesses in black velvet vestments of the Teraithian priesthood watched Andric approach. A glossy black and gilt coach, flanked by a pair of Seraphic Guard knights, waited in the courtyard. It was as grand as a royal carriage, and it was not difficult to guess it was the archseraph's. The knights and other guards all saluted and the clerics bowed as the prince's group dismounted.

"Your Highness," the senior priestess soberly greeted him, "you honor us with your visit." Her warm-brown skin indicated Kushaani descent, though her voice carried no hint of an accent.

"I am sorry it is under such unfortunate circumstances. And it appears I'm not the only visitor you have today," Andric said, glancing at the carriage.

"Yes, the archseraph has also graced us with his presence, and Captain Drandin of the city guard is here as well. They're inside with Seraph Prozint. May I show you to where they are?" With a gesture from Andric, the clerics turned and led them through the ornate, cast bronze doors of the temple.

Barak had only been inside one other Teraithian temple before; the one on the Mount of the Gods. He had asked Andric during their studies if he would show him each of the temples on the Mount, figuring he would get to see much more of them if accompanied by the prince. He had not been disappointed. They were each magnificent in their own way, reflecting in their design and decoration the values of their respective deities.

That had been an interesting educational experience. This was entirely different. Even as a guest of the prince, Barak felt out of place walking into the temple. He was not particularly astute at reading emotions, but even he sensed the tension running thick through the place.

They passed through a foyer into a large inner courtyard encircled with more guards. The gurgling of water from a beautiful marble fountain in the center of the courtyard felt irreverent in the heavy atmosphere. The acrid smell of smoke infused the area, though there was no visible sign of damage. Several wayward wooden buckets were haphazardly stacked near the fountain in the otherwise immaculate courtyard.

Another set of imposing double doors led into the temple's grand assembly hall. Beams of light streamed through the smoky air from large windows high overhead at the top of the octagonal central tower. Whisps of white smoke rose from piles of charred benches and tapestries. Barak's eyes were drawn to a number of red sheets covering body-shaped forms on the floor.

"The smell is awful," Barak muttered.

"It smells like sulfur," Andric replied, wrinkling his nose in disgust.

"Yes, some of the fires were started with brimstone, and others by the demon that was summoned," the priestess replied as she led them toward the group gathered near an enormous alabaster statue of Teraithia dominating the center of the hall. It was partially blackened from the smoke and fire, and one of its outstretched arms was broken off above the elbow. Although it held no religious significance for Barak, he was saddened to see a beautiful piece of artwork damaged that way.

The metallic salutes from the archseraph's guards as Andric approached drew the attention of the group standing by the statue.

The priestess leading the way stopped and bowed. "Your Eminence, the—"

"Prince Andric," the man at the center of the group interrupted. He inclined his head in a polite nod to the prince, while the others offered a more traditional greeting, placing their hands over their hearts and bowing. The high priest's distinguished sophistication was accented by the age lines at the edges of his face and the gray highlights in his otherwise dark, trimmed beard and immaculate hair.

"Your Eminence, it has been a while," Andric returned the greeting with a more formal tone than usual. Barak wondered if it was out of respect or caution.

"Too long, Your Highness. Your visit is a welcome surprise. We were just discussing how best to track down the criminals responsible for this vile act of desecration."

"Do you have any thought as to who might have done this?" Andric asked.

"I'm certain the Servari are behind it. They summoned an unholy creature from their gods' realm, which is what caused the fires."

"How do you know it was from the Holy Couple's realm?" Barak asked.

All eyes dropped to look at him.

"You must be the Acolyte Ve'Aurben I have heard about."

"Oh, I am not a priest, just someone who likes books. Otherwise you have it right though. But I believe you were about to tell us about the daemon." Barak knew manners dictated he should use one of the many honorifics for the archseraph, but he already didn't care for the man. Besides, a little disrespect might put him off just enough to get something useful out of him.

The high priest addressed his answer to Andric. "We have records with descriptions of flora and fauna of each of the deities' realms."

"Well, all except Akraharr of course," Barak interrupted.

The archseraph slid a thinly veiled annoyed glance in his direction before continuing. "The summoned creature shared certain features that are common to those in the realm of the Couple."

"Such as...?" Barak asked. He was genuinely curious but made his tone doubtful to needle the man a bit. He had to be careful though. Too much and he might embarrass Andric, or worse, be asked to wait outside.

"I believe Seraph Prozint," Charin gestured to the priest at his side, "is in the best position to provide those details."

Prozint drew in a breath, his brow furrowing dramatically, but Barak spoke first. "So you saw the daemon yourself?"

"No, but I have the descriptions from those who did see it, at least the ones who survived, and they were all very clear."

"Perhaps we could hear from them directly," Barak suggested casually, "if it wouldn't be too much of an inconvenience," he added as if suddenly remembering his manners. Barak caught a slight grin touch the corners of the city guard captain's mouth.

"I'm sure that can be arranged," the seraph said flatly.

Barak began to feel remorseful about his behavior. He glanced at Andric to see if he could gauge his friend's reaction. A couple of the Divinarim shifted uncomfortably. He must have been much more offensive than he had realized.

I really should apologize.

One of Divinarim spoke firmly, her raised voice echoing in the large hall. "It's my duty to inform you all that it is against the king's command to use benefactions or met'elan against a member of the royal family or their advisors."

Barak's guilt abruptly subsided and his thinking cleared. *Someone was dispositioning me,* he realized as anger replaced the guilt he had felt moments earlier.

"Yes, thank you for that reminder," Andric said, his words filling the awkward silence that followed the Divinar's pronouncement. "But as to the question at hand, maybe I can be of some assistance on this matter."

"Your Highness is gracious to offer. By all means..." the archseraph said with an accepting nod.

"Celestial creatures are imbued with the divinessence of the deities of the realm they are summoned from. I may be able to sense which realm this one was from."

"Your Highness can sense the Couple's divinessence?" Seraph Prozint asked, his brow furrowing again.

"At times, yes." Then Andric shifted his gaze to the archseraph. "And sometimes I can sense when someone is attuned to Teraithia's divinessence."

"Forgive me, but I don't consider this an appropriate time to jest, Your Highness," Prozint said, trying to strike a tone of polite disapproval.

Barak wanted to defend Andric's integrity, but this was a delicate matter and he might do more harm than good.

"Everyone other than Prince Andric and his companions will **wait** outside." the archseraph ordered abruptly. The clerics who had escorted

Andric in immediately retreated out of the grand chamber, followed by Captain Drandin and the archseraph's guards. It took a moment longer for Seraph Prozint to accept that the order included him as well. He gave a slight bow and followed the others out, the doors echoing softly as they closed behind him. Only the Divinarim and Barak remained with the prince and the archseraph.

"Your Highness should be more discrete in claiming to have such... an unusual talent, to sense the divinessence of a deity to whom you have not yet committed your full devotion. Most won't believe you, and some might even consider it heresy to make such a claim."

"I don't really care what they think."

"Of course you do. As well you should. 'Perception is the power that shapeth the world.'"

"I'll keep that in mind. Shall we see if I can put my perception to use?"

"I welcome any assistance you may render, Your Highness."

Andric looked around the assembly hall, walking first in one direction, then closer to a wall, then moving off in another direction. Barak followed, as much to stay close to his friend as to have some distance from the archseraph, always shying away from the cloth-covered bodies on the floor. He was not sure if it was the acrid smoke wafting through the air or being this close to death that was making him nauseous.

"What are we looking for?" Barak asked in a hushed voice, hoping to help speed things along so they could leave.

"Somewhere the daemon may have touched, especially long enough to start a fire or leave a mark."

"If we brought in the actual witnesses, they could probably narrow it down for us," Barak suggested.

"If we have to, but I'd like—"

"I would be happy to have the witnesses brought in if it would help," Charin offered. Barak looked back at the archseraph, still standing by the towering statue of Teraithia. He was surprised that he could have heard what they said at that distance. The acoustics must carry even a whisper to that spot. He noticed again the burned and broken arm.

"Look," Barak said, pointing at the pieces on the floor.

"You might be right." They walked back to the center of the assembly hall and approached the statue.

"No luck?" the archseraph asked, sounding almost pleased.

Barak wanted Andric to succeed if for no other reason than to put a dent in the man's smugness. It was a petty instinct, but one he could not immediately push aside. Andric bent to examine the stone arm lying on the ground. It was partially blackened, and three of the fingers had broken off, but otherwise it appeared intact. Barak guessed it had been elanticly hardened to have remained mostly whole after such a fall.

Andric ran his hand along the polished alabaster, then stopped at a particular spot in the blackened area. He closed his eyes in concentration. Barak was familiar with the process Andric went through to put himself in alignment with a particular divinessence. He usually recited some memorized sacred text that crystalized for Andric the aspect of that god the prince's heart and mind most responded to. Barak had made many attempts to do the same, but try as he might, the only divinessence he ever felt was Viance's.

"Archseraph, may I ask you to please move back some distance."

"Have I offended Your Highness in some way?" The high priest's voice was stiff, sounding more slighted than apologetic.

"You're too strong a source of Teraithia's divinessence. It's making it difficult to sense the traces left by the daemon."

"I see," he said smiling, apparently pleased by the prince's words, and somehow managed to look regal and relaxed at the same time as he strode several paces away. Barak knew that he would never have that kind of bearing, but was glad not to suffer from the arrogance that usually seemed to go with it.

Andric finally nodded. "It is indeed the Holy Couple's divinessence," he said, rising.

"Remarkable," the archseraph said as he returned to the statue. "So you really can sense more than one deity's divinessence. How many can you sense?"

"Is this really what we should be discussing at the moment?" Andric asked.

"If Your Highness would indulge my curiosity for just a moment."

Andric sighed. "All of them, though Akraharr and Sykoria are a bit more challenging."

"I should hope so. Still, I don't think I have ever known anyone who could sense more than one without first converting. How long have you been aware of this gift?"

"All my life, I suppose, though I didn't really understand it until this last year. Master Ve'Aurben has been instrumental in assisting me. Now, about the attack on the temple—"

"Forgive me, Your Highness. One last question if I may. Are you able to attune to the divinessences, to perform benefactions with them, or just sense them?"

Something in the way the archseraph asked the question stirred caution within Barak. He seemed... hungry for the answer.

"I don't generally practice benefactions, but yes, I can attune to the divinessences. At least, to those I've tried. As I said, I haven't put much effort toward Akraharr or Sykoria."

The archseraph stared intently at Andric for just a moment, then looked down at the statue's arm lying on the ground, changing the subject. "So, what are we to do about the Servari attack?"

"Do you have any idea who may have done this? Were any threats made against the temple?" Andric asked.

"Oh, there are always gnats buzzing about, but I don't pay them any mind. At least not until they infest my house. Then they must be dealt with."

"Archseraph, tensions in Teris are already high. I do not believe it would be prudent for the Church to involve itself in this matter. Please ensure your people cooperate fully with the city guard, and I will ensure that our best resources are directed to bringing the culprits to justice."

"You expect us to sit by and do nothing? That would be an affront to Teraithia's teachings. That is the path of the weak and helpless."

"Taking actions that weaken Teraithia's influence in the world is also an affront to her teachings, isn't that right?" Barak asked.

"So you fancy yourself a theologian as well, I see," the archseraph said condescendingly. "It's true that every action taken by her disciples should be designed to bring Our Lady greater glory."

"Which is why you issued a Writ of Divinity calling for all Teraithians to bring souls into the faith or let them 'burn in a hail of brimstone and fire' I believe were the words." Barak knew from Scholar Idduak's lecture that the Writ was laced with phrases from the Ultideic Prophecies.

"I fail to see what that has to do with this situation."

"If your grace would indulge my curiosity for just a moment."

The archseraph's eyes tightened, betraying his irritation at having his words parroted back to him. He looked at Andric, perhaps hoping the prince would put Barak in his place. Barak was grateful when Andric held his gaze steady, waiting for an answer.

"The Writ was intended to inspire greater fidelity and action in spreading Teraithia's truth in the world."

"And do you think it's possible that some of your followers took the words of the Writ to let those who reject such efforts 'burn in a hail of brimstone and fire' literally, and were involved in setting the fires at the Dorothi and Servari temples in the past few months?"

"You dare accuse me of instigating the attacks on the other churches!" The archseraph's voice echoed loudly in the smoky air. Barak felt an oppressive weight fall on him like a hand threatening to extinguish his life. Two Divinarim stepped forward, halberds lowered. The others seemed hesitant to threaten their spiritual leader.

"Your Eminence, it is forbidden," the same Divinar admonished, her words measured but hard as stone. The pressure evaporated, leaving Barak shaken but more determined to forge ahead.

"Perhaps it—" Andric began, but Barak cut in.

"I am not accusing you of anything. But someone is."

"What do you mean?" the archseraph asked.

"You think it's a coincidence that the attackers used brimstone and a daemon to set fire to the temple?"

The archseraph looked around the assembly hall, though what he was looking for Barak could only guess. Perhaps he was buying time to consider the idea. "An interesting theory," he finally said. "One I'm sure you will share with Captain Drandin. Now, unless Your Highness needs anything else from me, I'm afraid I have pressing matters to attend to back at the Mount."

Barak could not help himself. "Forgive me, Your Grace. One last question if I may. Do you believe we are in the time of the gloaming of the gods?"

"If we are, Teraithia help us all." With that, the archseraph strode from the assembly hall. The sound of his hard-heeled footsteps echoed loudly in the grand chamber.

"I don't think he'll be inviting you to dinner anytime soon," Andric said.

"I thought that went rather well, all things considered."

"You certainly know how to get under some people's skin," Andric replied with an amused tone that told Barak his friend was not bothered by how things had transpired. "Anyone else you'd like to perturb before we go?"

"I had hoped to hear the description of the daemon from the firsthand witnesses, but honestly, I'm just eager to leave."

"You don't want to have a look at the bodies or something?"

Barak shook his head and started for the door, hoping Andric was joking about the bodies. He was relieved when the prince followed.

"If you really want to talk to the witnesses, I can arrange for it later," Andric offered.

"If the city guard will be making a report of the statements, could I just get a copy?"

"I'll see what I can do."

Andric stopped briefly to inform Seraph Prozint and Captain Drandin of what he had found and assure them they had the full support of the crown. By the time they made it out to the steps of the temple, the sun was high overhead and glinted brilliantly off the archseraph's carriage as it headed toward the front gates. Andric quickly mounted and kicked his horse into a canter. The iron-shod hooves clacked loudly on the cobblestones as they hurried to exit through the gates held open by the temple armsmen. The city guards in the street cleared a path through the crowd for the archseraph, and the Divinarim led Andric the same way. Once they had moved past the crowd, Andric directed them down a different street.

"I want to get out of the city. Let's go see the fairgrounds," Andric said.

Barak wanted to get back to the comfort of the library, but he knew his mind wouldn't soon let go of the events at the Temple of Venerate Alscome. Perhaps it was better to accept the distraction of a ride. Besides, he didn't want to have to endure Andric's attempts to pressure him.

"All right."

"Really? Just like that?"

"I want a preview of where you're going to have your royal hide thrashed tomorrow."

Andric barked a laugh. "I don't know about that. You'll have to be there to see for yourself which way it goes."

Andric chatted about his sword training and the competitors he hoped to face this year. Barak only half-listened, distracted by thoughts of the attack on the temple. He could not relate to people who chose violence to express their grievances. What good did it do—had it ever done? Did they really think it would change the way the Teraithians believed or acted?

Soon they were on the Grand Avenue, passing beneath the colossal Hightowers' Gate, the main way in and out of the inner city. The fortification consisted of a series of massive portcullises with six towers that rose high over the tunnel running through the massive city wall. The stone appeared seamless and impossibly smooth but did not look entirely natural, having been constructed before elantir perfected their craft. That men could accomplish such a feat of engineering left Barak in awe.

Beyond Hightowers' Gate, the Grand Avenue was called Dunnigan's Highroad. A sprawling outer city had spilled beyond the bounds of the massive city walls. No one had attacked Teris in over two centuries, and security had given way to growth. The outer city was an odd mix of poverty and wealth, with filthy slums and extravagant estates. Originally, the shanties of beggars and other undesirables had surrounded the city's mighty walls. Slowly at first, then like an avalanche, shops and homes appeared that were too poor or too large to be built within the inner city. They had started close to Dunnigan's Highroad, but now they surrounded the entire city. Without strict confines to work within, the streets and districts of the outer city followed no rhyme or reason. Most of the crime in Teris occurred in the outer city. Two years ago, King Laconeus had ordered it cleaned up and reconstructed with a sense of order. Most of the ongoing work could not be seen from the Highroad anymore.

Behind the prince's party, the mid-day peal of bells from the Grand Temple of the Holy Couple tolled out from the Mount of the Gods, their perfectly tuned notes carried to every ear for miles around. Barak had been fascinated to learn the elantic principles that enabled the sound to propagate over such distances without having to be louder at the source. Elantir at the temple surrounded the bells with a field of elan attuned to the yldrath modality, which slowed the dissipation of the vibrations. Knowing how things worked helped him appreciate them so much more. He enjoyed the sound and wished they rang more often, but they only sounded on holy days. At dusk, all the bells in Teris would peal in a glorious cacophony.

"I can't believe it's the second tolling already," Andric said. "We don't have much time. I have to be back by the third."

They picked up the pace toward the fairgrounds just beyond the outer city. Hamoth's Field and the surrounding lands were kept clear of any settlement by law dating back to the time of King Hamoth himself. Barak was grateful to have an area of untouched nature to enjoy on occasion. The manicured parks and gardens of Teris were beautiful, but there was something about being in an untamed forest Barak found particularly rejuvenating. He sighed, wishing that was their destination instead.

The fairgrounds were teaming with people making the final preparations to set up booths, pavilions, contest areas, stands, stages, and a multitude of other areas for activities Barak could only guess at. Noticeably absent were the delicious smells of cooking food Barak always enjoyed. His empty stomach growled in anticipation of tomorrow's festivities. He knew that not everyone observed the privations of Preparations Day fasting, but today it was prohibited to sell food at the fairgrounds.

"It might be difficult to come see you for a while," Andric said casually.

The Divinarim had formed a wide circle around Andric and Barak, giving them some semblance of privacy. Barak sensed something was on Andric's mind, and guessed that he was about to hear what it was. He remained quiet, giving Andric time to get the whole matter out at his own pace.

"The Kushaani slave raids into Remalia have been increasing, especially in the Vastan Province. My father intends to put a stop to it."

Barak nodded his head, realizing that Andric was revisiting a previously discussed topic.

"It will be interesting to see what resistance my father receives over the next few days from the nobles. I think he's expecting a fair amount of maneuvering, if not outright opposition."

"He must be planning a fairly extensive campaign," Barak observed.

"What makes you say that?" Andric asked, cautiously looking around for eavesdroppers.

"Well, if he intended to just stop the raids, he could simply increase border security. The Kushaani lands along the border are relatively poor, and therefore not particularly attractive from an economic perspective. Taking them has some small strategic advantage to stop the border raids, but that can only be a strong motive for your cousin and the crown, not nobles from most places in Remalia, and therefore not a source of much contention. On the other hand, if he intends to go after the slavers, that means invasion." Barak's mind raced ahead to the implications of his own words. He saw in his mind's eye the maps he had studied in tutoring sessions with Andric.

Barak continued explaining his reasoning that had led to his conclusion. "The central and southern tribes are the primary markets for slaves, so to the extent your father intends to shut down the slave trade, he has to shut down those markets. They're also the richest lands in Kushaan, making them far more attractive targets. However, that will require Remalia to push far into Kushaani territory, which is terrain that will significantly slow your troop movement and require a much larger force and a greater proportion of foot troops than Remalia's traditional unit composition. Also, if taking spoils was Remalia's intention, again your father wouldn't anticipate much difficulty, so he must intend to conquer and hold those lands, which would of course give rise to contention over who gets to control them. But doing so will significantly increase the complexity and scope of the campaign."

Andric shook his head in amused wonder. "Maybe I should suggest to my father that he appoint you as an advisor."

Barak grimaced. "No thank you. I fear I would lose my mind if I had to be occupied by the inanity of politics. My studies are enough for me."

"Gee, thanks," Andric replied with a touch of feigned injury.

"If my guess *is* correct, you would have either had to already be amassing troops in the borderlands, or you would have to deploy a vast number of troops very soon if you're going to have enough time to secure a foothold down in the Strappatka territory before the next storm season sets in."

"Are you a spy? Or maybe you've secretly changed your studies to military strategy?" Andric joked.

"Hardly, on either count. Curritan is sparsely populated, and Kesh is dense jungle. The Strappatka lands are the most productive agricultural region anywhere near your targeted territories. The food will be critical if you're going to be that far from Remalia. And the Strappatka are the nearest of the large tribes, putting you on one side of the other large tribes' lands so you limit the number of fronts you can be attacked from and position yourself to conduct a more systematic and measured campaign. It seems the logical choice."

Andric accepted the futility of keeping anything from his friend. "Stephir has been developing foodstuffs in the Vastan Province, and he has slowly been building our forces at key strategic locations. Unless there's some major problem with the nobles, my father will start moving the bulk of our army within a week, with additional forces from the other nobles to follow."

"Maybe Scholar Idduak was right."

"She said we were going to war against Kushaan?" Andric asked.

"No, she said a major war was imminent, and it would involve all quarters of the world."

"Taking over the world may be a bit heavy-handed just to stop the slave raids," Andric joked. "I think my father misses leading a big army. It's a chance to relive his glory days. Alas, I have not heard of plans for worldwide conquest. Not a bad try for a dusty bookworm, though."

"Are you certain?"

"About you being a dusty bookworm? Absolutely!" Andric laughed.

The wheels in Barak's head churned. "So when do you leave?" Barak continued as if it was nothing out of the ordinary, though the implications of Andric's departure for their friendship were significant.

"If all goes according to plan, this coming Restday."

Only four days? A mix of emotions surged through Barak. He was going to miss his friend. At least there was little chance of Andric dying in the war. But he would certainly be different when he returned. Would they still be friends?

"We should probably head back. My father will kill me if I'm late." They left the fairgrounds and returned to the road. Many more people were moving in both directions, and Andric had difficulty keeping the quick pace. By the time they reached Hightowers' Gate, the sky was tinged with orange and pink as the sun dipped below the Lithowen peaks in the east. Andric instructed two of the Divinarim to accompany Barak to the temple. Barak's instinct was to decline the offer, but he thought better of it. After what he had seen today, he was glad to have the protection.

"I'll see you tomorrow at the tournament grounds. Wager against me at your own risk," Andric said boastfully.

"I'll see if I can fit it into my schedule," Barak joked back. Andric smiled, then hurried up the Grand Avenue toward the Mount of the Gods. Barak turned toward Selmarine, his thoughts churning over everything that had transpired. His mood slowly darkened, matching the deepening shadows of late afternoon in the narrow city streets. Try as he might to focus his attention elsewhere, one thought kept returning to the surface and he knew he would have no rest until he had followed it to its conclusion. He needed to delve into the Ultideic Prophecies.

At the temple's gates, he bid the guards farewell, then hurried to stable Steed. He wanted to find Scholar Idduak before the evening devotions started and ask to read her discourse. It seemed the best place to start.

The third tolling of the bells began before he left the stables, their chimes filling the air with ringing. He usually paused to savor these occasions, but tonight the chaotic chorus seemed to underscore the trouble in the world. He chuckled sardonically. There was no way Andric was going to make it to the devotions. The prince was surely feeling dread at this moment, though for a completely different reason than Barak.

He remembered tomorrow might be the last chance to see his friend for a long time, and an aching loneliness suddenly gripped his heart.

Not right now. I'll have time to feel lonely later.

Now it was time to see if he could peer above the glass and glimpse the plans of the gods.

CHAPTER IV
STEPHIR

S tephir knelt next to his father, King Jevorak, in the royal sacellum, the Laconeus family's private chapel in the palace. Unlike the grand temples on the Mount, the close confines of the sacred room helped him feel a deeper connection to the Holy Couple. The white stone of the palace halls was replaced with warmer desert granite walls and amberwood benches worn smooth from generations of use and hand-polished to a glowing sheen. The lone stained-glass window at the peak of the far wall, just above the velvet-covered alter where Stephir knelt, was framed on either side by the alabaster statues of Yonvaar and Kerail. The warm sunlight cascading through the geometric pattern in the glass mirrored the dancing lights from iron candelabras encased in seven vacant alcoves around the sacellum.

The third bells had tolled, and Stephir knew his father was upset with Andric for being late to the Preparations Day evening devotions. On any other day, it would have simply been a breach of etiquette. Today though, his father was taking a step Remalia hadn't taken since before he and Andric were born; he was convening a war council. This year's devotions weren't the usual ceremonies. This was the last opportunity to plead for the gods' blessings before Remalia declared war. For Andric to miss this was irresponsible and insulting.

As the crown prince of Remalia, Stephir knew his duty required unwavering support of his father's decision, but his prayers for success in the war rang hollow. Stephir believed this war was ill-advised, and he had said so on more than one occasion, but the king had made his decision. The time for debate had passed, at least as far as Stephir was concerned. The nobles were another matter.

There could be no dispute that Remalia needed to send Empress Arrdiwat a clear message—slave raids across their borders would no longer be tolerated. Kushaan had always traded in slaves, though they had mostly avoided forays onto Remalian soil since the Laconeus family had taken control of the crown so many generations ago. Remalia had established somewhat peaceful relations with their neighbors to the south, enjoying the prosperity brought by thriving trade between the two nations.

The Kushaani Empire was far older than Remalia, its history stretching back thousands of years. The Empire was a loose collection of several dozen tribes and provinces spread over the vast Kushaan territory. Internal strife, at times bordering on outright civil war, was a constant fact of life for the Kushaani, and most of the slaves sold by Kushaan were their own people. There had always been the occasional report of Kushaani raiders making small incursions into Remalia to take a few captives.

Not all those taken as slaves were to be sold. Some tribes took slaves to be held only for a limited time before allowing them to become full members of the tribe or released to return to their homeland. Stephir had a hard time imagining anyone wanting to live with those who had forced them into slavery, but apparently it was not entirely uncommon.

The slave raids over the past several months, however, were beyond anything Stephir had heard of before. The Vastan Province had been hit the hardest, though some of the distant West Marches had also been raided. The Velspar Mountains, which ran nearly the length of the border between the two nations, were an almost impenetrable barrier that probably kept the raids from being worse.

Empress Arrdiwat had clearly miscalculated Remalia's tolerance for such actions. At first Stephir's father was willing to allow for the possibility that a rogue tribe or province was responsible. However, when Remalia's diplomatic envoys were rebuffed, Remalian trade caravans were raided, and Kushaani traders stopped the flow of goods to Remalia, it was clear the long years of peaceful relations were over.

Still, Stephir did not believe outright war was the best response. He preferred increased border security and ongoing diplomatic efforts. Perhaps the empress would soon be deposed, or at the very least convinced by her people to reverse course. After all, the cessation of trade hurt Kushaan just as much as Remalia. In the long run, Remalia could survive a trade freeze better than Kushaan.

Alas, Stephir had not prevailed. Jevorak and his closest advisors hoped to gain much from the war. But Stephir knew there was another reason, which his father hadn't shared with anyone. The king wanted his son, more than anything, to grow into the crown. A noble ideal to be sure, but he was determined to make this happen the only way he knew how—on the field of battle, just as he had.

Stephir lifted his eyes to look at the faces of Yonvaar and Kerail, masterfully worked into the polished white stone. Stephir had gazed upon those faces hundreds of times and was as certain now as he ever was that the Holy Couple knew the true desire of his heart. He prayed they would keep his doubts hidden from everyone else, especially his father.

Ilyanara put her hand on his shoulder, signaling she was ready to leave. Stephir silently nodded but remained where he was. He had already told his wife he expected he would be staying longer than usual. He gave a warm smile to his daughter, Crown Princess Shannyth, and signaled her to go with her mother. He listened to their quiet footsteps retreat while he remained kneeling next to his father.

The king was not a particularly spiritual man, but he observed all religious devotions and duties and expected his two sons to do the same. *Where is Andric?* Stephir wondered again. At this point, it was probably best he didn't come at all. Stephir hoped for Andric's sake he had a good excuse for his absence.

His father continued his devotions long after Stephir wanted to be done, but he would not rise until the king was ready to leave. Stephir again looked up to the stone face of Yonvaar. The royal family was not supposed to have a patron deity; it was expected that they make room for the worship of all the gods. But Stephir's mother had been a devout Servari, a true disciple of the Holy Couple, and had asked that the statues of the other deities be removed from the royal family's private sanctuary. After she died, Jevorak never had them put back. The empty pedestals were a reminder of the void left in their lives by her passing.

Stephir could not remember another occasion when his father had spent this much time kneeling in the chapel. No doubt he had a lot weighing on his mind and was preparing himself for the impending ordeal of trying to garner the support of the high nobility. As king, it was Jevorak Laconeus' right to command the nobles to follow him into war. However, commanding unwilling men and women to put blood and treasure at risk was never ideal. The king needed to receive their full support. That was going to take persuasion, negotiation, strong-arming, and perhaps some divine intervention with a few of the more recalcitrant nobles.

At last, the king rose, and Stephir gratefully got to his feet as well. His knees ached, but if his father was not complaining, Stephir certainly was not going to. Stephir had inherited the Laconeus physical stature, tall and well-built. Jevorak was yet a half-head taller than his son with a broad chest and shoulders. His coarse hair, longer than the current fashion that many nobles of the king's court, had long since turned gray, though the faded brown of yesteryear remained in a few places. Years of softer living had made him a bit heavier around the middle as well, but he was still an imposing figure. Stephir walked at his father's side through the half-deserted palace to the large council chamber near the Throne Hall. The uncanny resemblance between the two was striking, though Stephir's short-cropped hair was a darker brown than his fathers had ever been.

"Do you think they have already assembled?" Stephir asked more to fill the silence than to receive an answer. The high nobles were almost certainly waiting or were on their way to the palace after making an appearance at their preferred deity's temple for their private devotions before the crowds were granted access in a few hours to the Mount of the Gods for the public devotional services. Stephir wished more chose the Holy Couple. Maybe this war could be avoided if they embraced the Servari teachings of universal familial love, service, and harmony.

"We'll see soon enough," his father answered with an uncharacteristically clipped tone.

Because of Andric or the war council? Stephir wondered. Stephir preferred not to be added to that list, so they walked on in silence until they arrived at the king's entrance to the chamber where, to Stephir's surprise and relief, Andric waited.

"My sincere apologies for missing the devotions, Father. Things took much longer at the Temple of Venerate Alscome, and—"

Turning to his chamberlain, the king cut his son off. "Is everyone gathered?"

"All but Duke Markham, though I understand he passed through the White Gate some time ago. Shall I send runners to bring him?"

"No. I can guess where he is. Let's not keep the rest waiting."

Andric kept a stoic expression, but Stephir could tell their father's words stung. Not that Andric didn't deserve it. The chamberlain opened the door and the murmur of conversations abruptly stopped as everyone rose to their feet. Stephir gave a knowing nod and placed a quick, reassuring hand on

Andric's shoulder as he passed by, and the brothers followed the king into the council chamber.

The great room was already full, though there was certainly room for others to join. The assembled nobles stood in a silence that sharply with the severed silence of hanging conversation. Even the blazing fire in the open hearth at the far end of the room seemed to hush as the king greeted the nobles with a nod.

A large table, solid and unadorned, stood at the head of the room with a trio of chairs, the largest in the center befitting the king. Two long oak tables ran through the center of the room with a dozen chairs for the kingdom's high nobles. The pungent scent of pine filled the overly warm air. Fresh-cut pine boughs were draped along the inner edges of the tables. The traditional Charge Days decorations commemorated the scant coverings Hamoth's troops had in their impoverished conditions.

The king took his place in front of the large chair at the center of the head table. Stephir moved to the seat on his father's right, and Andric made his way to the chair on the left.

"My lords and ladies," Jevorak began, his baritone voice and face firm and serious, "greetings, and I thank you for coming. Good Charge Days to you all. Please, be seated," he said, gesturing to their chairs. Stephir took his seat and looked at the twelve faces focused on their king. Ten of them were the most prominent nobles in the kingdom. The other two were High General Gul Kuymon, commander of the Remalian armies, and High Consul Hadana Penrossart, high priestess of Sharin Dara.

Even though the crown recognized no official state religion, the clergy of Sharin Dara were involved with so many aspects of the governance of Remalia that one might suspect Sharinism was the official church of the kingdom. The goddess espoused moderation, tolerance, and diplomacy as tools to bring about the greatest good for the greatest number of her children. This made many of her clerics well-suited to positions as ambassadors, judges, and, in the case of the high consul, close advisor to the king. It had already been decided that Hadana would continue to serve as chief counselor to Stephir's wife, Princess Ilyanara, who would act as head of state in the absence of the king and his sons. Stephir was confident his wife was equal to the task, but he knew some of the nobles of the court would try to take advantage of her inexperience. High Consul Penrossart's guidance and support would be crucial to successfully dealing with those challenges.

The gathered nobles were from every corner of the realm. Many had journeyed for weeks. Those from the Western Marches had traveled the farthest, sailing east through the Inland Sea of Calavia, then up the Cocunn River to the Trilumen Lakes before journeying by carriage the final days to Teris.

The journey this time of year could be challenging, with late-winter storms causing delays and the last melting snow turning some of the roads into quagmires. Stephir's sister, Princess Hilenne, was expecting her fourth child and was due to deliver any day, so she had remained at her estate in the great coastal city of Tennury on the Inland Sea rather than risk the journey back to Teris this year with her father-in-law, Duke Elel Markham, and his entourage. For Duke Macen Frendic, Lord of the Great Plains of Remalia, who had assumed the dukedom just four months before after losing his father to the shaking fever, this was only his second time in the capital city. Some of the others came every year for the Charge Days. The king always assembled the nobles during the celebrations, but it was usually for the grand feast on Victory Day, not the Preparations Day devotions. Their day of fasting (for those who kept the observance, which Stephir suspected was not many) might make for short tempers during the war council.

Jevorak surveyed the assembled nobles as they settled into their chairs and gave him their undivided attention. "These are difficult times we live in. I have reports from all corners of the kingdom that the long peace we have enjoyed is failing. Temples burn, zealots attack pilgrims and other travelers, the people indulge in Sykorian vices as never before, children turn against their parents, and neighbor fights neighbor. It's as if Akraharr himself walks the earth, sowing his seeds of chaos.

"These disturbances are disconcerting, to be sure, and must be dealt with. Were these alone the extent of our difficulties, it would be a daunting task. However, as you are all well aware, for the past several months, Kushaan has violated our security and slapped away our extended hand of friendship. Clearly she has no desire for peace." There were a few nodding heads in the room, and Barron Marstoff looked like he wanted to interject at every other word, but he knew better. He was by far the lowest-ranking noble in the room, but ironically one of the most influential as well, particularly in this matter.

The baron was the younger brother of Countess Resmannery, who had married Stephir's uncle, Grand Prince Deuric Laconeus, brother of Jevorak. Upon the death of both the grand prince and the countess, the dukedom had passed to their only child, Stephir's cousin Osten. The young duke was only eight years old at the time, not old enough to assume the legal authority that went with his peerage. So the king had appointed Barron Marstoff, Osten's other uncle, as the viceroy until Osten was old enough to assume full legal rights of the dukedom.

Vastan Province was in Osten's dukedom, placing the focal point of the Kushaani conflict under Marstoff's control. Of course, as a viceroy and baron, Marstoff was in no position to argue with the king on any issue, which was exactly what Jevorak had intended. This ensured Stephir's father had a free hand to start the war he wanted. But the baron had significant resources at his disposal and didn't hesitate to use them to increase the dukedom's influence.

"We have allowed this to go on long enough," the king continued gravely. "We cannot sit idly by while our enemies do these wrongs." He looked around the room as he let his words sink in. The king had not called the Kushaani enemies in many years. "We have tried both diplomacy and defense and have received only more attacks for an answer!"

Stephir watched his father's fist clench in emotion.

Jevorak took a deep breath, and his voice shifted to that of an exasperated parent. "I would not enter into this lightly. We have truly exhausted all other options." It was a point over which Stephir strongly disagreed with his father, but he was not going to say anything to the contrary now. "We have tried to settle this without bloodshed. But it seems bloodshed is the only message they are prepared to hear. Perhaps they feel Remalia has gone soft in our years of peace and plenty."

This had been an undercurrent of this concern among certain nobles and generals for some time, and one of them took the bait. "She's not soft, Your Majesty. They will find the Stallions of Remalia will tread them under hoof." The metaphor was well played. The Laconeus family crest featured a rearing black stallion, and Remalia's army was built on the unquestionable strength of its cavalry.

The king nodded as if in deep contemplation. The crackling fire was the only sound in the room. Of all the nobles in the realm, these were the critical ones to win over. They commanded the loyalty of many of the lesser nobles and gentry throughout the kingdom, and without the help of these men and women, the campaign into Kushaan would be a short one.

It was one thing for the king to take his armies on the long journey to fight the Kushaani, but without the other nobles' support, there would be few reinforcements, limited supplies, and only the coffers of the crown to pay for it all. There were also those who would be tempted to make a play for the crown in the king's absence. It was only the threat of retribution from the other nobles loyal to the king that would keep them in check.

His father rose to his feet and leaned forward, pressing his fists to the table. "Too long we have turned a blind eye to the abuses of the Kushaani tyranny and their unholy practices. Justice will have its payment in their guilty blood, and we will bring mercy to her innocent children, and protect our own in this endeavor. Our course is set, and the gods will go before our faces and at our sides. What say you?"

Stephir knew his duty, despite his doubts. Before his father's words finished echoing off the chamber walls, he stood. "My lord, can there be any doubt that you have our allegiance in this? Ever have we been loyal to the crown, and if this is what Remalia requires of us, then we will gladly pay her due."

King Javorek smiled, and for a few moments, gone was the king of Remalia, leaving only a proud father.

"Yes, Father," Andric added as he stood, joining Stephir in solidarity.

Stephir cringed at Andric's breach of etiquette. He shouldn't have called him father in this setting.

"Speak what you would ask of us, and it's yours. We are yours." Andric glanced at his brother, and Stephir realized the younger prince was unsure of what he was required to do but wanted to show his support, nonetheless. He supposed the error could be forgiven, and Stephir was proud of him for speaking up when no one expected it of him.

King Jevorak raised an eyebrow at the sound of Andric's voice, but he warmly clapped both of his sons on their shoulders. "Every father should be so blessed as I have been." He squeezed their shoulders and the three retook their seats. The king looked expectantly at the seated nobles in the chamber.

Unsurprisingly, Baron Marstoff shot to his feet. "Your Highness, all that I have is at your disposal! All I ask is that we exact justice on the barbaric Kushaani savages," he said, practically spitting the last word as he leaned forward and pounded his fist on the table. "We will grind them under our fists!"

The baron seemed about to go on, but Archduchess Tra'en of the Western Marches rose gracefully from her seat. The baron knew better than to continue and bowed stiffly before sitting. Her words were sober and clear, regardless of the slight drawl of her accent setting her apart from the rest of the nobles. "My king, though our lands are far from here if you require us to make the journey, we will sail at once."

Unlike Barron Marstoff, support from the archduchess was somewhat unexpected since hers were the only other lands in Remalia that could readily be reached by slavers and she needed all her troops to protect her border. Perhaps she was counting on the king to tell her as much, allowing her to appear supportive with little chance of having to do more than continue protecting her own lands.

Quietly, Stephir's great-uncle, Grand Prince Emric Laconeus, came to his feet. Although his son, Archduke Irris de'Venneshen, was one of the most powerful nobles in the kingdom and deeply loyal to the crown, unrest in the Eastern Reaches made leaving Steadleigh impossible. He had designated his father to be his representative at the war council. Emric's face was unreadable, but his eyes were thoughtful and intently focused on his king. "King Jevorak, none of us like the prospect of war," he said, garnering a low growl from Baron Marstoff at his side.

Stephir's heart skipped a beat, knowing many would follow the grand prince's advice on many matters. He thought his father had already obtained the archduke's agreement, but this didn't sound like a good start. Emric was the grandfather of Stephir's second cousin and closest friend, Freydon de'Venneshen. Stephir tried not to imagine what might happen to their friendship if Frey's father opposed the king.

The grand prince continued in a measured tone. "We must weigh the good and evil that comes with such a cause. Do we want to see more innocent blood of our sons and daughters spilled?"

Is he playing for a stronger hand? Stephir wondered, trying to guess Emric's motives.

"There is never any question of our loyalty to you, great King. If one of us has been wronged, all of us have been wronged." The grand prince paused, looking around the room at the other nobles. "Ever has the Kingdom of Remalia stood united against her enemies." That was not exactly true, but no one was going to argue history with him at such a time. "My son, Archduke de'Venneshen assures Your Majesty that you have the Eastern Reaches' men and coffers, as you need them, my King."

Stephir breathed a muted sigh of relief.

One by one, the others in the room stood and voiced their support until only Duke Garamond remained. Stephir hadn't expected any of the others to outright balk, but he had expected far more questioning and discussion. Now he caught himself holding his breath as he waited for the Lord of Rookstone to speak. There was no love lost between Garamond and the king. His father had given the duke the honor of playing the part of King Hamoth in this year's reenactment of Hamoth's Charge in hopes of at least softening the man's opposition, but Stephir doubted the gesture would have much of an effect.

The broad-shouldered duke slowly slid his guarded gaze around the room at the nobles, almost imperceptibly shaking his head. Then, without rising, he turned to the king. "Your words are fairly spoken, my lord."

Andric and Stephir were the only people in Remalia allowed to use the familiar honorific with the king. The duke's usage was an intentional slight, but one that Stephir knew his father would overlook under the circumstances. No need to make things harder by getting upset over a lack of manners.

Duke Garamond paused, perhaps to build tension, or to choose his words carefully. "I am certainly not one to tell my noble peers how to conduct their own affairs."

That was a lie. Garamond bullied, bribed, and schemed to get his way wherever he could get away with it. He was a true Teraithian if ever there was one. Marchioness Miarsten grunted under her breath, revealing her feelings regarding the duke's statement. Stephir was worried Garamond's temper would ignite, but instead, he continued as if he had not heard anything.

"I am a peaceful man and abhor the thought of war." The duke opened his mouth as if to continue, then closed it again. After taking a deep breath, he tried again but seemed unable to speak.

A heavy, almost crushing weight filled the room and Stephir's vision momentarily blurred. He tried to gasp for breath, but it was as if the air had congealed. He desperately fought to draw a single, agonizingly slow breath. His ears filled with a terrible vibrating, though he could hear nothing. He shook his head, and when it cleared, Garamond was already speaking again.

"... required, then you'll have what support you need from me." The duke slumped in his seat, exhaustion etched on his face as if he had exerted himself beyond his strength.

What had just happened? Stephir glanced at the high consul, wondering if the priestess had somehow dispositioned those assembled, though it was hard to imagine anyone influencing so many minds at once. The high consul appeared as confused as Stephir, her eyes narrowed as if she was attempting to ascertain the thoughts of those in the room when she should have been overjoyed at their success. Had she felt that same oppressive presence?

The Divinarim were strictly charged with ensuring no benefactions were used in the royal family's presence without their express consent, so it seemed unlikely. Besides, the feeling had been unlike any dispositioning Stephir ever experienced. The prince tried to read the faces in the room for any sign of concern mirroring his own, or at least some reaction to the miracle of a unanimous resolution. The nobles could not reach unanimous agreement on the color of the sky, let alone a declaration of war, and without so much as a question. Stephir's reservations overshadowed what should have been gratification at the apparent show of solidarity. He studied his father, but the king's face was inscrutable. Andric also appeared to be lost in somber contemplation.

Stephir expected his father to offer High General Kuymon and High Consul Penrossart an opportunity to speak, but Jevorak once again rose. The king's voice was uncharacteristically subdued. "Lords and Ladies of Remalia, for your words, and certainly for your sustainment of our purpose, I thank you all. Tonight, attend to your Preparations services. Tomorrow, we will celebrate victories past and begin our plans for victories yet to come. May the gods drive our enemies before us as in times before. May they prosper our way. Until that day, go in peace, yet with firm resolution to our duties."

The nobles bowed their heads as the king left the council chamber, followed by his two sons. King Jevorak walked briskly, silence enveloping him like a cloak, brooking no interruption. Stephir, Andric, and their guards pushed themselves to keep pace. Stephir shot Andric a questioning glance, who answered with a slight shrug. The king should have been elated with the outcome. Did he perhaps know something he was not sharing with them? Stephir wanted to ask but thought better of it.

As they approached the corridor leading to the king's private quarters, Jevorak finally spoke without slowing or looking back at his sons. "I will see you at the services tonight."

Andric and Stephir stopped in their tracks and watched Jevorak turn the corner, surrounded by four Divinarim, leaving the brothers standing with the remaining guards in baffled silence. Stephir considered pursuing his father but sensed they both needed time to grapple with their thoughts. There would be plenty of time for discussions after the evening devotions. He continued toward his own rooms with Andric following at his side.

"You missed our devotions," Stephir observed for lack of anything better to say.

A cloud of guilt passed over Andric's face. "It was a busy day," was the only explanation his brother offered. It annoyed Stephir that his brother had been out enjoying the day, free of the cares that occupied Stephir's every waking moment.

"Why was father... well, you know...?" His brother stopped, apparently unable to put into words any better than Stephir could the confusion over their father's reaction to the war council. "Things couldn't have gone any better if the gods themselves had commanded it."

Stephir nodded but kept his thoughts to himself.

"You don't seem particularly happy either. What am I missing here?" Andric asked with confused impatience.

Stephir glanced at the guards. He could not very well voice his reservations in the open. "No, you're right. It was a miracle."

"That's not what I meant, but since you brought it up, you felt it too, right? It was like nothing I've ever felt before."

Stephir was relieved to know that he was not the only one who had been affected by whatever *it* was.

"Then you don't know what it was?" Stephir asked. Andric had always been the more spiritually sensitive of the two of them, though Stephir wished his brother would stop keeping one toe in each faith and devote himself wholeheartedly to the Holy Couple. Remalia's law allowing the worship of all of the gods was meant to foster a peaceful society, not be a pattern for personal living. Andric stopped abruptly and turned to the Divinarim.

Andric stopped abruptly and faced the Divinarim. "That was Teraithia's divinessence tonight, wasn't it?"

Stephir was startled at Andric's accusation but was equally eager to hear their answer. The holy knights were highly adept at preventing any benefactions from being used against the royal family. If a threat had been detected, they would have acted immediately to stop it.

"I swear, Your Highness, no one in that room was channeling divinessence," one said emphatically.

"But it *was* Teraithia's power," Andric pressed.

The knight glanced uncomfortably at his companions before speaking. "It... it felt that way, m'lord."

"Do you know what it was?" Andric asked.

The holy knight said nothing and shifted his gaze uncomfortably to the other Divinarim, who also remained silent. Getting no answer, Stephir started again toward his chambers where Ilyanara and his children were getting ready to attend the devotions at the Grand Temple of the Divine Couple. He had expected the war council to take much longer and was looking forward to spending a few unexpected moments with them. They might be some of his last for a long time.

"Well, at least we will soon be putting Kushaan in its place," Andric said, changing the subject as he matched Stephir's pace.

"That's certainly the plan," Stephir said with more uncertainty in voice than he had intended.

"What do you mean? The Kushaani don't stand a chance against the combined might of Remalia!" When Stephir didn't immediately agree, Andric pressed him. "You can't possibly believe they will be able to stop us."

"War never goes as you expect it to, Andric. If we were to fight the Kushaani on an open field, we'd come out the victor with few losses. But the Kushaani aren't liable to fight us in the open. They know their countryside, and they'll have plenty of time to prepare for us."

Andric smiled, though Stephir noticed it failed to reach his brother's sky-blue eyes. "I guess we'll see soon enough."

When they reached the doors to Stephir's rooms, the crown prince gave his younger brother a firm pat on the shoulder and forced a smile. "We had better see you at the temple first, or Father might ensure that the only thing you ever see again is Akraharr's dark realm."

Andric laughed sheepishly. "I'll be there," he said with a short wave as he continued toward his chambers. Stephir's smile faded and he hung his head, trying to collect himself before he entered his rooms. He wanted to be the loving husband and father the Holy Couple taught that he should be. With so much weighing on him lately, he often fell woefully short of that ideal.

Help me, Holy Mother and Father, Stephir prayed silently outside his door. *Give me the strength to be what my family and my people need.* So many expectations, so many duties. It felt like a mountain threatening to crush him. He wished he could be as carefree as Andric. He could wish all day, but he knew no relief would come. His only choice was to forge ahead. With a supreme effort, he lifted his head and forced a smile back onto his face, then entered his chambers.

CHAPTER V
STEPHIR

S tephir sat erect in the front row of the audience hall of the Grand Temple of the Congregation of Servants. Of the eight buildings that occupied the Mount of the Gods, the Grand Temple was second in size and grandeur only to the royal palace. But where the palace's immense space was filled with many rooms and corridors, works of art, and artifacts of history, nearly the entire temple consisted of the cavernous audience hall. Although the adornments were sparse, in keeping with the tenets of the Servari faith, the sheer enormity of the vast hall was itself awe-inspiring. Tonight, it held thousands of worshippers, more than Stephir had ever seen gathered in the Grand Temple.

Despite Patriarch Mielka's objections to having Teraithia's holy knights in the Holy Couple's temple, the high priest relented when the king suggested that perhaps the royal family should attend one of the other temple's Preparation Day ceremonies. Upon the royals' arrival with their contingent of Divinarim, it was clear many of the Holy Couple's faithful followers were uncomfortable with the holy knights' presence. A murmur of whispers and scowls irritated Stephir. He wondered if the people had forgotten the royal family's guards always attended them in the temple. The unusual degree of religious fervor among the populace was leading to more and more animosity everywhere one looked. Perhaps the war would give them something else to worry about.

Stephir was in his usual position on the king's right hand, and Andric was seated on the other side. Despite the king's somewhat improved mood, their father still had said only a few words to Andric. His brother had some atoning to do for his earlier absence. Princess Ilyanara sat two seats from Stephir's right with their son Jenden on her lap and their daughter Shannyth between them, making the entire royal family present. His wife had wanted to leave Prince Jenden at the palace, but Stephir had insisted their two-and-a-half-year-old son was old enough to attend the service despite the late hour. She had expressed her usual concerns that the boy would make too much noise for the service.

Having spent her whole life in Calavia before marrying Stephir, she was still terribly uncomfortable with noisy children at any ceremonies, especially religious ones. Stephir had tried to assure her many times that the Holy Couple wanted families to worship together, including noisy small children. Before coming to the services this evening, he hadn't felt like attempting gentle persuasion and had simply demanded it. Ilyanara's silent stiffness underscored how she felt about his behavior.

Their marriage had certainly been one of political benefit, though Stephir believed it had grown into something much more. Ilyanara was breathtakingly beautiful, but when he had first met her at a festival in Calavia, she was the daughter of one of the lesser merchant houses. Stephir's attention to her had been noted, and a bidding war to adopt her ensued among the navarchos, the rulers of the great merchant houses of the Calavian Consortium. Stephir never knew how much was paid to her house for the right to adopt her, but the investment had paid off.

Stephir's father had initially objected to the marriage, unwilling to look past her lowly birth. But the reality that her adoptive family was one of the most powerful houses in Calavia, and that Navarchos Gwendolyn Stenbar would be an important ally in maintaining open and fair trade relations with the Consortium, Jevorak finally relented. Stephir liked to imagine his father had also considered Stephir's happiness but suspected it was at best an afterthought.

Stephir fixed his eyes on the illuminated white-marble altar atop the raised dais a few paces from where he sat. He and Ilyanara had knelt there to be married just days after his sixteenth birthday. It had all been so romantic, but then the realities of being married had begun to intrude on the fairytale. At first, Ilyanara accommodated Stephir's every wish, no doubt living her own version of the fairytale. But when Shannyth was born, his wife began to grow into her station as a princess and someday Queen of Remalia. She showed an inner strength as she voiced her opinions and at times insisted on doing things as she saw fit.

Despite the growing pains of adjusting to their developing relationship, Stephir had grown to respect and even admire her. She was not always exactly what he had imagined or even hoped for, but in many ways, she was much more. He ventured a glance across the divide between them, and he again marveled at Ilyanara's unquestionable beauty. The elegantly smooth white silk gown was a striking contrast to her olive skin and green eyes. Her glossy black hair fell in loose curls around her shoulders, framing a face that had outgrown the features of a carefree young girl into those of an empowered and noble woman. Despite the painful loss of two unborn children in the nine years between the births of Shannyth and Jenden, Ilyanara had embraced motherhood gracefully, and with it gained a greater measure of supernal refinement. Stephir believed she would make an extraordinary queen. But at the moment he was troubled by the hardness of her expression and the determined set of her shoulders.

He tried to focus on the dais where the high priest and high priestess of the Congregation of Servants sat, waiting to begin the Preparations Day evening service. Although they were nearly a decade older than his father, they were still considered young to be the heads of the Church. But they were so kindly and good, there were few who didn't love them, and none who did not respect them. Stephir admired how they openly and unabashedly expressed their love for one another. He could not imagine anyone more qualified to represent the Holy Couple, and he basked in Yonvaar and Kerail's divinessence that radiated from the enlightened paragons of Servarism.

What would Patriarch Mielka do in my place? Stephir wondered, but he already knew the answer. He considered whispering an apology to his wife, but Patriarch and Matriarch Mielka stood to begin the services and the opportunity slipped away.

Stephir was close enough to hear as Patriarch Mielka whisper to his wife, "Would you like to offer the invocations, or shall I?"

She smiled and patted him warmly on the hand in reply, as she usually did, signaling that she declined his offer. Stephir had seen her surprise the patriarch from time to time and accept the invitation. Stephir understood that public speaking was Patriarch Mielka's strength, not hers. However, he always offered, and Stephir could not help comparing his behavior toward Ilyanara to the gentleness of the high priest.

Do they ever argue behind closed doors? Stephir wondered.

Patriarch Mielka bowed his head, and thousands of heads followed suit, clasping hands with those around them in unity before the Holy Parents. Stephir enclosed Shannyth's hand with his right hand and his father's hand in the left. Ilyanara stood Jenden on the bench between Shannyth and herself, each holding one of Jenden's little hands. The young prince swung his hands playfully, causing his sister to quietly giggle and try to settle him down. It was as close to an ideal picture of the royal family as Stephir could imagine. He wondered what people would think if they knew how things really were.

The high priest's strong, melodic voice permeated the vast hall. "Holy Yonvaar and Kerail, we your children and servants in this great Kingdom of Remalia do raise our hands before you with nothing to offer but our hearts and minds..."

Stephir glanced at Jenden, amused by his son's head bobbing up and down, bowing over and over with exaggerated movements, making a game of what was otherwise an act of reverence. He resisted the temptation to put his hand on the boy's head to hold it still.

"... your servant Jevorak Laconeus, King of Remalia, Defender of the Realm. Grant him continued wisdom and strength to rule this kingdom in justice and mercy..."

Stephir's mind wandered, imagining all the things in his life that were about to change: separation from his family, the inconveniences of life in the field, and perhaps worst of all, commanding men to fight and die. His father was finally getting the war he wanted, and Andric had only romantic ideas of what the road ahead held for him, though his younger brother would undoubtedly miss the comforts of palace life. Stephir felt he was the only one of the royal family being called on to sacrifice for this war. The thought felt selfish somehow, even though it had the taste of truth.

He was abruptly pulled back to the present. Something was wrong.

The high priest had stopped his prayer mid-sentence.

Stephir hadn't been paying enough attention to understand what was happening. He lifted his eyes and searched the congregants for signs of trouble, but they held their heads down respectfully. Andric glanced up as well and met Stephir's eyes. He looked as if he was about to whisper some witty remark, but Stephir silenced him with a stern look.

The high priest's voice resumed, resonating throughout the Grand Temple with a strange echo. "*Infiant so 'ulm Nii artuozak.*"

The brothers' attention snapped to Patriarch Mielka. Stephir was certain he had never heard those words before, but they somehow felt familiar. As he tried to replay them in his mind, emotions rose in his chest as the Holy Couple's divinessence washed through him. Love and gratitude became almost overwhelming. His breath caught in his throat as he tried to stave off the tears welling in his eyes. He could almost recall Mielka's words, but he somehow felt he grasped their meaning. *Our lost children will soon return home.*

If that was the correct translation of the words, they still made no sense. And yet, he longed for them to be true. He blinked back the tears and watched as the high priest, apparently finished with the invocation, took his wife by the hand and returned to their seats. Other heads slowly came up as the congregation began to realize the prayer was over. Hushed murmuring spread through the temple like a light breeze through tall grass. Stephir sensed with relief that he was not the only one confused. He stole furtive glances at his father and Ilyanara, but neither gave any sign anything was out of the ordinary.

A procession of white-robed clerics, alternating priests and priestesses, sang a hymn of supplication for deliverance as they slowly made their way up the center aisle toward the altar dais where the Mielkas sat. An elderly priestess approached the altar and lit two urns filled with incense. Within moments, thick white smoke wafted toward the vaulted ceilings, symbolically carrying the assembly's prayer to Yonvaar and Kerail in their holy realm beyond.

The Preparations Day service progressed as usual. Stephir tried not to be distracted by the hunger from a long day of fasting and the day's strange events. A group of priestesses sang a hauntingly beautiful song about the losses suffered in war as wives lost husbands and mothers lost sons and daughters, praying for Kerail to comfort all and Yonvaar to protect those who continued to fight so there might be no more suffering. It was a familiar song from Preparation Day services in the past, but this year it took on a whole new meaning. Stephir's heart was moved, wondering if Ilyanara and Shannyth would have to experience the loss they sang of. Most in attendance had no idea that as of an hour ago, the kingdom was officially at war.

If they knew, how many would feel as I do?

Patriarch Mielka stood to give the devotional. It generally followed the themes pronounced in the invocation, and Stephir was soon lost again in his thoughts until something in the priest's words brought his attention back to the ceremony.

"... isn't only in the world of men, but rages in the realms beyond creation. Peace will never be seen again in our world until that great war of the gods, which began before the world was even a spark in the heavens, is finished, and Yonvaar and Kerail, side by side, reign personally among the inhabitants of Baon in the final unity under one true Faith!"

Stephir shifted uncomfortably at the rise in Patriarch Mielka's voice, now echoing throughout the vast assembly hall. This was behavior he would have expected from one of the crazy zealot street criers, not from the loving high priest.

"We will stand within the protection of their unmatchable power or perish as dry stalks consumed by an unquenchable fire! The day of that choosing is upon us all." Suddenly, the characteristic love and deep emotion returned to the high priest's voice and countenance. "Choose well, my brothers and sisters. Serve one another in faith and lift those who have fallen or are downtrodden. Go in the love of our Holy Parents."

Stephir was again filled with a deep sense of the love and devotion of which the priest had spoken. He sat in his seat long after the services ended and others had risen, vaguely aware of the hushed voices around him. He longed to sit in solitude without having to stand and face the reality of the impending war.

Ilyanara broke the trance by calling his name, pulling him into the present. He put on a smile for Shannyth as he stood and retrieved Jenden from Ilyanara's arms, then offered his hand to help his wife rise. He was grateful she took his hand with a smile and wondered if she too had experienced some of what he was feeling. Perhaps an apology wouldn't be necessary after all.

The crown prince held his young son in one arm as he faced the crowd of nobles and prominent citizens of Remalia. Those seated immediately behind the royal family commented politely on how well-behaved his children had been throughout the services or how radiant he and his wife looked. Stephir did his best to patiently thank each of them for their kind words, but all he wanted was to return to his quarters and find the quiet solitude he was craving.

A hand on his shoulder turned his attention to Patriarch Mielka, who had descended from the dais to give his personal greeting to the royal family, as was custom. Stephir's father offered his thanks to Matriarch Mielka for the beautiful service. The high priestess smiled warmly and thanked the king for his kind words. With the courtesies having been observed, the king called Shannyth to his side and turned his attention to the nobles standing nearby, waiting for a moment of personal attention from the king. Shannyth would inherit the crown upon Stephir's passing, and he and his father both knew how critical it was to include her in building and strengthening the relationships and alliances that would ensure the Laconeus line would continue to rule Remalia. Archduchess Tra'en was the first to receive Jevorak's attention; a small sign of her importance to the kingdom. The distant

Western Marches were some of Remalia's wealthiest lands, and without her support, the campaign against Kushaan would have to be significantly scaled back.

"Patriarch and Matriarch Mielka," Stephir said, bowing as well as he could with Jenden in his arms.

"Your Highness," the couple replied respectfully in unison, returning a deep bow.

Stephir took Matriarch Mielka by the hand and kissed it reverently while her husband greeted the prince. "It's good to see you, Prince Stephir. It has been a while since we have spoken." The engaging sincerity of the priest's manner reminded Stephir why he had such a fondness for the man. He was like the ideal uncle he wished his actual uncles could be. He used to wonder how much of their influence was attributable to having reached enlightenment, but eventually decided it didn't really matter. Either way, he truly desired to emulate their holy example.

"And you too, Prince Jenden," added Matriarch Mielka with a motherly tone, extending her hand to the young boy who tightly held to his father's shoulder. The child glanced from the extended hand to his father questioningly. Stephir nodded at him, and the boy released his grasp and grabbed the high priestess's offered hand. He gave it an exaggerated shake and Matriarch Mielka laughed in delight. "What a young lord you are, my prince."

Stephir thought he saw a slight expression of puzzlement cross Ilyanara's face, but it was gone before he could be certain.

"Just like his father, I would imagine," Patriarch Mielka added with a sly smile and a wink. With their faces next to each other it was clear where Jenden had inherited his sandy-colored hair and square jaw, but Stephir was certain the high priest hinted at some of Stephir's less flattering moments from when he was younger.

Before becoming the Servari high priest, Patriarch Mielka had been one of the prince's tutors in theology. A memory surfaced of when Stephir was thirteen and didn't want to have their weekly lesson. He had shoved a stick into the lock and broke it off, preventing Mielka from unlocking the temple room for their lesson. Hilenne had sworn not to tell Father Mielka if Stephir did it, but with a stern look from the priest Hilenne had confessed all. The reprimand from Jevorak had been quite stern.

Stephir smiled, graciously accepting the compliment. "Oh, hopefully much better than his father." As if in defiance, Jenden squirmed to get down from Stephir's arms. When unsuccessful, he squawked in frustration.

"Nope, exactly like his father," Patriarch Mielka said with feigned disappointment. The three of them laughed, and even Ilyanara smiled despite her obvious embarrassment at her son's outburst.

"I'm afraid it's well past his bedtime," she said apologetically, reaching for Jenden.

"Of course," Matriarch Mielka answered. "Brennon gets this way when it's past his bedtime as well," she said, patting her husband on the arm as he nodded, a look of feigned guilt on his face.

"Thank you, Mother," Ilyanara said with a polite tone that told Stephir she didn't feel comforted. Turning to Stephir with a look that was almost entirely polite, she asked, "Shall I take him home now?"

"Yes, that would be fine," Stephir said. He pursed his lips together, realizing he sounded like he was granting permission instead of sounding grateful. He tried to apologize with his eyes, but she didn't look at him. He would have to make it up to her when they returned to the palace. Stephir tried to make up for it a little by saying, "Leave Shannyth with me. I'll make sure she gets home safely. I might be late, so please don't feel you need to wait up for me."

Ilyanara replied with a cold smile and bowed.

Ouch! Stephir cringed inwardly. Anyone who was not close to the royal couple wouldn't have understood that the gesture was as close to a slap in the face as Ilyanara was ever likely to give him in public. Stephir had insisted from the beginning of their marriage that he wanted them to be equals. It had taken her some time to grow comfortable with the idea, and Stephir had not always stuck to his side of the bargain. Tonight was turning out to be one of those occasions.

Ilyanara set Jenden down, keeping a firm grip on his hand, and curtsied to the high priest and priestess. It was a gesture only a Servari would make to the leaders of the Church. Ilyanara had grown up without any devotion to a particular deity, as was the norm in Calavia. When she learned that Stephir's mother had worshipped the Holy Couple, Ilyanara adopted the Servari religion as her own, first out of duty, but increasingly out of sincere devotion.

"Good night, Matriarch and Patriarch Mielka. I'm sure we'll see you again over the next couple of days." Matriarch Mielka must have sensed something was upsetting the princess, and she broke protocol by stepping forward and enfolding Ilyanara in a warm embrace.

Someone behind Stephir sucked in a quick breath. He could do nothing but stand there awkwardly as the high priestess continued hugging his wife. He heard the priestess whisper, "Kerail loves you, child."

Ilyanara's stiff shoulders relaxed and she released Jenden's hand to fully return the loving gesture. Prince Jenden tried to make a break for it, but Andric caught him and swept him up, pinning him in the air. The young prince squealed again, this time in delight. At last, Matriarch Mielka released the princess and Stephir thought he saw a hint of tears in his wife's eyes. A pang of guilt flashed through him as Ilyanara retrieved Jenden from Andric.

"Would you care to use our private entrance to leave the temple?" Matriarch Mielka offered kindly. "No need to fight your way through the crowd to the front doors." With a complement of Divinarim to clear the way for her, Ilyanara would have had little difficulty going anywhere, crowds or not. But the high priestess's protective care would ensure the princess wouldn't have to endure any further pressures tonight.

"Yes, thank you," Ilyanara said in a thin voice. With Jenden in tow and flanked by four guards, Ilyanara followed the high priestess around the dais and through a side door to her quarters.

"She's a wonderful woman," Patriarch Mielka observed casually.

Stephir was not sure whether he meant Ilyanara or Matriarch Mielka. "Yes, she is," Stephir responded, playing it safe with the continued ambiguity. He wanted to change subjects before Patriarch Mielka could go any further down that path. "May I ask you a question, Your Grace?"

"Of course, Your Highness."

To Stephir's surprise, Matriarch Mielka came back through the door, much too quickly to have taken Ilyanara out of the temple. *Is something wrong?* Stephir worried, but the matriarch's gentle smile put any concern out of his mind. She probably had another priestess escort his wife. As the high priestess returned to stand alongside her husband, Stephir's mind tried to formulate the questions tumbling in his head all evening, but he could not quite find the right words.

"I see that look in your eye, Stephir," the patriarch noted, turning serious and leaning closer. "It was the same look you had as a young man when you wished to challenge me on a point of doctrine but weren't certain of the propriety. So, what is it now?"

Stephir would still have hesitated in his younger days under the same circumstances. The intervening years as crown prince had driven that tendency from him. "What did you say at the end of the invocation?" The brief hint of shock on Patriarch Mielka's face gave the prince a moment's pause, then he pushed on. "At first I thought I had simply not heard clearly, but throughout the service, I could not escape the feeling my hearing was not at fault. I gather there is something... out of the ordinary?"

Matriarch Mielka shifted her gaze from Stephir to her husband, who had dropped his eyes to the floor. After a moment, Patriarch Mielka lifted his head and looked intently into the prince's eyes. "I wish I could tell you exactly what was spoken through me." Stephir thought it was a peculiar way of describing the event, especially for one as down to earth as the high priest, who was not given to turning even unusual events into something mystical. "The truth is, I simply don't know. I am certain of its source, however, because I have had similar experiences in the past." He paused for emphasis, glancing at his wife, either for support or confirmation.

"It was certainly different from the divine presence that manifested earlier this evening," the high priestess said thoughtfully.

Patriarch Mielka gave her an odd look Stephir could not guess the meaning of, then said flatly, "Yes, that one was not the Holy Couple's influence."

Stephir realized they must be referring to the oppressive presence that manifested during the war council. *But they weren't even there!* his mind protested. "You felt that here at the temple?" Stephir asked with surprise.

"I dare say it was felt by many here on the Mount, maybe even out in the city."

"Do you know what it was?"

"You would perhaps need to ask Archseraph Charin to be certain, but my best guess is that Teraithia extended her hand in a way I have never witnessed before."

"I thought you told me that the gods do not directly intervene in the affairs of men. You said that it would destroy the world."

"That is a simplistic version of the truth.; of two truths actually. First, if any of the gods were to appear in our world while it is not yet fully aligned with their divine essence, Baon would burn—literally disintegrate under the intensity of their glory. In a much smaller way, this is what happens when a creature from the realms of the gods is summoned to our world."

"Like what happened at the Teraithian temple that was attacked last night," Stephir said, watching Patriarch Mielka's reaction for any hint the high priest might know something about who was behind the attack.

"Exactly. Which is why there have been no theophanies since the Great Cataclysm over eight millennia ago." The cleric seemed to completely ignore the double meaning of Stephir's question as he continued. "But the second truth is much more complicated. The gods are their own source of the divinessence accessed by those who adhere to each god's respective doctrine. The greatest aspiration of each god is to inspire so much devotion to their doctrine among the people of Baon that the world becomes sufficiently aligned with that deity's divine essence to allow the god or goddess to personally manifest here without destroying the world."

"You're talking about the end of the war of the gods," Stephir said. "When only one god remains."

"Yes, that is the central theme of the Ultideic Prophecies. But here is the complicated truth to which you alluded: the power that accrues to the gods from our devotion depends upon the free exercise of our will to give such devotion. Therefore, the more directly the gods involve themselves in the affairs of the world, the more it weakens our capacity to freely choose such devotion; it could destroy it if they interfere too much. I can't imagine the incredibly complex calculations the gods must perform to weigh the benefits to their designs against the destructive influence on our freely given devotion that their interventions will cause. For this reason, their interactions are almost always subtle, a small nudge here and whisper of an idea there, leaving as much room for individual and collective agency as possible."

"Well, there was nothing subtle about Teraithia's hand earlier tonight," Stephir observed darkly. "But what about the words you spoke in the invocation? Is that not the Holy Couple intervening in the affairs of the world?'

Patriarch Mielka gave a slight smile. "It's a very insightful question, and one to which I do not yet have a perfect answer. However, I might have a guess about it if you promise to take it as such," he said with a twinkle of excitement in his eyes. "Can you remember the words?" he asked the prince.

Stephir shook his head no.

The high priest looked at his wife, who closed her eyes in concentration. "*Infiant so 'ulm Nii artuozak,*" she recalled quietly.

"Verine has an incredible ear for sounds. She can hear a tune once and know it as if she's heard it her whole life. Or, in this case, the words you heard tonight. A marvelous gift." Matriarch Mielka smiled softly. "Now, if I remember correctly," Patriarch Mielka continued, "there is a passage in the Canticle of Ulmen, which is purportedly taken from an ancient text long lost to the world. It is perhaps the oldest of the Ultideic Prophesies. It recounts the first time one of the gods personally manifested on our world. There are many versions that I'm aware of, and all remarkably consistent in the basic story of that theophany, except, of course, the detail of which god it was. I personally believe it was Yonvaar, but Grandmaster Riddard will surely tell you it was Vai Doroth.

"Now, the name Ulmen itself may be a clue. It comes from either the root word *yulma*, meaning *chosen warrior*, or from *hulme-en*, meaning *divinely appointed messenger*. As far as I'm aware these words first appear in that text, which was later translated by the great high priest Gilrath-Han. That is the version most widely accepted today." Matriarch Mielka cleared her throat gently, and Patriarch Mielka caught the hint, hurrying toward his point.

"It's believed by some that the original text was written in the language spoken in the realms of our Holy Parents, including the name Ulmen itself, which may be a name-title for a valiant spirit chosen from among the dead to serve the gods as an archangel. If that's true, then perhaps what we heard today was a revelation in that tongue spoken in the realms of the gods." The high priest finished with some excitement.

Having captured their full attention, he pressed on. "There is something else. There's a part of that holy text I have never understood and admittedly still don't. It's supposedly a prophecy about the gods and all Creation returning to the beginning or beginning again; almost like a rebirth. There are horrible depictions of universal war, suns and moons and stars dying, and even the end of the gods themselves. Many believe it is merely allegorical.

"One passage of the Canticle I always found especially curious says, 'In the dusk of that day when the *hulme-en* walk toward the beginning, and are come *Nii*,' spelled N-i-i, which I had always thought was an error in translation, but perhaps it wasn't, 'art thou, the Will, made manifest.' I know that it's quoted out of context but trust me that it doesn't make any more sense in context. I think it may have something to do with some chosen one, or perhaps the children who walk toward the beginning, being a messenger or a warrior. I wish I knew what *Nii* means, but I don't."

"Do the words, *'Our lost children will soon return home'* mean anything to you?" Stephir asked. Patriarch Mielka considered Stephir intently for a moment before closing his eyes. Stephir knew from experience this meant the high priest was searching his memory or seeking inspiration from the Holy Couple; or perhaps both.

Before he answered, Matriarch Mielka answered. "There is an obscure Servari poem called The Lay of the Departed. Most versions have the line, 'And the dead shall be yielded from their grave.' However, one version I recall had the line as, 'The children lost before shall return as if from the tomb.'"

As the words left the priestess's lips, Stephir felt a thrill run down his spine.

"I have the strong impression that there is a touch of prophecy at work," Patriarch Mielka said in a reverent tone, "and that some part of it is close to being fulfilled. For whatever reason, the Holy Couple has given voice to some aspect of that through us tonight."

The priest seemed to hesitate. Stephir had respected and even admired the patriarch for many years, but he had never known him to be hesitant. He eagerly awaited to hear what the cleric would say.

Finally, the patriarch looked around, leaned forward, and spoke in a hushed voice. "Perhaps *you* are the Voice from the Stones of which the prophecies speak, my lord. I know you do not wish to go to war and have said as much to your father. Yours is not the voice of thunder or of trumpets, but it pierces to the quick. No monarch of Remalia has been more devoted to the Holy Couple than you are. Yours could be the voice rolling from the mountains to finally bring peace to the world."

The high priest suddenly straightened, and Stephir felt a discord in the air as two Teraithian holy knights escorted Shannyth back to him. "My lord," she said formally, "Grandfather requests you attend him as soon as you are able."

Stephir cast his eyes around the nearly empty temple and realized the king and many others had already left the audience hall. It was strange that his father hadn't said anything before leaving. He decided he had best go find him. No doubt there were more difficult discussions ahead of the prince tonight.

"We will talk again soon, Your Highness," Patriarch Mielka said, smiling and patting Stephir's arm.

"It was wonderful to see you and your family as always," Matriarch Mielka said, bowing to the royals.

Stephir bid them both a good night and made his way out of the temple to return to the palace. He walked at a measured pace to accommodate Shannyth's shorter strides.

"Anything interesting happen while you were with your grandfather?" Stephir asked his daughter.

"Uncle Emeric seemed annoyed with one of the nobles, Earl Chennel I think, but I couldn't figure out exactly why. The earl turned red at some remark Uncle made about the earl sleeping with the empress of Kushaan, and then he stormed off." Stephir could guess what the insult was and understood why the earl would be upset. "Other than that, it was pretty boring, as usual."

They continued to chat as they walked, but Stephir's mind was only partly engaged in the conversation. He knew the war effort would be the only thing on his father's mind tonight, and he tried to focus on what lay ahead, but his thoughts kept revisiting Mielka's words.

The Voice from the Stones.

It seemed impossible that the ancient prophecies could include him. He shook his head, trying to anchor himself in reality. *You are the Crown Prince of*

Remalia. That should be more than enough for anyone. Leave the fantasies to Andric.

He nearly laughed at the thought of Andric being part of the prophecies. *He barely even showed up for the war council!* He wondered if his brother had been summoned by the king as well. Not that it made much difference either way. Stephir knew the burden of this war was going to be put squarely on his shoulders. At best, Andric would just be along for the ride.

Stephir forced himself to listen more attentively to Shannyth as they climbed the palace steps. He hoped it would fend off the apprehension that weighed him down more and more by the moment. He was going to miss these times with her while he was away. He needed to make the most of them when he had the opportunity. He wished he could go with her back to their rooms, but duty called. He kissed her forehead and sent her off with her guards.

He didn't dwell on the twinge of jealousy over Ilyanara's time with their children. He quickened his pace as he headed toward the king's council chambers, trying not to be too discouraged at how long of a night he had ahead of him.

CHAPTER VI
ANDRIC

Andric woke in the dark hours of the morning to the gentle shaking of one of the servants. "I'm awake," Andric said, surprised to realize it was true. Two early mornings in a row, and he felt alive.

The prince silently vowed to the gods (except for Akraharr, who accepted no vows from mortals) that this would mark turning over a new leaf. Then he laughed derisively at himself. Now that Remalia was at war, he wondered if he would have many days of sleeping late, even if he wanted to. He doubted it, but that was a small price to pay for finally getting to be in a war. While growing up, he imagined countless times the glories that would be his, leading troops into victorious battle. At last, the chance to fight against the heathen Kushaani was here.

Master Ronnil knew Andric was to be awake early and had ordered everything to be ready for the prince's preparations. All entrants into Hamoth's Tourney had to register before dawn, another commemoration of Hamoth's Charge launched in the pre-dawn twilight more than four centuries ago. Andric would certainly have been granted an exception if he entered late, but he wanted to at least appear to abide by the same rules as everyone else.

Andric felt nauseous, though whether from not eating since yesterday's breakfast or his nerves about today's contests, he wasn't sure. *Both*, he decided. It would be cold this early in the morning, so Andric donned heavy winter clothes lined with silver fox fur, and set about the task of making himself the image of royalty. His newly tailored Charge Days clothes weren't well-suited for the cold, but they were the latest fashion and quite flattering on him. He had arranged for them to be waiting for him in his tent set up next to the tourney grounds—a welcome luxury for the royal family that allowed him to wear finer clothes than the other nobles participating in the Tourney.

Except, of course, Baron Arcroft. The baron always came to the Tourney in his finest clothes, then changed in the open, stripping to nothing for the eyes of the whole world. Arcroft may have been a fine specimen in his youth, but his bulk had gone soft, and his thick black hair grew in patches on his otherwise pale body, making a distasteful sight. Andric had to suffer seeing it only once, a few years earlier. It was a sight he fully intended to avoid today.

When Andric was satisfied he was suitable, he left his room and headed for the stables. His guards fell in behind him and smoothly matched the prince's quick pace. Andric held himself erect, wondering if he looked princely from the guards' perspectives.

The chill of pre-dawn morning wrapped around him, but he was dressed warmly enough that he could almost convince himself the cold didn't bother him. He looked up at the darkened sky, free of clouds on the crisp spring morning. The two moons, Fenthal and Silmal, looked as if they swam through a sea of stars. It was a sight Andric didn't see often, at least not this early in the morning.

It was not long before the prince was astride Wind, making his way past the temples, lit always by thousands of lamps, torches, candles, and the beaming beacon light atop the temple of the Holy Couple. Despite his best efforts, the sight of the fires sent a shiver across his body. Andric was eager to reach the tourney grounds, and the slow pace of his escort having to walk grated on him. It also gave him time to realize he was hungry, and the prospect of ending his fast in a couple of hours was small comfort. His stomach growled in agreement. When they arrived at the White Gate, his escort finally mounted their horses and they were on their way.

On any other day at this hour, the Grand Avenue would have been virtually empty, but today there were already crowds on foot, on horseback, or in carriages, all making their way out of the city for the Charge Day festivities. Many workers and soldiers slept in the fields near the pageantry grounds; there were too many things to be taken care of to waste time moving in and out of the city. At least everyone was moving in the same direction. With his guards around him, there were few obstructions to his progress and it was not long before he passed through Hightowers' Gate into the outer city.

The sky got lighter and Andric was worried he might not make it in time to arrive before dawn. He spurred Wind to a full gallop along Dunnigan's

Highroad, the Divinarim matching his speed in a thunderous procession. He raced past the growing river of people who quickly moved out of the way at the sound of the galloping hooves of the prince's escort and the frequent shouts from his guards to move aside.

The sun crawled its way from behind the horizon in the west, and he pushed Wind as fast as she would go. *Racing the sun!* thought Andric to himself, taking pleasure in the exaggerated vision in his imagination of racing through the sky to beat the sun.

Dawn burst over the world as he covered the last paces to the Registrar's area. He knew he had technically missed the deadline, but he was too pleased with the dramatic fashion of his arrival and the smiling bows and enthusiastic greetings of the small crowd of tourney competitors milling around to worry about it. Andric and the Divinarim dismounted, their horses steaming and lathered. Andric handed the reins to one of the guards and proudly marched to the raised platform of the master registrar. The Laconeus Coat of Arms was posted on the platform and the royal colors of blue and white adorned the banisters, posts, and other furnishings. It was brilliant in the bright dawn light.

Andric declared himself confidently, trusting the master registrar wouldn't make a fuss about the late registration. "Prince Andric Laconeus, second son of Jevorak Laconeus, King of Remalia, humbly requests admission to Hamoth's Tournament."

"Of course, Your Highness," the master registrar answered smoothly. "For what contests do you present yourself?"

"Arms and jousting." He didn't stand any chance of winning either event, but he had been training hard and thought he might do well. Jousting was not his strongest event, but it would look worse if he didn't participate. The other contests included various horse-riding skills, archery, and grappling, none of which appealed to Andric.

The man marked his list, nodding. "Gods grace, Your Highness."

The rest of the royals weren't due to arrive for a little while, so Andric turned to find his friends. Marquis Freydon de'Venneshen, oldest son of Archduke Irris de'Venneshen and someday heir of the dukedom, stood amid a group of nobles and other hangers-on. Frey had won the sword fighting contest the last two years and was favored to win again this year. Add to that Frey's high station in the nobility, his familial ties to the crown, his close friendship with the crown prince, and a reputation for amorous adventures and extravagant parties all made him a luminary among his peers, and a favorite with the commoners.

The crowd parted as Andric approached. Despite his family home being in the great coastal city of Steadleigh in the Eastern Reaches, the de'Venneshens had ensured that Frey spent a good deal of time at court in Teris, bonding with his cousin and closest friend, Crown Prince Stephir. Frey had always treated Andric as a friend as well, which allowed him to get away with a degree of informality not shared by many others.

"Prince Andric!" Frey exclaimed with exaggerated enthusiasm. "I had dared to hope I might finish well today, but alas..."

"As if you ever had a chance!" Andric played along, hoping he pulled it off. Frey had a wicked sense of humor, which was not Andric's forte. At court, Andric had heard rumors that Frey did not bring his wife Myral and their children to Teris this year because he was tired of her complaining about his Sykorian habits. Andric decided to play on that rumor. "Too bad they haven't made whoring a contest yet—you'd be unbeatable." Andric was relieved to see everyone laugh. His father wouldn't have approved of the crass jest, but having everyone's approval mattered more to Andric at that moment.

"But I keep practicing in case they ever do!" Frey always managed to one-up everyone.

He wondered how Barak would deal with him. *Probably just ignore him,* thought Andric. That wasn't an option for Andric or even something he wanted to do. He liked Frey and looked up to him in many ways, though not the way he looked up to Stephir, who seemed nearly perfect. He had no hope of being as good at anything as Stephir (at least not by any measure that mattered), but Frey seemed within the realm of the possible. Frey was also a lot more fun. The contestants continued their banter, and Andric moved easily among them, enjoying himself.

Stephir did not participate in the tournaments. As crown prince, the risk of serious injury or death, as slight as it might be, outweighed any esteem he may have garnered by participating. Some of the nobles were privately critical of Stephir's lack of participation, claiming it was cowardice or weakness. Stephir knew of their opinions, but he never seemed to be troubled by them. He knew his strength was in governing, not soldiering, though he was more than capable with the blade. Stephir's absence allowed Andric to stand on his own rather than in Stephir's shadow for once.

It didn't take long before Andric realized from the veiled questions and comments that at least some of the other nobles knew more about last night's war council than they should have.

"Will your father and brother be able to join the festivities this year?"

"We're glad important matters didn't keep you away from the tourney."

"Is it safe to assume that tomorrow's grand Victory Day feast will still be held at the palace?"

"I wonder what next year's Charge Days will be like."

Andric was tempted to join in, pretending their questions meant nothing out of the ordinary, but dropping a few well-placed hints to suggest he knew everything. Instead, he kept the matter in confidence as his father had insisted. When Andric was tired of dodging the matter, he excused himself to prepare for the day's activities. Andric's squire, Jase Couvor, stood unobtrusively to the side with the other squires, waiting until their services were required.

Jase was Andric's cousin, the second son of his mother's twin sister. Upon the death of the queen, Jevorak had promised Andric's aunt she wouldn't be forgotten. She had called upon that promise two years ago and asked that Jase be given a position in Teris. Jase was two years younger than Andric, but he was a bright young man, if a bit shy. Jevorak appointed him to be Andric's squire. That, of course, required granting Andric's previous squire some other position, and the king bestowed a commission in the Remalian army. Andric was unhappy with the change at first, but it had worked out all right.

Andric liked Jase well enough, and he was a good squire. Being the son of a woman who looked just like their mother endowed Jase with a strong family resemblance to the two princes, and Andric sometimes wondered what it would have been like to grow up with another brother. Jase wouldn't have been Andric's first choice, though. Andric would have picked Frey.

The prince excused himself and made his way to his tent. He caught Baron Arcroft calling for his squire as he began unfastening buckles and buttons, no doubt to be followed by the rest of his clothing. Andric shook his head in disgusted mirth. He could never decide if the man was drunk this early in the morning or simply ridiculous, though he strongly suspected the latter.

Andric entered his tent and found everything laid out for him. The fine mail, forged and finished by the finest smiths in the kingdom, shone brightly from polish and oiling, as did the plates beside them. It was far from his best armor and nothing like the fancy ceremonial suits he wore in processions. This was battle armor, made of the finest Remalian steel, plain and unadorned, except for a faint gold inlay at the edges of the plates. The only other ornamentation was the horses embossed into the leather straps and behind the breastplate.

It was not his favorite set, but he could appreciate the workmanship, nonetheless. He had decided that his favorite armor would only be worn in the coming war. Any scratches and dents would be earned in the heat of battle, not in the Charge Day festivities. Jase and Andric's guards waited outside the tent while Andric changed into his under-armor clothing.

Andric was famished. This was the first year he had made it through the entire fast without eating, and he was proud of himself despite the discomfort. Technically, the fast was to be broken with the traditional breakfast before Hamoth's Charge of a hard biscuit, a little cheese, some dried frostberries, and a cup of water—a last reminder of the deprivations suffered by King Hamoth's men.

However, when Andric saw the platter of sweet cakes, fruit, and salted pecca intended for later, his willpower collapsed and he shoved a piece of sweet cake in his mouth and chewed happily. The morsel was moist enough, but in his dry mouth, it turned into a paste that was difficult to swallow. He grabbed one of the bottles of wine and poured himself a glass, downing it in a few gulps. As the cool liquid descended his throat and hit his empty stomach, he instantly knew it would go straight to his head, so he resisted pouring himself another. The small snack was enough for now. He wiped the evidence from his face and called Jase to assist with donning his armor. Jase gathered the chain shirt and lifted it over Andric's head, then helped settle it onto his shoulders.

They were securing the last straps on Andric's greaves when shouts erupted outside from the growing crowd. It only took a moment to realize the noise was in reception of his father and brother. Jase quickly ensured Andric was perfect before Andric stepped confidently out of the tent and approached a magnificent black charger tied to a nearby post. He wouldn't be riding Wind for the Charge or jousting. Wind was a beautiful horse and wonderful for comfortable riding and speed, but today's activities demanded the service of Kobo, one of the finest warhorses in all of Remalia. Even though he was not participating in the tourney, Stephir would be riding Kobo's brother, Havvoron. The two horses were named after the mythical warrior brothers who defeated the monster Trestiks, the fabled companion of Akraharr. It had been one of their favorite stories as children.

Jase ensured Andric was securely mounted, then wished him godspeed as Andric went to find his family. They weren't hard to locate, he only had to follow the shouts of "Hail the king!" and "Long live House Laconeus!"

Andric directed his escort to where he hoped he would intercept the king's path. He didn't want to appear to be chasing after his father and brother. His guards had to push their way through the crowds until he found the route cleared by a large contingent of Divinarim. Their gleaming armor and weapons formed a moving ring of men and metal around the royal family.

Stephir rode next to their father, followed by the royal carriage that carried Ilyanara, Shannyth, and Jenden. The open carriage was covered with a royal blue canopy that dripped with white fringe to shade the princesses from the bright morning sun. Prince Jenden stood on the seat next to his mother, waving his small hand energetically to the crowd. Shannyth sat much more demurely, looking every bit the noble young lady she was raised to be.

With a word, Andric was permitted to pass into the open space around the king. One of the guards, his red-gold armor and winged helm the only thing that distinguished him from the other Divinarim, faced him as he approached, his halberd lowered as if it was a lance, prepared to charge. When Archpaladin Nophet, head of the Order of the Divine Flame, recognized the prince, he nodded a curt greeting and motioned for the other Divinarim to widen their circle to make more room for the prince to address the king. Jevorak halted at the disturbance, allowing Andric to move to an appropriate distance to greet his father.

Andric bowed as well as his armor and saddle allowed, which was not much, with his fist over his heart. "Good Charge Day, my lord!"

Stephir broke into a broad grin at the sight of his brother. Their father smiled slightly.

At least he's thawed a bit since last night, thought Andric, not sure if it was true but willing to hope.

"Good morning, son. It looks to be a fine day for the festivities. What contests did you present for?" Jevorak already knew the answer since they had discussed it a couple of times during the last few weeks, but it was small talk made for the benefit of the onlookers.

"Arms and jousting," Andric announced with confidence. Jevorak nodded his approval. The trumpets sounded, announcing the impending commencement of the Charge reenactment.

"Excellent! To battle then." The king spurred his horse forward and gestured subtly for Andric to fall in next to him as the procession began moving again. Andric had intended to take his place with the other riders for the Charge, but he was not about to refuse his father's direction. He greeted Ilyanara and Shannyth as he positioned himself next to the king. They rode together toward the royal pavilion next to Hamoth's Field where the king would watch the reenactment.

"You'll do well at the contests today," his father said.

Andric wasn't sure if he meant it as encouragement or a command, but he was pretty sure it carried the unstated demand that Andric conduct himself well. "I'll do my best, my lord."

"I'm certain you will. Good luck."

"Yonvaar grant you his strength, Andric," Stephir offered. Andric bowed in acceptance of the benediction.

"You're joining the Charge, aren't you?" the king asked Andric.

"Yes, my lord. With your leave, I should..." Andric almost said, "... be there already," but he didn't want to indicate he was more irresponsible than his father already thought he was, so he finished with, "... make my way there soon. No doubt they're expecting me." His father simply nodded. Andric bid the rest of the royals another good morning, then made his way out to the field to prepare for the charge.

Dew on the vast field glistened in the morning sun, masking the weeds and grass trampled flat over the last few days of practice. The air was filled with the sound of a thousand horses stamping and neighing in the brisk air, their riders sitting quietly as they had been instructed. Hamoth's Field was two miles long and over a mile wide, but the Charge reenactment only covered the southern end of the field.

This year's Charge was the largest in Andric's memory. Nearly ten thousand foot-soldiers dressed like the barbarian Chaldmeres stood on the opposite side of the field, though almost half of them were commoners who were allowed to participate if they wanted to. Andric understood that having so many was in no small part an excuse to stage large numbers of supplies and troops ready to leave for the Kushaan border as soon as the Charge Days were over. It was also a great recruiting tool for the army, to give young men a chance to put on some armor, hold some weapons, and go out onto the field in mock battle.

After the reenactment, there were areas around the tourney grounds for people to take a few swings with a sword at practice dummies, shoot arrows at targets, and try on some real armor for a taste of the excitement of being a soldier. No doubt this year's efforts would encourage more to enlist. It would be a shock tomorrow when those who enthusiastically enlisted found out they were going to war. They might be conscripted eventually anyway, but for now, recruits were enough to provide the numbers they sought.

The large stands of wooden benches erected on the west side of the field for the nobility, gentry, and special guests, were filled to capacity. Commoners found places wherever they could, many choosing to watch from the east side of the field. It was not a great spot since the morning sun shone directly in their eyes, but at least they didn't have to look over hundreds of heads to watch the event.

Andric rode along the line of horses, mostly ignoring the salutes from the hundreds of men he passed, until he arrived at the midpoint of the cavalry line. Frey was already there, picking at a small bag that held the sparse pieces of the traditional breakfast. As Andric took his position next to Frey, a serving boy ran up to him and handed Andric a small bag of food and a cup of water. Andric accepted it with a nod of appreciation. The prince took a small bite of the cheese followed by a handful of the dried frostberries. He was especially happy to have the cup of water.

"Not feeling well, Your Highness?" Frey asked, gesturing to the bag of food that Andric left largely uneaten.

"I'm fine, thank you," Andric said dismissively.

Frey leaned closer, his voice an exaggerated hush. "You have a few sweet cake crumbs on your cheek."

Andric immediately reached a hand up to wipe his face, embarrassed he had been caught.

Frey chuckled. "Thought so!" he teased, then whispered, "I had three."

The prince shook his head and he stifled a laugh.

Trumpets blared across the field and Andric watched his father walk to the front of the king's balcony built in the center of the stands. Duke Garamond rode out alone, dismounted, and dropped to one knee as he approached the king, head bowed. Jevorak took off his crown and placed it on Garamond's head. For this morning, Duke Garamond was *King Hamoth*.

The trumpets sounded again and Matriarch Mielka stood and made her way toward the king to invoke the Holy Couple's blessings upon the proceedings. Andric was confused when Archseraph Charin also stood and was quickly followed by Creator Zandrin, Grand Master Riddard, and the elderly Master Scholar Commersome. Usually, only the head of one church was invited to offer the invocation. It was difficult to tell from this distance, but Matriarch Mielka appeared to be as confused as Andric. The high priestess began her prayer, but the other clerics simultaneously commenced with their own benedictions.

"What in Akraharr's hole are they doing?" Frey asked, sounding wryly amused by the unfolding scene. The barbarians across the field shouted and made obnoxious noises and gestures while the high priests and priestesses pronounced their competing blessings upon *King Hamoth*, King Jevorak, and all those present. Andric could not remember anything like the growing roar of angry shouts that filled the chill morning air from thousands of bystanders. Andric shook his head in disgust at the disrespectful breach of etiquette. He felt certain this was yet another sign of the religious turmoil spreading throughout the kingdom.

Before the prayers finished, Andric saw his father say something to Garamond, who rose and mounted his stallion. The king then gestured for the clerics to return to their seats while *King Hamoth* galloped across the field to take his place in the center of the cavalry forces. The duke may have been old, but he certainly looked impressive in his gleaming gilded armor mounted upon his chestnut stallion. When he was in position, with Andric on one side and Frey on the other, the line of horses moved forward.

"What was all that about, Your Grace?" Andric asked.

"Your father should send the lot of them to go proselytize in the Kolrathi Wilds," Garamond replied angrily. The duke drew his sword and lifted it above his head.

On the far side of the field, ten thousand voices roared and the horde broke into a wild charge. It was an impressive sight, and Andric wondered what the real Hamoth's Charge looked like as they charged across the vast field toward ten times that number. The horses stamped impatiently, knowing from the practices it was time to charge. Duke Garamond held his sword, waiting.

Andric was getting nervous. *What is he waiting for?*

The two forces were supposed to meet in the middle of the field in front of the king's balcony. If Garamond waited much longer, the infantry would be too far across the field. He was about to say something to the duke when his sword fell forward and four thousand hooves tore across the field, nearly drowning out the riders' war cries.

Garamond sped toward the opposing force at full speed, and others followed suit. At this speed, they would certainly close the distance quickly enough, but it was also more dangerous for everyone involved. They only had moments before the horses would crash through the ranks of the foot soldiers.

"Slow down!" Andric yelled at the duke, to no avail. Both sides had practiced dividing into tight columns, allowing the horses to ride safely between troops. The choreographed moves allowed weapons to swing harmlessly over their heads. At this speed, the columns weren't forming cleanly or quickly enough. Someone was going to get hurt or killed.

Andric swore under his breath and pulled on Kobo's reins to slow him down, hoping others would do the same.

Garamond rode ahead of the rest of the force and sped through a column that barely opened. Men several ranks deep jumped aside in their haste to get out of *King Hamoth's* way, disrupting the adjacent rows. Screaming erupted from where Garamond pushed through with a column of riders on his heels. It was difficult to tell if the screams were part of the reenactment or if anyone was injured. Andric didn't have time to stop or to slow the columns of riders down the line as he focused on getting his column of riders safely through the troops.

After the first charge, more than half of the barbarian force lay dead in the field. After the second, the cavalry dismounted and finished off the barbarians in hand-to-hand combat. The whole reenactment took less than half an hour.

King Hamoth remounted his horse and rode across the field of victory to return the crown to King Laconeus. A roar of cheering and applause went up as the two men bowed to each other, the crown held momentarily between them, symbolic of the respect and gratitude tying past and present.

Soldiers and riders made their way off the field while others were busy setting up the lists for the jousting and other contests. Andric watched as some of those who had played the *barbarians* were taken to the physicians' pavilion. There was no doubt plenty of blame to cast, but Andric directed most of his ire at Duke Garamond. The man had always been a stubborn, meddlesome thorn in his father's side, but to senselessly vent his injured pride on common soldiers helping with the reenactment was asinine and petty.

As Andric rode to where they would hold the Contests of Arms, he tried to shake off the irritation he felt for Garamond's behavior. It was not yet mid-morning and the sun was already hot on Andric's armor, not helping to cool his anger. He did his best to dismiss the brooding mood that threatened to overtake him. Instead, he focused on the contests ahead but was distracted by the sweat trickling in the few places not pressed in by his clothes and armor (which weren't many, he noted uncomfortably—a small price to pay for ensuring his royal person was not seriously injured in the contests).

Due to the cavalry being the backbone of Remalia's military strength, jousting, and the other equestrian contests were performed in front of the king, as well as the final match in each of the other contests. The combat-at-arms rings were on the north side of Hamoth's Field, too far for the king to watch. Andric knew Stephir would want to watch Frey fight, so Andric rode to the small pavilion next to the main ring.

Jase was already waiting when Andric arrived. The squire took Kobo's reins as Andric dismounted. Andric's eyes asked the unspoken question, *"Who is my first contest?"*

"Sir Vanth Parrik," Jase said casually.

Andric cringed inwardly, hoping his face didn't betray how he felt about his first opponent. He kept his thoughts to himself as he made his way under the pavilion and sat as best he could in one of the cushioned chairs. All the cushions in the world weren't going to make much difference when sitting in full armor. It was not as heavy or bulky as some of the knights wore, but it was not exactly lounging attire either.

Frey was the first to join Andric, not bothering to wait for an invitation to take the seat next to the prince. They ate hungrily from a tray of food that a servant had brought. After a few choice remarks about Garamond and the reenactment, the conversation turned to who they thought would do well at the various contests and whether they could get away with inviting the attractive daughters of Lord Malder to come sit with them. Other nobles greeted Andric and offered well wishes for the festivities and luck for the competitions. No doubt some of them would have appreciated an invitation to join Andric and Frey under the pavilion, if for no other reason than simply to have the honor of doing so. However, Andric found he was not much in the mood for small talk with those who didn't have anything interesting to say, nor did he wish to be questioned about the war by those who probably did.

Stephir soon arrived with Ilyanara, Jenden, and a few others in their retinue. They exchanged the usual greetings and congratulations on the reenactment.

"Look who I found wandering around the tourney grounds," Stephir said pleasantly, gesturing behind him. No one out of the usual was behind Stephir, and Andric looked confused.

Stephir turned to look for whoever was supposed to have been there, then he shook his head in amusement. "Master Ve'Aurben!"

Barak.

A moment later the diminutive scholar came out from behind the tent, not looking the least bit concerned at having kept the royals waiting.

"Did you know there are several uses for horse urine?" asked Barak matter-of-factly as he strolled into the pavilion. Without waiting for anyone to indicate an interest in hearing them, he elaborated. "They use it to accelerate the greening of new copper used on roofs, so it doesn't look out of place. There are medicinal purposes as well, such—"

Ilyanara and her lady-in-waiting had disgusted looks on their faces. Andric was amused and was tempted to let him go on but cut him off.

"From the smell of him, our beloved Marquis de'Venneshen here uses it to bathe in," Andric teased.

Frey smelled himself in mock self-consciousness.

Andric was again relieved that many laughed, including those hovering outside the pavilion, trying to stand as close as the Divinarim would allow.

They all took their seats. Andric was less careful than he should have and felt his armor leaving a heavy scratch in the chair. He had a fleeting thought to call for a backless chair but decided he didn't care enough to bother. Stephir asked who he and Frey were fighting in their first contests. Frey was fighting Earl Ferrisen's oldest son, Corran. The man didn't stand a chance against anyone, let alone Frey, so they were a perfect match. Frey got an easy warm-up, and Corran was allowed to lose to one of the best swordsmen in the kingdom, thus saving his pride.

"Who are you up against in your first match?" Stephir asked.

"The Bear," answered Andric, trying to sound confident.

Stephir nodded politely as if Andric had said nothing more noteworthy than the sky was blue, but Frey was not so circumspect. "Ouch!"

"Thank you," replied Andric, his voice dripping with sarcasm. Sir Vanth Parrik, often referred to as "The Bear", was the third son of Barron Hovath Parrik of Massonly, a vassal of Duke Garamond.

Frey laughed. "Don't worry. He's a brute, no doubt about it. If he hits you, it's going to hurt, but he's slow and he always favors a crosscut from the left. And if you really piss him off he'll start swinging erratically. Easy pickings."

Andric rolled his eyes. "And how do I do that? Insult his mother?"

Frey pretended to consider that, then answered with feigned seriousness. "I think his mother was actually a she-bear. Hard to come up with a good insult for that. I'd stick to just slapping his arse with the flat of your sword—quite humiliating." The three chuckled.

"Well, he's certainly got plenty of arse to aim at. Good chance I'll hit something," Andric jested, eliciting a good laugh. He hoped his comment didn't get back to The Bear before the match.

Soon Frey was called to the ring nearest the pavilion and they all wished him luck. He made a good show of looking like he was trying against Corran, but it was obvious to anyone who knew what to look for that Frey was just playing. After the bout, Frey joined the brothers under their pavilion and watched the other matches. Frey would occasionally give Andric tips to watch for with some of the better competitors.

When Andric's name was called, the crowd around the other rings turned to watch the prince's match. Watching him fight The Bear was far more entertaining than anything else happening. Andric felt a wave of nervousness wash over him as he waited for Jase, who helped situate his helm and gauntlets, then handed Andric his sword. The contest swords weren't sharp and were rounded at the tip, but could still leave some good bruises. They had even been known to break a bone or rattle a skull.

A loud cheer went up as Andric stepped into the ring. He raised his mirror-polished sword in a show of much more confidence than he felt.

Then the Bear stepped into the ring, and Andric felt the circle shrink by half. The man's armor, heavy plates buckled over chain, seemed to be blackened a bit, dulled to reduce any luster. His ruddy cheeks and the thick, mud-brown beard sprouting from his open-faced helm were the only splash of color on the man.

The Bear carried a huge, dull black sword. It looked more like an iron beam with a handle and was made solely for heavy bashing. Andric regretted not calling for his shield, but doing so now would only make Andric appear frightened by his opponent. Besides, a shield would only make him less agile. He had been working on parrying in training, but only against another arming sword. He was not sure a parry would work for a weapon meant to batter you to pieces.

They barely saluted when The Bear, true to his reputation, lunged forward and swung his sword in a wide, powerful arc aimed at Andric's left flank. Andric easily stepped out of range and circled left. He caught himself holding the sword up in a blocking position—as if he had any chance of stopping one of those heavy strikes. He dropped the tip of his sword, ready to make a glancing parry. It was a dangerous move if he didn't get his footwork right. He wanted to slip in for a quick strike, but he wouldn't be able to retreat quickly enough to avoid being hit by the cross-cut counterstrike, and he knew he would come out on the short end of that exchange.

Although Frey had been joking about slapping his behind, Andric decided to try and maneuver himself into a position to step in behind Sir Vanth and take his leg out. They poked the tips of their swords at each other, took small swings, testing each other's reactions as they circled each other. In anyone else's hands, The Bear's massive sword would have been slow and easy to slip past, but Sir Vanth was so strong that he moved it as easily as Andric wielded his arming sword.

On one of The Bear's test swings, Andric made a strong parry and lunged well inside Vanth's reach. He intended to step to the off-arm side, but The Bear slammed the pommel of his sword into Andric's chest. The prince's armor kept the blow from causing much damage, but he felt the air driven from his lungs.

Fortunately, the blow also knocked Andric stumbling back far enough to give him space to deflect the downward strike, giving him time to regain his footing and his breath. The opponents reset their stances, ready for the next exchange. Test and counter. Poke and evade. Circle and press. Andric barely heard the cheering of the crowd.

Keep your breathing calm. Ignore the sweat tickling the side of your face, Andric coached himself silently.

The Bear took another arcing swing at Andric. Instead of dodging this time, Andric lunged forward with his sword blade down to receive the blow. If he had stood his ground, the blow would have crushed Andric's guard. Instead, Andric let the force push him into a spin that landed him behind The Bear. Andric swung his sword in a tight circle around his body and brought it down across the back of The Bear's knee. If his sword had been sharp, it might have severed tendons, but the strike was enough to buckle The Bear's leg. Andric punched him hard in the back of the head. It was perhaps a bit unsportsmanlike, but Andric was willing to play a little dirty against The Bear. He was too outmatched in a toe-to-toe contest.

Sir Vanth fell forward, putting an arm out to catch himself. Andric kicked his arm out from under him and The Bear fell to the ground and rolled onto his back. Impossibly, he brought the massive sword up in a blind swing toward Andric's legs.

He's so damn strong! thought Andric as he barely got a clumsy block up in time. The Bear kicked hard and knocked Andric's left leg out from under him. Andric went down, arms flailing wildly.

Just keep hold of your sword! Andric tightened his grip on the sword in his left hand, anticipating hitting the ground hard. *Roll away to the right and get to your feet fast.*

Andric heard a cry of pain as he partially landed atop Sir Vanth, but ignored it as he went through his maneuver, coming to his feet, though somewhat less gracefully than he would have hoped. The Bear remained on his back with his gauntleted hands covering his face, his muffled curses filling the air. When the man didn't try to reach for his sword or get up, Andric dared hope that somehow the match might be over.

"Yield?" Andric yelled at The Bear, keeping his distance.

The Bear growled in pain, and Andric still had no idea what had happened. Sir Vanth rolled to his side and took his hands from his face. He spat blood and what may have been a couple of teeth. His nose was bent in a grotesque angle, and his face was spattered with crimson.

"Yield!"

The Bear nodded weakly.

The crowd roared their approval. Sir Vanth's squire and another knight stepped into the circle to help him stand. A cloth was pressed to his face, covering the damage and stanching the flow of blood.

Andric held up his sword with as much energy as he could muster, but his arms and legs were shaking, so he quickly stepped out of the ring amidst cheers and applause. Jase took Andric's sword, helm, and gauntlets. When Andric reached his pavilion, he dropped into his chair. "Wine!" he called to no one in particular, figuring someone would respond to his demand.

Frey slapped him on the shoulder with a broad smile. "Well done! You knocked his teeth right out of his head! That Bear will lose some of his bite from now on," Frey laughed.

Andric wanted to laugh but could only manage a half-smile. He had no idea what had happened, but he was not about to admit that now.

"That was quite a show," Stephir said with what sounded like approval in his voice.

Jenden stood in front of Andric with his tiny arms held out. "Up!" his nephew demanded.

Andric didn't feel like holding him after the fight, but he relented after Jenden demanded again. He patted a small hand on Andric's armored shoulder and bobbed his head smiling. "Good, good, good, Andic!" Then he was done and scooted off his uncle's armored lap.

Andric smiled despite himself. Jenden was a cute little boy most of the time. A servant produced a cup of wine for the prince and offered some to the others.

Barak leaned in from behind Andric and said in a low voice, "Did you really have to knock his teeth out? That didn't seem terribly sporting."

Andric shook his head and drank the wine. He would ask Barak later what happened. For now, he was content to have survived.

CHAPTER VII

ANDRIC

Andric was bone weary as he rode along Dunnigan's Highroad with his family and the tourney victors. The tourney had finished as a cold wind carried heavy clouds over the area, shrouding the sky. The king had announced that he preferred to return to the palace early rather than risk getting caught in the rain if the weather decided to take a turn for the worse. Andric had made no objection.

In keeping with tradition, the king invited *King Hamoth* and the tournament winners to return with him to the Mount and be his guests at the palace for the night. Tomorrow they would be guests of honor at the king's Victory Day feast. Naturally, they all accepted, and Andric found himself riding next to his father with Duke Garamond on the king's other side. Behind the king, Sir Ovell Leighton, winner of the Joust, rode alongside Lady Belevay of Quibbin, winner of the Contest of Equitation, and a soldier from the scout corps who won at Archery in an upset after a default was called against the four-year champion, Captain Grissar. Frey had won the Contest of Arms as expected, and he and Stephir rode behind the other tourney winners next to the royal carriage bearing Stephir's family.

Charge Days traffic was heavy along the Highroad, and their pace was slow even with the Divinarim clearing the road ahead of the royal procession. Andric recounted the details of his matches to his father and the duke. He had won his second match against a soldier he didn't know, Lieutenant something-or-other, but lost his third match against Sir Cadelle Monat. Even if he had beaten Monat, he still would have had to win at least three more matches to face Frey in the final contest. He had also won his first match in the joust by unseating his opponent, but lost by a single point in his second match.

The king commended his son for his progress in his training, and Andric hoped he had done well enough to convince his father he should be given a command position with one of the combat units. Now was certainly not the right time to bring it up; perhaps tomorrow after the Victory Day feast.

The wind picked up, driving the cold through Andric's fine Charge Days clothing. He wished he had changed back into his warmer clothes from the morning. He considered it, but vanity had gotten the better of him. He was tempted to sit in the royal carriage with Ilyanara and the children and huddle under their blankets. Again, his vanity won out. He didn't want to look ridiculous, so he ignored the cold as best he could.

Andric tried to follow the conversation between his father and the duke. He knew they were talking about the war, but it was like listening to parents talk in front of their children using half-veiled words and unfinished sentences to hide their true meaning. His mind drifted back to the day's contests.

Barak had furnished him with the details of his fight with The Bear. When Sir Vanth had kicked the prince's leg out from under him, Andric had fallen on his back with his arms splayed, his gauntleted fist smashing into The Bear's face. Andric still wondered if everyone knew it was just dumb luck or if they thought it had been intentional.

He recalled losing to Sir Cadelle. His wrist still hurt where the knight had chopped with a well-aimed blow, causing Andric to drop his sword and end the match. Andric's gauntlet had prevented the strike from doing serious damage, but it would definitely be sore for a few days. He looked forward to Sister Merranine's ministrations. The chief royal physician, an elantir and Servari priestess who was head of the royal physicians, worked wonders for the infirmities of the body.

Andric hardly noticed when they passed through Hightowers' Gate, but was grateful as he realized it was not as cold within the inner city. Teris' massive walls shielded them from the worst of the winds. It still seemed to take forever to make their way up the Grand Avenue to the White Gate, and Andric found himself frequently fighting to stifle a yawn. A hot bath, a hot meal next to a warm fire, and a warm bed were all he wanted.

"Marquis de'Venneshen," the king called to Frey as everyone but the royals dismounted in front of the White Gate.

"Yes, Your Majesty," Frey replied, striding forward as quickly as his horse would follow. "How may I be of service?" he asked, making the slight bow look elegant and respectful.

"Would you care to take my place riding with my family to the palace? I fancy a walk, and who better to take my place than the champion swordsman of the realm?"

Andric could not remember anyone other than the royals ever riding on the Mount. Was his father even allowed to make such an exception? *Why not,* thought Andric, *he is the king.*

Frey hesitated for just a moment, probably asking himself the same question. It was the only time Andric had seen Frey hesitate about anything.

Frey gave a deep bow. "Your Majesty is most gracious. It would be my great honor." He remounted, and the two princes, with Frey in the lead, rode through the White Gate. The royal carriage followed, surrounded by an escort of the Divinarim on foot.

When they were out of earshot of the king, Stephir laughed. "How does it feel?"

"It's about time," Frey answered with a feigned mild annoyance as casually as if he were discussing a dinner course being served late. "Next I expect he'll be asking me to take up the crown."

"Over my dead body," Stephir scoffed.

"That *is* how it usually happens," Frey pointed out with a sagely cautionary tone.

"If you please!" Ilyanara interjected with displeasure.

Andric had almost forgotten she was there, enjoying the banter between the two friends.

Frey beat Stephir to the apology. Turning in his saddle, he gave as much of a bow as he could manage. "My sincere apologies, Princess Ilyanara. I fear your husband brings out the worst in me."

They all knew it was the other way around. She simply inclined her head curtly in acceptance of the apology. The wind was stronger up on the Mount of the Gods, and the hundreds of points of firelight illuminating their path did nothing to warm him. As they wound their way through the palace gardens, a particularly strong gust of wind blew through the trees, causing the branches to sway and creak. Andric shivered. The stables were in sight, and he was tempted to jump off his horse and head straight into the palace.

Just a few more minutes, Andric thought, not wanting to appear too soft in front of his family.

When they reached the royal stables, the attendants were nowhere to be seen, no doubt trying to stay out of the cold. *Can't blame them,* thought

Andric despite his impatience. One of their guards whistled loudly, calling for the stable hands as the royals and Frey dismounted. Stephir helped Ilyanara and Shannyth out of the carriage, then lifted Jenden and threw him into the air. Jenden squealed in delight.

Watching his brother with his family, Andric caught himself wishing he had the same thing. Those thoughts seemed to come more frequently these days. Just then, he felt a hand on his shoulder.

"He's leaving us, isn't he?" Frey asked forlornly. Andric was not sure if he was talking about Stephir's imminent departure for Kushaan or his growing attachment to his wife and children. "Running off to fight the Kushaani without us."

Andric was surprised. It was the first time Frey had said anything about the war. His grandfather must have told him after the war council last night.

"I thought you would surely be going?" Andric asked.

"Me? No!" Frey exclaimed. "I'm needed here to comfort and uplift the spirits of the fair maidens of Remalia!"

Andric laughed, shaking his head. Ilyanara shook her head as well, without a laugh. Most of the time, Frey acted as if his wife at home in Steadleigh didn't even exist. Andric knew Ilyanara, as a devout Servari, found Frey's behavior particularly disgusting.

Andric grew impatient, and he scanned the stable yard to look for the stable hands. Several of them came running to retrieve their horses.

Finally! He held the reins out gratefully to the approaching servants.

Frey shoved Andric hard to the side.

Andric cried out as a blinding pain drove into his shoulder. He spun on his heels and staggered into Kobo, falling to the ground. He gritted his teeth against the fire in his shoulder. He lifted his hand and was surprised to see it smeared with blood. He had been stabbed. He struggled to push himself to his knees, trying to regain his bearings.

Footsteps rushed past him as he heard the clash of steel nearby. A woman's scream came from behind him, though it seemed strangely distant. With extraordinary effort, he struggled to his feet. Divinarim halberds lay on the ground next to two of the holy knights, their lifeblood spilling from their slit throats.

Another scream of agony pulled his attention. A stable hand lay on the ground, tunic and the flesh on his back gaping open. A maelstrom of blue stable hand tunics, mirror-polished armor, and clashing weapons churned near him. Shannyth was screaming and Andric feared the worst. *Stephir?*

The unfolding scene seemed impossible. Andric looked past a Divinar trading blows with another stable hand in a blur of attacks. He felt a wave of relief when he finally caught sight of Stephir. His brother stood in front of his wife and children, sword out, desperately fighting to keep two attackers from reaching them.

I'll burn them to ash!

He tried opening his center to draw on elan, but he struggled to focus. He had never tried to perform met'elan in a fight and was dismayed when nothing came. Andric shook his head, abandoning the effort, and reached instead for the hilt of his sword. His fingers felt thick and numb. He wanted to pull his blade out. He wanted to jump to his brother's defense, to strike down those who had dared to attack them, but he couldn't move.

"Andric!" Frey's voice screamed at him from somewhere, cutting through the fog in his mind that rooted him in place.

The prince turned to look and somehow his sword was in his hand, blocking a short, curved blade arcing toward his throat. *His hands are tattooed*, a part of his mind noted as he deflected a reverse cut from the attacker. He didn't remember ever seeing a stable hand with tattoos before. Andric wasn't holding the sword tightly enough and felt the sting of the blow vibrating through his aching fingers.

His sword was so heavy. He tried to cut across his attacker's stomach, but he couldn't lift the sword high enough and only managed a swing just above the man's knees. He felt resistance as his blade bit into flesh. His opponent's face contorted in a grimace as he fell to the ground, writhing in pain. Andric drove the point of his sword through the man's heart.

The stable hand's eyes widened and his mouth fell mouth open in a soundless scream, then the writhing stopped.

Andric yanked his sword free as another stable hand rushed toward him. He feared he wouldn't get his sword up in time. From out of nowhere the head of a halberd streaked through the night air, the spike on the end driving through his assailant's throat. Andric lunged forward, driving the point of his sword into the man's torso.

He turned back to his brother, ready to jump to his aid as two attackers rushed from the side. In a blur, Frey stepped behind them and drove his sword savagely into one would-be assassin's back. The blade erupted out of his chest, red spray painting Ilyanara's face.

A Divinar grabbed the other attacker by his hair and pulled him away from the princess so hard that the man flew off his feet. The knight's blade was already arcing down and sank deep into the man's stomach just as he landed on his back, nearly cutting the man in half.

Andric moved forward, legs shaking. Arms shaking. He was so cold.

Frey fought the last attacker, a dark-skinned woman with a wicked curved blade in each hand, cutting high, then low. The woman spun and Andric's breath caught in his throat, certain her blade had found its mark, but Frey was somehow not there. Andric had seen Frey fight numerous times, but he had never seen him move so fast.

Frey cut high and dodged to the right. The woman dove forward, tucked into a roll, and cut fast and sharp at Frey's leg. Frey leaped above the swinging sword and came down with a knee smashing across the woman's face. Her head jerked sickeningly sideways. Frey pulled his blade in a smooth line across the exposed jugular and was awash in a shower of red. In one fluid motion, he was up and scanning for the next attack.

A shock of pain and panic hit Andric as a firm grip seized his arm just below his wounded shoulder, propelling him forward. He cried out and tried to wrench away, then noticed it was one of his guards, grim-faced and moving him toward the others. Andric stopped fighting and let himself be guided into the protective ring of the remaining Divinarim.

Andric tried to sheathe his sword, but his arm was lead. He looked down at his hand and couldn't feel his numb fingers, red with blood, wrapped numbly around the hilt.

Just keep hold of your sword! His gaze wandered over the area. Three armored bodies and what must be a half dozen stable hands lay motionless on the ground. Even in the dim light, he could see dark pools around the bodies. *So much blood.*

He heard shouts all around them as several Divinarim from the palace secured the area, searching for any other enemies. He looked at Stephir next to him. Shannyth clung to her father, terror written on her young face. Stephir's free arm was wrapped around Ilyanara, who held Jenden tightly to her chest. Andric hoped none of the blood on them was their own.

Andric was shaking and cold. He was surprised to feel tears on his face. *What's wrong with you?* he scolded himself. He reached up and wiped his cheeks with the back of his forearm. A familiar feeling pressed on his mind, like a headache without the pain. Someone was trying to link to his mind in communion. Practicing the divine benefaction with the Divinarim had been part of his training as a member of the royal family, and he reflexively opened his mind to allow the link.

"Your Highness, we need to get you out of here, now." The Divinar's words formed almost as thoughts in Andric's mind. Andric stared numbly at the

man and simply nodded, not having the energy to send words back through the communion link.

The knight's eyes narrowed as they scanned the prince. He suddenly stepped forward to look more closely at Andric's shoulder. *"You're injured. We need to get you to safety."* He reached down and carefully took the sword from the prince's weak grasp.

Andric gave it up gratefully. His mouth felt like it was full of cotton. *"I'm fine,"* Andric said the simple words through the link. He again felt tears on his face. He was embarrassed, but too tired to fight it anymore. The link disappeared as the Divinar ordered someone to run ahead and inform Sister Merranine. The knight stayed at Andric's side as the royals were quickly ushered the short distance through the gardens and into the rear of the palace amidst a bristling ring of protective guards.

Andric's mind kept playing pieces of the scene over and over, jumping out of order, making the memory feel fragmented and surreal. Some part of him knew they had entered the wing of the palace where the royal family lived. In a brief moment of clarity, he watched as Archpaladin Nophet strode toward them along with a contingent of Divinarim. His face was set in stone, but a palpable aura of righteous indignation radiated from him.

He spoke to Stephir as his piercing eyes darted to each member of the royal family. "Your Highness, thank Teraithia you are unharmed." His eyes narrowed as his assessing glance stopped at Andric. "Why didn't anyone treat that?" He yanked a cloth off a decorative table on the side of the hallway and the beautiful vase resting on top crashed to the floor. He firmly pressed the cloth to Andric's wound.

Andric winced as pain shot from his shoulder along his arm and through his chest. It felt like his knees would buckle, but he stubbornly kept them locked. Andric sensed Teraithia's divinessence coalescing around the archpaladin. Anger and determination replaced the cold numbness, making the pain diminish in importance.

"Was my father attacked?" Stephir demanded, anger resonating in his voice, as they started moving through the palace again.

"No, my lord. He is waiting in his apartments. We will get you all to your rooms, then I will have someone escort him to you." They moved again, and Andric tried to shut the world out.

So much blood.

Frey's voice cut through the haze with a single word.

"Kushaani."

It took Andric a moment to realize it was the answer to a question from

Archpaladin Nophet—the question swirling under the surface of his consciousness since the attack began.

Who?

Now there was just one thought left as the fiery indignation continued to course through him.

They're going to pay.

CHAPTER VIII
STEPHIR

"You can't go, Ilyanara." Stephir's commanding voice was edged with frustration born of concern for the safety of his wife and child. "It's hard enough to leave as it is. It will be far worse with you and Jenden in the open. Not today." Just three days after the attack on his family, Stephir's nerves were on edge, and he looked with suspicion at everyone who came near. Ilyanara and Jenden had not left the palace since that night, and he didn't want them leaving today either, even if it was the last time he would see them for months. It was better to say his goodbyes within the safety of the palace walls.

"We have to do this," Ilyanara replied with firm resolve. Her steady gaze radiated a regal calm. "You know we do. You've said so yourself many times."

Stephir had relented yesterday and agreed she could come to the grand procession with the king and his sons leading the Remalian army. However, he had since changed his mind. He could have commanded her to stay, but he didn't want to leave her on those terms. She had to go out in public sooner or later. With the other royals gone from Teris, Princess Ilyanara would be the face of the crown.

Ilyanara bent to help Jenden put a small toy knight back on a wooden horse Jenden was using to slay a silver dragon figurine. "You know this isn't easy for me either, love." Ilyanara rarely used the term of endearment, and it made Stephir feel more guilty about leaving her. "I worry about taking Jenden out among so many people. I worry Teris might not be the haven it has always been. I worry the people might learn my fear. I worry I'll never see

—" Her voice broke and she turned away, her hands trying to smooth the front of her emerald-green dress. The nervous habit only manifested when she was upset.

Stephir gently took her shoulders in his hands. Bright morning light streamed through the large windows in their apartment, shining on Ilyanara's lustrous black curls, but it did nothing to lighten his mood. "I don't care about the people right now."

Ilyanara took a deep breath and held it for a moment before slowly letting it out, then turned to face Stephir. "Yes, you do." The words hung in the air. "I love you too, but we have other duties we must put ahead of ourselves right now."

Stephir nearly whispered, making a last feeble attempt to keep her within the safety of the palace. "Yes, the people need to see us, but they need us at our best. I won't be at mine if I'm constantly worried about your safety."

"Do you really have such a low opinion of yourself?"

Stephir had no response.

"You will do what you are best at—doing what must be done. And right now, the people need to see you strong."

He pulled her into his arms and held her.

"I need to see you strong," she whispered into his chest.

The discussion was over.

Stephir's mind ran through all the activities ahead of him today and started inserting Ilyanara into each of them. Anxiety gripped him, but he forced it down into a tight knot that wound itself around his heart. Jenden was bored and began to fuss, wanting to be held.

Stephir gave Ilyanara one more squeeze, and she hugged him back. They both bent to pick up their son and laughed. It was the first lighthearted moment since the attack. Ilyanara stepped away, allowing Stephir the opportunity to be with their son.

He lifted Jenden and tossed him in the air. It was one of his son's favorite games.

"'Gain!" the young prince demanded as he always did with a broad grin on his face. Stephir obliged, but only once. It was time to go. His father had insisted the family share a last breakfast.

"'Gain!"

"Nope," Stephir said with a smile and gave Jenden a tickling poke in the ribs. Jenden squirmed and laughed. "Time to go have breakfast with Grandpa!" Stephir slung the boy over the hip opposite his sword. "You're getting so heavy!" He wondered how much his son would grow by the time he returned from war. He took Ilyanara's hand and walked to the door, opening it for her with a slight bow. She put on a brave smile and stepped into the corridor.

Four Divinarim snapped to attention. The guard for the royal family had been doubled after the attack. It helped Stephir feel somewhat safer, but it only went so far. As they made their way to the king's quarters in silence, he thought about the royal guards slain in the attack. He was deeply grateful they had performed their duty so admirably and had willingly sacrificed their lives for his family.

"Where's Shannyth?" Stephir asked.

"Already attending the king, Your Highness," one of the guards replied.

"Stephir!" Andric called from behind. Everyone turned and waited for his brother to join them. The usual greetings were exchanged as they walked along the bright corridors of the palace.

"How's the arm this morning?" Stephir asked. Other than the sling, Andric showed no visible sign of the wound he had suffered in the attack.

"Sister Merranine can work wonders. She has the gentlest hands."

Stephir silently chuckled. He knew Andric had always harbored a secret crush on the physician despite being nearly old enough to be his mother. She was not altogether unattractive, but Andric's fondness for her made no sense to Stephir. There was no shortage of suitable young ladies of the court, any of whom would have been more than happy to receive Andric's attention.

The royal physician's healing was, of course, aided by her skills as an elantir and the divine power of the Holy Couple, but she also knew the art of herb lore better than anyone Stephir knew. She had even studied under a few of the Kushaani masters when times between the nations were peaceful. Suspicions of Sister Merranine possibly being a spy for the Kushaani flitted across Stephir's mind. *Don't be ridiculous*, he scoffed at himself. If the priestess had a mind to kill any of them, she could have done so many times over.

They soon arrived at their father's private dining room, the huge double oak doors already open. The Teraithian knights stepped aside to admit the royal family then closed the doors behind them. Jevorak and Shannyth were already seated. Shannyth stood and curtsied to her parents and uncle while the king greeted them with a warm smile.

"Good morning! Come, sit." They all bid the king a good morning as they took their seats around the white linen-covered table. Jenden climbed up on his grandfather's lap. The king gave the boy a tight squeeze, patting his leg affectionately. The food smelled delicious, and Stephir was grateful his appetite was returning. He had not been particularly hungry the last few days.

He had hardly touched his meal at the Victory Day feast the day after the attack.

Stephir was surprised at the amount of food spread before them. Fresh fruit, exotic cheeses, sweet pastries, sliced ham, and several other dishes he could not wait to dig into. Stephir was even more surprised to see the table set with fine porcelain dishes edged in gold, jewel-cut crystal goblets, and elaborately crafted golden flatware. He looked at his father with puzzlement.

"What's this?"

Jevorak's smile faded slightly, a faint sadness touching his hazel eyes. "They were your mother's."

A lump formed in Stephir's throat and tears sprang to his eyes before he could hold his emotions in check. His father hadn't mentioned their mother more than a handful of times since Stephir was a boy. He knew why today was different. He kept his head down and clenched his teeth to keep the tears from spilling. Ilyanara took his hand, and it was no use. The world blurred away.

They sat in silence, no one moving. Stephir hadn't felt the sorrow this deeply since his mother's passing. He wished desperately she was here today, but he was comforted knowing she was waiting for him in the Holy Couple's celestial realm.

Ilyanara finally broke the silence. "They're beautiful."

Jevorak cleared his throat, his voice strained with emotion. "Yes, she loved beautiful things. I thought today was a good day to bring them out." Jenden reached for one of the pastries and whined when he couldn't reach it. "The boy's right! Let's eat."

Stephir wiped his face with his napkin and looked across the table at his brother. Andric smiled and raised an eyebrow. It could have meant any number of things, but Stephir was not going to ask. He simply smiled back and reached for the sliced ham. He had already finished several bites before he noticed Andric struggling to manage his breakfast one-handed. Stephir walked around the table and helped his brother get his food situated, then returned to his seat. Ilyanara patted his hand affectionately.

Stephir said little throughout the meal, grateful Andric was feeling particularly chatty today. The king had originally intended Andric's first command to be over a supply battalion, but the recent events had changed his mind. Andric had fought for his life and done well, killing two of the Kushaani assassins. The king was extremely proud (after his rage had subsided) and granted Andric command of an infantry battalion under General Westwren.

Andric was thrilled until he learned that his battalion was not due to leave

Teris for another three weeks. Andric had balked, complaining it was too long to wait. However, his disappointment was short-lived, and this morning he peppered Jevorak with a hundred questions, all of which their father seemed pleased to answer. Stephir was pleased to hear Shannyth interjecting questions of her own. While she may have occasionally interrupted a bit too much, he preferred that to the opposite problem.

When the meal was over, they sat making small talk, none of them wanting the precious moment to end. Jenden's impatience was never going to be satisfied in the small dining room, so they stood and agreed to reunite in front of the palace within the hour. Stephir instructed Shannyth to prepare for the day's ride and meet them on the palace steps, then he and Ilyanara returned with Jenden to their quarters.

Once again alone behind closed doors, Stephir was uncertain how to begin his goodbye. He tickled Jenden playfully. "Please, let's leave Jenden here." It didn't take any argument. Ilyanara simply nodded.

Stephir gave his son a firm hug and kiss on his cheek. "I love you," he whispered. When he was done with his brief goodbye, Ilyanara took Jenden to the nursery to leave him in the care of his nursemaid.

Alone in the room, Stephir fell into a heavily cushioned chair. He sighed, feeling... *what? Sad, worried, homesick already?* Yes, but more than anything, he simply felt alone.

Sometimes Stephir envied his brother. His life was so much simpler; no burden of always having the expectation to be a ruler, without the right to rule; no obligation to measure up as a husband or father. He was free to be himself, to live *for* himself. His thoughts shifted to Frey, who lived his life in Teris as though he did not have a wife and two children at home in Steadleigh. As tempting as their lives appeared sometimes, he knew it would feel empty to him now.

Ilyanara returned to the room, her lips set in a tight line, no doubt trying to show Stephir she could be as strong as he was expected to be. His eyes drank in her beauty, trying to burn her image into his memory. She stood tall and proud, willing to be the center of his attention. A fierce desire welled within him. They hadn't made love since before the Charge Days.

Stephir approached her, his eyes fixed on hers, silently seeking confirmation that she felt as he did. He moved closer until he felt the energy between their bodies connect. She leaned against the wood-paneled wall, her face lifted to hold his gaze. He brushed his fingertips against her chin and gently kissed her forehead, tracing his way to her cheek and her neck with his lips.

Ilyanara's eyes closed, accepting his affection.

Stephir lifted her chin and kissed her lips. The tension between them melted. Her fingers entwined in his hair, and she pressed her lips against his with an intensity that matched his yearning.

Their passion grew and he pressed himself against her, pinning her to the wall. Ilyanara wrapped her arms around his neck as he lifted her and carried her to their bed.

For a time, he knew nothing else.

CHAPTER IX
STEPHIR

S tephir stepped onto the steps of the palace, squinting against the bright morning sunlight. Ilyanara respectably held his arm, but her grip was tighter than usual. His hand pressed hers affectionately in return.

His armor reflected the early spring sun. It was not his full set of battle armor; that was packed away for his journey toward Kushaan. Still, the breastplate and other pieces of gilded armor affixed to his arms and legs made him look like a warrior out of the old tales. He liked wearing it.

There had been a fair amount of discussion regarding Ilyanara's attire. She wanted armor as well, a sign of her strength as the remaining member of the royal family. Stephir didn't think it was appropriate for a noble lady to wear armor and wanted her to wear a gown. She did not want to ride sidesaddle, thinking it made her look weak. When Stephir raised the issue with his father, the king laughed and refused to get involved.

In the end, they took the recommendation of High Consul Penrossart to compromise. Ilyanara wore a beautiful, long flowing skirt of deep blue silk that shimmered as she walked, and a light breastplate of polished bdellium over a white blouse with a high, stiff collar, and long, loose sleeves with lacy cuffs. She wanted a weapon, but Stephir had gone as far as he was willing, and she did not press. As they walked to the steps, Stephir noticed with a smirk a slender dagger hilt peeking from beneath her belt.

Stephir had been shocked when his father visited them in their apartments just as they were preparing to leave and presented Ilyanara with the crown Stephir's mother had worn. Some may have questioned the propriety of a princess wearing the queen's crown, but it hadn't been seen by anyone in nearly twenty years, so there were few who would recognize it, let alone consider the propriety of the decision. And none would question the king on the issue now. She was absolutely radiant, with the deep blue sapphires and white starstones set in into a delicate, swirling latticework of gleaming platinum perfectly complimenting every inch of his regal wife.

Hundreds of Divinarim lined the palace stairs and the length of the Grand Avenue to the White Gate. Stephir had never seen so many at one time. He guessed every knight in the order must have been present. The only others allowed on the Mount today were the hundreds of clergy who stood in front of the grand temples in the attire of their various priesthoods and offices.

The priests and priestesses of Yonvaar and Kerail, in their robes of white and gold, contrasted sharply with the somber disciples of Vai Doroth dressed in their loose-fitting vestments of black linen with white trim. The Viancian scholars wore simple earth-toned robes, the masters set apart by their red and black tams. Yerin's followers (hardly eligible to be called priests; more a loose community of painters, poets, musicians, sculptors, and the like, who congregated to bring to life beauty in all its forms) had no discernible clerical attire, each man and woman free to express themselves in every color and style imaginable. Sharin Dara's clergy resembled nobility more than clerics, though their kemrelacs, the distinctive short capes draping their left shoulders and arms in black, blue, or purple, denoted their particular order as Justicars, Diplomats, and Domesticants respectively. The Teraithians were the fewest in number by far (unless one counted the ranks of Divinarim along the Grand Avenue). They were dressed in immaculate black of the finest velvet, satin, silk, and leather, and many wore some semblance of ceremonial armor.

The assembly awaited the king's arrival in silence, giving the Mount an unexpectedly reverent atmosphere.

Andric was already in the wide courtyard with the horses, needlessly checking buckles and straps on Kobo's saddle as best he could with one hand. His wounded shoulder prevented him from wearing armor. Instead, he wore his new officer's uniform, looking quite sharp in the royal blue with white trim and black piping. Andric was doing a good job of putting on a strong face in public, but he made up for it with plenty of whimpering in private. The worst injury Stephir had ever suffered was at twelve when he sprained his wrist falling off his horse, so he was willing to give his brother some slack.

An enormous fountain occupied the center of the courtyard, water splashing pleasantly over the gracefully carved marble statuary of horses at play. Like the royal stables, the fountain originally had been erected in the days of Hovac Laconeus. Stephir once saw a drawing of the original fountain. Its design was far more ornate than the current one which he felt was more consistent with the solid, practical Remalian architecture. It was still a feat of Viancian engineering and met'elan to have any kind of running water on the Mount.

Stephir and Ilyanara descended the stairs and joined Andric next to their horses. Ilyanara's horse was a beautiful white mare named Arilin, and Stephir would ride his magnificent black charger, Havvoron.

"Where is Shannyth?" Andric asked.

"Probably with Father," Stephir answered. The two had been spending a great deal of time together over the past several days. Stephir felt a tinge of jealousy, wishing for more time with his daughter, but he was still grateful she was finally getting the opportunity to strengthen her bonds with her grandfather. Stephir had already promised to take her with him on a trip when he returned, and she had beamed with delight at the prospect.

The three made small talk while they waited for the king to arrive. Shannyth appeared through the enormous palace doors and gracefully descended the white granite steps to join her parents.

"Where is your grandfather?" Ilyanara asked.

"Right behind me," Shannyth answered quietly.

As if on cue, Jevorak stepped through the front archway onto the colonnaded porch at the top of the stairs. The metallic clash of hundreds of Divinarim snapping to attention filled the air, arms across their armored torsos, gauntleted fingertips resting against the upright hafts of their halberds. It was an impressive scene—one Stephir had never witnessed before. Perhaps it was a Divinarim tradition reserved for sending a king off to war.

Although arrayed in much the same fashion as Stephir, the gold crown that ringed his polished steel helm like a divine halo set him apart as the royal sovereign of the kingdom. The other royals bowed as Jevorak descended the stairs. No other movement was detectable on the Mount. The world seemed to hold its breath out of respect as the king walked toward destiny and certain victory.

"I have been looking forward to this day for a very long time," Jevorak said earnestly as he looked at his sons, clapping them both on the shoulders. Andric winced, and Stephir winced for him. Their father was quick to apologize. "Ooh! I'm sorry, son. I forgot." Stephir could not remember the last time his father had apologized for anything.

"I'm fine, my lord." Andric put on a brave face, but Stephir could hear the strain in his voice. "It's nothing compared to what we will bring down on the Kushaani soon enough."

Their father smiled with an apology still playing on his lips. "Well, let's not keep them waiting."

Stephir was not sure if his father meant the Kushaani or the throngs that awaited them outside the Mount. The royal family mounted their horses, but Andric struggled, having only one arm. The knight that held the reins for Stephir stepped quickly to help Prince Andric into the saddle. The task was better suited to a servant, but under the circumstances, it was a noble act of service. Andric looked chagrined.

"Gods' mercies, Andric," Stephir said with a measure of amused disbelief. "They nearly cut your arm off a few days ago." It was a deliberate exaggeration to keep the edge off the criticism. "Don't be so hard on yourself." Andric nodded as they fell in behind their father, riding silently amidst gleaming knights, grand temples, and holy clerics. Stephir had trouble imagining a more awe-inspiring sight, and for a moment, he felt hope.

Only the staccato clacking of their horses' hooves on the paving stones of the Grand Avenue interrupted the reverent hush over the Mount. *What an appropriate metaphor*, thought Stephir. *The sound of riding to war destroying the peaceful quiet of my life.* He looked at Ilyanara hoping to connect with her, but her eyes were fixed ahead. He could not bring himself to make a sound to get her attention, so he cast his gaze ahead toward the White Gate.

He felt time slip away from him moment by moment. *She said she needs to see you strong*, he chastised himself silently. *They all do. At least pretend you're pleased to be going.* He touched the memory of the attack on his family a few nights ago, and the anger was as close to resolve as he could muster. It would have to be enough. He straightened himself in the saddle and tried to strike the right balance on his face of confidence and satisfaction about marching to war.

As they neared the White Gate, the noise of the throngs crowding the streets outside the Mount penetrated the silence, and he steeled himself against the anxiety of a hundred unseen threats within the waiting crowd. *You can do this,* he thought. *You must do this.*

The hard-eyed Archpaladin Nophet, the only person not in line with the other holy knights, stood centered on the White Gate. He saluted sharply as they approached, and silently gave the signal to open the gates. As one, the Divinarim behind them stepped to the middle of the Grand Avenue, then sharply turned to fall in line behind the royal family. The heavy sound of their synchronized movements felt like a door closing behind him, even as the White Gate opened in front of him.

A roar of cheering burst from the crowd as the king rode forward, his hand raised in greeting to his people. Stephir could not see his face, but he guessed he wore a wide smile. *He has the benefit of actually wanting this war.* Stephir tried not to sound so derisive, even if it was only in his thoughts.

Commoners were held back by the city guards lining each side of the Grand Avenue outside the Mount, leaving room for the high nobility and generals who had the honor of riding through the streets of Teris with the king. The army was represented by a small contingent of soldiers from each fighting corps (cavalry, archers, and foot soldiers). The bulk of the Remalian forces were already moving along Dunnigan's Highroad outside the city.

The king's high council was present, though only a handful of them would go south with the king. Stephir was surprised to see High Consul Penrossart, holding the reins of a striking chestnut mare. He could not remember ever having seen her on a horse. He had only ever known her to ride in a carriage on the rare occasions she left the Mount. This would be entertaining.

Stephir was happy to see Frey there next to his grandfather, Grand Prince Emric. As only a marquis, Frey wouldn't normally have the honor of riding so close to the king, but Frey enjoyed certain exceptions and was more than happy to take advantage of them all. He never let it go to his head though, which was one of the things that endeared him to Stephir.

The nobles bowed as the king approached, and Jevorak warmly greeted them in return. He dismounted and spent a moment mingling among his peers, giving them firm pats on the back or arm, and taking Archduchess Tra'en's hand in both of his. Stephir had rarely seen his father display this disposition. He liked it, but couldn't help wondering if it was an act or if he was genuinely in a happier place.

Stephir rode to Frey and dismounted. They hadn't spoken since the night of the attacks, and Stephir did not know what to say about it, especially here in the open. He decided to stay in safe waters. "Since when is the rabble allowed to ride in the king's company?" he asked in mock scorn.

"Well, it seems your father thought I did some good in that little scuffle we had the other evening. Something about coming to the rescue of Your Highness's ugly hide, or something like that," Frey said with a wink to Ilyanara. Frey's lighthearted banter was betrayed by the taught set of his shoulders and his pursed lips. Stephir had the impression Frey was just as tense about the battle as the rest of them, or at least more than he was letting on.

"He told you, that, did he?" Stephir raised a mocking, dubious eyebrow.

"In those exact words, I think," Frey looked skyward in feigned contemplation. "Your royal hide might be improved by a few scars, but I wasn't about to let them sully our lovely princess." Frey offered a playful bow to Shannyth.

"All right," Ilyanara chimed in, a thin smile of waning patience playing on her lips. "Can we please not talk about that?" She turned to her husband, who nodded in reluctant agreement.

Frey didn't seem to give her any heed. "You did rather well in the fight yourself, Prince Andric."

Andric, still seated on his horse, looked a bit embarrassed and shot a glance at his brother and Ilyanara before replying. "Not really, but thank you for saying so. If I had perhaps acted a little quicker, maybe—"

Frey cut him off, leaving no room for dissent. "Nonsense! You did a great job with some of those parries, and I saw you get at least one blow in at the end, there. They were well-trained fighters. You can be proud of yourself."

Andric shrugged, apparently unconvinced, wincing with the motion.

Frey must have noticed it as well. "How's the shoulder?"

"No permanent damage, I'm told. The healers were able to close the wound, but said it would take some time to regain full use of it."

"Yes, Uncle Andric almost managed to cut his own breakfast this morning," Shannyth teased, something she attempted with increasing frequency lately, though often with too much mean-spiritedness for Stephir's liking. They all laughed politely, but Stephir made a note to say something about it to her later.

Without any fanfare, the king mounted his black warhorse and everyone followed suit, cutting their conversations short. The Divinarim had already mounted, and Archpaladin Nophet gave a subtle sign to the king that the royal guards were ready. Stephir expected his father to ride in front and moved to fall in behind, but Jevorak invited him to ride at his side. Stephir was surprised but honored his father would allow it. Part of him wished he could stay with Ilyanara, but he dutifully directed Havvoron to move next to the king.

Stephir and his father spoke little as they made a straight course down the Grand Avenue toward Hightowers' Gate. The crowds continued to cheer, and some threw flowers onto the street in front of the king. Occasionally he glanced back at Ilyanara, who rode next to High Consul Penrossart, probably discussing their respective roles in managing the affairs of the kingdom. He caught her eye and smiled, and she smiled back. Recognizing his father had caught the backward glance, Stephir returned his attention to the road ahead.

"I never loved your mother as much as I did when I was leaving for war." The comment hung heavy in the air between them. Stephir had so many questions but now was not the time. "Except when you and your brother were born," he added as a wistful amendment to his first statement. "Do you remember her?"

Of course I remember her! Stephir wanted to scream. *Today, of all days, to start talking about her again.* Instead, he answered, "It has been a long time. Sometimes I don't know if what I remember is real or just my imagination." He seized the opening to ask at least one question he had always wondered about his father. "Why did you never remarry?"

Jevorak remained silent, not even bothering to acknowledge his subjects who still cheered him. Finally, he spoke, his voice low. "Anyone I considered always fell short of my expectations after being with Serenne." After a heavy sigh, the king's face took a harder edge, but he quickly put on a smile like a mask as he returned to acknowledging his people as he rode past.

Stephir took the cue from his father, waving to the crowds, but he was lost in thought. They passed under the shadow of the massive Hightowers' Gate, and he took some comfort knowing Ilyanara would be safe behind the massive walls of Teris.

"My lord, would it be all right if I rode the rest of the way with Ilyanara?"

"Of course. I should have been more considerate."

Stephir wondered if his father was troubled and might need his conversation more than Ilyanara, but the prince was not going to question the allowance. He thanked him and moved aside to wait for his wife.

Grand Prince Emric took Stephir's place next to the king. Emeric would not be riding south with the army. Jevorak was relying on him and his son, Archduke de'Venneshen, to help keep the remaining nobles throughout Remalia in line during the king's absence.

Ilyanara and the high priestess stopped their conversation as Stephir moved to his wife's side. "Good day, Your Highness," High Consul Penrossart inclined her head respectfully to the prince.

"Forgive my intrusion," Stephir said politely. "I was hoping to take a moment with the princess."

"But of course, Your Highnesses." She bowed in the saddle respectfully to Ilyanara and turned her horse, finding a place in the growing company of nobility and officers that trailed the royals.

"Is everything all right?" Ilyanara asked casually, though Stephir could hear the subtle strain in her voice.

"Absolutely!" he exclaimed cheerfully. She laughed at his exaggerated enthusiasm, and they shared a smile at the private joke in light of their difficulties over the last few days. They chatted idly as they rode through the outskirts of Teris, the warm spring sun shining down on them. It was nearly a perfect day, and he tried to savor every moment of it. He should have appreciated these moments all along and vowed he would do so when he returned.

It was well past noon when they reached the main army. A pavilion had been set up for the nobles to take some refreshment before pressing on. As they entered the cool shade of the pavilion, Earl Sumtin suggested to the king that it was getting late in the day and perhaps they should just stay here for the night, striking out early in the morning. The king would not hear of it. Stephir was disappointed but not surprised and did his best to enjoy himself.

Too soon, it was time to say goodbye to those returning to Teris. Under other circumstances, Stephir might have had several people wishing to give him their farewells, but most of his peers were going with the army and were busy saying their goodbyes to their families and other friends. He was left in peace to say goodbye to Ilyanara, Shannyth, Frey, and of course a brief godspeed to Andric who would be following in a few weeks.

Stephir found Shannyth talking with some other young nobles and led her aside to a spot of relative privacy. He had already said most of his goodbyes the previous night and simply wanted to give her a last parting kiss, but she had already launched into a question.

With a voice laced with annoyance, she asked, "Baethon Ovelle told Nimmond Rheseus that you had his uncle sent to prison for saying we were going to lose the war. Is that true?"

"No, we are not going to lose the war."

"No," his daughter rolled her eyes, a recent habit Ilyanara had been trying to train out of her, "I mean about you sending Sir Ovelle to prison."

"Sir Ovelle was arrested for trying to kill a man he was having a drunken argument with. What he said before that is irrelevant, though I'm sure the Ovelles prefer their version of the story."

"I knew Baethon was a liar."

"And suppose he *was* lying. What do you think his motive is?"

"I don't want a lesson right now," Shannyth complained, rolling her eyes again.

"You can't afford not to see and think clearly about these things. So, what do you think?"

"I don't know. There could be a million reasons. Trying to win points with Nimmond and the others. Or maybe he was just trying to make me look bad because I told him Adelaine would never marry him."

Stephir smiled. "Yes, those sound like reasonable guesses. Or maybe he wasn't lying at all but was simply repeating things he has heard his elders saying. In which case, the same question applies—what are their motives?" Stephir paused to let that thought sink in. "But you're right, no more lessons for today. I could hardly believe how grown up you looked riding with the other young nobles. I can't even imagine the lady you'll be by the time I return."

"But I thought you'll be back before winter?"

"Yes, I'm sure we will. But a lot can change in so many months. Who knows, by then perhaps Grandfather will even let you sit in on a council meeting." He meant it in jest, but her eyes lit up.

"Do you really think so?"

Stephir laughed. "If you ask nicely." He bent down to give his daughter a gentle kiss on the cheek, then whispered, "I love you, princess."

Shannyth suddenly threw her arms around his neck and squeezed, pressing his throat into the lip of his gorget.

"Careful," he said, choking, "or you might inherit the throne sooner than you thought!"

"Mother says you shouldn't tempt the gods by joking about that."

"I'll do my best to heed her words. See that you do the same."

Shannyth curtsied, then took her leave to join her friends. Ilyanara was nearby, so Stephir wandered in her direction. Andric and Frey were both talking to others, leaving him as much privacy with his wife as he was going to get amid the crowd. He didn't have anything left to say that had not already been said, and he'd never been one for public displays of affection, but he did not want to let her go.

He took her hands in his and pressed them to his lips. "I'll be back soon," he promised gently.

"I'll be waiting."

He kept her hand in his and escorted her toward her horse.

Before they left the pavilion, the king called out loudly. "Stephir!" They both turned to see his father striding toward them. "You weren't going to let my daughter-in-law leave without saying goodbye to me, were you?"

Stephir felt chagrined he had not even thought about it.

Without waiting for a response, the king stepped close and spoke to Ilyanara. "Do keep the home fires burning, my dear. I'll have your husband back before you know he's gone. Trust me, these times pass quickly."

"Of course, Your Majesty," she said with a slight curtsy.

The king took her face gently in his hands and pulled her forward to kiss her forehead. "You will be a wonderful regent in my place."

Stephir didn't know if other onlookers thought this was anything out of the ordinary in the royal family, but he could not have been more surprised if the Holy Couple themselves had come from the netherworlds to pronounce the benediction upon her.

"Thank you, my lord. Gods preserve and keep you until you grace us again with your presence."

Jevorak smiled and put an approving hand on Stephir's shoulder, then turned his attention elsewhere.

"I think you're starting to rub off on him," Ilyanara said when the king was out of earshot.

"I think someone has replaced my father with a doppelganger—and not a very convincing one."

Andric intercepted them and asked with amused incredulity, "Did Father just kiss your wife?"

Despite her olive skin, Stephir could see Ilyanara was blushing. Stephir wanted to make light of it but didn't know how Ilyanara would take it, so decided instead to take the opportunity to bid farewell to his brother. "You just worry about bringing reinforcements. And take care of that shoulder. We need your sword arm in working order by the time you make it to the front."

"I'll do my best. And take care of Father. I'm afraid he's so angry with the Kushaani, he's likely to ride straight to Kushaan and try to take on the lot of them by himself." Stephir smiled, then Andric added, "Or at least I thought he was before today."

Stephir embraced his brother as gently as he could while wearing armor. "Gods speed you, Andric."

"You too."

Stephir led Ilyanara to her horse without any further interruption. Before she mounted, she quickly turned to Stephir and moved to embrace him but was met with the clanking of her breastplate against his.

"Maybe the armor wasn't such a good idea after all," she smiled sheepishly.

"No, it was perfect." He kissed her cheek and helped her onto her horse. He held her hand for one more moment. "Goodbye, my love."

She responded with a brave smile, then turned her horse away, flanked by four Divinarim, to join the others who were gathering to return to the city.

Stephir scanned the crowd for Frey and found him casually leaning against a nearby tree, trying to look like he was not watching Stephir the whole time. Stephir strolled to his friend and slapped him on the arm. "Nice of you to wait for me before heading back."

"Well—"

"Listen," Stephir cut him off, "I have a favor to ask. Please check in on Ilyanara and the children from time to time. I know she doesn't always appreciate your finer... well, if you had a finer quality, she would have a hard time seeing it." Frey gave a sarcastic bow. "Seriously, promise me you'll look after them as best you can."

"I can't do that," Frey said soberly.

"Why not?" Stephir asked, trying to determine where this joke was heading.

"Because I'm coming with you."

"What?" Stephir asked, unable to keep his surprise and skepticism from his voice.

"Apparently your father insisted that my grandfather persuade me to come. Something about keeping you out of trouble, or some such nonsense."

"Keeping *you* out of trouble, more likely." Stephir gave an exaggerated sigh. "Very well, I suppose you can tag along."

"Your Highness is too kind." They laughed, and Frey put a hand on the prince's shoulder as they looked for their horses. "Let's go see how many Kushaani arses we can thrash."

CHAPTER X
ANDRIC

The cold, gray sky matched Andric's mood as he slowly rode Wind across the Mount of the Gods. Taking command of the battalion assigned to him had been exciting at first, but the luster of the tasks his duty required had quickly dulled. As the day of his departure neared, even the few fun parts like training drills and sparring had given way to packing lists, gear inspections, supply requisitions, and myriad other details he just couldn't bring himself to care about. Not that he personally had to attend to most of it, but he was expected to receive reports and status updates from his junior officers and pretend any of it mattered to him.

He was long past due at the warehouse district, where his soldiers were no doubt wondering where the prince was. He had been procrastinating all morning, finding any reason to delay attending to his duties. Andric knew his officers would manage things just fine until he arrived.

He paid little attention to the magnificent temples that flanked the Grand Avenue until he neared the Temple of Teraithia. Seeing the towering structure reminded him that Archseraph Charin had requested an audience twice in the past week. Andric guessed the high priest wanted to discuss the investigation into the attack on Venerate Alscome's temple. Andric had meant to ask for an update before meeting with Charin, but now any option other than heading to the warehouses sounded more appealing, even giving a half-informed report to the august cleric.

"I need to speak with the archseraph before we continue into the city," Andric announced to the Divinarim escorting him.

"Where were you scheduled to meet him?" one of the guards asked, sounding as if this request was nothing out of the ordinary.

"It isn't a planned visit. I was hoping to find him in his offices."

With only a nod to acknowledge the prince's new instructions, the Divinarim altered their course toward the temple. It looked like his guards intended to lead him around the temple to the archseraph's quarters in the rear.

"I prefer to go through the temple today," Andric instructed.

Part of him wanted to waste time taking the longer route, but another part hoped that seeing the monumental statue of Teraithia in the Ascension Hall and feeling the goddess's divinessence would snap him out of his melancholy. The guards adjusted their trajectory again and soon arrived at the wide walkway leading to the temple's entrance. After dismounting and handing the reins to one of his guards, Andric made his way between the towering statues of celestial sentinels that flanked the tightly fitted cobblestone path to the wide front steps.

The diffuse morning light made the temple's grayish-white granite feel even more imposing. Streaks of golden morning light slashed through a sudden break in the clouds, casting shadows across his path, before disappearing a moment later, leaving the world feeling more bleak than before. Only the royal family and Divinarim were allowed to be armed on the Mount, but Andric knew the uniformly clothed clerics stationed along the path to the temple were well-trained in unarmed combat, perhaps surpassed in skill only by Vai Doroth's monastic disciples.

As he approached the temple steps, Andric took note, as he always did, of the names of the other gods chiseled into the riser of each step. As a young boy, he had been curious why Teraithia would pay homage to the other gods by carving their names on her temple. His tutor had explained it was meant to show the lesser gods' proper place as one stepped over them to ascend into Teraithia's exalted presence.

Two clerics stationed at the front doors to receive visitors bowed as the prince approached. He nodded a casual greeting but stopped short when the two enormous bronze doors swung inward. They were rarely opened except on certain Teraithian holy days. Visitors instead used one of the smaller doors set within each of the massive doors. Every head inside the temple turned in his direction, no doubt just as curious as he was about the unusual reception. Andric was used to people watching him wherever he went, but this felt different. The Divinarim moved before he did, and he almost felt caught in the pull of their motion before remembering he was supposed to be moving with them.

Andric held himself erect and strode forward with an air of authority befitting a Laconeus prince. The gray light flooding into the temple from the open doors began to diminish as several black-clad priests pushed the gigantic doors closed again until the temple was once again illuminated solely by the light emanating from the translucent golden columns around the perimeter of the wide-open space. Temple patrons were spaced sporadically on the outer concentric square steps that rose toward the colossal statue of Teraithia towering in the center of the Ascension Hall. Andric felt the goddess's divinessence radiating from her majestic likeness, dispositioning him with a subtle sense of awe and unworthiness to approach. For those whose lives were sufficiently aligned with Teraithia's doctrine, the dispositioning made each step increasingly difficult as one moved toward her statue.

He noted that some of the patrons were dressed in the finest ceremonial garb, some looking like legendary warriors in gleaming armor, some arrayed in royal finery befitting the king on Hamoth's Feast Day, and others were adorned in elaborate priestly attire similar to Archseraph Charin on high holy days. These symbolic vestments were provided to Teraithian disciples in the final stage of their Ascension Quests just before entering the Ascension Hall. Each was attended by a cleric at their side who occasionally whispered something to their charge as they attempted to approach the statue. The opportunity to come and test one's fortitude against the awesome power of Teraithia's visage on the Mount of the Gods brought her most devoted followers from across Remalia and beyond. Wealthy Teraithians could afford the sufficiently large donations required to repeat the pilgrimage, but for most, it was a once-in-a-lifetime experience.

Andric watched as an elderly woman, leaning heavily on a bejeweled staff, struggled to ascend the third step. The tanned, leathery skin beneath the finery marked her as a commoner, but she could otherwise almost pass as the matriarch of a noble family. He admired her effort as she slowly straightened herself into a dignified posture on the edge of the step. It might take her hours more to make it to the next. He was half-tempted to see how close he could get, but it seemed sacrilegious when he wasn't a true disciple of the goddess. Besides, there were limits to how long he would allow himself to delay attending to his duties.

He silently wished the old woman a divine fulfillment of her quest then continued through the Ascension Hall toward the archseraph's offices. He paid little mind to the masterpiece sculptures and paintings lining the corridors. His mind was occupied with rehearsing responses to the archseraph's most likely requests concerning the investigation, the king's progress toward Kushaan, and similar matters.

The prince had never been to the archseraph's offices before, but he was certain they had arrived when they entered a grand hallway where several of the Seraphic Guard stood at attention outside a pair of large, glossy black-lacquer doors. Gray light filtered through large windows on one side of the hallway, and the high vaulted ceilings and polished marble floors felt as grand as the royal palace.

The black doors opened and a middle-aged priestess escorted two guests into the hallway. Andric recognized both men but only knew the name of the portlier one. Magister Hillsath, guildmaster of the stonemasons. He was pretty sure the other was a magister of one of the guilds as well, even if he couldn't quite place him. Their expressions turned from annoyance to surprise upon seeing the prince.

They both quickly bowed in greeting. "Your Highness, what a pleasure to see you."

"You as well, Magister Hillsath. I hope I'm not interrupting your appointment with the archseraph."

"His Eminence is pleased to receive you, Prince Andric," the priestess answered before the magisters could. "If you would care to follow me."

Andric bid the guildmasters a good morning and followed the priestess through the doors. They crossed a large antechamber illuminated by beautiful silver alchemical lamps and furnished with a writing desk and some deep-cushioned chairs. A pair of guards opened a matching set of glossy black doors for the priestess and her charges.

Inside the next chamber, Andric was surprised to see rich wood-paneled walls, wood flooring, and wood on the ceiling. All he had ever seen in Teraithia's grand temple was stone. Bookshelves lining one long wall were filled with neat rows of leatherbound books and the occasional curiosity or small decoration. A fire burned in a large fireplace on another wall, while a third bore a tapestry of the largest map of Baon Andric had ever seen. The last was a wall of tall windows that overlooked the temple's beautiful gardens, green buds on the trees and bushes showing signs of spring finally taking hold in Teris.

Charin was just outside one of the windows, speaking with another priest.

"May I offer Your Highness some refreshment? A glass of wine or perhaps tea and cake?"

"No, thank you. I did not have an appointment to meet with the archseraph. I simply stopped by because he had requested to meet with me. If now is not convenient, I would be happy to see him another time."

"The archseraph is grateful you took the time from your busy schedule to visit him, my lord, as I'm sure he'll tell you himself in just a moment."

Andric wondered if Charin and the priestess were in communion and if she was conveying everything the prince said. Andric had been taught about such tactics in his diplomacy training. He had even been required to practice them on occasion with his Sharinist tutors. Most of the time, he considered such measures beneath him, preferring instead to be direct with people. *Let others play their games if they need such a crutch.*

"Would it be all right if I took a closer look at the map?" Andric asked politely. Assuming the answer was yes, he stepped toward it.

"Of course, Your Highness. The archseraph enjoys studying it as well."

Andric immediately found Teris and visually traced the path Stephir and his father had taken toward Kushaan—the same road Andric would be following a few days from now. He scanned the provinces and cities of Kushaan, wondering which ones the would-be assassins had come from. He wondered how much of the map would become part of Remalia by this time next year. Stepping back to take in more of the map, he left Iuventia and looked across the Auroric Ocean to the other of Baon's major continents, Vestura. He found Celendria and Eastgate and other lands he had barely heard of. Seeing the whole world spread out before him in a beautifully crafted tapestry made the prince feel small, insignificant.

The sound of the door opening pulled Andric back from his visual journey to the archseraph's office. Before he turned around, a wave of Teraithia's divinessence washed over him, bringing with it a sense of awe and empowerment. Andric immediately recognized the effects that accompanied the archseraph. It had been rumored for many years Charin had achieved enlightenment, and the prince was convinced the effects he felt were evidence of it. Andric had considered asking Charin directly, but the timing to broach such a sensitive topic never seemed quite right. Perhaps today would be different.

"Forgive me for keeping Your Highness waiting. Do you like my map?" Charin asked with his usual gravity. "I find it gives me a healthy sense of perspective."

"Yes. In fact, I was just considering having a similar one commissioned upon my return from Kushaan to show the new borders of the kingdom after we've won the war."

"I hope to be afforded the opportunity to see it when it is finished, my lord. I am more pleased, though, to have the opportunity to speak with you before you depart. I was not certain it would happen. To what do I owe the honor?"

"I apologize for the delay. Preparing my troops to leave has consumed all my attention these past couple of weeks. I was on my way to my command post this morning when I realized there might not be another opportunity to speak with you, so I decided to take a chance I might find you available. I hope I didn't interrupt anything important with the magisters."

"Not at all. I'm certainly glad you came. Are you in a hurry, or may we sit for a few minutes?"

Andric answered before his guilt could persuade him otherwise. "I can't stay too long, but I would be happy to chat for a few minutes, Eminence."

"Your Highness is gracious. I would not normally ask a favor so abruptly, but circumstances appear to be conspiring to foreshorten the usual etiquette. May I press upon your indulgence and ask that we have everyone else wait outside?"

Andric was pleasantly surprised at the unusual request. It was rare that someone of Charin's stature would ask to speak with Andric privately. The prince felt an upwelling of pride but schooled himself to appear as if this was nothing out of the ordinary.

"Of course," Andric replied casually and nodded to his guards, who saluted and followed the priestess out the way they had entered.

Charin gestured to a set of deep leather seats.

"I'm afraid I don't have much new information to report about the investigation into the attack on Venerate Alscome's Temple," Andric apologized as he unbuckled the belt holding his scabbard. He leaned his sword against the bronze table next to his chair before easing himself gracefully into the soft seat.

"Oh, then you must not have received the latest reports. We found the ones responsible and reported everything to Captain Drandin, as you requested. I believe arrests were made just yesterday."

Andric didn't know if he was more surprised the culprits had been caught or that Charin had followed Andric's directive not to seek retribution. "That's excellent news. Who was it?"

"Servari militants calling themselves Yonvaarians. I should think the crown will want to investigate further into the group's activities, but I will be satisfied with seeing these criminals receive the king's justice."

Andric seriously doubted that would satisfy Charin in the least, but he played along. "I couldn't agree with you more, Eminence. I wonder, though, if they are connected to the previous attacks on the Servari and Dorothi temples, or are there more necks that deserve the headsman's axe? I suspect the latter; in which case, I hope those culprits are brought to justice as quickly as these Yonvaarians so we can put this unpleasant religious turmoil behind us."

"While I share Your Highness's hope for such justice, I'm afraid I am somewhat less optimistic it would bring an end to the unrest. I have reports from all over the kingdom of growing religious strife. And it appears to be the same in Calavia, Celendria, Eastgate, Qelasaar."

"Do you think we are in the time leading to the gloaming of the gods—the gathering of the armies of crown and sword?" Andric asked, recalling his discussions with Barak and Stephir regarding the Ultideic prophecies.

Charin canted his head and studied Andric for a moment. "You seem to have more familiarity with the prophecies than most, Your Highness. Do you see any evidence of the people coalescing into just two factions?"

Andric scanned his memory of several reports he had received of such incidents, searching for any kind of polarity, but couldn't recall any. He wondered if Barak would be able to see something. "Not that I can think of."

Charin nodded. "The world is in a constant cycle of peace leading to prosperity, leading to complacency, leading to abuse, leading to turmoil, and reemerging into peace. Every generation experiences the turmoil phase of the cycle and wonders if it is the end of the world. Whether we are in that time or not, my principal concern is foreshortening the period of turmoil and restoring the peace we enjoyed for so many years under your father's steady hand. And I believe you may have a unique role to play in that restoration."

Andric's interest was piqued. *Is this what Charin wanted to see me about?* "I certainly hope to help with that in our war against Kushaan. Once we win—"

Charin interrupted, "Do you think defeating the Kushaani will lessen the religious conflict in Teris, or at Rookstone, or Steadleigh?" Andric didn't answer, so Charin continued. "Do you know why temples to all nine gods were built on the Mount?"

The question seemed to be a non sequitur, but Andric answered anyway, trying not to sound confused. "To offer thanks for the gods helping King Hamoth defeat the Chaldmere hordes."

"Yes, but what aid did the gods provide to merit the temples? And why all of them?"

Andric didn't know where Charin was going with this and didn't want to appear ignorant. He played it safe and answered, "I'm sure each of the gods played a role in our victory."

"You think Akraharr took our side in the fight?"

Andric had never thought of the question before. Technically there was no temple to Akraharr on the Mount, just an empty plot of land where a wild wood had grown for centuries, unattended by anyone. Andric had hidden in the grove as a child on a few occasions when he managed to sneak away. It had been frightening the first time, but he eventually learned to appreciate the raw beauty of a place untouched by human intervention.

"I suppose not. Perhaps King Hamoth didn't want to offend Akraharr by leaving him out."

"Offend the god who shuns the other gods by not offering him a temple site alongside theirs? I imagine Akraharr would rather prefer it that way. No. Did you ever learn of the Nine Ecclesiastics?"

Andric shook his head, wondering if Barak had any idea what Charin was talking about.

"I'm not surprised. I had only a vague recollection of the story myself before our discussion a couple of weeks ago. I've had my top archivist combing through the Church's records, and even at the Great Library," Charin said with a note of distaste, "searching for information about any others with your gift."

A flurry of thoughts and feelings suddenly swirled through Andric. He was flattered but perplexed. *Why is he taking such an interest in me?* Confusion slipped toward curiosity. *What did he find?* Apprehension filled him. *Is there something wrong with me?* Sharp anxiety sliced into his thoughts. *What will Father say if he finds out?* A growing undercurrent of pride rose to the surface, overshadowing his doubts. *Am I truly destined for greatness?*

Andric finally managed to utter a response. "You didn't need to trouble yourself on my account, Eminence."

"To be honest with you, I was somewhat disappointed, though not entirely surprised, by how little we were able to find. The story of a mystic who could journey through the realms of the gods; a rumor of a holy child who could bend time; an ancient account of a woman who could change the course of rivers and move mountains. There were very few details about their ability to attune to multiple divinessences or how such feats were performed. It was probably little more than myth and superstitious exaggeration in most cases, but the accounts of the Nine Ecclesiastics have proved to be quite intriguing.

"Facing overwhelming numbers of the Chaldmere forces, King Hamoth gathered his clerics and elantir to determine whether there was anything they could do to weaken the enemy. Do you know what they did?" the archseraph asked.

"The elantir created a storm of lightning and thunder for three days to strike the enemy camp."

"Yes, that is the common account. Do you know any more details?"

Andric had always enjoyed imagining that scene and was surprised to realize he had never given it any critical thought. Knowing what he knew today about met'elan and benefactions, it seemed very unlikely. He shook his head.

The archseraph continued, "It seems it wasn't actually lightning and thunder, at least not based on any natural phenomena. They replicated the light flashes and thunderclaps, but there was no actual power in it. Apparently, that was not their intent though. They wanted to distract the enemy, instill fear in them, deprive them of any rest."

"All useful for weakening the enemy," Andric acknowledged.

"No doubt, but that's not the interesting part. Do you know where the elantir and Ecclesiastics were while they were performing their feats?"

"If it was all just elantic effects, I assume they would have to be near the enemy camp, or even among them. Did they disguise themselves to blend in with the horde, or somehow cloak themselves to remain unseen?" Andric's imagination raced with wild ideas about what secret powers the ancient Remalian elantir may have wielded.

"No. It is far more incredible, if I understand correctly and if the account holds any truth at all. They were here, on what is now the Mount of the Gods."

Andric scoffed, but Charin's expression remained unchanged except for the hint of an underlying intensity in his steady gaze that the prince found unnerving. *That's impossible*, Andric thought, resisting his instinct to believe the archseraph.

"I could hardly believe it myself."

"But how? The amount of elan it would take to cause any effect at that distance... let alone... it just wouldn't be... that can't be right."

"I have found more than one record. Of course, we can't be certain if they are true, but they agree that a ritual was performed by the Nine Ecclesiastics on the Mount, and the elantir were with them. However, there is a clue in a journal we found, hinting at a possible explanation." Charin's words began to quicken from their usual measured pace. It was the closest thing to excited Andric had ever seen the man get.

"The journal states the Nine were joined in unity for three days, without interruption, while the elantir worked their met'elan."

Andric nodded, pretending to follow Charin's point, straining to find the answer before it had to be spoon-fed to him. Charin paused, though for exactly what purpose Andric didn't know. *Is he waiting to see if I figure it out? Come on, think!* He remembered the last time he had combined elan and divinessence in the Library of Selmarine, with Barak. He still didn't fully understand technically what he had done to unlock the doors, but offering any plausible answer was better than sitting in silence, looking stupid. "Did the Ecclesiastics fold the world on itself?"

"Why do you say that, my lord?"

"The distance is the problem. The enemy camp would have been at least five or six miles away. No one can channel elan that far. That must have been what the clerics were doing."

Charin raised an eyebrow and nodded approvingly. Andric's pride swelled at having impressed the archseraph. "Do you have any idea how they would do that?"

Andric considered the problem for a moment but couldn't begin to guess. "Were there any other clues in the records?" he asked, trying to buy some time.

"No, but you might find it useful to know that in those days, the word they used for the benefaction we now call unification was 'unity'."

"You mean, they were able to harmonize all eight divinessences simultaneously?" Andric asked skeptically.

"Nine, technically, if I understand correctly. Apparently Yonvaar and Kerail each contribute a unique aspect of their unified divinessence, which the Servari once believed should be attuned to separately. I'm obviously no expert on all the permutations Servari doctrine has undergone through the centuries, but that is somewhat beside the point. Other than, perhaps, to be instructive of the idea that the divinessences can apparently work in unison and that doing so unlocks unimagined powers."

"I think if that were possible I would have heard of it before now," Andric said, his mind reeling with the implications.

"Can you imagine how difficult it must be for nine individuals, each sufficiently devoted to their respective deities that some say they had each reached transcendence—or enlightenment, or whatever the others call their version of it—even agreeing to work for a common purpose, let alone one that requires them to find a balance and harmonize with one another? I have tried to imagine it a few times since reading the accounts, and I confess I would find the idea abhorrent. To desecrate Teraithia's holy essence by blending it with the whore goddess, or the god of chaos, or the servile gods, would be such an affront to Teraithia's divine will that even the attempt would make one unworthy to channel her divinessence, thus making it impossible."

"So you don't believe the accounts?"

Charin kept his gaze fixed on Andric for a moment before quietly answering. "I wouldn't have before I saw what you did at Saint Alscome's." The archseraph's words hung heavy in the air. "It shouldn't be possible, but I saw what I saw. You seem to possess the ability not only to sense but to actually attune to most or all the divinessences." Charin forced the words out with some difficulty. "Have you ever tried attuning to more than one, blending them together?"

"No, it's hard enough to attune to one at a time. Attuning to more than one seems even more difficult than modulating elan to more than one modality at the same time."

Charin laughed. "Your many talents apparently include understating difficulties." The amusement disappeared, replaced by a stony calm masking a subtle but unmistakable intensity. "I want to help you, Andric. I want to help you realize the great potential of this gift, and help keep you safe until the world is ready to see who you really are."

For as long as Andric could remember, he had yearned to capture the attention of the powerful; to be taken seriously—to be one of them. Not because of his titles or his connection to the crown or the favors he could do, but for who he was. The ferocity of his desire to accept Charin's offer nearly took his breath away. The subtle but ever-present feeling of being drawn toward the archseraph, no doubt the effects of being enlightened with Teraithia's divinessence, suddenly intensified. At first, Andric suspected he was being dispositioned, but that wasn't quite right. There was no way of knowing, of course, since Charin seemed to be continually attuned. The power of Teraithia's mouthpiece must be immense.

Can divinessences really be harmonized? Andric wondered. He wished Barak was here to discuss it. Thinking of his friend led him back to the memory of unlocking the sealed door at the Library of Selmarine and folding the world. Without thinking, he attuned himself to Viance's divinessence. It was the one he was most practiced with, and it fit his craving for knowledge in this moment. He felt his orientation shift as his connection to the divine strengthened. It was nothing like Teraithia's divine radiance—powerful, dominant, demanding. Viance's essence coaxed toward exploration of the unknown, whispered to look deeper.

Dominion and knowledge. Andric reached for Teraithia's divinessence. He knew it was always there, waiting to be perceived by anyone sufficiently aligned with the goddess's will, ready to answer those worthy of it.

It will not share you with another.

Are you so certain that you're not even willing to try?

Andric exerted his will to connect with the second divinessence. He could sense Charin's attunement, beckoning him into the same union. *I can do this!* he insisted.

Demanding to get your way is not alignment with Her will, his inner voice mocked, even as Viance's divinessence faded.

The prince shook his head, frustrated and disappointed. "I don't think it can be done."

"One attempt and you are ready to give up?" Charin's tone was uncomfortably similar to the mocking of his inner voice. "Stay in Teris. I do not believe you were put on Baon to simply live out your life as other men. Your destiny is greater than that. Let's work together to find out how much greater."

Why does he want this so much? The question was a memory of one of his tutors, a priestess of Sharin Dara if he remembered correctly, though her name escaped him. *Everyone wants something.* The thought suddenly made him cautious.

"Your offer is most generous, Your Eminence." Andric found himself rising to his feet and reaching for his sword before he realized he had decided to leave. A spark of fear flashed through him at the possibility of offending Charin and losing the opportunity offered by the archseraph. "My duty to Remalia must come first," Andric said, then rushed to add, "but I'm sure our victory will be swift, and I shall be home before winter. I would be pleased to discuss this with you further when I return."

Charin reluctantly smiled with a hint of displeasure behind his gaze. "As Your Highness wishes. Please allow me to reiterate my prior word of caution. Be careful with whom you share knowledge of your ability. Most will not understand it, and for any who do, I fear it will make you a target of their ambition, or worse. If you need to discuss this with someone while you are in

Kushaan, consider confiding in Archpaladin Nophet. He has my complete confidence and can do more to keep you safe than anyone."

"I will. Thank you, Archseraph."

"Teraithia guide your path until you return, my lord."

Andric inclined his head in response. "And yours, Eminence," he offered, then made his way from the room.

There was nothing sluggish about his steps now, though whether he was rushing away from something or toward it, he couldn't tell.

CHAPTER XI
BARAK

It was late morning when the young acolyte handed the sealed message to Barak with a bow, then departed. The scholar set aside the scroll he had been reading and looked at the folded paper in his hand. He was pleased to discover the message was from Andric.

It had been almost three weeks since the king had marched his armies toward Kushaan, and nearly that long since his friend had come to see him. He was not surprised though; Andric was not the sort to keep in regular contact unless it was convenient. With as many things occupying the prince's mind these days, Barak was glad to receive any word at all. He had started to worry Andric would leave without saying goodbye at all.

Barak rarely received written messages from Andric. Their friendship was one of convenience, meaning Andric reached out or visited when it was convenient for him. Barak carefully opened the folded paper, guessing it was probably a goodbye note. He felt a twinge of disappointment his friend hadn't taken the time to visit him in person. He was surprised to see a short message scrawled on the white parchment. He scanned the words quickly, then went through it again more carefully.

My dear friend Barak,

I am sorry that my contact comes so infrequently. I find that my position requires much more attention than I had anticipated. I leave tomorrow for the front with a battalion of reinforcements. I don't foresee being able to get away to see you. Would you please come to see me this evening at my quarters in the western warehousing district, E section? Just ask for me and someone will direct you to where I am.

Sincerely,
Prince Andric Laconeus

Barak wondered at the formal title with which his friend signed the note. *Is Andric getting full of himself?* After a moment he thought better of it. More likely his royal friend was finally settling into his position of office, as he always should have. He was glad to see maturity setting in. It would be nice to observe firsthand what these weeks had done to Andric, as well as see his friend off. He picked up the scroll he had been studying and resumed reading.

The evening meal, which by most standards was simple fare, was nevertheless very well prepared. While many in Remalia were having to adjust to the wartime rations, the disciples in the Library of Selmarine went on as they always had. Barak was too anxious to sit through the whole meal. That was the ordinary course for him, although it was usually his studies that drew him away from the dinner table. He left the hall after excusing himself to Headmaster Gowend and made his way to the small stables just outside the temple walls.

The sun had already passed below the towering city wall, and the warm, spring sky was backlit by a deep amber. Barak had never been to the western district, but he had a good mind for remembering maps and was confident he could find his way with little difficulty. He avoided the open market district entirely. Not that there would be many people there, but the merchants would be busy closing up their stands and packing away their goods, all to be brought back and put out again tomorrow. Instead, he took a route through the northern housing district. Being in proximity to Hightowers' Gate, it was one of the safer areas to pass through at night, which made it worth going that way even if it took a little longer to get to his destination.

It was well past dusk when he arrived in the western warehouse district. The stars glittered brightly in the night sky, and it was easy to imagine there was no war in the realms above. However, Barak suspected differently. It was the realm of the gods after all, and were they not the source of contention? *No. Not all of them anyway.* It was strange to be having these kinds of thoughts now. His mind began to trace the line of thought to its source, then he stopped himself, realizing he had no idea where to find Andric.

There was not much activity here—mostly city guards on security patrol. Barak stopped a couple of soldiers and asked how to get to section E. Following their directions, he soon arrived at the specified location. Insects fluttered around a multitude of lamps that illuminated the area for soldiers double-checking the orderly line of wagons packed and staged for the next day's departure. Barak found it necessary to ask another soldier where he might find his friend.

"The prince, suh, oughtta be in the building jus' the other side o' tha' warehouse there," the young man said with a heavy country drawl, pointing down the street.

Barak thanked him and made his way to the small building, which was little more than a converted storehouse. Four Divinarim stood post outside the doorway, halberds in hand, the light from inside the building glinting off their armor through an open window.

One of the guards stepped forward and addressed the small Cannessi. "State your business, please."

Before Barak could answer, one of the other Divinarim spoke. "Master Ve'Aurben, the prince is expecting you."

Dismounting was somewhat of an acrobatic feat for Barak, especially when wearing his priestly robes, but he had done it enough to avoid completely embarrassing himself. After tethering his horse next to the others, he followed the knight inside. They walked past the two open rooms comprising the front half of the building, one on each side of the hallway leading to another closed door. The man again opened the door for Barak, who inclined his head in acknowledgment as he passed by. He normally skipped the formalities, but decided it was best to follow protocol. He didn't want to give anyone an excuse to doubt or question the prince because of the friends he kept.

When he entered the room, Andric was seated behind a plain pine desk;

fitting for a warehouse he supposed, but still surprised the prince settled for using it. His friend looked up from the pile of papers he was reviewing with another officer and gave a weary smile of recognition. Barak took a seat against the right wall, opposite Andric, waiting patiently.

Two other soldiers also occupied the room; one taking down the prince's orders while the other sat at a tiny writing table, rifling through another pile of documents. The room was well lit by large oil lanterns that hung on thick chains from the ceiling in the four corners of the room, as well as by a plain but sturdy alchemical lamp near Andric's desk. The light attracted several insects, mostly moths, that fluttered around the lights. Barak had the sudden realization that he never saw moths in the temple. Strange, he had never noticed before. He made a mental note to look into it later.

Within a few minutes, Andric stood and dismissed the two soldiers from the room. After a healthy stretch, (Barak noticed it wasn't for show—he could always tell the difference) Andric grabbed a chair and sat down next to his friend.

"Thank you for coming to see me on such short notice, Barak."

"Of course. I will always be glad to come see you," Barak answered sincerely. "How's the shoulder?"

Andric rolled his arm in a circle, slowing and wincing slightly as it reached the high point. "It's much better, but not quite back to normal. I wish my father hadn't taken his physician."

"Yes, I'm sure you miss her ministrations," Barak said with a hint of amusement. He knew why Andric missed Sister Merranine.

Andric stretched both arms and changed the subject quickly. "You don't know how good it is to talk to someone I don't have to give or take orders from. Not that I mind, of course," he added quickly. "It's just tiring, that's all. Anything new at the cave?"

Andric liked calling the Library of Selmarine 'the cave.' He adopted the nickname when Barak had first taken up residence there and Andric tried to get his friend to move back to the Mount.

"No, nothing much is new." Barak sensed something was troubling his friend and decided to find out using the indirect approach—boring him until he opened up on his own. He inwardly chuckled at the thought of it, wondering how long it would take the prince to interrupt. "I did recently discover, though, a fascinating work on the subject of energy conservation in matter transmutation."

Andric raised an eyebrow but said nothing, so Barak continued. "The book deals first with elantic protections against the dangers of traversification, such as susceptibility to elantic siphoning and disembodied souls possessing the traversifier's body while the soul spark is absent." Barak wondered when the prince was going to cut him off as he usually did, but his silence persisted. "The first step is to set up a protective shield around the body to keep disembodied souls at a safe distance through a benefaction called *shrouding*. It is something like creating an artificial aura around the traversifier.

"Next, an elantir must imbue the shroud with elan to protect the traversifier's body from having its elan siphoned. This requires a great deal of concentration and elan, often leaving little of either to do anything else. The problem lies in how to modulate the elan in a way that it will infuse the shroud, which is essentially a structure of pure divinessence, offering nothing for the elan to naturally bond to. The implication, of course, is that..." Barak had begun to get caught up in the subject. Fascinating as it was, he mustn't do that right now. This was long past when Andric would normally have interrupted, so Barak decided to give his friend a pass. "But you didn't ask me to come here just to hear about my latest studies, did you?"

"Actually, I miss discussing things other than the mundane details of shipping manifests, harvest projections, and supply routes." Andric stared at the floor for a moment then smiled. Looking up, he continued. "I like overseeing the martial training of the soldiers, but so many tasks feel like I'm just a glorified stock clerk."

"Well..." Barak said with an exaggerated drawl.

Andric punched him in the arm. "I met with Archseraph Charin yesterday. He tried to convince me to stay in Teris."

The prince's statement seemed to come out of nowhere, but Barak's wary interest was immediately piqued. "He's just trying to use you to get back in my good graces."

Andric laughed. "Odd that your name didn't come up at all in our conversation." Andric's eyes slipped back to the ground as he laced his fingers together. Barak kept quiet, and several moments passed before Andric finally spoke again. "Have you ever heard of the Nine Ecclesiastics?"

"Not that I can recall."

"They were a group of clerics, one for each of the gods, who helped King Hamoth defeat the Chaldmere hordes. Evidently, they performed some version of unification, but instead of amplifying one deity's divinessence, they were somehow able to harmonize all the gods' divinessences. Have you heard of anything like that?"

Barak's curiosity deepened and he combed through his memory for any information he might have come across, though he was fairly certain he had never heard of anything like what Andric had described. *The implications though.... Master Iadis might know something about this.* "Why were you and Charin discussing ancient history?" he asked with a fraction of his attention, trying to stay engaged in the conversation while his mind searched for pertinent information.

"He thinks I might be able to do the same."

Andric's simple words brought Barak up short, all of his attention focused on his friend. "You mean, with others... or by yourself?"

"We didn't get into the details, but I think he meant myself."

"And he wants you to stay in Teris so he can bring you under his wing and explore his theory," Barak said flatly, jumping to the obvious conclusion.

"I already said no," Andric said reassuringly, though which of them he was trying to convince, Barak wasn't sure. "Obviously my duty as a prince must come first."

Barak nodded. "I'm sure that's for the best. Still, it's an intriguing concept. I'll research the topic and let you know what I discover when you return."

Andric nodded, then suddenly changed the topic entirely. "Do you ever imagine what you would be doing if you ever went to war?"

"Yes, I have thought about it very carefully, and I decided the best way I could support the war effort is to stay *out* of the way," Barak answered in all sincerity.

"You can't tell me you never once imagined the thrill of riding into battle in full armor and coming out on the far side of the enemy ranks victorious."

"Of course I have. I've imagined myself Barak Quer-tav at the battle of Torgradden, or Draeden Lianador-aian when he drove back the Te-gor."

"Who?" asked Andric.

"Have I never told you the legend of Draeden and the Te-gor?" Andric shook his head. "Oh! It's one of the greatest tales of heroism among the Cannessi, at least of the split kingdoms. You see—"

"Is this going to take long?" Andric interrupted.

Barak was relieved to see a little of his friend remained intact, even if it meant missing a great story. "I suppose it would be best to save it for another time."

"How about tomorrow?" Andric asked with a restrained pleading that perhaps only Barak was able to recognize.

Barak thought he understood what the prince was asking, but it was almost unbelievable. "Will there be enough time before you have to leave, or do you want me to follow you for a morning ride to tell the story?" he asked, purposefully ignoring the intent of his friend's request.

Andric did not let him off that easily. "What have you got to lose? You've said you would like to experience firsthand the things you study. This is the perfect opportunity."

"I don't think telling you the legend of Draeden and the Te-gor is going to quite satisfy me."

"Quit being obtuse, Barak. I want you to come with me tomorrow to Luresh. That's where the mass of our force is staging. My battalion should arrive within three weeks. Come with me at least that far. There are always companies returning to Teris. If you change your mind at any time, you can come back with one of them."

"I don't want to run off and play soldier, Andric," Barak said patiently.

"But you don't have to be a soldier at all. You wouldn't go anywhere near the fighting. I want to take you on as a personal counselor. Many general officers have priests on their staff."

"I'm not a priest." It was a weak objection. Barak wondered why he had used it rather than simply declining his friend's absurd request. Before he could make a more solid declination, Andric jumped on the opening.

"That's a pathetic excuse, and you know it. No one would know the difference, and even if they did, I'm not asking you to come for your ability to officiate in religious duties. You're smarter than I am, and I could use your advice and counsel."

"Honeyed words won't get you anywhere with me," he said lamely. Barak knew he was already stuck. Perhaps he really wanted to go, despite his conscious objections.

"Besides," Andric pressed, "you know how I'm always getting myself into trouble. You would never forgive yourself if you don't come now and something happens to me."

"That's a hollow argument, Andric. But I'll tell you what... I'll sleep on it tonight, and if I decide to go, I'll be here in the morning."

"I knew you'd come," chided Andric.

"I haven't made up my mind either way. I said I would think about it."

Barak expected to be pestered until he promised, just to get Andric off his back. No such display was forthcoming though.

"Fair enough," the prince replied.

"When should I be here?"

"We leave before dawn, so if you're coming you should pack as quickly as possible and come straight back here. If there's enough time to sleep before we leave, I will arrange a place for you."

Barak abruptly got to his feet. "You sure don't leave one much time to prepare, do you, my lord?"

The prince smiled. "Welcome to war, my friend."

"Hmph!" Barak grunted as left the room.

CHAPTER XII
BARAK

An hour before dawn, Barak returned to find the 'E' section rather crowded with small groups of sleepy men leaning against the wagons covered with heavy canvas tarps. The preparations had been completed hours ago, and now they stood awaiting the order to assemble and move out. Their packs and bags were neatly lined in rows of four interspersed with the wagons in the middle of the road. Many men were either on the young or older end of the acceptable age for soldiers.

Barak made his way to the offices where he had met with Andric the previous evening. The prince stood in front of the building with his back turned to the approaching Cannessi. Barak waited patiently for his friend to finish, wondering how he would fit in among the soldiers being the friend of the prince. He didn't have to wait long before Andric turned his attention to Barak.

The prince maintained a hard, business demeanor as he greeted his friend. "Good to see you made it back in time. We are just getting ready to move out." Andric looked behind Barak and sized up his belongings. The few things Barak had brought were well packed in a fine pair of saddlebags, with a bedroll and backpack also tied to his small horse. "I didn't know you had traveling gear. I had some brought for you, but I see that won't be necessary. Where did you get it by the way?"

"The temple keeps some supplies on hand for whoever may need it, traveling research and such," Barak answered. "Where do I need to be while we are marching?"

"For now, you will stay close to Lieutenant Stetter, the one you saw earlier in my office at the small desk. I have already told him you're coming as my advisor, which means that unless I give orders otherwise, you don't have to ask for permission from anyone to see me." Andric paused for a moment and added almost apologetically, "I hope I don't sound like I am trying to make myself more important than I am. I'm just trying to give you an idea of the things I would be wondering about if I were in your place."

This was a surprising change. *Genuine humility in Andric?* Barak wondered. He smiled approvingly, "No, my lord. I appreciate your consideration."

"Good!" Andric exclaimed with a great expulsion of breath he had been holding. "Wait here and Stetter will come get you. We'll have plenty of time later to talk about all the details. Is there anything else I can get for you in the meantime?"

"No, my lord. I'm sure that I'll be fine." It felt a bit strange constantly using formal forms of address with his friend; he usually only did so when being sarcastic. He was tempted to allow himself some informality but decided better of it. It was probably best to keep up the pretense he was actually the prince's counselor rather than his friend. That distinction would undoubtedly be important at some point.

"I'll see you later then," Andric said as he disappeared around the corner of the building. Barak moved his horse aside and waited for the young lieutenant. The pre-dawn light began to highlight the western sky in the distance by the time Stetter came for him. The young officer wore his new uniform rather sloppily and didn't look especially enthused about his present circumstances. *Perhaps it was the long night*, Barak thought, and suddenly yawned wide and long. He had been awake this long before, having spent more than one sleepless night immersed in a scroll he could not put down, but he could always sleep when he finished. Now he dreaded the long day ahead of him. He hoped the sleepiness would pass by sunrise, especially once they got moving.

"I'm sorry for the delay, Master Ve'Aurben," Lieutenant Stetter greeted him. Barak felt a twinge of guilt about receiving the honorific of an ordained disciple of Viance, and a master no less, but it was not worth amending now. "Just the usual last-minute hang-ups. My name is Caermon, but you can call me Cae."

Barak decided it would be best to keep things formal for the time being. "Thank you, Lieutenant. Are we leaving soon?"

Stetter's face slumped in disappointment at the scholar's obvious declination of informality, but it passed quickly. Barak doubted the man cared one way or the other. He was too young an officer to have come through the common ranks, and he didn't appear to be here of his own volition. Barak assumed he was the son of some ranking member of either the military or gentry, undoubtedly counting the days until he would be through with his duty as a soldier and could return to his life of leisure.

"As a matter of fact, we're leaving now. If you'll follow me, sir." Stetter turned his horse and they made their way to the main street where everything was staged for their departure. A few officers rode up and down the column, taking last-minute accountability checks. Barak and his escort fell in behind the small group of officers at the head of the company, bemoaning the softness of Remalia's army compared to the old days.

Barak recognized Andric's squire next to an older man in plain clothes who stood out from the others in military livery and guessed it was another of the prince's servants. "Good morning, Jase. It's good to see you again."

"And you as well, Master Ve'Aurben. I didn't know you were joining the prince's company."

"That makes two of us," Barak replied under his breath.

An officer rode to the head of the column and reported to Andric that the battalion was ready. The prince barked the order for them to move out. Barak heard the order repeated several times down the column behind him as they began their slow march to war. There was little talking as the company moved through the quiet streets of the warehouse district toward the Grand Avenue. Soon, the traffic picked up as merchants, farmers, and anxious customers went about their daily routine of bringing the market district to life.

Sunrise broke just as they entered the Grand Avenue near Hightowers' Gate, and Andric cursed. "We couldn't even get out of the city ahead of the sun's rising," he said with disgust. Barak guessed some of the officers would assume the prince blamed them for the delay, but he knew better. Andric took it as a personal failure when his plans didn't work out as he had hoped.

The prince's tendency to always take his failures personally was a double-edged sword. On one hand, it kept the prince from unfairly laying accountability for failure on other's shoulders. On the other, Andric was often too harsh with himself and seldom held others accountable for their actions. To minimize the potential for failure, the prince did his best to keep control close at hand. This had worked in the past because he had never been given this much responsibility. Barak knew this tendency would no longer be manageable. *Perhaps it is fortunate I'm coming along after all*, Barak mused.

As they passed through Hightowers' Gate, Barak marveled (as he always did) at the wonder of its construction as city guards saluted and a few shouted words of encouragement that echoed loudly off the walls. Once under the open sky, a cool spring morning breeze blew from the southern mountains.

Before long the battalion passed beyond the outer city and followed the Highroad west beyond the outlying farms. The bright morning sun blinded them as they followed the hills dressed in neat rows of freshly planted vegetable fields and fragrant fruit trees beginning to blossom. Barak had been over this stretch of road before and was content to let his mind wander to the long journey ahead. Within a week, their road would turn south into the Myranthin Valley and take them through the Worrin Gap, one of the only passes through the Velspar Mountains into Kushaan.

It was not in his disposition to second-guess himself, but neither was it his nature to run off to war. His mind turned over in the same cycles of thought, never getting anywhere. He guessed that the seeds of a sleepless night were beginning to grow in him, nourished under the warmth of the sun and the rhythmic sway of his little horse. Shaking his head vigorously, he decided that even boring conversation with his companion would be the best way of fighting off his sleepiness.

"So how is it that you came to serve in the army, Lieutenant?"

By the look on his face, the question had intruded upon some dazed reverie the lieutenant was enjoying. After a moment of hesitation, Stetter answered. "It's nothing terribly exciting I'm afraid. My uncle is Baron Glawtar of Haetter. My mother wanted to get rid of me and asked him if he might be able to find me a position in the army. Here I am."

Barak second-guessed his decision to engage in the conversation but decided to give the young man a chance. He opted for the blunt approach. "So what's wrong with you that would make your mother want to get rid of you?"

The look on his face loosely resembled indignation, but was far too apathetic to get all the way the way there. "I suppose it's because I'm too lazy. Most people here think I'm a little slow sometimes, but you should've seen me before I began my tour in the army," he answered with an edge of self-deprecation.

Barak was surprised by the honesty of the reply, and he wondered if there were some deeper issues, so he changed the subject. "What would you rather be doing?"

"Oh, I'm happy where I am."

It was not a response Barak would have expected. He wondered if the answer was intended to cater to the prince's counselor, but before he could question him on the point, Stetter continued.

"You see, believe it or not, I enjoy having something constructive to do. I'll be the first to admit that I'm not the best soldier or the best officer, but I can do my job well enough. I can't really see myself doing anything else for the time being."

Barak was forced to amend his earlier assessment; perhaps in time, he could help the young officer improve his outlook on things. In the meantime, he decided to allow a bit of informality between them. "So, what do you like to do when you're not soldiering?"

"Nothing much really. I suppose I enjoy sleeping a lot." Stetter replied somewhat offhandedly.

Barak laughed. "Perhaps you have the soul of a *daxtant*, and the gods accidentally put you in a human body," he said, feigning seriousness.

"A what?" Stetter asked.

"A daxtant. They're something like furry slugs the size of small bears. They are rare creatures that live in the heavy jungles of Colbatta, in Kushaan. They sleep for days or weeks at a time and move very slowly when they're awake. They leave a slime trail, as do other creatures from the snail family; theirs, however, is highly sticky and traps their prey. It also contains a slow-acting poison that sedates whatever gets trapped. Later, when the daxtant comes across the food, it positions itself on top of the prey and secretes a powerful acid that dissolves its food. The daxtant then absorbs the food through its soft underbelly."

Stetter squinted and he curled his lip. Barak sensed the lieutenant was bothered by something more than the disturbing description, and waited for his companion to respond.

"Please forgive me, Master Ve'Aurben, if I am out of line in saying so, but it doesn't seem appropriate to speak of the gods as capable of making mistakes of any kind. Especially not of the nature you're suggesting."

Barak didn't know whether to be annoyed that Stetter was narrow-minded and missed the point, or pleased that he believed in something strongly enough to suggest to a priest (or someone he believed to be) that his pronouncement was *inappropriate*. He was about to retort when a halt was called for the battalion. Barak realized he had lost track of his surroundings and was surprised at how far they had traveled.

Barak remarked as they dismounted, "It must be near midday. It's amazing how quickly time passes when you're enjoying yourself, wouldn't you say, Lieutenant?"

"Yes, sir," Stetter answered in a clipped tone.

Bark guessed Stetter might be worried that he had offended the prince's counselor and wanted to put that fear to rest, but stopped as Andric came riding up.

"How are things here?" the prince asked. "Has Master Ve'Aurben worn you out with lectures and questions yet, Lieutenant?"

"No, Milord. Rather—"

Barak cut him off. "Rather, we were having a stimulating conversation about the possible theological similarities between the ritual cannibalism of the ancient Elginfir Cannessi, and the ancestral worship common to the Cannessi of the Tessuddex tribe of the Fire Range Kingdom."

Andric smiled. "Lieutenant, I will see what I can do about awarding you with a medal of commendation for this difficult assignment."

"It's my pleasure, Milord."

"We'll see how you answer after a couple of weeks," the prince jested. Barak was glad to see Andric in better spirits than when they were leaving Teris.

"Yes, sir," Stetter answered.

"Master Ve'Aurben, have you rested sufficiently to join me for a while?"

"Of course, Your Highness." Barak climbed back onto his little horse. His stiff back and legs protested the missed opportunity to rest. He knew the use of a court title would politely convey the message to his royal friend. "It appears that we'll have to finish our conversation at a later time, Lieutenant Stetter," Barak said in as friendly a voice as he could.

"Of course, Milord."

Barak sensed a hint of unease from Stetter but ignored it and followed his friend. The battalion had halted in an area shaded by tall cottonwood trees with newly sprouted green and glossy leaves. Hundreds of birds chirping in the trees floated above the low din of the soldiers chatting as they rested in the wild grass at the sides of the road. The men broke out some rations of bread, cheese, and dried meat, taking the opportunity for a midday meal.

"I wanted to ride through the battalion and ensure everything is still in order," Andric explained. As soon as they were out of Stetter's earshot, Andric chuckled. "Ritual cannibalism. Really? Is Stetter going to be all right? I know he lacks a bit of... uh... enthusiasm at times."

"Of course. He's not a bad young man."

"Barak, he's older than you are."

"Age isn't everything. You should know that as well as anyone. He chooses to remain an adolescent in many ways." Barak didn't worry he might hurt Stetter's career by talking this way to the prince. If anything, Andric might try to help him.

"It must be nice," Andric stated in a more somber tone.

"You would prefer to be ignorant of the world, driven by currents beyond your control or understanding?" Barak asked.

"You think any of us truly have control or understanding? I feel carried along by the currents in the world just as much as Stetter or anyone else."

"Maybe at the grandest scale, but you're in a position to shape the world more than most." Barak's words came out more lecturing than he intended.

"Not that it seems to make much difference in the end." That was a loaded statement, but Andric stopped to issue instructions to one of the sergeants. When they resumed riding down the line of soldiers, the prince continued. "Did I mention they captured the ones who attacked Venerate Alscome's temple?"

"See, you do make a difference."

"There was another attack on a Sykorian temple two nights ago. I haven't changed anything. It just keeps getting worse."

Barak did not have a good reply. They rode to the front of the battalion under the weight of a heavy silence. *Was there any point in coming on this fool's errand?* Barak wondered darkly.

He suspected the answer was no.

CHAPTER XIII
STEPHIR

Luresh would recover.

Indeed, it seemed hardly to have sustained much damage at all. The Kushaani siege equipment that now lay abandoned and broken on the fields surrounding the city was crude and largely ineffective other than to chip large holes in the white plaster covering the red-brick city walls like bloody wounds on a great white bear.

Luresh was the provincial seat of Stephir's cousin, Duke Osten Laconeus. Once part of the Kushaani empire, their grandfather had conquered it many years ago. Two generations under Remalian rule had seen it built up to become the largest city between Teris and the great port city of Kashpur on the Fragrant Coast in southern Kushaan.

Still, Stephir had a hard time imagining the reason the Kushaani had attacked Luresh in the first place. It certainly made sense as a strategic target, but the Kushaani could never have hoped to take the city with the forces and equipment they had fielded. Perhaps they had simply not anticipated the Remalians arriving when they did, or maybe they had underestimated the difficulty of taking Luresh. Whatever their reasons, Stephir was grateful for the victory.

When word had reached the king after leaving Balinth's Fortress that the Kushaani had invaded Remalia and were attacking Luresh, the army pressed south with all due haste. Of course, it hadn't been fast enough for Baron Marstoff, who stood to lose his home if the city fell, not to mention his wife and nephew ('the king's nephew as well,' the Baron never tired of pointing out). However, the report spoke of only a few thousand troops, primarily light infantry—hardly a serious threat to Luresh. The king had decided that arriving in four days instead of six was as much as he wanted to push his troops; any faster, and he would risk losing stragglers, stretching supply lines, and wearing out the men before they arrived.

From the look of things, the king's calculation had worked out well. Luresh had withstood the assault. The Kushaani forces were lightly armored and lightly mounted—no match in direct battle with Remalians, and had been routed with ease. The Folkerk River that ran next to Luresh was somewhat swollen with late spring runoff, and the Kushaani had collapsed the bridges, buying themselves some time.

Remalian archers kept the riverbanks clear with a rain of arrows while foot soldiers across the Folkerk and began pressing the Kushaani back. Once Remalia's cavalry was able to cross, Stephir quickly mounted a charge on the enemy's flank, shattering their ranks (such as they were). The battle was over in moments. Chaos took hold of the undisciplined Kushaani and they scattered like crickets under hoof.

The easy victory had left the soldiers elated and the commanders confident the future battles would be just as easy. Stephir knew that wouldn't always be the case, but he was willing to simply enjoy the victory for now.

The prince rode alongside his father amidst the ever-present Divinarim, followed by the usual tail of armored nobles, knights, and generals. They surveyed the battlefield as they made their way toward Luresh's gates, congratulating the men and graciously receiving their cheers as they passed. As they neared the gates, the young Duke Lachoneus rode out of Luresh with his aunt and an entourage of lesser nobles and guards to greet the king.

It had been a few years since Stephir had seen Osten. There was not anything particularly noteworthy about him. He was a rather plain-looking young man despite the finery he was decked in. As the two groups approached each other, Osten and those with him dismounted and dropped to a knee.

"Thanks to Your Majesty for saving our city. We are forever in your debt and your service." Osten's voice was a rich baritone that was at odds with his youthful appearance.

The king gestured for them to rise. "I only wish we could have been here sooner to keep them from your walls in the first place. No matter. They won't be back, I assure you."

Lady Marstoff chimed in. "Will Your Majesty do us the great honor of residing with us at the palace?"

"I wouldn't have it any other way." Jevorak directed an easy smile toward Osten. "I've been wanting to hear all about my nephew's plans for the future of these lands."

Stephir laughed silently at the small jab at Baron Marstoff, who was off surveying the damage to his fair city. Perhaps the Baron had annoyed his father more than the king let on. Stephir asked the king's leave to attend to matters outside the city, before joining them later. The king invited Osten to take Stephir's place at his side, and the large group headed into the city.

Stephir broke away with his commanders to see to the needs of the army. He gave orders to find the city's chief engineers and elantir with related skills to start work immediately on repairing the bridges. Some troops were tasked with salvaging whatever they could from the field (which Stephir guessed probably was not much) and hauling the rest into piles to be burned.

The Remalians had taken several hundred Kushaani soldiers captive. It was possible that over a thousand had fled into the densely forested country-side, and twice that number lay dead, or near enough for his men to do them the mercy of hastening the inevitable as they cleared the field. The captives were put to work collecting their dead and burying them. Kushaani tradition called for the burning of their dead and to leave the enemy's dead to rot. Stephir wouldn't normally care one way or another what his army did with the enemy's bodies, but the people who lived in Luresh wouldn't appreciate rotting or burning corpses outside their city, so this time they would all be buried. Fewer than one hundred of his men had died, and only a few of rank. Each would receive individual burials or be returned to their homes if their families could afford such honors. The Kushaani bodies were being placed in mass graves.

Having seen as much as he wanted of the battlefield, Stephir made his way to the army's camp on the north side of the city near the river where the army's. After nearly a month of marching from Teris to Luresh, they welcomed a couple of days to recover before pressing south into Kushaan. By all accounts, his father had been a great battlefield commander in his day, but Jevorak had never fielded an army this large. To manage the sizable force required planning and discipline that few officers and fewer nobles had the mind or patience for.

But Stephir had delved into the matter whole-heartedly. He poured over historical accounts of campaigns, scholarly treatises on logistics, and had even traveled to Eastgate two years ago on a diplomatic mission to strengthen trading ties for the Western Marches. Such a mission would normally have been beneath the attention of the crown prince of Remalia, but his ulterior motive was to observe the Eastgatian military's logistics discipline, which, as far as Stephir could tell, was the finest in the world.

Upon returning to Remalia, Stephir had pressed his father to let him take full charge of the Remalian army's logistics. To say the king was less than enthusiastic about the idea was an understatement. Jevorak insisted the task was beneath Stephir's station. In an attempt to appease Stephir, Jevorak had suggested they put that task in Andric's hands, but Stephir persisted, and the king relented.

Once in place, Stephir aggressively instituted sweeping reforms. He ordered a separate Quartermaster's Corps be established, with designated officers and soldiers. In preparation for potential threats, stockpiles of weapons and equipment, foodstuffs, livestock, wagons, and a myriad other supplies were incorporated into a five-year plan. Granaries and warehouses, with small garrisons to protect them, were strategically planned across Remalia.

Stephir also changed the way they organized the troops on the march. Jevorak had refused when Stephir requested uniform weapons, equipment, and clothing for their entire army. 'It's far too expensive,' the king had insisted; they would continue with the system that had been in place for generations, with each soldier's liege lord providing much of what was needed, and the rest was either purchased by the soldiers, gathered from the battlefield, or handed down from father to son (if anything was high enough quality to last that long).

Stephir was disappointed. Remalia hadn't been in any real war in over twenty years and the old system was inadequate to accommodate the king's plans for war. Jevorak had made a small concession and allowed Stephir to provide the entire army with uniform livery and a decent weapon for every soldier.

There were many places in Remalia where Stephir's vision remained yet to be realized. However, the plans for supply depots along the Spice Road from Teris to Kushaan had been largely implemented. This allowed the army to move far more quickly since they weren't required to forage or carry large amounts of supplies with them. Alas, the storehouses south of Luresh would only provide another week of support at most. Beyond that, the army would be in enemy territory and would have to resort to other means of supply.

Today was the first time the entire army would be in one place for more than a night, and Stephir was eager to see that his orders were carried out as he intended. The terrain through the Worrin Gap and the Neral Valley was not well suited to the large, geometric patterns of camp order that Stephir had pictured. Most days the troops spread haphazardly out over a mile or two.

There had not been much he could do about it before, but now it was time to instill some much-needed discipline.

Some commanders were trying to follow Stephir's instructions of establishing neat rows of bedrolls, with campfires at even intervals, and horses tied in long lines of posts. However, many of the men plopped down anywhere they could find an open spot out of the way, and nobles sought decent locations for their tents to be erected. The chaos grated on Stephir's nerves. Wherever he rode, he insisted on order.

"Those latrines are being dug too close to the camp. Move them out there. And don't forget to fill in the holes you already started!" "Get all those bed rolls in line. No, twenty to a row. Not sixteen; not twenty-two. Twenty. And the gaps between them should be five men wide." "I'm sorry, Earl Rhingstorf, but you must move your quarters to the east end of that line or out beyond the latrines if you prefer. Those are your choices." "Where are the wheelbarrows for hauling the horse manure out of camp? What do you mean we don't have any? Well, get some men and build some or you'll be carrying it out with your bare hands!"

Frey hadn't said much for some time but finally quipped, "Well, I am *so* glad I came with you instead of going to the palace with the rest of the sane people. It is far more entertaining listening to you make sure the horse shit is taken care of."

"Careful, or I'll have them put it next to your tent. Then you can decide whether it's important to take care of," Stephir retorted.

Just then, Quartermaster General Fenishol rode in Stephir's direction from the east side of the camp. Stephir liked the man well enough, and he had almost as much of an eye for detail as Stephir did.

"Your Highness," Fenishol greeted the prince with his usual flat expression.

"Quartermaster General, how do things proceed?"

"About as well as you suspected they would, my lord. But we'll have them disciplined well enough by day's end, even if day's end doesn't come until tomorrow."

Stephir knew Fenishol meant it, which was in no small part why Stephir had selected him for the position of quartermaster general. While Stephir had addressed a handful of issues, he could guess Fenishol and his officers were having to deal with dozens of details, large and small.

"Is there anything I should be aware of?" Stephir asked, hoping there wasn't, but he was committed to whatever it took to make his vision materialize.

"No, Your Highness. It's all being taken care of. As I understand it, the royal pavilions haven't been erected due to the expectation that you and your father will be staying in the city." Stephir nodded his confirmation, the quartermaster went on as if he was discussing nothing more important than barrels of horseshoe nails. "If you'd like to take some refreshment, my command pavilion is set up due east toward the city walls."

Frey chimed in before Stephir answered. "Excellent idea, Fenishol!" Stephir did not like the disrespect to the quartermaster general by dropping his rank, but Frey did that to most officers, and Stephir was not going to reprimand him—at least not in front of everyone. "I'm famished and could use a stiff drink after today's fun. Your Highness, shall we?" Frey asked as if the decision had already been made.

Stephir had myriad thoughts spinning through his mind, but he hadn't eaten in several hours and neither had those with him. They could all use a moment's rest and some food. "Of course, thank you, Quartermaster General. We'll make our way there now."

Fenishol bowed his head and two of his men turned their horses and galloped away to make the arrangements. Stephir nudged Havvoron into a practiced canter and the prince's his way through the camp toward the city. Calls of "Hail, Prince Stephir!" and "Stephir the Conqueror!" were shouted as he passed.

"I wish they wouldn't call me that," Stephir mumbled to Frey while attempting to look pleased. "We didn't conquer anything, and it was hardly a fight at all."

"Well, it's hard to blame them," Frey said, casually glancing at the men erecting tents and arranging equipment. "We won, for Akraharr's sake! The day is ours. They can be forgiven for being a little exuberant after a battle like that, can't they?"

A smile crept onto the corners of Stephir's mouth. Indeed, they had won, just as the king, nobles, and generals had predicted, and with more ease.

They soon arrived at the quartermaster general's command tent. It was not as stately as the king's field pavilion and command tents, but it was spacious and would hopefully be cooler in the shade of the city walls. Stephir and his entourage dismounted, tethering their mounts to the horse lines. Stephir handed Havvoron's reins to his squire, Gaeten Pouley, and followed the two Divinarim that preceded him inside the large tent. A couple of soldiers immediately stopped what they were doing and stood straight, saluting with their palms facing the ground, fingertips at their hearts, the universal salute when not carrying a weapon.

His eyes had difficulty adjusting to the dim light, and the air was hot and heavy. *So much for cooler*, Stephir thought with disappointment. He was used to the elantir keeping his quarters and the command pavilion at a tolerable temperature. "Continue," he commanded without much thought. The men bowed and returned to their work, quickly setting up additional chairs and small tables for the prince and his company.

Gaeten helped Stephir remove the heavier pieces of his armor and the other nobles and officers followed suit. They tried to relax as best they could, considering the impromptu accommodations. Food and drinks were eventually served, and the men joked, laughed, and bragged their way through the next hour. The prince was relieved to realize someone must have summoned an elantir when the tent became noticeably cooler.

Stephir listened to General Cadaer recount an amusing story from years ago when he punished his men for leaving their post to sneak into a nearby village in the Western Reaches by making them strip down to their small clothes and march through town with the rest of the squad. Stephir laughed until he felt a sudden presence behind his shoulder. He instinctively flinched, knocking over his wine glass while reaching for the sword that was no longer on his hip before he even realized what he was doing.

"Vance!" Stephir yelled, angrier than he should have been. "Don't sneak up on me!"

"My sincerest apologies, Your Highness!" Lieutenant Vance said earnestly, regret written on his weather-worn face. A servant was already at Stephir's feet, cleaning up the spilled wine. Stephir tried to laugh it off, and Frey was more than happy to help.

"Your Highness didn't get enough fighting out of your system today. Be patient. There will be plenty more to come!" Frey chuckled.

Stephir appreciated his friend helping to deflect his embarrassment. "So," Stephir said, facing the junior lieutenant, "was there a reason you needed to stop my heart, or were you just trying to help my son ascend to the throne a little sooner?" It wasn't particularly funny, but the other men in the room laughed as a courtesy. Stephir hated that. He was not as good at humor as Frey or even Andric. It had been that way his whole life, which was why he usually tried to avoid attempting it altogether.

All eyes were on Lieutenant Vance, who withered under the attention. "Again, my apologies, Your Highness. Alscan requests a moment of your time."

"*Commander* Alscan," Stephir corrected sternly; while he may put up with some of the nobles and generals failing to use appropriate titles, he didn't tolerate it from the soldiers. It was hard enough getting anyone to accept the elantir as part of the army, including many of the elantir themselves, and insisting they be given equal courtesies was an essential part of making that change. "Well, don't keep the commander waiting. Show her in."

"Of course, Your Highness." The lieutenant held the tent door open as a slender, middle-aged woman strode confidently into the room. She wore twin braids, one at each temple, holding back a cascade of sandy-brown hair behind her shoulders that framed her pleasant face, which was cast in a sober expression. She was clad similarly to the scouts, although she carried herself with a great deal more poise. Her soft leather boots were laced up to her mid-calf and folded down at the tops. Dark blue breeches were barely visible behind strips of oiled leather weighted at the end by metal disks. Her leather breastplate was simple but functional and hardened to turn a stray blow.

Commander Alscan stopped in front of Stephir and saluted in the peculiar manner of the elantir, left hand open, palm up, and the edge held close to her body, the heel of her right hand resting in her open palm, fingers pointing toward the sky. Then she moved her hands in a circle, parallel to the ground. Stephir understood the meaning behind the salute, even though few others did, or even cared. Stephir inclined his head, acknowledging her greeting.

"Commander Alscan, to what do we owe this pleasure?"

"Your Highness, forgive my intrusion. I have something I would like to discuss with you in private if you will permit it."

Stephir respected Calinda Alscan. She was the highest-ranking elantir serving in the army and a brilliant woman. Months ago, and at the suggestion of High Consul Penrossart, Stephir had selected her to command the army's elantir. They had occasionally discussed the role of the elantir. She believed that they could serve a far greater role if provided the opportunity.

The elantir had their uses, to be sure. Their abilities ranged from offering conveniences like heating or cooling the air in the tents, strengthening the construction of buildings and bridges, and providing the means to communicate at great distances. Legends were told of great elantir in ancient times who could reshape Baon itself to their wills. 'If you could do that, I'd be very interested,' Stephir had said with mild irony.

'Perhaps if Your Highness would let me know what you would like us to do, we could work on it," she had answered sincerely. Stephir had promised to give it some thought, but more immediate needs always seemed to demand his attention.

Stephir wanted to stay in Fenishol's pavilion and relax a while longer, but there were still many things to attend to, and the commander's request was as good an excuse as any to get himself moving again. Seeking a private audience with the crown prince was an unusual request from the commander. Stephir worried she may have received word something had happened to Ilyanara or one of the children and was anxious to hear what she had to say.

Addressing the others in the tent, he politely asked, "Would you all please wait outside while Commander Alscan and I speak? I will be with you shortly." Everyone quickly rose to their feet and bowed. Stephir motioned to Frey to remain seated. "Marquis, you will please remain." The others continued their conversations as they exited the tent, leaving only the three of them in Fenishol's pavilion.

"Commander, I don't know if you've had the pleasure of meeting Marquis Freydon de'Venneshen, eldest child of Archduke Irris de'Venneshen." Frey and Alscan exchanged greetings and the marquis retook his seat.

When everyone else had left, the commander bowed her head in a moment of concentration. Stephir felt the slightest pull on his elan and knew Alscan was performing some elant. Most people didn't recognize the feeling of their elan being drawn unless it was significant, but Stephir's few months of training with Master Bellubont as part of his tutelage had sensitized him to it so he at least knew what it was.

The ever-present background noise of the world that blended into the subconscious background of life suddenly went silent, and he knew she had created a space where no sound could penetrate or escape. It was useful for ensuring their conversation remained private, perhaps even from the Divinarim that remained inside the tent.

Stephir took the opportunity to ask a question he had wondered about in the past and occurred to him again now. "Why do you block the sound in both directions? Is it possible to let us hear the sound around us, but prevent others from hearing us?"

The commander smiled. "An astute question, Your Highness." Unlike many of the nobility and others that Stephir had to deal with, Alscan never gave false praise or patronized him. "Yes, it can be done, but it's much more complicated and would be difficult for me to maintain the elant while conversing. A group of us could do it easily enough I suppose, although I don't know why we would."

"Safety," Stephir replied without hesitation. "If something were happening outside the tent, an attack for example, it would be advantageous to hear what was happening, don't you think?" He hoped he didn't sound paranoid.

"Of course, Your Highness. I shall instruct the elantir to consider that in the future."

"And what's so urgent to warrant all of this?" Stephir asked, trying not to sound worried.

"Something is impairing our clairaudient capabilities."

"Your *what*?" Frey asked as if she had said something distasteful. Stephir knew him well enough to recognize when he was mildly annoyed. He probably thought the commander was purposefully using words he didn't understand just to be insulting.

"Our ability to use met'elan to communicate with others over distance, Marquis."

Stephir felt an immediate sense of relief that the concern had nothing to do with his family. He also knew what a serious matter this was. Without the ability to communicate on the battlefield, it would complicate how they managed their tactics.

"Do you know what's causing it? Is it just us or is Teris having the same problem?" Stephir had many more questions, but he chose to tackle one problem at a time.

"Your Highness, we cannot contact Teris either."

"How is that possible?" Stephir asked, anxiety slipping into his voice. He took a deep breath to regain control before continuing. "Did something happen to the Bonded?"

He hated thinking about the elantir who allowed themselves to become living communication links. Through some arcane process, a group of Viancian scholars had devised a way to divide an elantir's body in half, from the top of their head down through the torso, then fuse each half of the body to a giant blood-red crystal. It left the elantir in somewhat of a half-life, neither dead nor entirely alive, but it allowed communication to occur between the two halves.

The Viancians had explained vaguely that the spirit still inhabited each half as one body, two parts of a still-living whole, or something like that. In one location, a pair of Keepers, an elantir and a priest, could lay their hands on their half of the body to open a link with Keepers touching the other half, allowing people in both locations to speak to one another. Such living links were called the *Bonded*, and they were regarded as heroes for their ultimate sacrifice. Of all the met'elan Stephir had seen, these disturbed him the most.

There were six Bonded in Teris: one linked with Balinth's Fortress, one with the great port city of Deock in the Western Marches of Remalia, one at each of the ancient cities of Tennury, Banbridge, and Steadleigh on the northern coast of Remalia on the shores of the Inland Sea. The final one had been brought with the army. The Bonded were eminently useful in aiding the king and his government to stay in constant contact with key parts of his kingdom, but it chilled Stephir to think about those who had sacrificed themselves for such a gruesome transformation, regardless of the benefits to the kingdom.

To communicate with his commanders in the field, the elantir used similar communications using divided parts of a tentacled ocean creature instead of a human. The only thing he knew about the fachim was that its brain was spread throughout its whole body, including its tentacles, which was necessary to create the link. However, the creatures rarely lived more than a day or two after being divided and bound to the crystals, and the distance was limited to a few miles. The human links didn't seem to be limited by distance, and they could exist for years if properly sustained and dispositioned.

The commander continued circumspectly. "We have yet to determine the cause. As you can see from my elant," she said, making a sweeping gesture, indicating the silent space they were in, "other met'elan is working as it should. It appears to be limited to our clair—" she stopped herself, "to our communications with the Bonded and the fachim. We are currently unable to use the Bonded at all. Communication with the fachim appears to be..." Alscan seemed to search for the best word, "... inconsistent, though we are only in the preliminary stages of our investigation. I assure you, Your Highness, my experts are diligently working on the matter, but I thought it best to keep this information contained at this time.

"As for whether this is just affecting us or is a more widespread phenomenon, I can't say. I believe it would be wise to dispatch soldiers with some elantir back to Balinth's and south to Penniven. This will allow us to determine whether Balinth's Bonded is affected as we are, or if this problem is limited to the immediate vicinity of Luresh. We have begun working on an alternate system of communicating in case this problem persists."

"How do you know it's an elantic problem and not the divinessence?" Stephir asked.

"Truthfully, the priests have little to do with communications and aren't used with the bonded fachim at all. Their role is primarily to disposition the source to keep them at ease. It is the elantir who extend the lines of communication through the link."

"Ok, but can we go back to the question of why this is happening?" Frey interjected with the same tone one might use with a servant who failed at some simple task and had not given a satisfactory explanation. "I mean, you must have *some* idea."

The commander kept her steady gaze on Frey, no doubt choosing her words carefully. "While it is very delicate work to create the Bonded in the first place, once accomplished, the link is incredibly stable until the source is lost."

"The source?" Frey asked, sounding as if his patience was wearing thin.

"The living creature through which the link is created," the commander answered flatly.

It bothered Stephir that she referred to the elantir who had made such a sacrifice in such an impersonal way, but maybe it made it easier for her to deal with. He honored those who would forfeit the rest of their conscious lives to become a link for communication even though it left him with a hollow feeling in the pit of his stomach.

"The fact that this is the first time any of us have even heard of this phenomenon, that it occurred while we were performing this particular elant, and that it's occurring immediately following the battle with the Kushaani, leads me to believe they may have something to do with it. That is, however, merely circumstantial conjecture, and offers no help in resolving the issue."

Stephir's mind raced through the implications of this news. He was certain of only one thing: he needed to tell his father.

Frey's voice cut Stephir's musings short. "She's right. We should send out riders. The commanders need to know what's going on, and we need to know if the other Bonded are having the same problem."

"Not yet. I need to speak with the king." Stephir rose and the normal sounds of the world returned. "Commander, please send word to me at the palace if there's any further news. Marquis, you'll come with me."

Alscan bowed and left the tent.

"Your Highness, a thousand pardons," Frey said with exaggerated obsequiousness, "I have a matter with my men that needs attending to."

Stephir was certain his friend meant he wanted to join the victory celebrations with the other young nobles. Stephir shoved a twinge of jealousy aside. He envied the freedom Frey enjoyed, but parties and celebrations weren't Stephir's favorite pastime anyway. He didn't want to let his friend off that easily though. "Is it more important than informing the king of this grave threat?"

Frey's scowl was nothing more than a slight contracting around his eyes. "Of course not, Your Highness," Frey answered sarcastically. "I would be ever so grateful to listen to you deliver this news to your father."

"Marquis," Stephir put his arm around his friend's shoulders as if about to lay an even greater burden there, "I'd sooner see a fire swallow caged than drag you into the torture chamber of my father's war council. Go with the Holy Couple's blessing and attend to your men."

Frey bowed low with arms spread wide. "I'll ride with you for a bit, Your Highness, at least until we enter the city."

A wry smile touched Stephir's lips despite the disconcerting news he was tasked to relay to his father. The prince squinted against the glaring sunlight as he exited the dimly lit quarters to join the others who had waited outside the tent while the commander gave her report. They mounted their horses and rode directly for Luresh's main gate. Along the way, he gave orders for a variety of tasks needing attention, and the men split off to see that they were carried out.

Stephir's impatience got the better of him and he kicked Havvoron into a gallop, Frey at his side and the others following. No one challenged them as they rode through the open city gates. They were forced to a crawl through the crowded, narrow city streets that twisted haphazardly. The people of Luresh shouted their thanks and offered the gods' blessings upon Stephir for saving them. As the Divinarim worked to clear a path, Frey took the opportunity to excuse himself from Stephir's company.

"Don't do anything I wouldn't do," Stephir advised his friend.

"Then I apologize in advance for disappointing Your Highness."

Stephir shook his head and laughed.

Luresh may have been the largest city in the Vastan Province, but it was dwarfed by Teris, and Stephir quickly arrived at the ducal palace. Several of the city soldiers guarded the large plaza in front of the palace. The elaborate structure was not at all to Stephir's liking.

The smooth plaster finish of the sculpted walls was the color of tanned leather. Cylindrical towers along the palace walls were dotted with many small but beautiful stained-glass windows. Wide steps ascended from the plaza to a large, peaked archway sheltering two royal blue doors. The upper floors of the palace were lined with enormous open windows occupied by guards who watched the plaza below.

Stephir dismounted and handed the reigns to a young attendant, demanding to be taken to the king. Two Divinarim accompanied Stephir as a pair of house guards ushered him through the gilded royal blue doors. They walked briskly along the corridors, and Stephir noted how much more lavish the décor was than most Remalian houses, even among the nobility. It had probably been that way when it was originally built by the Kushaani before being conquered by Remalia, but Baron and Lady Marstoff had not shied away from the style in their years managing Osten's estate. Perhaps the Marstoffs secretly worshipped Yerin, who espoused the virtues of the creative arts and beauty in every form. Either way, he guessed their patronage had provided full employment for many artists who dedicated their lives to the tenets of Yerinism.

Stephir knew he had arrived when they turned a corner and he saw six Divinarim standing guard. They were already at attention and snapped sharp salutes in unison as Stephir approached, then opened the door for the prince while Stephir's escorts joined their ranks. Heads in the room turned, and those who sat came to their feet when Stephir entered, except for the king.

For just a moment, Stephir locked eyes with Jevorak and recognized fatherly pride. But it was quickly replaced with the king's usual stern public demeanor. Stephir bowed to his father and Jevorak nodded a greeting. Maps covered a large, polished wooden table occupying the center of the rectangular room. Troop markers were set in their customary places each time the maps were brought out. Stephir was grateful he had missed the usual repetition of their war plans.

Jevorak regarded Stephir seriously. The king said nothing, and the long silence in the room became awkward. Stephir resisted the urge to shift self-consciously as the moment stretched on, trying his best to appear confident to the rest of the assembled nobles and officers. Keeping his eyes fixed on his father in patient expectation, he saw a few of the nobles fidget uncomfortably in the king's uncharacteristic silence. Stephir was unsure of his father's expectations, and he shuffled through possible responses.

Fortunately, the king finally broke the silence. "This may be the first time I have participated in a battle since I was a child where the victory was not mine, but belongs to another." King Jevorak spoke to no one in particular, but he kept his careful gaze on Stephir. "This victory belongs solely to my firstborn son, and future king of Remalia."

The assembled nobles, priests, and officers began to applaud loudly. Several of them offered their congratulations, but Stephir heard none of them. His father rose from his seat and approached with outstretched arms. Stephir had nowhere to go but to accept his father's embrace, returning the affection as best as he could manage under the scrutiny of the nobles.

His normally stoic father grabbed him by the shoulders, pulling him in close, and whispered so only Stephir could hear amidst the still cheering nobles around them. "Today you became a king in their eyes, Stephir. Remember the power of perception." With a couple of quick affectionate pats on the shoulder, his father released him and stepped back, beaming with pride.

Stephir cleared his dry throat as best he could before speaking. "Thank you, Your Majesty, but the victory belongs to everyone."

Jevorak gave a slight sigh, though Stephir could not discern what thoughts might have triggered it. The prince finally glanced at the others in the room as the applause and commotion died down. Osten was by far the youngest one in the room and sat silently next to the king's place at the table.

Baron Marstoff was not as reserved. "As I was saying, Your Majesty, Luresh's hospitality is yours for as long as you require it. But certainly we should press our advantage. We could be at Nanjab within four days and—"

"Only if we press the troops at the pace we did to arrive here," interrupted High General Kuymon, absently smoothing the ends of his mustache into his beard with his thumb and finger. "Those were exigent circumstances, and it took a toll on the men. They should rest for another day or two before we move on, and then only in the ordinary course."

"Well, with the supply shipments replenishing our stocks, I suppose..." Marstoff trailed off. Stephir knew the baron's real concern; he didn't want his resources depleted by feeding the whole of the Remalian army.

"Stephir?" his father sat in his place at the table and directed the attention of the room to his son.

The prince wanted to use the opening to give his father the news, but he needed to demonstrate that he was a commander first and foremost. His father had made it clear several times that he was to take charge of the army. He had already considered their argument and was ready with a response.

"We no longer have a single objective," he said, approaching the maps on the table. "We must reinforce the borders here, here, and here," he said, pointing to small fortresses marked with carved stone towers. "Two thousand men, including one hundred mounted, will be assigned to each. They will leave tomorrow morning. That will keep any Kushaani from slipping into Remalia after we have moved into Kushaan. The men can rest when they arrive at their posts."

Barron Marstoff nodded. Stephir was sure the man was pleased to have at least a portion of the army off his doorstep, even if was only a fraction of the vast host.

"Osten, you will retain all of your forces here." Stephir continued.

Baron Marstoff inhaled sharply, ready to object, but Osten's response was too fast. "Whatever you command, my lord. It shall be done." Marstoff's face turned red, but there was nothing he could say about it now. No doubt he would make a private plea later.

"The day after tomorrow our remaining forces will march for Nanjab. However, as soon as we are over the border, General Premmet, Duke Frendic, and Marchioness Haedep will take their troops and march south to circle east of Nanjab," Stephir moved the markers to illustrate his plan. "Our main force will move slowly enough to give them time to get behind Nanjab before we attack to cut off their retreat."

Jevorak nodded his approval, and the nobles hammered their fists on the tabletop in acknowledgment of the commands.

"Now, I need the room to speak with the king, so if you will all excuse us."

Jevorak's face was inscrutable. If he was surprised by Stephir's actions, he didn't show it. "High General Kuymon, you should stay." With the meeting adjourned for the time being, the other nobles, priests, and officers filed out of the room, their own conversations resuming before the doors were even closed.

"So, what news?" Jevorak asked.

"The elantir have lost their ability to communicate," Stephir answered.

"Well, at least we won't have to listen to them complain about their place in the war anymore," the king quipped. The high general stifled a chuckle.

"Through the Bonded, and sometimes using the fachim as well," Stephir continued more gravely.

Jevorak's face fell. "Do they know what's causing it?"

"Commander Alscan suspects the Kushaani are somehow interfering with the met'elan, but hasn't yet discovered the cause. We need to send men to Balinth's and Penniven. We also need to plan for an alternate means of communication in case this is permanent."

"The scouts will do it," High General Kuymon stated. "Of course, with our forces spread out, we'll need a lot more scouts. Perhaps we can press Baron Marstoff's men into the scout corps."

The three of them snickered. Had Marstoff heard, he would be downright apoplectic at the insult.

"General, see that it's organized tonight. I want groups moving at first light. The scouts should move ahead of everyone else. Coordinate with Commander Alscan for the groups that will have elantir with them."

"Yes, Your Majesty." The high general stood to attend to the matter.

"Good enough for now," the king said with finality. "It's time to go celebrate our victory!"

CHAPTER XIV
QUARIAN

Quarian tethered his horse to a tree in a dense copse of towering silver pines a half-hour's climb below the ridge line. His mount was trained to keep silent, as were all scouts' horses, but Quarian didn't take unnecessary risks. The wind in these mountains could easily carry an errant sound to the enemy's ears, and that could spell disaster for a scout's work. Quarian ordered Teek to remain with the horses as he and Dain followed Vai up the mountainside to a safe vantage point to see for himself what they had discovered just three days ago.

Quarian had hardly believed the report of a massive Kushaani army moving east through the Velspar Mountains toward Teris. The Velspars were a vast mountain range, and many areas were impassable this early in the year. With soaring peaks, weather that could turn deadly without notice, treacherous glaciers, and the risk of avalanches and rockslides on the steep slopes, even the scouts did not venture far into the mountains.

For the past three months, Quarian commanded the scouts patrolling the areas along the mountains west and south of Teris. Previously, he had spent ten years patrolling the lands of Remalia bordering Kushaan south of the Velspars. He was good at his job, and despite being Sa'ari, he had been promoted to captain of the southern borderlands scouts three years ago. He had shaped them into some of the best scouts in the Remalian army, for all the good it did them. Scouts were generally disdained by the rest of the army, who viewed them as too cowardly to do any real fighting, slinking through bush and shadow like mangy thieves. Many of the officers knew their value but didn't hold them in particularly high regard either.

Quarian had trained his men well. Due in large measure to Quarian's efforts, the scouts were organized into independent units with their own command structure. Before his leadership, the scouts were a ragtag mix between messengers and eyes and ears out in the wilds of Remalia and beyond.

Three months ago, without any explanation, he had been reassigned to patrolling inside Remalia. As he became aware of the impending war, he deduced that the Kushaani border patrol was now a more respected position. He had effectively been demoted, and it bothered him. He suspected it was because he was Sa'ari, but he would never speak of it to anyone; it wouldn't be the first time since arriving in Remalia. He just hoped that with time and hard work, the reassignment would prove to be only temporary.

It was late afternoon as Quarian and his men crouched behind rocks and small brush in a safe vantage point overlooking the next valley. Spring may have finally arrived in the lowlands, but up in the mountains snow and ice still held a tight grip on the world. The icy wind whipped the few loose strands of Quarian's raven hair around his golden, weathered face, but he gave no sign it had any effect on him. He focused on the hundreds of human figures moving swiftly through the snow, rocks, and sparse trees in the shadowed valley below.

He carefully pulled out a blackened bronze spyglass to get a better look. He shaded the glass lens with his hand to ensure the sunlight would not reflect off the glass and give away their position. Most scout officers carried spyglasses, but Quarian's was a treasured possession from his homeland, far superior to Remalian craftsmanship. He watched unmoving for several minutes, taking in every detail with his keen eyes.

These soldiers were different from any Quarian had encountered before, in physical appearance, dress, and weaponry. He kept looking for any clue that would allow him to figure out where they came from. The only answer that made sense was that they were Kushaani forces that had somehow made their way through the mountains further west, but it felt wrong. Kushaan covered a vast territory, and while Quarian had familiarized himself with the details of the most common (and a number of the less common) Kushaani tribes, there were admittedly some that he was not familiar with. If Empress Arrdiwat had decided to invade Remalia, she would no doubt pull troops from every corner of the empire.

Quarian took more time than he was comfortable with to determine that the shadows weren't playing tricks with his eyes. These Kushaani were gray-skinned, and their clothes were slate gray, blending in with their skin and the surrounding rocky terrain. Most were heavily built but bore light weapons—curved knives and short javelins. And they were adept at moving swiftly through the mountainous terrain.

He wondered how they were provisioned, seeing no wagons or pack animals. There was some game in the mountains, but foraging for such a large force was out of the question. Each soldier carried a large pack, so he assumed they carried their rations with them, but he wondered how long they could survive with that. He suspected they must have had mounts and other supplies until relatively recently to have made it this far across the Velspars.

But it was their size that made Quarian question his senses. He was skilled at assessing people and objects, even from a distance, but if his eyes were to be believed, these warriors stood at least a head taller than most Remalians and weighed half again as much. He watched for a long time, repeatedly comparing them to their surroundings to gauge if he was correct. He had seen many Kushaani in his time, but never any that looked like these.

Finally, Quarian decided he had seen enough. He carefully stowed his spyglass and signaled his men to follow him back to their horses. His quick mind was already laying out every detail of his next steps. Once back at the horses he broke the silence.

"I think you were right, Vai," Quarian addressed the older scout who had first reported the news about the troops. Quarian had brought Vai with him when he was reassigned from the borderlands patrol. Vai was an excellent scout and, more importantly, was skilled at making other scouts good too. "They must be Kushaani of some kind, though I've never seen their likes before."

Vai and his partner, Teek, nodded in agreement. They had tracked this group after they split off from the main Kushaani force, which had turned north. According to Vai's report, the main army was approximately twenty thousand strong, though that number seemed impossible. Kushaan was a strong empire, but to have secretly gathered such a large force in addition to the troops fighting the king and his army in eastern Kushaan was unlikely. Quarian was perplexed by how they had gotten into Remalia without anyone knowing about it. A force that big could not have come through western Remalia without being discovered. They must have found a route through the mountains further east.

Quarian wished he had time to catch up with the other scouts tracking the main force so he could see for himself, but there was no time. It had been two days since Vai had intercepted him in the Worrin Gap, which meant he would be racing to get word to Teris and Balinth's Fortress ahead of the possible attacks.

Quarian spoke with his men as he prepared to leave. "Dain, how many do you estimate they are?" At only seventeen, Dain was by far the youngest of Quarian's men. The captain included him as an equal in their discussion, as he did all his men. Among many other things, Quarian's fairness earned their love and respect. There had been some who assumed his equitable treatment meant they were *actually* Quarian's equal, but it rarely occurred anymore. Quarian let the other men straighten out anyone who got the wrong idea, leaving Quarian free to develop his scouts, not keep them in line.

After a moment's concentration, Dain ventured a guess. " 'bout five or six hundred, I'd say."

Quarian knew it was imperative to get this news into the hands of his superiors, but it could wait a few moments to give some instruction to the young man. "And how did you come to that number?" Quarian was not trying to embarrass Dain, but he needed to get the boy to think methodically. He knew Dain, like most of his men, had almost no education before becoming a scout. Quarian required all his men to learn reading, writing, and simple math, but Dain was still too new to have gotten very far in those studies.

Quarian could see on Dain's face that he immediately recognized his answer should've been based upon more than a mere guess and now was unsure how to respond. Quarian didn't have the time or the disposition to leave Dain in this awkward position. "I can see you've already understood the point. Vai, what's your estimation?"

" 'bout a thousand, give or take maybe fifty," Vai answered coolly.

"And how did you come to that number?"

"They're spread fairly evenly over 'bout two miles or so. I marked off some space on the ground that looked 'bout ten parts in a mile. I tried to get a count of how many men were in that space at a time. It seemed to be 'bout fifty. Ten of those in a mile would be five hundred men in a mile, and two miles... a thousand men," Vai managed to state matter-of-factly, without any smugness.

Quarian appreciated Vai's humility. However, he knew Vai was secretly pleased with himself, as well as he should be; as recently as a year ago Vai could not have performed the same feat. He made a mental note to commend Vai in private later. Vai would be embarrassed if Quarian praised him in front of the others.

Quarian knew Dain was completely lost, but that was fine. He didn't need him to follow the arithmetic or the logic right now, he just needed to adjust his mindset. "Don't feel bad about it, Dain. We'll teach you how to do the same. You've got good instincts, but we expect much more of ourselves in my patrols. Prepare to use your mind as much as your instincts."

Quarian mounted his horse and the others followed suit. He had one more lesson to impart to Dain before they split up. "I saw when you realized it was wrong to guess at the enemy numbers, but you didn't immediately own up to it when you recognized your mistake. That's a much worse mistake. I don't expect you to be perfect, but I do expect you to have the integrity to take responsibility for your mistakes. Problems are easier to fix when they're out in the open." Quarian paused to let that sink in, then finished, "Scouts live by trusting each other, and there's no faster way to lose the trust and confidence of those around you than by failing to own your mistakes or to earn their respect when you do.

"Vai, you and Dain stay on this group," he ordered. Quarian kept his scouts in pairs, usually with the same partners for a year or more, and didn't change things lightly. But he had good reasons to leave Dain with Vai. Remaining to track the troops was more responsibility than returning with Quarian, and he wanted to show Dain that he didn't hold anything against him. More importantly, Quarian had to move as fast as possible, and in this treacherous terrain he could move faster with the grizzled but experienced Teek. Quarian turned his horse and he and Teek began the journey out of the mountains.

If the enemy kept their current pace and stayed in the mountains, they would be at Balinth's Fortress three days from now. With any luck, Quarian and Teek could be there tomorrow night. Quarian pushed them as quickly as he could without unduly risking the horses' safety. The last thing they needed was a crippled horse. Stopping for a short rest at dusk to feed and water the horses, they ate a light meal of dried fruit, nuts, and some dried venison, then pushed ahead on foot, leading their horses through the deep darkness beneath the thick pines. It was tedious work, but every mile they moved meant more time to prepare for an attack, assuming that was the enemy's intent.

They traveled for several hours before stopping for a bit of sleep. They woke as pre-dawn light cast a pale rosy glow on thin wispy clouds high in the sky, though the light had not yet penetrated the darkness of the narrow valleys of the Velspars. After another few bites of food, the pair set off on foot again until it was light enough to safely ride. The light was short-lived, however.

Dark, heavy clouds blew in overhead from the west, promising that rain was soon to arrive.

It could be to their advantage if they arrived in the open valley quickly enough. It would slow the Kushaani considerably, especially if it was warm enough to rain instead of snow up in the mountains. It was not long before a light rain began falling on their heads; not enough to be more than a nuisance, but if it got any heavier, it could become a problem for the horses.

They pushed ahead as an icy wind blew from the steep mountainsides behind them, whipping the spring showers into a cold downpour. Quarian found it a relief that it was at their backs instead of driving into their faces. *Small favors.* Streamlets crisscrossed their path, making the way more treacherous in the low light of the valleys.

Several hours passed before they abruptly broke free of the soaring peaks into the broad valley a hard day's ride north of Balinth's. The wind was less severe here, but the rain was heavier. It had taken them longer to arrive than he had anticipated, and it was going to be well after dark before they got to the fortress.

The miles passed as they pushed south along the road. Although hidden behind the clouds, the sun had passed its zenith; they only had a few hours before dark would once again descend. Quarian felt the tension build as each delay cut away their lead on the enemy.

Teek signaled to Quarian to look at the ground.

Quarian nodded. Tracks of a sizable force were written in the muddy earth. There was no way to tell their numbers or who they were though. Quarian would be surprised if it was anyone other than Remalian troops heading south. They would keep a sharper eye on the road ahead, but he could not afford the delay of leaving the road.

Nearly an hour later, the rain abruptly ended. Rays of sunshine beamed through the occasional break in the clouds, softly touching the golden peaks around them, but unable to reach the floor of the steep valley. Despite the circumstances, Quarian found himself taking a moment's pleasure in the beautiful scene, fleeting as it might be. As they rounded a sharp mountain spur jutting into the valley, they abruptly came upon Remalian troops moving south toward Balinth's. Quarian's full attention returned to the urgency of the situation.

The two scouts rode past the supply wagons that rolled sluggishly along the muddy trail. Dunnigan's Highroad was well-maintained, hard-packed, stony ground, so the mud didn't pose much of a problem for them. The rain-soaked soldiers marched grimly through the mud as well, the respite in the weather bringing little comfort. Soldiers glowered at the two scouts as they passed. Quarian guessed they were envious that those they considered *lowlifes* had the great luxury of being mounted. A couple of hours of daylight remained, so their marching was not nearly over. Quarian knew that once his news was delivered to the commander, their marching day was likely to get much longer.

It was only a single battalion, so it didn't take long for them to make their way to the head of the column. He was surprised to see the royal guard there. A young officer broke away from the main group and stopped the two men. "What business do you have, scouts?" the young lieutenant casually asked, not bothering to acknowledge Quarian's superior rank.

Quarian ignored the slight. "I need to see your commander immediately."

"If you'll tell me what this is about, I will convey the message to him."

Quarian didn't bother answering the young man. He had no time or patience for games today. He pushed his horse forward toward the other officers. The lieutenant spun his horse and tried to pull in front of Quarian but Teek cut across his path.

"Out of my way, *scout*," the officer barked contemptuously.

The commotion drew the attention of the officers and the royal guards, who spurred their horses into a protective formation around one of the officers. From all appearances, Quarian assumed it was Prince Andric. He had been informed that the prince had left Teris and was moving through the valley to join the rest of the army at the front. Quarian was unsure of the proper protocol in Remalia for reporting with a royal in the group, but he would rather slight a commander than a noble, so he chose to deliver his report directly to the prince.

Two Divinarim and their captain moved in front of the prince, with three more flanking him on each side. Quarian was about to ask for permission to speak to the prince but decided to skip the formalities. "M'lord, I have dire news that you must hear immediately."

The prince looked at an officer to his right that Quarian guessed was the commander of the battalion. Turning his attention back to Quarian the prince answered. "What is it, Captain?"

Quarian was dismayed at the prince's casual response. It could only mean that his scouts had not delivered their news to those at Teris yet. "Might I suggest that we discuss this at a small distance?" The prince's guards sat forward in their saddles and their hands tightened their grips on weapons. It probably didn't help that he was a foreigner. "Please, m'lord. This news should be heard privately."

"Very well." The prince, along with his contingent of nine guards, the commander, and his second, followed Quarian and Teek as they turned to move a bit further down the road. Quarian noted how the prince's guards moved into an hourglass-shaped formation around the prince. Quarian's mind tested the formation against different attacks if he and Teek had meant harm to the prince. It was quickly apparent that it was a highly effective formation to handle any tactic they might have tried. He thought a circle may have been better if it was just the two of them, but bringing in a knight on each side of the prince made a shot from a bow much more difficult. Quarian stowed away that information as he reigned in his horse and faced the prince.

"Your Majesty has not had any news from Teris then?"

"It is '*Your Highness*' or '*My lord*', not '*Your Majesty*'," the commander corrected him snidely.

"Thank you, Commander," the prince cut in. "I'm sure the captain meant no disrespect to the king." He again regarded Quarian and answered pleasantly. "Teris is two weeks behind us, and we've had no word since then. What's going on, Captain?"

Quarian was not sure which news to convey first, but after a slight pause, he decided it didn't matter and pressed on. "There's a force of approximately a thousand Kushaani troops moving through the mountains in this direction. They are only a day or two behind us." He noted the confusion and shock that played across the faces of the prince and two officers and thought he noted some slight reaction on a few of the faces of the prince's guards. "That's not all. There's a much larger force moving northeast through the mountains. We can't be certain, but they're likely heading toward Rookstone or perhaps toward Teris."

"What! How? How many are there? When will they reach Rookstone?" The prince shot the questions at Quarian in rapid succession.

Quarian answered much more calmly. "My men report that there could be as many as twenty thousand."

Again shock flashed across the men's faces. "That's not possible!" the prince exclaimed, his concern edging toward anger.

Quarian knew he needed to keep that anger from being misdirected at him and his men and instead focused on solutions. "Some of my men are tracking the main army, but I have seen the smaller force with my own eyes just yesterday. We were very fortunate to have discovered them before they broke away. In those mountains, they could easily have passed undetected until they attacked."

"Attack what?" the commander scoffed. "Teris? Balinth's Fortress? Ridiculous!"

"Who have you reported this to, Captain?" the prince asked, ignoring the commander.

"You're the first, Your Highness. We were on our way to Balinth's Fortress to give this report when—"

"Have you sent word to Teris?" the prince cut in tersely.

"My lord," the commander interrupted, pleading with the prince. "We can't possibly take these reports seriously on nothing but the word of a couple of scouts. Perhaps the Sa'ari just—"

"My father would never disregard this kind of information, no matter who it's from, and neither will I," Prince Andric said, cutting off the commander's protest.

Quarian appreciated that the prince didn't appear to entirely bear the usual prejudices against the scouts. "My men are following the main force and have dispatched riders to report to Teris as soon as they are able. Balinth's Fortress was much closer and I thought it would be faster to ride there and have their elantir contact Teris directly, then they could send riders to take word to the king."

The prince mused aloud to himself. "Twenty thousand is a strong force, but even so, they're only on foot. Without siege equipment, it is unlikely that even that many Kushaani could take Teris. Maybe their intention isn't the capital. But what else would they intend? Rookstone? Even if they could take it, they could never hold it. Maybe simple pillaging? None of it makes sense. And how did they get through the Velspars?"

The commander jumped into a moment's pause. "If this larger force really exists, then it's certainly the greater threat. A thousand men foraging through the mountains could never take Balinth's. The real question, my lord, is whether to send the battalion back to Teris or continue to the fortress. I suggest we have them return and reinforce the city. Teris won't fall, but we don't want these Kushaani raiding the countryside and burning the fields."

The prince nodded slowly, though whether in agreement or merely acknowledging the commander's words, Quarian couldn't tell. He knew his opinion on the matter was not welcome, but he hoped they would overlook the intrusion under the circumstances. "Perhaps it isn't my place to say, but I believe those men would be put to better use defending Balinth's Fortress."

"You are correct," the commander said with feigned pleasantness. "It is not your place."

"Let him speak, Commander," the prince said firmly.

Quarian was surprised. This was not the spoiled, shallow prince he had heard stories about. Prince Andric had some steel in him. "Your battalion would be lucky to make it back to the city before the enemy arrives there. Even if they did, what difference are they going to make?"

The edge in the commander's voice made it clear he didn't appreciate being second-guessed by anyone, especially some scout, captain or not. "You make it sound as if Teris is already lost. The city has never been conquered, and I don't intend to see it happen during my lifetime. We have reduced the numbers in Teris to push most of our forces to Kushaan. If there is a viable threat, we should have every available man defending the city."

Quarian didn't want to be argumentative, but he wanted to finish making his point. "What concerns me, sir, is that it makes no sense for those forces to attack Rookstone or Teris. Either they have another trick in store, are acting as some sort of distraction, or the cities are not their target. They could intend any kind of harm in the north country, in which case this battalion isn't going to be of much use against such a large force. Either way, a sizable portion of our army is going to need to return to stop whatever it is they intend to do. But if the fortress is captured, that could become problematic. It would be costly in time and men to retake that fortress from the southern side."

The commander took in a breath, seemingly intent on continuing the argument, but the prince cut him off. "Thank you both for your counsel, but I must agree with Commander Fenlan. Balinth's Fortress has withstood tens of thousands of Kushaani before. It has a contingent of eight hundred defenders, which is more than enough to hold off a mere thousand. Teris is our highest priority. Commander, please gather the troops and make all haste back to Teris to defend her against the enemy."

Quarian didn't like how this was unfolding at all, but he felt powerless to change it.

"Of course, Your Highness," responded the commander, sounding insufferably satisfied the prince had followed his advice, but also somewhat surprised at what the prince's order implied. "You don't intend to return to Teris with us?"

Quarian saw the subtle signs of self-doubt play across the prince's face and wanted to persuade him to reconsider, but this was a level of politics far beyond his depth, so he simply remained silent.

"I intend to find my father and brother and aid them however I can. Teris is in good hands, Commander. As you said, it seems impossible that such a force could ever take the city, and your men will help ensure that remains true. Send riders as you go to alert as many nobles as you can, and have them

raise all the troops they can muster. I will bring aid as quickly as we are able."
Then the prince addressed Quarian. "How soon can we reach Balinth's?"

"If we can ride straight through and the weather remains clear, we should
be there by the time Silmal zeniths." Quarian was not used to working with
anyone other than scouts, nor was he used to someone else being in charge.
And he certainly had never imagined he would be riding in the company of
royalty. *Such are the odd circumstances of war.*

"Knight Captain," the prince addressed the captain of his guard, "we
need rations to last until morning. And please inform Master Ve'Aurben that
he'll be joining us." The captain nodded to two of the Divinarim who
galloped away to retrieve the supplies for the group. Quarian had never seen
the Teraithian holy knights up close, but he had the sense they would be quite
fearsome in battle.

"Gods speed and keep you," the prince said to the commander.

"May the gods keep us all, Your Highness." The commander rode away to
inform his men they were returning home, although it was under worse
circumstances than any could have imagined when they left Teris a couple of
weeks ago.

Quarian glanced over his shoulder at Teek for the first time since the
exchange began. The corporal slightly raised an eyebrow but gave no other
indication of his thoughts. Quarian had only met Teek a few times before
yesterday and hadn't spent enough time with him to tell from his look what
he was thinking. Vai vouched for him as a solid scout, if a bit rough around
the edges. The man had a reputation, though, for being too quick to speak at
inopportune times and having a rather sharp disdain for nobility, neither of
which showed through in this instance. Perhaps the reputation was
undeserved.

Quarian turned back as the prince began speaking again. "You said the
other Kushaani force is a few days behind us?"

"If we are lucky." A few days was not at all what Quarian had said, and he
was surprised the prince was so far off. In these circumstances, those seemingly small differences could prove to be a matter of life and death. "It's more
likely they are only a day behind us. Two at the most," he corrected.

The prince shook his head, and Quarian could imagine what he was
thinking. Discovering his kingdom had been invaded; his home, the capital
city, under threat of imminent attack; the key stronghold between his army
and the enemy might soon be under attack; and he was the only person positioned to warn the king. It would be a lot for anyone to digest, and under-
standably more so for a young and inexperienced prince.

Quarian felt hunger gnawing at his stomach. They hadn't eaten since before dawn, but need drove them to forgo food. He hoped they would eat something before they arrived at the fortress. *What does one eat when traveling with a prince*, Quarian wondered to himself. He pulled out his waterskin and took a long drought. The cold water hit his empty stomach, and he hoped it would take the edge off the hunger until they departed, then he would forget all about being hungry.

Quarian and Teek waited in silence until the knights returned. They were followed by someone that Quarian assumed was this *Master Ve'Aurben*. If he hadn't known better, he would have guessed it was a young boy due to his size. Even more discouraging was the small stature of his horse. Quarian felt frustration fill his empty stomach; this would surely add more delays when none could be afforded. But it would be worse than pointless to say as much to the prince, so Quarian remained silent.

Teek, however, failed to follow his example, muttering half to himself, "His *Highness* may just as well have brought the whole damn army for as much speed as we're gonna make now."

Quarian's heart clenched in fear that the prince had heard the remark. Whether he did or not, Prince Andric made no response. Quarian shot the scout a withering look. Teek shrugged. Apparently, the corporal's reputation was well deserved. Quarian would have to address this later.

One of the holy knights whispered to his captain, who nodded then addressed the prince. "Your Highness, Master Lonset and Squire Couvor have inquired whether they should come with you?"

"Well of course Jase should come!" the prince exclaimed with exasperation but then appeared to struggle for a moment. Finally, he added with even more annoyance in his voice, "I suppose Lonset should come as well. Tell him that only the barest essentials should be brought."

One of the royal guards rode back to the battalion. Quarian tried to suppress his growing impatience. He could wait quietly for several hours while scouting, but sitting in this silence was painful. The minutes seemed to stretch endlessly, and the rest of the battalion was reversing course when at last the Divinar returned followed by two young men. One was clad in light armor—Quarian was certain he was the prince's squire—and the other was a heavy-set man with short blond hair and ruddy cheeks. He led an extra horse with saddle bags and small boxes tied to its back. He must be some kind of personal attendant of the prince.

"Lonset, I said essentials!" the prince exclaimed in exasperation. At least Quarian was not the only one.

"Forgive me, Your Highness. I was not sure what your lordship considered essential, so I took the liberty of packing a few clothes and other necessities."

Quarian looked and saw that, unlike everyone else, the prince had no saddlebags or other personal effects with him. *Of course he wouldn't,* Quarian chastised himself. The prince probably had an entire wagon full of personal effects. Master Lonset must have had an awful time trying to narrow it down to just a few items.

"Leave everything but one or two changes of clothes and the cleaning gear," the prince ordered.

It took a few minutes to rearrange everything. Quarian glanced at Teek again, who simply shook his head and spit to the side, out of the way. Quarian considered chewing sourleaf a disgusting habit, but Teek was not the only soldier to do so. The scout captain could not quite tell if the grizzled scout's expression was one of amusement, disbelief, or disgust, but Quarian had all of those emotions turning in his stomach. Or maybe it was just the hunger.

"Let's go," the prince finally said as he spurred his horse into a gallop.

Quarian was unsure where his place should be in the group, so fell in line with the royal guards who spread out to flank the prince. Heavy darkness descended as night overtook the valley. Not long after, rain overtook them as well; a steady drizzle to accompany their slow pace.

It was going to be a long night.

CHAPTER XV
ANDRIC

Andric had stayed awake all night before, but it was always for fun with friends and parties—not like this. Weariness wrapped around his mind like a cold, wet towel and ached deep in his bones. It was just after dawn when Balinth's Fortress came into sight between the steep, towering walls of the narrow canyon that soared overhead. The diffuse morning light filtering through the clouds and incessant rain made the enormous granite structure gray and dull. Andric had only seen the fortress once before on a trip to visit his aunt and uncle in Luresh when he was twelve years old, before they had gone to their god's embrace. It looked as imposing now as it had then, perhaps even more so now that he could appreciate its significance.

How could only a thousand men hope to take this fortress, especially without siege engines, mining equipment, or food to sustain them? No, their intention must have been to catch him unawares, to overtake his battalion within the confines of the canyon. He let out a slight sigh, satisfied he had made the right decision to send the battalion back to Teris. Andric assumed the scout captain either had never seen Balinth's or was no tactician to have thought the fortress was in danger from such an insignificant force.

The fortress silently slept until they were within bow-shot of the gates, then the muted sound of chains and gears rattling inside the walls began echoing up the narrow canyon. Slowly the portcullis raised, and the iron-bound gate doors swung inward. A score of mounted soldiers, with the fortress commander at their head, rode out to meet the prince and his party.

Andric was within speaking distance and was about to instruct the commander to take them inside when the large man spoke first. "Prince Laconeus," he said, bowing slightly in his saddle. "Your Highness's arrival is most welcome, but also unexpected at this hour." The commander's demeanor was firm and well-polished.

Andric didn't know him, but the prince could tell that he came from an excellent heritage. His mostly gray hair, showing signs of having been black in his younger years, was cropped short and combed flat with practiced care. His pinched nose and tightened expression were at odds with his deep, baritone voice as he addressed the prince. "We were informed you were to be expected yet another few days hence, else we would have—"

Andric interrupted, "Yes, thank you, Commander. We rode all night to arrive here. Perhaps we could get out of this rain to discuss the matter."

"Of course, Your Highness. Forgive my thoughtlessness," the commander said bowing again., He turned his horse and led Andric and his men around the other garrison soldiers, who waited for the newcomers to pass before falling in behind. In minutes, they were entering the northern gate into the stone-floored fortress, a cacophony of horse hooves clacking and echoing off the tunnel walls. The commander led them through a series of hallways and tunnels that Andric guessed took them into the canyon wall itself. It was good to be out of the rain, but the air was even colder than out in the open, and Andric shivered as it pierced his soaked skin.

At last, they stopped in a long, open chamber. The commander dismounted and the group followed suit. Several young men took the reins from Andric and the others. The prince took a moment to give Kobo an appreciative pat on his powerful neck.

"Your Highness will, of course, want to change into dry clothes, have a meal, and perhaps get some sleep," offered the commander. "I will be happy to escort you to your quarters."

Andric longed to accept the commander's hospitality, but it would have to wait. "Please make my men comfortable, but we must speak immediately."

Knight Captain Lindthen selected two Divinarim to escort the prince. Barak raised his eyebrows, wordlessly asking Andric if he required his presence. The prince shook his head. The ride had no doubt been harder on Barak than anyone. Andric turned to the raven-haired scout captain. "Captain Min, you will join us as well."

Min was much easier for the prince to remember than the captain's full last name, which was too long and foreign for Andric. Minalsum, or some such name. It sounded Sa'ari, as did his accent, but the prince had no inclination to inquire into the man's background. He was just grateful the captain had offered an alternative that was easier to pronounce.

They followed the commander up a narrow, winding staircase carved from the rock of the mountain. Andric's healing shoulder ached from the long, wet ride. His legs were stiff and sore too, but it felt good to be using them again, even if it was to climb stairs that seemed to go on forever. They passed three more floors until finally the commander exited the stairwell that continued to climb the fortress heights. He led them across a roofed stone bridge spanning two enormous semi-circle towers built into the mountain walls on either side of the canyon. There were two such bridges between the towers, and he guessed they were crossing the lower one. The bridge had small openings on each side, looking north and south over the canyon pass. Tunnels ran throughout the canyon walls, and openings at various places along those walls high above the canyon floor provided unreachable positions from which to attack the enemy.

The main fortress extended below them, filling the entire canyon like a dam. It once represented the southernmost point of Remalia, but the kingdom's borders now extended nearly a hundred leagues south. Although there were no records of who built the fortress or when, the kings of Remalia had always held it in defense of their homeland against the Kushani. It had never fallen since the earliest days of the kingdom, and Andric was sure it would not fall now.

Andric noted it had stopped raining. It was his kind of luck, he thought to himself, that it would stop raining just after arriving at the fortress.

"Forgive the long route, my lord, but Balinth's Fortress was built almost entirely for defense. The few comfortable accommodations are just through here." They passed through a doorway at the end of the bridge into the west tower and into a large antechamber, which had passages disappearing into the darkness beyond. The commander continued across the chamber to a large wood door flanked by two guards, who immediately pulled it open and saluted as their commander passed and entered a larger room. Delicious warmth washed over Andric as he passed through the doorway. A fire blazed in a large fireplace on the south side of the circular room. Andric immediately made his way closer to the fire and carefully stretched his aching shoulder. He vaguely heard the commander instruct the guards to add two chairs to the ones already near the fire.

"May I offer you a drink while we wait for your breakfast to be brought?"

"No thank you, Commander. I'm afraid it would put me to sleep."

Turning to his two companions, Andric extended the commander's invitation. "Captains?"

"No, thank you, Your Highness," the two men answered in unison.

"Let me get straight to the point, Commander," Andric continued. There was a great deal to say, and Andric was not sure how to prioritize, so he just jumped into it. "Captain Min..." Andric stopped as he realized no introductions had been made, and he still didn't know the commander's name.

"Forgive my manners. I should have allowed for proper introductions. Commander, may I present Knight Captain Wreyn Lindthen of the Order of the Divine Flame, son of Lord Gareth Lindthen of Wainsford." Knight Captain Lindthen saluted the commander, arm across his waist, fingertips at his sword hilt. "And Captain Min of the Scout Corps I have just recently met, so I will let him introduce himself properly."

"Captain Quarian Minanthsolum, sir," the scout said with his fingertips resting just above his almond eyes. "Or Captain Min is just fine if you prefer."

Andric had always found the salute of the scouts a bit odd, but it made sense. The scout's weapons were his eyes, so where else would their fingertips go?

"A pleasure to meet both of you captains to be sure. Minanthsolum. That's a Sa'ari name, is it not?"

"It is, sir. I came to Remalia nearly ten years ago from Qelasaar."

Andric was pleased to have been correct about the origin of Captain Min's name. He liked the sound of it but knew he would never remember the whole thing. He waited a moment, but when the captain offered no additional information, Andric turned to the commander. "And please forgive me for not knowing your name, Commander."

"Not at all. Your Highness cannot be expected to know the name of every man in all of Remalia. I am Commander Winvelle Tra'en of Deock, son of Duke Braedel Tra'en." The commander saluted, fingertips at his sword hilt.

"Oh. Archduchess Tra'en is your sister then?"

"Half sister, Your Highness. My mother was Lady Caran of Bin'sha, my father's second wife."

"I saw Her Grace at the Charge Days in Teris. I know my father very much appreciated her earnest support for this campaign." It felt awkward with the four of them standing, but he didn't feel like sitting and the others would never accept an offer to sit while the prince remained on his feet, so he pressed on. "Would that we were more at our leisure, but I am afraid we come with critical news." His conversations with Barak were affecting his manner of speaking, but he liked sounding more serious.

"Captain Min and his scouts discovered a force of Kushaani soldiers moving through the mountains northwest of here. He estimates nearly a thousand will be here in the next day or two."

The commander squinted in consideration of the prince's words, but he didn't seem overly concerned. "One thousand troops... through the mountains?" Andric understood the commander's skeptical tone, but he didn't want to rehash the discussion about whether Captain Min's report was to be believed. He was relieved when Tra'en moved on. "Do you have any idea what their intentions are? Does this have anything to do with why our communications with Teris have been lost?"

Confusion and panic fought for dominance inside Andric's weary mind. "What do you mean? Your elantir aren't able to communicate with Teris? Has something happened to the Bonded?"

"Yes, two days ago," Commander Tra'en answered, confirming Andric's fears. "We sent messengers to the king, but we haven't had word back."

Andric was disappointed. "While we don't know the cause, we may know the reason. Another force reported to number twenty thousand are also traveling through the Velspars toward Rookstone and perhaps Teris." The commander's face finally registered some shock at this news, and Andric continued. "Your loss of contact with the city leads me to believe it may already be under attack. Balinth's is likely to be next."

"But surely a thousand men on foot can do little against this fortress? And Teris? Even twenty thousand against her defenses cannot possibly prevail. What can they hope to accomplish?"

"Again, Commander, we don't know. I am confident that you and your men are more than capable of dealing with whatever the enemy has planned for Balinth's, but we thought it worth hastening to alert you."

"Of course. Thank you for your efforts, Your Highness. I will inform my men to prepare immediately. Should we expect the battalion you were leading to arrive soon?"

"No. I thought it best to send them back to ensure that word of the threat was spread to the areas en route to Teris and to help defend the capital. However, I had hoped to send word to Teris from here, but I can see that's not..." he let his words trail off in thought. *I should have immediately sent riders ahead to Teris*, he chastised himself. He felt his shoulders slump. They had lost another day or two.

"My apologies," the commander began hesitantly. "I can summon one of the elantir if you wish. Perhaps they could shed more light on the difficulties with the Bonded."

"That won't be necessary, but we need to warn Teris. I hope they are already aware of the threat, but I want messengers sent at once just to be sure."

"As you command, my lord. And what does Your Highness plan to do next? How may we be of service?"

"If I may impose upon your hospitality a bit further, I believe my men and I will take a few hours of rest from our travels before we press on. I must reach the king and my brother with all haste and inform them of this news."

"It would be our great pleasure, Your Highness. The breakfast I ordered for you should arrive here soon, but if you prefer to take it in your rooms, I could show you there immediately and have the food sent to you instead."

Andric was impressed that the commander managed to be solicitous without being obsequious. It was a balance he did not see often. It seemed to come most easily to those of humble but firm confidence. Andric was glad to see a man of Commander Tra'en's caliber in command of Balinth's Fortress.

"I think I will be able to enjoy the breakfast a bit more if I'm in some dry clothes."

"As I said, there aren't many comfortable accommodations here at Balinth's, but I would be deeply honored if Your Highness cared to stay in my quarters."

Sleeping in a real bed for a change sounded magnificent, but he wanted to show that he was not the spoiled prince some people seemed to think he was. "Thank you, Commander, but I prefer to stay with my men. A simple bed for a few hours of sleep will be more than sufficient."

"If you'll follow me then." The commander stopped briefly to issue instructions for their food and to have the commander's captains meet him in some other area of the fortress, then led them back across the bridge and down two floors and out into the main fortress structure. It was not long before they arrived at the quarters where Andric's party had been given accommodations. The commander showed Andric and the two captains to private rooms adjacent to the common barracks rooms, then continued to a small eating area with wooden tables and benches where his guards, Barak, Jase, and Lonset were all eating some hot food. A couple of the fortress soldiers were in the room as well, though not eating, just there to give help as needed.

"Your food will be down soon, I'm certain. Is there anything else I can do for you, my lord?"

"No, thank you, Commander Tra'en. I believe we have everything we need for the moment. We will find you again after a bit of rest."

"Of course, Your Highness. I'll take my leave then to prepare for these little rats that think they can sneak into our house," the commander said with a chuckle. He saluted again, nodded to the captains, then returned the way he had come.

It only took a few minutes for their breakfast to arrive. He was not sure if it was just the fatigue, cold, the circumstances of the past day, or if Balinth's had an excellent cooking staff, but the food was delicious, and it was all Andric could do to maintain his manners and not devour everything in sight. He made plans with Knight Captain Lindthen to leave mid-afternoon. Andric didn't see the need for another all-night ride, but it would be late before they stopped to sleep. With any luck, they could be at Luresh by the day after tomorrow.

He bid them a good morning and went to his quarters, where he found that Lonset had set out a change of clothing and had some hot water and his cleaning gear waiting on a simple stand with a small metal mirror. These accommodations were nothing like what he was used to, but he was too tired to care. Upon further reflection, after he changed his clothes and got cleaned up, he started to feel somewhat like a real soldier for the first time. He took some satisfaction in that as he fell into bed.

As soon as he closed his eyes, there was a knock at the door. *Ugh! Couldn't they let me get a few moments' rest?*

"Yes?" he called out testily without opening his eyes.

"Forgive me, Your Highness, but it has been five hours," Master Lonset called plaintively through the door. "I was told that you would want to be wakened."

Andric sat bolt upright. *How could that be? We should be leaving now.* "Yes, come in." Andric was still not entirely awake and needed Lonset's help to ensure he was presentable when he joined the others.

Lonset was already apologizing as he entered, bowing low. "I knocked an hour ago, but you told me to go away."

Andric didn't remember anything of the sort, but neither was he surprised. "It's fine. I should have been up an hour ago. Are the others ready?"

"Yes, Your Highness. They're waiting in the dining area."

Damn! thought Andric. *This is not going to help earn anyone's respect.* Between the two of them, they got Andric looking presentable in no time, and Andric made his way quickly down the hall, trying to appear as if everything was as he intended rather than showing how sheepish he felt. His men stood as he entered the room, except for Barak who remained sitting at one of the tables.

"Knight Captain Lindthen, is everything ready for our departure?"

"It is Your Highness. Shall I send word to Commander Tra'en that we are leaving?"

"Yes. Ask him to meet us at the horses." Andric caught a glimpse of a page as he ran to inform the commander.

The Divinar captain nodded and the other Divinarim left the room. Andric heard them moving along the corridor toward the stairs leading down to where they had left their horses, though Andric noted one of the knights posted themselves just outside the door. "There's some food here Your Highness. We will wait with the horses for your arrival."

"Thank you, Captain. Do we have the additional provisions we'll need for the trip to Luresh?"

"It's all been taken care of."

"Very well, I will join you momentarily." Knight Captain Lindthen saluted and turned to leave, but Andric stopped him. He hadn't seen the two scouts. "Where is Captain Min?"

"I believe he's with Commander Tra'en, my lord."

"Really?" Andric was surprised. He hoped the scout wasn't making a nuisance of himself.

"I believe so, Your Highness," Lindthen confirmed.

A yawn caught Andric by surprise before he could answer, so he simply nodded and waved Lindthen away. The Divinar saluted again and departed. Barak was the last one left in the room, watching Andric with a bemused look.

"What?" Andric asked defensively as he joined his friend at the table and reached for some bread, cheese, and fresh fruit.

"Sleep well, my lord?"

"Oh stop," Andric said curtly, glancing at the door where the royal guard waited. "How's the sunburn feeling?" Andric inquired sympathetically.

Barak already had fair skin, but remaining inside with his books all the time had left him ill-prepared for the constant exposure to the unforgiving sun during their travels from Teris.

"It's feeling better. The salve I got from your physician has helped." Barak took a drink of water, then changed the subject. "You know, I keep thinking about Captain Minanthsolum's description of the soldiers in the mountains. Do you really think they sound like Kushaani?"

"Who else could they be? Kolrathi maybe? They are supposedly darker skinned, but these numbers would be more than all the tribes put together, from what I understand. They know how to live off the land though, so it might explain how they made it so far without more provisions."

"No, I don't think they're Kolrathi."

"Spit it out. I can tell you have thoughts rattling around in your head."

"While I can't be certain, there are several points of similarity with descriptions I have read of the Kuldrith."

"You mean the Kuldrith who the Eastgatians all but wiped out five hundred years ago?"

"It wasn't the Eastgatians. It was the Byanthine Empire. The Eastgatians have just been fighting the Kuldrith more recently. But the description from Captain Minanthsolum fits the Kuldrith better than any other group I can think of."

"Barak, they are a small handful of people scratching out living in caves halfway around the world. How and why would they come all the way to Remalia?"

"I don't know. I'm just trying to keep an open mind." Barak paused, absently pushing the food around on his plate. "I keep thinking about Teris getting attacked by... whoever they are. I try to imagine what it would be like to be there now, the fighting going on outside the temple. Part of me wishes I was there to help, but part of me is glad to be far from there, out of harm's way. I'm afraid you have a bit of a coward for an advisor."

Andric was surprised by Barak's candor and didn't quite know how to respond. "Don't worry. Nothing is going to happen to Teris or your books. If the Kushaani are foolish enough to siege the city, they'll still be waiting when we return to crush them against her walls."

Barak shrugged, then continued more seriously. "I'm slowing the group down."

Andric knew it was true and had thought about it more than once last night. It had never been a problem while traveling with the battalion, but it was a factor when speed was essential. Regardless, Barak was here now. Andric couldn't send him back to Teris, and he was not about to leave him here in the fortress with the Kushaani coming, real threat or not. So, he had to come with them. Besides, he was still one of the only people Andric was completely comfortable talking to, which alone made him one of the most valuable people in the world to the prince. He hadn't needed Barak's advice as much as he thought he would, but he was still grateful to have him along.

"A few hours more or less isn't going to make any difference in the big scheme of things, so don't worry about it. Besides, you're the prince's advisor; who's going to question whether you're worth the extra trouble besides me?"

Barak grimaced. "I'm glad you can make light of it."

"What else can I make of it? You only weigh about ninety pounds." They laughed more than the joke merited, but it felt good. Andric finished a few more bites and drained his cup, then he and Barak left to join the others, followed attentively by his Divinar protector.

As they arrived once again in the close, cool chamber at the foot of the stairs, everyone was making final adjustments to their saddles and bags. He was relieved to see Captain Min was already with the horses. Kobo and Steed stood ready for their riders. Andric needed something to do while they awaited the arrival of Commander Tra'en, so he double-checked the saddle fittings. No need, of course. Jase had already taken care of it, as he always did. They finished securing their gear and waited. Uncomfortable in the silence, Andric spoke with Knight Captain Lindthen and Captain Min about the journey ahead of them to Luresh, even though he knew well what to expect.

At last, the commander strode along one of the corridors toward the chamber. "Forgive me for keeping you waiting, my lord," the commander said apologetically as he entered the room. "I see you are ready to leave. Is there anything else I can provide for you?"

"No, thank you, Commander. We must be on our way."

"If you will follow me then." The commander mounted his horse and led them down the corridor he had just come from. They rode through another series of narrow passages, the sharp clicking of shod hooves on stone echoing loudly in the tight space. Soon they arrived at the massive granite wall on the south side of the fortress, easily half again as tall as the north side and twice as thick. They rode directly for the south gate, the only way in or out of Balinth's from the Kushaani side of the fortress.

The gate was made from a solid piece of granite three feet thick and twelve feet wide. Andric recalled some old history lesson about the operating mechanism to raise and lower the gate, with a complex series of pulleys and counterweights that still required twenty men to open. Andric's tutor had said it could have been designed to be opened by a single man, but the builders appeared to have specifically made it to require more so that a single spy or saboteur could not open it for an enemy army. However, a single man could close it. Commander Tra'en was right; everything in Balinth's Fortress was designed for defense. The gate was open in anticipation of their departure.

Andric bid farewell to the commander. "We appreciate your hospitality. I expect you will have many of our troops moving back this way within a couple of weeks. Gods bless you in the defense of Remalia."

"And you in your journey, Your Highness."

Andric spurred Kobo out of the fortress, followed by his men. Unlike when they had arrived, a bright afternoon sun shone in the sky above the shaded canyon. Even with only his riding clothes on it was warm, and Andric began to sweat. His guards must have been uncomfortable in their armor. He was happy to have men so dedicated.

It was not long before they left the steep canyon, though the soaring peaks on either side kept them in shadows throughout the afternoon. They passed the occasional farmer's wagon or handful of merchant wagons, but for the most part, the road was theirs. Their pace did not lend itself to conversation, and Andric's mind wandered as the hours passed. As the sky began to dim, the prince noticed the terrain was changing. The valley widened and grew greener. Tomorrow, they would descend from the mountains into the deep basin of the fertile Neral Valley, and if they were lucky, they could reach Luresh within a couple of days.

They only had an hour or two of daylight left, and Andric tried to decide how long they should push into the night before stopping. He had no intention of making another all-night ride. He knew Knight Captain Lindthen had no idea where to make a suitable camp, so he called for Captain Min.

"Yes, my lord?" the scout captain asked once alongside Andric.

"I was considering how long to ride before we make camp for the night. I know your patrol is north, but I thought perhaps you might have some idea."

"Until a few months ago, my patrol was here in the south for several years. I spent most of my time in the borderlands, but I have been through here a few times. Do you wish to stop before sundown, or do you intend to push on in the dark?"

Captain Min didn't follow all the proper protocols for addressing royalty, but one could not expect too much from a scout. Still, he was much more... Andric could not quite put his finger on it, but he was more than Andric would have expected from any scout, captain or not, leaving Andric somewhat puzzled why Min would have been transferred away from the front just when the war started. He seemed perfectly suited to lead the scouts when they were most needed. Andric guessed Captain Min had asked to be transferred to remove himself from harm's way. It was just one more example that intelligence and charisma did not necessarily equal solid leadership. Andric was slightly disappointed.

"I think it best to ride two or three hours past sundown. I intend to reach Luresh by noon the day after tomorrow."

"If my memory serves, I believe there is a small side valley a little over three leagues from here. It has a few streams for watering the horses and trees which should provide us suitable cover."

"That sounds fine, Captain. Please inform me when we have arrived."

"Of course, my lord. We'll scout ahead and find a suitable location." Captain Min saluted then signaled for his other scout to follow him as they moved quickly down the road.

They traveled in silence. Barak's presence forced them to keep a moderate pace, which was probably for the best, especially as the long shadows fell across the valley before deepening into darkness as evening became night. Andric was anxious to get this news to his father and Stephir, but what he had told Barak was true: a few hours would not make a critical difference. No good would come from unnecessarily wearing out their horses, or worse, stepping wrong and having to put down a mount. Still, Andric had to fight his growing impatience to let the horses run unrestrained. Fortunately, Fenthal, the larger of the two moons, was nearly full, and Silmal was half full. Their light reflected off the snow-capped peaks, affording plenty of light to maintain a decent pace.

Andric felt fatigue wrapping itself around him, dragging him toward welcome slumber. He strained to keep his eyes open, shaking his head to wake himself. A cool evening breeze blew from the valley into their faces. It helped for a while, but sleep was threatening to overtake him when the sound of an approaching horse jolted him awake.

Captain Min rode beside him. "Your Highness, we are here. The valley runs in over there."

Even in the bright moonlight, Andric could not see what the scout was talking about. Maybe it was because he was so tired. "Lead the way."

Without a word, Captain Min led them off the road. They crossed a wide field surrounded by the gentle susurrus of the tall grass as they passed, then dropped down a slight decline under the shelter of the wide, tangled branches of a few mighty banyan trees. It was much darker under the thick canopy of leaves and tangled branches, and much slower going. The air was filled with a chorus of chirping river frogs that nearly drowned out the sound of the nearby stream. Captain Min dismounted and walked through the stony and root-tangled undergrowth until they reached a decent clearing alongside the stream.

"Will this do, Your Highness?" Captain Min asked quietly.

"Yes, it's fine. Thank you." Finding a suitable spot to comfortably sleep fourteen men was no easy feat, especially in the inky shadows of the evening.

The men attended to their horses and prepared a simple camp. Jase took care of Kobo, and Lonset prepared the prince's bedroll. This would be a first for Andric, sleeping without some sort of roof over his head. Even traveling with the battalion, his tent was set up each night. He supposed that as long as it didn't rain, it should be all right. At least for a few nights. Soon he would be in Luresh with the Remalian army, and everything would return to normal.

A small fire was built, and a decent meal of roasted goose, pan-roasted potatoes, and carrots, salted to perfection, was prepared for the prince. Andric noticed that the others made do with some cured meat and hard cheese. This was why the nobility did not eat with commoners. Some small talk was made, but they mostly ate in silence. Andric was famished and didn't quite get his fill, but decided against asking them to prepare more food. It was too late. Besides, sleep was even more inviting.

As he settled into his blankets, a few of the men laughed in hushed tones at some shared remark around the campfire. Andric hated being left out of the camaraderie enjoyed by his men. Barak was Andric's only friend here, but the prince never felt entirely comfortable with their relationship when others were around. Officially, Barak was his advisor. Their different stations made being friends... well, awkward.

He had never cared about that before, but he realized that Barak understood the difficulty long before Andric did. Now that the prince was constantly looked to as a leader, something had changed. Andric wished he had a friend like Frey was to Stephir. Someone close enough to his station that informality wouldn't seem improper. The sudden aching loneliness in his chest kept Andric suspended between smothering fatigue and longing not to be alone, until a restless sleep finally claimed him.

CHAPTER XVI

ANDRIC

Andric woke to the sounds of his men preparing to depart. It was still dark, and he had no idea what time it was. The pungent, sweet smell of the large rhododendron tree he had slept under invigorated his mind more quickly than most mornings. His first night on the ground had been almost unbearably uncomfortable, and he had slept little. His injured shoulder forced him to lay on just one side, resulting in an all-night struggle to find a comfortable position. Despite longing to be asleep, it was more of a relief to get up and start moving.

Just one more night, he told himself. Tomorrow night he would sleep in comfort in Luresh. The thought brought only a thin satisfaction, as he knew they might not make it in time to avoid another night of discomfort while riding at a pace Barak could manage.

They ate a small breakfast of salted eggs, hard-boiled for the road, a fine Rodestein cheese, and warmed flatbread, then made preparations to leave. In short order, they were in the saddle making their way out of a small grassy glade amid tall, leafy trees to the road. Andric again took the lead and set as strong a pace as he thought Barak and Steed could handle. Dawn found them nearly out of the forest and making their way through the wide, green Neral Valley. Frequent farms and orchards dotted the landscape throughout the rolling hills. There were small villages between the pass and Luresh. They were quaint, but nothing to hold Andric's attention.

The few villagers who happened to be along the main road watched with curiosity as the party passed by. Andric knew they had no idea they were seeing a prince of Remalia ride through their midst. Some part of him wished he could have made his way here with the battalion as originally planned. These villagers had probably witnessed the vastness of the Remalian army pass just weeks before, but it still would have been fun to bring something interesting to lighten their otherwise mundane lives.

When Andric's grandfather expanded the kingdom to include this province nearly forty years ago, Remalian settlers were granted land holdings to encourage migration to the area and bring it more securely under Remalian control. It was interesting to see the mix of Remalian and Kushaani influences in the architecture, dress, and many more things he didn't particularly care about as he rode quickly past the common folks living out their simple lives.

The air grew hotter and more humid in the lower lands as they pushed southward. The only breeze to speak of was the little air that stirred around the group as they rode along the hard-packed road. What had been Dunnigan's Highroad through the Worrin Gap was now called the Spice Road south of Balinth's Fortress. Stretching from the stone gates of the fortress down to the great port city of Kashpur on the Fragrant Coast, the road was the primary trade route between Remalia and Kushaan—or at least it had been before the war began.

Andric took note that while his men showed little sign of fatigue and no sign of complaint, their red and sweating faces told him they could use a break. Barak looked absolutely miserable. Andric had probably pushed them too hard. He slowed the pace and spoke with Captain Min, who informed him they should be passing through another village in a few miles. Andric ordered them to stop there for a short rest.

They passed a few farmers tending their fields while children played together. Andric imagined them being captured by Kushaani slave raiders, the father resisting and being cut down, and a small child left standing alone crying in the doorway in the middle of the night; it was to protect these people that he and the rest of the Remalian army were here. But now the raiders were descending on the heart of Remalia. They could never carry captives back across the Velspars to Kushaan, of course, but what horrors might they inflict on the people in the Remalian countryside who were unable to retreat behind the protective walls of Teris?

A few minutes rest won't change anything, he reminded himself as he fought the rising urge to leave the others behind and rush to deliver the news to his father.

The village sprang from the landscape as they rounded the next hill. The road turned west, placing the late-morning sun in their eyes, although it was climbing to its zenith too quickly for Andric's liking. Several nearby fields were dotted with workers tending to whatever crops they grew. Andric slowed Kobo to a trot as they left the main road and entered the village proper. The sounds of a smithy rang out in the warm morning air. A cobbler's shop windows were open, and Andric noticed a younger man, probably an apprentice, working at a bench inside. Soon the fourteen weary men converged on the village square, nearly filling it. A large tree commanded the center of the square with signs of having been charred by a recent fire.

The sudden smell of freshly baked bread caught Andric's attention, and his stomach rumbled. They quickly found the bakery and Andric instructed Master Lonset to buy some bread and cheese. Andric looked for a trough for watering their horses but didn't see one at any of the buildings.

"Captain," Andric said as he continued looking around the village, "find out where we can water the horses."

"Of course, Your Highness," both Lindthen and Min answered in unison. Andric had meant to assign the task to the scout. He turned and nodded at Captain Min, who rode toward what appeared to be a small inn and signaled the other scout to look in the other direction. Andric and the others dismounted and led their horses toward the burned tree. A few wooden benches were set around the broad trunk, and a couple of weathered old men rose as the group approached. Andric nodded and they nodded back, touching their foreheads in a respectful greeting.

Lonset and Captain Min returned to the group at the same time. Min informed Andric there was a place to water the horses behind the inn. Andric nodded, and Jase took Kobo and followed the scouts and a few Divinarim to take the horses for watering while the rest waited under the tree. Barak had already taken a seat on one of the benches and leaned back against the trunk with his eyes closed. Lonset distributed the bread, cheese, and some cured spicy meat. Andric ate with satisfaction. The bread was as delicious as it smelled.

Andric noted that the two old men were still standing, casually watching the new arrivals. Other villagers around the square either stopped to look or slowed their pace, shooting glances at their unusual visitors. Andric addressed the old men.

"There's no need to stand. Please, sit." The old men sat in unison without a word. Then one, with tanned wrinkled skin and a wreath of white wispy hair finally ventured to start a conversation.

"Oo d'ya be, lords? From the grea' ci'y no doubt."

"Indeed, we are," Andric replied as graciously as he could, though he inwardly cringed at the thick accent and lack of social etiquette. He did his best to hide his distaste. "I am Prince Andric Laconeus," Andric said, feeling an odd mixture of beneficence at engaging in conversation with a commoner at all and bemusement at the absurdity of it. The men looked at each other briefly, then stood and bowed low. Andric almost laughed at the unnecessary gesture but appreciated it nevertheless.

"This village is Tieka, is that right?" Andric knew it was correct, having studied the maps of this region several times in recent weeks, but he didn't know what else one spoke about with commoners.

"Yes, m'lord." The old man didn't offer more, probably having even less idea what one said to one of the nobility than Andric had speaking to them.

"And have you lived here your whole life?"

"No, m'lord. Me an' me brother...," he said gesturing with his head to the man next to him, "we came here aft' the king, bless 'im, took this land from the Kushaani savages too many years 'go ta count. We been farmers 'ere 'er since."

"How has your village faired in recent times? Have you experienced any difficulties from the Kushaani?"

"Aye, they's gave us trouble, though not like they has other folk further down south from whuh we 'ear told. Only stole some livestock and the like from us. They asn't run off with any of our folk."

"Well, we are here to ensure that never happens again. Did they burn this tree too?" Andric assumed it was a simple enough question, but the brothers looked uncomfortably at each other, then one dropped his eyes to the ground as the other answered.

"Truth told, m'lord, none 'ere rightly knows whuh it was fired 'at tree. Some says it was Vai Doroth's wrath for our sins. Others says it was one o' them rovin' Teraithian cults punishin' folk for too much believin' in the wrong gods."

"Your Highness," Lindthen interrupted from behind Andric.

The prince turned to face the captain, who gestured to a middle-aged woman with curly, shoulder-length auburn hair with white starting to show at her temples. She was dressed in a quality, forest-green skirt that ended below the knees where black leather boots met the hem at mid-calf, and an embroidered white blouse untied at the top, leaving the light material fairly open. *Not altogether unattractive*, Andric thought to himself.

"Your Highness," the woman said with a slightly awkward curtsey. "Welcome to our humble village. I am Mistress Bowen, Headwoman of Tieka. How can we be of service, my lord?" Andric thought she was well-spoken for a commoner. He had never heard of a village having a headwoman, but these were practically the borderlands and she seemed composed, so he supposed it was not too strange.

After washing down the food in his mouth with a drink of water, he replied. "Thank you, Mistress Bowen. We are here to water our horses and take a moment's rest on our way to Luresh. We will not be here much longer. These good men were just acquainting me with your village. I am glad to hear you've been relatively untroubled by the Kushaani."

"Kerail has blessed us with peace," the headwoman said sincerely. It was not often that only one half of the Holy Couple was invoked without some connection to the other. Andric knew some people chose to focus their worship on one or the other, but that seemed a contradiction of their doctrine of unity exemplified by their eternal companionship.

Motion from the side of the square caught Andric's attention. His men were returning with the horses. "I regret that we cannot stay to enjoy your hospitality further, Mistress Bowen, but we must press on."

"Of course. We are grateful you chose to stop here, Your Highness. Kerail speed and protect you," she said as she curtseyed again.

Andric hadn't eaten his fill, but was anxious to be off, so he handed his remaining food to Lonset as the men mounted their horses. "And you as well," Andric said politely with an incline of his head. Andric led the men out of the village square to the main road. He turned south toward Luresh and spurred Kobo into a trot. It was fully mid-day, and the bright sun bathed them in uncomfortable warmth.

Mile after mile seemed to be the same as the previous ones, marked by seemingly the same farms, small villages, trees, grassy hills, and a bridge over the occasional stream. The mountains behind them shrank into the distance. As evening approached, the Spice Road turned southeast toward Luresh. The sun set behind the eastern mountains, and a dim pink light filled the sky when Captain Min suggested a spot to set camp for the night.

The routine was much the same as the previous night, with the gathering of wood and kindling for a cooking fire, tending the horses, fetching water, and clearing spots for the bedrolls. Lonset was solicitous of Andric's needs, laying out a blanket for the prince to sit on for his meal. Everyone carried out their assigned tasks while Andric sat and watched. It was nothing out of the ordinary; he was used to others beneath his station taking care of the mundane tasks, but something was different tonight. He felt... he was not sure what; not useless exactly, but uncomfortable with being the only person without a task. He didn't like imagining what the others might think of him.

He could have helped with the horses or gathered firewood, but those chores seemed too boring. He didn't have the first idea how to cook, so that was not an option. He had never started a fire from scratch, but it sounded fun, *and how hard could it be*? Captain Min appeared to be preparing a spot for the fire, so Andric interrupted. "Min, I'll take care of the fire."

The scout captain looked at him with just a moment's hesitation, then quickly stepped out of the way. Manners dictated he should have bowed and offered a proper acknowledgment of Andric's order, but again, one could not expect too much from a scout, and a foreigner at that. Andric was conscious of Min hovering, and it felt as though the man was judging his work. He was sure he could figure out the fire, but he wanted to be left in peace to do it. Andric was tempted to order Min to fetch some more firewood. *He would certainly hate that!*

Min had already gathered little piles of different-sized sticks, dried weeds, and bark. Andric guessed that he needed to burn the small things before the flame would catch on the larger sticks. He took the dried grass and leaves and placed them in a pile, then started stacking increasingly larger sticks on top until he had a nice mound. Thankfully, Captain Min left to go do something else. Lonset and the other scout brought more wood for the fire, but they stayed to watch.

You'd think they had never seen anyone make a fire before! Andric griped to himself. He looked around for the rock and metal bar he had seen others use but didn't see them. He didn't know what they were called, but he decided to ask for them as best he could. "Lonset, I need the fire starters." He purposely avoided eye contact, not wanting to see their reactions if he had gotten the term wrong.

"Of course, my lord." Lonset hurried to his gear and untied one of the small boxes. Captain Min made a clicking noise and the other scout left. Soon Lonset returned with a small, lacquered wood box and handed it to the prince with a bow.

"That will be all," Andric said dismissively. It was heavier than he expected. He opened it and found some black cloth, some short pieces of rough rope, a shiny piece of steel, and a dull reddish-gray bar of metal. He was not sure what to do with the rope, but the cloth looked like it could be useful, so he wadded up a piece and stuck it near the bottom of his pile next to the grass and leaves. Andric took the two pieces of metal and struck them together with a loud clang.

Nothing.

He tried harder, but still nothing. He tried rubbing them together without results. He desperately wanted to avoid asking for help, but he knew it was no use starting the fire this way. He opened his center to draw in a small portion of elan. Creating a flame was a simple matter of attuning the elan to two modalities, thet and vis, and blending them in an amplified harmonic.

"If you'd like to learn how, I'm happy to show you," Captain Min offered. "It takes some practice before anyone can do it well."

Andric was grateful the Sa'ari scout did not sound condescending or like he was trying to kiss the prince's backside. Andric was tempted to decline, but he thought having some idea of how to start a fire without elan might be useful someday, so he swallowed his pride and accepted the offer.

"Thank you, that would be appreciated." Min knelt next to the pile Andric had made and took it apart as he explained the essentials of fire building. Andric was particularly interested to see how the metal bars came into play. Min commented that the ones Lonset had supplied were of particularly high quality, and the captain showed Andric how to easily produce sparks. Getting the black ash cloth to light, however, was another matter entirely. Soon they had a respectable fire going, and the warmth was pleasant despite the heat of the day lingering in the evening air.

Lonset replaced Andric and Captain Min at the fire to attend to the cooking, and Andric checked on Jase's progress with the horses. Andric liked Captain Min (*what was his first name, Coorain or something like that*) and was curious to learn more about him. *What brought him to Remalia? What does he think of the war?* But Andric was concerned with what the others would think about the prince having personal conversations with a scout, even if he was a captain. Perhaps Barak could be persuaded to initiate the conversation. It would be perfectly natural for a Viancian to be inquisitive about his traveling companions. Barak was reading one of the books he had brought (Andric was sure it was the third or fourth time since leaving Teris), so he left his friend alone for now. He would mention it later.

Despite his hunger, Andric was rather disappointed with the plain meal and dreaded the thought that each bite took him closer to attempting sleep on the impossibly uncomfortable ground again. He could endure one more night of misery, he told himself wearily. The soldiers in the army would have to do this every night for months. He thanked the gods he had been born into better circumstances.

After bedding down for the night, it didn't feel long enough before Andric woke to Lonset shaking him, with apologies on his lips before Andric knew where he was. He felt aches and pains all over and was surprised he had managed to sleep through the night. The sleepless nights must have caught up with him. He was chagrined to see everyone ready to travel. He hadn't expected to sleep much at all, and especially not until everyone was practically already on horseback. Lonset was ready with Andric's breakfast, steaming water, clean gear, and a change of clothes. The prince declined to change his clothes but washed quickly with the warm water and ran a comb through his sandy brown hair. There was only so far royalty should allow their appearance to slip. He took some of the food he could eat in the saddle and mounted. Everyone immediately followed suit, and the group again headed south for Luresh.

Farms and villages slipped past without Andric giving them a second thought, and Andric was pleased to see they were making much better time. They would make it to Luresh by nightfall after all. They only stopped twice at small garrisons to water the horses before pressing on. Andric was surprised to hear that Luresh had been attacked by the Kushaani, although the reports were clear that the Remalian army had routed them with ease. Andric said nothing about the force invading northern Remalia but wondered what the Kushaani could be thinking to attack on multiple fronts.

It was late afternoon with the sun slipping toward the horizon, painting the sky ember-red, when they at last approached Luresh. Construction was underway, repairing bridges and damage to the city wall. Andric was surprised not to see any troops camped around the city. He had understood that his father would stay in Luresh and manage the campaign from there while Stephir led the troops in the direct assaults, but surely a fair contingent of soldiers would be kept in reserve to secure Luresh while the king was there.

Andric didn't slow down as he rode toward the large entrance to the city. Soldiers wearing Luresh's colors stood guard at the main gate and atop the city walls. No one else was on the road as they entered through the gates. Andric paid no attention to the soldiers who saluted sharply as he rode past. His only thought was to find his father.

His memory of the city from his one previous trip so many years ago didn't give him any idea how to get to the ducal palace that housed his cousin Osten and Baron and Lady Marstoff, but he didn't think it would be too hard to find his way. It was easily the tallest structure in the city and could be seen from any but the narrowest streets. The Divinarim moved into a tighter formation around him, though there were not many people on the streets this late in the day. The few city guards they encountered saluted as they rode past. Unlike Teris, Luresh had no main thoroughfare. The streets meandered in a haphazard way, which took Andric away from the palace as often as toward it.

Most of the buildings were either white or various shades of tan, with smooth plaster on the exterior walls. The doors were recessed into the walls, concealed partially by towering archways pointed at the top. The city was a sprawling expanse of one- or two-story houses and shops and open work-spaces built for the warmer climate this side of the Velspars. The ducal palace loomed over the rest of the buildings and streets, easily two or three stories higher than the surrounding buildings. A wide plaza opened before the palace, creating a staging ground for assembling in front of the wide steps leading to the entrance. It was nothing as spectacular as what one would find in Teris, but it was pleasantly situated overlooking the city and appeared as well built as anything this side of Balinth's.

The palace was smaller than Andric remembered. Numerous torches lined the top of the walls, and two large braziers burned brightly on either side of two thick iron-bound wood doors barring the way. The light glinted off the armor and weapons of the half-dozen soldiers standing guard at the steps. A conversation among the men came to an abrupt halt as all attention turned to Andric and his men. The knights preceding him moved aside to let Andric move to the front. The gate sergeant looked surprised but seemed to quickly recognize Andric was a member of the royal family. No doubt he had seen enough of the Divinarim guarding the king and Stephir to understand who Andric was.

"Sergeant," Andric said firmly as he stopped in front of the guards, "are the king or my brother inside?"

"No, m'lord. None of them have returned since they left for the war," the sergeant said somewhat apologetically.

"And Baron Marstoff?"

"No, m'lord."

The urgency and anticipation of delivering the news to his father that had sustained Andric through the long trip drained out of him in an instant. All he felt now was exhaustion and deep disappointment. "I assume my cousin Osten and Lady Marstoff have remained here. Show me to them at once."

"Yes, Your Highness," the sergeant saluted as the other soldiers called for those inside to open the doors.

Andric and his men dismounted. "Knight Captain Lindthen, Captain Min, Master Ve'Aurben, come with me." Lindthen selected two other Divinarim to attend them as they were led into the palace. Andric knew the others would be shown where to go to take care of everything, so he hardly gave it a thought. The men were led down a long straight hallway with high arched ceilings that ran directly from the front doors to the great hall. Oil lamps and great candelabra bathed the corridor in light, showing the paintings, tapestries, and sculptures lining the hallway.

They stopped in the large foyer from which ran two corridors, while the wall opposite the entrance held another set of doors Andric remembered opened to the great hall. The guard said someone would be with them any moment, then returned the way they had just come. When they were out of earshot, Andric sighed heavily.

Barak was the first to speak. "I assume we will be leaving in the morning," he said flatly.

"Yes." Then, reading more into Barak's words, Andric added, "You can stay here if you like. We will undoubtedly be back in a few days, and you can rejoin me for the return to Teris."

"I'm at your disposal, Your Highness."

Andric could not tell if Barak meant he was coming or staying. He would have to clear it up later. Andric contemplated what to do next as they waited in silence. Part of him wanted to leave immediately for wherever his father was, but he knew he didn't have it in him to continue tonight without some sleep. He could send Captain Min ahead to take word to his father, but Andric wanted to be the one to deliver the news. He wanted to be involved when decisions were made about what they would do. He knew it was a bit selfish. How many times could he tell himself a few hours wouldn't make any difference before the hours became too many? He would leave first thing in the morning and refused to dwell on the decision any longer.

Soon the presumed headmaster arrived from a side corridor with two servants in tow. Andric's hand instinctually flew to his sword, his heart beating heavily, before he realized what he was doing. It took another moment before the anger and fear in his mind crystallized into a coherent thought. *They're Kushaani, wearing servants' clothes; just like that night at the stables.*

"Your Highness, welcome to Luresh," the man said with a grand flourish and deep bow, followed in kind by the other two. "Please forgive the wait, my lord. We had not expected Your Highness."

Andric nodded, wary of any sign of a threat.

"What service can we offer, my lord? Lady Marstoff will be happy to meet with you immediately in her salon... unless Your Highness would prefer to take some rest and refreshment after your journey. We can have a meal prepared if my lord desires."

That was a lot of 'lords' and 'highnesses', thought Andric, almost wanting to laugh at the contrast between the obsequious manners and his fear they might be assassins. *Of course they have Kushaani servants*, the prince chided himself, releasing his grip on his sword. Luresh was part of Kushaan not long ago. His heart continued to beat heavily as he focused on answering the head-master's questions.

What to do tonight? He didn't want to see Lady Marstoff with three days of filth on him. He was sure they were all an unpleasant group to be close to. It would be terribly rude not to see her, but the thought of taking the time to become presentable, then meet with her, then wait for them to prepare the meal that no doubt under normal circumstances he would be more than happy to eat, exhausted the last of his patience. All he wanted was to sink into a bed and sleep. He remembered his father's words spoken numerous times, 'It is precisely when we least feel like acting nobly that doing so defines our nobility.'

"I would be pleased to meet with Lady Marstoff after I have had an opportunity to make myself presentable. A meal would also be greatly appreciated, though I have had a long ride, so perhaps Lady Marstoff wouldn't be too offended sitting with me while I ate."

"Of course, Your Highness. I believe your things have been directed to your quarters. Will your men be staying with you, or shall I have them shown to their quarters, my lord?"

Oh, for crying out loud! Andric thought to himself. *Do I have to deal with every detail?* He forced himself to think it through. Barak ought to be invited, although he might be grateful if he wasn't. He was sure neither of the captains would be offended if they weren't invited, and almost certainly the scout would be out of place.

"While I am sure they would all enjoy Lady Marstoff's company, please inform her that I will be the only one joining her. Meals for all my men would be appreciated, though."

"As you wish, Your Highness," the man said, bowing. "Lady Marstoff will be delighted."

"Is my cousin available to join us? I would be pleased to see him."

"I believe so, Your Highness. I shall pass along your desire to see him. Does my lord require anything else for the moment, or would you like to be shown to your quarters?"

"No, that will be all for now."

"Very good, my lord. These two will show you and your men to your respective accommodations, and I will inform Lady Marstoff and Duke Osten immediately." The headmaster bowed again, then returned the way he had come.

The young servants invited Andric and the others to follow them down another corridor. After a couple of turns, one young man directed the others to follow him down a separate hallway from Andric. Knight Captain Lindthen sent the Divinarim who had come with him to follow Andric, while he, Captain Min, and Barak were shown to their quarters.

When Andric arrived at his rooms, he was somewhat surprised. Although only a guest room, it was more lavish than any room at the palace in Teris. His uncle certainly had more extravagant tastes than his father. Lonset was already laying out his things.

"May I be of any further service, m'lord," the servant who had escorted him asked politely with only a hint of Kushaani accent.

"No, thank you. That will be all," Andric answered.

The servant bowed and then left, closing the doors behind him. Andric was surprised when Lonset informed him that a hot bath was waiting for him and asked how they had managed to put together such a luxury so quickly.

Lonset hesitated before answering, "They filled the bath with cold water, and it was heated by someone who I am guessing was an elantir."

"Really? What a strange thing to have an elantir do. Still..." Andric undressed and got into the bath. It was wonderful. He rested for a few minutes with his eyes closed, then jolted when he felt a hand on his arm. He opened his eyes to Lonset standing over him.

"I'm sorry to disturb you, my lord, but you seemed to have fallen asleep."

Again? Andric chided himself. He cupped his hands and brought them full of water to his face, trying to wake himself up.

"Shall I leave you and perhaps inform Lady Marstoff that you would prefer to see her tomorrow."

"No. I would rather get this over with tonight so we can leave first thing in the morning."

"As you wish, my lord. I have your cleaning gear and your clothes ready."

"Thank you. I'll be out in a moment." Andric finished washing, then stepped out onto the cold stone floor and hastily put on the bathrobe waiting beside the tub. With Lonset's help, he was soon ready. A servant waiting outside the room led him to Lady Marstoff.

When he arrived at Lady Marstoff's salon, Andric was happy to see Osten was waiting for him as well. Hamoth's Charge Days a year ago was the last time Andric had seen his cousin, and the boy had grown at least a couple of inches and was starting to fill out a bit. His Laconeus heritage showed in his stature.

They sat down to the hot meal already waiting for him. After several days of road fare, the food tasted delicious. Andric was keenly interested in hearing the account of the Kushaani attack on Luresh and the battle when the Remalian army arrived. He had intended to keep the information about the Kushaani forces in Remalia to himself, but Lady Marstoff was a shrewd woman, and he was tired. She managed to pull most of it from him before he finished his second plate. Osten asked a lot of questions, but Andric had no more answers than he did when he first heard Captain Min's report. They chatted about the plans for the war, but despite his best efforts, soon he was having a hard time following the conversation.

"Prince Andric, our apologies. You're exhausted!" Lady Marstoff said sympathetically. "We should have met with you in the morning."

"No, I must leave first thing in the morning to get to my father."

"Of course. I will have everything arranged for you."

"Thank you, Lady Marstoff. Osten, it's good to see you again. Perhaps we'll have more than a few moments to talk when I come back this way."

They bid each other goodnight and Andric was shown back to his quarters. He changed for bed and slipped into a dreamless sleep.

CHAPTER XVII
STEPHIR

Stephir and his commanders sat in their saddles looking through their spyglasses at miles of Kushaan territory from atop a high bluff. From this vantage, Stephir could see a sweeping arc from south to west to north. There was not much to see westward except the tops of the dense, lush forest stretching northward toward the soaring Velspars that were barely a smudge on the distant horizon.

Below him, a broad valley stretched between the high hills from north to south. A small river meandered along the valley floor, and tall pecca trees were scattered across the grassy fields. A gap in the thick forest canopy to the south-west on the far side of the valley marked the Duntai Ravine where scouts had reported a large hidden Kushaani force.

One end of the ravine emptied into the valley. Stephir had sent troops to make their way through the forest to the other end of the ravine, intending to drive the Kushaani south into the valley, where he planned to crush them. But he needed Miarsten and Wenstak to be in position between the hills on the east side of the valley, and from his vantage point, he could see they weren't.

"Tell them if they go any further into the countryside, they'll all be demoted to scouts! They can watch the rest of us do the fighting." Stephir's patience was running paper-thin, but he still felt a small twinge of guilt for snapping at the lieutenant. Frey coughed and Stephir took a deep breath as the junior officer galloped away to deliver the prince's message to Lord Miarsten, Duke of Glastony, and General Wenstak.

"Your Highness will eventually have to make good on the threats to demote someone to a scout, or everyone might think your threats hollow," Marchioness Haedep stated coolly.

Lady Haedep was one of the few noble women who participated in the fighting, preferring to command her soldiers herself. She was about the same age as Stephir's mother would have been, and her years of experience made her a capable commander and a voice of reason amidst other spoiled and arrogant aristocrats. Stephir regarded her as a strong ally. She was a handsome woman, with deep-blue eyes and blond hair now slipping toward a beautiful silvery gray. More than once, he had considered suggesting his father marry her, but he already knew how that conversation would go, so he didn't bother.

"Any recommendations on who I should start with?" Stephir asked.

Lady Haedep looked around coolly at the others in the company. "I have a few ideas, but perhaps it would be best to discuss it later, my lord."

Stephir nodded. He liked the idea of keeping everyone guessing at their sincerity.

"This is the third time in two days I've had to stop those two from running off to chase some phantom enemy."

Stephir had been certain that once they moved into enemy territory, fighting the Kushaani would not be as easy as the battle at Luresh. Until now, he hadn't had a chance to test his theory because each time his men located Kushaani soldiers, the enemy fled before he could mount a strong offensive. The enemy appeared content to harry his flanks, drawing small groups away from the main body of the army for isolated skirmishes. Both sides lost few soldiers this way, but it was having its effect on discipline and morale, especially among the nobles, who wanted to prove their valor in grand battle.

It had been a long time since Remalia had truly been at war with Kushaan, but these tactics were nothing like their reputation as fierce warriors who would fight to the death. Even at Nanjab three days ago, there had been little fighting. The few brief battles they had fought along the way appeared to have been nothing more than a delay tactic to slow the Remalians while their people escaped. By the time they were at Nanjab's walls, the city was largely abandoned.

The king had remained in Nanjab, claiming he desired to oversee securing their first conquest in Kushaan, but Stephir knew his father wanted him to take command of the army without the king present to detract from Stephir's honor. Besides, his father and dozens of their people had taken ill the day after entering the city. Many suspected it was some kind of dark Kushaani met'elan. The king had promised to catch up when Nanjab was secure and he returned to full health.

If Stephir could ensure no sizable Kushaani force was behind him, there would be nothing keeping him from pushing further south into the Kesh Province as his father wished. The lack of substantial resistance had given the king a renewed vigor for a major conquest, possibly driving to the thriving city of Sarkesh, or perhaps even all the way to the Fragrant Coast. If the entire eastern end of Kushaan beyond Dhramas to the vibrant port cities of Kashpur and Rishakesh could be captured and held, Remalia might become a foreign trading power rivaling Calavia.

It would be a serious blow to the Kushaani empire and its slave trade, much of which passed through the two southern ports. Stopping the slave traffic would be a strong moral victory. The prospect was almost enough to convince Stephir the war would have been worthwhile. Making it a reality was still a long way off, despite the confidence of most of the other commanders.

"Look there," Frey said, pointing to the south end of the valley.

Stephir quickly raised his spyglass. He could not make out individuals, but he watched the dark mass of his troops who had left before dawn spread across the gap. If Miarsten and Wenstak got into their places, the Kushaani forces would be trapped in the valley. Now there was nothing to do but wait.

The sun beat down on them like a smith's hammer in a forge. Stephir missed the cooler climes of Teris. Even the nights here were hot and oppressive, though he did find the verdant landscape beautiful. Perhaps winter (or whatever passed for winter in this country) would be tolerable. He might conquer the land and make it part of his kingdom, but it would never be the Remalia he knew and loved.

Heads turned as a rider galloped up the slope to the top of the bluff. Captain Fashir. "My lord," the woman said, addressing Stephir. "We just received word from Commander Elorin of the third cavalry. General Bascon is already pushing through the ravine. Unless the Kushaani hold their position, he should reach the valley within two hours."

"Any report of how many enemy troops we should expect?" High General Kuymon asked.

"No sir. Scouts have continued their attempts to get above the ravine to have a look, but the Kushaani have too many men in that forest. The scouts can't get close enough. No doubt the General's soldiers will remedy that shortly, but for now, we have nothing more to report."

"Tell Commander Elorin to move his men there," Stephir instructed, pointing to the farthest point north in the valley that was clear of trees. The ravine continued to wind its way north for many miles, but the forests covered much of it, making it worse than useless for his cavalry to fight there. The captain saluted and galloped away to deliver the message.

"I wish the elantir would fix the problem," High General Kuymon remarked offhandedly. It was becoming a daily mantra for him. *The problem* was their inability to communicate through the elantir. The short-distance communications through the tentacled fachim worked most of the time, but if they could not be counted on every time, they were useless in battle.

Stephir and his commanders had discussed several options for alternate means of communications, but most entailed some kind of visual and audible signals that could be received at long distances, which meant the enemy could pick up the same messages. In the end, they opted for human messengers. It was painfully slow and meant Stephir had to trust his commanders to exercise independent judgment when he normally might have preferred to be in control.

The one good thing to come from their predicament was that he had finally given serious consideration to additional uses the elantir might have in the war effort. Commander Alscan had some interesting ideas, at least in theory. Many, however, were beyond the scope of anything their elantir had attempted before, including softening the ground to make it the consistency of mud, causing a concussive blast to disorient the enemy, or creating noxious fumes that induced vomiting. There had been a few unpleasant accidents in camp, though thankfully few permanent injuries.

Stephir was encouraged by the ideas and was determined to remove obstacles to their progress. The greatest hindrance came from many of the elantir themselves, particularly among some of the more senior soldiers drafted from the Elantic Order. The order was the largest elantir guild in Teris, and it was second only to the merchants' guild in its power and influence in Teris and other parts of Remalia. They had fought as hard as they dared to prevent their members from being pressed into the king's service, but ultimately, Stephir had won. However, they still hoarded their secrets and remained a self-imposed faction within the ranks of the elantir corps. More frustrating to Stephir and Alscan was their members who subverted efforts to develop new elantic techniques and applications. As a result, the corps had made only marginal progress in their endeavors so far. They had only been at it for a couple of weeks though; Stephir was willing to give them time.

Frey had told him privately that some soldiers were testing new monikers for the prince: *the Sorcerer King, Stephir the Elantir*, and *the Met'elan Monarch*. Stephir had been inclined to ignore it, but allowing the mockery to go unchecked, even if it was meant in good humor, could turn poisonous, especially if the war became difficult. He required Commander Alscan and her top elantir to give daily reports during his evening war council. It hadn't stopped some from criticizing him, but it got many of the real concerns and ideas, good or bad, out in the open where they could be dealt with. Some had even started coming around to the idea that perhaps the elantir could be more useful than they had been in the past, even if communication continued to be a problem.

A pair of servants brought the prince and his entourage food and drink. He was tempted to ask them to set up a pavilion so he could get out of the sun while he waited, but he was not going to allow himself such a luxury while his men waited to face battle, and possibly death. His discomfort reminded him that his soldiers weren't just markers to be moved around on a map and not just stones to be thrown at the enemy. His father had told him a king could not afford such sentimentality, so Stephir never shared these thoughts with anyone, but he refused to change his mind. He knew the Holy Couple approved, and that would have to be enough.

"What is that?" Frey asked while peering through his spyglass, his simple words laced with something more than curiosity. He pointed toward a dark slit in the forest near the ravine. Stephir looked but saw nothing out of the ordinary.

"What are you looking at?" High General Kuymon asked, obviously seeing nothing more than Stephir did. Of course, Kuymon's aging eyes were not what they once were.

"The gap seems to be getting... I don't know, *bigger*? Darker maybe?" Frey answered.

"My dear Marquis," the Earl of Attathan said with a teasing tone, "I thought you could hold your wine better than that. A few sips and already the world is turning black." A few others laughed, but Stephir saw an edge in Frey's face. His friend wasn't joking. Stephir scanned the forest tops until he found what had caught Frey's eye.

"What *is* it?" someone else asked, no longer laughing. Silence fell over the group as they tried to make sense of what they saw. The trees near the gap seemed to be darkening, as if under a shadow, or as if being burned, but there was no cloud in the sky, and no sign of fire. The darkness slowly spread both along and away from the ravine. Whatever it was, it was not natural.

"Bring Commander Alscan immediately!" Stephir barked to no one in particular. He heard horse hooves speed away but refused to take his eyes off the ravine. Certain it was some form of met'elan, Stephir could not imagine what it was or why anyone would want to blacken the trees. It did not move evenly but seeped a little here and spread a little more there.

"Look at the birds," Marchioness Haedep directed. There were more birds in the air than usual, but nothing worth—*wait, they're all flying away from the ravine*. A knot formed in Stephir's stomach. "Should we do something?"

"Maybe they summoned a daemon? That might explain the blackening," High General Kuymon offered.

Stephir shook his head doubtfully, his brow furrowed in thought. Anything was possible, but it seemed unlikely. He recalled Andric's description of the fires at the Teraithian temple in Teris. He said there were scorch marks on whatever the divine creature touched. However, no smoke was rising from the ravine, and there was just too much of the spreading blackness for that to make any sense.

Stephir scanned the sprawling Remalian camp behind him, looking for a sign of Alscan. His eyes darted haphazardly, and he realized he was searching for any hint that something similar might be happening to the camp. Everything seemed normal, and at last he saw a group of horses racing toward them. *Finally!*

He returned his attention to the ravine, hoping to see something different. The only change he saw was the darkness continuing to spread. He looked where his men were positioned in the valley and was relieved everything seemed in order. Even Miarsten and Wenstak had found their place between the eastern hills. Commander Elorin's forces still hadn't left the forest on the north end of the valley, and Stephir felt the knot in his stomach tighten. He hoped nothing was wrong.

The blackening had not spread to the area where the commander was waiting, and it was possible he hadn't yet received Stephir's last message, so the prince stopped himself from jumping to dark conclusions. He considered sending for Father Daemmer, just in case this was some sort of previously unknown daemon, but he waited to see what the elantir had to say. All heads turned as Commander Alscan and her escort came to a hard stop, horses breathing heavily in the heat.

"Where?" she asked abruptly.

The only hands that remained still were the Divinarim's as everyone quickly pointed. The areas where the blackness had spread were now easily seen, even to the naked eye. She watched in silence for several moments before turning to one of her attending elantir. "Lieutenant Azeliun, I require your assistance."

Others moved aside, making room for the stocky, middle-aged man to maneuver his horse next to the commander's. Stephir would have guessed by the lieutenant's armor he was a soldier, not an elantir. *They* are *soldiers*, he corrected himself.

"I need to reach down there, but I need your elan." Commander Alscan said.

"Of course, Commander."

High General Kuymon moved his horse a bit further away, a look of unease on his face. Alscan put a thin hand on the lieutenant's arm and closed her eyes. Stephir tried to sense the met'elan she was performing, but he only felt the vague currents of the elan swirling around Alscan. Andric would have a better idea of what she was doing. Moments stretched into minutes, and the smallest noises sounded harsh in Stephir's ears: horses adjusting their stance, creaking saddle leather, the annoying buzz of a few flies refusing to be shooed, and the occasional errant sound from the camp.

Suddenly the commander sucked in a sharp breath through her teeth, and she cursed under her breath. Such language was out of character for the disciplined elantir commander, which did nothing to calm Stephir's growing anxiety. She showed no other sign of breaking her concentration, but her heavy breathing and the beads of sweat forming on her face and soaking the edges of her silky brown hair spoke of the strain she was under. Stephir grew impatient and wanted an explanation, but he forced himself to keep his mouth in check for the moment.

When Alscan finally spoke again, her voice was hoarse. "Your Highness," she began but coughed. Stephir handed her his waterskin. She sipped a bit, then again before handing it back. "Thank you, my lord."

He waived it off, letting her keep it. "What is it?" Stephir asked. He could hear the worry in his own voice and inwardly chastised himself; he needed to convey strength and confidence, not fear.

"Put simply, something is drawing off so much elan from that area, the plants are..." she seemed to be searching for the right words, "... decaying, I suppose, is the closest word to put it simply." She looked at the other elantir as if for confirmation, but his head hung down. She shook her head, though Stephir could not read what emotion was behind the gesture.

"I assume it's the Kushaani elantir doing this?" Stephir thought of the large number of elantir he ordered to accompany General Bascon's force into the gap, and he wanted confirmation it was not his people causing the blackening.

"Almost certainly," she replied.

"But why? Are they trying to kill the forest?"

"Oh, I doubt that. The blackening is simply a consequence of draining the plants' elan. I could not tell what form their met'elan is taking, but I could feel it..." again she paused, "... being pushed into the area. Whatever they're doing, it's very dangerous, both for themselves and anyone else down there."

"We have troops in the ravine. Can you discern what is happening with them?" He knew the answer before he asked it, but he had to ask.

"No, Your Highness. I cannot make those kinds of distinctions from here. It is too far, and there is too much life down there."

"Your Highness, perhaps my plan should be reconsidered." High General Kuymon interrupted. He had preferred to push troops from both ends, trapping the Kushaani in the ravine and crushing them between the two forces, ensuring they could not escape but at greater risk. Stephir briefly reconsidered their strategy but held to his decision. He felt the familiar sensation in his mind of a request to join in communion. He was almost certain, it was Archpaladin Nophet. He thought it was odd, but perhaps the Divinar commander sensed some threat.

Stephir accepted the link, and Nophet's words penetrated Stephir's thoughts as if they were his own. The link with the Teraithian knight brought the familiar dissonance of having a foreign divinessence in his mind.

"Your Highness, forgive the intrusion, but may I suggest that a prayer of supplication to Teraithia is warranted."

Stephir was taken aback by the suggestion. Communion between the Divinarim and the royals was for official matters only. He could not remember a single time the man had ever spoken other than to carry out his duties. At a loss for words, Stephir collected his thoughts before responding. *"Is everything all right? Is there a threat?"*

The holy knight's words resonated in his mind with authority. *"Our Lady is the champion of the mighty. She rewards power with power. She is pleased with our victories. I know she will aid Your Highness in fighting this corruption."*

Stephir felt a desire to believe Nophet's words, to act on them. The world seemed heavier, pressing on him. His mind teetered on the edge of accepting Nophet's suggestion, then he felt a calm strength flowing into him like a breath of fresh air, releasing the pressure. He severed the communal link and heard himself say aloud, "Thank you, Lord Nophet. I shall think upon your suggestion." The words felt strange in his mouth.

From the corner of his eye, Stephir noticed several heads turn in his direction, confused looks on their faces, but the prince hardly paid them any attention. He tried to clear his head, and he hazily wondered if someone was dispositioning him. The benefaction was practiced by many priests to influence the hearts and minds of others, but this felt different—insistent, heavy.

The Divinarim wouldn't allow anyone to disposition me, thought Stephir. *But what if it's Nophet? Would they stop him?* More than ever, Stephir wished he had Father Daemmer with him. The priest would be able to advise him as to what this might be. Without fully clearing the daze, he addressed High General Kuymon. "Send reinforcements to the northern end of the ravine, but I don't want them going in there. I just want to ensure the Kushaani don't come back out that way."

By the looks on their faces, the implications of his words weren't lost on the others. Frey voiced what Stephir was sure everyone was thinking. "There is no way the Kushaani could get past four thousand soldiers. General Bascon has enough men to fill the entire ravine."

"Then the extra troops will, at worst, be bored," Stephir retorted impatiently.

"No, they'll at worst be killed by the same thing that's happening to the trees," Frey shot back, forgetting his place in the public setting. Stephir didn't object to others expressing opposing views. On the contrary, he tried to encourage it. But there was a time and place, and this was not it.

"That would be nearly impossible, Marquis," Commander Alscan stated with an even voice that nevertheless conveyed the full weight of her station. "As I have explained before, the more elevated the life form, the more difficult it is to siphon its elan against its will. With humans, it is, well... nearly impossible." Her voice was edged with condescension.

Stephir put an end to the discussion. "My order stands. High General, make it happen."

High General Kuymon nodded to one of his junior officers, who left to carry out the order. Stephir hadn't anticipated issuing so many dispatches to the field from atop the bluff. With so many scouts and junior officers carrying out his orders, Stephir would have to start carrying his own messages if messengers didn't return soon.

"There's a fire in the ravine!" someone shouted in alarm. Thick white smoke billowed from the treetops in the ravine, nearly a mile from where it opened into the valley near the blackened trees.

"Is that our doing or theirs?" Stephir asked Alscan.

"I can't tell from here, my lord."

Stephir sighed and continued watching, alternating between his spyglass and his natural vision. The smoke spread rapidly south along the ravine. He hoped the fire was pushing the Kushaani toward the valley, but he could not decide which side of the smoke he hoped his men were on.

His attention was drawn to Commander Elorin's position. The cavalry's right flank suddenly churned in chaos. Men and horses fell long before their distant shouts climbed through the air to his ears. A volley of arrows from the tree line gave him all the explanation he needed. A third volley arced higher, hitting deeper into their ranks.

Shields up! Pull back! Stephir wanted to shout but knew it was futile. Horn blasts sounded, signaling the order to right face and form ranks. By the time the fourth volley flew, the army faced their enemy and charged. Stephir could not imagine what they intended to do. They couldn't charge through the trees. He watched in powerless frustration as his men did just that, slowing, but riding straight into the forest.

Yonvaar, preserve them, Stephir prayed silently.

As more of Elorin's forces disappeared into the trees, he caught sight of Kushaani pouring from the ravine into the valley, the smoke close on their heels. A single flaming arrow shot in a high arc from a high hill near the south end of the valley, signaling the rest of his forces to move into the valley and engage the enemy.

It's too soon! They should be further into the valley. Like it or not, his trap was sprung and would now run its course.

Commander Elorin's forces jammed up at the tree line, the natural result of the forward ranks having to slow as they reached the trees. The war horns signaled a left face, form ranks.

He's sending the rest south. Stephir was pleased. *Elorin is an excellent commander. He knows what he's doing.*

The men were well-practiced at mounted maneuvers and formed quickly. Another signal was given to move forward at a canter. It took a great deal of discipline to keep the men from charging the enemy from a distance, but it was critical to maintaining formation and keeping the horses from being tiring before they engaged. They would be at a full charge soon enough.

Duke Miarsten and General Wenstak were spreading out to form a wide blockade on the eastern side of the valley. Stephir hoped they didn't rush in before his forces from the north and south closed the envelopment.

A blanket of heavy white smoke poured into the valley from the ravine, obscuring his view of the battlefield. He suppressed a curse. *Teraithia wouldn't care if you cursed.* The random thought bothered him. He fought the urge to debate theology with himself. *Focus!*

Frey cursed, and Stephir almost smiled. *He'll never hold back.*

Stephir squinted, attempting to see through the thick white smoke. A stream of Kushaani spilled from the ravine, but it was impossible to gauge their numbers, or how they were composed, or if Bascon was at their rear. *Just hold back and wait for the smoke to clear. Don't be in a hurry.*

The smoke blocked his view of General Verindas's troops on the south end of the valley. Horns sounded a halt, and Commander Elorin's cavalry stopped short of the smoke, veering from the trees on his right. They were not completely out of bow range, but they were at least at a safer distance than before.

Patches of black smoke began to mix with the white along the top of the ravine as the blackened, decaying trees caught fire. If the flames atop the ravine spread quickly, thousands of Stephir's soldiers could be trapped. He hoped the lush forests were wet enough to prevent the fire from killing his men. *The fire won't spread quickly*, he tried to reassure himself.

Duke Miarsten's forces started moving, and Stephir feared the impetuous man was mounting an assault.

"What is he doing?" Kuymon asked, sounding aggravated. Stephir watched as Miarsten turned his men south while General Wenstak held his troops in place. It was still a sizable force, but Stephir feared a strong push by enough Kushaani could break through. If that happened, Commander Elorin would have to ride blindly into the smoke if he wanted to hit the Kushaani flank.

"M'lord," Kuymon said, facing Stephir. "We should send reinforcements to Wenstak. It could be too late, but at least we would already have troops moving to hold the Kushaani from escaping the valley and give the rest of our forces time to attack from the rear."

"I agree. Who do you recommend?" Stephir asked.

Before Kuymon answered, Frey jumped in. "I'll go. I'll take my two hundred mounted, and if you give me another three hundred, I can be there within a half hour."

"I can go as well, Your Highness," Marchioness Haedep said. Other nobles and officers eagerly volunteered as well.

"Marquis, Marchioness, you'll both go. Lady Haedep, you will have command." Frey stiffened. Their ranks may technically have been of equal as designated heirs to a royal title, but being the heir of a dukedom gave Frey a higher station than Lady Haedep, who was in line to inherit an earldom. Frey was certainly the better fighter, but Haedep was a superior tactician, and more level-headed. Stephir made a mental note to smooth things over with his friend later.

Addressing Kuymon, Stephir continued. "Send word that everyone in those forests is to pull out and move into the valley behind Elorin."

Stephir turned his attention to the battle. The smoke thinned as it drifted throughout the valley. It no longer seemed to pour out of the ravine, but it continued to rise high into the air like a misty shroud. Bodies were strewn on the ground among scattered groups of soldiers fighting.

Stephir wrinkled his nose at a faintly acrid smell carried on the wind. He turned to Alscan, "Can you do anything about—"

The sound of the horns signaling a charge cut him short. All eyes watched as nearly two thousand horses charged into the smoke.

Stephir's breath caught in his chest. The faint clashing of metal mingled with the distant shouts of soldiers was the only indication of the veiled scene playing out beneath the white shroud that covered the valley.

"Go!" Stephir commanded Frey and Haedep. The sound of galloping hooves quickly receded down the slope. The sounds of battle in the valley grew fainter. *They must be moving south,* Stephir thought.

And then there was only silence.

CHAPTER XVIII
ANDRIC

Two days south on the road was two days further than Andric had ever been. The endless vibrant green sea of tall wild-grain grasses broke against the occasional island of trees or a village. The distant mountains rested along the north and east horizons. Initially, the gentle beauty of the land had put Andric somewhat at ease, but that was gone. Yesterday, they began passing wounded and sick making their way back to Luresh and then to their homes throughout Remalia. Andric had stopped to talk with some of the people they passed, but the stories were essentially the same, so now he simply rode past them without a word as he pressed on toward Nanjab.

Remalia had won a resounding victory, driving the Kushaani out of the borderlands, but the king hadn't stopped. He had pushed into Kushaan and conquered Nanjab, apparently with little difficulty. Although Andric was pleased with the resounding success of the campaign, the army needed to return to Remalia but kept slipping farther away with each victory. That would all change when he reached Nanjab though.

Under the heat of the noon sun, Andric and his men approached the high, arched city gates. He was surprised there were no signs of the city having been sieged and conquered less than a week before. The soldiers standing guard informed him that the king could be found in the first grand estate along the main street leading into the city. Andric and his party rode under the wall's shadow and into the winding streets of Nanjab.

Andric saw no Kushaani in the vicinity of the gates, which made sense.

The inhabitants of the city had no doubt been cleared from the area to provide room for Remalia's soldiers and to prevent any counterassault on the gates if the Kushaani forces returned. Squads of soldiers moved along the streets, performing some duty or another, but Andric thought there should have been many more. There hardly seemed to be enough to hold the city against another Kushaani attack.

As they rode further into the city, Andric became more disquieted. The hot, still air became increasingly devoid of any signs of life. Apart from the small contingent of Remalians, the city was uninhabited.

The street abruptly opened into an expansive walled courtyard with large trees growing here and there, seemingly at random. Long beds of once vibrantly colored flowers wound through the courtyard, though they were badly wilted and dying. The horses' hooves clicked loudly on the sandstone-paved path leading to a beautiful house plastered with a gleaming white finish that reminded Andric of the Grand Temple of the Holy Couple in Teris. The building looked like it had once belonged to a wealthy merchant or local noble. The white walls were contrasted by a deep turquoise painted on the inside recesses of the windows and archways. The vibrant color splashed against the stark white in an impressive contrast.

Andric hardly spared a thought for the surrounding aesthetics as he reined in his mount to a halt. Soldiers stood at attention in front of the wide steps leading into the estate. "My father is here?" he asked brusquely.

"Yes, milord," answered the barrel-chested corporal.

"Take me to him at once." Andric dismounted, and his men followed suit. Without looking back, he climbed the few steps to the covered porch. The shade was a welcome relief from the heat. He followed a guide through the front door to a large round foyer. Open windows flooded the space with sunlight. Six Divinarim barred a short set of stairs that led down to the main floor of the house. At the sight of the prince, all of the men snapped to attention and saluted.

"Your Highness," one of the knights greeted him, then added an acknowledgment of Knight Captain Lindthen with a slight incline of his head. "Knight Captain."

Before Andric could give his orders, Lindthen spoke to the young man. "Good to see you, cousin. We'll talk later. The prince wishes to see his father at once."

"Of course." The knight led Andric down the short flight of rug-covered red marble stairs. Divinarim were posted at regular intervals along their route. After a few turns and hallways, they rounded a corner into a spacious circular foyer. Large windows set into a domed ceiling arching overhead provided all the light they needed. A large round table covered with beautiful bouquets of bright flowers dominated the center of the chamber.

Four Divinarim guarded large double doors with gold and mother-of-pearl inlaid with patterns of flowers and birds. Andric didn't care. The holy knights snapped to attention as Andric approached. Master Dathalin, the king's chief minister since leaving Teris, stood from behind a small desk that looked out of place in the well-appointed chamber.

"Your Highness," the man greeted in a hushed tone, bowing low. The gesture from the usually arrogant man, who always seemed dismissive of Andric, set the prince's nerves on edge. "We did not expect you for several days yet."

"I have an urgent matter to discuss with my father. I understand he's here," Andric said as he looked at the closed doors.

"Yes, my lord. Have..." he paused, then started again. "Has Your Highness been told about the king's condition?"

"I heard that he might be sick. Is that true?" Andric fought the urge to burst through the doors and see his father as a nagging fear grew in his heart.

"Yes, Your Highness. The king is attended by priests and physicians at all times. Perhaps it would be best to speak with one of them before entering."

Despite the heat, Andric felt a chill run down his arms. "How bad is it?" He was surprised at how flat his voice sounded.

"Your Highness, permit me to retrieve the physician. She will be best suited to discuss this matter with you."

"Fine," Andric said without inflection. His mind raced in confused circles, and fear swelled inside his chest. He knew better than to assume the worst, but his mind didn't always follow the rules he outlined for it. *Wait for the physician*, he chided himself. Master Dathalin disappeared through the double doors but returned before Andric realized any time had passed. He had a hard time focusing on the physician's face until he realized it was Sister Merranine, then she had his entire attention.

"Prince Andric," Sister Merranine said softly as she elegantly curtseyed. As chief royal physician, it was natural that she would attend the king, but it simply hadn't entered Andric's mind that she would be here.

"How is my father?"

"Come walk with me," she said taking him gently by the arm and leading him across the foyer. She gently guided him into a large open garden in the center of the house. It was surprisingly cool here. The sweet smell of flowers filled the air, but it was the intoxicating scent of Sister Merranine that made Andric's head spin. He had always loved the way she smelled.

At last, she spoke, her voice laced with amusement. "Do you remember when you broke your arm falling off the garden wall?"

Andric nodded.

"You whined and carried on so!" Andric could not imagine what this had to do with his father. It didn't seem an appropriate time to be teasing him. "You've grown considerably since then. I think you can handle pain much better now."

Andric felt a sudden sinking feeling in his chest as his breath escaped him. He instantly clamped down on his swirling emotions, fighting for calm, remaining silent.

Sister Merranine turned to face Andric. He stood a full head taller than her, and it felt strange to look down on the woman who at this moment seemed to be the only person holding up his world. "Andric, your father is dying."

He felt nothing, but he could not stop his thoughts from racing out of control. *How did...? What is life going to...? Where is Ste—? What's that spice I always smell on her...? Should I find Stephir or stay with...? What is life going to...? Who can I tell...? Where is Stephir?* He couldn't break into the whirlwind in his head.

"Andric?"

He strained to focus on her face. Her face. Some corner of his consciousness told him to snap out of it, to stop being childish. He finally forced out a single word in little more than a whisper. "How?"

Sister Merranine placed her hand on his arm. "We don't know exactly. It started the day after we took over the city. We knew some of the Kushaani fled, but when we arrived, only a few stragglers were left behind, mainly the old and the sick who could not flee. I thanked our Holy Parents there was no bloodshed. Your brother left the next day to pursue the Kushaani. Several of our people had suddenly fallen ill, but it was no illness any of us had ever seen. There is no fever, no pain, no stomach sickness, just complete fatigue. No one else has gotten sick after that first day. Within two days we could see that those who were sick were wasting away. It was as if the body was consuming itself. The physicians have found neither cause nor cure. Some elantir believe it's some form of Kushaani elant, but no one knows for sure."

Andric heard every word, but as if from a great distance. "He could get better though. You could still cure him." Even his own voice sounded distant and muted.

"A few people have already died. No one is getting better. Jevorak is strong, but..."

"I must... Can I...?"

"Of course. Come with me." Sister Merranine took Andric by the arm with her warm and gentle hands, leading him back through the garden into the house. "I must warn you. His body is practically a shell. He has no strength left, even for talking." After a pause, she added, "But I know he will be comforted to see you."

Knight Captain Lindthen and the others watched Andric as he approached the king's quarters, but he could not look at anyone, even Barak. He kept his eyes on the ground. His conscience screamed at him, *This is no way for a prince of Remalia to act. Hold your head up!* His body refused to respond.

Inside, the room was open and bright. Sister Merranine guided him to the side of the wide bed. Andric stared blankly at the pile of skin and bones propped up by pillows, a thin crimson-and-gold blanket laid over the frail figure that was supposed to be his father. He scarcely recognized the withered form before him. Everything and everyone seemed so far away.

At last, Andric mindlessly sat on the edge of the bed without removing his eyes from the faded visage.

No thoughts. No feelings.

Andric felt a light hand on his shoulder. Sister Merranine. He wondered if she would allow him to bed her. *What is wrong with you? Your father's dying right before your eyes and you're thinking about sleeping with a priestess, a married woman, who is twice your age?*

Another voice, his own but one that rarely surfaced, came rushing to the surface. *Yonvaar, Kerail, help me. Save me.*

The other voice, the harsh one, retorted. *Stop thinking of yourself.*

The gentle, pleading voice obeyed. *Holy Couple, bless my father. Heal him. We all need him. I need him.* Andric reached out and took his father by the hand.

A different voice, immovable as a mountain, yet gentle, rose from beneath his scattered thoughts. *You may say goodbye.*

Suddenly, all other thoughts fled from his mind and he was left with only a feeling of a strength beyond himself, bearing him up.

His father opened his eyes.

"Andric?" his father's voice rasped out, barely more than a whisper.

Andric couldn't breathe. He nodded. A single tear ran slowly down his cheek. His mind focused on it, followed its warm path as it moved across his skin.

"What are you doing here? You should be at the front with Stephir." Even on his deathbed, his father hadn't changed—and Andric loved him more in that moment than any time in his life. The dam holding back the emotions, the tears, the pain, broke loose and a racking sob tore from Andric's chest. He slid off the bed to his knees. He rested his forehead on their joined hands and let his sobs disappear into the pillows under him.

Stop crying. You're embarrassing yourself, the harsh voice chastised.

You are showing love for your father. There's no shame in that. Others will find it touching.

Always worried what others think of you. Have you no genuine bone in your body?

"Andric, come here, boy," his father invited weakly.

Andric could not look up for a few long moments, but with some effort he raised his head. The sight of his father's sunken face nearly overwhelmed him again, but he clamped down on the emotions and rose to sit next to his father again.

"What day is it?" the king asked.

"Crestday, the fourteenth day of Solsticeswell."

Jevorak nodded slowly, closing his eyes. Andric feared his father had slipped away and felt panic rise, but the king spoke again, opening his eyes slowly.

"I miss Serenne." His father had not spoken of Andric's mother for years until the morning he and Stephir had left Teris. "I wish you could have known her. She would have adored you. You're so much like her; spontaneous, impetuous even; carefree and full of life. I miss her, Andric."

Andric had never seen his father like this. He didn't know how to respond. "Father, how do you feel?"

"Wonderful." His father strained to draw in breath. "Put me on my horse and point me toward the enemy," Jevorak said with a wan smile tugging at the corners of his dry lips.

Andric couldn't help smiling.

"Listen, Andric." Jevorak's breath rasped in his throat. "You must do something for me."

"Anything, Father. You have but to ask."

"Find a good woman and love her forever." Andric wanted to laugh. It was an absurd thought at a time like this. "And have babies... lots of babies...

like your sister. I wish I could see her again. So beautiful. Just like her mother."

Andric glanced away and his eyes strayed to Sister Merranine, who returned his gaze with a soft, sympathetic smile. *Eleah. Her name is Eleah,* he thought. The prince's cheeks flushed, and he quickly looked back at the king. "Of course, Father."

"And another thing. Tell Stephir that I am proud of him. He'll be the greatest king Remalia has ever had." Jevorak closed his eyes. He drew in a shallow, ragged breath. Without opening his eyes, the king whispered, "I love you, boy."

Andric strangled a sob that threatened to escape, but he couldn't stop the tears from streaming.

"Father?" He squeezed his father's withered hand. "Father!"

Sister Merranine knelt beside the prince and put her hand on the king's head. "He's only sleeping, Andric," she said gently, moving her hand on top of Andric's for a moment before moving to a seat across the room.

He sat there for several minutes, unmoving. He realized at some point that the tears had stopped. His eyes burned and his body ached, but he didn't want to move. At last he could no longer stand the discomfort. He laid his father's hand across his shrunken chest and stood, rubbing his eyes. They felt like he had come through a sandstorm. He wanted to sleep. He wanted to stay with his father. He wanted to ride to Stephir. He wanted to go home.

He crossed the room and opened the door. "Knight Captain, please summon Captain Min. And find the ranking officer in this city and send for him as well."

Lindthen saluted, his eyes lingering on Andric for just a moment, then turned and walked briskly down the hallway. Andric returned to his father's bed and moved a chair within arm's reach of Jevorak, but folded his hands in his lap. He was startled to notice two men standing silently in a corner of the room. Embarrassment and anger intruded upon his calm. Who had the audacity to invade his privacy in these intimate moments with his father?

He remembered what Master Dathalin had said about priests and physicians attending the king day and night. Andric tried to shut them out as he gazed at his father. He hated the Kushaani with a renewed passion for what they had done to him; for what they were doing in Remalia; for every atrocity they had committed against his people; for being Kushaani.

He stifled a yawn and felt guilty for being weak. Stephir would never have been tired at a time like this. Then a grim thought occurred to him; Stephir might never see their father again. Andric hung his head, fighting the dark mood threatening to drown him. He forced his mind to walk through everything that needed to be taken care of before he could give all of his attention to his father. It was not long before the doors opened and Master Dathalin entered a few steps into the room.

"My lord, Captain Minan... sadum is here to see you."

Despite his black mood, Andric was amused Dathalin couldn't pronounce Captain Min's name any better than he could. "Tell him to come in." Andric mused again on the fact he felt no distaste at having to speak with a scout at this moment. He appreciated Captain Min's quiet confidence. He would have made a good line officer. Maybe he would say something about it to someone.

"Your Highness," Dathalin said with the tone of a counselor as he stepped into the room and closed the door behind him. "If I may, we have been cautious, allowing only a handful of people to see the king in this state. Word has spread that he is not well, but it would be best if we keep the severity of his illness private for as long as possible, not only for his sake, but there are other considerations as well."

"I understand," Andric conceded, nodding. Once word got out that the king was possibly on his deathbed, things would get much more complicated for everyone, especially Stephir. "I will be cautious, but I trust this man. Please send him in." Master Dathalin bowed and exited the room, leaving the door open.

A moment later, Captain Min took a step into the room and saluted. "You summoned me, Your Highness?"

"Yes, Captain. Come in."

Min took a few more steps into the room, and a Divinar closed the door. Andric saw him glance around the room, his eyes pausing for a moment at sight of the king in his bed. "My father isn't well. I need you go on ahead and find my brother. Tell him about the Kushaani."

The scout captain's expression softened, and he appeared to suppress a smile. Annoyance flashed through Andric at what he assumed the expression was amusement, but he reconsidered as he recognized it as more patient and compassionate.

"Of course, my lord," Min responded gently. "May I suggest that perhaps if I were to deliver a written message from you it might meet with more success in reaching Prince Stephir. I don't know that a foreigner scout will be admitted to His Highness in the middle of the war."

He was probably right, but Andric wanted Stephir to hear the news first-hand from Min. Andric ordered the men in the corner of the room to bring him paper and writing instruments. They gestured toward a small writing table near the bed that had what he needed. He sat at the desk and took up a quill pen, dipped it in the inkwell and stared at the paper. There were so many things he wanted to say. He probably could have written all day. He opted for a simple introduction for Captain Min and urged Stephir to move with haste. He considered saying something about their father, but instead he signed the letter and folded it.

Andric held his breath for a few moments, then let it out slowly. It wouldn't be right to tell Stephir nothing. He took up the pen again and haltingly wrote a second note. It was equally brief, but it was all he could think to say.

I am here in Nanjab with Father. I do not know how long he has to live. I hope to see you soon.

Andric sealed the second note, then handed the first one to Min. "This letter states that you are to be admitted directly to my brother. He'll listen to you." Then Andric handed him the second note. "Please deliver this to my brother as well. It's for him alone. No one else need see it."

"I understand, Your Highness," Min said firmly.

"Gods speed and keep you."

"Thank you. And you as well." Captain Min saluted, then left the room.

Andric returned to the chair by the bed. His father had said that he loved him, but he was proud of Stephir. He wished he had been someone his father could have been proud of. There were so many things he wished he had done differently: paid more attention to his lessons, been more involved in the affairs of the kingdom. His mind wandered through memories of his father. Too many times he saw Stephir by their father's side, but not himself.

The silence in the room was starting to bother him. He wanted to talk to someone, but he didn't know who. Sister Merranine would be happy to talk to him, but he wouldn't know what to say.

Barak.

Without getting up, he spoke to no one in particular. "Please summon my advisor, Master Ve'Aurben." The door opened and Andric listened as his order was conveyed to those outside. He heard Master Dathalin sigh quietly, but the prince didn't care.

It had been several hours since Andric had eaten breakfast, but he had no appetite. *Something to drink, though.* He cast his eyes around the room. There were armoires and other cabinets along the walls, and he rummaged through them. Most were empty and one contained his father's neatly hung clothes. Nothing to drink.

"Is there any wine in here?"

"I don't believe so, Your Highness," answered the shorter man in the corner. "Shall I have some brought?"

"Yes. Strong wine."

The man bowed and left the room. Andric glanced at Sister Merranine, who sat watching him. "What's being done to find an answer to the sickness?" he asked. "Has anyone tried to capture a Kushaani elantir to extract the information? Someone must know what this is."

"We have exhausted all our knowledge. Others are working with those who are sick to see what can be discovered. I heard that some were sent to find answers among the Kushaani."

She has such a comforting voice, Andric thought to himself. "How many are sick?" he asked.

"Hundreds."

"In one day? How is that possible?" Incredulous anger was welling up inside him, but he wouldn't let himself direct it at Sister Merranine. Anyone but her.

The door opened and Master Dathalin announced Barak's arrival. Andric motioned his friend to enter. Barak scanned the room, then looked intently at Andric. "How can I be of service, Your Highness?"

"No formalities, please. You've heard about my father? About all the sick?"

"I heard he's not well." Barak's glance shifted to the king, then back to Andric. With intense sincerity, he quietly said, "I'm sorry."

Barak's words made everything seem so much more real. Andric returned to the seat next to his father. He wanted to talk about his condition, but he didn't know what to say, especially with others in the room. "I've sent Captain Min to find Stephir and tell him about the Kushaani."

"That's probably the best choice."

"Look at him, Barak. He's hardly recognizable." Andric gave an ironic chuckle. "Strange. If Captain Min had not come along with the news about the Kushaani, I wouldn't have raced here to find my father. I might never have seen him alive again."

"The ways of the gods are a mystery."

"Too many mysteries. It seems this sickness is a mystery that no one can figure out." Andric longed for simpler days. "You don't happen to have the answer tucked away inside that head of yours, do you?"

"Maybe."

Andric spun in his chair, staring at Barak. This was no time to joke, but he could see no sign of amusement on his friend's face. The men in the corner edged forward, intense interest on their faces.

Sister Merranine spoke with tension in her voice. "You know what this is?"

"I'm not sure, but I have an idea," Barak answered calmly.

Andric was incredulous. "Why didn't you say so sooner? Damn it, my father's dying!"

"Yes, he is. I don't know how to change that. I have only read an account that described something similar."

Sister Merranine had composed herself, her voice calm again, but merely masking an underlying intensity. "Anything could help, Master Ve'Aurben. Please tell us everything you know."

"During The War to Break All Oaths, the Kul-a'durith delved into met'elan that altered their bodies, making them stronger, faster, their skin harder."

One of the priests interrupted Barak, "Who are the *Kul-a'durith*?"

"Today they're more commonly known as Kuldrith." The man nodded, so Barak continued. "The Kul-a'— Kuldrith began changing as many of their soldiers as they could, but the process was slow and painful. It involved infusing several modality configurations into the muscle, bone, sinew, blood —every part of the body to make it work together. Make the muscles too powerful and they'll rip from the bone, so you have to strengthen the sinew, and so on. The Kuldrith called these elanticly augmented warriors the *ultha an'katar*, "the hands of death." Well, literally it means "the hands of slumber", but in this case 'slumber' was a euphemism for death."

"Barak," Andric interrupted. He had little patience at the moment for his scholarly friend's endless tangents.

"I'm getting there. Even with far greater numbers, Aerion Dar-ka'Surth's forces were outmatched by the ultha an'katar. The Byanthine elantir tried to find a way to undo the elants that were woven into them, but they had no knowledge of such body alteration. They considered it a corrupt and evil practice."

"So what are you saying? This is some form of ancient Kuldrith met'e-lan?" Andric asked impatiently.

"No. Aerion's elantir couldn't reverse the elants. However, in studying the problem, they discovered a way to add to the flows already anchored in the ultha an'katars' bodies. The new infusions caused hyper-acceleration of some of the body's processes. It caused their bodies to consume themselves. The description of what it did to them is very similar to what appears to be happening now."

The quiet room erupted in questions as everyone spoke at once, but Sister Merranine's voice silenced the rest. "Do you know the elants? Our elantir have searched and found nothing. Can you search the bodies of the sick to help us find the solution?"

Barak slowly shook his head. Andric knew this was the greatest source of sadness and frustration for his friend. "I don't have any ability to perform met'elan. I study the theories, the histories, I sense elan all around us, but I can do nothing with it."

"Did you learn what the elants were? What modalities they used?" the older of the two men asked anxiously. "Any clue as to what we should be searching for?"

"No. I have some ideas, but I was forced to piece the history together from obscure texts. The Byanthine at the time were delving into forbidden knowledge. They felt it was justified, I'm sure, considering they were facing the destruction of their entire people, but there is no record I have found that gives any detail of their work. Even if they did write it down, which is doubtful, they would have either destroyed it after the war or hidden it away to keep anyone from gaining access to the destructive power."

There was silence in the room for several moments. Andric returned wearily to his father's side. Barak took a seat at the writing desk, no doubt uncomfortable with all the scrutiny, while Sister Merranine and the two men resumed talking quietly on the other side of the room. The bright moment of hope Andric had felt when he thought that Barak might have the answer now left him in a deeper darkness in its absence.

After fidgeting for a few minutes, Barak got up from his seat and joined the others. The three turned to look down at the little man with skepticism. Barak spoke too quiet for Andric to make out his words, but the others appeared to be listening intently to what he was saying. He wondered if he wanted to hear his friend's ideas, or if he would even comprehend that level of elantic theory. He wished he had been allowed to study met'elan more; perhaps it would have allowed him to help now.

Andric turned his back on them, determined not to get his hopes up. He opened his center and let it fill with a small measure of his elan, not wanting the others to sense what he was doing. He gently reached out to feel for his father's life essence, expecting it to be as weak as his body looked. Andric was surprised that it instead felt frenetic and chaotic. Barak's description certainly seemed to fit what he felt. Andric was no physician, but he was certain there must be some way to fix this.

He released his elan and joined the others to listen to what Barak was discussing with the healers.

Barak spoke in a hushed tone. "... have nothing to lose. They're going to die if you don't do something."

"But what do we alter?" asked the silver-haired man. There was no rank insignia on his white robes, and Andric surmised he was an elantir in the service of the Holy Couple. "The heart rate? Their breathing? Body temperature? Nothing appears out of the ordinary. Even if this could work, it would likely take us weeks or longer to find the right combinations to keep them alive. They will probably all be dead by then." The man glanced guiltily toward Andric. "Forgive me, Your Highness. I meant no disrespect."

Andric simply nodded.

Returning to the discussion with Barak, the priest opened his mouth to continue his argument, but Barak cut him off. "Do it all. Slow down everything in the body as close as you can to shutting down completely. It may well prolong their lives a bit longer, which buys you more time." Barak said emphatically.

"But it could also kill them," the second man chimed in.

"Like I said, they're going to die for certain if you do nothing."

After a moment of contemplation, Sister Merranine finally broke the silence. "Thank you for your suggestions, Master Ve'Aurben. We will see what we can do." She gestured for the others to leave the room with her.

As the three stepped out, two Divinarim entered carrying platters with assorted fruits and cheese, and a tray with wine and glasses. It was amusing to see the armor-clad knights perform the duties of common house servants. It would have been almost surreal if he had not just spent days riding south with them. Andric had seen them perform all the same mundane tasks as anyone else, making them seem more... normal. They placed the items on a table and left the room.

"Finally," Andric sighed heavily. "Do you want something?"

"No," Barak answered.

Andric filled a glass with chilled wine and took a long drink. It was not as strong as he had hoped, but the flavor was rich and full. No doubt it was a good selection to pair with the fruit and cheese, but he was only interested in the wine for the moment. He finished off the glass and poured himself another.

Barak had taken a seat and stared at the floor.

"What's on your mind, Barak?"

Barak didn't answer immediately, but instead slowly shook his head. After several moments, Andric was about to repeat the question, but Barak finally responded. "Do you know why I've never taken the vows?"

Andric knew he meant the vows to become a priest of Viance. Barak rarely spoke about his faith. Andric felt a bit uneasy, but he didn't have anything else he wanted to discuss, so he followed his friend's lead. "Because you like to study but don't want to be tied down to the duties of a priest."

Barak shook his head. "I am never going to be useful."

Andric was confused at the response. "What are you talking about? Just having you here helps me a lot. And you have given more help to Sister Merranine and the oth—"

"That's not what I'm talking about." Barak interrupted.

Before Barak could elaborate there was a knock at the door. He was about to tell whomever it was to go away, but he was first a prince of Remalia who had duties that must be attended to with the king on his deathbed. "Sorry, Barak. Just give me one moment," he said sincerely. "Come in!" he ordered.

Master Dathalin stood in the doorway. "Your Highness, Intercessor Shiralla Henden begs a moment of your time."

"Tell her I'm busy, and I'll speak to her another time."

"Forgive me, my lord, but she says she has an urgent message from Consul Rellat."

Andric failed to suppress an exasperated sigh. "Send her in."

"Your Highness, perhaps it would be best if—"

Andric cut him off. "If an intercessor can't keep a state secret we're in serious trouble. Just send her in."

Dathalin bowed and stepped out.

Andric was surprised when a woman who appeared to only be in her late twenties strode purposefully into the room. Certainly she was far too young to be an intercessor already. Her deep-red hair and fair skin were accented by the viridescent flowing dress expertly tailored for her slightly plump physique. She curtseyed deeply, arms spread wide with the cape-like *kemrelac* draped over her left arm. The white lining of her kemrelac was the same as those worn by all of the Sharinic clergy, while the outside was blue, showing her service in the foreign diplomatic corps. Her elegant movements revealed she was a priestess of Sharin Dara as much as her title and clerical vestments did.

The formality of the visit was apparent to Andric and he hoped to bring it to an end quickly. He stood as she rose from her curtsy.

"Your Highness, please forgive my intrusion at this difficult time. No doubt you wish to spend time with your father in privacy, but Consul Rellat urged me to see you as soon as we learned of your arrival."

"What can I do for you, Intercessor?"

"Thank you, Your Highness," she said with a perfect blend of politeness, gentleness, and business. "Two Kushaani emissaries from the Vanassi Province arrived in Nanjab two nights ago; they are requesting an audience with his majesty, the king. We have attempted to ascertain their purpose, but all we have learned is that they wish to discuss a treaty on behalf of the Vanassi. We did not want to let them know the king's condition, but they refused to discuss their business with anyone else. Consul Rellat fears that they will misconstrue this treatment as a refusal to treat with them and will leave. An agreement with the Vanassi could be very beneficial, Your Highness. If they agree to treat with you in the king's stead, gods preserve him, would you be willing to meet with them?"

Andric didn't know much about the Vanassi. They lived over sixty leagues west of Nanjab in the jungles below the Velspar Mountains. They were probably one of the most independent of the Kushaani tribes. Perhaps they wished to separate from the empire. Part of Andric's mind acknowledged they could be of some use, although he was more inclined to order their executions than to treat with them, after seeing his father's wasted condition.

"Can't this wait until tomorrow?" he asked impatiently.

"We can certainly ask them, Your Highness. But the Vanassi are... well, somewhat impulsive. That they've remained here this long says something of their desire to discuss this matter."

Andric sighed. This was one of the reasons he was relieved Stephir was to be king instead of him. He liked being involved sometimes, but he had no desire to bear these responsibilities all the time.

"Very well. I will meet with them after dinner."

"Your Highness, if I may offer a suggestion," the Intercessor said firmly.

"Of course."

"The Vanassi custom when making peace pacts is to do so during a meal. If Your Highness waits until after the meal, they might take it as a sign that you're not truly interested in what they have to offer."

"Well, they came to us. They should learn what our customs are!"

"Andric," Barak said quietly. The prince looked over at Barak, who simply raised one thin eyebrow.

Andric sighed again. "Fine. Invite them to dinner. You and Consul Rellat will, of course, be there."

"As you wish, my lord."

"Master Ve'Aurben will be in attendance as well." Andric flashed a mischievous grin at Barak, who subtly scowled in return. "Also, I still haven't heard who is in command here?"

"That would be General Obannern. He has spoken with the Vanassi emissaries already, though only briefly. Does Your Highness wish to invite him as well?"

"Yes, thank you. Where will we have dinner? I assume there's a dining hall in this manor?"

"Yes, Your Highness."

"Very well, Intercessor," he searched for her name but realized he had already forgotten it. *Oh well, nothing new.* "I shall see you at dinner."

"Thank you, Your Highness," she said with another deep curtsey, arms outstretched, then left the room. *Sharinists are always so formal,* Andric mused for a brief moment before turning his attention back to his friend.

"Sorry," Andric said apologetically. "You were going to tell me why you're useless?" Andric hoped to lighten his mood with the jest but knew immediately it was in poor taste over something as personal and sensitive as Barak's faith. "Sorry, that didn't come out right."

Barak smiled a thin, empty smile. "That's ok. We should probably get ready for dinner anyway. We'll continue our conversation later."

Andric wanted to push his friend to talk but knew better, and his mood was black enough without creating a rift between them. "Perhaps after dinner."

Barak put a hand on Andric's arm, gently squeezed, then left.

Andric went to the bed and took his father's frail hand in his own. He longed for a return of the sense of stability his father's dominant spirit had provided throughout his life. True, he had balked at times when it felt too much like domineering. Now all he wanted was a little more time to find a balance between those touchstones.

Some part of him sensed that time was the one thing none of them had enough of.

With a sigh, Andric kissed his father's hand and left the room.

CHAPTER XIX
ANDRIC

Andric's quarters in the Nanjabi estate were not as large as his father's, and nothing compared to his rooms in the place in Teris, but they would suffice for now. He was pleased to discover that Master Lonset already had everything in order, and happier to see wine had been provided. He poured a glass and took a drink. It was strong, which he appreciated, but had a slightly bitter aftertaste. He wasn't going to enjoy drinking too much of this, and probably just as well. In his current mood, he was likely to overdo it. The last thing he needed was to show up intoxicated to a diplomatic dinner.

He floated through a fog of swirling thoughts and concerns, hardly noticing what his body did as he washed away the dirt and sweat of the day. He wished he could clean himself on the inside as easily. His thoughts were interrupted by a knock at the door. Andric looked down and realized he had been dressed and sitting on the edge of his bed for some time.

"Your Highness?" Lonset asked.

"Come in."

"My lord, dinner will be served shortly. May I be of any service?"

"Is everything in order?" Andric asked as he turned so Lonset could examine him.

Lonset adjusted Andric's white shirt under his black vest embroidered with gold thread. "Your Highness appears well in order."

"Thank you. Is everyone assembled already for dinner?"

"Yes, Your Highness."

Andric had hoped for a different answer and sighed. "I had better not keep them waiting." The prince left the room and followed his guards through the halls to the other side of the house. The sun had dipped below the horizon into dusk, casting burnt orange light through the windows. He glanced out at the wispy clouds high in the darkening sky, wishing he had the same carefree existence, carried wherever the wind took him.

Servants flanked a large, open archway into the dining room. The Divinarim preceded him into a long, rather narrow room with high ceilings. A long, dark wood table with matching high-backed chairs dominated the center of the room, leaving only enough space for a servant to walk behind the chairs once people were seated. Oil lamps with red silk shades shone dimly in sconces set in the mahogany-paneled walls. The dark sky, the dark room, the dark furniture—they all suited his mood.

Andric was surprised to see he was the first person to arrive for dinner. Through another open archway at the opposite end of the room, he could hear hushed whispers from the foyer. He stood next to the head chair as servants ushered the other guests into the room. General Obannern was first, followed by Consul Rellat, two holy knights of Sharin Dara in gleaming armor, then the two Kushaani emissaries, the intercessor he had spoken with earlier, and finally Barak. The room was too narrow to have a comfortable greeting space. Andric made do with greeting them politely from where he stood.

General Obannern reached Andric first. He saluted casually with his hand across his somewhat large belly to the sword hilt at his hip. At sixty-two, he was the oldest active general in Remalia's army. He had been through every war Andric's father had fought, and the two men remained good friends despite the Obannerns being one of the oldest noble families in Remalia, and had long held ambitions to take over the throne. Their aspirations had never resulted in open rebellion, but no love was lost between the families.

"It's good to see Your Highness's safe arrival." The general glanced slightly over his shoulder, then locked eyes with Andric. "I'm sorry your father isn't disposed to join us tonight. We'll talk together later." Andric knew it was important to keep the king's condition vague. Word was bound to get out sooner or later, but probably later was better, after Stephir had the opportunity to prove he was a king to be reconned with. Andric thanked the general, who made his way around the other side of the table to stand by his seat.

"Your Highness," Consul Rellat greeted Andric solemnly, bowing with his arms stretched out, a gesture made somewhat difficult by the tight quarters.

"Consul, it's good to see you again." Andric forced a smile as he greeted the priest. "I feared I would arrive only to discover that you had negotiated an end to the war and the surrender of the entire Kushaani Empire. I'm glad you've left some work for the rest of us." The words were more for the Kushaani, who remained behind the two men guarding the consul. Sharin Dara's holy knights were a spectacular sight, but they didn't have a reputation for being especially skilled at fighting. They certainly were no match for the Divinarim.

The consul's lips remained fixed in a straight line. He was always a serious man, which made joking with him all the more fun, even if it was a bit sadistic. "Your Highness, it is my honor to introduce to you Bejurn sud-Ta, emissary of the Vanassi Tribe."

The two knights stepped past the consul to make room for a tall man with long, jet-black hair and chiseled features. Andric was tall, but this man towered over him. The close quarters made the height difference even more disquieting. The man raised his dark hands to his face and touched his fingertips to his eyes, then his ears, his lips, his heart, and finally he extended his open hands toward Andric.

"It is a deep honor to meet you, Prince Andric Laconeus."

Andric had expected a deeper voice, not the warm tenor that flowed from the man's lips. His accent was thick and lilting, with an almost musical quality to his intonation.

"And you as well, Bejurn sud-Ta," Andric had been saying the name over and over in his head since the consul had first said it, and he was happy to remember it through the strange greeting. "I am looking forward to our dinner together." Andric watched the tall man move next to the general.

Having the man at his back made Andric a bit nervous. Images of the Kushaani assassins' attack at the royal stables flashed through his mind, and his heartbeat accelerated. *These are the people responsible for my father's death*, Andric couldn't help thinking. *These are the people attacking my home as we speak.*

"And may I also present—"

Andric turned to look at the other Kushaani visitor and his breath caught in his chest.

"—Jalanti san-Rivva."

Andric watched transfixed as she came forward and offered the same greeting as her tall companion. Andric was certain he had never seen a more exquisite woman in his entire life. Her smooth and flawless skin was the color of deep caramel, like the ones served in the palace on Winterscrest. Her hair, ebony and shining, almost blue where the light danced delightfully on its surface, cascaded in a gentle flow around her shoulders. Her eyes were deep pools of brown with hints of yellow and hazel that contrasted subtly with the seamless color of her skin.

She glanced downward demurely, something Andric normally found more annoying than attractive, but in her it was somehow different, more alluring and mysterious. Her smooth and unadorned shoulders peeked through a wide neckline in the white form-fitting gown that was barely opaque. The gown accentuated the turn of her neck, the suppleness of her waist, and the curves of her chest.

Andric told himself to focus, but that proved impossible when the woman smiled warmly, as if she understood what he was going through and sympathized with his efforts at self-control. He vaguely heard himself respond to her greeting, then watched entranced as she moved next to her companion. He finally wrenched his gaze away from her when he realized Consul Rellat was speaking to him.

"...believe you already have met Intercessor Shiralla Henden."

Andric regained his bearings and answered, "Yes. Hello again, Intercessor Henden."

The priestess curtseyed as low as she could, given the tight quarters. Andric struggled to keep his eyes wandering back to Jalanti. He longed to look at the Kushaani woman again. Was she really as beautiful as his first impression made him believe? He forced himself to observe his manners. "And may I introduce to you all my personal advisor, Master Barak Ve'Aurben."

Barak bowed and disappeared behind the chairs. Even standing upright his eyes were barely higher than the back of the chair. It was almost comical to see Barak flanking the man nearly twice his height. Andric risked another glance at the Kushaani woman and felt his heart lurch in his chest. Her beauty was unearthly. He gripped his chair. "Please sit."

The table was long enough to easily accommodate twice their number, making the room feel lop-sided. Servants filed in and filled their glasses with wine, and placed succulent and savory dishes from both Remalia and Kushaan on the table. The scent of sizzling roasted ducks and racks of lamb still sizzling from the ovens wafted through the warm evening air. Curried meats and unfamiliar spices assailed Andric's senses, somehow blending into an appetizing harmony for the suddenly hungry prince. Bowls of vegetables, some of them freshly cut and some grilled, covered the table. Andric hadn't paid much attention to the conversation as they ate until General Obannern asked him about his unexpected arrival.

"I'm afraid I grew a bit impatient with the pace of traveling with the battalions." The plural was an exaggeration, but he wanted to make their force sound as menacing as possible to the emissaries. "I was anxious to join my father and brother."

"I know what you mean," the General laughed, helping himself to a generous portion of roasted duck. "I have often wished for the freedom to mount my horse and ride to battle alone. But any battle fought alone is surely to be your last."

The artful opening seemed designed to invite the consul to direct the conversation to its main focus. "Yes, it's wise to have companions in such endeavors. One can never fully guard every side," Rellat said carefully, glancing at the tall Kushaani.

Andric turned to look at Bejurn, but Jalanti was seated between them and he could not help glancing at her. Their eyes met briefly before he quickly averted his eyes to the pieces of roasted lamb on his plate. He felt her look sideways at him through her thick, dark lashes. *This is impossible.* He absently placed a piece of the succulent meat in his mouth, but he barely tasted it.

"It requires a great number of men to guard each side when you fight out in the open," Bejurn said, gesturing widely. "In my home, there are many trees. With few warriors, when we must fight, we do it among the trees. The trees guard our sides and our backs. They do the same for our enemies, but we know the trees, so they protect us more."

What is he talking about? Andric wondered, absently sipping his wine, hoping for a swift end to this ordeal. He wanted to invite Jalanti to the garden with him, and he felt guilty and angry at himself for desiring the company of the enemy.

"What do you do when it's necessary to fight among your enemies' trees? When the trees protect them?" the general asked.

"If we can, we find someone from among the enemy and make them part of our tribe. Then the enemy's trees become ours also."

"You're talking about slave raids into your neighbors' lands." Andric knew his words were not very diplomatic, and probably outright rude, but he didn't care. The man had admitted to slave raiding as if it were nothing more than inviting a neighbor to dinner on a feast day. Thick tension filled the room. Jalanti broke the strangled silence, the first words she had spoken since greeting Andric. Her velvet voice was almost too soft, and the prince had to strain to hear her.

"I was taken by a Vanassi raiding party when I was ten years old." Andric was shocked and angered to think of Jalanti as a slave. "I was scared, but I was also excited. My father was a Vanassi before he was captured by the Tan'nikin tribe. He told me stories of his days as a Vanassi. Many days I dreamed of leaving my village to see other places in the world. Life as requital is not what you may think. They work alongside other members of the tribe. The most menial tasks are left to them, but they aren't abused or maltreated. The period of requital rarely lasts more than four or five years. It's a time to assimilate as a full-fledged member of the tribe. Some choose to escape and return to their previous clans, but most remain with their new tribes. I'm a Vanassi now, and I am happy. I returned once to see my old family. This practice may seem strange to you, but it's a way of life we are happy with."

Andric recalled hearing this perspective of Kushaani slaving, but it didn't excuse the atrocities committed against his people. "If you want to make slaves of one another, that is your business, but we will not stand by when you violate our borders and steal our people. And those who have been taken and sold into a lifetime of slavery, treated as animals or worse—they would certainly disagree with such a rosy picture."

Without any apparent anger, Bejurn took up the argument. "Yes, the Kushaani have always practiced the corruption of which you speak, but that is not how the Vanassi—"

"Are you not Kushaani?" Andric fought to keep his voice steady.

"The Kushaani are a tribe, just like the Vanassi, Tan'nikin, Strappatka, or other tribes. But they have always desired to dominate the other tribes, and have succeeded many times. For that reason, all our tribes have come to be known to the outside world as Kushaani; but no, I do not consider myself Kushaani. I am Vanassi."

"I see. And what have you come to discuss with us?" Andric knew his tone was too sharp.

"We have come to offer our help in your fight against the Kushaani."

Andric was surprised and tried to soften his tone. "And what do you propose to do?" Andric studiously avoided looking to the other side of the table. He didn't want to give the consul an opening to interrupt him. He had always imagined himself negotiating like this—cutting through the diplomatic double-speak and getting straight to the point.

"From what we have observed, you do not intend to stop at the border of your Remalia. We believe our best service might be to act as your guides as you pursue the Kushaani."

"In exchange for what?" Andric leaned forward.

Bejurn's voice registered some surprise of his own at Andric's question. "For whatever you might choose to offer us in return."

The Kushaani's words made Andric's suspicions come alive, and anger welled up inside him. It was not the fiery anger of outrage, but the slow-burning embers of rage fueled by insult piled upon grief and pain. "You offer to lead the Remalian army deeper into Kushaan when another Kushaani force is marching on our capital city even as we speak. Forgive me if I don't jump at the offer."

Andric now glanced around the room and saw shock register on every face. Andric's grim satisfaction at their reactions was tinged with self-doubt. He wondered if he had revealed too much, but it didn't matter, so he pressed on.

"Maybe your offer is sincere. I don't know. However, if you want to help us, you will have to find another way. Show us a sign that we can trust you; then we will see what Remalia has to offer in return." Andric thought about his father, the king of Remalia, lying on his deathbed. *It should be their empress on her deathbed!* "You could start with killing Empress Arrdiwat. That would certainly do the trick."

Andric stood and the others followed suit. "Forgive my early departure. I must see my father. Please enjoy the rest of your meal." Looking once more at Jalanti, he added, "Safe journey to you both."

Andric held himself erect as he marched from the room.

CHAPTER XX
QUARIAN

The drumming of the hoof beats pounded on endlessly as Quarian watched the scenery blur past him in a steady stream of trees, brush, and the lush forests he was familiar with from his time patrolling the Kushaani borderlands. The hot, humid air clung to him like a wet blanket as he and his companions rode on. He pushed them hard, but the horses had a long way to go.

With the letter from Prince Andric, Quarian had little difficulty obtaining fresh horses at the occasional garrisons. His horse was well trained for his needs as a scout, and he was loath to leave him behind in Nanjab, but speed was more important now. He wished they had been riding with the same haste all along, but it had certainly been a unique experience traveling with the prince. He even kind of liked the young man; the prince had an unexpected strength to him.

An added benefit of their pace was the respite from the heat as the breeze rushed past him. Quarian almost missed the chill of the mountain passes that were leagues behind him. But his desperation to return there had nothing to do with his own comfort. The enemy hidden in those mountains soured any pleasant memory he might have harbored. He had longed to return to his patrols in Kushaan for the months he had been assigned to the northern mountains, but not under these circumstances.

He was grateful to leave the prince and his entourage behind, allowing the scouts to travel with the haste their message required, though he felt guilty for thinking such a thing. The news of the king's health had seemed to be hard on the young prince. From what he had heard of the strange sickness, how it wasted a man's body to a dry husk, it was nothing Quarian would wish even on his enemies. His thoughts briefly drifted to his own family, his father and mother in distant Qelasaar, and he wondered how they were and what they were doing. Were they alive and well? Would word of an illness affecting his home ever reach his ears here in Remalia? He doubted he would ever know. It was a bitter thought, but it was probably for the best. Qelasaar was no longer safe for him, and his family was better off without him there.

Briefly taking his eyes from the road ahead, he glanced at his traveling companions and briefly nodded encouragement to them. Teek was a much better rider than Quarian would have guessed, and the captain already knew Sander to be capable in the saddle from their days serving together in the borderlands. While Sander, who joined them in Nanjab, had always seemed a little lackluster and the unkempt, and Teek was more than a little unpolished, they both had the makings of fine soldiers and scouts.

Seeing the familiar landscape after being gone only a few months felt somewhat like returning home. A flash of annoyance once again crossed his mind at the thought of having been sent away from the front lines simply because he was not Remalian by birth, but he quickly brushed the thought aside. Perhaps being sent back to Remalia had been for the best after all. Would another captain have been as far-reaching into the mountains with his scouts as Quarian had? Would they have discovered the Kushaani armies deep (*impossibly deep*, he thought) within Remalian territory? Quarian doubted Teris would have been given as good a chance at being warned had his men not found them and acted so quickly. He hoped Teris had been warned.

He reviewed countless times how so many troops could have gotten past their scouts without any word of such a large force out in the field. It made no sense, and he had been dealing with armies and warfare for much of his life, both in his homeland and during his years serving Remalia. He had seen strange things, but nothing had baffled him as much as this. Had he not seen them with his own eyes, he would be like the prince and so many others, doubtful and dismissive.

Even after seeing the Kushaani troops for himself, there were still so many questions left unanswered. Where did they come from? How had they crossed the expanse of the Velspars? Why did they look so different from any of the Kushaani he had ever seen? Quarian had overheard the prince's Cannessi advisor say something about them possibly being Kuldrith, but that was just the wild guess of a scholar who obviously didn't have much experience with the real world. He feared the truth would come to light only after battle and bloodshed.

Drifting smoke could be seen in the early morning light over the hill they were approaching, no doubt rising from the cook fires being stoked for breakfast preparation. The muggy morning made the thought of campfires and cooking far less appealing than his empty stomach told him they should be.

They had passed patrols and other scouts along the road with barely a word, and now Quarian sped past the lookouts as the horses galloped over the crest of the hill. Their mounts were still riding strong, but he guessed they had another half hour left in them; better to exchange them now.

The small unit only comprised about one hundred and fifty soldiers by his estimate, many of them just starting to wake for the day's duties, leisurely stretching and walking about. They behaved as if they were still within the borders of Remalia. It grated on Quarian's nerves when he saw such complacency anywhere, but it was almost unforgivable here in the midst of war. The soldiers didn't appear to be part of Remalia's regular army but were perhaps part of some noble's provincial force, which would explain why they weren't on the front lines. Rather than slow their pace to keep from alarming the sleepy camp, Quarian decided to instill a sense of urgency in their situation. He could just as well have been bringing news of an imminent attack, and they should be prepared for anything. He had dealt with the Kushaani for many years, and he knew they were far more cunning than the Remalians gave them credit for.

He spurred his mount into a hard gallop as they approached the camp. The guards seemed to barely react with mild interest as the scouts approached. Their attention quickly turned to alarm as Quarian sped toward them, reigning his horse in only at the last second. A satisfying cloud of dust from the three halting riders enveloped the guards, causing muttering and waving of hands.

"Where's your commander?" Quarian opted to skip any semblance of formalities.

The guards, still batting at the cloud of settling dust, looked beyond Quarian toward his companions and the empty road behind them. Others in the camp wandered toward the commotion.

"Where's the rush, scou'? The Kushaani hot on yer tail, eh?" A young, tall, and fair-skinned guard spoke, his skin peeling on his face from a fair bit of sunburn. Another guard with a slightly bulging waistline chuckled at the remark and lowered his spear.

"Your commander, soldier! Now!" Quarian longed to drive home a lesson in the lackluster guard, but he needed haste more than satisfaction. Besides, he would never see the man again and knew it wasn't worth his breath, though a change in attitude might save his or someone else's life someday.

The guard's chest puffed out in apparent indignation at being barked at, but a glance at Quarian's rank kept him silent. Before the situation worsened, the guards saw their commander strolling toward them and simply waited. The young lieutenant was no doubt the son of some lord. Quarian hoped the man was at least reasonably competent.

"You there, scout! See that you treat my men with more courtesy."

Apparently not, Quarian lamented to himself.

The lieutenant gathered himself as he approached, ready to dish out more of a rebuke, but he also paused upon his discovery that Quarian outranked him. He instead ordered the guards to return to their duties before addressing Quarian with a more measured tone. "What brings you so urgently to the front?"

Quarian caught the unspoken insinuation that they were coming from the safety of behind the lines, but he refused to allow himself to be baited. "I bear a message that must reach Crown Prince Stephir with all haste. I need fresh mounts as quickly as you can ready them."

The lieutenant studied him with no small degree of suspicion. "What news? Perhaps I can send fresh riders from among my men and save you the journey. Have the Kushaani crept in behind us?"

"I am on an errand from Prince Andric."

"Ahh, so the Prince-Who-Would-Play-Soldier is finally in the field?"

Quarian had been aware of Prince Andric's reputation, but now he had firsthand knowledge it was not well founded. The prince was an earnest young man who would make a fine leader with experience and maturity. Captain Quarian gave the lieutenant a warning look; he was in no mood for games. The lieutenant waved dismissively, chuckling at his private joke. "No matter. I'm afraid my men need all their mounts as they are. You see, we've been fighting Kushaani forces in the area and they're likely not beaten yet. There are a few scouts over on the far side of the camp, however. You're welcome to trade mounts with any of them if you like."

"Thank you." Quarian turned and mounted in one fluid motion. With a quick heel to his horse's flank, he spurred him into a gallop, ignoring the protests from the insufferable officer. He hastened around the edge of the camp, Teek and Sander following closely behind. They rounded the far side and Quarian saw a welcome sight as four soldiers stood to greet them as they approached.

"Captain Min! Ain't you a sight for sore eyes, indeed!"

"Corporal Tans! It's good to see you again." Quarian was happier than he would have expected at seeing his men again. He had worked hard to overcome the stigma of being an outsider and worked even harder to help them overcome their own beliefs about being scouts and their second-class status in the army. "How are you faring these days?"

Corporal Tans was a weathered soldier, wiry and fit. His sandy blond hair had turned a steel gray at the temples, and age lines around his eyes spoke of years of hard service. He stood at attention and snapped a salute above his brow. "We'd be better if you was here, sir. Captain Jaspen don't seem ta know what ta make of us, which is fine by us. Fordric pretty much runs the unit in his place, though I don't know if ya heard about the problems with the elan-tir." Quarian nodded. "Now that they ain't able to talk with each other, the generals and nobles seem to want to just use us as messenger boys rather than scouts and soldiers." He seemed to want to say more but held his tongue. Quarian remembered a time when the corporal could not hold his tongue to save his hide. He needed Teek to learn that lesson.

"We know, Corporal. How are the Tamdaari foothills? Any word from there?"

Tans shrugged. "Nothin' that I've heard. Not a peep from them, though they's a long ways from the action. Why? Some Kushaani get past us?"

Quarian shook his head. No news was bad news. "Corporal, I need your horses." He intended to explain, but Tans was too quick to reply.

"They're yours!" He spun on his heels and shouted orders to the other three scouts. "Prepare my horse, as well as Spirit and Highstep. Quickly!" He strode to a few saddlebags hanging on a pole lashed between two trees and pulled out provisions for them, including a small round of cheese, hard bread, and three skins of water.

Quarian was grateful for the consideration, but much more for the corporal's unquestioning obedience. He knew he should have expected it, but he'd been away for a while and wasn't quite sure what to expect. "We don't need much, Corporal. We're only going as far as the prince's camp and hope to be there before midday."

Tans nodded as he stuffed the hastily gathered supplies in a coarse sack for transport. "You'll be hard-pressed ta make it that far by nightfall, sir. Prince Stephir is drivin' south down the Spice Road toward Taljir Mar. We heard they won a great victory over a large force o' the Kushaani army and are pushin' south. Word is they're aimin' fer Dharmas." He tossed the sack to Quarian. Jamner and another scout Quarian didn't recognize brought three new horses as Teek and Sander made the exchange.

"Thank you, Corporal," Quarian said, swinging into the saddle. He could tell it was a good horse, lean and fast. He tucked the sack of supplies in the saddlebag behind him. "Ours aren't scout-trained, but they're good horses with plenty of stamina. They need a rest, though. We'll try to get yours back to you if we can. I regret we don't have more time to catch up, but I hope we will get the chance soon. Keep up the good work." With no other word, he spun the horse and spurred it toward the southern road.

The morning stretched into mid-day and the sun climbed higher into the sky. They pressed the well-conditioned mounts as much as they could without over-taxing them. As the day progressed, patrols and supply carts with escorts became a frequent sight.

The Spice Road extended south through the eastern provinces of Kushaan and into the Fragrant Coast with its prosperous southern ports. It had been a well-beaten trail for centuries, but a hundred years ago, merchants from both Kushaan and Remalia decided they needed a suitable road for all their trade. They paid a significant portion of the cost but saved money by building much of it with Kushaani slave labor. Now it made for an easy and clear route for the armies marching southward.

Quarian and his men chatted amiably in the brief moments they stopped by a brook or other spot to rest or water their mounts before another hard ride. It mostly consisted of the other two answering Quarian's questions about their lives. He liked knowing his men, but few ever asked much about his past in return. He preferred it that way.

After midday, they swapped mounts once more with a group of scouts carrying less urgent messages from the front to forces scattered over the leagues behind them. As they pressed into the afternoon, they encountered more carts laden with wounded Remalian soldiers followed by lines of Kushaani captives under heavy guard, lumbering northward in numbers that would have been alarming if Quarian didn't know just how many troops both armies had.

At last, he saw the haze of the evening cookfires floating in the distance and he knew he was approaching the main camp of the Remalian armies. As they crested a small rise and got a glimpse of the army spread before them, Teek gave a low whistle, and Sander stopped altogether. With a quick signal from Quarian, they spurred their horses back into a gallop toward the sprawling tent city.

The sight was more than impressive. Rows of orderly tents in various shades of white carpeted the shallow valley from one end to the other. Quarian, in all his experience leading soldiers, had never seen such an assembly of troops in one location. He had heard they numbered nearly sixty thousand, but his mind hadn't grasped what a force that size would look like spread out before him. Armored patrols on horseback swarmed the outskirts of the valley, and soldiers were busy at work gathering wood from the nearby forests, slowly pushing back the edges of the concealing trees, fueling the fires that fed war.

Quarian slowed his pace somewhat as they approached the edge of the camp. Quarian had no idea where he would find the prince or his generals. He had figured he would find the largest tent, but the camp was so large it was difficult to tell where the command pavilion would be. One of the mounted patrols with weapons lowered cautiously intercepted the threesome before they got within bowshot of the tents.

"Hold there!" the patrol leader ordered with such an excess of seriousness that it was almost comical. He was a large man, imposing in the width of his shoulders as well as the girth of his belt. The good quality of his armor and mount indicated he was from some noble house. "What business do you have?"

"I have urgent news for His Highness from his brother, Prince Andric. If you would be so kind as to point the way..."

The pillowy man squinted with profound skepticism. "What commander do you report to?"

"None here. I am to deliver the message to the prince directly. Now if—"

"You think they're going to allow a filthy scout an audience with His Highness?" the man said with dramatic incredulity. "And a foreigner to boot."

Quarian stiffened when the other men gripped their weapons. Why were these things never easy? Quarian had half a mind to spur his way past the man, but it would end with more trouble than it was worth, so he took a calming breath and withdrew Prince Andric's letter of introduction, wordlessly handing it to the fool. In one respect, he was lucky the man was from a noble house—he could read and would probably recognize the Laconeus seal fixed to the bottom. The patrol leader read it through twice then returned it to Quarian.

"Follow me," he said begrudgingly.

The three scouts rode behind the man while the other patrolmen fell in line behind the group. Teek issued a colorful curse under his breath. Quarian felt the same way, so he would let this one go without any word of reprimand. The casual canter of the patrol as they passed row after row of tents was agonizingly slow after the frantic journey. The soldiers in the camp paid them no heed as they passed. Quarian was impressed to note there was little downtime among the troops. Each soldier was busy, setting up the last of the tents, tending to the weapons, or hauling water for the rest of their unit. Gone was the laughter and carelessness that had been the state of the Remalian army in recent years. Fighting for your life will sober a man quickly.

At last, they finally neared an enormous pavilion set up amid several large blue and white striped tents. Quarian knew instantly from the many Divinarim surrounding the area that this was where he would find the prince. They were allowed to pass a guard point still some distance from the royal pavilion without challenge. As they drew near to the next guard point, their escort dismounted. The three scouts followed suit.

"Stay here," the man ordered. He handed the reins of his horse to one of his men and lumbered toward the holy knights. Even several feet away, the man was loud enough for Quarian to hear him recount the encounter and the purpose of Quarian's presence. One of the royal guards called for Quarian to approach.

Leaving his mount with Teek, Quarian hurried to the Divinar, who asked for the letter of introduction from Prince Andric. Quarian calmly passed it to the man, who instructed them to wait, then turned and disappeared into the throng of people milling around the pavilion.

Quarian took the time to assess his surroundings. The camp was organized and well laid out, with no wasted space. The rows of tents were spaced to provide walkways no wider than four could move abreast. Weapons were stacked neatly, upright, and at the ready. This spoke well to the readiness of the units. He grimaced as he thought of the camp from earlier that day. This one showed far more readiness and purpose, despite their weariness from recent battle.

Now that he was standing still with no wind in his face from speeding on horseback, the heat even in the waning day was intense. He wiped the sweat from his forehead and dried it on the seat of his pants, trying to keep the front of him as presentable as possible after two days' hard ride. At last, the knight returned with an officer.

"Captain Minanthsolum?"

Quarian saluted sharply. "Yes, sir." He was surprised the commander knew his full name. The note of introduction from Prince Andric had only stated his name as Captain Min.

"Well met. I am Commander Haresh." Quarian recalled meeting the commander a few years ago, though it was hard to imagine the commander would remember the brief encounter. He had liked the man and had heard favorable accounts of him from others since then. "Come with me."

Commander Haresh led Quarian away from the pavilion to a nearby cluster of large tents. Quarian was a bit confused as they entered a tent guarded by regular soldiers. Surely the prince would only be guarded by the Divinarim. It was hot and stuffy in the dim light of the tent. No one was inside. The commander gestured toward a tall stand near a wall of the tent.

"There's water in the basin and a towel. You need to clean some of the grime off you before you see the prince," the commander said good-naturedly, not as a criticism. Quarian shook his head in disbelief but walked to the stand and began washing off the dirt. It was refreshing to have the cool water rubbed over his skin. "Believe me, it isn't for the prince's sake. He's anxious to speak with you. It's just one less thing for the other nobles to get worked up about."

Quarian nodded. "I understand, sir."

"So, do you want to give me an idea about what news is so urgent that Prince Andric gave a scout, even one with as good a reputation as yourself, a letter of introduction to the Crown Prince of Remalia?"

Quarian faced the commander as he continued washing, surprised at the remark about his reputation. Under other circumstances, he would have probed a bit, but he let it pass. "It isn't good, I can tell you that. I would be happy to let you take the news to the prince if I hadn't been given explicit instructions by Prince Andric to personally deliver the news to his brother."

Commander Haresh shrugged and nodded. Quarian placed the dirty towel back on the stand next to the wash basin, frowning at the quantity of dirt he had rubbed off his face and hands. He brushed off his clothes and straightened them as best he could.

"Ready then?" Haresh asked.

"As I'll ever be under the circumstances, I suppose."

The commander smiled and led Quarian out of the tent toward the royal pavilion. As they passed under the cover of the pavilion, Quarian was amazed at how much cooler the air was. He looked around the area but found nothing to account for the difference in the temperature.

The commander smiled and said, "Elantir. Being near the prince does have a few perks."

Quarian scanned the area to see if he recognized anyone, but these men and women were far removed from anything in his life. Or, at least they were until a week ago. Haresh wove his way through the maze of people toward a group on the east side of the pavilion. Divinarim stood near the group, so it was not hard to guess Prince Stephir was among them, but Quarian didn't see anyone who particularly stood out as the prince. None wore armor, and most were dressed in the finery of nobility, with a handful of officers among them. A Servari priest stood next to a stoic woman with the trappings of a Teraithian cleric, who Quarian thought were an odd pair to be conversing together.

Commander Haresh signaled Quarian to stop as he pushed his way into the group. He stopped next to a man whose back was to Quarian and spoke quietly in his ear. The man's head perked up and turned in Quarian's direction. The resemblance to Prince Andric wasn't overwhelming, but enough to confirm they were brothers.

Quarian felt a sudden drop in the pit of his stomach when Commander Haresh signaled for him to approach. Quarian rarely felt uncomfortable around others; he was never terribly impressed with titles or rank, but even after having just spent days with a prince, there was something unnerving about this situation. Perhaps it was that conversations in the group tapered off as eyes began to focus on him. He shouldn't have been surprised. Scouts were probably never admitted this close to the prince. Their information would be passed up the chain of command before reaching the nobles' and generals' ears, as his would undoubtedly have been under any but these strange circumstances.

Haresh's voice seemed slightly louder than necessary. "Your Highness, may I present to you Quarian Minanthsolum, recently appointed captain of Commander Rovan's scout corps, formerly captain of Commander Epmon's scout corps."

The prince eyed Haresh with a slightly puzzled look. "Why the reassignment?" he asked.

Quarian wondered if the prince was concerned that the reassignment to a less critical patrol was due to some incompetence.

"I believe it was so that Lord Maensen's son could be given a command near the front, Your Highness." The prince sighed and nodded slowly. Haresh added, "Perhaps it was the providence of the gods, though, my lord. From all accounts, Captain Minanthsolum is the finest scout captain in Remalia."

Quarian's chest tightened with emotion at this high praise in front of the prince and other nobility.

The commander continued, "Perhaps he was meant to discover whatever it is that Lord Andric has sent him here to tell Your Highness."

An unsettling silence had fallen over the group, though the noise of other conversations and orders being issued around the pavilion still buzzed in the background.

"So, Captain Minanthsolum," the prince said with controlled intensity, "what dire need drives you all the way down here to us?"

Quarian caught himself holding his breath. He had gone over this moment the entire ride south, but no words seemed adequate or believable at the moment. *Just give them the facts* he told himself. After taking a breath, he said, "A week ago, my scouts discovered a large force of Kushaani southwest of Rookstone in the Velspars, moving due east as if to bypass Massonly and head toward Teris."

Heads shook and whispered comments swept through the group. Quarian was slightly annoyed to hear a snort of derision and a low chuckle. He ignored it and pressed on. "We estimate their numbers to be as many as twenty thousand, possibly more, and they are..." His words were lost in the cacophony that erupted from the nobles and officers.

"Twenty thousand? That's not possible!"

"How in Akraharr's name could...!"

"We must return to Remalia immediately!"

"This must be a prank by Lord Andric," a voice behind Quarian commented quietly.

The outbursts continued, but Quarian blocked it all out, focusing his sober gaze on the prince. He expected Prince Stephir to react as his brother had, with almost indignant disbelief, but he was surprised the prince returned his steady gaze amidst the commotion. The two men said nothing, each considering the other. He knew his words were difficult to believe; if he hadn't seen them with his own eyes, he too would be skeptical.

Prince Stephir raised his hand, and everyone went silent. Reluctantly, the group fixed their attention more intently on the two men at the center of the ring of onlookers. Stephir regarded those circled around him, a reproachful tone entering his voice. "I hear whispers that this is merely a joke played by my brother." His pause left the words hanging in the air like an unspoken challenge. "I know him better than that. This is not something he would ever joke about." Turning his attention back to Quarian, he ordered, "Tell me everything."

"They travel quickly, with no significant supply trains or siege enginery that we saw. Some of my men left immediately after discovering the invaders to warn Teris, though I have been unable to confirm whether they made it through because Balinth's Fortress is unable to communicate with Teris."

This comment elicited more murmurs. Stephir promptly held up a hand to silence the assembled nobles while his eyes remained patiently on Quarian.

Quarian continued, "Others of my men tracked a smaller force of about a thousand that broke off from the main force and traveled through the mountains. They appeared to be heading toward Balinth's Fortress, so I left men to continue tracking them and made my way to warn Commander Tra'en." Another wave of head shaking spread through the group, but no outburst followed this time. "We came across Prince Andric leading a battalion about a day's ride north of the fortress. He ordered the battalion to return to Teris to ensure its safety, then he rode with us to deliver the news to Commander Tra'en, then to Luresh, and finally to Nanjab to warn your father."

Quarian considered commenting about the king's condition but decided against it. "When he discovered you weren't there, Prince Andric stayed with the king and sent me to deliver this news to you."

Quarian was confused at what appeared to be a slight look of pleased satisfaction playing across Prince Stephir's features as he cast his eyes at the ground, but it was quickly replaced with seriousness as he looked at Quarian again. "Have you any idea how they came to be on that side of the mountains or what their intentions may be?"

"I'm afraid my speculations wouldn't be any more valuable than anyone else's, Your Highness."

"Is there anything else, Captain?" the prince asked.

Quarian considered whether any of the other details about the strange Kushaani were pertinent, then decided against elaborating. "Just this from Lord Andric." Quarian pulled out the letter and handed it to the prince.

Prince Stephir broke the seal and read the note. His eyebrows furrowed and concern passed over his face. He reread the brief note, then looked back at Quarian. "Remalia is grateful for your dedicated service, Captain." Turning to a short, silver-haired man at his side, the prince firmly ordered, "General Marishet, please see that Captain Minansola receives a proper commendation."

Quarian could forgive the prince for mispronouncing his name. At least he had tried.

"Of course, my lord," the general answered, nodding at Quarian.

Quarian felt somewhat guilty at the thought of receiving a commendation for having done no more than see the enemy and act as a courier for the information, but he understood the value of a leader giving merited praise. "Thank you, Your Highness."

"Holy Couple speed and keep you, Captain."

Quarian saluted, and Commander Haresh said, "I'll walk you out, Captain."

Quarian turned and followed him back through the incredulous crowd. When they were out of earshot of the prince and his advisors, the commander signaled Quarian to walk at his side. "This is going to change everything. What do you intend to do now?" Haresh asked.

"Return to my men." It was a simple but sincere answer. What else would he do?

"At this point, you could ask for the command of any scout corps in Remalia and get it. You could even probably take command of a combat unit if you wanted it."

This day kept spiraling out of proportion. The idea of being in command of troops again after so many years was a tempting proposition, but he was not clear-headed enough to make any decisions at the moment. They left the pavilion and Quarian was hit with the lingering heat of the day. He had forgotten the air was cooled under the shade of the prince's roof. Sweat instantly beaded up on his forehead.

"Thank you, Commander. The idea merits some serious reflection, but at the moment I think I need to get my feet back under me." Quarian stifled a yawn.

"Perhaps getting a bed under you would be more in order," the commander said with a chuckle. "I don't suppose you've made any arrangements for sleeping or food?"

"No, but I'm sure I can manage."

"Nonsense. I'll take you to my second's tent. You can get some sleep and then join us for dinner."

"That's a very generous offer, sir. Normally, I would be happy to accept, but I have men with me whom I need to make arrangements for as well. I believe some of my old scouts are around that I would like to see again. I'm sure we can find accommodations with them."

"Gods, I wish we had more men like you!"

Once they reached the checkpoint, Quarian scanned the area to see where Teek had gone.

Haresh added, "If you need anything, Captain, let me know. Gods speed and keep you," the commander said, giving him a firm pat on his arm.

Quarian saluted. "And you as well, Commander."

Haresh turned and headed back to the pavilion. A loud whistle drew Quarian's attention over his left shoulder and he watched Teek and Sander walk toward him leading their horses.

"That was a long report. Did they make you kiss their arses first?" Teek asked, always colorful in his speech.

Quarian laughed. "Not exactly. Let's go find something to eat."

CHAPTER XXI

STEPHIR

Stephir had always wondered how he would respond in a true crisis, but he never imagined it would come so early in his life. He was finding it difficult to follow one of his father's cardinal rules in dealing with the nobles in a crisis—let them have their say first. 'Know their thoughts and concerns as well as you can before you act.' Stephir had said little in the minutes since the scout captain had delivered the heavy news.

And the note from Andric.

It sounded completely preposterous, but Andric would never have sent such a message unless it was dire. Stephir could not imagine anything worse—his father was dying, perhaps already dead. Remalia was invaded, and Teris was probably under siege. *Could it possibly be taken?* The thought of Ilyanara and his children captured, perhaps killed or taken as slaves, put his stomach in a knot. It was moments such as this that he had prepared his whole life. He used that knot to focus on the task at hand. As those around him continued to argue, and deny, and blame, Stephir walked through each piece of information in his mind, stepping back and further back to try to see the bigger picture.

The increased border raids, the assassination attempt, the easy victory in the borderlands, the abandonment of Nanjab, the loss of communications between the elantir; perhaps these had all been carefully orchestrated to pull Remalia further into Kushaan to give the Kushaani forces the opening to invade. How they could accomplish such a thing was beyond him. If he didn't know better, he would have guessed they had been spirited there by the gods or some dark power. Stephir shook his head. Translocation was just an old fairytale.

They had to have crossed the Velspars on foot using some passage they discovered. *But how on Baon's sweet soil could they ferry twenty thousand men that far? And why? What could they hope to accomplish?* Perhaps they had invaded Remalia to draw Remalia's armies back home, out of Kushaan. It was a risky strategy to commit so many troops to what was essentially a diversion tactic. *Either way, they will pay for their mistake with their lives.* It was time to end the discussion. It was time to act.

"My lords," Stephir said in a hushed voice. When Stephir wanted people to be quiet, he got quieter, not louder. "My lords," he repeated quietly. Those nearest him heard his words and began silencing the others. It took a few moments, but when he had their undivided attention, he spoke. "My lords, thank you for your counsel." Turning to General Marishet, Stephir issued his first command. "General, you will have five thousand infantry and one thousand cavalry with which to secure our gains here in the south."

Voices began to comment, but Stephir ignored them and directed his next words to Ambassador Sepheus, the ranking priest of Sharin Dara in Stephir's camp since Consul Rellat had remained in Nanjab with his father. Thoughts of Jevorak wasting away caused Stephir's throat to constrict, but he refused to allow such things to get in the way of his decisions before the assembled nobles. The Sharinists understood the hereditary lines, titles and holdings, and politics of the Remalian nobility as well as anyone and better than most, so Sepheus would be an invaluable advisor in matters of peerage. Of course, Consul Ullara in Teris was the true expert and Keeper of Peerages, but she was currently beyond Stephir's reach, so Sepheus would suffice.

"Consul, please work with General Marishet to prepare any recommendations you might consider for the long-term security of these lands." This was Stephir's way of asking him to make a plan for dividing the newly conquered land among the nobility and the potential granting of new peerages. They had discussed this once or twice in the last month, but he hadn't anticipated needing to make it happen this soon. Only the king could grant the titles and holdings, but that might fall to Stephir far sooner than he would have liked.

"High General Kuymon, I want the rest of our forces to depart first thing in the morning to return to Nanjab."

"As you wish, my lord," the general said, a single nod the only indication that he approved.

Archpaladin Nophet, as always wearing his full suit of gleaming red-gold armor with elaborate platinum inlays of flames in the emblems of his deity and holy order, stepped from behind Stephir into the space surrounding the prince. "Your Highness, may I be permitted to speak?" The request was so out of place for one of the Divinarim, even if he was the archpaladin.

Stephir was alert to any indication that Nophet was influencing him. Ever since the incident with Nophet's breach of protocol at the Neral Valley, he had become more wary of the commander. "What is it, Lord Nophet?"

"Surely Your Highness does not intend to turn your back on this cause that Teraithia herself has blessed? You have crushed the Kushaani beneath the fist of Remalia's might at every turn! Victory is all but guaranteed. Even if the report from the scout is true, the heathen Kushaani will impotently beat themselves against Teris's walls. We all heard they have no siege equipment and no supply chains. They cannot hope to prevail. We should drive a lance through Kushaan's heart once and for all, then return in victory and sweep up any vermin we find. This would be fitting for the great House Laconeus!"

Nophet had never inserted himself into politics before, and now he sounded more like Archseraph Charin than the Divinar commander. But he spoke the mind of many of the nobles, and Stephir had to deal with this now or it would continue to fester. "Lord Nophet, you speak the words that are half of my heart. But if a scorpion crawls inside your armor, you don't leave it there while you kick the dog. There is plenty of time to kick the dog after you get rid of the scorpion."

"Forgive me, Your Highness, but if the dog continues to bite your children while you chase the scorpion, should you not kill the dog first?"

What is he doing! One of the bedrock tenets of the Order of the Divine Flame was that they were to remain out of all state affairs. It was written into their very charter! Their sole duty was to protect the royal family and the Mount of the Gods in Teris. Stephir had been surprised when the archpaladin chose to leave the king in Nanjab to travel south with him. His prime duty was to ensure the king's safety. If he was breaking this tenant of their oaths, why not do it through communion like his last attempt? Whatever the reason, he was here and Stephir knew he and Nophet could exchange metaphors all day and not get anywhere.

Before he could end the exchange, an uncharacteristically angry Frey cut in. "Enough Nophet!" Stephir winced inwardly at Frey's insult, dropping Lord Nophet's title. "The crown prince just issued a command and reiterated it in picture words for you." Oh, this was going from bad to worse. "And if you—"

"That is enough Marquis de'Venneshen," Stephir cut in sharply. He could not remember the last time he had addressed Frey by his formal title.

Stephir's eyes pierced Nophet as a tense silence settled between them. Stephir knew it was a useless exercise. Whether by nature, training, or divine gift, Teraithia's archpaladin was impervious to intimidation. But Stephir needed everyone to see that he was just as immune. Calm and unflinching authority was the only thing that would serve now.

"Lord Nophet, if you would prefer to stay here and fight the Kushaani with *your* men, I am willing to release you from your duty to my family." It was a heavy-handed slap in the face. "But tomorrow, *my* army returns to Teris." Stephir wished he was in a position to dismiss everyone from his presence; it would have felt better than walking out himself. He could have done it, he supposed, but it would look ridiculous. Instead, he turned and strode from the pavilion amidst bows and salutes.

"Admit no one," he ordered the Divinarim guarding his private tent. Although relatively spacious, especially since it was sparsely furnished, the tent was hot and stuffy, but he did his best to ignore it. He sat down in the one luxury he allowed himself, a deeply cushioned seat he had found in the manor his father had taken in Nanjab. It was the most comfortable chair he had ever sat in. He sank into the cushions and closed his eyes, extending his legs and crossing his ankles on the ottoman. He was going to love having it back in his apartments in Teris, holding Jenden cuddled in his lap. That was a direction he wouldn't let his mind wander.

"My lord," Master Selaren said quietly. Stephir opened his eyes, annoyed that the guards had failed to follow his orders. "Is everything all right? Can I get you anything?"

Perhaps having Selaren here was not so bad after all. "Some chilled wine. Strong wine." Selaren bowed and left the tent. Stephir replayed the evening's events in mind, beginning with the report from the scout captain. *Twenty thousand Kushaani marching on Teris!* Never could he have imagined such a thing would happen in his lifetime. If the king wanted his sons to be forged in the fires of war, he was going to have his wish fulfilled many times over.

Was his father even still alive? He would find out soon enough when they passed back through Nanjab. This brought his thoughts to Andric. The scout's report sounded as though Andric had done very well. Their father would be proud. Stephir was proud.

Selaren returned with wine but was stopped by the guards. Stephir thought it was strange, then it occurred to him that Selaren must have been in his bed chamber in the adjoining room of the tent earlier, and had never passed the guards in the first place. He called out for them to let the man pass.

His attendant entered, unfazed. He handed a glass of wine to Stephir, then stepped back out of the tent.

Stephir smiled. He was sure Selaren was just outside the tent in case he needed anything. He knew why his father had never allowed them to have personal servants at home. It was tempting to want them to do everything for you. His thoughts were interrupted when his guards turned someone away.

Frey's voice rang out loudly, "Tell His Royal Highness it's me. He'll want to see me."

Stephir didn't want to see Frey at the moment, but it would be even more awkward later if he didn't, so he swallowed his annoyance and called out to the guards to admit his friend. *What must the Divinarim think of me, giving the order to allow no one and then making exceptions for everyone who showed up?*

"So this is how you treat your friends?" Frey asked.

Stephir could not tell if Frey meant silencing him in the pavilion or giving orders to keep everyone out. He let the remark go without comment on either. "There's some chilled wine there on the table," Stephir offered. Frey wordlessly poured himself a glass as Stephir drained his own and held it toward his cousin. "Would you be so kind?"

Frey took the glass and returned it filled. "How soon do you think we can get back to the city?"

Stephir sighed. "It depends. If we divide the army and take just a small force of light cavalry, assuming we don't run into any difficulty along the way we could probably be back in three weeks, maybe a little sooner."

Frey groaned, and Stephir agreed. Three weeks to siege a city as fortified as Teris was no great concern. But any attacks on other targets throughout Remalia could be devastating. Weeks sounded like an eternity. Based on the scout captain's report, the Kushaani troops might already be attacking Teris or Balinth's, or both. Even with such a large force, the city should be able to withstand their attack, especially without siege equipment. However, the fact that they had no siege equipment made him nervous. Maybe their intention was not to take Teris. Maybe it was a massive slaving raid through the country.

"But I don't think splitting our forces is a good idea," Stephir continued. He was grateful as he felt the air begin to cool. The elantir usually had his tent cooled before he arrived, when he kept to his usual schedule.

"Stephir, we have to get troops back there as fast as possible. If you wait for the whole damn army to make it back, it could take two months. Teris could be ashes by then."

"I know, but with twenty thousand Kushaani running around, it would be dangerous to send only ten thousand cavalry, even ours. We need the bulk of our force together. I'll leave another five thousand troops to secure the borderlands and keep the Kushaani from harassing our rear. And don't forget there are a thousand Kushaani somewhere in the Gap. That could be a major nuisance."

"I hope they attack Balinth's," Frey said hotly. "Then we won't have them to worry about."

"What are you talking about! The fortress is built to keep the Kushaani from coming north. If they attack from the Remalian side, they might actually cause problems."

"They don't have any siege equipment! What do you think they're going to do, hurl curses at the walls?"

"They did in Nanjab," Stephir said poisonously.

"Which is why we never should've left Remalia in the first place! You should have stopped this stupid war a long time ago!"

"You didn't seem to mind while you were having fun killing Kushaani."

"And now the Kushaani are going to have fun raping your kingdom."

"Get out." It took all Stephir's self-control to not hurl his glass at Frey.

"What, you can't—"

"Out!"

Frey threw his glass down on the table, shattering it, and stormed past the Divinarim who rushed through the door of the tent, halberds leading, concern visibly written on their faces.

"It's fine," Stephir told the guards, waving them out dismissively.

Master Selaren entered on the heels of the guards. Seeing Stephir was okay, he knelt to clean the broken glass.

"Later. Just keep everyone out," Stephir said.

Selaren bowed and retreated from the tent. Stephir's heart was pounding as he rubbed his forehead. His fingers were wet from the cold condensation off the glass, but it did little to cool his anger. He could not remember the last time he and Frey had argued. There would be time to fix things later. Right now, he needed to get his plans laid out. He forced himself to walk to the door of the tent. He pushed a flap aside, and the holy knights turned to face him.

"Please summon High General Kuymon, General Marishet, Commander Chamdon, Duke Miarsten, and Commander Alscan."

"Of course, Your Majesty," the Divinar said as Stephir let the tent flap fall closed.

Despite his efforts to stay focused on what needed to be done to get back to Teris, he could not keep his mind from wandering back to thoughts and worries about Shannyth and Jenden. If anything happened to his children, he would kill every last Kushaani he could find. The intensity of his emotions took him by surprise. He clenched his fists as he leaned against the long table. Hanging his head and closing his eyes, he tried to get himself under control before his advisors arrived. *Just breathe*, he told himself over and over.

He reached for the wine, then stopped himself. He didn't want refreshment, he wanted to quiet the storm of emotions threatening to shatter his calm. That would have to wait until after he tended to these matters. He scanned the maps on one end of the table. He knew all the territory between here and Teris with his eyes closed, but it was a simple place to start focusing. He saw in his mind's eye as his army marched north to Nanjab, then northeast toward Luresh, then north to Balinth's Fortress. Hopefully, they would encounter no difficulty getting through the Warrin Gap, then up Dunnigan's Highroad, past Rookstone, and finally to Teris.

Then what? He hated being blind. Not for the first time, Stephir cursed the loss of the elantic communications. Just then the tent door was pulled open and Commander Alscan entered.

"Your Majesty," she said, nodding at Stephir as she positioned herself across the table from him. She eyed the broken glass and raised an eyebrow but said nothing. In that moment of silence, Stephir appreciated her more than ever.

"Commander, any thoughts about our situation?"

"Plenty of thoughts, but none that seem particularly useful. The next several days involve primarily logistical matters, which do not generally fall within my purview."

"We are possibly facing the greatest threat to Remalia in over..." Stephir tried to think of the last time Remalia faced such a threat. Nothing came immediately to mind since King Hamoth's day. He skipped the thought and went on. "We need to marshal every resource at our disposal to ensure victory."

"I wish I could give you the news you want, Your Highness, but we aren't any closer to solving the communication problem."

"That's not what I meant. The Kushaani elantir have silenced us, stricken us with illness, and caused the very forests to attack us. What can you do to *them*?"

She considered for a moment before answering. "The elantir have never been permitted to train in any combat applications of met'elan." General

Marishet and Commander Chamdon entered the tent while she spoke. "And your troops have not been trained in the inclusion of elantir in their strategies or actual maneuvers. At a minimum, it adds a new level of complexity and could prove as much a hindrance as help.

"Or worse," General Marishet said flatly, eyebrows furrowed.

Stephir knew what he meant. The generals and nobles had been willing to tolerate Stephir's experiments with the elantir after Luresh, but the near disaster in the Duntai Ravine several days ago had revived old prejudices and soured all but the most progressive thinkers. But where others saw danger Stephir saw possibilities.

The Kushaani elantir had pulled elan from the plants and trees in the surrounding forest, which had been the cause of the blackening, and infused that elan into the plants in the ravine, making them grow wildly, intertwining into a dense blockade and choking off the Remalians' ability to push them toward the valley. General Bascon had ordered his men to burn the dense vegetation, but the fire merely smoldered in the fresh growth. Then he asked the elantir if they could make it burn faster. They had succeeded.

The fire had blazed through the thick wall of twisting trees, vines, and other plants, filling the ravine with thick white smoke. The elantir had even managed to force the smoke to blow through the ravine, driving the Kushaani into the valley and Stephir's waiting army. However, the fire had ignited the surrounding deadened forest and nearly entrapped General Bascon's men. The elantir's efforts to control the fire just made it worse, more erratic. By the Holy Couple's grace, they escaped the forest, but not before nearly one hundred died in the flames, and many more suffered burns and smoke in their lungs.

In the end, Stephir had won a major victory over a force of nearly eight thousand Kushaani. He tried to put the elantir's efforts in the best light possible, giving them the credit for driving the Kushaani into Stephir's trap, but tensions had run high since then.

"Please go on," Stephir instructed the commander.

She sighed but did as he asked. "We have made progress on things that can affect the enemy's senses: lights shining in their eyes, wind blowing in their face, noises in their ears, illusions to confuse them, heat and cold as appropriate. They will have some impact on our men as well. As I have said before, training is necessary to teach them what to expect and how to cope."

"Lights and noises," the General said shaking his head. "Not worth the time I should think. Can you kill them? Break their weapons? Hold them still so we can do it? Any of those would actually be useful."

Commander Alscan's voice took on a hard edge. "There hasn't been any reason to study those areas of met'elan because we have been told for generations that such skills were forbidden, too dangerous, even immoral. Perhaps in time my troops could develop those abilities." It was the first time Stephir had heard her refer to the elantir as 'troops'. He felt surprisingly proud of her for it.

Alscan addressed Stephir. "But this is more than learning a few new tricks. This is a fundamental restructuring of what we do—of the very nature of who we are. That kind of change will not come quickly or without conflict, for the elantir, your commanders, the soldiers, the priests; everyone. We will do our best to learn to burn and freeze, to strike and hold, but it will take time, Your Highness."

They didn't have time for old divisions to get in the way. Stephir needed to create a cooperative relationship between the two if this was to work. Marishet was an excellent general, but Stephir knew he would never be open-minded enough to make the most of the elantir. Commander Chamdon was another matter. Sometimes brash and too much of a risk-taker, he was still a brilliant tactician and was always open to trying new ideas.

This was going to take a bit of careful finessing. He needed to get Marishet to agree with the overall program but leave the details to Chamdon without signaling to any of them that Commander Alscan or her elantir deserved anything less than the highest respect and consideration. Stephir looked at the tent opening. High General Kuymon and Duke Miarsten should have shown up by now, but Stephir was glad they hadn't. He had intended to have this discussion at a later time, but it was happening now, and adding those two to the mix would just complicate matters.

"General, I appreciate your concerns and understand the risks laid out by Commander Alscan as well. I won't have our men put in any undue danger, but I want to explore every possible advantage we can gain to make our people safe, as I'm sure you do as well. Perhaps we can ask Commander Alscan and Commander Chamdon to work together to develop strategies and other ideas for our consideration." He wanted to watch Chamdon to read his reaction, but he kept his eyes fixed on Marishet. The general's face was unreadable as he returned Stephir's steady gaze. Stephir waited patiently.

"Of course, my lord," Marishet said at last. Turning to Chamdon and Commander Alscan he said politely, "I look forward to hearing what you're able to come up with to help make the greatest army in the world even better."

Stephir knew it was the general's way of saying he didn't think he needed any help but was willing to go along for now. That was as much as Stephir suspected he was going to get for the time being. The prince looked to Commander Alscan, who simply nodded, then to Commander Chamdon who smiled and said, "Thank you, my lord. I look forward to the challenge."

"Good. Now to our most immediate needs. General, how quickly do you think we can have our men back to Teris?"

"Barring any unforeseen hindrances, I would say we could be there in five weeks and still have the men in fighting condition." His assessment matched Stephir's estimation. High General Kuymon entered alone, but Marishet continued, "I don't mean to question your commands, my lord, but have you considered maintaining a sizable force here to continue the campaign and sending a smaller force to handle the invaders? They could be gone before you ever get back, or are perhaps already defeated. I hate to see our work here be for naught. Besides, a smaller force could move more quickly."

"As I said earlier, I plan on leaving five thousand infantry and one thousand light cavalry in the south to guard our rear against harassment and secure the borderlands. I will not risk the kingdom for any amount of gains in Kushaan."

"As you wish, my lord."

Kuymon took the opportunity to insert himself into the discussion. "I will leave Commander Sikethet in command of the forces here in the south."

"My lord, perhaps it would be advisable to send a force of light cavalry ahead to ensure Balinth's Fortress is secure and the Worrin Gap is clear," Commander Chamdon suggested. Stephir knew what Chamdon really wanted was to have some of his men be unfettered from the slow-moving main army.

"Cavalry won't do any good at Balinth's or in the Gap," Kuymon stated flatly.

Stephir wondered whether the high general was merely making an observation, or agreed with his decision. He would try to find out later in private. "We stay together. Dispatch messengers back to my brother in Nanjab instructing them to be ready to march when we reach the city."

The four advisors caught the finality in his voice and bid their farewells before leaving the tent. Stephir filled a new glass of wine and took a long drink. He heard someone approach his tent as he settled into his seat. The tent flap was pulled back and Duke Miarsten, Lord of Banbridge of the Glastony Province, entered.

"Lord Miarsten," Stephir greeted the duke without standing. "I'm afraid you missed the festivities, but there is wine if you care for some refreshment." He pointed with his glass to the bottle resting on the table.

"No, thank you, my lord. Forgive my absence. Is there any matter on which I may offer Your Highness my services?" The duke's voice had an edge of annoyance, probably at the thought of being left out of their discussions more than having been summoned in the first place.

"Nothing in particular. I confirmed that I want the army on the march back to Remalia first thing in the morning. I'm leaving five thousand foot and a thousand horse here in the south to hold our gains and guard our rear. I would be grateful if you would add a thousand of your men."

The duke pinched his lips together and took a deep breath before he spoke. "What does the king think about this?"

Stephir wasn't sure it was advisable to tell anyone what Andric's letter said. Things were complicated enough; he didn't need issues of succession clouding matters. "My father has left this decision in my hands."

"May I speak plainly, Your Highness?" Stephir waived him on. "Archpaladin Nophet may have spoken out of turn, but he voiced the thoughts of a number of the nobles. If you take the whole army back to Remalia and it turns out to be nothing, you might lose too much support to return and finish this campaign."

"And if I don't take the whole army back and Remalia falls?"

"I'm not saying you should do nothing, but consider sending part of your forces back while you press the advantage here. Retreating now sets a bad precedent for our enemies."

Isn't there anyone who agrees with me? Stephir wondered. *Are they right? Am I overreacting?* He wondered if he was using this as an excuse to stop a war he didn't want in the first place. If a number of the nobles and officers felt he should keep fighting, what would it cost politically to go home now? Could he afford to fight a war on two fronts?

His father had told him repeatedly that being a king meant making decisions in the face of no clear right answer, and sometimes despite others' contrary opinions and second-guessing. But Stephir never expected to be facing a choice upon which his very kingdom hung in the balance.

"How many men do you think it would take to hold the new territory here in Kushaan?" Stephir asked.

"It's hard to be certain. Based on what we have seen so far, two thousand cavalry and eight thousand foot would probably suffice. Of course, taking the Curritan Province would make things easier, keeping the Kushaani from our backs. Regardless, that means you would be marching back with nearly nine thousand cavalry and thirty-five thousand foot soldiers. But why? Half that number would be more than enough to take on twenty thousand Kushaani, and that doesn't take into account troops that are already there."

"I don't intend to abandon our gains, but I will not risk having too few men to secure our home. I'll leave twenty-five hundred cavalry and ten thousand foot soldiers."

"Well, that will probably be enough to convince the nobles that this hasn't been a wasted endeavor, but many had their hearts set on larger holdings."

"Maybe I should leave them all here to keep fighting while I return with my troops," Stephir said sarcastically.

Whether the duke failed to pick up on it or chose to ignore Stephir's tone, he took the suggestion seriously. "I, for one, would be in favor of that. I wouldn't stop until Dhramas was ours."

Stephir was tempted to let him. It would certainly be simpler to leave all the nobles here. However, regardless of the outcomes here in Kushaan and back in Remalia, that would cause more political instability than he wanted to deal with. "We have secured our borders and increased our lands. Once we defeat the army in Remalia, the Kushaani will have lost nearly thirty thousand troops. They will no longer pose a threat to us, and we can decide any further course of action at that point."

"And have you thought about how your father should divide up the land, Your Highness?"

Ah! Now we are getting to the heart of the matter. He was sure this was the first of many more questions along this line. He wanted to tell the duke to leave him alone, but a few minutes to frame the discussion would pay far greater dividends later.

"We only have time for two choices until a more permanent resolution can be determined. All of Remalia's lands south of Balinth's are part of Ostin's dukedom. We could keep it that way for now, with Baron Marstoff managing it for the time being. Or we could appoint a new regent protector over our new holdings. Do you have a preference?" Stephir expected the duke to make a play for the latter. It didn't make sense for him to take the position himself, but perhaps one of his sons.

"May I offer an alternative?" Miarsten's voice shifted into politicking mode. The duke wanted something. "Make everything south of Vastan a new dukedom. Lord Osten will keep his current holdings, and the new land will be placed under an appropriate peerage. A new dukedom will incentivize the nobles to vie for the title, and you can leverage that into getting someone who will commit enough resources here to prosecute your war further while your remaining forces are free to return to Remalia."

Miarsten's proposal was bold, to be sure. The duke was one of the few obvious choices, having the largest force aside from the crown in Kushaan. Osten's force was perhaps larger, but he was in no position to rule what would be the largest dukedom in Remalia if the new lands were given to him. Baron Marstoff wouldn't be happy with that, but his usefulness was nearing its end.

"It's a very interesting proposal, Lord Miarsten. We'll have to see what my father says, but I am confident he will give your proposal due consideration." Stephir was not at all confident. He suspected his father might be more inclined to reserve the new dukedom for Andric, but Stephir needed Miarsten's immediate support.

A broad smile broke across the duke's face. "Excellent! Excellent!"

"I need the nobles to be convinced that returning with our main force to Teris is the right move."

"I will give whatever voice I have to your command, my lord."

It was a surprising relief to finally have garnered the support of at least one man. His influence with the other nobles would be valuable in the coming days. Stephir stood and poured two glasses of wine. Handing one to the duke, he lifted his own.

"Holy Couple guard and speed us," Stephir toasted as he and the duke drained not the last glass of wine of the night.

The news was spreading through the camp like wildfire. This was sooner than the thoughtful figure leaving the command tent would have wished for. She wanted to suppress the news, but that was no longer possible. Everything about their plan hinged on the element of surprise, and she had hoped to stretch out that moment of discovery as long as possible. However, that stone was rolling down the mountain, and there was no putting it back.

A brisk wind, following on the heels of predawn light, whipped the tents as they were taken down in preparation for the army's departure, making the soldiers' task more difficult. She needed to make all haste in getting the message to its destination. She would have preferred an elantic communication, but the Remalian elantir might detect it as they fumbled for a solution to the loss of their own clairaudient capabilities. She cursed the need to use mundane methods of communicating, but any device she could carry would have a limited range, and the risk of being discovered far outweighed any benefit.

She strode among the enemy, confident in her disguise, knowing she would never be caught. She had been at this for several years now, and her role in the plan had become second nature. She had not been chosen for her knowledge of the Remalian customs or her ability to blend in but for her considerable experience with met'elan. These foolish and ignorant people were oblivious to the vast powers in the world around them. They would learn, but only after some punishing lessons.

She reviewed the day's developments. The Remalians knew, but it didn't matter. It was already too late for them; nevertheless, she needed to send word. The note she had written was simple and concise, though the true message would be hidden even if the note were intercepted. Only the receiver would know what it meant.

We have been making strides in breaking the communication barrier. We are doubling our efforts. Our work is known. We have explained to the prince what our elantir intend to do to break through. We must make haste; the prince marches to Teris. The efforts will require more supplies, so send what you can. Remalia must be secure.

I will keep you apprised of our progress.

She knew it seemed innocuous, but like all their communications, only the third, fifth, and seventh sentences held any true meaning. Creativity was never her strong suit, so she stuck with a basic topic and didn't embellish her writing. Her pace quickened, but she resisted the urge to jog as she made her way to the nearby scout camp. She sealed the note while she walked, a minor elant melting the small wax disk in place and imprinting her seal without any break in her stride.

For so many years she worked toward this day, making victory possible for her people. So many years of coddling these people, aiding them, disguised as one of their pathetic elantir. They had such a narrow view of what she knew could be a much greater power. Someday soon, their eyes would be opened;

she only hoped she was there to see it. Teraithia willing, she had earned that right at the very least!

She was pleased to finally see the posted standard emblazoned with the insignia of the scouts snapping in the wind. Their camp was busy with preparations as well. She hoped she could find someone quickly to carry her message to Nanjab. Two mounted men rode through the midst of the camp toward the main road behind her. When they neared, she recognized with some surprise the Sa'ari captain who had brought the news yesterday to Prince Stephir. She smiled at the irony of having the same man carry a message back to one of her fellow conspirators, warning them the Remalians were aware of their invasion forces.

She waved at the scouts as she called out, "Captain!" The man looked around, then turned his horse toward her. "Captain, do you happen to be traveling back to Nanjab?"

"We are, but we have no time to add another traveler if that's your desire." The captain looked weary but carried himself as one who had born such hardships before and was resigned to doing so again.

"No, I simply have a message I would ask you to carry if you're willing. It is of utmost importance concerning the problem with the communications."

The captain sighed. "Do you have it with you?"

She held the sealed note out to the scout. "Deliver this to Captain Eskett of the elantir corps. He should be easy to find." The scout captain nodded as he reached to receive the message. "This must be given directly to Captain Eskett and no one else."

The Sa'ari captain nodded. "Have you had any luck in solving the problem?"

"We continue to work on it. I hope we will unravel the mystery soon."

"Best of luck in your efforts, Corporal," the captain wished her sincerely.

Luck had nothing to do with her efforts. "God speed you, Captain."

She would not normally wish Teraithia's blessing upon the enemy, but he was now on her errand after all, so it seemed permissible. She watched the scouts as they rode north, then strode back through the camp. She despised having to spend a few more weeks in this charade and looked forward to the time she could finally assert her rightful dominance over these people.

She was confident the end was near.

CHAPTER XXII
QUARIAN

Mid-morning on the second day after leaving the Remalian army camp, Quarian and Teek rode north on the Spice Road toward Nanjab. The sun shone brightly overhead, but a warm rain fell on them. Quarian knew the rain clouds trailed behind and the wind carried the rain to them. Despite any discomfort from riding wet, Quarian loved these rare occurrences. He was certain from the grumbled curses that Teek didn't feel the same.

Despite the urgent need he felt pressing on him to return to his patrol, especially with twenty thousand Kushaani traipsing around gods-knew-where, he had avoided setting too strenuous a pace on the ride north. It was not normally in Quarian's nature to be slow about getting back to his duties, but after so many days of urgent riding and the weight of the news he had carried to Prince Stephir, a few days' easier riding could perhaps be forgiven. Somewhere in the back of his mind, though, he knew there was more to it. The words of Commander Haresh ran through his mind. *Any post you want.*

Did he want his old patrol back? Did he want to get out of the scout corps and in command of combat troops? The possibilities were appealing. If he was to capitalize on the opportunity, it was best to strike while the iron was hot. If he waited to decide until he had returned to his current assignment, he could be there a long time. But was that such a bad thing?

He enjoyed the challenge of putting another patrol in order, and his men showed the potential of becoming a decent group of scouts. More importantly, his current duties put him squarely in the middle of possibly one of the greatest threats Remalia had faced in its history. It was not his homeland, but Remalia had treated him better than Qelasaar had, and he had grown to care about his adopted home. Quarian had a chance now to make a significant difference. He knew he needed to decide before he left Nanjab, and after two days of running it over and over in his mind, he was fairly certain what his decision would be.

Several miles slid by before the earth-colored walls of Nanjab were within sight. It was beautiful in the glow of sunlight shining down on the city which was quickly becoming an island of light in a sea of dark clouds rolling in from the south. Quarian knew the clouds meant a heavy summer storm was going to wash over the city in a torrent. Lightning flashed brightly to the west.

"Cap, can we pick up the pace a bit?" Teek asked plaintively. "I've already had enough of a bath for the day. Ain't 'nough dirt left on me ta make me want to be out under that storm."

Quarian answered by spurring his horse into a trot as a faint thunder rolled over them. He tried to gauge the speed at which the clouds were moving in, and it soon became apparent they wouldn't reach Nanjab before the clouds overtook them. The rain-slicked roads made the ground too dangerous to push the horses to a faster run, so he resigned himself to an even more thorough soaking. In moments they were thrown into shadow as the sun disappeared behind a veil of heavy, dark clouds. Nanjab grew bigger by the moment, then suddenly disappeared as the world became an impenetrable shroud of water. The downpour was a physical weight on Quarian's head and back.

A blinding flash turned the world white, and a deafening crack of thunder rattled him from head to toe.

His mount veered sharply to the right and slipped in the mud. Horse and rider went down hard. Quarian rolled away from the horse and onto his feet. He hurried to his mount as it clambered to stand and grabbed the reigns before it could bolt. Teek appeared next to him, his face invisible behind a veil of water pouring down over his deep hood. Quarian ran his hand over the horse, searching for damage. Finding none, he walked the horse several paces along the road and was relieved the horse could walk without any sign of injury.

"Everything okay?" Teek's voice yelled out from the hood, sounding distant and hollow through the ringing in Quarian's ears.

The captain winced at a dull pain on his side as he remounted. He was pretty sure nothing was broken, although certainly bruised. He would be sore for a few days. Mud caked both sides of his cloak from his boots to his thighs, but the downpour was already starting to wash away the evidence of the fall. "Fine!" Quarian yelled back as he tried to get his bearings. "Let's go!"

He waited for Teek to turn his horse, then followed him as they made their way more slowly up the road. Time seemed to stand still as they blindly navigated through the downpour. Another diffuse flash of light surrounded them, followed moments later by a rolling peel of thunder. Quarian could feel his mount tense beneath him, but he kept a tight rein as he patted the horse's neck reassuringly.

A dark shape appeared ahead, looming over them, and he was grateful they had finally arrived. He longed to change into dry clothes and plant himself in front of a roaring fire with some hot spiced wine and a hot meal. The gates stood open and shadowed figures huddled under the arched passageway beneath the city walls. Quarian and Teek were inside the gateway before one of the guards moved to stop them.

"What's your business?" the young soldier, who could not have been more than sixteen, called out over the pounding rain.

"We're scouts from the front, looking to get out of this weather," Quarian answered wearily.

"Pull your hoods back," the soldier ordered. Quarian knew the boy was merely doing his job, but the captain had little patience for it. Nevertheless, he pulled his hood off, then removed a soaked leather glove and wiped the water from his face.

"I'm Captain Min and have just returned from delivering a message for Prince Andric to Prince Stephir. I have business that needs to be attended to immediately."

The young soldier considered the words for a moment before one of his older companions barked at him. "Don't be daft, boy! Let 'em pass." The young man looked downcast as he moved aside to allow them entry.

"Is there an inn or somewhere else we can stay?" Quarian asked the older man. Normally Quarian would have gone straight to the scouts' quarters, but with everything soaked, he hoped he could find other accommodations for at least one night.

"No inn, unfortunately, least none that's got any folks ta run it. Just the houses left 'bandoned. Take yer pick."

"Thanks," Quarian responded flatly as he pulled his hood back over his head and urged his horse into the unrelenting torrent. Streamlets of water rushed beneath their mounts' hooves as they trudged through the brick streets, looking for a suitable place to stay. The only signs of life in the city were dim lights shining through shuttered windows. At last, they found a darkened house. Quarian handed the reins to Teek as he dismounted. He splashed through ankle-deep water toward the front door, only to find it unyielding. He walked to the next house, followed by Teek, and tried again. This time, the door swung open into a dark foyer.

Quarian stepped outside, closing the door to keep the water out, and walked around the corner and down a small space between the two houses to the rear of the house, hoping to find a place to shelter the horses. The rain prevented him from seeing more than a few strides ahead, but a brief search revealed nothing useful, so he returned to the front. He considered looking further, then shook his head as he removed his saddlebags.

"I'll be right back," he yelled, going inside. It took a few moments for his eyes to adjust to the darkness barely penetrated by the dim gray light filtering into the room through the door behind him. Slowly, silhouettes of furniture took shape. Quarian placed his saddle bags on a small table that stood in a corner of the narrow foyer. Even in the darkness, Quarian knew exactly where to find what he was looking for in his meticulously packed bags. He pulled out a small tinder box wrapped in an oilcloth. A warm, flickering glow filled the room as he lit a candle.

He could not make out many details in the candlelight, but it was enough to see where he was going. He felt like a thief as he slowly made his way further into the house. From what he could see, the former inhabitants had been moderately well-off. There were no alchemical lamps on the walls, but he found a few oil lamps in the room and hallway. Had the owners been merchants, or perhaps a magistrate's family? He wondered how they would feel seeing him walking through their home now.

It was not a particularly spacious house. There were no interior doors, but dark wood-paneled walls with arched openings divided the ground floor into three rooms. Quarian had seen enough for the moment. He could look around the rest of the house once Teek got out of the rain. He dripped some wax onto the top of a small cabinet and stuck the end of the candle into it, then went back to the front door. Stepping out into the rain, he took the reins from Teek without a word and led his horse into the house.

The large animal nearly filled the small entryway, but Quarian continued into the first open room, followed closely by Teek. Water pooled on the tiled floor beneath them as they removed saddles and bags from the horses. The horses breathed heavily, their muscles tense, so Quarian removed two apples from one of the bags and fed them to the horses, trying to put them at ease. Teek fetched two large basins of water while Quarian prepared their feed bags.

"Is there a fireplace somewhere? Blankets? Anythin' to get warm?" Teek asked. His tone bespoke focus and efficiency. For whatever shortcoming he had, Quarian knew Teek was a good scout and a reliable man to have with him.

"I was thinking about leaving you out there while I looked around a bit, but I figured the rain has washed off about as much stink as it's going to, and I didn't want the horses catching a cold."

Teek snorted his amusement as he shook his head. "Oh, I 'preciate it. But a few more minutes in the rain would have been just fine if it meant comin' in to a nice fire, some roast pork, maybe a steamin' bath. D'ya think ya got time to scare up those things now?"

It was Quarian's turn to laugh. "Finish with the horses and let me see what I can find. Do you have another candle?" Teek dug through one of his bags and handed Quarian another small candle. Quarian lit the wick from his candle on the cabinet, then began looking around, pushing his cloak clear of his blade, just in case. It only took a moment to explore the ground floor of the residence. The next room had four low, metal-framed chairs with plush cushions surrounding a low, round table in typical Kushaani fashion. Quarian had never liked sitting so low to eat. He preferred sitting up properly, but anything was better than how he ate most of the time out in the wilds, sitting on the ground or a log.

The next room was the kitchen. No food had been left behind, though some random bowls and dishes remained. A bin with a few pieces of wood stood next to the stone ovens, one over the other. Quarian had only seen single ovens before and was impressed by its ingenuity. He returned to the first room and told Teek to get a fire going while he looked upstairs.

The narrow spiral stairs took him up to the second level where the rain on the tiled roof was louder. The candle's flame flickered as he walked from room to room. There were the things one would expect to see in a rich house: hastily abandoned beds that looked comfortable, empty dressers, a particularly large metal sculpture of a peacock in flight hanging on a wall, a broken vase that appeared to have been dropped and left behind in the rush, things too big to move quickly or not worth taking. Otherwise, the place was empty.

When he returned downstairs, he found Teek in the kitchen blowing a nascent fire to life in the lower oven. They did not have many provisions, but they wouldn't starve until morning when they could get more supplies. Quarian brought their bed rolls into the kitchen and hung them from hooks in the ceiling. The oilcloth cover had done its job, but in this kind of rain nothing was impenetrable, so they would dry them out as best they could. It was still late afternoon, so they had a few hours before it would be time to sleep.

"I need some more small pieces of wood," Teek said between breaths as he worked on the fire. Quarian looked in the bin, but Teek had already gotten whatever was there.

"It looks like you got it all."

"Well, sir, how 'bout you go get some from the other room."

"I didn't see another bin."

Teek looked over his shoulder then rose, shaking his head. Quarian followed him into the other room. "Right here," Teek said, gesturing to one of the cabinets.

"But—"

Teek smashed the delicate cabinet with a strong kick.

"What are you...?" Quarian began to ask in surprise.

"I don' think they're gonna miss it," Teek interrupted as he picked up splintered pieces of wood. Quarian shook his head but followed Teek's lead. Soon they had a good fire burning in the oven. Quarian was somewhat disappointed to see that the oven was well designed to keep most of the heat inside; undoubtedly a useful feature in these warm southern reaches, but not exactly what he was hoping for when soaked. He changed into dry clothes then checked on the horses.

They needed more food, but he would have to see to it in the morning. He refilled their water basins, then joined Teek for dinner. After eating a decent meal of fried duck eggs and a bit of sweet potato they had on hand, they went upstairs. It was still early, but it had been a long day, and the promise of a couple of extra hours of sleep in comfortable beds sounded inviting to both of them.

"Do you think they'd let me keep this house for myself?" Teek asked Quarian.

"I don't know. You mean you would trade the open road and sleeping under a tree for being stuck in a boring life with soft beds, hot meals, and a roof over your head?" Quarian asked mockingly.

"For a life like these people had? Sure. In a heartbeat," Teek answered with a sincerity Quarian rarely heard from Teek.

"Well, you're friends with the prince now. I'll bet he would happily give it to you."

Teek snorted before bidding Quarian good night as he went off to the other bedroom to sleep.

A bright halo of light beamed around the edges of the shuddered window of the bedroom where Quarian slept. *What hour is it?* he wondered lazily. He rolled onto his back in the plush bed and stretched muscles that were more relaxed than they had been in weeks, but he was still tired from too much sleep. Where was Teek?

Quarian forced himself out of bed and walked to the bedroom where Teek had slept, but there was no sign of him. He opened the window to see what time it was and was surprised that it was mid-morning. Quarian got himself dressed and went back down to the main floor. Apart from some dung on the floor, there was no sign of the horses, but the saddles and gear were where they had placed them last night. Only the bridles and reins were missing. Teek must have taken them outside somewhere. Quarian wandered back to the kitchen and found breakfast that had long since gone cold. The fire had mostly burned down to embers, but he put the ceramic plate in the oven on top of the remaining coals to warm the food.

He peered out the front door to see if he could locate his companion. There was no sign of anyone, though Quarian hadn't expected any. They had ridden pretty far into the abandoned city. Most of the Remalian soldiers were in buildings close to the front gate and along the main avenue with the large estate where the king and Prince Andric resided. He went back in and ate his breakfast, then looked for something to clean the dishes with. The water barrel was practically empty and he didn't want to search for the cistern, so he forced himself to leave them dirty. He returned to the front room and was packing the last few things in the saddlebags when he heard the horses in the front and Teek's heavy footsteps echoing as he passed through the small foyer.

"So, the dead have woke up," Teek jested.

"Why didn't you wake me?" Quarian asked casually, though he was happy he had been able to sleep so long.

"No offense, Cap, but a few hours to myself sounded pretty good for a change."

Quarian smiled as he lifted his saddle. "Make any good use of the time?" he asked as he headed for the front door.

"Actually, yeah," Teek answered, picking up his saddle and following Quarian. "I found out where that elantir Eskett is like to be found. Seems they have taken up a couple of big houses right near the main gates, one with a couple of statues of naked ladies in the front," Teek said with an amused leer on his face. "Supposed to be pretty easy to spot."

The scouts saddled their horses with practiced efficiency, gathered the saddlebags, and soon were mounted and on their way. The late-morning air was warm and heavy with moisture from the night's rain. They soon found streets bustling with soldiers who were packing wagons and readying other supplies to move. Quarian was curious about the unexpected activity, so he stopped to ask what was happening.

"All's I know is we has got orders to pack everything and be ready to march first thing t'morruh."

"March for where?" Quarian asked.

"Gods only knows. We just pack and wait for more orders."

Quarian and Teek exchanged looks and moved on through streets that were similarly occupied by soldiers and Kushaani captives preparing to leave. *Are they going to abandon the city again?* Quarian wondered. It seemed such a waste. As they approached the city gates, Teek's information proved correct; the grand houses were nearly impossible to miss. Now that he saw them, Quarian remembered seeing them when he had first arrived in Nanjab with Prince Andric.

He and Teek dismounted and tied their horses to iron rings fixed into the reddish-brown brick wall in front of the larger of the two houses. A tall gate was unlocked and they made their way through a luscious garden that smelled deliciously fresh after the rain. Quarian knocked on the front door, but when no one answered after a few attempts, they entered.

They were greeted by a spacious foyer graced with marble statues and a grand double staircase leading to the next floor. Two rooms flanked the foyer. Faint voices came from the right, so he walked toward the murmurs.

The first room they passed through was large and open, with few furnishings. Several windows lined the outside walls of the house. In the next room, several iron-bound chests formed neat rows being packed by a few young men and women under the supervision of a middle-aged man with receding blond hair and a thin, severe face. After directing one of the young men who carried some unidentifiable cloth-wrapped object to one of the chests, the man noticed Quarian and Teek.

"Yes?" he asked tersely.

"Excuse me, but do you know where I might find Captain Eskett?" Quarian asked politely.

"The magister is a busy man. What do you want?"

"I was given a message for him by an elantir at Prince Stephir's camp."

"Leave it with me, I'll see he gets it," the man said impatiently.

"I'm sorry, but the lady was insistent that I give it directly to Captain Eskett and no one else."

The man gave him a stern look, then summoned a girl who was dressed in an apprentice uniform. "Take these men upstairs and have them wait while you inform Magister Eskett. You understand?"

The girl curtsied quickly. In a sweet voice, she invited the scouts to follow her. Quarian saw a small staircase leading directly from the room to the next floor, but instead the apprentice led them to the front foyer then up to the second floor using the grand staircase. The first few rooms they passed appeared to be inhabited but were currently unoccupied. Toward the rear of the house, they approached a room with closed doors.

"Please wait here," she instructed politely, then went inside the room and closed the doors behind her. Quarian and Teek quietly waited, admiring the rich decorations. The place was not as opulent as the grand estate where the king stayed, but it was a wealthier residence than most Quarian had seen. At last, the girl opened the door and beckoned them inside.

As Quarian stepped into the large room, a few of the twenty or more faces turned toward him. Mouths moved as if speaking, but he heard nothing. They must be silencing the area somehow. Then a man spoke, penetrating the silence.

"I am Magister Eskett. You have something for me?" The man was taller than his companions, with a broad chest and muscled physique, resembling some ideal picture of a warrior than what Quarian usually thought of when it came to elantir.

"Are you *Captain* Eskett?" Quarian was not familiar with the title Magister. Perhaps it was some special rank for the elantir.

The man rolled his eyes dramatically, a look of disgust on his face. "Yes, I suppose so."

"Then this is for you," Quarian said stepping forward and producing the note. The man impatiently took the note and turned it over to examine the seal. Quarian could not be certain, but he thought he saw the magister's eyes narrow ever so slightly. The elantir captain broke open the seal and read the note. It must have been a short one because in just a moment the magister folded it and tucked it into a pocket.

"You've come from the front."

"Yes," Quarian replied.

"The army is returning to Remalia. Do you know why?" There was little inflection in the elantir's voice.

Quarian wondered whether he should say anything but figured they would all know soon enough. He had heard word of it spreading through Remalia's camp before he left. It was only a matter of time. "A large Kushaani force was seen over a week ago marching toward Teris." Quarian had expected the same reaction he had received to his previous deliveries of this news, but these men and women didn't respond other than a few sideways glances. "There was also a smaller force moving through the mountains heading toward Balinth's Fortress."

"How did you hear this information?" the captain asked.

"I saw the troops with my own eyes." Again, the elantir's eyes moved with the slightest narrowing. "At least the ones moving through the mountains. My men reported seeing the others in the northern foothills."

"You say they were Kushaani," Eskett stated flatly. "Are you certain?" The question struck Quarian as odd. Perhaps because in his other reports, no one had bothered to ask the question he had struggled with himself. The elantir seemed impatient with Quarian's hesitation. "Well?"

Quarian kept his doubts to himself. "Who else could they be?"

"Yes, well... thank you for your service. May I impose on you for another?"

"We are returning immediately to our assigned area of operation north of Balinth's Fortress. If the task can be done without diverting us from that duty, I would be happy to assist."

The elantir captain considered for a moment then nodded. "I would like you to take one of my elantir with you as far as Balinth's Fortress. I need him to examine the Bonded there, and it appears to be more urgent than I realized. Will that be acceptable?"

Teek sucked air through his teeth, something he usually did when he was annoyed.

Quarian asked, "How quickly can they be ready to leave? We have to report to Prince Andric before departing, but I expect to leave Nanjab within the hour."

"I will have them ready to depart immediately. Should I have them meet you at the city gates?"

"That will be fine. No extra pack animals, just a well-conditioned traveling mount and enough provisions for two days. We'll resupply along the way." Quarian stated.

"Excellent," the elantir said without enthusiasm. "Thank you again for your service, Captain...?" He left the question hanging.

"Captain Minanthsolum." Quarian didn't feel like giving the arrogant man the convenience of a shorter name.

Without taking his eyes from Quarian, Eskett addressed the apprentice, who waited on the outskirts of the group. "Alayda, please show these men to the door. Teraithia speed you."

Quarian and Teek followed the girl to the front door then made their way out through the garden. "He was a pleasant fellow," Teek said, his voice heavy with sarcasm, spitting to the side of the path on their way out. Quarian agreed but said nothing.

The pair found their way to the estate to find Prince Andric and report on the completion of his assignment. They were stopped by the Divinarim guarding the residence. "State your purpose," one of the guards demanded.

Quarian was about to respond, but one of the other knights answered first. "This is the scout captain that rode with Prince Andric."

Quarian thought he recognized the man as one of the knights that had guarded the prince on their journey south, although he could not be certain with so much of his face covered by his polished helm. "What do you need, Captain Min?"

"I was returning to report to Prince Andric on the assignment he gave me."

"Unfortunately, the prince isn't here at the moment. You may be able to find him with General Obannern. I understand they're at the headquarters building near the city gates."

Quarian thanked the guard and headed back toward the city gate. With a few inquiries to soldiers along the way, they found the building with little difficulty. It was tall, but only a single story with thick, white plastered walls. A wide, shaded pavilion covered in climbing vines formed a canopy in the front of the otherwise plain building. Regular soldiers stood guard outside the front doors and Quarian wondered if he had missed the prince again. He was pleased to be informed the prince was inside. After another exchange with the guards and a bit of waiting, Quarian was directed to the prince, who greeted him with a thin smile.

"Captain Min, good to see you again. I understand you were successful in delivering your report to my brother."

Quarian was surprised the prince was already aware of what had happened. Maybe messengers had been sent back to Nanjab that same night, or perhaps the elantir had solved the communications problem. "Yes, Your Highness. Everything was presented as you requested."

"Well, now we are preparing to return to Teris to deal with the Kushaani invaders," the prince said with some satisfaction. "What are your orders now?"

Quarian had no orders, and this was the moment of decision that would put him on one path or another, at least for the foreseeable future. Despite his mixed feelings, he didn't hesitate with his answer. "I am returning to my post in the Velspars to see what we can do to ensure you know as much about the enemy as we can tell you."

"Excellent! I'm sure we are all glad to have you there."

"Is there any other way I can be of service before I leave, Your Highness?"

"No, thank you. You've been of great service already. Gods keep you, Captain."

Quarian saluted sharply, then turned and left the building. Back in the busy street, they mounted their horses and trotted to the gate. He needed to find a quartermaster to restock his supplies before taking to the road. It didn't take long to find what they needed, and by noon they approached the city gates.

Their new traveling companion was easy to spot. The middle-aged woman in her elantir uniform sat comfortably atop a beautiful chestnut Remalian Plainsbred. Quarian was surprised that a common elantir would be provisioned with such a fine horse. At least he wouldn't have to worry about her slowing them down.

"Captain Minanthsolum?" the elantir inquired.

"Yes," he said, impressed she pronounced his name flawlessly. "And you are?"

"Sergeant Evva Lascombe."

"This is Corporal Teek Arrell," Quarian said, introducing his companion.

"Teek's fine," the scout added quickly.

"You have everything you need, Sergeant?"

"Ready to go, Captain."

Quarian nodded and led them through the open city gates.

CHAPTER XXIII
QUARIAN

Quarian had ridden a horse most of his life, but he doubted he had covered as many miles in the saddle in such a short amount of time as he had in the last few weeks. He loved riding, the freedom he felt, the power to move so much faster than men could alone. But as the miles slid past him, his enjoyment slid away as well. The frantic pace of their journey southward was a sharp contrast to the steady determination of their monotonous trip north. The landscape blurred into a single wash of brown, green, and gray. They ate occasionally and slept when it was dark. It was all mechanical; all except his thoughts about whether he had made the right decision and whether he would ever have another opportunity like Commander Haresh's offer.

A few farmers and local merchants were the only traffic along the Spice Road, moving a few miles here or there between villages or farms. There were no caravans or groups of wounded soldiers heading home. Strangely, there were no soldiers at all other than a small patrol they met near Tieka, who had nothing of interest to report. This was how the world should be—if a war were not going on days behind him. Now it was cause for concern. Were the Kushaani blocking the pass, stopping traffic from getting in or out of Balinth's? A thousand Kushaani would be a difficult obstacle in the confines of the canyon walls, but the sheer numbers of the Remalian army would over-power them in no time.

It was mid-afternoon when they approached the valley leading to the Gap and eventually up to Balinth's Fortress. Quarian welcomed the thought of getting an update from Commander Tra'en and the first night in a bed in six days since leaving Nanjab. A sharp exclamation from Teek pulled him out of his thoughts. Teek pointed some distance up the road. Quarian followed his gesture and caught sight of a figure running into a copse of trees to the side of the road.

"Could you tell who it was?" Quarian asked as they rode forward cautiously, scanning the landscape for any sign of threat.

"Well, it didn't look like one of them strange Kushaani, but other than that I couldn't tell."

"I want them taken alive, whoever they are. I will go in after them. Stay here," Quarian ordered Sergeant Lascombe. "Teek, ride ahead and cut off any route going north."

Teek nodded as they kicked their mounts into a gallop. Quarian quickly found the trail of crushed grass where the man had run off the road and was at the tree line in moments as Teek continued up the road. He sprang off his horse as he pulled his sword from the scabbard behind the saddle. He was one of the few scouts with any skill using a sword. Most preferred the bow and could use a knife well enough.

Quarian scanned the leaf-covered earth where the man had run into the trees. It was possible this was an ambush, but Quarian doubted it. He cautiously made his way into the dim woods. Apart from birds, there was no sound. He easily tracked the route through the undergrowth; bent grass from a footfall here, a broken branch there. Quarian moved quickly, his senses alert to any sign the man might not be alone. He hadn't gone far when the man jumped up from behind some bushes and started off at a dead run. The deep blue and white of his Remalian uniform was easy to follow.

"Stop!" Quarian called out as he raced after the man. "I just want to talk to you." The man kept running, but he was slow and Quarian caught up to him in no time. The man picked up a dead tree branch and rounded on Quarian, swinging a clumsy stroke with all his strength. Quarian danced out of range as the branch arced past him, then sprang toward the man and struck the branch from his hands with the butt of his sword. The man's eyes went wide and he turned again to flee, but Quarian swept his feet out from under him and the man fell. Quarian saw he was going to land on a tree root and quickly shoved him in the opposite direction, sending the man rolling clumsily away. He tried to scramble up, but Quarian drove his knee across his shoulders, pinning him face down in the leaves and dirt.

"Lie still. I don't want to hurt you. I just want to talk."

The man struggled for a moment, panting hard, and then suddenly he went limp, nodding feebly. Quarian stood up, and the man rolled onto his back, revealing a dirty face and leaves in his sandy-blond hair. Quarian offered his hand, but the young man scrambled toward the nearest tree, eyes wide and breathing heavily. He cowered with his back against the smooth bark, his eyes darting around like he might bolt at any moment.

"Who are you and why are you out here alone?" Quarian asked.

The man's head snapped toward the sound of Teek rushing through the trees toward them, a long knife with a serrated back edge in hand. "You always get all the fun, Cap," Teek joked as he stopped near them. The man closed his eyes and slumped, trembling against the tree. "Who is he?"

"He was just about to tell me," Quarian said, keeping his attention on the soldier. Quarian squatted so he was at eye level with the man. He softened his voice and questioned him with more care. He hoped he hadn't caught a deserter. "I am Captain Min, and this is Corporal Arell. What's your name?"

The man opened his eyes, then said simply, "Petten."

"All right, Petten. Now, what are you doing out here alone?"

He looked as if he wasn't going to answer, then finally answered quietly, "A bunch of us was in a company, headin'..." his voice caught in his throat and he stopped. Quarian waited for him to continue. "... headin' back home," he finished, his voice thick with emotion, and his eyes welling with tears. "We was comin' up ta the fortress and had just entered the gates when suddenly we was attacked."

Teek cursed aloud, but the man's eyes remained focused on something far away, remembering the scene. "There was nothin' we could do. We just ran, but they kep shootin' arrows down on us. Me and some others got away a bit, but they came after us. I run inta the forest and lied there, prayin' the gods wouldn't let 'em find me. I heard 'em..." Again his voice caught in his throat. "I heard 'em killin' the others."

There was a long pause, and Quarian was about to prompt him to continue when he resumed his account. "I lied there all night. Must 'ave fell asleep. In the mornin', I woke up and snuck off through the woods. When I got along a ways, I come out on the road and was makin' my way back to find some help. That's when I saw you and run."

A chill ran up Quarian's spine and he glanced up at Teek, but the scout simply looked at him with his brow furrowed. He knew what the soldier's story meant, but he had to ask anyway. "The ones who attacked you at the fortress, what did they look like?"

"They was strange lookin', that's sure. They was big men with kinda grayish skin, like they was dead or sunthin'. Their clothes was gray too. They wasn't like any Kushaani I seen before, that's sure."

"And they were inside the fortress? You're certain?" Quarian asked with a steely calm, cold dread gripping his heart as he waited for the soldier's reply.

"Yessir."

"Mother of whores!" Quarian shot Teek a warning glance, but the cursing continued. "Akraharr's balls, that could'a been us."

"Not helpful, Teek. It was somebody else. Somebody's friends," Quarian said, nodding his head toward Petten. Teek muttered a few more choice curses but thankfully kept them under his breath.

Quarian's mind raced through the implications. *Impossible! How could only a thousand Kushaani take Balinth's Fortress?* For now, how didn't really matter. The fortress that had never fallen was no longer in Remalia's hands. This changed everything. There was no route to get the army back into Remalia for hundreds of leagues in any direction. They could try crossing the mountains, but they were more likely to starve or die from exposure or other treacherous conditions than make it through.

Quarian offered his hand to Petten again, and this time the young man took it. Quarian looked at Teek as he pulled the soldier to his feet. Teek shook his head, and Quarian could guess his thoughts. "Petten, I'm going to need you to stay here with Corporal Teek until I return. Do you understand?" Petten nodded dumbly at first, then his eyes seemed to light with recognition, and he nodded more confidently.

Turning to Teek, he continued. "I'm going to have a look at the fortress. Don't let anyone past your position here. If I'm not back by morning, you are to make all haste for Luresh." He stopped and asked Petten, "Do you know how to ride a horse?" The young soldier shook his head. Quarian clenched his teeth in frustration but wasn't surprised. "Leave him at Tieka with instructions to stop anyone from coming north. Then find Prince Andric and give him the report. Spread the word to any troops moving this way."

Quarian was certain Petten hadn't been lying—the fear in the man's eyes was genuine. He just could not be sure if the soldier had been mistaken about what he saw. But how else could he describe the warriors Quarian had seen with his own eyes? He retrieved his horse and walked back to the road before mounting.

"Everything all right?" their elantir traveling companion asked.

"I'm afraid you may not be able to visit the fortress after all. Stay here with Teek. I should be back in a few hours."

"You sure you want to go up there?" Teek asked, jutting his chin toward the Gap between the looming peaks leading to the gates of Balinth's.

"Do I have a choice?" Quarian countered.

"I should come with you. I may be of use in keeping our approach silent," Lascombe suggested.

Quarian considered the suggestion for a moment, but decided he preferred to avoid the risk of approaching the captured fortress with someone he wasn't sure was skilled enough in the art of stealth, even if she could perform met'elan.

"I appreciate the offer, but your orders stand," Quarian said brusquely, then spurred his mount into motion. A cold, biting dread turned in the pit of his stomach, but he knew what his duty required. The last few miles slid beneath the blurred hooves of his mount as the sun crept further east, inevitably closer to sunset.

Too soon for his liking, he was at the mouth of the narrow canyon leading to the fortress. A warm air blew into his face, but he still felt chilled. He dismounted and tied his horse to a tree off the road. His need for stealth outweighed his desire for speed. His eyes were everywhere as he made his way up the canyon, spotting movement from a flitting bird, a lizard sunning itself on the canyon wall, or a dust cloud whipped up by the swirling currents of wind that frequently gusted through the canyon.

Quarian reached a bend in the canyon that looked like it would have been carved out by a river at some point in the distant past, and he knew the fortress was not far ahead. He crept along the edge of the canyon wall as stealthily as he could, doing his best to remain in the deeper shadows.

Soon the imposing walls of Balinth's Fortress came into view. He stopped and scanned the scene for any movement, any sign he was being watched. A bird soared lazily overhead, a hooded crow by the shape of the wings, but otherwise the area was quiet as a graveyard and just as foreboding. As each moment passed, the quiet became too unnatural. There should have been some signs of life, guards patrolling the walls or something. Then he caught sight of a flash, a glint of the waning sunlight off metal atop the parapets of the fortress, though he still could not detect any movement. He squinted, making out what appeared to be the tiny figure of a man atop the massive walls, but it was just too far to be sure.

He took his spyglass out of the pouch at his side and carefully extended it to avoid the clicking sound of the brass tubes locking into place. At this distance, it was difficult to scan the walls slowly, but he had been a scout for a long time and managed to hold it steady enough. Soon he found what he was looking for. A Remalian soldier stood at attention, helmeted head looking down toward the base of the walls. Quarian moved the spyglass down to the canyon floor, but there was nothing there. It took a moment, but Quarian got the spyglass back to the same spot. The guard seemed to be standing completely at attention, unmoving, though Quarian could not be sure because of the shaking of his hand. Finally, his mind accepted what his eyes were showing him. The head wasn't looking downward, it was slumped forward. The guard was not at attention, he was completely motionless.

Quarian continued to scan the walls and soon spotted another soldier standing impossibly still atop the battlements, then a third. All of them held a spear at the ready, adorned in armor, with their heads slumped forward. If only he could get his hand steady enough, he was certain he could see ropes around their shoulders.

Suddenly, he caught movement. It was brief, but he was certain he had seen it. There, next to the third body was... something. It was only a glimpse, but something gray passed behind an opening atop the battlements. He couldn't tell for sure what it was, but he knew in his heart he had seen it before. He remained focused on the opening and waited another minute, stretching agonizingly into two, and then he saw it a second time. A gray figure briefly appeared; it was the same shade he had seen in the Velspars.

They were atop the walls, inside Balinth's Fortress. The fortress had fallen.

A falling rock clattered nearby, and Quarian's head jerked from his spyglass, one hand shot to the hilt of his sword at his hip. He held stock still other than his eyes darting around, searching for any sign he had been discovered. When he was satisfied that he was alone, he carefully backed away in the direction he had come. He had seen enough. His duty as a scout was to deliver information, and he could not do that if he was captured or dead. When the fortress was a comfortable distance behind him, he moved away from the safety of the canyon walls to the clearer path and ran back to his horse.

Dusk had fallen over the valley, but he spurred his horse to a full gallop. He could not help glancing behind him every few minutes, looking for any sign of pursuit. His mind raced through all the implications of what this meant for Remalia. He tried to think of some strategy that might give them an advantage in retaking the fortress, but he had come up with nothing useful when he reached the small copse of trees where Teek, Lascombe, and Petten were hiding.

Quarian swung down from the saddle before his horse came to a stop, panting heavily from the exertion. "Time to move," he called out. A moment later, Teek emerged from the evening shadows beneath the trees, leading his horse and a haggard-looking Petten, followed by the elantir.

"Well?" Teek asked, looking nervously toward the darkening mountains to the north.

"It's them. I'll tell you everything on the road. Let's go." As much as Quarian wanted to race down the road, his mount was already tired from a hard day of riding. However, he was not about to sleep this close to the Gap, so they walked the horses down the road through the deepening darkness. He intended to walk throughout the night, but after just a few hours he was bone weary, so he finally led them to a secluded spot off the road. He gave Petten his bedroll and moved back to a spot along the tree line where he could watch the road. He only slept for a couple of hours at a time before worry of pursuit pulled him awake to check the road again. After waking the third time, he knew he would not find sleep again.

Time to get moving.

The miles carried them past the same farms and small villages he had passed just the day before, but they wouldn't serve his needs. It was nearly dark when they finally rode into the empty village square of Tieka. It seemed like only yesterday he had been here with Prince Andric on their way to warn the king. Now the threat had become a reality, he was on the same journey south again. He was tired.

They approached the small inn on the far side of the square to find accommodations for the night. They tethered their horses and entered the small common room to find the innkeeper and make arrangements for their stay. Despite the hour, Quarian hadn't expected the small common room to be completely empty.

"Hello?" Quarian called out.

"Coming!" a voice called from some back room. The lanky innkeeper appeared with a thin smile on his face. "How can I help you, sirs?" he asked politely.

"We need lodgings for the night, and for our horses."

"Of course, of course. How many rooms will you be wanting, sir?"

"Do you have any with four beds?"

The man looked a bit crestfallen. If the empty common room was any indication, he was hoping to fill four rooms. Quarian had the money, but he was a practical and frugal man, with no disposition for luxury. "Three beds in a room is the best I have there, I'm afraid."

"One of those and a single bedroom will be sufficient." After he paid for the rooms, Quarian ordered a hot meal for the four of them, then he and Teek tended to the horses. When they returned, the innkeeper had hot stew and some cold bread and butter with a bit of honey waiting for them. Petten was already seated, devouring the food. He hadn't said a word their entire trip southward, but he seemed to perk up at the prospect of filling his belly with a hot meal.

Quarian hadn't yet decided how much to tell the villagers, so he opted for caution. "It seems a bit quiet," he observed when the innkeeper came to fill their beer mugs with a dark, heavy beer. Not quite what he would have preferred on a warm night, but good nevertheless.

"Just a lull. Happens from time to time," the innkeeper said pleasantly.

"Seems strange that there should be a lull at this time of the year, especially with the traffic from the war. How long has it been like this?"

"Oh, about a week, maybe a bit more."

A week or more since the Kushaani had taken Balinth's, and this was the first word to make it south? That was a level of thoroughness Quarian didn't expect from Kushaani. He considered suggesting to the village headwoman that they flee south but decided against it. The Kushaani clearly meant to hold the fortress, and launching assaults south was probably the last thing they intended to do. But he needed to ensure that no one else went north.

"I must speak with the headwoman tonight. Can you take me to her?" he asked the innkeeper.

"Of course, of course," the innkeeper replied. "Or I'm sure she would be happy to come see you here. Mayhap I can fetch her while you finish your meal?"

Quarian agreed and the man left immediately. Quarian found it surprising that the man would leave four strangers in his inn unattended, but sometimes this was the way of small communities; trust was simply a way of life.

They finished their meal and Petten had nodded off when the innkeeper returned with the village headwoman. Quarian stood and Teek elbowed Petten awake as he and the elantir followed the captain's lead.

"That's the one who wanted to talk to you," the innkeeper said, pointing to Quarian.

"Good evening, sir. I am Mistress Bowen, Headwoman of Tieka," she said with a slight bow of her head.

"I remember you from our visit here nearly two weeks ago. I was in the company of Prince Andric," Quarian said, hoping the connection would lend more weight to what he had to say.

"How may I be of service?" she asked, her voice steady but betraying the tension behind her calm exterior.

Quarian thought about asking to discuss the matter in private, but word was bound to get out soon enough. "I'm Captain Min. My companions and I have just come from Balinth's Fortress. It appears a Kushaani force may have captured the fortress."

The headmistress stared at Quarian for a moment, eyes blinking, a blank look on her face.

"You haven't seen any troops move south for about a week, correct? That's because they can't get past the fortress."

"Or worse," Teek muttered under his breath.

Quarian shot Teek a withering glance.

"Kerail protect us!" Mistress Bowen exclaimed. "Are you...? How could...?"

"I am certain, Headmistress. I have seen it with my own eyes." The woman's jaw clenched and unclenched, but she drew herself up and nodded. "Corporal Arell and I must leave first thing in the morning to take word to the king. This is Sergeant Lascombe. She and Lanceman Petten will stay here in Tieka to ensure that no one, absolutely no one, goes north." Quarian stated it as emphatically as he could. He was tempted to add that he spoke on authority of the prince, but that was asking for prison or worse if anyone cared to take issue with it.

"What will happen to us? Should we leave the village and go south?"

Quarian admired the steel of her nerves. "No, the Kushaani will stay at the fortress. You will be safe enough here until the army returns. They're on their way now."

"But you said they don't know yet. Why are they coming back?"

Quarian admired her intelligence. "It's believed that a much larger force is somewhere near Teris. Crown Prince Stephir is returning home to ensure the city is safe, but they need to be aware that we no longer hold the Gap."

"Is there anything you need, sir?" the headwoman offered.

"We'll need some of your village folk to help watch the road to stop anyone attempting to go north." Quarian could see the concern written on her face. "Don't worry. You're not in any danger." He tried to sound reassuring but wasn't convinced of his own words.

"I'll do what I can. Unless there is anything else..." she paused long enough for Quarian to shake his head. "Then I bid you goodnight. Kerail speed and keep you."

"And you as well, Mistress Bowen."

The headwoman left, and the innkeeper showed them to their rooms. Quarian rarely took advantage of his rank, preferring to live and work as his men did. Tonight he was tempted to but decided to let Sergeant Lascombe have the room instead. Teek had been none-too-subtle in his efforts to seduce Lascombe, and although he had mostly kept himself in check after Quarian had ordered him to stop, he knew the sergeant would feel more comfortable in a room by herself. He told Teek they would be gone before first light, then spent several minutes explaining to Lascombe how she and Petter were to help the villagers secure the road. Quarian would have preferred to also leave Teek, but his message to the king was too important to leave in one person's hands. At least Mistress Bowen appeared to be a capable woman. She would help ensure the work was done properly.

When Quarian felt Lascombe and Petten understood their new duties, the captain bid the elantir goodnight and went to his room with Teek and Petten. It was a small room, but it was no doubt better than the ground. Despite his exhaustion, Quarian found it difficult to quiet his mind, especially with Teek already snoring loudly. Eventually, he fell into a fitful sleep.

It was still dark when Quarian forced himself out of bed. He roused Teek, and they quickly dressed. He left Petten asleep, and they descended the narrow wooden steps to the common room. Quarian intended to slip out quietly and was surprised to see the innkeeper busying himself with bowls and cups.

"I have some hot porridge for you if you care for it," the man offered pleasantly. Quarian was anxious to be on his way, but a few minutes to eat would be welcome and help sustain them. He thanked the man, who brought their food within moments. They ate hastily, then bid the innkeeper farewell.

Dawn found them miles away from Tieka. Quarian wished he could let the horses run full out, but even traveling light and with well-conditioned horses they still could only endure that pace for an hour or two at the most, so he set a quick but sustainable pace. Just before noon, they stopped at a small stream beneath some orange trees in a large orchard to water and rest the horses. Small oranges grew beneath blossoms, filling the air with their sweet aroma.

"Much as I enjoy doing something different from the same ol' patrol I've been doin' for years, I must say this up and down the same road here is gettin' a bit old."

Quarian laughed in agreement, then remounted his horse. He knew it wasn't the last time they would travel this stretch and tried to fight the oppressive weight of that knowledge and everything it meant for him and all of Remalia.

As difficult as it was to be this close to Balinth's Fortress without running straight there at the first opportunity, Sergeant Lascombe spent the day continuing to play the role of the dutiful soldier. She helped the villagers set up the watches on the road to keep the stray traveler from continuing up the Spice Road to their unsuspecting death that awaited in the Worrin Gap. She had been tempted more than once to kill the Remalian scouts and put an end to her waiting, but had decided against it. *Why bother?* The Remalians were already aware of their presence. The news that they already held the fortress would make no difference in the end. In fact, as gratifying as an ambush at the fortress would have been, she relished even more the thought of the gnawing fear the news would plant in their weak hearts.

After years of blending in among these pathetic people, she would soon be rewarded for her efforts and live like royalty among them, her considerable powers finally brought to bear to subdue them under the feet of the empire. That night, she waited until well into the second watch before sneaking out of the inn and through the farm fields surrounding Tieka before finally moving to the road. Each mile she traveled felt like a weight lifting from her shoulders, and she let herself smile.

It was nearly dawn when she approached the last stretch of the road leading to the imposing gates of Balinth's Fortress. She still needed to be cautious. Those holding the fortress were as likely to kill her as any Remalian approaching without leave. She dismounted and retrieved a small, ornate metal box from one of her saddle bags. With a small alteration to the elantic seal, the box unlocked and she withdrew the single object from inside—a dagger-sized crystal.

She drew elan from her horse, from the earth around her, and from herself until she had pooled enough for her elant, then began tracing an intricate pattern in the air with the crystal. There was no visible sign, but she sensed every thread of elan woven into the pattern. It grew tighter until it had formed almost a solid panel directly in front of her.

She put a reassuring hand on her mount, then spoke, her amplified voice reverberating off the stone walls of the canyon. "I am Viest-at Second Vanguard." It was good to say her name, to hear it ringing from the stones.

She often went months, sometimes years, without saying or hearing her true name. "I am known among the Remalians as Sergeant Evva Lascombe, of the Remalian Elantir Corps. I must report that Laconeus King is aware we hold Balinth's Fortress and that we are marching on Teris."

Her stomach knotted as she waited for a response. She was so close. She longed to be with her people again. She knew it was foolish to hold the elant in place while she waited, but it felt like a thread connecting her to those inside the fortress. She just couldn't bring herself to let it go despite the discomfort of continuing to draw so much of her elan. At last, the heavy portcullis in front of the gate rose. She felt relief as she released her elant, but it did nothing to ease the tightening knot inside her. She remounted and proudly rode forward, praying to Teraithia they didn't put a bolt through her after all.

One way or another, her old life was finally over.

CHAPTER XXIV
ANDRIC

"Care for him as if your life depended upon it." Andric sounded harsher than he had intended. He was concerned for his father, but that didn't excuse mistreating others, and he knew it.

"As always, Your Highness." Sister Merranine looked slightly injured as she supervised the transfer of King Jevorak from his plush feather bed in the lavish Nanjab estate to the bed in the large wagon outfitted to carry the king back to Teris. A pair of seasoned elantir stood nearby with heads bowed in concentration. Andric felt the flow of elan as the pair wove a tight cushion of air around his father, stabilizing and protecting him against any bumps or jostling. Andric was tempted to add his own flows to support his father to be sure nothing happened, but he knew it was a pointless gesture. The king was receiving the best care available in the world. Two Divinarim gently lifted him from one mattress to the other with ease.

Andric's eyes were locked on his father's gaunt face, anxiously waiting for the barely perceptible signs of his slight breathing. The king was covered with several white linen sheets to keep a chill away that did not exist this far south. Sister Merranine had explained that after slowing down so many of his body's functions, the king had difficulty keeping his temperature up. Barak's advice had seemed to slow his father's deterioration, but he was fairing no better. He clung to life as Andric would have expected him to—tenacious and unrelenting.

Andric still could not bring himself to believe this strange illness might defeat his father, but the memory of the weak voice coming from this once-mighty man brought the prince to the verge of despair. Andric ferociously shoved the memory away and clenched his teeth to maintain at least a semblance of calm.

They carried the king through the hallways to the rear of the house where they could load him into the wagon away from the eyes of all but those closest to Jevorak. Andric focused on the wagon that was to carry his father homeward and frowned. It was more of a house on wheels than any wagon Andric had seen before. Apparently, this was how important people traveled in Kushaan. It was ornately carved around the doorway and windows and brightly painted in blue and yellow, giving it a somewhat garish look. The wide double doors at the rear of the wagon allowed for easy loading of the king, and the metal struts were ingeniously designed to absorb the shocks of the road. It seemed like quite a privileged way to ride, yet somehow still not befitting the king of Remalia.

Andric remembered when he rode out of Teris with Stephir and their father. A few advisors had quietly suggested that the princes should encourage the king to travel in a similar manner, that horseback was getting hard on the older king, especially with the distances they were to travel. But none of the advisors dared broach the subject with Jevorak directly, and Andric and Stephir were equally wise. Andric knew well enough that his father wouldn't have tolerated anyone suggesting he was incapable of riding to war on his mount.

When the others had loaded the king and exited, Andric stepped past the Divinarim surrounding the royal wagon and climbed the few steps into the well-furnished interior. He was pleased to see his father resting peacefully in the bed. The quarters seemed a bit cramped, and the thick humidity was oppressive, but there were a surprising number of amenities.

A bottle of Jevorak's favorite wine imported from the Gallucia region of Calavia, clean water, and other necessities for caring for the sick were fixed to the side shelves. A shallow washbasin made of a deep blue stone was installed near the bed. There was a chair for relieving oneself behind an ornate wood screen, presumably with a hole leading directly to the road below. Andric thought it was crude, but he hoped it would get used as his father regained his strength. *He is going to get better!* Andric insisted to the part of his mind harboring his doubts.

"Prince Andric!" Barak called from somewhere out of sight.

Not now! The words were felt more than thought. Andric didn't want to deal with anything other than being at his father's side. A twinge of guilt cut through the resentment that was becoming his constant companion. It was probably thanks in no small part to Barak that his father was still alive. Most of the others who had gotten sick were already dead, and the rest barely held on, being tended to in much the same way as the king. Gods' graces, the sickness (or curse, or whatever it was) hadn't taken hold of anyone new since the first group of over six hundred soldiers.

"In here, Barak." Andric tried to sound positive as much as he could manage, but it sounded forced even to him. He was comforted on some level to see Barak; he just didn't feel like being pleasant at the moment. He was sure his friend would understand.

Barak didn't bother climbing into the wagon himself, and from the ground, his head was barely higher than the floor. He bowed formally to the prince, as he had taken to doing more frequently in public lately, but the upturned corner of his mouth reminded the prince how little his friend cared for it. Andric assumed he did it to avoid the judgment of others who considered such things important.

"Jase has finished packing your things, and everything seems ready for our departure. I thought you might like to ride out to the gates and watch Stephir's approach before we join the march."

"*You* thought I might like it, or General Obannern did?"

Barak was absently kicking the heavy mud from his boots. The streets had taken a turn for the worse with the nightly rains. "In truth, it was the general's idea, but he thought it best if I broach the subject with you first. Perhaps he's a bit intimidated by your... cheerful demeanor of late."

Andric laughed humorlessly. "Maybe you should be, too."

Barak waved off the comment. "I've known you far too long to let a foul mood get in the way. It will pass like it always does."

"Of course it will," Andric said flatly.

"I've heard you say that before, too."

Andric stared at the floor as his emotions began to stir again. He knew his mood would be tied to his father's fate, and the physicians' veiled reminders that his father would soon die if they could not discover a cure made it difficult to see any light at the end of the dark road.

Why did it have to be my father? It was such a random thing, to be infected by this mysterious illness like so many of the common soldiers. If perhaps Jevorak Laconeus were a lesser noble, Andric would find it more believable. His father was a good man and a great king. *It's unfair! How could the gods allow...*

Barak's voice brought him back to the conversation, soft and full of compassion. "I can only imagine what you're going through." His friend rarely strayed into sentimental topics, and he seemed about to go on, then retreated to safer territory. "With any luck, a cure will be found."

"Look around you, Barak. Look at this place." Andric's gaze rested on the raised garden in the center of the courtyard filled with plants of varying colors, all foreign but still beautiful. He could almost enjoy it here, but everything was tainted now. Arched doorways, delicate furniture, striking sculptures, all intricately carved by hands that had killed his people, and maybe soon his father.

"I should never have brought you here." He realized his words might be taken the wrong way and hurried to clarify. "It was selfish of me—"

"Nonsense, Andric. I am your advisor and your friend." Barak had dropped any pretense of formality. He lectured Andric in a way only he could get away with. "I'm sure appointing me as your advisor was just your way of getting me to come, but you're not going to change it now. An advisor has duties, and one of them is to remain with his lord through the difficult times and help him stay the course even when everything seems impossible." He paused for a moment, then his tone again softened. "And what kind of friend would I be to leave you alone now?"

Andric couldn't respond, couldn't move. His eyes were unfocused and he couldn't get his mind to grasp hold of any of the swirling thoughts that glanced and slipped away.

"I'm not going anywhere. Well, I suppose technically I'm going back to Remalia, but you know what I mean."

Andric knew Barack was trying to lighten the mood, but he could not make himself smile.

"Andric, you have people that need you here and now. Word is getting out of your father's condition. You can help provide stability in the face of uncertainty."

Anger welled up in the young prince. If the soldiers were finding out, someone must have said something they shouldn't have. They had all agreed to keep the king's condition a secret even after the emissaries left the city. He had known it was only a matter of time until word got out, but it should never have happened this soon. Andric was beginning to think the only person left in the world he could trust was Barak... and Stephir. His brother should be arriving at any time, and then Andric wouldn't have to be in charge of anything.

"No need to linger here any longer, don't you think?" Barak was deferential even in suggesting the obvious. Andric tried to nod but still could not force himself to respond. *Stop acting like a child! You're a prince of Remalia, for the love of the gods.* With a supreme effort, he raised his eyes to look at Barak. Then he was on his feet. Then he descended the wagon steps. He still could not make his eyes focus.

"Let's go," Andric managed to say woodenly. "Have Jase bring our horses."

"Already done. He should be here any minute."

Andric leaned against the side of the wagon, his gaze moved between his father and the ground. Barak reported on unimportant information to fill the silence, but Jase arrived before Barak delved into some obscure theory or history or whatever happened to cross his mind next. They mounted and rode out of the elaborate courtyard onto the wide and winding avenue back through the city. Andric was eager to be out of this cursed town, but he didn't want to leave his father, so he kept pace with the king's plodding escort as they made their way to the gates to await Stephir's arrival with the remainder of the Remalian army.

General Obannern and several other officers were already at the city gates, watching the steady and methodical approach of the coming force, stretching as far as they could see down the Spice Road. Andric was sweating as the sun climbed to late morning, pulling the moisture out of the heavy mud and wrapping them all in a smothering blanket of humidity. He didn't know which he wanted more right now—to be back in the more temperate Teris or to stay in Kushaan to avenge his father. With a Kushaani army waiting in Remalia for him to come and kill them, he might get the best of both wishes.

"Good morning, Your Highness," Obannern said with his usual stoicism and a polite bow from horseback.

Andric returned the greeting and nodded acknowledgment to some of the others with him as he fell in beside them. They kept their gaze fixed southward toward the marching army. Stephir rode with other nobles and general officers at the head of the column. Several scouts and outriders had preceded them to announce their coming. Behind Stephir, thousands of cavalry formed the first section of the army, with countless foot soldiers following. Hundreds of lumbering wagons were interspersed through their ranks, carrying food, tents, and hundreds of other items to supply the vast army.

Even after seeing Stephir and their father depart Teris, Andric was amazed at the sheer numbers approaching the city. Though most of their soldiers were beyond his sight, the approaching armored cavalry was more than imposing enough to deter any enemies of Remalia. Andric could not imagine anything withstanding their might. *If only they could defeat an illness so easily,* he thought but quickly shoved it aside. This was not the time for dwelling on dark thoughts.

Andric had the sudden urge to ride out to his brother, to greet him on the road, to turn everything over to him. All the responsibility, the grief, the worries, the concerns—they would soon be Stephir's. The thought was bitter-sweet, but he remained in place as his brother approached.

Stephir looked regal and strong, much more a future king than Andric ever could. Finally, he motioned his officers to stay behind him and rode out to greet his brother. Stephir's cape, the deep blue of the Laconeus family fringed in gold-threaded embroidery, caught in the afternoon breeze and flowed beautifully behind him as if the wind also acknowledged his divine right to be the next ruler of Remalia. Andric was both proud and jealous of his brother, though he felt a pang of guilt at the latter. This was no time to be thinking of himself. He spurred his horse and met his brother before the gates of Nanjab.

Andric intended to keep the reunion formal in front of the whole of the Remalian army, but Stephir dismounted as they drew near. Andric followed suit and offered his hand to Stephir, but his brother brushed past and pulled Andric into an embrace. Andric felt self-conscious with such a naked display of affection, but he returned the embrace, wanting all the onlookers to see the two brothers unequivocally united.

"So, how do you like Remalia?" Stephir gestured around him in a wide arc with a smile that did not touch his eyes. Andric couldn't tell if Stephir was teasing him, putting on a show for the onlookers, or if he was genuinely happy to have conquered the new territory.

"Well done." Andric offered his congratulations in mock sincerity. "You conquered an oven. I don't know how we could have lived without it." To Andric's relief, Stephir laughed.

The army was coming to a halt behind Stephir. Andric wanted them to keep marching so he didn't have to stay in Nanjab a moment longer, but Stephir needed to see their father before they continued. The king's coach waited in the shade beneath the arched passage of the city walls.

"I'm sure Father is eager to see you." Andric felt the lie weigh on his tongue.

"Let's not keep him waiting then."

They mounted Kobo and Havvoron and rode the short distance back to the gates of Nanjab. Sister Merranine met them beside the wagon as the two princes dismounted in a synchronized fluid motion. They had both learned horsemanship from Mistress Teer, and their skill was nearly matched.

"Your Highnesses," Sister Merranine curtsied to the brothers, though Andric knew it was really for Stephir's benefit. She and Andric had gotten past formalities in the days they had spent attending the king together. Stepping closer, she almost whispered, "Prince Stephir, how much do you know of your father's condition?"

Stephir glanced at Andric. "I gather he's very ill, but I haven't been told any details."

In hushed tones, Sister Merranine filled Stephir in about the sickness, much as she had explained it to Andric, though Andric was surprised she included a few of the conjectures Barak had made. Satisfied she had sufficiently prepared Stephir, she led them to the rear of the wagon. The two elantir who would ride with the king descended the steps and bowed to Stephir.

Sister Merranine followed the two brothers into the cool confines of the brightly colored wagon. Andric wished he could ride with his father, both for the sake of being with him and because it was so much cooler with the elantir carefully maintaining a comfortable temperature. Linen curtains were fixed over the windows, not heavy enough to keep out the light, but the difference from being outside in the noonday sunlight meant their eyes needed to adjust a bit before they could see clearly. The wagon swayed slightly as they made their way to where the king lay in his bed.

Sister Merranine warned Stephir that his father was probably unable to talk to him, but Stephir seemed not to hear. Andric couldn't blame him. He recalled the moments when he first arrived at his father's side. He could not be certain it was the Holy Couple's intervention that had given him a last chance to say his goodbyes to his father, but he chose to believe it was. He offered a silent prayer to Yonvaar and Kerail that Stephir would have the same opportunity.

Stephir knelt reverently at his father's bedside and grasped his frail hand. After looking at the king for a moment, his brother bowed his head. Andric guessed Stephir was offering the same prayer Andric had prayed a hundred times. Finally, Stephir looked up and called his father. His voice was clear and strong.

Jevorak did not stir. Stephir called again, but there was no response. His father's chest gently rose and fell, weak and unnaturally slow. The king remained in his perpetual slumber, restful and slowly withering away, oblivious to his son's plea for a moment of lucidity.

Andric felt a pang of guilt. Why had the gods allowed him the chance to talk to their father, but Stephir, the pious one, was denied the opportunity?

Andric had been certain his father would wake up when Stephir arrived at his side. Sister Merranine gently called for Stephir to leave him to his rest. Stephir gently kissed his father's hand, then rose to his feet and let it slip from his grasp. Stephir took a deep breath and drew himself up.

"Give me a moment." His voice was strong and commanding, his face unreadable. For a few moments, Stephir leaned his shoulder against the wagon wall, arms and ankles crossed, head bowed, taking slow and deep breaths. Andric wanted to go over to him, to lay a comforting hand on his shoulder, but his feet seemed rooted to the floor. He knew there was something more he should do, but nothing seemed to spur him forward. Somehow, Stephir's reaction to the situation seemed so much more regal and befitting his station than Andric had felt when he had been at his father's side for the first time.

"How many know it's this bad?" Stephir asked, his voice betraying a hint of strain.

Andric felt guilty he hadn't done a better job of maintaining the secret. "Only the physicians and Divinarim that attend him have seen him. Oh, and Barak I suppose."

"You brought Barak?" Andric couldn't tell what Stephir thought about it.

"Yes, he's been very helpful. He even offered ideas that have helped keep father alive." Stephir frowned and nodded, but said nothing, so Andric went on. "General Obannern and a few others as well. We did our best to limit those who saw him."

Stephir maintained a heavy silence. At last, with a nod to Sister Merranine, Stephir signaled he was ready to leave. Andric squinted at the noon sun flooding into the wagon when the physician opened the lacquered wood door. The three exited the wagon and the elantir climbed back inside to tend to the king on the long journey home.

After thanking Sister Merranine, the brothers greeted General Obannern and Consul Rellat. They exchanged a few pleasantries and offered Stephir their congratulations on the victories he had won. Stephir asked if there was anything noteworthy he needed to know before they departed Nanjab.

"No, Your Highness. You're already aware of the important things. The rest has been taken care of."

Andric hoped the meeting with the Vanassi envoy was not one of the things Stephir was already aware of. He was not especially proud of the way he had acted. Stephir didn't mention it, and Andric certainly had no intention of bringing it up.

Barak appeared from wherever he had been and Stephir smiled in greeting. "Barak, how did you let my brother drag you all the way down here?"

"Your Highness has it all wrong," Barak said after giving a half-decent bow. "I was hoping to gain a first-hand appreciation for the saddle soreness and heat stroke real soldiers endure, and Prince Andric was gracious enough to afford me that opportunity. It has been truly eye-opening."

"Well, I understand you've been a great help in addressing the illness affecting our soldiers. Thank you."

"Would that I could do more, Your Highness."

Stephir appeared as anxious to continue the march northward as Andric was. He declined the suggestion to have lunch before continuing the march, opting instead to eat in the saddle, and gave the order to get everyone moving again.

Andric felt a mix of pride and guilt as he rode toward the head of the column with Stephir and High General Kuymon. His noble birth gave him the right to be there, but he somehow felt out of place among these men who had earned their place in the world. He hadn't fought in a single battle or done anything noteworthy. He had missed his opportunity for glory and honor. He felt the resentment at having been left behind in Teris rise in his chest again. *You'll have your chance*, the voice in his head told him.

Andric's mood lightened when he saw Frey waiting with the rest of Stephir's retinue. The always-gregarious marquis would no doubt soon be regaling him with stories of the battles Andric had missed.

"Marquis, many thanks for keeping my brother's hide intact."

"Well, now that you're here, Your Highness, the job is all yours if you'd like it," Frey said with a smile, but Andric felt something was off.

He's probably just tired.

In short order, Stephir received word that the army was ready to move, and at last, Andric was riding at Stephir's side as he had always envisioned. Of course, his father lay dying in a carriage behind them, Remalia was invaded, and they were cut off from communicating with Teris or Balinth's—so perhaps not quite as he had always envisioned.

Stephir gave Andric the highlights of the last several weeks, with High General Kuymon or Frey filling in details when they thought it was merited, usually when Stephir was leaving out something about himself. Occasionally, some officer or another would approach and report on something deemed worthy of the prince's attention. Most of the time, Andric could not fathom why Stephir would want to hear about things like ore supplies or axle grease, but a report of Kushaani forces following a day and a half behind them received his full attention.

"Shouldn't we deal with them so we don't have them harassing our rear?" Andric asked, trying to sound like an advisor, not a little brother who was worried.

"This is what they do," Stephir answered casually. "They get close enough for us to think we should attack, but they fall back as we approach, pulling us away from our course. I've set forces to hold a line at key locations south of Nanjab. They won't be getting through that anytime soon."

Stephir laid out his plan for securing the newly held lands for Andric. Andric noticed he did not mention any plans for titles and land holdings. It was no doubt because he wanted to avoid a fight with the nobles for the time being. A part of Andric hoped Stephir's plans included giving some or even all the new lands to him, though as he considered what he would do if it were up to him, he quickly realized it was far beyond his capabilities to decide the best course of action. He was again grateful he was not in Stephir's shoes.

It was late afternoon when Andric's attention was drawn to a pair of riders approaching from the northern road, riding hard. He was surprised when four Divinarim rode ahead to investigate. He said as much to Stephir, who explained that the standard protocol in the army for anyone moving along the road was to ride wide of the vanguard. Whoever the riders were, they weren't part of the army. Andric could not see much detail from this distance but could at least make out that the riders were stopped, questioned, and then held as a Divinar returned to the princes. Andric assumed this was not standard protocol either, and he was curious who would merit the exception. He didn't have to wonder long.

"Your Highness, the riders we stopped are two scouts, one of whom is a Sa'ari who claims to have urgent news he wishes to deliver to you personally."

Captain Min? Again? A sense of foreboding rose inside Andric.

"He identified himself as Captain... Koran Minsolum." Andric smiled at the butchered attempt to pronounce the Sa'ari's foreign name. "What is your desire, my lord?"

Could he have already come back through the pass? Andric was eager to hear what news Captain Min brought back but deferred to Stephir.

"Let's go hear what he has to say." Stephir kicked Havvoron into a gallop. Andric was surprised Stephir would ride to meet the scouts instead of the other way around. Perhaps he wanted to receive the news of Teris away from the other nobles and generals. Andric wondered if he feared the worst as he did. Maybe he was just tired of the slow pace of being tied to the army and wanted an excuse to have some wind in his hair for a moment's respite from the heat of the afternoon sun.

Andric was not sure if he was supposed to join Stephir, but when Archpaladin Nophet and High General Kuymon followed Stephir Andric followed.

Captain Min looked wearier and more travel-worn than the last time Andric saw him. The bitter memory of when they had first crossed paths soured further with the certainty that seeing the scout again meant something else was wrong. Andric desperately hoped the battalion he sent back to Teris had reached the city before the Kushaani had.

The two scouts saluted Stephir and the others.

"Captain, I wish I could say it's good to see you again so soon," Stephir said in greeting, "but I'm certain whatever it is you have to report is not good news."

"My lords, the Kushaani have taken Balinth's Fortress."

"Akraharr's stones!" Stephir practically spat the words out. Andric hadn't heard Stephir swear since they were teenagers. It was unnerving but expressed exactly what Andric felt. "How is that possible?"

"We were unable to determine that. We found no survivors of the battle and encountered only one soldier just south of the Worrin Gap who escaped an ambush at the fortress. I got close enough to Balinth's walls to see for myself. They're staying hidden, but I spotted the same Kushaani we saw in the Velspars. They have killed the defenders and placed some of the bodies at posts on the walls to appear as if they're still standing watch." General Kuymon muttered something under his breath, but the captain continued. "I believe they've been making pretenses that the fortress is still open to lure troops inside. I couldn't see much, only what I could glean from a distance. There was no way to determine how many hold the fortress."

Balinth's is lost! Andric's mind struggled to find a handhold in the whirling doubts and fears. *How could such a force have taken it? There simply weren't enough...! The fortress has never fallen! Its fortifications are impenetrable! How could such a small force...? Would more defenders have helped? Could this be my fault? I could have saved them. I should've sent the troops there instead of having them return to Teris. But how could I have known? Captain Min recommended it! Why didn't I listen to him? What must he think of me now? Will he tell Stephir he advised me to reinforce Balinth's but fool that I am, I disregarded his advice?*

Andric's heart pounded against his ribcage. Any second Stephir would hear Andric could have prevented the fall of Balinth's Fortress. It would be better if Stephir heard it from Andric rather than a scout. It was the only honorable thing to do. *I should just say it now and let him know before he heard it from—*

"There is nothing to do but continue north and deal with whatever we find there," Stephir said with an impossible calm. "What should we tell the others?"

"Tell them nothing for now, my lord," the high general said emphatically. "It will be of no help, and will almost certainly hurt morale. Many of them already believe this war was cut short, and no doubt rumors have spread about the invasion and other problems we face. This will be a serious blow to them. Better to delay it as long as possible."

"Agreed. This remains among us."

"What would you have me do, my lord?" Captain Min asked.

"I hate to ask this of you, Captain," Stephir said with what sounded to Andric like sincere regret, "I know you've already made the journey between here and Balinth's three times in as many weeks, but I would ask you to return to the fortress once again and ensure no surprises are coming south. I will be sending twenty more scouts with you."

"As you wish, Your Highness."

Andric couldn't tell if Min was happy about having a full patrol of scouts under his command again. However he felt about it, he conducted himself admirably.

Stephir regarded him in silence for a moment, then went on. "I am also going to send one hundred Messian lancers with you. They will have a captain commanding them, but their captain will report to you. Do with them as you see fit."

Andric was shocked. Surely there had never been a scout of any rank in command of combat troops, let alone an elite cavalry unit.

"Your Highness," High General Kuymon said, concern in his voice. "It would be very unusual for one captain to be reporting to another captain. Perhaps a promotion is in order to avoid confusion among the men." The only detectable sign any of this was registering with Captain Min was his jaw muscles flexing as he clenched his teeth.

"A commander?" Stephir asked with mild skepticism in his voice.

"Perhaps not commander. We could establish an interim rank." Kuymon offered. Stephir frowned, clearly uncomfortable with the idea. Kuymon went on, "High captain?" Stephir shook his head. "The Calavians have a rank called a *santate*," the high general offered.

"That doesn't even sound real, and nobody would have any idea what it meant. It would make him sound even more foreign."

"Major captain?" Kuymon continued, throwing out another idea. Andric wanted to laugh at how the scene must appear to Captain Min, watching the crown prince and high general creating a new rank out of thin air, and he would be the first man in the history of Remalia to carry it.

The vanguard of the army had nearly caught up to the group. "Captain major. Major captain. Captain major. I like that one better." Stephir returned his attention to Min. "Forgive me, Captain. Remind me of your full name again."

"Quarian Minanthsolum, Your Highness." Captain Min sounded hoarse. Andric could imagine why.

"Quarian Minanthsolum, you are hereby promoted by my hand to captain major in the Royal Army of Remalia, in the four hundred and thirty-fourth year of its founding. You will—" The approaching army caused Stephir to stop. The men blocked the road, and Stephir was going to have to either get out of the way of his own army, order a halt, or get moving. "You will have to wait until later to receive word on the rest. Thank you again for your service, Captain Major."

Min saluted sharply, fingers over his eyes. Andric wondered if he would keep the same salute or adopt a new one. The scout (*is he still a scout*, Andric wondered) quickly moved his horse off the road as Stephir started moving again with the army, riding stoically with his steady gaze straight ahead.

Andric was struck with how similarly his brother carried himself to their father. He looked for all the world like Jevorak Laconeus' son, and Andric pictured him as King Stephir with the crown on his head. A full minute passed in silence, then High General Kuymon started laughing, interrupting Andric's thoughts.

"That was worth all of the trouble this is going cause, Your Highness," Kuymon said, still laughing.

Stephir seemed to try holding back a smile without success. "Find a solid captain that can handle reporting to a scout. Higher rank or not, that will not be easy to swallow."

Andric felt like he had been left out of some private joke.

"I think I know the right man. I'll speak with him myself."

"And make sure to arrange for him to be outfitted with proper armor and uniform."

"Stephir, what just happened?" Andric asked, a little bewildered. Was this some kind of joke Stephir was playing on somebody? If so, he hoped it was not at Captain Min's expense. "You barely know the man."

"Captain Min—Captain Major Min," Stephir corrected himself, "received high recommendations from Commander Haresh and others. I've been impressed with him. You know him better, and you gave him a personal letter of introduction to have him report to me directly. Do you think it was a mistake to promote him?"

"No, not at all. He's nothing like the typical scouts, but to give him command of a hundred Messian lancers..."

"Most scouts are decent enough men, and good at their jobs, no matter what other soldiers think of them. But when you find exceptional talent and character, you cultivate it. Besides, it isn't a permanent arrangement. I'm curious to see what he does with it."

"Maybe you should promote Barak too." Andric mused offhandedly. "He helped the elantir figure out a few things with father's illness, even if it only slowed—" He stopped short, not wanting to say too much with other nobles riding behind them within earshot.

"Maybe I should," Stephir said, sounding more serious than Andric had intended with his comment. "If he could fix the communication problem, I'd grant him lordship over the entire Kushaani lands we just conquered and give him a place at court." He chuckled and turned a wry smile to Andric.

Andric laughed aloud at the thought. "I don't think Barak would accept if you offered him half the kingdom. Besides, can you imagine Barak at court?"

Stephir's smile softened. "Oh, I've imagined it before. It would be infinitely more fun and more trouble than the promotion I just gave to Captain Min."

"Captain Major," Andric corrected.

"As long as you're making up new titles, I was thinking 'archmarquis' has a nice ring to it," Frey said with a restrained smile.

"Well," Stephir said with a gravely serious tone Andric recognized as teasing their cousin, "before the king would ever be willing to consider such an outlandish request, you would have to do something spectacularly noteworthy for the good of the kingdom."

"My feats on the field of battle aren't enough to have earned the honor?"

"True, you've dispatched more than a few Kushaani, but I think Lady Haedep is giving you a run for your money there. I'm afraid you'll have to do better."

"It's a contest then!" Frey announced. "Marchioness, are you game?"

"Always," the lady said with a fierce grin.

The light-hearted conversation helped Andric avoid darker thoughts as they continued toward the daunting tasks ahead. The sun was beginning to creep toward the horizon when Stephir called a halt to the day's march.

"We still have several hours of daylight. Shouldn't we keep moving?" Andric asked with some consternation. He feared he sounded accusatory.

"Andric, the forward army stretches back over ten miles. It will be hours before the last soldiers catch up. In the meantime, those in the fore will establish camp."

Andric felt abashed. It was a basic enough concept, and one he vaguely remembered hearing in some lesson in the past, but he had never had to think about it in real life. *How many more issues am I completely ignorant of?* he wondered. He swore to himself he would do his best to learn them all.

Stephir was going to be king, and Andric would be his greatest general.

CHAPTER XXV
ANDRIC

Despite the circumstances that reunited them sooner than expected, two days of riding with Stephir had significantly improved Andric's spirits. He thought he might be able to enjoy the holiday feast if it weren't for the infernal cacophony coming from outside the banquet tent. Andric had gotten used to the night sounds in the wilderness, and he was able to block them out most of the time, but this was almost unbearable. The roasted lamb with blood orange and stafa bean sauce and other dishes laid out on the table were delicious, but it was almost impossible to enjoy them amid such distraction. The noise inside the tent was reaching ridiculous levels as the assembled nobles, top-ranking officers, and clergy tried to make themselves heard in their conversations over the noise from outside.

"For the love of the gods!" the prince exclaimed in frustration. He signaled a nearby servant to approach. "Tell one of the elantir to come in here."

The young man gave a slight bow and exited the tent. In moments, one of the elantir entered the tent, scanning the faces seated at the dinner tables until he spotted Andric, then hurried over to the prince, giving the elantir's unique salute. "Your Highness summoned me? Is the temperature in the room not to your liking?" the middle-aged man asked humbly.

"No, the temperature's fine, but is there something you can do about this infernal noise? Block it out or something?"

"I cannot perform that elant, Your Highness, but I could let Lieutenant Lianalie know of your request."

"Tell her to take care of it before I lose my mind!"

The elantir bowed and left the tent.

"Your Highness," Barak said in a gentle but chastising tone, "you should learn to appreciate what we are experiencing." By rank or title, Barak had no business being at the banquet, but Andric enjoyed having him there anyway. The discomfort his common status and, even more significantly, his idiosyncrasies, caused in the other nobles just added to Andric's fun. He knew Barak didn't like being brought into these situations, so he tried not to subject his friend to it too often.

"I don't mind crickets usually, but this is ridiculous!" Andric complained.

"They aren't crickets, they're icewing passalids. They only make this sound for a few nights every year when they're mating."

"The daughter of Earlessa Amarifal makes the same noise," Frey offered with a wicked smile. Barak rolled his eyes and Andric laughed. Barak didn't care for Frey's ribald comments, which just made Frey do it all the more.

"Where is your brother, Prince Andric?" Marchioness Haedep asked with refined grace, not deigning to dignify Frey's comment with a reaction. Andric felt slightly guilty for laughing. "Will he be joining us?" Others at the table looked in Andric's direction for an answer to the question they no doubt had as well.

Tonight was the Feast of Da'vashin, a celebration honoring one's ancestors. If he had been in Teris, the day would have been spent visiting the royal catacombs deep in the Mount of the Gods and placing flowers on the sepulchers, sitting through a worship service at one of the grand temples, and a great feast at the end of the day. But today's observances consisted of marching, a brief benediction by Father Daemmer at mid-day, and finally the banquet.

The tables at the head of the pavilion where Andric sat were covered with white cloth and arranged in a gentle arc. Colorful paper boxes decorated with the symbols of the gods were set at each seat, representing the tombs where their ancestors were buried. After the feast, each person would take their box to a fire outside to be burned, the rising smoke and ashes symbolizing the journey of the souls of their ancestors to the realms of the gods.

"I'm sure he'll be joining us soon," Andric said, trying to sound reassuring. High General Kuymon, Father Daemmer, and Consul Rellat were also missing. Andric hoped everything was all right, or at least not any worse than they already were after the news about the loss of Balinth's. His mind wandered, thinking through the myriad implications of the fortress being controlled by the Kushaani.

Suddenly the voices in the spacious pavilion sounded like shouts as the noises of the world outside vanished. Everyone stopped talking, and a near-perfect silence settled over the room like a heavy blanket of thick snowflakes on a winter night. It lasted only a moment before people resumed talking, but it was enough for Andric to regain the measure of calm he desperately needed.

Conversations continued much as they did most nights, with the nobles sharing gossip of the day or any other number of inanities. The only thing that held Andric's attention was hearing about the battles others had fought. He was jealous and longed to have his own stories to tell.

Andric's attention was suddenly drawn to the entrance of the pavilion as the white canvas doors were pulled aside and Stephir entered, followed by High General Kuymon and the two priests. Everyone rose and bowed as Stephir made his way to the head table to sit next to Andric.

"My lords and ladies, forgive my tardiness. Please continue enjoying the feast," Stephir said with a smile that disappeared the moment everyone took their seats.

Andric leaned close to Stephir and whispered. "Is everything all right?"

"Nothing earth-shattering. We'll talk after dinner." Stephir tried to sound casual, but Andric could hear the tension in his voice. Something was bothering his brother.

"Why is it so quiet in here?" Stephir asked with a look of curiosity on his face.

Frey was the first to jump in with an answer. "Your brother doesn't enjoy the dulcet tones of a thousand lovers enjoying themselves."

"Actually," Barak said in the scholarly tone that came so naturally to the clergy of Viance, "they go silent when they're mating. The sounds are only used to call for a mate."

"Maybe they should try alcohol. It's much more enjoyable for everyone." Frey was perhaps the one person who could come up with a quip for anything the scholarly Cannessi might say. Barak was likely to lose his patience with the irreverent marquis, so Andric decided he had better step in.

"I asked the elantir to block the sound. It was ruining the banquet," Andric said in answer to Stephir's question.

"Well, at least they can do *that*." The comment was unusually derogatory for Stephir. Something was bothering his brother. Stephir picked at the food with little interest while the rest of the room dined and returned to their conversations. Soon he stood and called for attention. Everyone rose to their feet as well.

In the unnatural silence, Stephir's voice carried easily throughout the large tent. He held his goblet lightly as he spoke. "Tonight is the Feast of Da'vashin. Today, we turn our hearts to those who have gone before us and give them honor and thanks for this amazing world they built for us. It reminds us that the success of our lives will be measured not by the feasts we eat, or by the fine clothes we wear, or even by the friends we enjoy, but by the world we leave for our children. No success in any other endeavor will be worthy of honor if we leave a darker world for future generations than the one we inherited from our forbearers. *Da'vashin!*" Stephir raised his goblet in a toast to the dead.

"*Da'vashin!*" two score voices echoed the toast holding their goblets aloft. Cups were drained, and everyone sat after Stephir again took his seat. Andric looked forward to forgetting the cares of the world for one evening with the free-flowing wine that would finish out the night.

"Come with me," Stephir said, leaning close to Andric. Stephir stood and High General Kuymon followed him. Before people could rise to their feet again, Stephir waved them back into their seats. Andric was unhappy about the interruption but hoped whatever Stephir wanted wouldn't take long so he could quickly return to the festivities. Consul Rellat, who was seated at another table, met them near the entrance. Servants held the pavilion curtains open as the four men stepped into the night. Andric didn't know which struck him harder, the sudden heat or the chirping of countless insects.

Stephir turned to a Divinar. "Inform Archpaladin Nophet that I require his presence at my command pavilion."

Frey had told Andric about the words exchanged between Nophet and Stephir, and the tension between them since. It was subtle, but Andric could hear it in the way Stephir spoke to the arch paladin, or about him. Stephir took a few steps, then called to the holy knight, "And send for an elantir to keep it quiet in my pavilion as well."

The entrance curtain parted once again, and Andric expected to see Frey coming to join them, but it was Intendant Vestin who emerged. She was a short and stocky woman, the ranking member of the Teraithian faith in the army, regal in the way she held herself, but with a sternness that made Andric want to straighten his posture.

She nodded to Stephir. "You summoned me, Your Highness?"

"Yes, thank you for joining us, Intendant. Please follow me to the command pavilion." He strode toward the pavilion flanked by a pair of Divinarim, leaving the rest with no choice but to follow. Flickering flames in braziers lighted their path, although the silvery light from the moons would have been adequate. The sounds of celebration throughout the vast camp mixed with the song of the icewings into an indistinguishable whirlwind of sound. Guards at the command pavilion pulled the tent flaps aside and saluted as Stephir strode past them.

Andric was disappointed it was not cool inside. Hopefully, the elantir Stephir had summoned to deal with the noise would fix the temperature as well. Scanning the room, Andric was surprised to see the priestess of Sharin Dara he had met in Nanjab waiting with two of the gleaming holy knights of their goddess. Andric tried remembering her name. *Intercessor something*. She bowed gracefully as Stephir made his way past the various tables and chairs toward her. A commander Andric didn't recognize stood with them.

The small group waited near the high-backed, polished redwood seat reserved for the king. Andric wished he could see his father sitting in that chair. Not for the first time that day, he wondered if next year on the Feast of Da'vashin he would be placing flowers at his father's tomb. Stephir went to the seat, placed an arm on the back, and casually leaned against it. Consul Rellat stood next to the intercessor and had a quiet word with her.

The only noise filling the air was from the insects outside, barely muted by the thin pavilion walls. Andric felt a trickle of sweat roll down the small of his back. He tried to imagine what this was about, but each possibility took him down a dark path. Andric was grateful when the archpaladin finally entered the command pavilion and crossed the room to join the others. He saluted Stephir, arm across his waist, fingertips resting at his sword hilt at his hip.

"I'm sorry for interrupting your festivities tonight," Stephir apologized, sounding more weary than heartfelt, "but there is a grave matter to discuss. I received a report tonight that Warden Commander Tullare Sammet, the provincial warden responsible for securing the Northern Kesh Province, is accused of atrocities, including the massacre of thirty-two men, women, and children in a village outside of Tarsapta."

Andric's stomach lurched at the thought of such a despicable act; and perpetrated by a Remalian no less.

"This is not the first report of abuses by Warden Commander Sammet. She has received two previous reprimands. She is Duke Elel Markham's sister, making her a noble. She's also a highly accomplished commander with many commendations, which is why she was appointed as the provincial warden in the first place. Sammet's history, as well as the report of this latest incident, will be ready for you by morning."

Stephir then addressed Andric directly. "Because Sammet is a noble, you will preside over the inquiry. You will have a warrant issued by the crown giving you full authority in all matters, including conducting a tribunal, meting out justice in any way short of stripping her of titles and lands, and establishing a new provincial government if necessary. You will be advised in all matters by Intercessor Henden. If you determine to convene a tribunal, you will preside, but the intercessor will conduct the proceeding."

"Your Highness, if I may," the intercessor said with a tone of asking permission to speak.

"By all means, Intercessor," Stephir said politely, although his expression didn't invite questions. Andric still had a hard time believing the young woman had already reached the rank of intercessor, a position more appropriate for someone twice her age.

"I deeply regret that I have no experience as a justicar. I am, of course, at your complete disposal, but perhaps you would be best served by another who has the requisite knowledge of judicial procedures to ensure—"

Consul Rellat cut her off. "Intercessor Henden, His Highness is quite aware of your experience." Rellat's smooth but firm tenor stressed the decision was not open for discussion. "This matter requires a delicate touch, and you are perfectly suited to call upon Sharin Dara's blessing to that end."

The intercessor curtsied deeply with her head bowed. "Of course, Consul."

Stephir continued as though there had been no interruption. "Commander Kasten will accompany you with a company of Messian lancers under his command." Andric thought being given command over merely one company of men must seem like a demotion to the commander. "If you determine that it's necessary to remove Sammet as the provincial warden, Commander Kasten will take her place." Stephir's declaration made things obvious. Andric felt foolish for not understanding sooner. Barak probably would have grasped the situation immediately.

"There is a further complication. Warden Commander Sammet has apparently been taking it upon herself to establish security in the province by forcing the Kushaani to become Teraithians, by the sword if necessary. The reports accuse her of establishing a cult-like following among her soldiers, again based on her Teraithian beliefs. We don't punish our people for their faith, but I will not tolerate anyone forcing others into it either.

"This is a very delicate matter." Stephir paused and looked from one face to another. His gaze finally rested on the archpaladin. "Intendant Vestin, I know you're the highest-ranking Teraithian south of Balinth's Fortress. I would like to send someone of stature from your faith, but I prefer that you remain with the army. I would appreciate your input on the matter. Who would you recommend we send from among the Teraithian faithful that can help quell any religious dissension?"

The intendant deliberated for a moment, her lips narrowing to a thin line. Andric didn't know the woman well, but in all his interactions with the king's advisors over the last two days, he hadn't heard her offer one word of advice. She had been vigilant and attentive, but cold and distant. Her silence stretched on uncomfortably, and Andric was starting to think Stephir may have to press her on the matter, but then she turned to Nophet.

"Archpaladin, you're the next highest ranking in the Faith this side of the Velspars, are you not?"

"My authority is limited to the Order of the Divine Flame, your grace."

"But your position as archpaladin is higher than any other clergy here in the south."

Nophet studied the diminutive but imposing intendant for a moment before carefully replying. "I cannot speak for the Kushaani, but among the Remalians that is technically true as far as I am aware."

"Then I would ask you to lead the contingent of your men that accompany Prince Andric in this matter. You may be able to find out more about the truth of what's happening than anyone else, and your position should hold great weight with Warden Commander Sammet. If the problems Prince Stephir has so clearly outlined truly exist, you will be able to assist Prince Andric in rooting them out with as little difficulty as possible."

Stephir nodded slowly, and Andric wondered whether his brother had even considered sending the archpaladin. Stephir's next words answered the question. "I am glad to see we are of the same mind, Intendant." Andric could tell Stephir was being calculated with his words. "Tensions are no doubt high in the area, and I fear violence could erupt with any misstep. Having you there to prevent that if possible, and to help ensure Prince Andric's safety if not, is the best I could hope for under the circumstances."

"Your Highness," Nophet said with a note of caution in his voice, "my highest duty is to ensure the protection of the king of Remalia, which it is my great honor to do." He stopped short of saying the words, but they all knew what he implied. *You are not the king.*

"Lord Nophet, I will speak plainly. My father is gone. His body is barely kept alive by artifice. I would keep him alive in any way possible in the hope that our Divine Parents see fit to bestow new life on him. I may not wear the crown yet, but for all intents and purposes, and by right, I rule Remalia now. Do you wish to challenge me on this point?"

The cacophony outside was abruptly cut off, and a heavy silence permeated the tent. One moment stretched into another, and another. The air cooled, and Andric felt a shiver run up his spine. Nophet glanced at the intendant and then back to Stephir before answering with a crisp bow. "No, Your Highness. I will do my duty as a Teraithian and a Remalian, as you command."

"Then you all leave first thing in the morning. May the gods go with you." Everyone bowed in unison, but Stephir was already walking toward the pavilion entrance. Andric looked at the others, wanting to say something, but Nophet strode from the tent, an aura of palpable indignation surrounding the archpaladin. A slight smile played on the thin lips of the intendant as she, too, turned and left.

Well, this is going to be pleasant.

CHAPTER XXVI
VIKKIN

Vikkin woke in the darkness of his tent. Having a private tent was one of the privileges he enjoyed as archpaladin of the Order of the Divine Flame. It was nearly an hour before dawn. He knew exactly what time it was; he had awoken at this time nearly his entire life. He was up instantly with no sleepiness hanging on him. His morning routine was second nature, but every action was deliberate, precise, efficient. He untied a small flap next to his cot and let it drop to allow in the light from the torches burning outside his tent.

Soon he was washed and dressed, and he called for the Divinar standing guard outside to enter. The junior knight had the privilege this morning of helping him don the archpaladin's armor. The process required little of his attention, and his mind was absorbed reflecting on his exchange with Prince Stephir and Intendant Vestin the night before. The situation was complex and delicate. Complex he was well equipped to handle; delicacy was not in his nature. It had never been required to perform his duties before, but it seemed war had changed that.

Before leaving Teris, Archseraph Charin had summoned him to the Great Temple of Teraithia on the Mount of the Gods. It was a shame the other gods were allowed to have a presence there. Teraithia was the only god truly worthy of the honor, and the archseraph wanted to make that a reality. He had worked for years to increase their goddess's power in Remalia. Teraithia's faithful had been sent throughout the kingdom to bring more disciples into the true light of the Queen of the Heavens and all Creation.

However, the seeds of faith were too often choked by the weeds of weakness, with Remalia's people clinging like infants to the soft blanket of their lesser gods. He expected such frailty in peasants or even the spoiled and vain nobles. But to see it in the otherwise mighty King Jevorak and his sons was a constant source of disappointment for the archpaladin and outright frustration for the archseraph.

Oh, the king claimed to give each god their due respect, but the Sharinists had managed to insinuate themselves into nearly every aspect of Remalia's government. He would be impressed, if they had any idea what to do with that kind of influence. And the Laconeus family had long been spiritual disciples of Yonvaar and Kerail. Love, peace, forgiveness—these were the indulgences of those without the strength to bend the world to their will.

At least the kings of Remalia no longer allowed the Mount to be utterly defiled by permitting the Sykorians and followers of Akraharr to have a place there. Sykorian hedonism was nothing more than an excuse for every form of depraved gratification of the flesh. Her worshippers were the weakest on the face of Baon, and yet the whore goddess had immense power due to the vast numbers who succumbed to the seduction of lust, gluttony, and the oblivion of drugs. Worshippers of Akraharr valued individual freedom above all else. Theirs was a vision of anarchy and chaos. Teraithia could reward the mighty and cunning in such an environment, but there was far more power to be had in controlling and ruling others.

The Order of the Divine Flame, through unsurpassed martial skill and unwavering devotion to the kings of Remalia, had long ago secured for itself the honor of guarding the Mount of the Gods and many generations of the royal family. He loved that duty more than anything, which was why it had troubled him when Archseraph Charin summoned Vikkin to the Grand Temple and commanded him to do everything in his power to bring the Laconeus house into Teraithia's strong embrace; but above all, Prince Andric.

When Vikkin asked for an explanation, the archseraph had said only that war was a time of turmoil and upheaval, and the young prince might prove instrumental in magnifying Teraithia's glory beyond anything they could imagine, or aid in her defeat if lost to another faith. Charin had impressed upon Vikkin with the full weight of Teraithia's divine authority that the archpaladin must prevent that from happening by any means necessary.

Vikkin had been conflicted by the archseraph's commands. The oaths he had sworn to Teraithia many times over as he climbed through the ranks of his order demanded absolute adherence to her will. But the Divinarim also swore an oath they would never interfere with the affairs of the state. Not only was what the archseraph asked a violation of that oath, but if their intentions were ever discovered it would jeopardize the Divinarim's enviable position as guardians of the most powerful and holy place in the entire world. Surely they would all suffer Teraithia's inextinguishable wrath if that honor were lost.

With his armor secured, Vikkin dismissed Divinar Staneff. The archpaladin knew the details of every knight under his command. He walked to a small table against one wall of the tent and dropped to a knee before the golden statue of his goddess. Bowing his head, he whispered his oath of fealty to Teraithia, then asked for her guidance in his endeavor. As always, he gathered his thoughts, focused on understanding Her holy will, and attuned himself to Her divinessence. The presence of power and authority filled his mind, settling in his chest and giving him strength. The familiar feeling brought comfort, like a warm homecoming, assuring him that he was welcome in Her powerful presence. Profound gratitude filled his heart as his goddess's approbation settled over him. A tear escaped his eyelashes and slid down his cheek. He nodded in satisfaction and rose from before the altar to focus on the next task at hand.

Today would be his first real opportunity to spend meaningful personal time with Prince Andric, and he intended to use it as best he could to influence the young man's faith toward Teraithia. It would be much better if the Sharinic priestess was not coming, but that could not be helped. He would simply have to be more circumspect in his efforts.

No food was brought for the archpaladin, as was his custom. Many years ago, he had sworn a personal oath to Teraithia that he would never again eat before noon as a sacrifice and sign of his devotion. It was not an oath of the Divinar order, but now several of his men followed his example. He did not know if they did so out of devotion to Teraithia or out of respect for him. Either way, it pleased him.

He left his tent and made his way through the flickering torchlight to where his horse was being tended to by one of the Divinarim accompanying him in escorting Prince Andric to Tarsapta. He had no doubt everything would be prepared for his departure as he had instructed the night before, but he always personally ensured that every detail was satisfactory. The other Divinarim saluted as he approached, and he gave them a respectful salute in return.

He stepped near his mount and patted the jet-black destrier firmly on his shoulder. At nearly two hands taller than the other mounts in the staging area, the war horse towered over all but Prince Andric's black stallion, which was being prepared by the prince's squire, who bowed as he greeted the arch-paladin. Vikkin began inspecting straps and buckles, and within moments he was satisfied everything was in order.

He felt an unfamiliar restless energy and tried to set his mind to running through the details of what would be required in his absence to ensure nothing had been missed. Frustratingly unable to focus, Vikkin decided to do something routine. Perhaps with part of his attention occupied, he would find the clarity that eluded him.

He opted for a surprise inspection of the Divinarim guarding the tents of the two princes and the wagon housing the king. He had not personally inspected his men since the day before they departed Teris in grand proces-sion. It was difficult to believe almost two months had passed since then. *How things have changed.*

Vikkin waited patiently as Paladin Cantry ordered the men to line up for inspection. If they were surprised, they hid it well. He expected no less. A stoic absence of expression was an important aspect of their duty, and a Divinar was not allowed to guard the royal family until they had sufficiently demonstrated through rigorous training that they could maintain their bearing in any circumstances.

The holy knights were first and foremost warriors, and Vikkin did not expect them to be overly fastidious in the field. However, they were also the guards of the royal family and should be appropriately attired for any task, whether standing as sentinels in the king's court or escorting him on the road to war. He knew he would find them well-ordered, representing both the Order and the Faith with utmost distinction, but he could always find minor things to correct.

The commander stood at attention in front of the small group of knights and pronounced them ready for inspection. Vikkin nodded, acknowledging the efficient assembly of the Divinarim present, then proceeded to step in front of each of them, carefully inspecting every detail until he found at least one blemish. Finding something would not hurt their pride—that was a fore-gone conclusion. On the contrary, they would boast to each other in private about how long it took him to find something and how minor it was. The archpaladin pointed out the hem of a Divinar's cloak, slightly frayed from riding and the wear of the road, then moved on to the next man.

In the background, the muted sounds of soldiers chattering as they prepared their gear for another day's march rose into the cloudless sky, greeting the golden pre-dawn light. He noted as the Sharinists arrived in the staging area that the consul and intercessor were accompanied by their holy knights. They were little more than showpieces to accompany the clergy they were supposedly sworn to protect. From what he had seen, not one of them would qualify to join the Order of the Divine Flame.

Ignoring the Sharinists, Vikkin pulled on a buckle of the Divinar in front of him. The archpaladin's face hardened. A bit of dirt and wear in the field were to be expected, but a loose strap was just sloppy. He said nothing. He did not need to.

Vikkin listened to the princes inside Prince Stephir's tent taking breakfast together before they parted company once again. They would be finished soon enough, and they would be on their way. Commander Kasten arrived as well, alone. His men would undoubtedly be waiting by the road on the way out of camp.

The archpaladin was surprised as he reached the end of the line of Divinarim to see Prince Andric's friend and supposed advisor enter the staging area on his mount, ready to travel. The tiny young man was not worthy to be in the prince's company, let alone his advisor and one of his closest friends. Unlike many others, Vikkin knew the Cannessi was not even an ordained priest of Viance, never mind a *master,* despite others' insistence on using the misplaced title. He kept the matter to himself though—it was one among thousands of secrets he held. He did not see any use for the information at present, and he most likely never would, but he never knew when such things would give him an advantage, so he kept them filed in his mind for the day they might prove useful.

Despite his best efforts to stretch out the inspection so it would end when Prince Andric was ready to depart, the brothers were taking their time and there was nothing to do but dismiss the men to return to their duties. He nodded to Cantry and wordlessly strode from the assembled Divinarim as the paladin gave the orders. Consul Rellat was previewing the documents related to the inquest with the young intercessor. Vikkin normally would not have given them more than a cursory greeting, but there was no telling how long he would be waiting for Prince Andric, so he decided to see if there was any more information he could glean about the situation in Tarsapta.

He knew a little bit about Warden Commander Sammet, as he did many influential people in Remalia, especially those who were Teraithians. He had only met the woman on a few occasions, but she had a reputation as one of the goddess's great disciples. He could believe Sammet had been vigorous in promoting the Faith. But outright abuse of her authority, and even worse, committing a massacre, must surely be an exaggeration or outright vicious fabrication. He was not happy to be sent on this errand, but at least he could ensure that Sammet would receive a fair inquest.

"Good morning, Archpaladin Nophet," the consul greeted him with a slight bow. The intercessor curtsied with arms outstretched. The two holy knights behind them looked on stoically; one was a darker-skinned older man and the other a fair-haired woman, not unpleasant to look at. Vikkin returned their salutations with the formal salute of his office, fingertips touching his forehead, then his heart, then the hilt of his sword. He ignored the knights.

"Consul," he started, keeping his tone casual as he pulled off his gloves, "while we are waiting for Prince Andric, I was hoping you could fill in a few more of the details about the situation with Warden Commander Sammet."

"Was there anything in particular you were interested in?" the priest responded smoothly and noncommittally. The Sharinists were notoriously difficult to pin down on any subject, and more so on sensitive or controversial ones. Their persistent disposition to find the path that caused the least conflict, did the least injury, made them soft and slippery. Although many of the priests were unquestionably intelligent and skilled at their craft, Vikkin still found them annoying to deal with. Fortunately, his duties rarely required him to. Today, however, he was not so fortunate.

"What about the reports of killing the people in the village? Who made the claims? Are they substantiated? What were the circumstances?" Vikkin was well-practiced at disciplining his tone, dealing with facts, not emotions, especially with those outside the Order. He thought it best to keep his skepticism to himself for the time being.

"Intercessor Henden has the complete dossier. You are welcome to review it." Vikkin thought the priest would leave it at that, so he turned to the intercessor intending to request the dossier. The consul then added as almost an afterthought, but with a hard undertone, "I pray the reports are not true."

Another non-answer. Vikkin knew he would get nothing useful from the priest, so he changed the subject and addressed the priestess assigned to accompany them. She was not altogether unattractive, and her light blue eyes held an intelligence he could almost admire. It was highly unusual for someone her age to be an intercessor, but he had been the youngest Divinar appointed as archpaladin in the Order's history, so he was willing to allow for the possibility of exceptional talent. He would give her the benefit of the doubt, for now.

But he also knew that intelligence and talent were no substitute for experience, and he wanted to test her composure under a bit of pressure without alienating her completely. There was no sense in getting on her bad side before they even started. He noted she had replaced her blue kemrelac with a black one worn by the justicars.

"Intercessor," Vikkin kept his tone measured and neutral, "or is it Justicar Henden now?" Vikkin thought he detected a slight look of surprise on the intercessor's face as she looked to the consul.

"I suppose *Justicar* would be more appropriate under the circumstances —just until you return from this assignment," Rellat answered.

Vikkin suppressed a flash of amused pride at having caught them flat-footed on that point but permitted himself the indulgence of letting the hint of a smile show on his lips. "I see. Well, *Justicar*, you mentioned last night that you have limited experience in this area. I am curious what experience you do have?"

If she was shocked or offended by the blunt question, she did not show it. "I have had the standard courses in judicial procedure, evidentiary investigation, and dispute mediation. I also spent half a year serving as a judicial clerk in Presternol," she stated with an air of practiced confidence that belied the fact that they were nothing more than the minimum requirements of any cleric of Sharin Dara.

Perhaps her inexperience could work to his advantage if worse came to worst. "Presternol? I am certain there were weighty matters to be adjudicated between the noble farmers." He managed to keep the sarcasm he intended out of his voice. Truthfully, he knew little of the area other than it was at the heart of the Eastern Reaches and a modest crossroads for trade.

The intercessor shrugged, smiling politely. "Law is law, no matter where it is applied."

With a hint of annoyance in his voice, he pressed. "Yes, well..." he let the unfinished thought hang in the air. "I was curious if you had any experience with disputes of a religious nature."

"All the world seems to be experiencing religious turmoil these days, don't you think?" There was no good response to that question, and he wasn't going to give her the satisfaction of answering. She did not let the question linger between them for more than a moment. "But that is not much of an answer to your question, is it, Archpaladin? Yes, I was involved with many matters in which the question of faith was introduced by one or more parties. One man murdered his family and claimed that Kerail had spoken to him and told him it was a mercy to end their lives rather than making them endure the end of the world."

"And how did you ascertain the truth of his claim?"

"The justicars have been tasked with adjudicating matters according to Remalian law, not with divining the will of the gods. Therefore, it was not necessary to reach the question of what Kerail did or did not tell him. That was a matter we sent his soul to discuss with his deity in the divine realms."

So many things were implied in her answer. She may not have been a justicar, but she was shrewd. The conversation had ended its usefulness. "Excellent. Then we are in good hands. If you will excuse me." He nodded and abruptly turned away from the two clerics and went to take his place at the head of the Divinarim formation. He mounted his war horse and waited in stoic silence for Prince Andric to arrive.

The activities of breaking camp were underway when at last the young prince emerged from the tent, accompanied by Prince Stephir and the Marquis de'Venneshen. The crown prince said a brief goodbye and then left in another direction. The marquis was a more suitable peer and friend for the royal princes than *Master* Ve'Aurben, but Vikkin still did not care for the brash young noble. He was certainly passable with a blade, but his actions were more in line with a Sykorian than a Teraithian, which Vikkin found reprehensible. The archpaladin was just glad the marquis's behavior did not seem to drag the princes toward the whore goddess's ways.

"Barak," the marquis called out louder than necessary.

"Marquis. Your Highness." The Cannessi scholar bowed, greeting the two nobles, formal and timid as always. He could hardly be seen over the back of his diminutive horse.

"Prince Andric told me this morning something that I just had to hear for myself."

"How may I be of service?"

It was clear to Vikkin, as it almost certainly was to the marquis, that the Viancian scholar did not care for the princes' cousin.

"Well, we were discussing the Kushaani invasion, and his highness said that you believe they aren't Kushaani at all. You think they're Kuldrith?"

Ve'Aurben sighed and pulled himself a little taller. "Well, to be more precise, I observed that, based on the description given by Captain Major Minanthsolum, they sounded more like Kuldrith than Kushaani."

The marquis barked out a laugh. "That sounds even more ridiculous than the first time I heard it! And believe me, it sounded ridiculous even then." The marquis glanced at Prince Andric for agreement, but the prince was unusually stoic and looked at his friend thoughtfully. "How in the name of the gods," the marquis continued, "do you suppose an all-but-extinct race of mad men got to the middle of the Velspars from halfway around the world with supposedly a greater force than any of the Kushaani armies we've seen here in the south?"

"They're far from extinct. The Kuldrith were driven underground by—"

"Whatever," the marquis waved off the scholar's interjection. "You know what I mean. How in the name of Akraharr's dark hole do you propose any force of that size could sneak right up to our front doorstep without anyone noticing?"

Vikkin kept his face from showing his disgust at the marquis's crass language. If Ve'Aurben felt the same, he kept his opinion to himself.

"I do not propose anything, Lord de'Venneshen. I was merely suggesting one possibility that might fit the available information. While I'll admit that on the surface it would appear to be less probable than their being Kushaani, it wouldn't be entirely outside of the scope of possibility."

"Scope of possibility? Are you serious? It's absolutely ludicrous!"

Master Ve'Aurben shrugged, but Vikkin noticed his jaw tighten slightly. "I'm certain you are more of an expert on ludicrosity than I am, my lord. I will defer to your judgment."

Again, Vikkin glanced at the prince, but Andric revealed nothing. He still seemed to be thoughtfully considering the young scholar as if he was trying to solve a puzzle.

The marquis did not appear to take offense. Keeping his gaze on the Cannessi, he shook his head, his bemused smile making the doubt written on his face seem condescending. "No, please, pray tell—"

Before the marquis could continue, one of the nearby Sharinic holy knights spoke. "He's right. They are Kuldrith."

The interjection from such an unlikely source, stated so matter-of-factly, appeared to render everyone incapable of responding. It was the older of the two knights that had spoken. Vikkin's attention was momentarily swallowed up in considering the knight and his words, and he hardly noticed the others' reactions matched his own. Marquis de'Venneshen stood speechless, staring at the knight. Only a mirthless laugh escaped weakly from his lips. Andric looked puzzled, glancing from the dark-skinned knight to the scholar and back.

Consul Rellat was the first to break the silence. "Knight Defender Mar, perhaps it would be best to leave this matter to the prince's company to discuss." Vikkin knew the priest's use of the knight's formal title was meant as a subtle rebuke.

"If you have information about the invaders, by all means, speak freely," Prince Andric addressed the knight. He displayed more earnestness than

Vikkin thought the absurd claim merited, but it was good to see the prince conducting himself well.

"Your Highness, all I can say is that the reports clearly describe Kuldrith soldiers. And before you ask, Marquis, I cannot explain how they have been able to get such a force onto Remalian soil, yet here they are."

Vikkin wanted to admire the knight. He generally respected those who were willing to speak their mind, especially to those in power. However, there was something about the knight, something he could not quite place, that made him distrust the man. No, it was more than distrust. It was something much deeper. He was not sure why, but he was certain this man was a threat. Was he somehow undermining the prince, the royal family, or Teraithia herself? Maybe he was even in league with the invaders. The archpaladin casually maneuvered his horse nearer the prince, his senses alert to any threat the knight might pose.

"How do you know anything about the Kuldrith?" the prince asked with genuine curiosity.

"I have fought them long enough to know when I hear them described, Your Highness."

"You're from Eastgate? I couldn't quite place your accent, but you don't look like ..." The prince's voice trailed off in uncertainty.

"At one time."

"Well then," the marquis said, his voice heavy with sarcasm, "the mystery is solved!"

"You're welcome," the knight said stonily, seemingly unfazed by the marquis's antics.

"I am sure we will have time to discuss this further once we are on the road," the intercessor offered, "if Your Highness is ready?" Her tone was at once conciliatory and suggested that the decision had already been made.

The prince considered the knight for a moment then agreed. "Yes. It's time to go."

Vikkin was disappointed. He was not sure what he was hoping for; perhaps that someone would somehow prove the knight wrong and humiliate him in front of everyone. They were petty feelings and should have been beneath him, but he found them stubbornly difficult to set aside. With uncharacteristic difficulty, he turned his attention elsewhere.

The prince said goodbye to the marquis and offered a cursory *good morning* to the others gathered for the journey. Soon they were all mounted and riding through the vast camp. The prince asked the Sharinic knight to ride with him, no doubt wanting to probe the man about the Kuldrith nonsense further. Despite his nagging anxiety at the sight of the knight near the prince, Vikkin had to admit he was curious to hear what the knight had to say, but the archpaladin's place was at the head of the company. His men who rode near the prince would report to him later about what was said.

Tarsapta was due west, and the blinding rays of the morning sun beamed directly into their faces. It was a full day's ride to reach the town and Vikkin hoped he still had his eyesight when they arrived. The contingent of Messian lancers awaited them at the edge of camp and fell in behind the prince's company.

Two days of Kushaan heat had dried the surface water from the road, but thick mud still clung to the horses' hooves. Even this early in the morning the air was not what Vikkin considered cool, but he was grateful they had at least an hour or two before the sun began to beat upon them again.

Prince Andric asked the intercessor to fill him in on the reports' details. She explained she had only received the dossier just before their departure and had not yet had the opportunity to review it, but assured him she would do so as soon as she could. He told the priestess to share the documents with Master Ve'Aurben as well. Vikkin had a fleeting discomfort with the young scholar being given sensitive reports, but he pushed the feeling aside. He wondered how the priestess felt about it.

Soon, the two of them were engrossed in reading the documents, and the prince was left riding alone. Vikkin decided now was as good an opportunity to speak with Andric as he was likely to get today, so he slowed his pace slightly and gestured to Divinar Bremmel to take the lead. He was surprised to feel a twinge of anxiety at the thought of what he was about to do.

"Your Highness, would you mind if I rode at your side for a moment?"

The prince failed to keep the subtle signs of surprise from playing across his face. "Of course, Lord Nophet." The archpaladin bowed slightly in his saddle and maneuvered alongside the prince. "To what do I owe this unexpected occasion?" Prince Andric asked pleasantly.

"I haven't had the opportunity to ask how Your Highness's shoulder is recovering since we left Teris."

"Well enough, thank you." Andric moved his arm as if to demonstrate. "It's still sore sometimes, and I don't have the full range of motion yet, but I can swing my sword well enough. It could have been a lot worse."

"I thank Teraithia it was not. I know His Majesty the King was very proud of the way you conducted yourself that evening. You are a true warrior." Such sentiments were foreign to Vikkin, but he hoped it sounded sincere to the prince.

"I wish I had a chance to really prove that. So far the only thing I've done since that night is ride countless miles." The prince's words did not come across as a complaint, merely a simple and sincere statement of fact. It appeared the war was having the effect King Jevorak had hoped it would.

"Teraithia grants us opportunities to demonstrate our strength. Your chance will certainly come, Your Highness."

"I hope it comes sooner than later."

"Seek the Goddess's favor, and it undoubtedly will."

"I'm afraid that the next opportunity will be at Balinth's Fortress. That does not bode well for any of us, even with all the gods' blessings."

"Perhaps. Have you spoken to your brother about the possibility of you taking command of a portion of your army and continuing the campaign in Kushaan? Many of the nobles believe it may be premature to abandon our gains here, and would certainly support you." Prince Stephir had made it clear he was not interested in this idea, but perhaps the young prince could be successful where others were not. And even if not, persuading Andric to envision himself as the conqueror of Kushaan would bring him closer to Teraithia.

The prince remained silent. The sun was finally high enough not to be directly in their eyes, so Vikkin kept his gaze fixed on the horizon and prayed that Teraithia would magnify his words in the young man's mind. Vikkin was comfortable with silence when many others were not, and he waited for Prince Andric to speak in his own time.

He considered how different it was from riding with Prince Stephir, who was constantly talking with other nobles or his officers. Vikkin had always been impressed with the crown prince and believed he would make a great king one day. Everything he had seen since leaving Teris confirmed that belief, even if he did not agree with some of the prince's decisions.

However, he was concerned that his efforts to push Stephir toward the path of Teraithia had damaged his relationship with the crown prince and jeopardized his ability to carry out his duties effectively as archpaladin. He swore to Teraithia that he would do everything in his power to repair that rift before it got any worse. Doing his duty to protect and support Prince Andric on this mission was a necessary first step, and he would ensure it was carried out with honor.

"Stephir has made his determination, and I will not go against him," Andric finally answered.

Vikkin noted that the prince did not say he disagreed with the suggestion. Perhaps there was still an opportunity to persuade the young man to embrace his role as a leader. "Of course not. But circumstances in war change constantly. The crown prince has already proven his ability to adapt, and I believe will continue to do so. Teraithia blesses those with the strength to seize upon opportunities when they present themselves. All I wanted to suggest was that you be ready when that happens."

From behind, the young intercessor spoke. "Excuse me, Archpaladin Nophet. Would you be so kind as to answer some questions that may have some bearing on the task ahead of us?"

Vikkin was annoyed with the interruption and guessed her timing was not coincidental. He turned his mount and trotted sideways so he could stay next to the prince and face her simultaneously. He would not do it for long, but he merely intended to convey that she could not manipulate him out of his position if he did not want to be.

"That's a fine bit of horsemanship, Archpaladin," she complimented him smoothly with just a hint of dismissiveness. Somehow acknowledging it outright lessened the desired effect, which further annoyed him. "Now, how well do you know Warden Commander Sammet?"

"Not well at all. We were introduced once and have been in attendance at the same sacraments on one or two other occasions."

"Are you aware that Archseraph Charin has issued a Writ of Divinity to the church, commanding all adherents to, quote, 'make every effort to bring more souls to the embrace of Our Holy Lady, Teraithia, Goddess of All,' close quote?"

Vikkin was all too familiar with it. "Of course." He felt his mount tiring of the sideways trotting, so he reigned the horse forward, sliding back so he was halfway between the prince and the intercessor.

"Does that apply to you, Archpaladin?" The priestess's question hit too close to his own discomfort. Prince Andric looked over his shoulder at the holy knight. He had to tread carefully.

"Of course, but what does this have to do with the warden commander?" he asked coolly.

"I would like to understand as well as I can what might motivate her actions. Since we cannot yet ask her directly, I thought that perhaps understanding how you perceive the writ's application to yourself might shed some light on the question."

"Each adherent must show their faith in whichever way they are able."

"If the accusations against the warden commander are true, do you believe that her actions are consistent with the Writ of Divinity from the archseraph?"

There was no good answer to that question. He felt attacked and cornered. He would meet her aggression in kind. "Intercessor, I am not a justicar. Far be it from me to judge the actions of another, especially in questions of faith. Perhaps there is a lesson there for all of us."

The Sharinic knight who spoke of the Kuldrith tightened his grip on the reigns. It was subtle, but Vikkin knew how to read such signs well; anything that might indicate a potential threat.

"I didn't ask you to judge the warden commander's faith. I asked you to consider your own." The intercessor said the words slowly, as one might do with a half-wit.

Outrageous! He stopped abruptly and spun his horse to fully face her, forcing everyone behind them to pull up short. "Do not question my faith." He said it quietly, but his words carried every ounce of authority at his command. He could feel Teraithia's power flowing through him.

The intercessor's dark-skinned guard edged his horse forward, his hand now resting on the pommel of his sword. "She asked you a straightforward question. Perhaps avoiding it is all the answer you can muster."

Vikkin wanted to strike the man down—to show him what it meant to be a true holy knight! The intercessor gave a slight wave of her hand to signal the knight to stand down.

The other Sharinic knight cut in with a laugh as fresh and sweet as morning dew. "Sir Mar, are you certain you're in the right order? Perhaps Lord Nophet has a new convert?" It would have been a harsh reprimand from anyone else, but it was so light-hearted that it simply washed the tension away. He had not bothered to give any thought to the fact that she was a woman. Now it was unmistakable.

"I'm sure we are all just eager to get back to crossing swords with... well, not that any of us actually cross swords with anyone, but you know what I mean." Again came the laugh that said nothing should be taken too seriously.

Vikkin briefly wondered if the woman was somehow dispositioning them all, but quickly dismissed it. It was one thing to disposition a single person, but nearly impossible to affect the emotions of an entire group, especially without the Divinarim knowing it.

Prince Andric spoke with considerably less levity. "If you can't stay focused on our task, perhaps we can remedy that by sending you to go cross swords with the Kushaani at Balinth's Fortress."

Vikkin was not sure who that was directed at, but he feared he had made things worse with the prince. He let go of the last of his indignation, but the priestess was quicker to apologize. She even managed to sound sincere.

"Please forgive any offense I may have given, Archpaladin. I meant no disrespect to you or your faith."

"It was certainly my misunderstanding, Intercessor," Vikkin said with a bow of his head. He could not remember the last time he had apologized. It galled him. "With Your Highness's leave, I will take my place in the lead."

"Of course."

Vikkin turned his horse and galloped to the front of the long column. *That could not have gone much worse!* Was he failing his goddess, or had the archseraph been mistaken to give him this task in the first place?

That is a dangerous path, his inner voice warned.

Unfortunately, he had many miles of open road ahead of him to sit with those thoughts.

CHAPTER XXVII
VIKKIN

Wispy dark clouds were painted in shades of rosy pink and orange as the sun slowly dipped toward the horizon behind them when Tarsapta finally appeared in the wide valley below. The ribbon of a river snaked its way through the verdant fields of farms, radiating from the large town at the center of the valley. Reflections of the colorful sky glinted off the river, but something else drew his eyes. White billows of smoke rose from the ground, lighted with the orange under-glow of flames blazing in Tarsapta.

Vikkin raced back to the prince. "Your Highness, the town is burning."

"What! Where?"

"I could not tell for sure, Your Highness. We should go. Now."

Prince Andric called to those behind him. "Ride hard!" Over a hundred horses were spurred into a gallop, and they sped down into the valley. Hooves thundered over the stone bridge across the river and soon they passed the first buildings crowding in on the narrow, winding streets. The smell of smoke hung heavy in the air, but the fire seemed to be somewhere toward the center of town. The streets were chaos—people yelling or crying, running in every direction—but everyone got out of their way. Vikkin scanned ahead to ensure there were no threats to the prince's safety.

As they rounded a corner, thick smoke and flames billowed from a row of wood buildings. A large crowd of people filled the street. Vikkin expected to see a bucket line but instead was surprised that they were concentrated in front of one of the few stone structures he had seen so far in the town. Flames from the next building licked at its walls, but so far it seemed intact. That could only last for so long. He wondered if people were trapped inside. As the prince's company approached, heads snapped in their direction then most turned and ran.

Something is wrong.

A large black banner bearing two gold overlapping angles hung above the building's iron-bound doors—this was a temple of his goddess. He was surprised. The Kushaani weren't known to have temples devoted to a single deity; they built shrines to all the gods. There were several empty alcoves along the front of the building that looked like they once held statues, but he saw no signs of broken stone to indicate an explanation having anything to do with the immediate situation.

As men scattered he saw two black-clad bodies lying on the ground. They had to be clerics of the temple. Vikkin's blood surged. His sword was in his hand in an instant, and he bore down on those standing over the bodies. A few of the men stood their ground, their swords raised defiantly. The nearest man fell with a scream beneath the archpaladin's blade.

Despite the weight of his armor, Vikkin was well-practiced at dismounting without assistance and was off his horse before it had even fully halted. The curved blade of a halberd shot past him as one of his knights drove the tip through another man's chest. Realizing they were no match for the knights, others turned and fled.

Heat and smoke from the flames consuming the nearby buildings whipped around him, but would not hurt him at this distance. A tall, heavy-set man, bald with a thick salt-and-pepper beard, called for others to stand their ground. Pools of blood surrounded the fallen. This man's blood was about to do the same. Behind Vikkin, the prince called for him to stop, but this sacrilege had to be answered for.

"This is not your concern, knight!" the man yelled at him with a heavy Kushaani accent. Vikkin answered with a flat cut of his sword from the side. The man blocked with his bloody sword and snarled, "Back away! You're interfering with—"

Before he could finish he must have realized one of the new arrivals was royalty as more of the prince's company filled the street. He clamped his mouth shut, but his face twisted with venomous rage. Slowly, he dropped to one knee. "My lord." He bowed his head behind his hands gripping the hilt of his sword, the tip against the ground.

Vikkin kicked the sword out of his hands and was poised to drop his sword on the man's neck, but he hesitated. Would he disobey a command from the prince? A scream from inside the temple saved him from deciding. He dashed into the building, scanning the dark interior for any threat and the source of the scream. He heard metal on metal clash, echoing through the stone building. He wanted to rush forward, but instead he carefully made his way forward through the cella, past rows of wood benches. Seeing no one in the cella, he hurried toward an archway leading to what he assumed was the vestry. Shouting pierced his ears and another clash of metal confirmed he was headed in the right direction. A single set of heavy footsteps followed a short distance behind.

"Nophet, stop!" He could not identify the voice, but anyone who knew his name did not pose a threat, and no one other than Prince Andric had the authority to command him so he pushed on. He had to duck as he passed through the archway into the low-ceilinged corridor. The metallic sounds of his armor echoed loudly in the confined space. He turned a sharp corner and passed through another archway into a small room with a few pieces of simple furniture. An elderly priestess, trapped against the sacellum, held a sword defensively against two men with crude maces. One man watched over his shoulder and swore when Vikkin entered the room.

"...or we'll drag your carcass..." the other said, trailing off when he noticed what had elicited the curse from his companion. The priestess tried to use the opportunity to break away, but the man who had been yelling at her grabbed her sword arm and wrenched the elderly woman around, using her as a shield. Vikkin set his course for the man holding the priestess, belying his true target.

"Don't come any—"

Before the man was finished, the archpaladin swung his sword in a low cut across the other man's leg, just above the knee. He screamed and crumpled to the ground, his mace clanking along the stone floor as the man clutched his injured leg. Vikkin's eyes never left the man holding the priestess. He put his sword against the injured man's throat, intending to use the threat to convince his companion to let the priestess go in exchange for his friend's life. Then he would end them both.

"Step away from him," a low voice from behind Vikkin demanded. It was the one who had followed him. He recognized the voice this time. *The damned Sharinic knight from Eastgate with the intercessor.* Vikkin refused to take his eyes off the man who was about to die. Teraithia's divine indignation flowed through him and made this his domain to command.

"In the name of Sharin Dara, I command you to step away."

Vikkin staggered as a force smashed him from the side, nearly knocking him off his feet. He caught his balance on the desk and spun on his attacker. The knight stood in the archway, impossibly far away. *What is he doing? How dare he!* The thoughts raced through Vikkin's mind as he righted himself and quickly considered his next move.

"Do not invoke the name of your pathetic goddess in this sacred place!" Vikkin's voice carried a rage that he did not expect. A loud clang of metal striking the stone floor pulled his attention back to the priestess. The villain holding her had dropped his mace and was now pressing a knife against the old woman's throat.

This is all the Sharinist's fault! Save the priestess, then deal with the rest. Vikkin made his voice cold steel. "Release the Prior and you might live." The man looked at the Sharinic knight, as if with a plea. "He cannot save you," Vikkin warned.

The other knight took a few steps into the room and spoke to the man with a calm confidence that grated on Vikkin's raw nerves. "Let the priestess go and you *will* live."

The man nodded. He shoved the priestess toward Vikkin and slid toward his new protector. Vikkin lunged with the point of his sword aimed straight at the man's heart. The Sharinist's sword came from nowhere and parried the blow.

"Enough!" the dark-skinned knight insisted. The man that had held the priestess skirted behind him and ran from the room. Vikkin clenched his teeth hard to restrain his frustration. He felt Teraithia's demand that someone pay for defiling her temple. If this knight wanted to take the other man's place in that role, so be it.

"You will pay for your interference."

"No, I won't."

Even as the knight spoke the words, Vikkin lashed out with his sword. He saw the sword coming up for a block and softened his cut just enough to let the block propel his sword into a swift reverse cut. Vikkin's blade arced around but he was caught by surprise as the other knight stepped in quickly and bashed the Divinar commander in the side of his helmed head with the hilt of his sword. His other hand grasped the middle of his blade and Vikkin felt him sliding it behind his leg, intending to sweep his leg.

Vikkin was too unbalanced to resist the move, so instead he spun quickly, hoping to remain on his feet and reset his stance. But in the middle of his spin, the man shoved him hard in the back. Vikkin crashed against the wall. *This man does not fight like a knight! He fights dirty.*

The archpaladin's neck itched with anticipation of a blow cutting him from behind. He knew he would not be able to stop such an attack, so he relaxed as if in submission, relying on the Sharinist's moral code to restrain his hand. The blow did not come, and Vikkin drew himself upright. He turned slowly, his blade lowered.

"You fight like a coward." He felt Teraithia's divine will coursing through his veins, urging him to attack. He needed to create an opportunity.

"I fight like someone who doesn't want to have to kill you."

The man on the ground groaned, and the priestess stood silently in the corner. Vikkin masked his emotions as he kept his eyes fixed on the other knight. He needed to draw his opponent forward. Without hesitation, he stepped toward the man on the floor and slowly drove his sword through his chest. He felt the tip of his sword hit the stone floor beneath him. The man screamed in agony; blood filled his throat, and his scream turned into a gurgling cough.

The Sharinic knight did not move. Restrained contempt dripped from each word as he carefully said, "You're the coward, Nophet." Then he turned away.

Vikkin's sword rose as he sprang toward the knight. His mind could barely register what happened as he smashed into what felt like a wall that formed between them. *Is he an elantir?* Vikkin wondered.

"Teraithia, empower thy servant! Cleanse thy temple!" the priestess cried loudly. Teraithia's divinessence permeated the room. Every fiber within him felt alive, invigorated in a way he only experienced when close to her presence. Vikkin focused his will and attuned to the divinessence that suddenly flooded into him. He thrust himself into the unseen barrier and felt it start to give way. The Sharinist retreated toward the corridor. *Coward!*

Pressing with all his might in righteous fury, Vikkin staggered forward as the barrier abruptly disappeared. He attempted a wild reverse cut as he fought to regain his footing. The opposing knight spun and parried the attack, leaving Vikkin to stumble off balance again. The archpaladin quickly recovered and raised his guard before his grim-faced opponent could follow with another blow.

Shouts echoed from the cella beyond the corridor. Vikkin did not want anyone to interrupt his fight with the knight. Now that they were on equal footing, he was certain he could finish it quickly. Heavy metallic footsteps advanced toward them. They would be in the room in seconds. *Not enough time.* Vikkin glanced at the doorway.

The Sharinic knight kept his eyes locked on the archpaladin as two

Divinarim ran into the room with swords drawn and concern written on their faces. "Archpaladin, is everything all right?"

Before Vikkin could answer, the Sharinic knight stalked from the chamber. Vikkin's men scanned the room, assessing any potential threat.

"It is over. Dispose of that," he gestured dismissively to the still form lying on the ground behind him. Then he turned his attention to the elderly prior, who drew herself upright with grim resolution written on her face.

"Teraithia's strength be upon you for your service, sir." The priestess had a Kushaani accent, but not nearly as thick as many others.

Vikkin wanted to return to his duty ensuring the prince's safety, but he needed more information about the situation. The two Divinarim would not have entered the temple if they felt Prince Andric's safety was at all in question, so he could spare a moment to talk with the priestess.

"What has happened here in Tarsapta, Prior? Why were you being attacked?"

The priestess's eyes darted to the two Divinarim dragging the body from the room, painting the floor in streaks of blood. Vikkin could not read the old woman to determine how she felt about what had happened. It was probably best just to let her speak, as long as she did so quickly.

The priestess's eyes snapped to the archpaladin and she bluntly asked a question of her own. "Why have you come here?"

Vikkin was slightly annoyed at not being answered, but undoubtedly the woman had no way of knowing who he was. Clarifying that immediately should make getting the information he wanted much simpler.

"I am Archpaladin Nophet of the Order of the Divine Flame."

The priestess's eyes widened, and she bowed low with her hand across her chest. "My lord."

"My knights and I are in the company of Prince Andric Laconeus, and have only just arrived to find the town burning." Vikkin decided not to mention anything about the warden commander or their mission at this point. Best not to cloud the situation. "What is going on?"

"There has been growing... unrest here and in the surrounding areas ever since..." the woman stammered, attempting to find the right words, "ever since our lands were liberated by the great Kingdom of Remalia." It was an answer the Sharinists would be proud of. "Some of the people banded together and are attempting to—"

Vikkin understood and did not have the patience to wait for her to find the words to say what was already clear. The Kushaani natives were fighting back against the Remalian conquerors.

It was an insurrection.

"I see. And why were they attacking the temple?"

"As always, there are those who refuse to bend the knee before the Queen of Heaven. The Time of Rebirth is at hand. There are only two sides left to choose—to stand on Our Lady's right hand and be exalted, or fall with all others."

Vikkin was as devout as anyone, but he had no interest in this kind of doomsday rhetoric. He was certain he already knew the answer to his next question, but he needed to hear it from the priestess. He could not afford any incorrect assumptions or incomplete information. At least one life depended on correct action. The archpaladin spoke slowly with grave intensity. "But why were they attacking the temple?"

"The rebels refuse to accept the Faith and seek to erase Teraithia's presence from this land. We must not let that happen."

It was enough of an answer for the moment. Vikkin knew what he needed to do to get to the bottom of the matter. "Where can I find Warden Commander Sammet?"

"The provincial headquarters are in the town square. She is either there or at the barracks on the west end of town."

Vikkin was tempted to assure the priestess and temple would be protected, but his first priority had to be Prince Andric's safety, and he would need all his men with him to ensure that would happen.

"Prior, I suggest you lock the temple until order is restored." With a slight bow of his head, he left to find Sammet.

He hoped she was still alive.

Vikkin found the street empty except for a small contingent of Remalian cavalry and a handful of bodies lying motionless on the hard cobblestones. The Sharinic knight was nowhere to be seen. Flames continued to consume nearby buildings, filling the air with thick smoke. The two Divinarim who had been in the temple rode up, leading his horse.

"Where is the prince?" he asked as he mounted.

"We were told he has gone to the provincial headquarters in the town center, my lord."

He did not know where the town center was, and he did not care. That was not his destination. He did not need to explain where he was going to his men —they would follow him wherever he went. He spurred his stallion into a gallop, the iron-shod hooves clacking loudly as he sped along the street. If Warden Commander Sammet was at the headquarters, she was almost certainly already in the prince's custody, so there was little Vikkin could do for her anyway. The priestess had said the barracks were on the west end of the town, so he would go there first to see if he could find her before Prince Andric did.

And then what? he asked himself. He did not know what he intended to do. He was not accustomed to uncertainty, but he did not let it occupy his attention. He prayed for Teraithia to guide him. Before he reached the next street the fires were behind him, though the smoke still drifted everywhere.

To his right, over the tops of the buildings he saw the orange glow of flames from a second fire burning somewhere in the town. It was in the direction where he guessed the town center was. He hoped if the warden commander was not there that the headquarters was on fire. It would keep the prince occupied and give Vikkin more time.

Twilight descended over the valley, making the dark, narrow streets almost impossible to navigate. He and his men slowed to a trot and more than once turned onto a street leading to a dead end. This pace was maddening. He was relieved when they came to a wide street that took them in what seemed to be the right direction. More people were on this street, but he spurred his horse into a gallop again, not caring whether they got out of his way.

The street turned a corner and Vikkin saw what he assumed were barracks. It was impossible to miss. Torches burned brightly all around and atop the building that stood alone at the end of the street near another stone bridge crossing over the river flowing next to the barracks. Heavy iron bars covered the small open windows and large, arched double doors. A heavy contingent of soldiers stood guard atop the barracks, bows in hand and arrows nocked. Several bodies lay motionless in the street, telling Vikkin the temple was not the only building attacked.

Bow strings were drawn and arrows trained on him and his men as they approached. He slowed to a walk but showed no hesitation as he approached the barracks. He remained mounted as he called out loudly. "I am Archpaladin Nophet, Knight Commander of the Order of the Divine Flame. I must speak with Warden Commander Sammet at once. Is she here?"

A rock struck his back, clanging loudly on his armor. Arrows flew passed him and someone behind him cursed in pain. He was unharmed but annoyed; the rock would undoubtedly leave a mark on his armor. The two Divinarim with him turned their horses around, halberds lowered. They would watch his back for any further threats.

Multiple voices engaged in a discussion from within the barracks, then a deep voice gave the order to open the doors. Heavy bars were removed and the doors swung inward. A group of soldiers in the large antechamber with swords and shields in hand crowded behind the soldier who stepped forward to unlock the iron gate protecting the entrance. With a heavy creak, they swung wide.

Vikkin took it as confirmation the warden commander was indeed here. The tension in his stomach eased slightly. He dismounted and handed the reigns to Divinar Yehtel. "Bring the horses inside," he said

"Sir, you canno' bring yer horses in 'ere! We'll take 'em to the stables."

"No, they come inside" he stated emphatically as he ascended the three stone stairs and stepped inside. His commanding presence filled the antechamber and the soldiers stepped back to give him space. His men led the large horses inside and the soldiers had to back further away to the edges of the room. The gates closed behind him with a clang and were locked, then the doors were shut and barred.

"Take me to the warden commander at once."

"Of course, m'lord!" the lieutenant with the deep voice replied, bowing low with his and over his heart. The man was Remalian and should have saluted, not bowed. Vikkin wondered if it was a mistake, or if someone had been changing protocols. It would certainly fit with the narrative of Sammet making these men her own. Glancing around he noted the soldiers had a small black cloth bearing two gold overlapping angles tied to their upper arms. It was normally a patch worn by Teraithian guards at temples. It had no place on a Remalian soldier.

He followed as the lieutenant led them further into the barracks, then up a narrow set of stone stairs to the second floor and along a torchlit hallway. Two soldiers stood guard outside of an open doorway. The lieutenant stepped in front of the guards and announced Vikkin's arrival.

"Warden Commander, Archpaladin..." the man appeared to have forgotten his name, "...of the Divine Flame has arrived and requests admittance to your presence."

What in the name of the Queen of Heaven is going on! Vikkin wondered with concern. He wanted to say, '*I am not requesting anything. Get out of my way!*' But the delicate situation kept the words behind his clenched teeth. A chair scraped on the wood floor, and quick steps accompanied a woman's commanding voice. "Let him in." The guards moved aside and Vikkin stepped into the room.

Warden Commander Sammet was a thin woman of average height. Her sandy brown hair was pulled back tightly in a braid that fell down her back, making her sharp facial features even more pronounced. A hawk-like nose dominated her tanned face, and age lines creased the corners of her narrow eyes. She placed her hand over her heart and bowed.

The same greeting as the lieutenant. Not a mistake.

"Lord Nophet, Teraithia blesses us with your presence. To what do we owe the honor of your arrival?" Her demeanor was calm and collected, as if she was unaware or did not care the town was burning at that very moment and people were being murdered in the streets.

"I have come to Tarsapta with Prince Andric at the behest of his brother, the crown prince, to ascertain what is transpiring here." Vikkin's words were far more formal than he was accustomed to using.

Sammet raised an eyebrow. "The prince is here? That is indeed an honor." There was no sincerity in her voice. "Is he not with you?"

Vikkin raised his voice slightly for emphasis. "He is out there," he pointed toward the town, "trying to restore some semblance of order in this chaos. Why are you not doing the same?"

Sammet's eyes narrowed and hardened, then relaxed and she shrugged. "There has been unrest throughout the province. Many of my men are restoring order out there," she inclined her head away from the town, "which is no doubt why these vermin chose this opportunity to cause trouble. We are too few to safely go out in the streets tonight, so I am waiting until more of my troops return tomorrow."

It was a plausible explanation, and he was willing to give her the benefit of the doubt for the moment, but he needed her to let her guard down if he was going to get the information he wanted. He needed to build some rapport quickly. "The temple was attacked." He did not specify which temple; she would know which one he meant. "They killed some of the clerics."

Her face hardened again. He wondered if he had pushed her in the wrong direction. "Prior Elkolur? Was she hurt?" Her voice carried a mix of anger and concern.

"I do not know her name, but the elderly prior lives, though she was moments from having her life taken by a couple of the rebels." The warden commander nodded, a flash of relief passing across her face. "Why would they attack our temple?"

"They are angry people. They lash out at anything they don't like."

Patience, Vikkin urged himself. He felt like he was having the same conversation he had with the elderly priestess a short time ago.

"The prior is Kushaani. Why would they lash out at her?"

Sammet did not answer immediately but walked back to the chair behind her desk and slowly sat down. "Why has the prince come to Tarsapta?"

Sammet asked, remaining casual, though the archpaladin thought he detected a hint of stress.

Vikkin was unsure how much to say but thought it would help him if he was candid with her. "Serious accusations have been made against you, Warden Commander. Prince Andric was sent here to conduct an inquest into the matter."

She snorted derisively. "An inquest! Those fools have no idea what's really happening in the world."

"Take care how you speak of the royals." He meant it both as advice and a threat, for Sammet as well as the soldiers listening outside the room.

"I apologize, Archpaladin. I didn't mean the king or his princes in particular."

She was still walking a dangerous line, and Vikkin wanted to pull her back to safety. He closed the heavy wooden door, then walked around to her side of the desk and sat on the corner, hands crossed casually on his armored thigh. "Tullare," he said with an even tone. It felt unnatural to use her given name, but he hoped it would reach her more deeply. "I think you do not fully appreciate the gravity of this situation. You are accused of capital offenses." She kept her eyes on his face and remained silent. "I want to help you if I can, but we must be cautious."

"Vikkin, we have been cautious for far too long." He was surprised she knew his given name. No one called him that except his lovers and the arch-seraph. He had opened that door, so he let it pass, though how she knew his name was a mystery he would have to leave for later. "Teraithia cannot have us cautious if she is to win her war."

He did not want to debate theology with her and tried to move away from it. "Remalia is also at war, and our duty is to ensure its victory."

"Open your eyes! The petty squabbles of nations are but a moment. The war of the gods is rolling across the face of the world like never before. The end is near."

"The gods' wars are from eternity to eternity. They will never end," Vikken countered.

"Perhaps in the realms beyond Baon, but this world will see a victor. It must be Teraithia! She will have power over all, but we must deliver it to her."

"Yes, by being strong in our faith and inspiring others to do the same."

Sammet shook her head, seeming more sad than angry. "I used to think as you do. I tried to give Teraithia as much devotion as I could muster. I was disciplined and strived to be my greatest self. I shared my faith with others and tried to reason and persuade them. I grew in power and influence, and still nothing in the world changed. Do you know why? Because I was unwittingly living the doctrine of the other gods. Tell me how I was different from a follower of Vai Doroth in self-discipline, or Sharinist in reason and persuasion, or Yonvaar in serving others. I was a hypocrite and never achieved anything worthy of Teraithia's glory. But in a month of valiant effort, I have brought more souls into Teraithia's burning light than in a lifetime of false worship."

"Their bodies may have bent the knee under the threat of your sword, but that does not make them Teraithia's people. They hate you, they hate Remalia, and what is infinitely worse, they hate the goddess you profess to serve."

"Still you don't see. That passion, that desire to fight back, to regain power, by the sword if necessary—what is more Teraithian than that? Even as they pretend to fight against her, they live by her doctrine and she is strengthened in the world. Power begets power, and in that, Teraithia will be victorious!"

The unmistakable power of Teraithia's divinessence washed over him unbidden. He desired to feel connected to it, to be strengthened by it. He instinctively reached out to attune to it.

Sammet continued, passion filling her voice. "You see, I am aligned with her will. Her presence sustains me, as should you."

She is illuminating me, he realized. It was a bold gambit, if misguided. Vikkin was moved by her devotion, but dismayed by her delusion. She was beyond his help, though he desperately wanted to save her. Could he let her escape? He knew the answer before he had finished the question. He put a hand on her shoulder as he rose to his feet.

"Provincial Warden Commander Tullare Sammet, by my authority as Archpaladin of the Order of the Divine Flame and in the name of King Jevorak Laconeus, I relieve you of your command and place you under my control. You will come with me."

Suddenly, black-banded soldiers burst into the room with swords drawn and fierce determination on their faces.

"Stand down!" Vikkin barked. The men paid no heed, and he braced himself for a fight. He was about to call out for his two knights, hoping they would hear him. He reached for his sword, his mind already mapping out his attacks.

"Do as the archpaladin commands." Sammet's words were calm, and the men instantly stopped their advance, letting their weapons rest at their sides. They placed their hands over their hearts and bowed.

She has certainly inspired unquestioning loyalty and obedience from her men. Vikkin could not deny a degree of respect for her as he gestured for her to stand and come with him. Trying to force her would only test her soldiers' obedience, and perhaps cost them their lives.

"I will go with Lord Nophet," Sammet announced to her men, both inside the room and without. "If they wish to put our Faith on trial, let all who assemble witness our devotion to the Queen of Heaven."

Her men glanced from the warden commander to each other questioningly, but they obediently stepped aside for Vikkin as he led the prisoner from the room.

CHAPTER XXVIII
SHIRALLA

The faint smell of burned buildings hung in the hot, still air in Tarsapta's large central plaza as Shiralla followed Prince Andric out the front doors of the provincial headquarters. She could not recall ever feeling this nervous in her entire life. She wanted to throw up. What in the holy name of Sharin Dara had Consul Rellat been thinking to appoint her to act as justicar for such a weighty case?

They descended the wide, worn stone steps and then climbed the new wooden stairs of the small platform erected the day before on which they would sit during the public inquest. The crowd that was gathered in the plaza remained as still as the heavy air. Prince Andric took the large center chair and Shiralla sat at his right hand. Master Ve'Aurben sat behind the prince on his left. She was opposed to him being there since he had no official position, but the prince had insisted, and of course, she conceded. There were important battles to be fought, and this was not one of them.

Divinarim stood erect at each corner of the wood platform, and two more were posted on the ground in front. Archpaladin Nophet stood directly behind the prince. Her two Sharinic holy knights stood behind her chair. The armored Remalian soldiers posted along the perimeter of the circular plaza were an impressive force.

So much capacity for violence, she thought grimly.

There had been some debate as to whether any of the soldiers who had been under Sammet's command should be allowed to be present at the inquest. Commander Kasten wanted a mix of his own men and hers to demonstrate to everyone (including the soldiers themselves) that they were first and foremost Remalian soldiers and would obey the commands of the crown. However, Shiralla was concerned (and surprisingly, Archpaladin Nophet had agreed) that having any of Sammet's soldiers at the inquest was dangerous. It could spark the people to attack again. Or the soldiers, who were on edge after the uprising, might overreact and make matters worse. Or they might try to interfere with whatever justice the prince commanded.

Prince Andric had sided with Commander Kasten, and the Remalian soldiers who had served under Sammet were ordered to stand guard, but every third man was one of the elite Messian lancers who had arrived with Kasten. Shiralla was still uneasy with the situation, but again, it was not a battle worth fighting. In addition to conducting the inquest, she wanted to position herself as a trusted advisor to the prince, and arguing superfluous points would make that difficult, if not impossible. She had never been in a position of such influence, and if she performed well, it could open many more doors. Perhaps it would even help earn her an ambassadorship someday.

Once everyone was in position the prince signaled for Warden Commander Sammet to be brought out. Murmurs rippled through the crowd and all heads turned to watch four lancers escort her to a smaller plat-form on the left where she was to stand during the inquest. She wore her formal blue and white officer's uniform without armor or weapon. She held herself erect with no hint that she was at all concerned about her circum-stances or that this might be her last day on Baon. Shiralla didn't know whether it was enviable courage, pitiable delusion, or arrogant defiance.

She had questioned the warden commander yesterday, but Sammet refused to speak. Prince Andric suggested more aggressive interrogation methods, but Shiralla had prevailed in convincing him not to go down that path. She sensed the prince had suggested it simply because he thought that was what tough rulers should be willing to do. She gave him a way out by showing that the negative consequences outweighed any benefits they might bring. He seemed like a good-hearted young man and readily seized the opportunity to change his mind.

Shiralla finished her fervent prayer for Sharin Dara's blessing as the warden commander stepped into place, then the priestess rose to her feet. All eyes turned to her. Her white dress somewhat lessened the intensity of the hot sunlight glaring down on her, but the black justicar's kemrelac hanging from her shoulders and over her left arm made her feel like she was baking, which only made the churning in her stomach worse. She had applied dry-cream to her face to keep herself from sweating, but it was making her skin tingle and itch, and she wondered whether it was worth it.

Focus! She took a deep breath and spoke loudly, her clear voice carrying over the crowd. "By royal decree of His Highness Jevorak Laconeus, Sovereign King of all Remalia, authority and jurisdiction have been conferred upon Prince Andric Laconeus to conduct this inquest and dispense the king's justice."

Shiralla's nerves were already beginning to settle. Performing her duties always calmed her. She looked at Sammet. "Provincial Warden Commander Tullare Sammet, you stand accused of capital crimes against the Crown and atrocities against the people of the Province of Kesh, whom you were charged to protect." Shiralla tried to lock eyes with Sammet, to make this intensely personal for her and thus for everyone else as well, but the woman seemed to be looking somewhere above Shiralla's head.

"The counts are as follows: you are charged with inciting mutiny; you are charged with the subversion of military order; you are charged with disobedience to orders; you are charged with abuse of authority; you are charged with issuing unlawful orders; you are charged with the war crime of massacring the people of the village of Opar'upten, including ten men, eight women, and fourteen children..."

Shiralla had rehearsed these words many times, in part to get them exactly right, and also to try to diffuse the strong emotions that came with them. But now she felt the emotions rise unbidden, gripping her chest and tightening her throat—anger, heartbreak, disbelief, horror, loss. She had served as a diplomat among the Kushaani for the past three years. Sharin Dara cared about all Her children, and Shiralla had grown to appreciate and even love many things about the Kushaani as she learned to see them as her goddess saw them. These crimes were an affront to everything Shiralla believed in and held dear.

"You are charged with—"

"I know what I am charged with!!" the warden commander screamed, her voice echoing throughout the town center. "You have your pathetic accusations, but you cannot begin to imagine what I am charged with!"

"Warden Commander, you will remain silent until the charges are enumerated and you are given permission to speak!" Shiralla's voice carried conviction but was no match for Sammet's well-practiced command voice.

"No, *you* will remain silent while I speak my charges! I am charged with Teraithia's might! I am charged with being her sword on the earth. I am charged with destroying those who stand against her!"

The crowd hurled angry curses at the warden commander and shouted their own accusations against her. Shiralla was unsure what action to take and felt panic fill her chest. *What should a justicar do? I don't have the authority to command any of the soldiers. Should I have Mar and diGreven step in? What should...*

Prince Andric stood and ordered all to be silent, but no one listened. Someone must have issued another order because the soldiers around the town center moved toward the crowd with shields raised but weapons not yet drawn. The people quickly responded and the tumult dropped to an agitated murmur, leaving the warden commander's voice filling the air.

"... not suffer this generation to wallow in such filth! This world is sick with the infection of complacency, the plague of gluttony and self-indulgence, and the corruption of every natural strength with which we, Her people, are endowed."

"Silence her!" the prince commanded the soldiers guarding Sammet. Two soldiers grabbed her arms to pull her back, but somehow Sammet remained immovable. The other two soldiers seemed rooted to their spots, glancing at each other with uncertainty.

"The time is at hand when all will stand on the side of the Queen of Heaven and Earth or be trodden into the dirt beneath her feet!"

Shiralla hadn't noticed that Lord Nophet left his position behind the prince until he stepped onto the platform next to Sammet. Nophet held his sword, and Shiralla's heart skipped a beat, unsure whether he intended to use it on Sammet or on the soldiers tugging futilely on the warden commander, seemingly unable to move her from her position of preaching.

Nophet put a hand on her shoulder and leaned close to Sammet, perhaps whispering something in her ear. Sammet's mouth snapped shut, and the soldiers, freed from their grip on the warden commander, released her arms and stared at her dumbfounded. One shook his hands as if injured. The other two soldiers helped them off the platform, whispering. The archpaladin stood alone next to Sammet, his sword tip on the wooden platform and his hands resting calmly on the pommel of his sword.

A tense silence fell over the plaza.

Shiralla was again unsure how to proceed. To finish reciting the charges now seemed hollow. She was tempted to ask Prince Andric how he would like to proceed, but throwing her duty on his shoulders would be worse than making a mistake, so she opted to continue with the next step in the inquest.

"Captain Gaen Ilorus, come forward."

A soldier who stood to the right stepped onto another platform like the one Sammet stood on. He faced the prince and saluted sharply with fingertips against the sword hilt at his waist. Captain Ilorus was the man who had sent the report to Prince Stephir of the warden commander's crimes, and was to be their primary witness in the inquest. His account was quite damning if it was to be believed. With only one day to prepare, she had not been able to properly corroborate many of the facts with other witnesses.

"Captain—"

"Justicar," Prince Andric interrupted her.

Her stomach clenched. *What did I do wrong?* Her mind raced over the possibilities while she did her best to appear calm as she turned toward the prince. "Yes, Your Highness?"

"Do we really need to proceed with witnesses at this point?"

Master Ve'Aurben leaned forward so he was close to the prince. "Your Highness, perhaps this is a matter that should be discussed privately."

She thought the prince looked annoyed, but it might have been chagrin. She wished she knew him better. Distinctions like that could have profound implications. "Of course," the prince replied casually, as if that's what he had intended all along.

Shiralla was prepared to follow him to somewhere more removed, but he remained in his seat while the prince's small advisor got to his feet and stepped closer. *Apparently private means right here in front of everyone.* She stepped closer, keeping her back to the crowd, and bent over slightly. She tried not to be self-conscious about showing her backside to the world. She didn't consider herself to have the most flattering figure, and this was perhaps the worst position to be in that she could imagine. *Dignity is a state of mind*, she told herself. It was a mantra she had repeated countless times.

"She just admitted she's guilty," Prince Andric said in a semi-hushed tone. "Shouldn't we simply move to pronouncing our judgment?"

Shiralla was tempted to argue the question of whether anything Sammet had said actually constituted a confession, but thought better of it. "My lord, there is much more at stake here than simply rooting out one guilty person. Those whom the warden commander has oppressed, terrified, and robbed of innocence, need to feel that they are heard and understood. They need to see that you're not just judging her for the offenses against the king, but against his people as well."

"So do you propose that we spend all day parading out everyone who is just going to tell us the same thing that Sammet just said?" His tone didn't seem accusatory, just impatient.

"Of course not, Your Highness. But may I suggest that you allow Captain

Ilorus to recount his story so that the people can hear that not all the Remalian soldiers were aligned with Sammet, and that she treated them as badly for it." The prince seemed to be considering her suggestion, so she pressed on. "I also believe it would be wise to request that one or two relatives of those who were slain at Opar'upten bring their demands for justice. It's an important custom to the people, and it is in keeping with our own legal practices. It will go a long way in making them feel they are heard and respected."

The prince remained silent, and she was about to continue, but she waited a moment longer. Finally, the prince said, "My father believed that a great ruler needs to dispense swift and decisive justice. The people know the truth already. If we continue with the trial, it will seem that we are wavering."

Shiralla was about to reply, but Master Ve'Aurben was quicker. "And Stephir would have done exactly as Justicar Henden is suggesting. It doesn't matter what others would do. You are here and have the authority, so you should do whatever *you* believe is right."

Shiralla had noted in the last two days that the young scholar slipped in and out of formality with the prince. She suspected his role as the prince's advisor was a pretense for the prince to keep his commoner friend close, but he was unquestionably intelligent and at times quite astute. Perhaps most importantly, he said things to the prince no one else would.

"Very well, Justicar. Let the people speak. But don't dwell on things unnecessarily."

She bowed to the prince, then she turned to face the captain and the crowd. "Captain Ilorus, when we found you yesterday, you were imprisoned in a holding cell in the military barracks. Please explain why you were there." She had instructed Ilorus yesterday that his account was more for the townspeople than the prince. He needed to speak loudly. He didn't need to vilify anyone, only to recount the facts as he had in his report. He assured her he could do that.

"Commander Sammet had me thrown in the cells because I refused to follow certain orders."

"What orders were those?"

"There were a lot of things. She said we had to be Teraithia's warriors. She gave us armbands to put on and made us do things like they do at the Teraithian temples. She made us cut each other and swear blood oaths to obey her above anyone else."

Shiralla watched the reaction of the guards around the plaza. There was a surprisingly wide range of expressions on their faces, but she didn't have time to dwell on it. "And those were the orders you refused to follow?"

Ilorus shook his head slowly. *Say the words out loud!* she willed him.

"No, Justicar. I obeyed those. It was others..."

"Tell us, Captain."

The man's head hung low, then he drew himself up and looked across to where Sammet stood in silence. "The commander gave us standing orders to *discipline* anyone who didn't accept the sign of the goddess."

"What was the sign of the goddess?" Shiralla noted the effect Ilorus's words had on the townspeople. Their eyes filled with recognition of what he was talking about.

"It was just wearing some kind of token with the Teraithian star, like our armbands, or a piece of jewelry, or even just some stitching on their clothes. Harmless enough."

"And how did you discipline those who refused to wear such a token?"

"We roughed them up a bit. Sometimes we broke something of theirs or charged a fine. Really whatever we wanted."

Someone in the crowd threw a rotten cabbage at the captain, thankfully falling short. Guards moved in quickly and escorted the woman out of the plaza. Shiralla had asked Prince Andric to order the guards not to arrest or abuse anyone who committed such minor offenses. After some debate, he had acquiesced and ordered they were to simply be removed. She hoped it held today.

"So when did you refuse to follow the warden commander's orders?"

"Word had come in that the villagers in Opar'upten refused to accept the sign. Some soldiers had already been sent to discipline them but they still refused, so the commander ordered a brand to be made. If they wouldn't accept the sign willingly, we would have to make them accept it."

"And did you?"

"No Justicar. That's when I refused. I told Sammet that disciplining folks was one thing, but branding them, or worse, was criminal and evil."

"And what did she do?"

"She had the men brand me and threw me in the cells."

"Show us."

The captain went through the slow process of unbuttoning his jacket, then unlacing his shirt, and finally pulling his clothing aside to show an ugly, blistered red burn on the left side of his chest in the shape of two overlapping angles. Murmuring rushed through the crowd, but Shiralla thought she detected a slight shift in the tone. Was it sympathy? Maybe not that far, but anything in that direction was what Shiralla was hoping for.

"Captain, are you the one who sent the report to King Laconeus about the matter?"

"A couple of days later, yes Justicar."

"What happened a couple of days later?"

"I heard what happened at the village and knew Sammet had to be stopped."

"And what happened there?"

"I can only tell you what I heard from some others."

Shiralla knew anything he said at this point had no real evidentiary value, but in the interest of moving the proceeding forward quickly to appease Prince Andric, she let Ilorus continue. If Sammet objected, Shiralla could always call other witnesses. Unfortunately, there were many.

"Please Captain, what did you hear about what happened in Opar'upten?"

"The commander took a unit to go and put the mark on the villagers. When they arrived, the villagers had painted themselves in the symbols of all the gods except Teraithia and were prepared to fight. Sammet told them they had one chance to lay down their weapons and be branded with the symbol of the supreme goddess or they would be killed. No one surrendered, so she gave the order to kill them all."

"Was there anything else?"

"She ordered that their dead bodies be covered from head to foot with Teraithia's brand, then nailed to the walls of the houses. I heard it took two days."

"Even the children?"

"That's what I heard, Justicar."

"Thank you for sending word to the king of this horrific situation, Captain. It took great courage." Shiralla turned to Sammet. "Warden Commander Sammet, you have permission to ask questions of Captain Ilorus if you wish."

"You swore by your blood to serve Teraithia. She will have your life one way or another."

Shiralla was about to admonish Sammet that she was only to ask questions, but the woman apparently had nothing further to say. After confirming that Prince Andric had no questions, she released Captain Ilorus to return to his duties. She saw no need to call any other witnesses and decided to call upon any family members of the slain to come forward.

Shiralla was nervous about this phase of the inquest. She had only seen it done in cases where there was just one victim. In this case, half the town could be related to a victim from the village. Things could go badly in so many ways, but she still felt it was worth the risk. "Are there any who by blood have a claim on justice for those who were slain?"

The plaza erupted into a cacophony of incomprehensible shouts. Shiralla scanned the crowd to assess if anyone posed an actual threat. The Divinarim along the edges of the platform and the soldiers on the perimeter of the plaza did the same. Her eyes fell on the warden commander and archpaladin who appeared as calm as the surface of a lake on a still morning. *I need to be that calm.* But calm felt impossible right now. She held up her hand as a sign to call for order, but the shouting grew louder.

Walk out among them. You will know who should speak. It was that certain inner voice that spoke from time to time but did not feel like her voice. She had been told by others it must be Sharin Dara speaking to her, but Shiralla was not convinced. Perhaps it was nothing more than her intuition speaking to her in a way she could understand. Whatever it was, she had learned to trust it. She started down the stairs, motioning for her two knights to remain at their posts.

Prince Andric called to her, a touch of panic in his voice. She looked at him and smiled reassuringly, but said nothing as she circled to the front of the platform and out into the crowd. She listened to the tones of the noise. *So much anger. So much pain.* It assaulted her senses and she feared she would drown in it. Her heart raced, and she felt the panic constrict her chest. *What am I doing?*

Hands grabbed at her and she shrank away from them. *Don't touch me!* she wanted to scream. *This was a mistake.* She looked around for the platform. She needed to get back there. The plaza hadn't seemed very large, but already the prince was so far away. Maybe she should push her way through to the soldiers on the side, then she would be safe. She turned, looking for the shortest way out.

Something caught her eye, but she was not sure what it was.

She searched the faces. Something was there, just beyond the bodies surrounding her. She pushed toward it. A small man in his middle years stood silently, shoulders slouched; his eyes were dark, deep pools of sadness. The sun had turned his wrinkled skin to darkened leather. His plain clothes were threadbare and patched. The noise faded into the background, and she heard the voice.

His is the voice of the many.

Peace settled over her, and she approached the man. She reached out and rested a gentle hand on his arm. "You lost someone in Opar'upten." It was not a question. His nod was almost imperceptible. "Will you speak?"

Tears sprung to his eyes and wet his long, black lashes, and he dropped his gaze to the ground. One moment passed, then another before he met her eyes and nodded.

"Come with me." She kept her hand on his arm and escorted him to the witness platform. Now the crowd parted easily and the noise died down. She probably should have returned to her place on the inquisitor's stand, but instead she stepped onto the wooden platform next to him. "What is your name?" The question was just between the two of them.

"Venka," he replied quietly, his Kushaani accent heavy.

"Do you have a family name?" He shook his head. That was not all that uncommon among the Kushaani. "Do you live here in Tarsapta?" A nod in the affirmative. "And who did you lose?"

The people nearest the platform hushed those around them, causing a ripple of hushes to spread through the crowd.

"Aborani."

"Who was she?"

"My daughter—" his voice broke before he could finish the word.

"I am so sorry." She squeezed his arm reassuringly. "Are you ready to make your claim?"

His gaze again fell to the ground, but he nodded.

Shiralla looked out over the crowd, trying to read the mood. Anger still permeated their countenances, but it was tinged with curiosity. She hoped it was enough to make them listen.

"This man is Venka of Tarsapta," she spoke loudly to the crowd. She wanted all of them to know him. "By right of blood, he wishes to make a claim on justice!" She looked at him and whispered, "Go ahead, Venka." He kept his head down and tried to draw a deep breath, but it caught in his throat. "Tell them about Aborani. How old was she? What did she do in Opar'upten?"

He remained silent, and she feared he would never speak. The crowd murmured uncomfortably. When he finally spoke, his voice was thin and tight. "My daughter, Aborani..." a tear coursed down his cheek.

How many times has he said those words to himself? Shiralla wondered.

"She was so beautiful. Everyone loved her." Silence spread as the people strained to hear. "She wanted to be a healer. She went to Opar'upten to learn from the *mundungu*. She will never..." a sob racked his chest. "... heal..." Sobs shook him, and tears poured down his face. He fell to his knees and wailed. "Aborani!"

Shiralla felt tears come to her eyes. She needed him to say *justice*. She bent and put an arm around him. "Say *justice*," she whispered to him.

"Justice," he whispered back.

"Good," she encouraged. "Now say it to the woman who killed Aborani."

Shiralla helped him as he slowly climbed to his feet. He looked where Sammet stood. He managed to pause his weeping long enough to say the one word. It was as if all of creation went silent to hear his claim.

"Justice!" He hung his head again and sank back into his grief.

Shiralla patted him on the back, then returned to her position on the inquisitor's stand next to the prince. His face was long, his thoughts unreadable. She was tempted to give others the chance to speak their demands for justice as well but felt nothing more was needed.

"Your Highness, I feel we have heard enough against the warden commander. I recommend we move to the stage of her defense."

Prince Andric nodded without looking at her.

Shiralla addressed Sammet as dispassionately as she could muster. "Provincial Warden Commander Tullare Sammet, you have heard the accusations and claims against you. You may speak or call others to speak in your defense."

Sammet said nothing, but instead stared straight ahead. Shiralla didn't know what influence the archpaladin had exerted on her, but the priestess was grateful for it. The last thing she wanted was a repeat of Sammet's earlier tirade. "You offer no defense? Do you confess your crimes?"

Still no response. Shiralla waited a moment, then another. She turned slightly toward Prince Andric so the crowd could still see and hear her. "Your Highness, do you have any further matters you wish to review?"

"No." His answer was quiet, subdued. She wondered if everything was okay.

"Then as justicar of this inquest, I declare the questioning closed. We proceed to judgment. Do you wish to deliberate?"

"No."

"Very well, my lord. What is your judgment?"

"Sammet is guilty."

Many in the crowd shouted their loud approval. Shiralla waited for the rest of the words he needed to speak, but he said nothing. She was going to have to coach him through this. "Of which charges do you find her guilty, Your Highness?"

"All of them."

More cheers and curses were called upon Sammet's head.

"In the eyes of the gods and these people present, it is witnessed that Provincial Warden Commander Tullare Sammet is declared guilty of all charges against her. Are you prepared to pronounce a sentence, Lord Laconeus?"

Prince Andric's eyes were transfixed on Sammet but didn't seem focused. He stared blankly. Shiralla felt a twinge of anxiety and asked him again. Still there was no response.

Barak rose to his feet and spoke quietly to the prince. Prince Andric didn't move.

Is something wrong? Is someone dispositioning him? Could a Sammet loyalist perhaps be trying to control him somehow? The Divinarim were supposedly duty-bound to protect the prince against that risk, but perhaps for a fellow Teraithian...

The prince's friend called for wine to be brought. Out of the corner of her eye, Shiralla saw the prince's squire enter the headquarters building behind them. Angry murmuring spread through the crowd again. She didn't know how long they had before things would become dangerous. *What should I do?*

Prince Andric looked like an old man slowly pushing himself out of his chair to stand on his feet, still wearing that blank stare. He put a hand on Barak's shoulder until he was standing fully erect. His gaze remained unfocused, but he spoke loud enough for the crowd to hear. His words sounded as if they were pulled from him.

"How could you have done those...?" Emotion erupted from the young prince. "Look at me!!"

Sammet continued to stare straight ahead.

"Archpaladin, turn the prisoner to face me!" Nophet turned to face the prince and Sammet followed suit. Prince Andric walked toward Sammet, stopping at the edge of the platform. "You're not a champion of anything. You're evil." His face took on a hard edge. "Hear your sentence. You will be branded from head to foot with the symbols of every god except Teraithia. I hope you don't survive the ordeal, but if you do, you will live out the remainder of your miserable life as a living witness that your goddess will *never* rule this world!"

The crowd broke into clapping and cheering. Shiralla was revolted by the sentence. She wished she had insisted that they deliberate the sentence before it was pronounced, but it was too late. Sammet certainly deserved to die, but Shiralla did not believe in answering cruelty with more cruelty.

"Teraithia, take me now!" Sammet cried out, looking up at the heavens with arms outstretched.

"Teraithia cannot save you!" the prince replied.

Nophet suddenly stepped behind Sammet, his large sword in his hands.

He's going to kill her! Shiralla thought with horror, wanting to look away but feeling her duty required her to witness what transpired. Soldiers rushed forward, weapons in hand. Nophet raised the blade and swung hard. The blade swept past Sammet and came down on the first soldier's head, crashing sickeningly into the metal helmet. Nophet kicked Sammet's legs out from under her and she landed hard on her back.

Two more soldiers reached the platform, weapons raised, and others were rushing to join them. The archpaladin swung his sword again to block the attack of one of the soldiers who tried to cut at Nophet's legs. The other man stared intently at the fallen Sammet as he stepped onto the platform, but Nophet kicked him in the chest and sent him flying backward into the crowd.

The other Divinarim surrounded the prince, and the two Sharinic knights stepped close to protect Shiralla. Prince Andric yelled at his guards. "Help Nophet!"

Shiralla cringed at the prince's mistake. Before she could correct him, the two Divinarim on the ground sprang forward and attacked a pair of soldiers from behind, one cutting off a soldier's arm, blood spraying onto the ground, and the other driving his halberd into the other soldier's back. Shiralla looked away and squeezed her eyes shut, trying to block out the images that were seared into her mind. She gagged and feared she would wretch. Metal clashed, and screams and yelling filled the air.

"Stay down!" Nophet commanded.

Shiralla did not know if she could stomach seeing more violence, but she forced herself to open her eyes. Nophet breathed heavily, sword tip pointed at Sammet, who was on her knees in front of him. His two knights guarded him from any interference. Perhaps it was for the best that Nophet ended this quickly instead of carrying out Prince Andric's sentence.

"It is over!" the price declared loudly. "Your men could not save you from your sentence, and neither shall your goddess. Take her away!"

Shiralla watched with confusion as Nophet grabbed Sammet's arm and hauled her to her feet, then he and the Divinarim escorted her back to the headquarters.

"People of Tarsapta," the prince addressed the crowd. "On behalf of my father the king, I promise that all such offenses shall be swiftly and decisively punished. You will be protected. Commander Kasten," the prince called, looking around. The commander ascended the stairs and stood next to Andric. "Commander Kasten is hereby appointed as the new Provincial Warden. He was chosen because of his unwavering devotion to justice and goodness."

Shiralla didn't know if that was true, but the words sounded good. Then the prince spoke to the commander. "Commander, protect these people as you would your own family."

Kasten bowed low to the prince, then unexpectedly turned and bowed low to the people who had just been placed under his care. Shiralla tried to read the reaction of the crowd who watched in silence, but her mind was distracted, replaying the scene of the archpaladin fighting the soldiers and Sammet. Something was off. She would have to think about it later. The Divinarim led the prince from the inquisitor's platform, and she and the others followed suit.

She was grateful to be out of the burning sun as she stepped into the provincial headquarters building. She was drenched in sweat, but her face was untouched thanks to the dry-cream. Nophet and Sammet were nowhere to be seen as the group walked silently to the warden commander's office. Andric dropped unceremoniously into the chair behind the large desk.

Two servants poured chilled wine into silver goblets and distributed them. Shiralla sipped at hers, afraid that too much would push her stomach over the edge. Prince Andric drained his glass in a single drought, then held out his goblet for more. He took another drink, then leaned back heavily in the chair, eyes closed. If the prince did not wish to speak, no one was going to disturb the silence.

Shiralla felt uncomfortable in silence generally, but this was worse than usual. There were so many things she wanted to say, and so many things she did not want to think about that she could not keep from flooding into her mind.

She heard heavy footsteps coming down the corridor toward the office. The prince opened his eyes as the Divinarim outside the door snapped to attention and saluted. *The archpaladin.*

Nophet stepped into the room and bowed to the prince. "A number of Commander Kasten's men are escorting Sammet to the cells at the barracks. They will ensure nothing happens to her until her sentence is carried out."

"Thank you, Lord Nophet," the prince said grimly. "I greatly appreciate your valiant service today. It would have been a tragedy if her men had succeeded." Nophet wordlessly bowed again.

Of course! Shiralla was ashamed she had so completely misunderstood what happened. Nophet hadn't been trying to kill the warden commander, he prevented Sammet's men from circumventing the prince's sentence.

Prince Andric shifted his gaze to Shiralla. She steeled herself for his criticism. "And thank you as well, Justicar. I don't think anyone could have done better."

She was stunned but curtsied before realizing what she was doing. "Your Highness is too gracious."

"Now, unless there is anything else we need to do before we leave..." The prince looked around the room, waiting for any replies to his unspoken invitation. "Then we depart at once."

CHAPTER XXIX
STEPHIR

Pre-dawn light touched the ribbon of open sky above Stephir as he slowly rode up the dark, narrow canyon running through the mountain pass toward Balinth's Fortress. A trickle of sweat ran down his neck despite the early hour. In part, it was that summer was nearly upon them and it didn't cool down at night as much as he would like. It was also his nerves if he was being honest, though he hoped it was more the former. He tried not to think about how much hotter it would be in a few hours. In the mountains, it was much cooler than where he would have been if he hadn't decided to return to Teris. He would be more than happy to still be pushing his army into the heat of southern Kushaan if it meant he was not faced with the task before him. His stomach clenched for the hundredth time at the thought of what he was about to do.

The walls of the fortress loomed somewhere ahead in the darkness between the towering mountain cliffs. Balinth's walls had always given him comfort in their solid strength, in their immensity, in the way they filled the canyon to keep out the dangers south of the Velspars. Now that he was facing them for the first time as an obstacle, as an enemy, he realized how daunting they could be.

Scouts and engineers had ridden ahead, watching the fortress for several days, and some of the more daring had even climbed the steep slopes of the mountains to watch from high above Balinth's Fortress. A few odd things had been reported, including figures darting about in the shadows and greater activity in the night hours, but nothing useful. The scouts had found hundreds of small holes running down the cliffs above the fortress. These were not the arrow holes looking out from the tunnels running through the canyon walls (one of the many things he feared sending his men into); these holes were approximately the size of a fist and looked like someone had punched out the holes from inside the rock cliffs.

They found no bodies other than the corpses staged atop the battlements, nor any other signs a battle had taken place; nothing in the pass leading up to Balinth's, nor in the foothills where, by at least one account, some of his men had been hunted down and killed. Rain washing away blood and wild animals dragging away bodies may have accounted for part of that, but it was unsettling that there was nothing to show that good men had fought and died here. And no trace of the enemy.

He knew at least some Kushaani were still inside the fortress, although how many was a mystery. The elantir had done what they could to discover anything about the enemy. Their powers allowed them to sense living beings particularly well, though he had been informed it was difficult at a distance. A small group had managed to sneak close to the fortress walls, and although they had confirmed there were people in the fortress, something was interfering with their ability to distinguish where they were located or how many there were. They had tried to give some explanation of possible causes, but he didn't understand what they were talking about, and unless it gave him something he could use against the enemy, he didn't have the time or energy to think about it.

Consul Rellat and a small escort of Sharinic holy knights had been sent to the gates of the fortress to treat with the Kushaani but had received no answer at all. If he didn't know better, Stephir would have thought perhaps Balinth's had been abandoned. It was strange for the Kushaani to refuse to talk to the priest. They were a superstitious people and considered it bad luck to disrespect the clergy of any of the gods. That had been the last attempt to engage the Kushaani before today.

There had been a great deal of debate over the past two weeks as they traveled up the Spice Road about what should be the plan of attack once they arrived. Baron Marstoff had insisted that even if the Kushaani had managed by some dark power to take Balinth's (which he still was not convinced of, despite all evidence to the contrary), they could not possibly have enough surviving numbers to withstand a full assault.

'Perhaps,' Stephir had replied. 'But with even a few hundred soldiers, the Kushaani could kill thousands of my men before we retake the fortress. Tens of thousands.'

Some suggested turning around and finding a way through the mountains. After all, if the Kushaani had done it, certainly the Remalians could do the same. Others thought they should divide their forces and attempt multiple approaches, including sending some forces around by ship to ensure some made it to Teris, even if it took longer.

Those were all foolish ideas. If they could not get through Balinth's, Teris would get no help. Without the returning army, the city would be able to hold out two months, maybe three. Assuming, of course, there really was an army of twenty thousand Kushaani attacking Teris, which seemed impossible. Then again, losing Balinth's had seemed impossible until a couple of weeks ago—until a few hours ago... a few minutes.

Duke Miarsten spoke in the darkness behind him. It felt like his voice shattered the silence, although Stephir knew the duke was not speaking loudly. "This is a test of our resolve. Put your faith in the goddess."

Stephir noted that the duke did not specify which goddess, even though he knew Miarsten was a stanch Teraithian. Ever since reports of what had transpired in Tarsapta spread among the nobles, Stephir had heard much less mention of Teraithia's name. That suited Stephir just fine.

"Pray for victory," the duke continued. "We are Remalians, and no Kushaani force can withstand our might."

Stephir sighed and looked up at the heavens to silently pray one last time for Yonvaar and Kerail's blessings. He felt small and inadequate for the task ahead. He thought about his soldiers and wondered what they must be feeling. Theirs was probably the more immediate fear of taking a wound, or worse. That seemed like a simpler burden to bear. Still, they deserved to have him at his best. He forced aside the self-doubt and steeled himself.

In the dark, he could not see much more than the silhouettes of the two thousand soldiers filling the winding canyon behind him—five hundred for the direct assault, two hundred archers, and the rest as reserves in case they could be put to good use. Further down into the broad valley, the better part of his army remained asleep, but soon they would be busy preparing for battle. That was just to keep them busy unless by some miracle they retook Balinth's today. It was still unclear what kind of battle they would be preparing for. Would it be an all-out direct assault, sustained attacks with siege equipment, or a drawn-out siege to try to starve them out?

A siege seemed the most likely. He could not imagine the Kushaani having supply lines, especially all the way here to the fortress. But Balinth's was also well provisioned, probably enough to sustain a thousand men for a few months. Depending on the success of the army attacking Teris (or the surrounding countryside, if that was their target instead), it might be enough time for them to get additional supplies and reinforcements to Balinth's. That would be disastrous.

Not an option.

Building siege equipment seemed the best choice. Thanks to the forests around the valley there was plenty of material, and Stephir had every confidence in his engineers' abilities to provide whatever siege equipment he asked for. But what to ask for? Balinth's would not succumb to any but the heaviest catapults, battering rams, siege towers, and the like. But that kind of equipment was too massive to be hauled up the steep slopes to the pass. If he tried to transport the materials and assemble them in the pass, the enemy could rain down arrows and rocks from the fortress's own catapults. Lighter equipment could be brought, but to what end? And if he somehow managed to get the right siege equipment there, the canyon was too narrow to get enough of them together to do much good.

That left a direct assault; very, very costly if the Kushaani could make the best use of Balinth's formidable defenses. The Kushaani mostly used hit-and-run, draw-and-envelop tactics. They weren't used to manning fortified defenses. At least, Stephir hoped not. He was about to find out.

Andric, astride his mount at Stephir's side, nodded soberly. "The Holy Couple is on our side," Andric offered in an attempt to sound reassuring.

He knew Andric was not singularly devoted to Yonvaar and Kerail as Stephir was, but his brother invoked them for Stephir's benefit. The crown prince smiled, not quite comforted, but still glad to have Andric with him. He had sometimes imagined riding into battle together, although in his visions it was always under much better circumstances. Today would be the first, and possibly the last.

Glancing around, Stephir caught Frey looking at him. His friend smirked and raised his eyebrows but said nothing. They had discussed today's strategy numerous times and had both agreed it was the best of the bad options available. Frey liked it better than Stephir did, but Frey usually preferred brash and daring moves. The crown prince didn't have that luxury; brash could cost him too many men and possibly the entire war.

Stephir felt more alone than ever. Ilyanara, Shannyth, and Jenden were on the other side of this pass, and he might never see them again. He forced the thought from his mind and tried to ignore the pain clawing at his heart. He wished his father was here, but that was not possible. Everything rested on his shoulders. This was likely to be one of the defining moments of his reign, and he worried how it would end.

Ahead, a figure stepped from out of the deeper shadows to the center of the path and held up her hand. They had reached the designated staging point for the assault. The plan was to launch the attack before dawn broke, and Stephir was relieved to see they were just going to hit the mark. He did his best to take some small comfort in that as he rode the short distance to the scout who saluted as he approached.

"Anything to report?" Stephir asked.

"No, Your Highness. It's quiet, same as always."

Stephir was pleased there would be no more delays, though a part of him had secretly hoped there would be something that might postpone the inevitable. He was tempted to go have a look at the fortress himself, but there was no point other than his desire to put off giving the order he dreaded.

"High General Kuymon," Stephir said with a hushed voice.

"Yes, my lord." Kuymon waited for Stephir to give the order.

"It's time. Send them in." Simple words that in all likelihood meant the deaths of hundreds of men, perhaps more. But if all went according to plan, by the grace of the Holy Couple, Balinth's Fortress would be theirs by nightfall.

The high general nodded to one of his commanders who rode off to give the orders. Within minutes, foot soldiers were moving toward the final bend in the canyon. Captains were among them, but not on horseback. They would be too easily targeted by archers. Most carried tall shields painted blue and white, the Laconeus colors. Others carried long ladders, one for every ten men. Dozens more soldiers pulled small handcarts full of wood, brush, and leaves. When the soldiers had all moved to their positions, Stephir and his officers rode forward to watch the operation unfold.

Most of the first wave of five hundred soldiers stood on the sides of the canyon while the center was left open for the carts to move forward. The soldiers took the materials out of the carts and made large piles several feet ahead of the rest of the troops, then dowsed the piles with thick, grayish oil. Having finished their preparations, the men and carts retreated to safety. Twenty elantir strode forward and lined up behind the soldiers. It was difficult to see the details of their uniform in the dim morning light, but Stephir knew they wore blue and white surcoats over long, light chain shirts and black gambesons, black leather jerkins, and boots. Black sashes hung shoulder to hip. Stephir had grown to like the uniform of the elantir; simple but sharp. Of course, they could afford to wear things made to impress more than protect since they always worked from the rear.

Once in place, each elantir rested a hand on the shoulder of the elantir to his or her left. Stephir knew this helped them better use their powers in concert. In moments, inky black smoke rose in front of the soldiers. Stephir could not tell exactly what they were doing, but he understood the elantir used met'elan to light the piles on fire. They kept the fires from growing into flame, suppressing them to a level where the debris and oil merely smoldered. This kept the fires from burning through the fuel too quickly. More importantly, it maximized the amount of smoke the fires produced.

The perpetual breeze moving through the canyon should have blown the smoke back in their faces. Instead, the black billows moved in tight horizontal columns along the canyon walls toward the fortress, as if confined inside invisible tubes. It glowed eerily red, as if it carried some of the smoldering firelight with it. The five hundred soldiers were given the signal and moved forward, following the smoke at a distance, the ember light reflecting dully on their armor.

Stephir had to admit he was impressed. The concern had been raised in every war counsel over the last two weeks that arrows raining down from the tunnels in the canyon walls were one of the biggest threats they faced in retaking Balinth's. The idea of using smoke to cover their approach had been visited repeatedly, but knowing a nearly constant wind blew out of the pass eliminated it as a viable option. Cover of dark was their next best option. It would make it more difficult for the enemy archers, certainly, but it would be somewhat of a hindrance for his soldiers as well. Stephir had asked the elantir for any ideas. Their usual tactics of aiding communication, reinforcing and repairing equipment, and providing helpful comforts in the camp didn't seem particularly useful for this task.

Two days ago, Commander Alscan had offered this idea. At Stephir's request, the elantir had provided a demonstration, but with limited success. Alscan had assured him it would work much better in the canyon. He was gambling his men's lives on that thin assurance, but he didn't see any choice. As the lighted smoke moved unnaturally along the canyon walls, he liked what he saw.

He watched anxiously as the soldiers continued forward, blue and white shields raised overhead. Archers on the walls of the Fortress were one danger, but part of the design of Balinth's defenses were tunnels dug through the canyon walls themselves, with narrow openings for archers to fire at any unsuspecting enemies on the canyon floor. These tunnels gave the Kushaani defenders a clear view of the Remalian soldiers approaching the walls. Hopefully, the smoke preceding Stephir's forces provided cover, at least for the moment. Stephir could not tell if it was working from this distance, but the elantir planned to funnel some of the smoke through the holes into the tunnels. The idea was to obscure the Kushaani soldiers' vision. The smoke might even drive them out of the tunnels completely. Of course, that would mean more defenders on the walls, but with any luck, his men would already be on the walls by then. Stephir caught himself holding his breath and carefully let it out so as not to reveal his anxiety to those around him.

The soldiers were well within the killing zone now and quickly approached the walls. Was the smoke working, or was the enemy simply biding its time, waiting until his men were beyond the point of a quick retreat? From this distance, he could not be sure, but it appeared his men had reached the walls and were hoisting the ladders. Next to him, Andric let out a heavy breath. He realized the area had gone silent except for the sounds of the horses, and the creaking of armor and saddles as his men waited and watched.

Now Stephir was sure of his suspicions. Shadowy figures climbed the ladders and began moving atop the walls. *By the gods, they might actually do this!* He dared to hope just a little. Were the elantir wrong? Was there some trick and no Kushaani were in the fortress? That seemed unlikely. But the Kushaani had already proven themselves cowards, abandoning their cities and leaving disease and dark met'elan to do their killing for them. His mind darted to his father, on the verge of death on his sickbed back at the camp. It fueled his anger, but he forced his emotions into a tight knot in the middle of his chest and turned his attention back to his men still making their way up the ladders. It looked like most of them were already off the ground.

Still nothing happened. Stephir considered the possibility that the Kushaani had been too few to defend the fortress and had abandoned it. Stephir wanted to send the rest of his reserve troops rushing forward, but caution won out. *Just a little longer,* he told himself. Groups of men should be making their way inside the main wall to the rooms housing the mechanisms that open the gates. Then it would be time.

The passageway through Balinth's formidable wall was blocked by three barriers. Two massive stone slabs blocked either end of the tunnel, with a heavy iron portcullis in the middle. The mechanisms for raising the three defenses were each in a separate room on three different levels inside the walls.

Suddenly shouting echoed through the canyon, but Stephir could not make out what they were saying. "Can anyone tell what's going on?" he barked. Heads shook as a chorus of *noes* answered all around him. "Commander Alscan?" The elantir had her eyes closed in concentration, her hand inside the watertight bag at her side carrying the still-living body of a fachim with its tentacles severed and bound to the same blood-red crystals used to create the Bonded. The severed tentacles were carried by elantir, some moving with the advance soldiers and others waiting with the soldiers in the rear in case they were needed. This was something the elantir could do; at least, they could if their elantic ability to communicate through the bonded fachim didn't fail again. It had proven too unreliable on the battlefield, but here he had no other choice but to try.

After a moment, Alscan responded. "Yes, Your Highness, I can hear them." Stephir was both pleasantly surprised and anxious to hear what she would report. "There appears to be fighting inside the walls." Her voice sank. "It's an ambush."

All around him, voices broke into an angry and urgent cacophony. Stephir ordered silence and he was mostly obeyed. "General," Stephir began.

Baron Marstoff cut in, not to be kept quiet. "My lord, we must send more men now! We control the walls. The elantir have done their job. We must overwhelm them while we can."

"Thank you, Baron. I believe I can handle this," Stephir said, far more calmly than he felt. He almost sounded like his father. "General, order the second wave to move up and stand at the ready for my command." Kuymon instructed one of his captains to convey the order, but Stephir was already turning his attention back to Commander Alscan. "Anything further?"

"The same," Alscan said. Unlike many in her profession, the commander was not one for unnecessary words.

Renewed shouting from the fortress walls sharpened Stephir's focus, his eyes straining to see anything that would give him a clue as to what was going on. He didn't have to wonder long.

"Your Highness," Alscan said urgently. Stephir's stomach clenched, fearing the worst. "It sounds like the inner gate-stone is being raised."

Excited voices broke out in relieved chatter. "I told you the Kushaani were no match for us," came a triumphant exclamation from among his commanders. Was that Miarsten, again?

Andric's gloved hand slapped him on the back. "And you had us all worked up for nothing," his brother joked with him.

Stephir was not going to allow himself to celebrate until they had secured the fortress and cleaned out every last trace of the Kushaani. Within moments, he could see the outer gate-stone rising. Even if there were Kushaani forces inside Balinth's waiting to ambush them, there would be no better opportunity to get his men inside than now.

"High General Kuymon, get the men in there. If we can capture anyone, make it happen."

The high general turned his horse and shouted the order himself. Commanders repeated the order, and Stephir's soldiers began marching on Balinth's Fortress. The line of elantir moved to the side to leave the path clear for the soldiers. The smoke they had kept in place drifted away from the cliffs and swirled through the canyon. Stephir was annoyed the smoke now obscured his view of the fortress, but it was a small price for getting his men safely inside.

Stephir watched with satisfaction as his troops marched past him through dark shadows still clinging to the deep canyon. He was not usually prone to fantasy, but at this moment he wished the morning sun that bathed the soaring peaks above Balinth's in golden light would somehow shine down on his men, glinting off their armor and weapons as they recaptured the fortress.

Through the smoke came the sudden sound of battle—metal on metal, men screaming in pain and fury. The sounds were too distant to be the soldiers marching through the canyon. The fighting must have broken out atop the battlements. Had this all been a trap after all? Should he rush forward or proceed with caution? It was impossible to tell, and Stephir knew he had to make the decision now.

"Get to the fortress!" he shouted. He had to suppress the urge to charge to the gates himself. He would get there soon enough, but he was a commander before a soldier. He had to set the battle in order.

"For Remalia!" Baron Marstoff bellowed as he spurred his horse forward. Several nobles, anxious for a fight, followed the baron's impetuous example. That was not what Stephir had in mind, but he knew he wasn't going to be able to stop them now.

"Commander Alscan, can you do something about the smoke? Put it back on the walls or at least get rid of it?" Stephir asked.

"I'll do whatever can be done, my lord." The commander turned her horse and rode away just as Kuymon drew near.

"High General, get the men in there and keep those gates open." Stephir knew he neither needed to elaborate nor worry about the details. Kuymon knew his business. But Stephir had somewhat less confidence in Marstoff and the others, at least for this kind of attack. On the field, most of them could hold their own, but this was going to require tight control of the battle.

Stephir turned to Andric next. "We may need more men. Ride back to camp and bring five hundred more men as quickly as you can, and tell General Pavam to keep sending fists of five hundred as quickly as they can be mustered."

Andric stared back at him for a moment. "You're sending me as a messenger boy?" he asked icily.

"Messenger boy?" Stephir snapped. He bit back the rebuke he was about to lash upon Andric. That would be counterproductive in so many ways. Andric's full support was important to Stephir, and humiliating him in front of the commanders was only going to drive a wedge between them. Andric already did not have the strongest respect from these men and women. Stephir wanted to do whatever he could to change that. He reminded himself that Andric was still green. His heart was probably in the right place, wanting to be in the fight, but he had to learn that he was a leader first and foremost.

"I need you to be in command of the second wave. If things go badly, you'll need to help get us out."

"This is probably going to be over long before I get back with more men," Andric countered, somewhat less icily. "You've got two thousand more men trying to get to the fortress. Let me keep five hundred back as a reserve force that can be ready to respond immediately if necessary. I'll send someone else back to camp with the message. If more troops can get here by the time they're needed, so much the better."

Stephir was impressed. It was a better plan. He wanted to look around and make sure the others in his command retinue took note, but he feared it would look like he was seeking their approval. He didn't need it.

He smiled at Andric and returned the slap on the shoulder. "Good point. Maybe you should go in first and I'll cover *your* back," Stephir joked.

"Done," Andric replied, returning the smile.

Stephir couldn't be sure Andric had picked up that it was a joke. The noise of soldiers running past them and orders being shouted from commanders up and down the line forced him to raise his voice. "You'll want about one in five to be bowmen," he instructed.

"Thank you. I believe I can handle this," Andric said with feigned seriousness. Stephir shook his head at having his earlier rebuke of Marstoff turned against him. "Go," Andric said as his only farewell, then he turned and ordered one of the nearby commanders to follow him. They rode back along the line of troops to arrange for his five hundred reserve soldiers.

The sounds of battle intensified and drew Stephir's attention back toward Balinth's. He expected not to be able to see much, but a corridor of clear air opened as the smoke once again drifted unnaturally toward the cliffs. Much of it had dissipated, so it wasn't the heavy cover it had been a short while ago, but at least it was no longer in his way. The fortress was still too far away to make out details, but he could tell there was heavy fighting atop the walls. He could also see that the first ranks of the second wave had reached the gates. No more time to wait.

"Let's go," he said as he drove his heels into his mount's flanks. Dozens more followed his lead. With a thunder of hooves, they raced toward the fortress. He looked up to the arrow holes in walls above him and on the other side of the canyon, a thousand dark eyes staring from behind a thin veil of smoke. Being fired upon from above was still the biggest threat they faced. He took a moment to thank the Holy Couple for their mercy and prayed it would continue.

Sweat soaked the clothes under his armor and a trickle ran down the side of his face under his helmet. Archpaladin Nophet rode at his right side, leading the Divinarim forming a protective ring around the prince, ready to defend him at all costs. It was strangely comforting to have the stalwart Divinarim commander with him, despite the recent tension between them. Stephir gave Nophet a sharp nod of appreciation. The Divinar to his left moved aside to let another rider in next to Stephir. He glanced to his side and Frey smiled fiercely. The only surprise was that his friend was not already at the gates. Frey must have read his thoughts.

"Someone has to keep those Kushaani blades off your royal hide!" Frey yelled.

Stephir smiled. He was glad to have one of Remalia's finest swordsmen at his side. As they approached the walls, Stephir could make out the faces of his men atop the battlements. There was Earl Sothmore's son, fighting... what?

That was no Kushaani! For the first time, Stephir glimpsed the defenders and his mind reeled. The description given by Captain Major Min had not come close to painting the true picture of the enemy his men faced. Gray-skinned, jet-black hair, yes. And they were covered in some sort of strange, black-scale armor. But the power with which they struck, their stature, their faces that looked chiseled from stone—everything told him that these were not Kushaani. *Who then? Where did they come from?*

He didn't have time to ponder the questions. A shockwave washed over him. There was no sound, no fire, no exploding rock, but in a blur the front gate-stone fell, crushing men as it slammed sickeningly against the ground. Another shockwave reverberated through the canyon and he could hear the screech of metal that must have been the portcullis, and a second, followed by the sound of the inner gate-stone crashing closed. Loose rocks and dust showered down on them from the canyon walls.

"They've got to get those gates back open!" someone behind Stephir yelled.

"Those gates may never open again. The opening mechanisms have been destroyed." Nophet's voice cut through the chaos to Stephir. The prince wanted to wheel around and protest, to ask how Nophet could know for certain, but somewhere in the pit of his stomach he already knew it was true. Those stones were designed to be lowered to block the entrance, not to come crashing down. What else could have happened?

Stephir's mind raced with questions and conflicting impulses. "Get to the ladders! We can use them to get over the walls," Stephir ordered to no one in particular. He needed more information. He wished Commander Alscan was still with him, but he turned to the elantir who had taken her place. "How many enemy soldiers are up there and how many men do we have on the wall and inside?" As the elantir repeated the question through the bonded fachim, Stephir scanned the chaos and confusion among his soldiers who milled around outside the walls. "Get the men into lines against—"

Whistling in the air signaled that the worst was happening. The sudden screams of his men confirmed it. "Get the men against the walls! Two rows! Outer row shields overhead, inner row shields level. Order a retreat."

A bolt hit his armor at an angle and deflected off. A couple of horses shrieked as bolts sank into their flesh. A captain nearby went down with a bolt through his throat.

"Off the horses!" Stephir yelled as he slid off Havvoron. Were the shots coming from both sides or just one? It only took a moment to see it was both sides. This enemy knew how to make the most of the fortress's defenses. *Why couldn't these be like other Kushaani?* Just as he and his commanders moved out from behind the cover being provided by their mounts, one of the elantir stopped him.

"Your Highness," came a deep voice from the middle-aged man with brown hair that formed a ring around an otherwise bald head. "We estimate there are two hundred or more Kushaani on the walls and at least that many in the tunnels on each side of the canyon."

At least six hundred! This is going to be a slaughter. Both men ducked as a bolt hit Stephir's armor with a loud ping and ricocheted past their heads.

"Corporal, anything else?" Stephir asked urgently. A wild look of fear fixed itself in the elantir's eyes. Stephir grabbed the elantir's arm and shook him. "Corporal!"

The man quickly regained his composure and continued. "I'm sorry, Your Highness. As I was saying, they are also in the inner courtyard, but it's difficult to tell how many. Certainly hundreds."

Eight hundred or more Kushaani? They had to have received reinforcements. By the elantir's count, the enemy would have only lost a fraction of their forces taking Balinth's, assuming Captain Major Min's report was accurate in the first place. He didn't have time to dwell on this now. He pointed the elantir toward the nearest canyon wall and gave him a firm push. The deadly hiss of bolts from above were almost constant, as were the sickening thuds of bolts finding too many bodies.

"Get out of here! Move along the wall." Stephir turned his attention back to his men, some of whom had either received the order or figured it out on their own, racing toward the walls with their shields up. Commanders were out among the men, yelling and shoving to get them moving. The men were moving, but many abandoned the protection of their shields and ran, falling in the attempt.

Stephir pulled Havvoron by the reins as he ran along the lines, shouting instructions to keep their shields up. He staggered forward, startled by the shock of another bolt striking his shoulder from behind. There was little pain though. He guessed it hadn't pierced his armor. Most of his men were either against the walls or downed by bolts. He could not tell which numbers were greater. He would worry about that later. Most of them would be in the latter category if they did not get out of there now.

Suddenly Havvoron's scream pierced his ears, and Stephir was yanked backward as his mount reared, hooves hacking furiously at the air, narrowly missing Stephir's head. As his forelegs touched the ground, they buckled, again pulling Stephir off balance. Two bolts had sunk deep into his horse's side and neck. They must have torn his flesh as he fell because blood poured onto the ground, his legs kicking feebly. Stephir knew Havvoron would be dead in moments, and his heart ached at the thought of it. He knew he should seek cover, but he put a hand on Havvoron's head and prayed for the Holy Couple to give him peace.

A shadow loomed over Stephir, and the prince looked up to see another horse interposed between him and the nearest wall. "Your Highness," Nophet's voice cut through the din of the dying around him, and he offered a hand to lift Stephir from where he knelt. "We must go. Now!" Nophet's voice was calm but firm, though his eyes darted about in search of approaching danger.

Another Divinar led his horse to the other side, keeping the horses as shields against the rain of bolts coming from the walls. It was crude and sickened Stephir to use such proud animals in such a grisly manner, but there was no time to protest. Stephir had no better plan. He grasped Nophet's hand, his shoulder aching in protest as he was pulled hastily to his feet.

"You're wounded," the Divinarim commander said as he stepped behind the prince. Stephir ignored him and shouted for his men to keep moving. A few more minutes and they would be past the worst of it. "It got through a joint at an angle, but I don't think it penetrated the chain."

A dull pain shot through his shoulder as Nophet yanked on the shaft of a bolt sticking out of his armor, but it didn't come out. He wondered if the bold would have gotten through if his armor was not elanticly hardened. Nophet tried again and the shaft broke, leaving the metal tip beneath his armor, digging uncomfortably into his shoulder. "Leave it, it's fine!" Stephir said, irritated at the distraction.

He looked behind him and across to the other side of the canyon, searching for Frey, Kuymon, Marstoff, and the others. He caught sight of Frey on the opposite wall, driving men back the way they had come just as Stephir was. More men were felled by crossbow fire. Some of the injured were helped along by companions, but too many cried out for help where they fell, unable to get to their feet and keep moving.

A scream from the horse protecting him pierced Stephir's ears. The Divinar struggled with the reins for a moment as the beast staggered and then bolted. Releasing the reins, the knight raised his shield and took the animal's place protectively at Stephir's side, holding the shield above, leaving his lower body exposed.

Stephir could no longer see Frey, but further behind he was pretty sure he saw High General Kuymon with a bolt sticking out of his arm, shouting for retreat. Back at the fortress walls, his men were still fighting and shouting for them to return and save them. Someone leaped from the height of the wall to escape only the gods knew what. Stephir's heart fell like a stone as the man plummeted to his death.

By the time the prince rounded the bend in the canyon, Andric and his reserve force were already helping the more severely wounded soldiers onto carts to be carried to the Remalian camp. Stephir walked toward his brother, fury still burning in his bones.

"Is it as bad as it looks?" Andric asked.

"Worse."

"Your Highness, we need to get that bolt out of your shoulder," Nophet said, then called for a healer.

"You're wounded?" Fear washed over Andric's face as he jumped off his horse and ran to Stephir. Faces turned with mixed expressions of shock, worry, bewilderment, and some with numb curiosity, to see if the crown prince was injured.

"No, I'm fine," Stephir said loudly to put as many at ease as he could.

"But you've taken a bolt?" Andric asked, looking him over.

"I think it was mostly stopped by the chain. We can get it out later."

Nophet showed Andric where the bolt had gone through and they worked to get it out. Stephir scanned the faces of men streaming past, searching for his command retinue and trying to figure out how many men he had lost. "Have you seen Frey? Or Marstoff? I lost track of them in the retreat."

Stephir felt Andric put a hand on his shoulder and begin channeling elan. He worried Andric intended to try and heal him. His brother was no healer and might do more harm than good if he tried. Stephir was about to stop him, but he felt the bolt head move and the aching pressure on his shoulder was gone.

"Got it," Andric said as he handed the bolt tip to Stephir. "And no, I haven't seen them, but I'm sure they're fine," Andric assured him. "Let's get everyone back to camp and find out where things stand."

An elantir stood at Stephir's side, trying to examine the prince's shoulder as best he could. It was distracting and Stephir waved the man away, failing to keep his anger and frustration from showing on his face.

"Agreed. Then we can figure out how to make these bastards pay for what they've done."

CHAPTER XXX
BARAK

B arak leaned heavily to one side in the tall chair, resting his forehead in his hand, his feet dangling off the ground. It had bothered him at first, knowing it exaggerated his small stature, but he was past the point of caring. He was only with his two elantir companions, Corporal Askko and Lieutenant Krallip, and they seemed to be finally taking him seriously, even if his feet did dangle a bit. Scribe Yemana was also in the room, though the Viancian priestess hardly spoke. None of them believed the source of their lost ability to communicate with Teris through the Bonded had anything to do with divinessence, but Commander Alscan had asked the priestess to be present for their discussions in case there was anything she could do to help.

"I'm telling you, there's nothing there," Krallip insisted, a hint of frustration edging into his voice. His hands rested gently on the Bonded laying inside the gold and crystal reliquary on a low, heavy-legged table in the center of the room. Barak had been working with the elantir for days to try and solve the problem. But with no progress to speak of and the grim mood settling over the Remalian camp after the loss at Balinth's Fortress that morning, the tension was starting to show through the cracks.

"It has to be there," Barak said under his breath as he racked his brain for some other way to approach the problem.

"Well, I'm telling you, it's not," Krallip retorted.

I wasn't talking to you, Barak wanted to snarl at the man, but he held his tongue. The tent flap opened and his eyes snapped toward the entrance. No one was supposed to be admitted. He was surprised but somewhat relieved to see Commander Alscan enter. Barak had expected she would be dining with the princes, as she had been doing more frequently. He had noticed she and Prince Stephir had been spending more time working together, and the crown prince seemed to be taking a liking to her. Barak had asked Andric about it, but his friend dismissed it as his overactive imagination. Barak was not so sure.

"Commander," the two elantir straightened and saluted. Barak liked the symbolism of the elantir's salute. The left hand was held flat in front of the diaphragm with the palm up, representing the elantir themselves. Their right hand pointed up, with the heel of the palm resting in their left hand, fingers toward the sky, representing the elan they controlled. The hands moved together in a horizontal circular motion representing the connection and transmutation of the elan all around them through their met'elan. The salute was a bitter personal reminder that while he could sense elan, he was blind and deaf to the individual threads, and could not touch or control them if his life had depended on it. He pushed the thought aside as he greeted Alscan.

"Commander, I expected you to be at the banquet. Is something wrong?" Barak asked, concerned by her unexpected appearance.

"Nothing is wrong, I just wanted to see if you had any progress to report."

"No, Commander," the two elantir responded together.

"Master Ve'Aurben?" A few days earlier he had confessed to the commander that he was not, in fact, an ordained priest of Viance, and not deserving of the title of 'master.' She had continued to use the title anyway. It was probably for the best, but it had become a thorn in his side—one more indication he had no business ever leaving Teris. He felt particularly guilty receiving the honorific in front of Scribe Yemana.

"Master Ve'Aurben?" Alscan repeated.

He didn't know what he should say. He refused to give up the idea that there must be some extra thread of elan woven into the elants that created the Bonded, but he had no way to find it on his own, and Askko and Krallip hadn't found anything. He was not convinced they were up to the task, but he could hardly say that with them in the room if he had any hope of continuing to work together productively.

"No, nothing new to report," he said flatly, trying to keep his frustration out of his voice.

Alscan considered them for a moment, then said, "Very well, tell me what you have proven is not the answer."

The other two elantir looked confused, but to Barak, her words were a breath of fresh air. He adored her in that moment, and the concerns weighing him down seemed to slough off. He wanted to laugh with the sudden relief, but contained it to a tight-lipped smile he hoped did not look like a smirk. After an awkward moment of silence, it was clear neither of his companions had any idea where to start, so Barak jumped in.

"Without the other half of a Bonded, we have no way to be certain the connection is still in place. However, as we have noted before, Scribe Yemana has confirmed the Bonded are still experiencing emotions and visions, which would be impossible if the connection was severed. Moreover, vibration induction seems to be attenuating as we would expect, so it seems safe to assume the link is intact. We haven't detected any primary or harmonic reflection, so an elantic obstruction does not seem likely." Barak had been careful to use 'we' up to this point to be inclusive of Askko and Krallip, but he was stepping into his own theory now, which the other two didn't agree with, and he wanted to be respectful of that.

"I believe there is likely another flow, or perhaps several, in the elant, but we haven't been able to detect anything to that effect so far." Barak knew without looking that at least Lieutenant Krallip was doing his best to make clear without speaking that he considered this line of thought a waste of time.

"And why are you so convinced there is another flow?" Alscan asked, sounding genuinely interested. "We have been looking for weeks and found nothing of the sort. We have examined and re-examined every stream, every vibration. Nothing is missing and nothing extra is there."

"May'e the gods are doin' this ta punish us," suggested Corporal Askko in her thick western Remalian accent.

That kind of reasoning sounded like a cop-out to Barak, but he didn't want to outright deride her, so he chose a softer approach. "Even if that's true, we should at least understand *how* they are doing it."

"May'e they changed the laws of nature so that our met'lan does na work anymore. We'ud ne'er know the difference," Askko added.

The suggestion was absurd, but something about it hooked his attention.

"I don't think that—" Yemana began.

Barak cut her off. "Quiet! I need to think," he demanded. *'Maybe they changed the laws of nature,'* he repeated Askko's words in his mind. No, that wasn't it. He set that aside and considered her next words. *'We would never know the difference.'* Why did that strike a chord with him? *'... never know the difference.'* What could change without them realizing it? What can they not see?*

He recalled a question Master Weccom had posed to him one time. 'If everything in the world, in all the vast universe, instantly doubled in size, would we ever know the difference?' It had been an interesting discussion, but Barak could see no relevance to the present problem other than the words were similar, so he dismissed the thought and tried something else.

What has changed recently that I haven't seen? he asked himself. His first thought was about the defeat at Balinth's Fortress that morning. He hadn't been present, but it was the only thing anyone was talking about. Krallip and Askko had talked about the elantir trying to block the enemy's vision with smoke, but it hadn't worked. It should have been effective if they were Kushaani, but much less so if they were Kuldrith, as he had theorized. The Kuldrith lived and fought their whole lives underground, so they could probably manage reasonably well without clear sight. *Kuldrith.*

"They're Kuldrith," Barak said, focusing on the word, struggling to see why his mind was bringing it to the foreground. *What can we not see?*

"What do you mean?" Alscan asked, sounding confused but curious.

"The enemy at Balinth's Fortress—I believe they're Kuldrith, not Kushaani."

"Really?" Krallip scoffed. "Kuldrith? In Remalia? And here I thought you were an expert on military matters too! Perhaps this explains why they haven't appointed you to the king's war counsel yet."

Barak bit back several insults straining to escape his mouth. *Stay objective,* he urged himself. "Yes, Kuldrith. But what—"

Krallip cut him off. "The Kuldrith are a ragtag bunch of cave dwellers halfway around the world! They haven't had a military force worth spitting at in over three hundred years. The only reason they even still exist is because the Eastgatians don't want to get their hands dirty crawling around in holes to ferret out the last of them."

"Actually," Alscan said casually, "I heard Prince Stephir and Marquis de'Venneshen discussing Master Ve'Aurben's theory after the battle today. Apparently, what they saw has them considering that he may be correct."

Barak knew he was taking too much satisfaction in seeing the abashed look on Krallip's face. He forced himself back to the question of what, if anything, this had to do with their communications problem. *What am I not seeing?* He wanted to avoid the painful answer his mind proffered, but he forced himself to face the truth. *You can't see the flows of the elant.*

Neither can they! he said defensively.

And why can't they see them? his inner voice replied as if coaxing him toward an end it already knew. He didn't have an answer and escaped the difficulty by turning back to enjoy the thought of Stephir and Frey talking about the Kuldrith.

Correct, the voice answered.

Barak's thoughts were getting twisted into a knot. *I must be getting tired*, he considered, but knew that was not the truth. The silence in the room had passed into awkwardness, but he pushed on, feeling that he was close to... *something*.

Barak thought out loud, verbally working through the puzzle, talking more to himself than the others in the tent. "If the enemy at Balinth's are Kuldrith, then the force invading Remalia is almost certainly also Kuldrith. It would make sense that they would want the communications stopped. But how?" *What can we not see?*

"Can they intercept it somehow?" the priestess offered vaguely.

Barak tried to fit that idea with his instinct that there must be something extra in the elants, like putting puzzle pieces together that didn't quite fit. *Maybe I'm looking at this too closely*, Barak thought.

"What do we know about Kuldrith met'elan?" he asked.

It was a rhetorical question, but Krallip answered it anyway. "How, by Akraharr's wind, would we know anything about them or their dark secrets?"

"That's an interesting point," Barak said, ignoring the vulgarity and focusing on Krallip's reference to the god of anarchy. "Did you know that the Kuldrith believe there are nine elantic modes, not the seven we use in Remalia?"

"The Restani have nine as well," Commander Alscan said, attempting to be helpful. It was beside the point, but Barak nodded politely, then went on. "Some ancient writers drew a connection between each node and a corresponding god. For example, they have a node called *Kosek*, which corresponds to Akraharr and represents the chaotic aspects of elan and its ability to bind with—"

"Enough!" Krallip barked, anger darkening his face. "Speak no more of this!"

Barak knew all too well he was venturing into dangerous territory. He had encountered it many times in his attempts to delve into the occult aspects of met'elan. "I understand this may be a difficult matter to discuss, but perhaps that's exactly what the enemy is counting on. What if they've hidden their work in places they know you would never look because you believe it's taboo?"

"It isn't *taboo*," Krallip spat the word with disgust. "It is forbidden, sealed away by sacred oaths. And for good reason. It is dark and dangerous power, and the gods have commanded it should not be touched by humans."

"Viance hasn't commanded that at all." Barak countered. "On the contrary. She teaches that all knowledge is appropriate for her children to have. It's in the application of knowledge that good and evil are manifest, not in having the knowledge itself. And ignorance can enable evil to exist."

"Says one who is forever blind in this matter," Krallip said contemptuously. It was a slap in the face.

"Hold your tongue, Lieutenant!" Alscan barked reprovingly. Then, somewhat softening her tone, she said to Barak, "So, you're suggesting there may be additional flows in these other elantic modalities?"

Barak appreciated the commander defending him more than he cared to admit for fear his emotions might get the better of him. He didn't want to squander Alscan's goodwill or attention, so he pressed ahead with the line of reasoning. "I can't say for certain, but it occurs to me that we haven't even looked there. And if the Kuldrith are the cause of this, then it could easily explain why we have missed it until now."

"And how would you propose we begin to search for something we have no knowledge of?" She didn't ask it accusingly, but as a practical problem that needed to be addressed.

"Commander, I must object. You cannot—" Krallip's anger seemed tightly bound behind his words.

"Don't tell me what I cannot do, Lieutenant," Alscan warned with steel in her voice that matched the hard-set look in her eyes. "The prince has charged us with solving this problem, and I will not allow the guilds' superstitions to get in our way. Do I make myself clear?"

"You set your word above the gods?"

"The gods haven't told me any such thing. Do you claim to speak for the gods?"

"Their commands have been handed down from time immemorial!" the lieutenant said, his voice rising with exasperation.

"May'e this is the gods' way of tellin' us they 'ave new commands," Askko suggested quietly, almost timidly. Barak believed she was trying to be helpful.

Krallip turned his head and spat, a superstitious and derogatory gesture. Hot exasperation flooded Barak's cheeks.

"Regardless, we are going to figure this out one way or another," Alscan said, finality resting heavily in her words. "Master Ve'Aurben, do you have any suggestions on where we should begin?"

Barak had already been considering the question, but all he could offer was what little he had been able to glean from vague references in ancient texts, none of which seemed particularly useful. However, he wanted to be helpful if possible. "The obvious first issue is to become sensitized to these other modalities. Unfortunately, there is little I can do in that respect." He knew Andric had experimented with those modalities. They were dangerous and no one who might have been able to help teach him had been willing to be responsible if something bad happened to the prince, so his experience was limited. Barak didn't want to tarnish his friend's reputation for a hunch that had little chance of success.

"I may be able to help with that," Alscan said. "In my younger days, I worked for Calavian and Celendrian merchant houses and learned a thing or two about elantic practices from other places. Nothing about the Kuldrith, but as I mentioned, the Restani and others practice met'elan that occasionally includes the additional modalities. Perhaps what I know will be similar enough that with your help we can find what we are looking for, if indeed there is anything to be found."

Alscan thanked Scribe Yemana and excused her to return to her other duties, then began working with Krallip and Askko to guide them in their first halting steps into unfamiliar territory. Barak offered what little help he could, but their activities quickly moved into efforts that left the room in heavy silence, broken only by the occasional "No, you slid past it again," or "I just felt something. Was that it?" and more than one "Ouch!" followed by some cursing.

As evening deepened into night, Alscan ordered food to be brought for them, but Barak hardly touched his. Boredom and frustration stalked him as his thoughts wandered further from the task at hand. He wished for the hundredth time he was back in Teris with access to the libraries there. *And what good would that do?* he asked himself with reproof. Words like *impotent* and *fraud* sprang up like weeds, choking every path his mind turned to.

Barak fought back the only way he knew how—by facing the truth, embracing it, seeing it for what it was. *Truth*—he could not perform met'elan. *Truth*—he had not yet helped solve the communications problem. *Truth*—neither had anyone else. *Truth*—he had not yet helped solve the mystery of the king's illness. *Truth*—neither had anyone else. *Truth*—he was out of his element with the nobles and elantir. *Truth*—he was friends with Andric, who seemed to find some value in having him around.

Barak continued to list fact after fact, but despite providing moments of reprieve, the painful words lurked at the edges, ready to swoop in to fill any pause in his recitation. He considered those words more closely. *Impotent.*

Fraud. He reviewed their definitions, wondered about the origins of the words, tried to remember anything he had read where they were used. He considered every situation where they applied in his life.

The Remalians were impotent to retake Balinth's Fortress. Father Meyan, the priest of Yonvaar, who had until recently served the royal family, had proved a fraud and had been defrocked for violating his oaths and partaking of the illicit services of the Sykorian disciples on the outskirts of the Remalian camp. The elantir were impotent to fix the communications problem. Perhaps the Bonded itself was a fraud.

His mind latched on to that idea. They had thoroughly examined the physical Bonded for any trace of something out of order. The human half was alive and functioning and was bound to the red carnelian crystal as it should be. Perhaps the elantic flows themselves were frauds. *Is that even possible?*

"What if it isn't an *extra* flow" he said out loud, as if vocalizing his thought could help it make more sense. "What if one or more of them is a fake, disguised to look like the genuine flow but not?"

"You can't make elan appear to be what it isn't," Krallip said as if lecturing a dense student.

"But you can certainly make an impotent copy. Have you never created an elant that for some reason didn't work and had a hard time figuring out what was off because everything seemed to be correct?" Barak knew he was taking a bit of a shot in the dark, but it stood to reason this would happen on occasion.

"Yes, that does happen," Alscan offered when Krallip didn't immediately answer. "But we have been through the flows again and again."

"Can you replace the flows, one at a time?" Barak asked.

Alscan thought for a moment, then shrugged. "Some of them, maybe. But most of them are anchored on both ends of the Bonded. We could not reconnect a new flow without both halves together."

"But this problem didn't begin until we were south of Balinth's Fortress. Which means something changed that can be done to only one-half of the Bonded."

"Assuming your theory is correct," the lieutenant pointed out, "which is nothing but pure speculation."

"Oh, for the love of Viance!" Barak exclaimed in frustration. "Open your mind, Krallip!"

"Open your center," the elantir retorted bitingly.

Barak had never been particularly susceptible to insults, but that one struck his core vulnerability, the one thing he desired most. It stung.

"All right," Alscan said firmly. "That's enough. Let's..."

Barak didn't wait to hear the rest of her words. He got down off the chair and kept his eyes fixed on the exit as he stalked across the tent and out into the sweltering heat and oppressive humidity of the night. Barak didn't usually pay any attention to the weather, but tonight it felt like nature was conspiring with everyone else to magnify his misery. He wanted to be away from everyone, to find some seclusion, but fires throughout the vast camp spread out like a sea of stars in all directions. He felt trapped.

He wandered aimlessly for a time, his thoughts trudging through the same worn tracks over and over. No one in the camp paid him any attention as he passed, and the anonymity felt almost like being alone, but it was not the same solitude he usually welcomed; it was a lonelier isolation, tainted by the constant reminder that he had no real purpose for being there. Even the other Cannessi who traveled with the army and helped with menial tasks such as cooking, cleaning, and the like, had their place. As much as he usually hated seeing them relegated to such ignoble work, tonight he found himself feeling envious of them. At least their contributions were actually useful, and some of the Remalians seemed to appreciate their service.

He considered returning to help Commander Alscan, but he just could not bring himself to deal with Krallip and the whole situation right now. Fatigue and frustration finally drove him to his tent. It was small and simple, but at least it was his alone—one of the benefits of being the advisor and friend to the prince. He could not muster the will to remove his clothes, and instead, he simply sank onto the firm cot and let the darkness envelop him. He drifted toward sleep, but his mind would not allow him to fully surrender to welcome unconsciousness. He listened to every footfall that passed outside his tent and realized he was hoping one of them would bring some kind of good news.

One set of footsteps finally stopped next to the entrance, and Barak waited with anticipation as one moment stretched into the next. At last, the tent flap opened and Commander Alscan entered. She wordlessly knelt by the bed and stroked his hair, then kissed him gently on the lips. Barak kissed her back, and she pulled away with a laugh—not a mocking laugh, but a laugh of joyful playfulness. Barak wanted to pull her onto his bed, but when he took her hand, she spoke.

"Come with me," she said, pulling him to his feet. They stepped through the tent flaps into a dark cave tunnel. Lights floated in the air like tiny, disembodied flames. He wanted to study them, to see how they worked, but

Calinda led him by the hand. Her skin was warm and soft, and Barak contented himself to see where they were going.

They came to an immense chasm, dark and foreboding. Across the gulf, a beautiful woman sat on a bright, golden throne. He wanted more than anything to go to her, but it was impossibly far.

"Come on, let's fly," Calinda said, smiling, and began floating into the air.

"I can't," Barak replied plaintively, straining to keep hold of her hand that was slipping from his grasp.

"Of course you can. Just come to me," she beckoned as their hands parted.

Barak tried with all his willpower and began shaking from the effort, but his feet were hopelessly rooted to the earth. Tears fell from his eyes in frustration and disappointment as Calinda drifted further from him. She laughed at him like a mother laughs at the antics of an adorable child. Barak was afire with shame, but she floated back to him and kissed his forehead.

Power surged through him. Elan, sweet and raw and alive, rushed into him. He soared into the air, borne on the currents of living energy all around him and coursing through him. They embraced, and kissed passionately, spinning gracefully through the air. He felt exhilarated, filled with an expansive lucidity that opened his awareness to everything around him.

Barak cast his eyes down at the dark chasm below him, and suddenly he was falling. Dirt and roots and rocks were all around him. He scrabbled desperately for a handhold, but the black stone was too slippery.

He stood in a room with a black altar, and on the altar rested a gleaming sword. Andric reached for the sword. "No!" Barak shouted, but it was too late. Elan exploded from the sword. Barak pulled the elan into himself, more and more of it rushing into every fiber of his being until his flesh began ripping apart, searing his bones, evaporating his very soul. He screamed in agony.

Barak awoke in the darkness of his tent, shaking and sweating.

Someone pulled the tent flap open and called to Barak in the darkness. "Are you all right Master Ve'Aurben?"

Barak was still caught up in the terror of his dream, and it took him a moment to discern the shadow and voice belonged to Jase, Andric's squire. It was odd the young man was here at this hour. "Yes, I'm fine," Barak answered, his voice sounding dry and hoarse.

"I'm sorry to disturb you, but Prince Andric sent me to fetch you to his tent."

"All right," Barak replied, and sat up, trying to shake off both the weariness and lingering sense of dread from the dream. He took quick stock of his situation and realized he was still fully dressed. "I'm ready. Let's go."

They walked the short distance to Andric's tent, and Jase led the way inside as Divinarim held the tent flaps open. Barak's skin broke out in goose flesh and a chill ran up his spine as he entered the cooled tent.

"Oh good, you found him," Andric said, hardly sounding pleased. He slouched in his favorite chair with a silver cup in his hand. "That will be all for tonight, Jase. Please make sure our horses are ready at first light."

"Yes, Your Highness," Jase replied as he gave a slight bow and then left the tent.

Barak noted the young man seemed to have grown more comfortable interacting with the prince and others of higher social station. Not that Barak was exactly in Andric's social station, but he may as well have been as far as Jase was concerned. Barak supposed the familiarity bred by daily contact was an inevitable and even desirable part of the patronage system.

"We missed you at dinner tonight," Andric said in his too-casual voice that told Barak his friend wanted something but was making small talk first. Barak was not in the mood for pleasantries. He was still deeply disturbed by his dream and could not help feeling it meant something important, but he just had no idea yet what it was.

"How may I be of service?" It came out harsher than he intended.

"Is everything all right?" Andric asked.

"Yes... sorry. It has been a difficult day."

"Tell me about it," Andric mumbled with a heaviness that grabbed Barak's attention. The prince took a drought from his cup.

Barak had seen Andric in all sorts of moods, but rarely like this. He realized how much worse the day must have been for his friend and felt guilty for having been so focused on his own problems that paled in comparison. He didn't know what he could do to help Andric other than offer a listening ear. "Any decisions about what you're going to do now?"

"Decisions? No. Endless discussion and arguments? Of course!" Andric rubbed his temples with his free hand. "Your theory about them being Kuldrith came up as well. I almost sent for you so you could weigh in, but I saw no good reason to subject you to unnecessary torture."

"Thank you. And...?"

"And nothing. It was mostly closed-minded scoffing before everyone decided it didn't matter who they are and went on to other topics." Andric took another drink. "How about you? Any luck yet with the elantir?"

Barak wished he had something positive to report. "Endless discussion and arguments."

Andric snorted derisively. "It figures. That seems all anyone is capable of these days. And I have more good news for you." The sarcasm was thick in the prince's voice. "You get to accompany me on another mission tomorrow."

"Andric—" Barak began to object, but the prince cut him off.

"I already know you don't want to go, but I need you there."

Barak sighed but didn't want to add another debate to his friend's day. "What is it?"

"Captain Major Min has taken a member of the Kushaani royal family captive, and the Kushaani want to discuss his release. They've asked for the same delegation that conducted Sammet's trial to lead the negotiations."

"I suppose that makes sense. You did justice for the Kushaani against one of your own people. That has undoubtedly garnered you some trust."

"Oh, it's worse than that. Apparently, they've given me the nickname *The Firebrand*. The Kushaani think I'm their champion among our people or something." Barak chuckled at the double meaning of the word. "It's not funny. Frey has picked it up now, and it's spreading."

"You know, there is a tribe of plainsmen in the Nowgli wastelands who name each person by the most recent significant deed they have done. So, if you murder someone, you would be renamed for your crime, or if you do something heroic, you get a new name based on that act. So it could be worse. At least you officially get to keep Andric."

"Small comfort," Andric said with no apparent interest. Barak had always found the idea intriguing and hoped someday he would find someone who wanted to discuss it further. "We leave at first light. We should be back in a couple of days."

"Andric, do you really need me to go? I would prefer to stay and work with the elantir on the communications problem."

"If I'm stuck going, so are you. Besides," Andric said with feigned cheerfulness, "wouldn't you rather see the world with The Firebrand than be stuck in a tent with a half-dead guy and some boring elantir?"

"You have no idea how close of a call that is," Barak replied, and hoped Andric understood that wasn't a compliment. He was so tired, the thought of travel sounded horrible, but arguing with Andric and the prospect of more days in a tent with an irritable Lieutenant Krallip sounded worse, so he didn't fight it. "Fine, I will be here in the morning."

"What, just like that? No argument? Are you sure you're feeling all right?"

"Goodnight, Andric," Barak said as he turned and left the tent without another word.

CHAPTER XXXI
BARAK

Wind whipped Barak's curly black hair around his travel-stained face as they returned to the main Remalian camp. They had pushed their mounts hard for nearly an hour to arrive ahead of the impending storm. Soldiers and servants scrambled to secure tent lines, cover equipment, and put away anything they didn't want to get soaked or blown away.

The first heavy raindrops fell on Barak's head as they hurried past the Divinarim into the war council pavilion where they had been informed they would find Stephir. The gusting wind made the heavy canvas of the tent snap and strain against the ties and support posts. Barak took comfort in knowing that of all the places in the camp, this was the safest from the storm. Reinforced by elantir, the large pavilion would not come down on the heads of the kingdom's highest nobles and officials. He worried about how his own tent would fare, but there was probably nothing he could do about it now anyway. He would just have to hope for the best.

"Andric!" Stephir smiled and he rose from his seat on a raised wooden platform across from the tent's entrance. The dozen or so in attendance stood as well. Barak wondered if Stephir ever got tired of having his actions mimicked by those around him. He would have to ask him sometime. "I'm glad to see you're back before the storm hit!"

"Not as glad as I am, I assure you!" Andric agreed wholeheartedly after bowing slightly to his older brother.

Barak always viewed these brotherly reunions with a degree of envy. It was something he never had as an only child.

"Come, sit down and tell us how things went. Master Ve'Aurben, Intercessor Henden," Stephir said, acknowledging Andric's companions who had come with the prince to report to Stephir, "it's good to see you as well. You're welcome to stay while my brother regales us with the tale of his adventure. Can I have anything brought for you? Wine or food perhaps?"

"No, thank you, Your Highness," Intercessor Henden said with a deep curtsey. "It is gracious of you to offer."

Something to drink sounded good to Barak, but he was not going to be the only one, so he declined as well. Seating was adjusted to make a place for Andric near Stephir. Barak sat next to Andric and Intercessor Henden was provided a seat next to Consul Rellat.

Before she took her seat, the holy knight attending the consul pulled her chair slightly back, so that it was not aligned with the other chairs. Barak wondered if he should have done the same, or if it was something particular about the Sharinic priesthood protocols that a lower-ranking cleric sit further back. That would make sense given their involvement in so many diplomatic and other governmental functions. It made clear she didn't consider herself equal to anyone in the room. Such a small display made a powerful statement.

"Well then, tell me what happened with the negotiations," Stephir requested.

Barak only half-listened as Andric recounted the last few days to his brother and the rest of the war council. The prince included many details Barak considered superfluous and left out many others he would have included to make the account more cohesive and useful to everyone hearing it for the first time. He noted how much Andric made the story about himself rather than providing a comprehensive report to Stephir.

Barak was impressed at how skillfully Intercessor Henden managed to politely and casually add salient points Andric had skipped. He hadn't interacted with many Sharinist clerics before the intercessor, so he was unable to make any informed comparisons, but he was aware she was quite young for her position. After the events in Tarsapta and now with the negotiations for the release of the Kushaani royal prince, he had no doubts she merited that honor. It made Barak reconsider whether he should take the vows to become a priest of Viance. Perhaps once they returned Teris.

"It was strange how urgently they seemed to want Prince Ulatwi returned," the intercessor said, adding color to the part of Andric's story where they concluded negotiations with the Kushaani delegation.

"How so?" Stephir asked with genuine curiosity.

"As you may be aware, the Kushaani don't place as much importance on the individual as we do in Remalia. They consider most persons to be relatively fungible, at least within the same caste. So while Prince Ulatwi is more valuable to them than most of their people, he shouldn't be more valuable than, say, his dozens of brothers and uncles, who all are considered of the same social rank."

"Surely they value those who have proved their worth more than others," said Duke Frendic.

"My lord," the intercessor responded in a polite tone Barak was beginning to understand was her condescending voice, "while that is a sensical thought within the Remalian cultural context, the Kushaani see things quite differently. So, as I said, while it makes sense they would want the safe return of the prince, it's odd they were so direct and forthcoming in their offers. We went there expecting the negotiations could take weeks, not a couple of days."

"And what do you make of it?" Stephir asked.

"They were intimidated by The Firebrand!" Frey interjected, smiling.

Laughter momentarily lightened the mood which had been growing heavier with the worsening storm beating down outside the tent. Barak refused to laugh and glanced at Andric to gauge his friend's reaction. Andric laughed with the others, but Barak was fairly certain he didn't truly find it funny. Barak detested social norms that made people feel obligated to show a face that was less than genuine.

"I can't be certain, Your Highness," the intercessor answered Stephir's question, ignoring Frey's interruption. "Prince Ulatwi is the empress's second son, is not a stellar military leader, failed badly as the minister of waterways, and has a reputation as an abusive and deviant patron of the temples of Sykoria. There is nothing to suggest he would be worth the ransom the Kushaani agreed to pay for him."

"No luck in getting them to agree to surrender Balinth's?" Stephir asked with his understated humor.

Polite laughter scattered around the room.

"Because they don't control it," Barak muttered under his breath, growing impatient with having to sit through yet another meeting where his presence was irrelevant. Unfortunately, his words coincided with a momentary lull both inside and outside the tent, and they carried further than he intended.

"Master Ve'Aurben," Stephir addressed him warmly, "I understand from

Marquise de'Venneshen that you have a theory about the vermin in my fortress not being Kushaani."

"Forgive me, Your Highness; I spoke out of turn," Barak deflected, hoping the moment would pass quickly so he could leave and check on the progress the elantir were making with the problems Barak most cared about.

"Not at all," Stephir replied warmly. "Please, share your thoughts."

Barak looked to Andric to save him from this predicament, but the prince instead nodded for him to proceed. Barak sighed, deciding the fastest way out of this was to push through. "I have simply observed that the descriptions of the invaders provided by Captain Major Minanthsolum and from the battle at Balinth's Fortress match accounts of the Kuldrith people far more than any Kushaani. And one of the Sharinic knights apparently fought the Kuldrith while serving in Eastgate and concurs they're Kuldrith. And before you ask, I don't have any idea how they managed to get such a large force into the heart of the kingdom, or disable the Bonded, or take Balinth's Fortress."

Murmuring spread among the nobles. Barak could not hear exactly what they were saying, but it sounded like a mix of disbelief and impatience.

"They're the ones preventing us from communicating with Teris? Why wasn't I informed?" Stephir asked, sounding perturbed that he had not been apprised of developments with the communication problem.

"Perhaps I shouldn't have been so definitive on that count. We don't know that for sure. It was just a theory I was exploring with Commander Alscan when Prince Andric pulled me away for the negotiations."

"We've already been through this, Your Highness," Duke Miarsten protested with a slight roll of his eyes. "As I have said, I don't see how it makes any difference one way or another. Retaking Balinth's—"

Stephir raised his hand to silence the duke, then turned his attention back to Barak. "Do you know anything about the Kuldrith that might help us fight them?"

"I have read the account of Aerion Dar-ka'Surth's defeat of the Kul-a'durith, as I'm sure you have, Your Highness. However, that was over five hundred years ago. How much of that is even true or would prove useful today, I can't say. But if you haven't already done so, I suggest you speak with the Sharinic knight who accompanied us to Tarsapta. If he has personal experience fighting the Kuldrith, that would certainly be more helpful than anything I could offer."

"That's a good idea," Stephir said, nodding approvingly. "Consul, do you know who he's talking about?"

"Yes, Your Highness," Rellat confirmed, inclining his head. "Sir Lathon Mar. Shall I have him summoned?"

"No need to send people through the storm. It can wait."

"Very well, Your Highness."

"Does anyone else have anything to add?"

"I'm sorry, but may I first ask what our strategy is to retake Balinth's and get back to Teris?" Andric asked.

"The short of it is that we have decided using siege towers will be our primary strategy. The natural geography of the canyon will make it difficult to get anything large enough close to the walls, so we are working on modified designs to overcome that challenge. We are exploring mining options, but again, given the realities in the canyon, we aren't overly hopeful that will prove a timely solution. We have sent scouts to comb through the mountains for possible routes to get troops above the fortress and climb down or rappel into the fortress."

"And what about the larger force headed for Teris?"

"We have dispatched messengers by several routes to get word to Teris of our predicament and return with word as soon as possible."

"But that could take weeks, months maybe!" Andric said in frustration. "There must be something else we can do."

"If you have any suggestions we haven't considered, I am happy to hear them, brother." Stephir's tone was tightly controlled, but Barak could sense the crown prince didn't appreciate Andric's implication that they weren't doing everything they could. Tense moments of silence followed, with Andric finally conceding.

"I don't know."

Barak knew it was not his place to speak, but he could not pass up the opportunity to share his thoughts on the subject. He probably should have discussed it with Andric first, but what was the worst that could happen?

"If I may be so bold, Your Highness..."

"Speak freely, Master Ve'Aurben."

"Thank you, my lord. Given the amount of time that has passed since Captain Major Minanthsolum's scouts reported the two invading forces and the assumption that the larger force began an attack on Teris at approximately the same time as the other force attacked Balinth's Fortress, it seems there are three reasonable possibilities." Barak held up one slender finger. "They're planning on a long-term siege to try to starve out the city and force a surrender. Certainly possible, given that they attacked in the spring after our winter stores were largely depleted, especially since the army probably took a substantial portion of any available foodstuffs. My lords would know better than I, but it seems safe to say that even if food is strictly rationed, the city could only last another three to four weeks before starvation becomes a concern."

Some nobles shifted in their seats.

Barak held up a second finger. "They're building siege equipment. Assuming the enemy has the technology in the first place, or enlisted the services of engineers from elsewhere, and assuming they can muster all the resources necessary to do the construction, I would think they could begin attacking the city in earnest within a week. However, while I'm certainly no expert, it seems likely that the city would face starvation before they could breach the walls. If they are indeed Kuldrith, they likely have extensive experience with sieges and fortified defenses, having defended against Eastgatian sieges for so many years."

Barak tried to read their faces for signs of their reactions. As best he could tell, they were genuinely attentive, which was gratifying. He held up a third finger. "Or they have no intention of taking Teris. While impossible to know with certainty, it could be that they're merely hoping that the attack will draw some or all of our forces out of Kushaan, which of course is what has happened, whether intended or not. If that is, in fact, their intention, once we are able to get past Balinth's Fortress, they will probably retreat and use hit-and-run tactics, and those forces will continue to pose a substantial threat. Assuming they could be a mercenary force hired by the Kushaani, this may prove the most likely of the three.

"No doubt you have considered all of this before, my lords, so please forgive the repetition." Stephir remained expressionless, but High General Kuymon and others nodded. "Under any of those scenarios and in light of the challenge posed by Balinth's Fortress at the moment, our forces here are unlikely to be able to provide timely assistance to Teris. The only answer is to get additional troops from somewhere closer to attack the Kuldrith at Teris.

"A substantial portion of the soldiers that were available in eastern Remalia are already here with us. I understand the eastern provinces have been adding conscripts for two months, and some troops will have been arriving from the west and north, but probably not in numbers anywhere near sufficient to challenge such a large enemy force. So my suggestion is to look for troops outside Remalia. Calavian mercenaries are the obvious choice."

"Mercenaries," Stephir said, bitterness in his voice. But he was not rejecting the idea outright.

Will he actually consider it? One moment stretched into another.

Frey was the first to break the heavy silence, addressing Stephir. "I don't like the idea any better than you do, but he has a point. Where else are we going to be able to get enough troops in time?"

"We can raise sufficient troops from our *own* people," Marchioness Haedep insisted. "There's no need to seek foreign aid, at least not yet."

The voices began to roll more quickly by the moment, building like the storm outside. Andric leaned over and whispered. "Now look what you've done. You are scary sometimes."

"So can I leave now?"

"Oh no. Your punishment is having to sit through this until it's done. That'll teach you to speak up in war council." Andric meant it as a joke, but it was much closer to the mark than he probably realized.

Barak tried to get comfortable and prepare himself for hours of boredom. He was pleasantly surprised when a few minutes later, Stephir interrupted the discussion.

"My lords and ladies, we have been at this for some time already, and Prince Andric and our other guests went beyond the call of duty to come directly here to give us their account without so much as a moment's rest from their travels. It sounds like the storm has somewhat abated. We will take some refreshment and rest. I will summon you when we are ready to resume."

Everyone stood and bowed politely, then servants were admitted to provide cloaks and other preparations to keep the nobles protected against the weather. Stephir and High General Kuymon stepped aside and spoke alone, then Stephir approached Andric and Barak. "Well, that went in a direction I did not quite expect, but thank you for speaking up, Barak. It may not be a popular idea, but I'm afraid it's one we have no choice but to consider. I'm just not willing to do so on an empty stomach. Would you both care to join me in my tent for a more private lunch?"

"Yes, I'm starving!" Andric answered eagerly.

"I was actually hoping to go speak with the elantir about their progress with the Bonded, if that's all right with you."

"Barak, you're probably the only person in the entire kingdom who would prefer to work rather than accept an invitation for a private meal with the royals," Stephir said with a pleasant glint in his eye.

"Don't get me wrong, Your Highness. I'm sure that listening to Remalia's greatest sons talk about... whatever it is you two will end up talking about... would be the height of delectation. Alas, I fear my too-deep love for this great kingdom compels me to more mundane tasks at the sacrifice of such sweet indulgences."

"Why did you bring him along?" Stephir asked Andric, the hint of a smile playing on his lips.

"Entertainment?" Andric proffered with feigned guilt.

"Very well, Master Ve'Aurben," Stephir said with exaggerated disappointment, "you have good leave to attend to your other duties."

Barak bowed low, mimicking the flourishes used by the Sharinic clerics. He expected he looked a bit ridiculous, but they were the last ones in the pavilion besides the Divinarim, so he didn't care. The brothers' laughter was cut short as lightning flashed and booming thunder shook the air. *So much for the storm abating.*

It was going to be a miserable dash to Alscan's command post.

CHAPTER XXXII
ANDRIC

Andric wiped the last little pool of mint sauce off his plate with a piece of bread. Dinner hadn't been particularly satisfying this evening, but Stephir had ordered stricter rationing for the army, and if the soldiers had to eat less, the nobles would do with less as well. There had been more than a few objections to that, but Stephir had quelled any dissent on the issue quickly. They both knew some of the nobles wouldn't give up the privileges of their station easily, though they would likely keep it behind the walls of their tents.

Andric was happy to follow his brother's lead. It gave him a sense of pride to sacrifice some of his comforts to show the common soldiers that the nobles weren't unsympathetic to the difficulties being placed on them. Looking down at the empty silver plate, though, made Andric chuckle to himself; less food maybe, but he doubted the men had any mint sauce or ate their meals on silver dishes. He came to appreciate each day how different his life was than the common soldier's. He was grateful the gods had seen fit to bless him with a royal birth.

"What's funny?" Stephir asked.

"Nothing," Andric answered dismissively, leaning back in the cushioned chair, chuckling silently again at the further evidence of the disparity between his situation and that of the commoners. Andric wanted to find anything to discuss that would prolong their break from seemingly interminable war council meetings. And always underlying everything was a smoldering desire to rush back to Balinth's to fight the Kuldrith.

Kuldrith. He still could hardly believe that the enemy really was the remnant of some obscure, long-dead empire on the other side of the world. It made no sense, but Stephir had decided that until they could determine otherwise, they would move ahead on the assumption that, in some bizarre twist of fate, they were, in fact, Kuldrith, had somehow managed to capture Balinth's, were possibly responsible for putting the king on his deathbed, and, if Barak was to be believed, disabling their communications with Teris. For all Andric knew, they might be responsible for instigating the conflict with Kushaan in the first place. Whoever they turned out to be, they were an incredibly formidable enemy. That was enough to steel him for what was proving to be a relentless flow of reports, discussions, arguments, and more reports.

"Do you think Gwendolyn could convince the Navarchos Conclave to give us the troops we need?" After a long afternoon of more arguments and posturing, the war council finally decided they did not have any choice but to follow Barak's advice and seek foreign aid. He had also been right that Calavia was the obvious choice.

Princess Ilyanara was the adopted daughter of Navarchos Gwendolyn yon Darnan Stenbar, one of the most powerful Calavian merchant lords. She would give her support to Remalia, for a price. Everything from the Consortium came with a price tag. Ilyanara was the only free thing Andric had seen a Calavian offer, although he suspected Remalia was about to pay for it now. Andric knew Ilyanara's adopted mother had paid a king's ransom (or, as it were in this case, a queen's) to purchase her adoption rights and no doubt she would be thrilled to finally have the opportunity to see that investment begin to pay off.

"Well, if anyone can, it's Gwendolyn. But I suspect the conclave will be slow to respond. They will want to see whether it's a lost cause before they commit their mercenaries, even if waiting ensures that it becomes one." Stephir's voice became more bitter as he spoke. "I hate to imagine what their price will be. It might bankrupt the kingdom just to try and save it. I may retain the crown, but Calavia will own it."

"We don't have much choice," Andric said emphatically. Stephir leveled a look as if to say the words didn't need to be spoken. Andric held up his hands in concession and apology. "All right. Don't bite my head off. Will they take your commitment?" Stephir was not king yet, although it could happen any day now. Of course, they had been saying that for the past three weeks, and their father was still hanging on to life. There was still time for a miracle.

"Probably, although they will undoubtedly use father's condition as leverage to get a bit more skin off my back. My biggest worry is the time. By the time we can send an embassy to negotiate with them, reach an agreement on terms, have them marshal their forces on Remalian soil, make the march to Teris..."

Stephir left the thought unsaid, but Andric understood all too well. Even if Calavia committed its forces today, it might be too late. If the messengers Stephir had sent could reach the other provinces quickly, perhaps they could raise enough troops to harass the Kuldrith from behind and buy enough time for the Calavians to arrive and save his home. Or even if, Akraharr's hand stop them, the Kuldrith took Teris, if the Calavians were ready to join forces once he and Stephir could get past Balinth's, they would certainly have enough numbers to retake the city.

Too many *ifs*.

"Come on, let's get back to it." Stephir hid it well, but Andric heard the weariness behind his brother's voice. Stephir had suggested they take their dinner in his tent again, as they had for lunch. Andric suspected it was because he needed a break from the endless discussions as much as Andric did. Outside his tent, Stephir ordered runners to be sent to ensure the war council members were summoned to reconvene.

The air seemed fresher after the storm, but that was a poor tradeoff for the mess left in its wake. Soldiers were busy putting the camp back together. The mud and humidity made the walk back to the council pavilion miserable, and Andric was grateful to be back where it was cool and relatively clean, even if it meant having to endure more discussions. The tent walls were tied about a foot off the ground to allow air to move through, and numerous candles on large wrought-iron stands filled the space with flickering light.

Andric was surprised to see Intercessor Henden speaking with Consul Rellat. He also recognized one of the Sharinic holy knights standing with them. It was the knight who had accompanied the intercessor on their mission to Tarsapta. He guessed they were concluding some business before the council started, but he was even more surprised when the intercessor took a place in front of one of the chairs next to the consul. Stephir approached the king's seat, but no one objected. Stephir stood silently, waiting for the others to find their seats. Once everyone was at their seat, Stephir sat and everyone bowed and followed suit.

"Consul Rellat, I see you've invited the intercessor to join us again."

"With Your Highness's permission. Intercessor Henden has some experience with respect to the Kushaani which, in light of this afternoon's discussions, I thought might prove useful."

Stephir inclined his head. "Of course, you are welcome, Intercessor. And were you able to locate the knight from Eastgate that we spoke of earlier?"

"Your Highness, my lords and ladies, may I present Knight Defender Lathon Mar, of the Order of the Third Wave." Sir Mar stepped forward and saluted, right arm reaching across his torso, fingertips touching the hilt of the knightly arming sword hanging in a gilded scabbard at his side. Andric was not sure what was off about the man, but Sir Mar had never struck him as the typical Sharinic knight.

The Sharinists understood better than most the impact appearance can have on others and were highly disciplined in how they presented themselves. Sir Mar was different. He seemed too casual, or maybe relaxed was a better word. Whatever it was, he didn't quite fit what Andric expected, especially for a Knight Defender of the Third Wave, the elite corps of Sharinic knights that protected many foreign diplomats the world over.

"Welcome Knight Defender Mar. We have been most eager to speak with you."

"I am at your disposal, Your Highness."

"I understand you're from Eastgate, is that right?"

"I am not from there, but I spent some time there, yes."

"And you have personally fought Kuldrith?"

"Yes."

"Did you serve in the Eastgatian army?"

"No. Eastgate is not the only place that contends with the Kuldrith. But for years I fought them and killed more than I care to recount. They are the most fearsome enemy I have ever faced, and your kingdom now must deal with this plague. You have my deepest sympathies." The knight's dark words cast a pall over the council.

"Thank you, but I was rather hoping for practical advice you can offer in our fight against them."

"You must understand who this enemy is, down to their very core, if you are to have any hope of defeating them. The Kuldrith are fanatical disciples of Teraithia. Their entire lives are devoted to nothing less than establishing a global empire under a Teraithian theocratic rule. They have been rebuilding their strength for centuries in their underground realm, and now have found the means to burst forth upon your kingdom. The best advice I can offer you, young prince, is do not give them any quarter. Do not treat with them. Do not let them turn to the left or to the right. Grind them into dust as quickly and mercilessly as you can. And pray the gods favor your sword."

"Sir Mar!" Scorn hardened Consul Rellat's face. It was the first time

Andric had ever seen the cleric break his composure. "The council would know of the enemy's strengths and weaknesses, tactics, equipment, and supply. Do you have anything worthy of our time on these matters?"

Sir Mar did not answer immediately and, if anything, appeared to relax even more despite the rebuke. "Their emperor is Overlord Arku. He rules with a high council called the Mavin Tar. The worship of any gods other than Teraithia is outlawed, and the Teraithians have been systematically crushing any opposition to their faith for several years. Not unlike what we saw at Tarsapta."

Andric looked at Stephir to see how his brother was reacting to being reminded of that incident. Archpaladin Nophet stood behind Stephir, and Andric was surprised to see anger flash across the Divinarim commander's ever-stoic face. Andric wished he knew what the archpaladin was thinking.

"They believe they are the chosen people to fulfill the ancient Ultideic Prophecies and that the world will bow to Teraithia as the only true god, with the Kuldrith as her rulers on earth. They nearly succeeded in the War to Break All Oaths but were stopped thanks be to the gods and the sacrifices of the Khalari. They are undoubtedly trying again."

"And you think they intend to do that in Remalia?" Stephir sounded skeptical but not dismissive. "Why here?"

"I cannot answer that, Your Highness."

"And how did they get here from halfway around the world?"

"I cannot answer that either."

Marchioness Haedep attempted a different tack to get something useful from the knight. "When you fought the Kuldrith, what did you find was the most useful tactic against them?"

"You're asking the wrong question, Your Excellency. If cut by a sword, they bleed the same as anyone. If hurled into fire, they burn the same as anyone. If thrown from the battlements, they fall the same as anyone. You have all the swords and arrows and spears you need. The Kuldrith are deadly because there is nothing they will not do to win.

"They use forbidden met'elan to corrupt their bodies, to make themselves stronger and faster. They sacrifice their own people to draw power from their blood. They will be your friend and ally until it suits their purpose to betray you and stab you in the back. They are the purest embodiment of Teraithia's evil doctrine of 'obtain power at any cost'."

"Enough of your lies!" Archpaladin Nophet barked as he stepped forward to the edge of the raised dais, looming menacingly over Sir Mar, his hand on his sword. "Teraithia's holy knights have faithfully served and protected this royal bloodline for generations," he said, pointing at Stephir. "You are the ones who have insinuated yourselves into every possible position of power in this kingdom. And you dare to stand there and claim that—"

"Lord Nophet!" Stephir cut him off. "Stand down. You're out of line."

"Your Highness cannot listen to these lies! The Sharinists twist everything for their own purposes."

"You're dismissed," Stephir said without argument.

Nophet bristled with palpable indignation fueled by Teraithia's divinessence coursing through him. Goosebumps prickled Andric's skin, and he shivered. The other Divinarim took aggressive stances, hands gripping the hafts of their halberds, though whether to aid Nophet or protect his brother, Andric wasn't certain.

After a moment of tense silence, the archpaladin gave a cursory bow, then spun and, without a word, stormed past Sir Mar and out of the tent. Somehow, the Sharinic knight appeared completely unfazed, as if nothing out of the ordinary had happened.

"Sir Mar, thank you for your report. If we have any further questions, we will call you again. In the meantime, you're dismissed as well."

Andric was not sure it was appropriate for Stephir to dismiss Consul Rellat's knight defender, but no objection was raised as the holy knight saluted and left the pavilion.

Stephir stood from his seat, and everyone began to rise as well. "Sit, sit," he said, waving them back down to their seats. He walked to a small table along the tent wall, poured a dark liquid into a crystal goblet, and took a drink. Then he returned to his chair and stood with one arm resting on the high wooden back. His eyes scanned the faces of those present before he spoke.

"So, an ancient scourge has invaded our kingdom, and for the moment, we are cut off from being able to stop them. We will, of course, do everything we can to retake Balinth's, but I still don't see that we have any choice but to send a diplomatic envoy to Calavia to treat for a mercenary army. The question now is who to send."

Stephir looked around the room, inviting them to offer their thoughts before making his opinions known. He was much better at that than Andric was. Andric tended to rush to offer his ideas, in part because he usually considered them to be pretty good, but he also liked testing them by having people challenge him. He was perfectly willing to change his ideas or abandon them altogether in the face of a better idea. Stephir once pointed out that, as with sparring against a royal in tournaments, many people were reluctant to oppose them. That might be true, but Andric was not afraid to venture his opinion to Stephir. If his brother didn't like his ideas, he knew Stephir would not be bashful about saying so.

"I think you should go, Stephir," Andric suggested. Stephir's face was unreadable, so Andric pressed ahead with his reasoning. "Navarchos Stenbar is your mother-in-law. No one else's word will carry more weight with her and the other navarchos than yours. You will also be far better at rallying our nobles than the rest of us. And if you stay here, you may not get through Balinth's for a long time. At least if you go, you're sure to get back on Remalian soil to manage the counterattack against the Kuldrith."

Andric didn't look around the room to see how others reacted. It might make him look weak, like he was hoping for someone to back him up. He wanted to be seen as standing on his own two feet.

Out of the corner of his eye, he saw High General Kuymon nodding, as was Frey. Lord Palipen was frowning, but he always frowned. Stephir pursed his lips slightly, which meant that he was considering it, or at least pretending to consider it. Andric hoped it was the former.

Earl Haldeth, seated a few places to Andric's left, was the first to answer. "Those are all excellent points, Lord Andric, and well put." Andric was pleased with the compliment, but he knew Haldeth was going to counter him. Haldeth was better at countering people's arguments than coming up with any new ones of his own. It got a bit tiresome at times. "I would ask you to consider some few other thoughts. With the Kushaani at our backs, we are unlikely to find a safe route to the southern coast to take ship, or alternatively to find a suitable overland course. I am loath to put the crown prince in such dangerous circumstances. With the loss of the king..." he skipped a beat, "forgive me—with the tenuous health of the king—the loss of your lord brother would be a devastating blow to our already battered Remalia."

Andric tried not to take the earl's words as an implied insult.

"And while I can't fault your observation regarding the powerful influence Prince Stephir would bring to bear with the Navarchos Conclave, I believe one of Consul Rellat's priests, or priestesses," Haldeth added with an acknowledging nod toward Intercessor Henden, "would be an acceptable alternative."

The consul gave a slight nod but canted his head to the side, acknowledging the compliment but not indicating any agreement that he could provide an alternative to the crown prince.

Haldeth then addressed Stephir directly. "And while there is no question but that Your Highness's presence lends courage and strength to any force graced by your command, sufficient experience and capability remains in Remalia, or could be sent with the embassy, to manage the task of crushing the enemy beneath our fist." The earl gently pressed a fist against his other open hand.

"My lord," Father Daemmer addressed Stephir in a quiet voice that requested permission to speak.

"Speak freely, Father."

"Forgive me for dwelling on the painful fact of your father's condition, but if, Holy Parents preserve and keep him, the king dies, and you lie beyond our ability to communicate with you, it would make the matter of succession very difficult. And while it pains me to even countenance the thought, with an enemy who may well be attacking Teris as we speak, and no sure way to know the status of Princess Shannyth, if you were also beyond our reach..." The priest left the rest of that thought unspoken, but they all knew what he meant. "While I am certain Prince Andric would be a capable and worthy regent, an unresolved question of the propriety of such arrangements is not a state your kingdom should have to face if it can at all be avoided."

That was the kindest way Andric had heard anyone address the issue of his potentially taking the reins of power, even if only as regent. But he could tell which direction this was headed. Stephir would not be going to Calavia. In truth, he preferred that he and Stephir stay together. If Stephir did agree to go, Andric was going to suggest privately that they travel together.

Stephir addressed the room. "Thank you all for your wise counsel. It is not an easy decision, but I will remain here. While I have every confidence I would be leaving my men in the most capable hands in the world, I won't be seen as abandoning them in our direst hour of need. And I am hopeful of our ability to retake Balinth's sooner than I could get to Calavia and muster sufficient forces to deal with the Kuldrith from the other side. But if I should be proved wrong on that count, whoever we send to Calavia will not make Teris their first target." Andric didn't know what Stephir had in mind, but his brother had their attention. "One way or another, Balinth's Fortress will be ours before we face their greater force at Teris. An attack from the Remalian side of the fortress will certainly be successful. I know that seems a long way off. I don't believe there will be a quick end to this conflict. We must plan for the long-term victory, and I am convinced this is the best course."

Everyone nodded, even Lord Palipen. Whether the nods meant agreement or merely understanding and acknowledgment of Stephir's plan, Andric could not be sure. But if any of them had doubts or different opinions, Stephir had made it clear that his mind was made up.

"That still leaves us with the question of whom to send," Stephir said, leaving the question hanging in the damp evening air.

Consul Rellat was the first to offer an alternative. "I appreciate the confidence Earl Haldeth expressed for our clerics, and we are happy to serve in any way Your Highness commands. Apart from yourself, may I suggest that Prince Andric's voice will wield greater influence than any other."

The words sent a shock through Andric. *If Stephir is staying, I should stay too.*

"Not only with the Navarchos Conclave," Rellat continued, "but with the other nobles in Remalia as well. A member of the royal family has greater authority and right to command than any other. In light of the direction you have given regarding the order of the campaign, your brother is well suited as any to carry out your wishes."

Andric wished to object, but no matter what he said it would not look good, so he kept quiet.

Earl Haldeth, however, could not let an opportunity to opine pass. "An excellent suggestion, Consul. Supported by the right counselors, I have great confidence that our young prince would achieve success. The which to ensure, I offer myself to accompany him, with Your Highness's agreement, and Lord Andric's as well of course."

Andric sensed Earl Haldeth had his own purpose behind the request, but he remained quiet.

"Perhaps," Stephir mused.

Is he really considering this? Andric thought.

"What security contingent would you consider sending with this envoy, Earl?" Stephir asked.

Andric clenched his teeth to keep his mouth shut.

"I would have to consider the matter more carefully, and it depends on who else Your Highness decides should go," Haldeth hedged. "But I would expect a dozen of the Divinarim and a full company of my best knights would be appropriate."

"And Consul, who would you recommend as ambassador?"

"I suppose that depends on a few matters being resolved. What course will the embassy travel? Is negotiating with the conclave the only need, or will other diplomatic endeavors require Sharin Dara's blessings? What will be the roles of the various members of the embassy?"

Andric was beginning to fear this would be a long and complicated process. Of course, it could prove to be one of the most important diplomatic missions in Remalia's history. The thought caught Andric up short. It was possible this mission could mean the survival or downfall of Remalia. A wave of paralyzing self-doubt mixed with intense pride washed over him. He could picture himself with an army at his back, Stephir with an army at his, uniting forces outside of Teris to crush the filthy Kuldrith. He realized he had missed some of what was being said.

Frey was mid-sentence. "... still the best course. Forget a small force. Send ten thousand cavalry. We can only get so many into the Gap at a time, so the extra men won't do us much good here, at least not in taking the fortress, assuming we can do it at all. And cavalry are especially worthless up in the canyon, no offense to your men, High General." Kuymon waved the comment away; they all knew cavalry could not do anything against Balinth's. "Put them to work getting the group down to the coast to obtain passage for the envoy to Calavia."

"I must agree with Lord de'Venneshen." That must have been a hard pill for Haldeth to swallow. The earl had never liked Frey's father, and the animus flowed through to Frey as well. From what Andric had heard from Stephir, over the last couple of months Frey and Haldeth had developed an enmity all their own. "Or better yet, grant me command of a larger force, and I will conquer all the lands between here and Kashpur."

Intercessor Henden whispered something to the consul, who motioned for her to speak. She gave only the slightest pause, before doing as he bid. "Your Highness, if you don't receive additional supplies soon, starvation will set in before anyone can reach Calavia." She paused to let the bluntness of her statement take effect. "Duke Lachoneus's lands and stores are already overly taxed and will soon be depleted."

"I think that's an overstatement of the situation," Duke Miarsten objected mildly, as with a naïve child. "The rationing is simply—"

Intercessor Henden interrupted, "Forgive me, my lord, but Prince Stephir knows it's true."

Andric was more surprised by her abrupt interruption of the noble than her claim about their situation. All eyes looked to Stephir. The crown prince fixed his steady, almost piercing gaze upon the bold priestess. Andric wished he knew what was going on in Stephir's head. He felt discomfort twist in his stomach as a moment's silence stretched into another.

Finally, Stephir responded. "So what is your proposal, Intercessor?" It was obvious Stephir hadn't addressed her statement, but that was enough of an answer.

"Send two embassies. Let the first go south with as large a force as my lords and ladies deem appropriate. As Earl Haldeth feels that is the best course of action and has so graciously agreed to assist in this endeavor, perhaps he would deign to be the lead envoy."

"That is not—" Haldeth began, but the intercessor rolled over him.

"Send the other envoy west to Vanashar."

Andric could not put his finger on what it was, but something about her held Andric's attention captive. She had beautiful auburn hair and a pleasant enough face, but she was a bit too heavy for his taste, so it was not a matter of being attracted to her. There was something about her voice. He considered the possibility that she was dispositioning him, but that was not quite it either. Besides, the Divinarim would never allow that to happen.

"Two Vanassi emissaries came to Nanjab while Your Highness was pushing south," Henden continued. "They were seeking a peace pact and to offer their assistance. I think we should seek them out and see if such a pact can be arranged and obtain more supplies."

Andric suddenly remembered the dinner with the two Kushaani emissaries and silently berated himself for having forgotten their visit. He also remembered with chagrin that his conduct hadn't exactly been worthy of a Laconeus prince. True, he had just found out an hour earlier his father was on his deathbed, but it was still his duty. He was sure Stephir would not have failed on either count.

"Whether that effort is successful or not, the second embassy can continue to Calavia. I realize such an overland route may take more time, but it is probably also much safer. In general, the northern tribes along the Velspars are not especially hostile to Remalia, and with the first embassy pushing south, most of Kushaan's attention will be drawn in that direction, hopefully leaving an easy path to the Vanassi."

All eyes were fixed on the intercessor. She really did have a beautiful voice.

Stephir broke the silence. "What emissaries?"

Andric experienced a moment of panic. *Out of everything she said, that's what Stephir decides to focus on?* Andric's behavior so many weeks ago now seemed gravely immature. Better to try and manage this himself than wait to see what the Sharinists would say about it.

"I met with them," Andric quickly admitted, trying to sound as if everything was perfectly normal. "They wanted to lead us deeper into Kushaan territory, and they weren't asking for anything in return. It seemed too suspicious, so I declined their offer."

"If I may add some context to Prince Andric's account, it might help to make things a bit clearer," Consul Rellat offered. Stephir nodded and Andric dreaded what the consul would reveal about Andric's bad behavior. Barak had given him a strong chastising the next day, and Andric was still displeased with himself. "The Vanassi don't normally bargain for things, at least not initially. If they want a relationship with someone, they offer what they're willing to give and accept whatever is offered in return. They usually understand what is needed by the other person. A farmer will give food to his neighbors. There is no obligation to pay for the food or to offer anything in return. But his neighbors, if they value the relationship, which they almost always do, will give the farmer clothes, or meat, or something else that they have. Warriors give their lives to the tribe, and the tribe honors them with gifts of food, weapons, and so on."

Andric thought it sounded too good to be true. What if someone didn't do their part? What if someone offered more than someone else and got all the good gifts? He tried to imagine that system operating in Remalia but let the thought go so he could focus on the discussion at hand. He made a mental note to discuss it with Barak later. What he really wanted was to discuss it with the beautiful Vanassi woman whom he had met in Nanjab. It would almost be worth going with the second group just to see her again.

"So, the Vanassi came looking to establish a relationship with us, at least," the consul continued, with a gesture to Andric, "if they were to be believed. If that was, in fact, the case, they would not have bargained for something in return. Whatever we would be willing to give would be accepted. Of course, if we gave them nothing of value, it would show that we did not value the relationship, and it wouldn't last long."

"So what should we offer in return for their aid?" Stephir asked. "And you said that they generally know what their neighbor's needs are. How will they know that we need food? Can we simply tell them, or do we have to wait for them to discover it on their own?"

The consul turned his head slightly toward Intercessor Henden, which she took as a cue to answer. "There are ways to make it known without seeming rude. It might take a day or two, but they will get the message. The difficult question is what we will take as a gift."

Andric felt a bit defensive, and his words had a hard edge that he tried to hide with a forced calm. "What would they want? We don't have much to give them. We don't have food, spare supplies, money. About all we could do is to give them back the lands we took from them."

"Prince Andric," the intercessor replied with a tone of patience that was just shy of condescension. "The lands Remalia has captured in this campaign were Kushaani lands—or Keshi lands, to be more precise. The Vanassi don't consider themselves Kushaani or Keshi, so they would not see it as getting back their own lands. Moreover, the lands we have captured would not be useful to them and therefore not a suitable gift."

"Then what would you suggest, Intercessor?" Andric tried to adopt her same tone but feared he sounded more petulant than superior, and it made him dislike her.

"Soldiers, my lord."

"You want us to send more soldiers back into Kushaan?" Andric was incredulous. "How many? For how long? Are they going make slaves of them?" Anger tightened into a knot in Andric's stomach. He tried not to let it show on his face, but he could hear it in his voice.

"Andric," Stephir said his name firmly, but not unkindly. If Andric hadn't known better, he would have sworn it was his father speaking. "My brother has raised important questions, Intercessor."

"My lords, I am only trying to offer insights into the Vanassi mindset and customs to afford you the best opportunity for success. I cannot tell you for sure that soldiers are the best offering. I do know that the Vanassi want to resist Kushaani rule, but they cannot do it with their numbers and weapons. Remalia has both, and you share a common enemy. I know that your attention is focused on our homeland, as it should be, but I think it would be a valuable relationship to have under the circumstances. A small part of your forces does not seem too high a price for it."

"How small?" Stephir asked, repeating Andric's question.

"I cannot say for sure, Your Highness. Perhaps five hundred to a thousand foot soldiers and captains to command them. Maybe the Vanassi won't want them at all. That is why I believe Prince Andric should be the one to lead the second embassy. If we can discover a different need we can fulfill, we must be ready to commit immediately."

Andric had already been imagining himself going with the first embassy and was not keen to change course, especially if it was slower and required him to go to some backwater corner of Kushaan.

"And you think they'll have enough food to make it worthwhile?" Stephir asked.

"The Vanassi Province is rich in wild game, herds of domesticated goats, and many fruits and vegetables. Most grain we are used to, such as wheat, corn, and oats, is almost entirely grown on a subsistence basis, so you're unlikely to get much there. However, rice is the one thing that the Vanashar Province can continue to provide in bulk."

How does she know all this information? Andric wondered.

"My lord, it is unlikely the Vanassi can entirely solve our food shortage problem, but they may be able to prevent it from becoming a deadly one."

High General Kuymon added his voice to the discussion. "Sending troops south and west has the advantage of allowing them to spread out the foraging to other territory, and leaves fewer mouths to feed here. In addition to whatever force we send as part of our support for the Vanassi, we can use additional troops to secure the supply routes between here and there to ensure the Kushaani don't cut us off."

"But a large force moving west will draw more unwanted attention from the Kushaani and may even be seen by the northern tribes as a threat," Frey countered. "And it will slow the second group down. I say we start to move some troops toward Tarsapta to be staged there, but wait to see whether the Vanassi want them in the first place."

"Well, Andric, what do you say?" Stephir asked him.

All eyes shifted on Andric. He hated the thought of being separated from Stephir again, of having to go begging to their enemies, tribal distinctions be damned. However, he knew the decision was already out of his hands. He could embrace it, as he was sure Stephir would if their roles were reversed, or he could be ordered to go. The choice was not a difficult one to make. Living with it was likely to be another matter.

"I will do whatever it takes to save our kingdom. If this is what you think is best, then I am happy to serve."

Andric's words elicited an approving smile from Stephir. Andric remembered their father giving Stephir many of those, while they had been much less forthcoming for Andric. "Excellent. And Consul, you will, of course, send a diplomat to serve as counselor to my brother."

"We are at your disposal, Your Highness."

"And who else would you have accompany you, Andric?"

"Master Ve'Aurben, assuming he can be persuaded." Only Stephir and Commander Alscan laughed at the comment. "Also, I believe Captain Major Min would be an invaluable asset. He served for many years as a scout captain in the areas we'll be passing through." Andric had grown to trust and appreciate the Sa'ari in the short time since they first met. "And he has already proved himself a capable military leader as well. He can take command of a small force to accompany me, as the marquis suggested. Commander Alscan, I trust you can select two or three elantir that would be appropriate for this mission."

"Of course, my lord."

Andric addressed Consul Rellat quickly, not wanting to allow anyone to take the reins from him. "Consul, how many will you be sending?"

"An ambassador and two knight defenders will accompany you, my lord."

"And I think forty or so of our finest cavalry should be adequate," Andric concluded matter-of-factly, trying to focus on these details rather than the enormity of his mission.

"It's settled then," Stephir said with a satisfied sigh, leaning further back into his seat. "Holy Couple preserve us, I believe it's the best course of action we can take. Now, for the second embassy."

Andric tuned out the rest of the conversation, lost in thought at the turn of events. He felt strangely relieved. This was a great burden to be placed upon his shoulders, but it was somehow comforting to be given such an important assignment, despite the bitter fact it felt forced upon him. For too long he had not been able to make a difference. Finally, he had a mission that could affect the future of Remalia. This was a welcome change, despite the intimidation he felt.

CHAPTER XXXIII
STEPHIR

The clang of Frey's sword parrying Andric's attack rang through the air as he easily sidestepped the attack. "You're telegraphing with your shoulder again," Frey said, his voice echoing inside his helmet. "Keep your right hip engaged for that strike and it will help keep you from over-extending."

Stephir watched from the shade of the small pavilion as his brother and friend circled each other in the sparring ring. Andric narrowed his stance and Stephir knew he was about to circle to his right. Sure enough, Andric slid his right foot and Frey raised his sword in a high feint, then quickly reversed it when Andric tried to press Frey's sword. The strike made a thudding clang against Andric's helmet.

Stephir heard Andric growl in frustration. He knew all too well what it was like sparring with Frey. So many things in Stephir's life felt like that. Just yesterday he had returned from Luresh where he had attended the funeral of Baron Marstoff, and already some of the nobles were making overtures of marriage for the baroness's hand. The Vastan Province had always been prosperous, but now, given its strategic location in light of the situation with Kushaan, whoever controlled it was well positioned to turn it into one of the most powerful and wealthy provinces in the kingdom, rivaling Glastony or perhaps even the Eastern Reaches.

Osten was still too young to hold full legal lordship over the dukedom, though only for a few more years. In the meantime, Lady Marstoff would act as his regent. She was a strong woman and loyal to the crown, so Stephir was not overly concerned about losing control of Vastan, for now. But a lot could change once she remarried. With the funeral of her husband out of the way, the wolves were circling. He was half-tempted to press Andric to marry her; he knew his brother was sometimes attracted to older women and the lady was only ten or twelve years his senior and pleasant enough company. However, there were numerous reasons their union would be problematic. Besides, Andric would be leaving in a few days to lead the second delegation to the Vanassi, then on to Calavia. It might be fun to tease him about it in the meantime though. Stephir tucked the thought away for later.

"Yield!" Frey yelled after successfully defending against a flurry of attacks from Andric. Frey dropped his practice sword and held his hands up, pretending to plead for mercy. The marquis removed his helmet and bowed to Andric, sweat dripping from his head. "I yield, Your Highness."

Stephir knew Frey just wanted out of the heat of the sun. He had practically begged to have their practices moved inside a pavilion cooled by elantir, but Stephir insisted they work out in the heat of the day to condition themselves for the circumstances they would face when they fought again. In a few weeks, conditions in the mountains would be warmer, and soon it would be summer in Remalia as well. Stephir glanced up the hills to the shadowed opening of the Warrin Gap that led to the collapsed gates of Balinth's Fortress. The narrow canyon hid the fortress from view, but it was always in his mind, ceaselessly taunting him to try again.

"Prince Stephir, I name you my champion," Frey said in a woman's voice, "to fight for my honor 'gainst the ferocity of your brother."

Stephir stood up and his squires, Gaeten and Kot, helped him don his helmet and pin it in place, then handed him his practice sword and round shield. Stephir stepped out of the shade into the bright sun and instantly started to bake. Andric had lifted his face guard to take a drink offered by his squire, then dropped the visor into place. Jase handed Andric his shield, and the brothers stepped to the center of the ring to face off against one another. They saluted with their swords, then raised their shields to the ready.

They began circling and traded a few hearty but harmless strikes against each other's shields, getting the feel for the distancing. They had sparred so many times against each other that feeling each other out lasted only a moment before Andric launched an attack, sword raised to slide in over the top of Stephir's shield, the tip aimed at his face. Stephir raised his shield and cut at Andric's forward leg, but his brother was already retreating, and the strike swung harmlessly through the air.

On the next strike, Andric drove the edge of his shield toward the inside half of Stephir's shield, intending to pin Stephir's sword arm. Instead, Stephir let his shield pivot and stepped to Andric's weak side, driving the point of his sword into Andric's chest while Andric's sword scraped harmlessly down his own deflected shield.

"Oh, nice move!" Andric complimented his brother as they stepped back and reset their stances. Back and forth the brothers traded blows, striking and counterstriking. Andric made a strong inverted-grip strike that came down with a resounding thud right on the top of Stephir's head. The padding inside his helmet prevented it from doing any real harm, but it left him a bit shaken.

As Stephir reset his stance, he imagined himself atop Balinth's walls, finally able to sink his sword into the dark gray-skinned Kuldrith barring the way from going home, from getting to his family. They were in danger, and he could do nothing about it. He shoved hard with his shield and his opponent went down. Stephir stepped forward and struck viciously, again and again. *They'll pay for what they've done!*

Suddenly Stephir was seized by someone and he spun to the attack. His sword just missed Frey's head as he dodged out of the way then kicked Stephir squarely in the stomach, sending him staggering backward.

"Stephir, stop!" Frey yelled, hands held up and backing further away to create even more distance.

Stephir was panting and shaking. He searched through the eye slits for Andric but did not see him, then realized it was Andric on the ground.

"Get my helmet off!" he barked. Dellat and Kot ran forward and did as they were commanded.

Frey offered a hand to Andric to pull him up from the ground. "Are you all right?" he heard Frey ask his brother.

"I'm fine."

By the time his squires had removed Stephir's helmet, Andric and Frey were already under the shade of the canopy next to the ring. Many questioning eyes were on the crown prince, but he did his best to ignore them. "Andric, I'm—"

"Forget about it," Andric cut him off without looking at him.

Stephir took the white cotton towel from Kot and wiped the sweat from his face and neck as he sat rigidly on the high wooden stool. He watched as Marchioness Haedep stepped into the ring with General Premmet. Servants offered chilled wine to the two princes and Frey. Stephir accepted his thankfully and took a long draft from his cup.

"You know," Frey began slowly, "this war is getting a bit tedious." Stephir knew he meant it as an understatement. "Don't get me wrong, I'm as happy to kill Kushaani, or Kuldrith, or whomever, as the next man, but I've killed a few dozen now, and I think my time would be better spent flattering the girls at Trevven's Tavern."

"I would have called an end to the war a long time ago were it not for the long list of pleas from those ladies begging me to keep you away as long as possible," Stephir said, appreciating Frey's attempt to lighten the mood and trying to play along.

"Yes, well," Frey countered, "I think they've probably changed their tune by now. Since we've lost the ability to check in with Teris from out here, let's go and ask them in person."

"Maybe you could use that gilded tongue of yours to talk the Kuldrith into leaving Balinth's. Then I would be happy to oblige." Stephir felt a touch on his shoulder. He turned, expecting Andric, and was surprised to see Commander Alscan.

"Forgive the intrusion, Your Highness. Something has just come to my attention that I believe we should discuss."

Stephir knew she meant 'discuss immediately.' It was undoubtedly bad news if she was asking him to leave in the middle of training. He looked at Andric and they locked eyes. *Father?* The question passed between them unspoken but hung heavy.

The elantir commander read their concern immediately. "The king is fine, my lords. Please, we should move to another location. May I suggest my command post?"

Stephir didn't bother trying to hide his surprise. Calinda did not like non-elantir coming to her quarters. "Who else should come?" Stephir asked.

"I think it best we keep this between High General Kuymon and Your Highness for now, begging your pardon, my lords," the commander said glancing at Andric and Frey.

Without looking at them Stephir overrode her suggestion. "They will come also. Kot, run to the sparring ring over there and tell High General Kuymon to come at once." It took a few moments for the men to remove their armor, and the high general had arrived by the time they were finished. "Commander, please lead the way."

Calinda gave the slightest bow of her head, then led them through the camp toward her command post. The afternoon sun beat down on them even without the weight of armor, and it didn't help his mood as he replayed in his mind what had happened in the ring. He felt bad for losing control of his temper but was more concerned he had not realized what was happening.

He hadn't been sleeping or eating well for days. Maybe that had something to do with it. He had dismissed it as the pressures of ruling in his father's stead, but now he wondered whether there was something else. Perhaps he would discuss it with Sister Merranine later.

It didn't take long to reach the area where the elantir resided. Unlike most of the camp, which was organized into companies of long, neat rows of four-man tents, the elantir area had larger tents capable of accommodating eight to ten people each. These were situated in two concentric squares, all with their openings facing inward toward the huge central command post; enough to quarter the slightly more than two hundred elantir that made up the central corps. Some elantir were assigned as special attachments to various units, but that was only another score men and women. Many of the more powerful nobles had an elantir or two serving with their forces as well, though most of those were relegated to providing an additional measure of comfort to the nobility.

Stephir took note of several elantir who appeared to be practicing in their own sparring ring of sorts. He hoped they would prove more useful in the upcoming battle to retake Balinth's. Their use of the smoke in the first attack had seemed to work well enough, but maybe it had just provided a false sense of cover while the enemy waited to spring the ambush. Stephir was inclined to think it could only have helped, but there was deep skepticism among the officer corps about using the elantir. He and Calinda agreed that developing direct combat techniques for the elantir was an important area for improvement.

One of the contestants fell for no apparent reason. "What happened?" he asked the commander, pointing to the man on the ground.

"A simple tripping elant. I still have them practicing non-lethal ways of thinking and practicing together so they don't kill each other before they learn to control more serious attacks."

He knew, among other things, she meant using fire to burn the enemy. It seemed to have the most promise of everything they had tried so far, but it was dangerous for the elantir and anyone standing in the vicinity of where the fire was created. Calinda had learned a fair bit about using met'elan to control fire in her younger days working in the Calavian merchant fleets. Ships and fire didn't mix well. Most of her training had been in preventing or putting out fires, but she had learned some techniques for starting them in enemy ships as well.

Stephir had a difficult time being patient, but he trusted Calinda would push them as fast as she reasonably could. Master Bellubont, the princes' tutor in met'elan, had told them that in other countries where elantir learned such destructive elants, many injuries and deaths were suffered while the elantir practiced controlling such powers. Calinda's challenges were even more complicated. Most of the elantir serving in the army had been recruited from the Elantic Order, the elantir guild in Teris, and they had brought with them many of their prejudices and superstitions, including the belief that using met'elan to hurt another human being was evil. Stephir had spoken with Calinda about her struggles to get them to leave those old ways behind and become a cohesive fighting force. It was not easy, but she had been making some progress.

The looming command post stood as a stark reminder of such efforts. It was a huge cubic tent, always erected with its corners oriented to the four points of the compass. As large as it was, it seemed impossible that it could have such a flat roof, but Stephir knew it was supported as much by elants as by ropes or poles or stakes. Many elantir called it the Guild Hall in remembrance of the Elantic Order's headquarters in Teris. But Calinda had pushed to get them to call it the command post, or *the post* for short, with some measure of success. No one openly called it the Guild Hall anymore, although Stephir had heard some call it *the Hall* when the commander was not around. One correction from Stephir had put an end to it once and for all, at least as far as he was aware.

Four elantir were posted as guards at the entrance. They wore the elantir uniform of a blue and white surcoat over a light chain shirt. They usually wore the chain over black gambeson, but the punishing heat of southern summers made overheating a greater risk than any attack they were likely to face, so they had stopped wearing the heavy padded armor. Stephir ordered his Divinarim to remain outside, but Calinda suggested some be allowed in. That was a sign something was seriously wrong. Stephir had given her his word weeks ago that no other soldiers, including the Divinarim, would be allowed inside the post without her permission. Two guards were quickly selected and joined the group that followed Calinda inside.

Despite being full daylight outside, bright white alchemical lights hanging from the support beams shone in the dim interior of the command post. Calinda led them down a long central corridor formed by curtains of heavy, white fabric hanging from the wooden beams high overhead dividing the interior into rooms and passageways. They had only gone about ten paces when Calinda turned into a small room on her right.

The only furnishings in the room were cushioned chairs along the tent walls. A few had been moved into the center of the room to face each other.

Two of the seats were already occupied, and the two men stood as Stephir entered. He was shocked to see Barak. He knew Barak liked to spend his time with the elantir when he was not with Andric, but Stephir could not imagine what the young scholar was doing at a supposedly confidential meeting of only the highest-ranking people in the kingdom. His mind flashed again to his father. Barak had been trying to work with the elantir to discover a cure for his father's illness. *Is this good news? Have they found the cure?*

Commander Alscan spoke first to the other man who had been waiting in the room, instructing him to add a couple more chairs to the circle. As they took their seats, Andric sat beside Barak. Stephir could hear him ask in a whisper, "What's going on?" but Barak merely shook his head. Stephir could not tell if that meant Barak didn't know or that he was unwilling to answer. "Please put up a ward," the commander ordered the other elantir. The man bowed his head, eyes closed in concentration, fingers making intricate motions as he concentrated on his crafting of the wards to protect them from eavesdropping.

Without hesitation, the commander began. "My lords, we have discovered," Stephir's heart skipped a beat, "what was blocking our communications, thanks in no small part to the ideas of Master Ve'Aurben, which is why I felt it appropriate for him to be here."

Smiles spread across the faces of the men in the room. "That's great news!" Andric said in a rush of enthusiasm, slapping Barak's arm in congratulations. "What was the problem?"

Stephir's smile faded as he looked at Calinda's face. He heard the words, and they should have brought joy, but something was wrong. She nodded to Barak, inviting him to explain.

"It's a form of sabotage."

"Sabotage?" Andric furrowed his brow as he looked at his friend.

Stephir noted the unusually grim look on Commander Alscan's face. "By whom?" he asked.

"It's being done by some of our own elantir." Barak paused, his words hanging heavy in the cool, still air. "Someone is corrupting the flows of the elants in the Bonded, but masking it to appear as if everything was as it should be. The additional flows create something akin to excessive harmonic resonance in the conduit that results in a diffusion of the energy after some distance. Quite ingenious really." Stephir had no idea what Barak was saying. "And it bears some conceptual resemblance to the sickness at Nanjab, leading me to believe that those who set that one on us have a common background with whoever has been disrupting our communications. Unfortunately, we haven't yet been able to solve the king's condition."

Stephir had a thousand questions running through his head. He wanted most to ask if they had made contact yet with Teris. Was the city under siege? Were Ilyanara and the children safe? He forced himself to take this one step at a time. He didn't want to overlook anything, and if the answer about Teris was what he feared it would be, he was likely to get distracted. He almost wanted to laugh at his own understatement. "So we have one or more traitors or infiltrators in the elantir corps?" It was not asked accusatorily. He was just trying to be clear.

Calinda answered, "There are undoubtedly a handful of them. I suppose it's possible one or two of them could also be from outside our ranks, among the noble houses perhaps, but it's very unlikely. Affecting the flows from outside the channeling group, especially without being noticed, would be practically impossible. I'm afraid we must assume they're among us. I will ferret them out." Her voice was quiet but hard and cold—calculating.

Stephir knew she did not need any help in that task. "Fine. Bring them to me once you have them." Stephir didn't know what he would do with them. Their treason had caused so much damage. *Are they also the ones responsible for the sickness in Nanjab? Do they know how to heal Father?* "And you know what they've been doing. Can you fix it?"

"Now that we know the cause, we can protect against it. There should be no further difficulty."

"Excellent. Then we should contact Teris at once." There was an all-but-imperceptible shift in Calinda's face, but Stephir knew what it meant. "You already have."

"Teris is under siege."

"Akraharr's stones!" Frey spat out the curse, hot fury in his voice and face.

"Why didn't you tell us that immediately?" Andric asked harshly.

Stephir kept his emotions under tight control. "Who did you make contact with?"

"Just the Bonded Keepers at Falan's. They have already dispatched runners to summon Commander Kalvarne."

"What information about the siege were they able to provide? How long ago was Teris attacked? How many troops do they have?"

"The attack began nine days ago." Captain Ambersol, Calinda's second in command answered with a deep baritone voice. All eyes shifted to the man who spoke. His short-cropped hair was salt-and-pepper gray, and the age lines at the corners of his eyes, combined with his stately demeanor, gave him an air of authority. "The city is still well defended." A wave of relief washed over Stephir, and General Kuymon let out a slow breath. "We didn't get any other details. Most of the time was spent explaining what has happened here and why we have been unable to make contact until now. It appears the communications were only lost with Balinth's Fortress and with us, but haven't been affected anywhere north of the fortress. They had no idea why they lost contact with us."

"How soon can we contact them again?"

"The Keepers are always available of course, m'lord, but I don't know what more they can tell us until Commander Kalvarne is contacted."

"Very well. We'll wait until we hear from them." He glanced around the circle at the faces he had come to know so well in the last couple of months. "I would like to say that we don't need to worry, that Teris can hold her own. But after what we saw at Balinth's, I fear we may already be too late. Even if we had taken the fortress, I don't know. But now..." he let the thought remain unspoken. They all knew what the current situation meant for their ability to return to Teris quickly.

Stephir tried to put some humor in his voice. "If any of you have any brilliant ideas you've been holding back, now would be a good time to let them out." Only High General Kuymon gave a short chuckle in response to his attempted levity. The others sat in silence, their expressions ranging from pensive to consternated to inscrutable.

Andric was the first to break the silence. "If the Keepers in Teris can contact Tennury or Banbridge, perhaps they can send an ambassador to Calavia now," Andric suggested. His face lit up as he realized how close their sister, who lived in Tennury, was to Calavia. "Perhaps Hilenne should go. She could get there weeks before Earl Haldeth's embassy. As a royal, her voice carries as much weight as mine would. I may not even need to go at all!" Andric's excitement rose in his voice.

"Perhaps. Let's not get ahead of ourselves though. Let's wait until we see what Teris has to say." Turning to Calinda, Stephir asked, "Commander, how do you intend to find the traitors?"

"Performing met'elan entails using one's own elan, at least in part. Whoever was working those elants may have left traces of their elan behind. The elants Master Ve'Aurben spoke of are of a nature Remalian elantir don't use and should be possible to isolate and trace. Unfortunately, that is a technique I'm not familiar with. But I believe the Elantic Order possesses that knowledge. I intend to find someone who knows how and obtain their assistance."

"And how long will that take?" Andric asked, voicing the impatience Stephir worked hard to mask. "Let's have Commander Kalvarne drag the guildmasters to Falan's and make them tell us."

"We have to be careful, Andric," Barak answered. "There's no telling what other problems the traitors could create, especially depending on how many there are. We will catch them as quickly as possible. But we need the element of surprise, so none of you should speak of this outside of this room."

Barak was right, if a bit careless in the way he spoke to his superiors. Before Stephir could reply, another elantir entered through the heavy curtain into the room. The commander motioned for her to step closer so she would be inside the warded area.

"My lords, Commander," the young woman said, giving the elantir's salute. "We are linked with Commander Kalvarne at Teris."

"Finally! Let's see what he has to report," Stephir said as he rose quickly and strode toward the young woman. The others followed them into a much larger room across the corridor. Just as in the room they had left, the same cushioned chairs lined the white-fabric walls. In the center of the room, Keepers stood next to the gold and crystal reliquary in which the Bonded lay. Viancian iconography was etched or inlaid with precious stones into the gold casing. Stephir felt it was a fitting honor for the Bonded and his sacrifice, though his stomach still turned at the sight inside.

The Keepers, whose hands were inside the reliquary resting on the Bonded as always, had their eyes closed and did not move as the others entered the room. Calinda instructed one of the other elantir in the room to be the voice, which Stephir vaguely understood meant that his job was to take the elantic vibrations transmitted from the Teris side and turn them into sounds those on this end of the link could hear. It took the man a few moments, then he nodded.

As Stephir scanned the faces, he wondered if any of them could be one of the traitors. How did Alscan know they could be trusted with managing the communications, let alone hearing the sensitive information discussed? Doubt, that hellish by-product of the poison of treachery, seeped into his thoughts. Nothing to do but go forward. He prayed to the Holy Couple that Calinda would find the traitors quickly.

"When you are ready, Your Highness," Commander Alscan said softly.

"Commander Kalvarne." Stephir said the words in a conversational tone as if speaking to someone in the room with them. When he had first used the

Bonded to communicate, he raised his voice, practically shouting, as if the extra volume would help get his words to the other end.

"Holy Couple's grace, it is good to hear from you, Your Highness!" Stephir knew Kalvarne worshipped Vai Doroth, but he was politically savvy enough to invoke Stephir's preferred deities. "How may I serve milord?" The disembodied voice of Commander Kalvarne was tinged with a slight echo but was otherwise clear.

"Just start from the beginning," Stephir commanded, trying to sound calmer than he felt.

"Of course, milord. We received word about three weeks ago that an army was marching east toward Teris through the Velspar foothills. It was hard to believe, but we prepared as best we could before the attack. The scouts tracked them all the way here. They attacked us on the twenty-third day of Solsticeswell in the third hour of the third watch, during Silmal's eclipse. First, they came at us from the east side near the warehouse district. We heard sounds like small rocks hitting the walls but weren't too worried until we saw the bastards climbing the walls without ladders. Now we know they were somehow making small holes in the wall, about the size of a man's fist. Nothing even close to breaching the walls, milord, but they can climb the walls using those holes."

Stephir suddenly understood what the holes in the cliffs above Balinth's meant. Frey leaned forward, seemingly reaching the same conclusion, but a quick motion by the prince quieted his friend. "Please continue, commander."

"While we were fighting off the first wave, a second attack came over on the southwest side near the Forlows District. They came out of the foothills where they had more cover. They still had to cross the open fields, so there was a bit of time for more men to get to that side by the time they were climbing the walls. A few of them made it into the city that first night. The men fought well, pushed them back, and killed all those who got in. Still, I know that no army has ever gotten past Teris's walls, and I'm ashamed the first was on my watch. I understand if Your Highness gives my command to another."

"No, of course not Commander Kalvarne. The Kuldrith have been more difficult than any of us could have imagined. Teris still stands. You have performed your duties admirably. I only wish Balinth's had fared as well. What has happened since?"

"So you're certain they are Kuldrith then? We weren't sure, but it was one of the ideas being rumored about."

"We believe so."

"They're unlike anything I have fought before. Too many men died trying to kill the few dozen or so that breached our defenses. But what is this news about Balinth's Fortress milord?" Stephir knew the news was going to be as hard on Kalvarne as anyone. No doubt he was counting on reinforcements returning to Teris as soon as possible.

"The Kuldrith have taken the fortress. We tried getting through days ago, but it was impossible."

"I see." Kalvarne sounded troubled, or perhaps he was measuring his words carefully; sometimes the subtlety of voices was lost in the communications through the Bonded.

"So, tell me where things now stand."

"Of course, sire. We haven't been able to get an accurate count because thousands of them are out in the countryside and still in the foothills, and they're most active at night. The scouts who tracked them here estimate their numbers between fifteen and twenty thousand, maybe more. They have no siege equipment that we've seen and don't seem to be building any. We can't determine how they are supplying themselves other than foraging. They don't have wagon trains or other long-distance supply lines we have discovered. We have no idea where they came from. They seem to have come through the Velspars from somewhere, but that doesn't make sense. They'd never be able to make it over the mountains, and certainly not without a strong supply line; unless they're in league with the Kushaani, I suppose.

"Regardless, they've cut us off from any supplies coming into Teris, and that's the most difficult part. Before the attack, we sent as many folks as we could convince to other cities, and they were mostly from the outer districts. Not too many from the city proper would leave, which means we've got all those mouths to feed. We have already started strict food and water rationing. Even then, I don't think we'll last more than a month or two without replenishment. We've already had a couple of minor riots, but we've locked things down pretty tight. We have also put as many to work as we can, managing the defenses and other support activities. I just don't know which will give out first, the food or the defenses." The commander gave his report matter-of-factly, but it was a grim picture.

"What word do you have of any other Remalian forces being mustered for a possible counterattack?" Stephir asked. "Steadleigh or Banbridge or Tennury?"

"We've contacted all of them and Princess Ilyanara called for their immediate action to defend Teris, but so far they..." Kalvarne hesitated, probably choosing his words carefully, not wanting to speak poorly of any of the nobility, especially not knowing who might be with Stephir, "they haven't committed to any specific course of action."

"Anything else, Commander?" Stephir asked.

"My lord, if I may ask, what are your intentions?" The simple question wrenched Stephir's heart.

"To do everything I can to get help to you, and do what we can to retain Remalia and Teris. You have my word. For now, that is only to offer my prayers, but I hope to be able to provide more soon. May I ask a personal favor, Commander?"

"Of course, milord!"

"Please convey to Princess Ilyanara that I am well and hope to be with her and our children again soon. They are all faring well, I hope."

"Yes, Your Highness. She's a great woman, and the princess is her mother's daughter!"

"Gods' blessings upon you, Commander."

"And upon you, Your Highness."

Stephir put his face in his hands for a moment, and silence filled the room. Stephir was so tired. No one would blame him if he waited until morning to reconvene his counsel; no one but himself. He drew himself up, taking a deep breath.

"High General, please send word to convene the war council."

He knew there could be no sleep, even if he tried. This was going to be a long night, and his patience already felt razor-thin.

CHAPTER XXXIV
EVIR

L ight glowing around Evir pushed back the ever-present darkness. His people could not survive without light. Not like air or water—one would quickly die without those. But without light, there was no direction, no movement. Perhaps that was not death, but it was not exactly life either.

The gentle glow emanating from the crystalline orb hovering in the air just over his shoulder was constant, unwavering. It was not like fire that writhed like an eyeless serpent, consuming, destroying, killing. This light was created by met'elan. He was no elantir, but he knew enough to understand what they created was very different from the miracle of creating actual life. Dae'yen had shown him part of that miracle with the birth of their children. How interesting, he mused, that he could help create a whole new life, a servant of the Kuldrith people, but he could not create the simplest *lumen*.

Many living on the surface of the world above took light for granted. This very element the Kuldrith treasured so much, the rest of the world lived with all their lives. It gently shined over them as they slept and blazed before them when they woke. Evir had lived for a time with a ceiling of clouds and glaring sun instead of stone. He remembered waking without the need for a *lumen*. He remembered lighting a fire without fear of it poisoning the air. It was a luxury to be sure, but a luxury that made the surfacers soft. Remalia would never prove to be a match for the Kuldrith.

Evir reached up and gently grasped the glass-like lumen, smooth and cold despite the light fading at his touch. His eyes quickly adjusted to the dimmer glow of the stone chamber he was in. A red luminescence emanated from thick crystalline veins winding like rivulets of magma through the polished stone walls of the small room. Evir knelt on the stone block before the clear crystal altar, atop which stood a gold statuette of their goddess, Teraithia. One of her arms bore the *v'kar,* the angular bladed shield used by elite Kuldrith warriors, her other arm outstretched, palm up as if to receive an offering. Other gods demanded sacrifices of food, money, or even blood. Teraithia accepted only the total devotion of one's life.

His quarters were meager compared to those that would normally be granted to one of his rank, but his current assignment in Kierden required that he assume an identity with the rank of only an intendant. Despite that, Evir was fortunate that even this rank permitted him to have a private altarene in his family's chambers for worshipping Teraithia. He came here often, though not out of any particularly strong devotion to the goddess. Oh, he played the part well enough in public. One had to show devotion to succeed in Kuldrith society; he could not have climbed to his current elevated station in life otherwise. But these moments he spent in his private altarene were for himself—a respite from the flood of details that possessed his every waking thought. It was a place to drop all the intrigue, politics, plotting, and secrets, to only focus on his thoughts and feelings. Self-reflection was an attribute often missing among his people today.

The soft padding of approaching footsteps, whispering in the absolute silence surrounding him, invaded his privacy. He kept his eyes closed. He recognized the measured lightness of the steps as one of his slaves. The rank of his assumed identity also allowed him to have household slaves. Not many in Kierden did. Most of the slaves in this remote location under the mountains were consigned to working in the mines or smelting or some other form of labor for the empire. Haisi was a slender woman from the surface, a Restani taken in a raid more than a decade ago. She was consigned to spend the remainder of her life down here in the darkness, serving Evir's house however he wished. But that didn't mean she was beyond deserving courtesy.

"Good morning, Haisi. Is breakfast already being served?"

"No, *p'ku,*" she said humbly as she entered the pool of light from the lumen. She was dressed in the simple, undyed clothes of all slaves, but her shirt sleeves and pants were longer than most, almost extending to her wrists and ankles. Her hair was cropped short, as was the custom for the Kuldrith slaves. Haisi hesitated at the corner of the passage. She never entered the altarene; not because of any reverence for the Kuldrith goddess, but out of respect for Evir and Dae. "Javinth Intendant sent an urgent message for you."

Evir sighed. *Work already.* Being pulled away from his reverie always came too soon. He remained on his knees in quiet repose. "Go ahead."

"He said that your presence is needed immediately at the temple treasury." Evir felt like he had been punched in the gut. True, he had hoped this news would come eventually, but the timing had too many terrible implications.

"Thank you, Haisi. Tell Maer to reply that I will be there shortly."

Evir listened as Haisi retreated, her hand sliding along the wall as her footsteps receded. She no longer stumbled as she had years ago when she was first given to Evir's family. She had even grown comfortable enough in the darkness of Evir's world to stop carrying a lumen everywhere she went. Many surfacers didn't transition well to a life of servitude below. Evir was certain his wife's approach to helping their slaves feel like part of the household was largely responsible for Haisi's success.

Evir sighed again and for a moment thought about making the clerics of the temple wait, but he knew that would accomplish nothing. If he didn't already know what he was walking into, he would have rushed to the temple at the first mention of trouble there. However, this trouble was partially of his own design, although the fact it was happening now confirmed that the treason he was there to ferret out also involved at least one of his superiors. And just when he had dared hope he might have been mistaken in that belief.

He rose with natural grace and stepped off the *kanthis* rug. The stone floor was cold beneath his bare feet. He missed the warmth and other small luxuries of Stierve, though there was no use dwelling on it. He was a long way from the heart of the empire. A little over half a year ago he had received the assignment to come to Kierden to root out and crush the rebellious factions that had gained a foothold in this remote city. His success at doing the same in other areas of the empire had earned him a strong reputation among his superiors in the empire's intelligence vein, the Obsidian Door.

It had also earned him the high rank of inquisitor. Only the four overseers and Malithir Lord Overseer back in Stierve held a higher position within the Door. The lord overseer answered only to Arku Overlord and the ruling council, the Mavin Tar. Now having proof that one of the five overseers was a traitor left Evir with a cold, empty feeling in his stomach. He would have to deal with that in time. For now, he needed to focus on the task at hand.

Kierden was proving a more difficult challenge in many ways than his previous campaigns against the Dorothi and other rebel groups. That was, in some measure, his own fault. While he had been very effective at breaking up factions and driving them out of whatever place they had tried to infiltrate, he hadn't yet been successful at cutting the heads off all the serpents and ending them once and for all. His strategy this time was to slowly infiltrate, to let them believe they were safe, to find the leaders, and finally take them all out at once.

Of course, this strategy had met with no small measure of criticism and, at times, outright hostility. However, Qin'acht Overseer supported his approach, and for now, that was enough. The incident at the treasury would hopefully bring him one step closer to successfully ending the most difficult group, the worshippers of Vai Doroth. Completing his work here in Kierden would mean he could finally return home. Dae would be happy when that tide arrived.

He lifted the lumen and its white light filled the room. Releasing the globe, it floated to its usual position above his right shoulder. A lumen attuned personally to him, let alone one that could hover and follow him, was another of the luxuries afforded to few in the empire. He put on the slippers waiting for him just outside the altarene and made his way into the adjoining chamber. He moved gracefully for a Kuldrith. The years had yet to take their toll on him, but he knew it was only a matter of time. Being in his forty-ninth year, he was young enough to still move quickly when needed, but he also knew his limitations.

He touched the crystal vase resting on the side table, and instantly it added its golden light to the white of Evir's lumen, giving the room a warm glow. The light glinted off the sliver cord woven into the thin braid of steel-gray hair hanging shoulder length at the right side of his face just in front of his ear. His otherwise short-cropped hair accentuated the angular features of his face, which were at odds with the smooth curvature of his stone world where corners and angles were the rare exception. His ashen-gray skin seemed at home in the world of stone and darkness. The fabric of his tunic was nearly the same color as his hair, and of the same silky texture, and his pants were a velvety, jet-black material. Both were lined with a fine layer of *xanath* wool to keep him warm. However, he knew the events this tide required more formal attire, so he donned an outer robe of silk nearly the color of charcoal, sweeping gracefully down to his ankles. He looked regal and imposing, befitting his station, though not his preference.

The room itself was sparsely furnished. A long, tiled table commanded the center of the chamber. A few pages of thinly rolled copper were stacked neatly on its reflective surface. Besides the table, the only other furnishings were a deep, cushioned divan and a couple of chairs set next to an exquisitely sculpted stand upon which rested his most cherished possessions, books.

These valuable objects were rare in this underworld and were some of the only possessions Evir had brought with them when they left Stierve so many months ago. Nooks and alcoves of various shapes and sizes honeycombed the walls and served as shelves for maps, writing implements, and the few figurines that were the only other decoration in the room.

It may have been modest by surfacer standards, but life below, near the heart of Creation, was a much harsher existence. By the standards of his society, he was very comfortably situated. The only other chambers in his private quarters were the adjoining eating room, a washroom, and two bedchambers —one for his slaves to share, and the other was his, where Dae still slept.

It was an early tenth-tide, but it was Evir's practice to be up long before most others when he could enjoy the time for himself. The smell of the food being prepared by Haisi and Takir caused his empty stomach to rumble in anticipation, but pressing matters wouldn't allow him to wait for breakfast. He rarely did anyway. Too many things were coming to light, and he wanted to ensure there were *no loose rocks in the ceiling*, as the saying went.

By the time Evir had finished dressing, Haisi dutifully returned with his usual fare, a warm slice of meat and some flat tavva bread covered with ghena paste. He smiled in appreciation as she backed from the room. In truth, it was not the most flavorful of meals, but it would suffice. It could be eaten as he walked and would sustain him for the next few tenth-tides while he poured over details of a theft that shouldn't have happened yet. He would remember to seem duly surprised and concerned when the high priestess reported the details.

He put the lumen on its pedestal as he left his residence, then proceeded down the narrow tunnel. He wouldn't need the light on his journey. All the main public areas had lumens at regular intervals. The staccato of his footsteps echoed off the stone, surrounding him like a familiar song as he strode toward Kierden's central cavern. The arched doorways of the residences of other high city officials slid past him. He paid them little mind other than the caution he took regarding his surroundings at all times, which by now had become second nature. He was trained to be alert to any threat that those who served in the Door might encounter.

The stone floor of the tunnel had been worn smooth more by generations of booted feet walking the same path day after day than by careful craftsmanship. Not like the paving stones in Stierve, which were maintained by the elantir stoneshapers. He continued his brisk stride from each sphere of light mounted into the wall alongside the walkway to the next. Most of the tunnels and corridors in Kierden were old mine shafts, and each step through the rough-hewn, monotonous stone felt the same as the one before.

The occasional passersby, usually some messenger or short-haired slave, were the only ones sharing his path this early in the tide. The road would be much busier a tenth-tide or two from now when exhausted foundry crews, smiths, and other craftsmen would shuffle to their residences and fresh workers took their places for their next shift. Evir had been surprised to see how many of them were *requited*, former slaves who lived as free members of Kuldrith society. Most requited earned their freedom through faithful military service, though it could also be granted for other valuable service to the empire, such as informing the authorities about slaves plotting rebellion or their master's corruption. Evir rarely saw requited in Stierve, and he had assumed it was relatively rare until seeing how many there were in Kierden. It was a sad commentary on how little opportunity there was for slaves to become requited.

Of course, war and struggle were the constants of life for his people. It hadn't always been so, or at least that is what his wife asserted, but she was a student of ancient history. He dealt in the present, with all its dangers, both from within the empire and without.

The tunnel opened into an expansive cavern and merged with the wide and nearly vacant concourse winding around the heart of the city. Kierden was a familiar sight to him by now. He had found the city ugly and brutish when he first arrived, but like with most things for Evir, familiarity had engendered some degree of appreciation for the place. He could make out rough shapes in the darkness, those few buildings contained within the expanse of the cavern. A multitude of glittering lumens shining in the darkness were Kierden's version of stars in the night sky in the world above. While it was nothing like the Grand Chasm of Stierve, it was still impressive.

Nearby to his right, under heavy guard, were the entrances to the storerooms where the foodstuffs were kept. The temple complex, with its white and red lights shining brightest, stood at the far end of the cavern to his left, past the refineries from the mine operation that were carefully vented to avoid poisoning the breathing air they all depended upon. He could even see Ettin's Veil from across the cavern, bathed in mist and filling the cavern with the ever-present susurrus of the gently cascading waterfall pouring from the wall into a pool hidden from his current angle. He would have seen it soon enough if he had taken his normal route to the Regent's Hall and ultimately the Obsidian Door's offices, where Evir was the highest authority in Kierden, even if many were unaware of it.

He turned abruptly onto a ramp that doubled back and dropped to the cavern floor, connecting him to an avenue leading to the temple and the treasury vaults that he was about to be informed had been robbed. He strode confidently, scanning the shadows around him for any sign of movement. In this world of stone and darkness, his ears often told him things before his eyes saw them; but the noise from the nearby foundry and the distant falls overwhelmed the subtle clues that would have been useful to him, like the sound of breathing, the scrape of a boot on the stone, or the soft hiss of a metal blade being drawn from a sheath. He didn't reach with his hands, but he mentally felt for the long knife hidden at his waist and the smaller one tucked into his vest. He doubted he would ever need them, but one could not be too careful.

The layout of the city still felt unbalanced to him. In Stierve, all roads led to the temple, which rested in the center of everything. Here in Kierden, the temple stood at one end of the central cavern, out of the way for most of the people. His path took him past tradecraft and merchant areas until the avenue veered to the right and opened into the wide plaza surrounding the temple, bathed in red and white light from hundreds of lumens floating overhead.

As always, several kieresta-atan, the warrior-priests of Teraithia, stood guard with swords at their sides, the overlapping edges of the polished stone tile lamellar armor dully reflecting the temple lights, as if they were covered in the scales of some great earthen reptile of legend. Teraithia's holy symbol was etched in gold on each stone tile of their armor, adding to their imposing presence. Today, their duty was not simply to guard but also to prevent anyone from approaching. There were many more than Evir had seen in the plaza before. He was aware the Church had quietly ordered additional priests to be sent to Kierden due to the growing unrest here. The high priestess was putting them to use today.

Evir continued walking along the path toward the temple as if he had every right to be there. Arguably he did, but that was a complex issue he was sure would be unnecessary to address. His long surcoat should have signaled Evir's superior status to the two towering guards blocking his path, but he saw no indication they cared who he was. He wondered if it was intentional, or just a symptom of the tension at the temple.

For all their size and strength, the warriors were young, only a handful of years older than his son. Of course, few of the kieresta-atan reached even their middle years. The alterations they made to their bodies as part of joining the warrior class of the priesthood were not conducive to longevity of life.

"The temple is closed. You must come back at a later time." The guard on the left spoke, an imposing woman of intimidating stature. The second glared menacingly with a hand resting comfortably on the hilt of his sheathed blade.

Evir stared at them flatly. *I came here this early, and they didn't have the decency to inform the guards?* He reached quickly into a pocket, causing the guard on the right to flinch, his hand switching from the pommel to the hilt of his sword. Evir produced a small, thin slab of obsidian, calmly showing it to the guards, a slight frown playing purposefully on his lips.

The glassy stone was no bigger than his palm, squared on the bottom and rounded on the top, with no markings whatsoever. The kieresta-atan shifted on their feet uncomfortably and glanced at each other, seemingly uncertain about what to do. The towering woman with hard-set eyes and chiseled features flinched as if reflexively forming a salute but stopped herself before any show of respect was formed. With the stress of the day's events, Evir was willing to look past the slight as the guards shifted uncomfortably at the sight of the ebony stone in his grasp. Many in the Obsidian Door would have taken pleasure in their hesitancy upon seeing the symbol of the secretive order. Evir did not. He was simply impatient with the delay.

"I am here at the request of Jt'alin Kavartha-akai. Please show me to her at once." These two almost certainly didn't have the authority to take him directly to the high priestess of Kierden, but at least they could get him moving in the right direction.

"Follow me," the woman instructed. Evir followed her, and the other atan fell in behind him. The other kieresta around the plaza were watching him. *Undisciplined*, Evir thought. He made a mental note to have that brought to the attention of their kieresta-akai.

The strides of his escort were longer than Evir's, but he kept his own pace, forcing them to adjust to him rather than him matching theirs. It was a small detail, but that was Evir's craft, and he was a master at it. In a few moments, they were across the plaza and approaching the temple. The facade of the structure was built into the cavern wall but was mostly obscured from view by three staggered rows of colossal gray granite columns. The grand temple of Stierve was much bigger, but he still felt dwarfed as he ascended the wide stone steps leading up through the columns to the doors of the temple.

Several of the consecrated warriors were posted among the columns, their augmented stature lost in the scale of the portico. At last, they approached the two massive iron doors that barred the way into the temple. Doors were uncommon in their underground world, and the Teraithian temples were some of the few places they were regularly used. Kierden was renowned for its metalworking, but Evir was amazed that the iron doors could have been so intricately sculpted. Met'elan must have been employed to create such lifelike bas-relief scenes depicting the goddess's victory in battle and ruling her people in glory.

Four kieresta stood in front of the temple doors, and Evir was certain there would be more inside. "The Obsidian Door is here at the summons of Jt'alin Kavartha-akai," his escort announced. If this young warrior had any idea who she was keeping out on the steps, she would have chosen her words more carefully and acted with far more urgency. But this was not entirely her fault. She could have asked him his station, but that may not have been the best choice either given his claim to be with the Door, and she had no way of knowing if he told the truth.

One of the guards banged a gauntleted fist on a heavy metal door. Evir heard the scrape of metal on metal, and the door swung inward a fraction. There was some whispered exchange, then the door closed and the metal bracing bar was put back in place. Before Evir could finish the curse under his breath at yet another delay, the bar was hastily removed again and the door swung open. A middle-aged man stepped out and bowed quickly to Evir. He wore the deep-red, high-collared cassock telling Evir he was a kavartha-atan, a priest of the governing order of the Church.

"Forgive me, Watchkeeper. I didn't mean to cause a delay."

"Intendant," Evir lied, maintaining the pretense of holding a lower rank as he walked past the guards. The priest nodded with a frown, no doubt dissatisfied that the Obsidian Door had not seen fit to send someone of a higher rank, then quickly schooled his face and looked away nervously. The priest appeared flustered and motioned for Evir to join him at his side as he turned to lead the inquisitor into the temple.

The common citizens of the empire knew very little of the Obsidian Door and would have had to wade through a great deal of rumor and fear to find the truth. Not that the Door did anything to dispel those stories, even though some of them were quite horrific. On the contrary, many of those rumors had been started by the Door itself. It often benefited their investigations when those who came under scrutiny did not know how far the Door would go to find the truth or to root out the enemies of the empire. The truth about the Door's day-to-day activities was usually far more mundane; but in certain cases, the rumors didn't begin to approach the truth.

As they descended into the lower levels where the vaults were located, the beautifully tiled floors gave way to plain paving stones or even bare rock. From his time here in Kierden, he guessed it was more a statement about the level of devotion of its people than an indictment of the way the Church was run here. Not that Evir particularly cared what the floors in the temple looked like, but it was his duty to root out disloyalty, unrest, rebellion, and treason against the empire. He was good at it precisely because he noticed trends and details in things as mundane as flooring, or that the lumens on the wall were almost a decade old, their light having gone flat and wan. One of the corridors had a seepage of moisture appearing near the floor, a sign of a structural defect in the rock and something that could lead to serious problems if left unchecked. He also noticed several hive crickets scurrying along the floor. That was most unusual here in the temple, but in this case not unexpected.

Evir noticed the priest who led him into the bowels of the temple was carrying a small weapon, probably a dagger, hidden beneath his robes at his waist. From its location on the right side, he guessed the man was left-handed, and the way he walked a bit too stiffly probably meant that he was not comfortable walking armed. All of these, or most of them, were superfluous facts, and Evir filed them in the back of his mind. They would be sorted through later for relevance.

They came to another set of heavy metal doors, the only ones Evir had seen inside the temple. Doors here were an obvious necessity in the treasury. Two imposing kieresta-atan guarded the entrance. There was no hesitancy this time as they stepped aside obediently. He hoped none of the guards were punished too severely because of the break-in and theft. It was not entirely their fault.

The kavartha-akai waited with her arms folded beneath her breasts, a frown creasing the slate-gray skin of her face. She wore a deep-red cope with a pattern of overlapping angles embroidered in gold thread along the outer edges, a mark of her higher station as the ruling priestess of this temple. Beneath the cope, she wore a long white dress, simple in style but extravagant solely due to its color. It was difficult to keep any clothing white for long, especially in this city where mining and smelting left nearly everything covered in dust and soot.

"Evir Intendant," she said before the kavartha-atan could announce him. "It's a pleasure to see you again, though of course I wish it was under different circumstances. My apologies for disturbing you so early. I was actually expecting Zideth Watchkeeper."

Evir knew she didn't need to be so pleasant or formal given her station relative to his assumed rank. The Church had immense, almost preeminent power in the Kuldrith Empire, and many in the priesthood felt they were above all other authority. In Stierve, the currents of power were much more complex and often subtle. He appreciated her open cordiality and smiled warmly in response.

Evir greeted her with the appropriate salute to a higher-ranking person, hands held out wide to his side, palms facing the high priestess while bowing low, eyes toward the ground. Jt'alin returned the salute with her right hand held out in front of her, open palm up. As Evir rose, she brushed back some silvery hair from her face, tucking it behind her ear, and smiled briefly, though there was little warmth behind the gesture. He wondered if it was a nervous tick, or perhaps something else.

"It's not a bother at all, Jt'alin Kavartha-akai. I usually rise earlier than most. I'm certain the watchkeeper will be in touch with you soon, but your request sounded urgent, so I felt it was best to see to your needs immediately."

"Please, no need to be quite so formal. Just Akai will be fine. Or Jt'alin if you're feeling a bit daring." Evir was surprised at her sudden degree of informality. *Is she teasing me? Or perhaps testing me?* His mind quickly went to work analyzing which path to pursue. The akai motioned Evir to follow her as she led him further into the chamber. "The uninitiated, of course, are usually not allowed into the temple vaults. Customarily, only the kieresta and I are allowed to enter. These chambers were sealed by the Church's elantir. It takes both an atan and an elantir to open the seal."

"Forgive me for interrupting, Akai, but I am familiar with the Church's treasury procedures. Why do you need the assistance of the Obsidian Door?"

Jt'alin looked a bit surprised but didn't appear offended. That was good. Evir meant no disrespect, only to speed the conversation along. "Well, someone..." she hesitated a moment, her face tightening as if she were loath to utter the words. The corner of her mouth turned down as she continued, "Someone has broken into the vaults and desecrated Our Lady's holy house. I would like the Door to help us find out who they are, and I will blot them from the heart of Creation." She spoke in a matter-of-fact tone, her voice devoid of the emotions her face could not entirely hide. A less adept observer they might have believed this meant no more to her than if she was ordering an infestation of insects removed from the premises.

Evir stopped in his tracks with a carefully calculated pause. "Here?" He raised an eyebrow slightly, an expression meant to convey surprise, not doubt.

"Yes," Jt'alin said with a hint of her annoyance coming through.

"Was anything stolen?" Evir asked, still feigning surprise. The kavartha-akai simply nodded. Evir looked around at the chamber as if trying to grasp the implications of her revelation. Then he looked both ways along the corridor to the kieresta-atan at the entrance they had come through and at the other vault doors. He carefully measured his voice. "How many know about this?"

"There were some who heard it before I could lock it down." The akai shrugged. "I assure you they will not speak of it outside these walls."

Evir frowned. "How many vaults were robbed?"

"Just the one. The others remain intact with no sign that any attempt was made to enter them."

"Show me the vault," he said, adding as an afterthought, "if you please, Akai." The breach of manners was not an accident, but an attempt to appear flustered.

The priestess frowned slightly and parted her lips as if to say something, but let it go. "This way." She strode confidently toward the end of the passage to the second door on the left. Evir followed behind her, keeping his steps even.

The doors at this end of the treasury differed greatly from the others he had seen in the temple. These were made of heavy iron, rough and raw, but appeared to be untouched by age or any sign of rust that reached everything in Kierden. The edges of the doorway were encased in brass, polished to a glowing sheen, and inlaid with elantic runes. A blackened group of crickets at the threshold made their deadly effect obvious.

The kieresta-atan at the door parted obediently for the high priestess as she approached and strode through without a second glance at the imposing guards. Evir followed a measured step behind as he entered the vault.

It was the first time he had ever set foot inside one of the vaults in any temple, and the gesture of confidence from Jt'alin was not lost on him. He ducked slightly as he passed underneath the runes above the doorway, as if instinctively, though he knew there was no need. The runes were there to prevent unintended entry but were harmless to those who had been invited.

The floor of the hallway was made of interlocking stone blocks, but the inside of the vault seemed to be one solid piece of stone as if carved by a river. There were no visible joints and no seams in the stonework. Floor flowed into wall flowed into ceiling, where a trio of lumens gave off a pale white glow. A pair of the kieresta-atan stood at attention just inside the doorway, and another set of guards stood at the far side of the room next to a gaping hole, no higher than Evir's waist, extending off into the darkness.

Evir instantly noted several things: the absence of debris in the room; the subtle stress on the faces of the guards next to the opening; the way the smooth lines of the room were marred by the jagged edges where the new passage breached the vault wall; the scrapes on the floor from where some large object had been moved near the new tunnel. Several crates and chests remained in the room. One was smashed, spilled coins of blue gold and palladium scattered on the floor, apparently ransacked in haste. He thought it odd for the temple to hold coins in its treasury vaults; they were only useful for spending in foreign lands where currency was used as a basis for trade.

Jt'alin was talking, and Evir dutifully turned his attention to her. "... elantir assures me the enchantments still hold. The wards in place weren't broken, yet the stone they were tied to was, well..." She gestured to the hole in the wall as the only explanation needed. "Some of the elants should have warned us the instant anyone began excavating anywhere near this vault or if met'elan was used on the stone. It's unbreakable by any normal means, whether physical or—"

Evir interrupted her. "You said those who are aware of this have been instructed not to speak of it with anyone?" That was not exactly what she had said, but it was a fair deduction.

The kavartha-akai replied, "You can trust they will keep this within our walls."

"I'm sure they will. Please have them separated and await my questioning, if you would, Akai." Evir kept his tone measurably polite, leaving his comments somewhere between a request and a command. He wanted to leave no room for mistakes in the investigation.

"You don't seriously suspect any of my people, do you?" Jt'alin's voice held both incredulity and strained patience.

"I don't suspect anyone at this point, Akai. I simply want to make sure I can gather all the information and judge the facts."

"I assure you, my vaesh'katir are very thorough. If there are any relevant facts to be found, they will find them."

"Akai, I am confident the vaesh'katir are more than capable of rooting out heresy and traitors to Teraithia in all corners of the empire. Their abilities aren't being called into question. It is my job, however, to see the pieces of the puzzle others miss, to look for the trends and signs of outside involvement, to track the information to its source." Evir doubted Jt'alin had any idea of why he was in Kierden, and he needed to ensure the Church continued to remain in the dark until he had finished his mission. Then they could conduct whatever conversion efforts they were inclined to pursue. "I can find who would dare to intrude on Her Majesty's house, to desecrate Her private vaults, to steal from Her and from us all. But I need to do things my way. Will you allow me to do this?" Evir was sincere in his request and kept his eyes on the kavartha-akai while she weighed his words.

Finally, she nodded begrudgingly.

"Excellent. Clear the room."

"Clear the...?" Jt'alin was noticeably taken aback. "But, we need to maintain security of the remainder here in the vault." She looked at the gaping hole in the wall.

"Akai, anyone who has the capability of doing this will know they can't come back anytime soon. Probably never. We aren't in any danger from that direction. I assume you already sent your people into the tunnel?"

Jt'alin nodded.

"And they found it closed off, probably collapsed?"

"How did you know?" she asked suspiciously.

"I have seen something similar before. It's the easiest way for the criminals to prevent pursuit. Have the guards remain outside, but seal the door. You and I need to discuss matters best left to our ears alone."

The akai frowned but ordered the kieresta-atan to leave and close the door to the vault. Evir waited patiently as they stoically took their leave, never questioning the high priestess. The inquisitor had always appreciated their dedication and blind obedience. When the door had closed, Evir smiled pleasantly.

"Thank you, Akai. I know you and your atan are very capable and letting outsiders in is no trivial matter. In this case, though, it's not possible to be overly cautious. You said this was the only vault breached?"

"It was. The others are untouched, their wards are still intact."

"Are there other valuables in the remaining vaults?"

"Yes, we have finished taking an inventory and everything else remains untouched, it would seem."

"What was stolen?" Evir asked, then added, "If I may be so bold?"

Jt'alin waved the deferential comment aside. She had invited him down into the sacred vaults, after all. He was already in her confidence. "There were a few articles of value and a fair amount of coin taken, but there was also a priceless artifact. It is called the Katharis Pool."

"A pool?"

"More like a bowl the size of a small table, made completely out of what looks like marble. I was told that if you carefully watch the pattern in the stone, you can see the lines shift and swirl like water. I watched it for several minutes, however, and saw nothing of the sort."

Evir raised an eyebrow. "A bowl? Why would someone steal a bowl?"

"It is an artifact of considerable power, albeit somewhat limited in its usefulness. For an atan capable of the benefaction of telesthesia, it aids in their ability to focus their sight."

Evir already knew of the pool's general powers, but it might raise suspicion if he didn't ask. "Telesthesia? You mean far-seeing? That's something like a Synoptic Stone, but shows images instead, correct?" Evir asked, referring to the large, flesh-colored crystals that were bound to halves of elantir who had been sacrificed to allow the empire to communicate over unlimited distances. The Obsidian Door in Stierve kept all ten of the empire's bonded crystals, with the other halves at key strategic locations where communication was most critical. One was even here in Kierden.

"Yes, something like that. I have never practiced telesthesia myself, but the specialists who came from Stierve with the pool tell me that with its aide they may be able to search all of Kierden without ever leaving the temple."

Evir nodded as though impressed. "That would certainly be something worth stealing. What were you searching for, if I may ask?"

"Enemies of the Faith, of course."

"You can determine that just by looking at them?"

"You can if they happen to have contraband from an apostate faith or are practicing forbidden rituals."

"Have you found anything useful?" It was too much to hope that she would have found the Dorothi leaders and could tell him who they were and where to find them, but maybe there was something that could help him.

"We have found some souls to bring into Teraithia's light, but never as many as we would hope." It was the kind of non-answer he expected.

"But one could see anything? Say, for example, spying on the overlord, or looking inside another temple vault?"

"It's not that simple. As with other benefactions, it only links to other souls. In the case of telesthesia, one cannot see where a person is not present. And it can't target a single mind. Instead, it feeds the priestess the images of what everyone within a sphere centered on the priestess sees. For a small diameter, that may not be overwhelming, but it isn't terribly useful either." Evir could think of several ways it could be useful in his line of work, but he didn't want to sidetrack the conversation. "The larger the radius of the sphere, the more chance you might see something useful, but the more inundated you become with an overload of images."

"And what exactly does the pool do?" Now Evir was genuinely interested. This was more detail than he had been given by his informant within the temple.

"It limits the reception of images to a cone instead of a sphere and reflects the images into the pool. Again, whoever uses it would have to be able to attune to Teraithia's divinessence and perform the telesthesia for the pool to be of any use, and there are very few who have those capabilities."

"So you suspect one of the Teraithian clergy stole it?" He was goading her slightly, but he wanted her to be the one to articulate her suspicions.

"Intendant, I can assure you my priests are loyal and would never betray Her trust. They know the consequences." She didn't need to say what would be done to someone who betrayed their Faith. That would be worse than blasphemy, for which the penalty was death. "I think we both know it had to be the Dorothi heretics. This is the last straw. I intend to stamp them out once and for all and retrieve the Katharis Pool."

"You may be right, but there are other traitors who also would benefit from having an artifact like the pool. It's too early to rule anyone out. For now, I just need all the facts, Akai. How many people knew of the pool's presence here?"

She appeared skeptical but answered his question. "Besides myself, only six people knew it was in this particular vault. However, I can't be certain how many people at the Grand Temple in Stierve knew that the pool was sent here."

"I see. The investigation may eventually lead us back to Stierve, but in the meantime, I will need to speak with all those here who knew that it was in this vault. Do any of the other vaults contain artifacts of similar value?"

"We have nothing else remotely comparable at this temple; in fact, nothing in all of Kierden. That is why I need the Door's assistance to help recover it immediately."

Evir nodded and sighed as if that was what he expected. "Tell me all you know about the situation. How did the Katharis Pool come to be here? Why was this vault selected to hold it? Which elantir helped seal it? Who was allowed access and on what basis? I assure you, no detail is too small."

Evir halfway listened to her answers but nodded as she detailed everything her priests had discovered. He already knew how information regarding the pool had been leaked. Evir himself had reported it to Malithir Lord Overseer and Qin'acht Overseer several weeks before (and may have exaggerated its capabilities to locate the Dorothi), though he never told them he was planning to use it as bait to catch the Dorothi leaders.

True, after weeks of no sign of a traitor in the Door he had finally been forced to leak the information about the pool to the Dorothi so they would steal it and he could track it to their hidden temple; but that was only nine tides ago, much too recently for them to have planned and executed this theft since then. He wished he had waited just a little longer so he could be even more certain, but the timing made it clear enough to Evir that the information must have first been provided to the Dorothi by one of his superiors. Now he knew he was playing the most dangerous of games, and he was balancing on a delicate spider's thread.

The kavartha-akai would certainly have been outraged anyone would dare to use the sacred vaults of the temple in such a plot, even if she could have been convinced there were bigger forces at play here than the sanctity of a building. The vice-regent of Kierden had connections to the Dorothi rebels and had been courting them to join him in leading Kierden to secede from the empire. Evir knew he only had maybe a few weeks before it would be too late for him to succeed in using his own methods, then the overlord would turn the matter over to Ski'va General to put Kierden under martial law; or worse, the kavartha-akai could take matters into her own hands. At that point, everyone would be treated as a rebel unless proven otherwise. For too many that proof would come posthumously, if at all. The difference between traitors and innocents in such cases often only determined whether they received death rites or not.

Covert politics and plots were Evir's playground, and he knew there were few who could see as well as he could the complex threads woven throughout the fabric of the empire, and how small vibrations in one part could have dire consequences in another. This was the primary duty of the Obsidian Door, but it was also a passion for Evir. He truly believed his people were destined for something greater, that they had the potential to be so much more than they were in their current state. If any of these rebellions were allowed to take root, they would lead to great death and destruction among his people. Evir may not have been the most devout follower of Teraithia, but he was completely devoted to the people of the empire. Many Kuldrith saw the Church and the Crown as one and the same. To Evir, there was a vast difference.

Showing due respect and devotion to the kavartha-akai, Evir collected every scrap of information from the high priestess and sincerely thanked her for her cooperation. He inspected the vault, taking careful notes on a slate tablet, which drew curious looks from the guards who had been ushered back in once Evir was through with his questions. Usually, Evir committed such things to memory, but sometimes he found it useful to make a show of taking notes. In this case, he wanted to impress on everyone who saw him how serious he was taking this matter.

For almost an entire tide, Evir stayed at the temple complex, talking to everyone who might have any information related to the theft, isolating each witness and giving them his full personal attention. In part, it was an act designed to convince the clergy everything was as it appeared to be. But now that he had such unprecedented access to the clergy, he took full advantage of the opportunity to see what else he might uncover. More importantly, he needed the rebels to believe they were not yet discovered, and so he played his part meticulously.

There was only so much he was willing to tell the kavartha-akai. Even if she could be convinced to forgive his role in facilitating the crime, he could not be sure she could keep up a convincing pretense of this being an unexpected theft. As Evir said his goodbyes, Jt'alin pressed him for information.

"I'm afraid I have nothing conclusive at this moment, but there are some threads that we will follow to see where they lead. I assure you Akai, I will let you know as soon as I have anything solid to report."

He left the temple weary, but he knew his work was just beginning. He made his way back to the main concourse running along the perimeter of the large cavern and followed it toward the Regent's Hall at the end of the cavern opposite the temple. There were many more people on the road than when he had first gone to the temple. Many of them walked in silence, their heads hanging low as they numbly went about their daily duties working in the mines, foundries, or some other equally monotonous task. Unfortunately, most felt no real connection to how important their labor was in producing the materials and goods so critical to the empire. This was the fertile soil of dissatisfaction in which rebellion grew. Evir could not fix that problem, so he focused on what he *could* do.

He passed Ettin's Veil, the waterfall pouring into a large reflecting pool next to the concourse. The bright lumens placed behind the falls made the water look like molten silver from this vantage point. Onyx gravel and golden sand were spread on the ground in a wide arc around the pool, providing a striking contrast to the falls, as well as serving the practical purpose of keeping the stone floors from becoming too slick. It was the one sight in Kierden Evir found truly beautiful. Today, though, it failed to make any impression. His mind was too preoccupied with meticulously reviewing the day's events, combing through the details. Before long, he found himself at the entrance to his destination.

The Regent's Hall was an extensive network of connecting chambers running like a hive through the cold stone of the earth. Various governmental functions occupied the chambers, including the Obsidian Door. Evir left the concourse and entered the first large chamber. There was nothing noteworthy about it except for the sixteen soldiers, eight on each side of the chamber wearing the metallic scaled armor of the regent's guard. Other than Teraithia's temples and a few of the residences and offices of the highest imperial officials, the Kuldrith rarely spared the resources for luxury or ornamentation. Everything was weighed against its utility in furthering the good of the empire.

By now every watch captain knew who Evir was, so he was not challenged as he passed through the chamber into the tunnels leading further into the Regent's Hall. Corridors branched, some sloping upward or downward, taking him past several chambers where people were going about their various tasks. He carefully passed a few people in the narrow corridors. If they had known who he really was they would have quickly moved out of his way and let him pass. Sometimes he missed the small perks that came with his rank, but it had its benefits as well. Sometimes receiving the endless courtesies from others was more tedious than having to perform a few of them himself.

The Obsidian Door's chambers were in a remote area of the Regent's Hall to ensure they had as much privacy as possible. Soon he arrived at a large antechamber with a short tunnel that led to the base of the steep stairs up to the Door's chambers. There were few places in their underground world with more than a handful of steps at a time. The enormous twin pyramids in Stierve's Grand Chasm, one the Great Temple of Teraithia and the other the seat of the overlord, each had a grand spiraling dual staircase running up through their centers reaching all the floors. The inquisitor missed seeing that beautiful sight.

Evir's legs were weary as he climbed the steps. The two gray-clad guards standing on the landing at the top of the stairs bowed slightly in the confined space and stepped aside as he passed. They weren't nearly as imposing as the kieresta at the temple, but what the Door's soldiers lacked in physical stature they made up for in unparalleled skill and a willingness to stop at nothing to fulfill their purpose. A blackened stone door barred the way, lacquered with an ebony coating to make it appear like the glassy stone of the Obsidian Door's namesake. A slab of genuine obsidian large enough to make a solid door was extremely rare, and Kierden simply didn't warrant such an extravagance.

The door swung effortlessly as Evir pushed his way inside. It may have seemed unremarkable to anyone else, but there were only a few people for whom the door would open. Many of the Empire's most sensitive secrets were kept by the Obsidian Door, and the secretive organization meant to keep it that way. Besides Evir, only his assistant, Javinth Intendant, and Zideth

Watchkeeper had the door personally attuned to them. Otherwise, only the guards posted at the door could grant access. It was not the same level of security the vaults of the temple had, but it was enough to stop, or at least slow, anyone from entering without authorization.

A narrow corridor ran a short distance straight back from the door. Evir passed a large chamber on his right where a dozen or so people worked at narrow stone tables, reviewing documents or talking together about one matter or another. The corridor came to an intersection and Evir turned left. After passing another chamber on his right where the Door's soldiers trained and sparred, the corridor finally ended in a chamber where an elderly man and a woman in her middle years leaned over a stone table, their attention fixed on a map. The man looked up as Evir entered the room and nodded a casual but respectful greeting. His silvery white hair hung just past his ears, framing the chiseled features of his ashen face. The years had been kind to Javinth, but they had also been many.

"You enjoyed your stay at the temple, I presume," Javinth said with a smirk. He was slight of frame, bright-eyed, and several years Evir's elder. The greens and grays of his clothes were in a style produced more than a generation ago and did not match anything currently being made in the empire. Javinth could have requisitioned new clothes, but he lived Kuldrith frugality to the extreme.

"They were as cordial as one would expect, given the circumstances." Evir was eager to get to business. "Where are we with finding the Katharis Pool?"

"I see you dusted off the formal attire. Trying to impress the locals, are we?" Javinth apparently was not ready to let the subject of Evir's time at the temple drop so easily. With a hint of sarcasm, he continued. "I'm surprised the kavartha-akai did not invite you to stay for dinner."

"She did offer to let me call her by her name."

Javinth raised an eyebrow. "Did she? Perhaps she wanted you to stay for more than dinner?"

Evir chuckled but opted not to reply.

"Are we going to talk about what this means?" the woman asked, her voice laced with the same anxiety Evir had been under all day. Kiavi was a talented elantir and one of the only people in Kierden who knew Evir's true identity and his plan for the theft of the pool. Evir had to keep his circle of trust as small as possible, considering the implications, and he needed an elantir to accomplish part of the task.

Javinth's lips creased downward and his fine, white hair waved as he slowly shook his head. "You were right... about everything."

Evir's stomach knotted, though only slightly. He had come to grips with this turmoil already. "I wish I wasn't. We're out over a chasm with this now. I just hope we can end it without any further bloodshed, especially ours."

"How did the information slip through our fingers?" Javinth asked. They all shared his frustration, but Kiavi took it as an accusation.

"I executed the plan exactly as we decided. It was impossible to cover all threads."

"We know you did, Kiavi," Evir jumped in to ease her back from the ledge. "The odds were always against us catching the mole red-handed. At least this is strong confirmation that there is a traitor. We'll just have to figure something else out."

"There is still a chance the plan will work," Kiavi mumbled as she glanced at a handful of blank slate tablets on the table. The plan they had devised weeks ago was relatively simple. In addition to allowing auditory messages to be transmitted over long distances, the Synoptic Stones also allowed the Door's elantir to inscribe elanticly sealed messages onto copper sheets on the other end of the connection. Such messages were usually sent to or from one of the overseers, though it was not uncommon to provide the service for a mavin tar or a high-ranking cleric.

A sealed message was the only way that made sense for the mole to get word to the Dorothi. Kiavi had devised a way to have the messages inscribed onto two plates instead of one. It was a major violation of security protocols, but given what was at stake, Evir had agreed. They could not unseal the messages without the exact elantic key, but the plates carried a trace of elan unique to the elantir who sent the message in the first place. If they were able to identify the correct plate, Evir could go back to Stierve and use it to track down the elantir and, hopefully, the traitor. They traced as many messages as they could, hoping one would lead them to the Dorothi and give them the means to eventually find the mole. So far, all their efforts had proved futile.

Evir shook his head. "We have more immediate issues to deal with. If we don't find the pool, they'll feed us to the thoss."

Kiavi sighed. "Nothing yet," she said as she glanced at the tablets again. Each was elanticly bonded to a second tablet carried by a Door operative in the field. Anything written on one tablet instantly appeared on the other. The bonding faded within a tide, so their range was far more limited than that of the Synoptic Stones used to communicate with Stierve, but they had their uses. At this moment, elantir from the Door had the matching tablets and were out scouring Kierden for signs of the pool.

"Have the hive crickets stopped coming after you?" Evir asked Javinth.

"Next time you get to extract the scent glands from the queens. I must have killed hundreds of those pests by now."

Evir laughed this time. "Didn't you say it would only take a week or so for it to wear off?"

"Yes," Javinth groaned, "with constant washing. The soap they have here is too fine. It seems nothing is as strong as I need."

"Kierden is full of miners and foundry workers; they have the strongest soap in the empire!"

"I know," Javinth said flatly. "I even tried burning the gloves. You might think that would have helped a great deal, but I think it only made things worse."

Evir chuckled at the disgust on Javinth's face.

Javinth had made a paste from hive cricket queen scent glands, and their spy in the temple had applied it to the bottom of the pool. While in the temple vaults, the wards would keep any hive crickets from reaching it to give away the secret, although he had seen a fair number of dead ones in the hallway outside the vaults. Hive crickets had an unusually large amount of elan, which made them useful as sources for the elantir to draw from. Now that the pool was out of the vaults, there should be a strong enough concentration of them for the elantir searching Kierden to determine the pool's location, if they could get close enough. At least that was the plan.

Evir stifled a yawn.

"It must be difficult getting old," Javinth teased.

"Just wait until *you* get here," Evir joked back to his friend who was nearly twenty years his senior. "And Artencu?" Kierden's vice-regent was in league with the Dorothi. Some thought they should have arrested him already for conspiracy to commit sedition, but Evir was afraid it would spook the Dorothi and he would lose his chance to apprehend them.

"Nothing interesting yet."

"Very well. I will be in my residence. Inform me as soon as we have anything actionable."

Kiavi saluted while Javinth offered a conspiratorial wink, his usual breach of protocol, as Evir turned and left the room. He was tired and needed to try to get some rest before the trap was finally sprung.

CHAPTER XXXV
EVIR

In an instant, Evir was wide awake. Lying in the dark next to Dae, he was gripped by a sense of urgency threatening to overwhelm him. Something was wrong. His mind groped for the source of the feeling, but it seemed to be on the fringes of his consciousness, like trying to remember a dream receding just out of reach. He was inclined to dismiss it as the anxiety that naturally accompanied his position, especially being on the verge of the final thrust of a crucial operation.

This felt different. He needed to be up and moving. He could not say exactly why or where he needed to go, but he had learned the hard way the consequences of ignoring these impressions. He gently kissed Dae's silky hair, then carefully backed away to avoid disturbing her. No sense in both losing sleep.

"What are you doing?" she mumbled dreamily.

Evir cringed. Not as stealthy as he would have liked. "I need to go."

"Already? You just came to bed."

He knelt next to her and kissed her cheek. "Go back to sleep," he whispered. "I'll be back when I can."

She reached an unseen hand to his face in the absolute darkness and caressed his cheek. "Be careful my love."

Evir nodded and smiled. Rising, he put on his outer clothes and shoes, then took his lumen and activated it in the corridor as he quietly made his way to the kitchen. The urgency was pressing him to be out of his chambers and find the problem, but he didn't know when he would be able to take another meal, and he was feeling the weakening effects of not having eaten regularly for several tides. Better to find something simple to take with him now.

Most Kuldrith received their meal rations at one of the many food commons located near the residences, but a private stocked larder and kitchen were benefits of Evir's rank. He was surprised to find a small basket of cherries, apricots, and radishes. These would not have been too out of the ordinary back in Stierve, but Kierden was deep below a remote area of mountains and didn't usually have easy access to fresh produce brought down from the few Kuldrith settlements on the surface. His empty stomach rumbled in hungry anticipation, and he was glad he hadn't chosen to skip eating. He put some of the food in his pockets, took several drafts from the water crock, then left his chambers.

Evir headed for the Obsidian Door in the Regent's Hall. He felt certain whatever was bothering him was not there, but since he didn't know where he *was* supposed to be, it seemed his best alternative for now. As he neared the main cavern, he heard voices coming along the wide road circling its perimeter, unusual this early in the tide.

Evir slowed, much more cautious than usual, and stepped closer to the wall. It was best not to call any undue attention to himself. *Probably just some porters delivering goods,* he chided himself. He didn't like being on edge like this. He was surprised to see shadows on the tunnel wall at an odd angle. That meant the group had an independent light source. *Not porters.* A group of soldiers turned into the tunnel, stopping abruptly at the sight of Evir on the side of the path.

"Inquisitor," Javinth said with a mix of greeting and curiosity, then saluted, hands out to his side and chin raised. His attendant's use of his actual rank in front of the other soldiers could only mean one thing—the trap was sprung. The others looked confused for a moment, then quickly bowed, hands out to the sides as well. Their armor was lusterless, meant for field use, unlike the polished stones used in the kieresta armor. Four bore the steel scale armor of the regent's troops, while the other four wore the mottled-gray stone lamellar used by the Door. Evir extended his hand, palm up, the return salute to subordinates.

Vekk-oth, one of the Door's elantir, was standing beside a large, glowing glass jar held by straps lashed to two poles being carried by a pair of soldiers. The light was emanating from a swarm of bioluminescent hive crickets held inside the jar. Bringing an independent light source could be useful on an operation, especially against the Dorothi, who fought better in the dark than most. More importantly, the crickets were a ready pool of elan for the elantir to use if needed. Stone was a poor source, in general, so the elantir had learned the value of bringing stronger elantic sources with them.

"We were just coming to find you. Did someone already inform you?" Javinth asked.

"No, I was just on my way to the Door." Evir didn't feel like explaining what had spurred him out of bed at this hour. "Inform me of what?"

"The Church has started a purge in the residence quarters."

"Akraharr's dark hole!" Evir cursed. A dozen questions surged through his mind. "Do they know the location of the Katharis Pool? Are they after just the Dorothi or is it broader?"

"We can't tell exactly what their intentions are. The reports say they are questioning everyone and putting some to the sword."

Evir wondered whether he should go to Jt'alin Kavartha-akai and ask her to stop the purge. It would be faster and safer, assuming she agreed; but if she refused, he would be losing precious time. That could prove disastrous for his objectives.

"I should also tell you Artencu Vice-regent mustered his own forces and went to the I'fa residences just before we got the report about the purge. Trayvik was following him. Unless he veered from his course, he should've arrived there just before the purge started."

"That must be where the Dorothi masters are. Did he know about the purge? Was he trying to warn them?"

"Your guess is as good as mine." Javinth's voice sounded casual, but the fact he didn't make a joke told Evir his friend was feeling the same anxiety twisting itself through Evir's chest like a horned viper.

Evir tried to decide what to do as Javinth handed Evir his *ess'at*, the curved sword favored by the Kuldrith. Evir belted it to his waist and ran through his options in his mind again as if he didn't already know what he needed to do. Evir waived off the v'kar Javinth offered. Evir still trained with the bladed shield, but he felt he projected more authority without one, and authority was the only weapon needed. At least, he hoped so.

"Let's go," he ordered. He was not in the mood to eat but pulled a radish from his pocket and forced himself to take a bite while Javinth continued to brief him. The sudden sharpness on his tongue helped bring his other senses into focus.

"About two tenth-tides after you left the Door, we received reports that groups of kieresta and vaesh'katir were seen leaving the temple, moving toward the Otpon, Gai'da, I'fa, and Gu-Tir residences."

"Four residences at once? How many warriors?" Evir asked between bites.

"Our best estimate is over three hundred."

"Three hundred! How is that possible? Their numbers were nowhere near that many."

"Apparently the kavartha-akai has been receiving more reinforcements than we were aware of."

"I wouldn't have guessed they had even half of that from what I saw."

"We'll look into it." Evir just nodded, so Javinth went on. "With so many swords moving on the residences, we decided it probably meant just one thing."

A purge.

"We immediately gathered half of the regent's guard and every hand from the Door that could carry a blade."

"That won't be enough if we have to fight them." He chose not to be more specific about who *them* was. He would never suggest publicly they would harm the Teraithian priests; that might be considered to border on blasphemy. However, his objective to capture the rebel leaders was paramount, and if the priests threatened the success of his mission, he would do what he had to. Of course, he also expected the Dorothi to resist capture, and with Artencu possibly making a power play, this might end up a very bloody day.

Evir was grateful the purge hadn't come into his residential sector, where the prominent members of Kierden's society lived. That might have slowed him down too much.

"Any indication the Katharis Pool is there?"

"You mean like a thousand hive crickets milling about? Not that we've seen. Maybe I killed too many when they came after me."

Evir grimaced involuntarily before realizing his friend was exaggerating. Evir had hoped to remain inconspicuous. Now, too many crickets were the least of his concerns. He fought the urge to run. He used the act of eating an apricot to help keep his pace steady, even while his mind raced.

They passed a tunnel to the Gu-Tir residential quarters where many Dorothi lived. Evir thought he heard some commotion echoing from the area, but he didn't allow himself the time to worry about it. He had to stay focused on his mission of capturing the Dorothi leaders. It was all guesswork, but Evir would not have risen to where he was unless he guessed well.

Of all the rebel groups Evir had to contend with, the disciples of Vai Doroth had proven some of the most difficult. They were not principally motivated by a desire for power or wealth but by a genuine desire to be left alone to follow the dictates of their faith. Of course, that had placed them increasingly at odds with the demands of the Church and overlord that all Kuldrith adhere to the one true Faith. He knew there were many among his people who secretly harbored some devotion to one or another of the lesser gods. That was not Evir's concern, but he *was* tasked with ensuring such inner deviances did not coalesce into threats against the empire.

However, the Dorothi were difficult stones to break. The tenets of their Faith espoused the virtues of self-mastery, patience, and autonomy, all of which made them problematic to control. To complicate matters, many Dorothi priests were masters of a secret combat style that had taken the lives of more than a few of Evir's men over the years. That would have made today's operation difficult enough and justified putting every available sword in the field. But now he had to contend with the kavartha-akai's purge and possibly a coup attempt by the vice-regent. He again lamented that he hadn't been allocated more of the Door's soldiers in Kierden. Having to rely even partially on the regent's troops left a bad taste in Evir's mouth.

The white lights of Kierden gave way to the amber lumens of the large tunnels branching away from the central cavern. The smooth path of the passage wound downward in a steady, wide spiral as it descended in alternating bands of light and shadow, leaving behind the echo of the falls and the industrial sounds of the city. They passed a line of a dozen slaves hauling handcarts bearing food and other supplies from the warehouse chambers to some of the nearby residences. He had a momentary urge to warn them but decided against it. The people still needed to eat, so the porters had to complete their deliveries. More importantly, he didn't want to lose a moment getting to his destination.

"How much food did you stuff into your pockets?" Javinth teased him as he spat a cherry pit to the side of the tunnel. Evir silently offered his last cherry to his friend, who shook his head. Evir shrugged and popped the delicacy in his mouth, enjoying the sensation of the smooth skin against his tongue before biting into the juicy flesh. What little food he had brought with him had taken the edge off his hunger, but he wouldn't have minded having another handful or two.

There were three routes down into I'fa, and they had decided on the way that using the children's school chamber was their best option. It was the entrance furthest from the central cavern and would take longer to get there, but it would bypass more of the residences. Now it might have the added benefit of avoiding the worst of the purge if they were lucky. It was the middle of I'fa's sleeping tide, so normally the common areas would be empty, but if the kieresta were rousting people from their chambers, anything could happen. When at last they arrived at the gently sloping passage taking them down to the residences, Evir's only thoughts were of the mission and the dangers they were walking into.

Not all of them were suited for such dangers, however. "Javinth, I need you to return to the Door and prepare for any emergencies."

"You may need to negotiate with the vaesh'katir. I can help—"

"Your assistance would indeed be helpful, but we may have a greater need for a hasty departure from I'fa. Gather additional forces to help get us out if things turn ugly." Evir knew Javinth was willing to face the conflict alongside Evir, but the man was long past his years of battle. He needed the intendant on the outside. Even if I'fa was far better than they feared, even if they could avoid violence and bloodshed, they would almost certainly need assistance extracting themselves, especially if they managed to capture the Dorothi masters. "I will do my best to handle any confrontation with the vaesh'katir with diplomacy."

Javinth grimaced and seemed about to protest, but a reproachful glance from Evir brought the matter to a conclusion. "As you wish, Inquisitor," Javinth replied formally, with a sharp incline of his head. The man was offended, but only marginally. Evir could live with that. "Teraithia's blessing and speed be upon you."

"Let's hope so." Evir turned from his friend and motioned the others to follow. The amber lights of the large corridors above were replaced by the dull purplish-white glow of the inferior lumens lining the paths in the lower residences. The metallic and sooty smell of Kierden's air was now made even worse by the smell of unwashed bodies and refuse. The city had grown rapidly in recent years, in part due to the influx of Dorothi fleeing the Obsidian Door's operations in other cities. Kierden's residences had been filled beyond capacity, and Morizhin Regent had been forced to authorize the hasty construction of new residences in many of the old mining tunnels near the city.

Bad planning and worse luck had landed I'fa near the main composting caves. Evir was vaguely aware there were plans underway to reconstruct several of the outlying residences and auxiliary support locations, but the growing unrest had kept those plans from moving forward yet. Between the purge and Evir's operation, today was bound to be a turning point for Kierden one way or another.

The narrow, sloping passage corkscrewed down several feet and ended in the large school chamber. Evir's stomach clenched at the sight of five kieresta knights on the opposite side of the chamber, their v'kar raised and swords at the ready.

One of them barked an order at Evir. "In the holy name of Teraithia, drop your weapons and kneel!"

The kieresta were well disciplined, but Evir's trained eye saw the subtle signs of tension and anger written on their faces. He technically had the authority to reverse the command on them, but he was on loose stones and had to be careful. To convey he was neither a threat nor subject to their authority (and to keep some distance from them as the rest of his soldiers entered the chamber) Evir casually scanned the school.

The lumens here were brighter than in the corridors, a small benefit of being a newer residential area, so the light from the jar of hive crickets didn't make as much of a difference as it had in the tunnels. Twenty or so mats made of woven kanthis fibers lay on the floor in neat arcing rows facing the chairs for the teachers on one end of the room. Shelves carved into the stone walls held various school supplies: stone-framed clay tablets for writing practice, a water bin for keeping the clay moist, a pile of shredded kanthis stalks for one project or another, a weights-and-measures set, and other items Evir brushed out of his consciousness. It only took a moment to look, but it was long enough to have the desired effect.

"Drop your weap—" the holy knight began repeating his previous order.

"I heard you the first time, Kieresta-atan," Evir said, abruptly cutting him off, adding a hint of steel to his measured tone. "I am Evir Inquisitor of the Obsidian Door. I am acting on the direct orders of both Jt'alin Kavartha-akai and Arku Overlord himself. Now stand down and get out of my way."

Evir walked briskly forward as if he expected them to be out of his way by the time he crossed the school chamber. Vekk-oth and the others followed closely behind. Despite the uncertainty on a couple of the knights' faces, they stood their ground and hardened their stances. *Not a good sign*, Evir thought grimly, but he did not slow.

He had eight with him, so they slightly outnumbered the Teraithian knights, but four of his were regent's soldiers, still using antiquated metal scale armor and lacking the elantic enhancements of the Door's armor. They were no match for the kieresta. Fighting his way past them was a worst-case scenario without any guarantee of success.

"I won't tell you again, Inquisitor."

Evir stopped just out of sword range. He made a subtle sign to Vekk-oth with his hand and opened his center to make it easier for the elantir to draw on the inquisitor's elan. All the Obsidian Door's elite operatives were trained in how to make themselves sources for the elantir, as well as how to prevent the enemy from drawing on their elan.

Evir did his best to balance the diametrically opposed tasks of relaxing the focal points in his head, his chest, and below his navel to allow his elan to flow to Vekk-oth, while maintaining his intense focus on the kieresta, who might attack at any moment. Fortunately, the elantir had other sources to draw upon, and the brightening glow from behind him meant that Vekk-oth was drawing on the crickets' elan. He felt a slight tug on the focal points inside him and hoped the kieresta were unprepared for what Vekk-oth was doing to them. He just needed to keep them occupied for another few moments.

"Who is in command of your... operation, Kieresta-atan?" Evir asked, giving his words a conciliatory tone.

"Teraithia guides our every step." It was a non-answer that would have annoyed Evir if he had actually cared about the information. Now it just gave him more time to stall.

"May she reign forever from on high." It was unusual for anyone other than a priest to utter the short glorification, and Evir hoped it would distract them from the dizziness Vekk-oth was working in them. Evir only had a rudimentary understanding of what the met'elan entailed—something to do with moving the fluid inside the ear to simulate the effect of spinning around. It was not a common tactic, especially on multiple targets, and Evir hoped it would be enough.

A scream echoed in the corridors behind the heavy curtains covering the entrances to the school, though it seemed to be louder from the one on the other end of the chamber. It put Evir's nerves even more on edge.

"I hope there hasn't been much need—" Evir stopped as a kieresta suddenly bent over and retched from the motion sickness she was experiencing. Another one shook his head to try and clear the effect. It was a bad choice and the action sent him stumbling backward, crashing heavily into the stone wall.

"What have you done?" one of the kieresta demanded angrily, struggling to hold his sword straight, then dropped to a knee and leaned heavily on his sword to keep himself upright. The knight next to him lurched toward Evir, sword raised to the attack. Evir sprang back, drawing his own sword in one smooth motion. The kieresta-atan lost his balance and veered off to the side, trying to keep his feet but tipping over and crashing to the ground. He struggled to get up but fell again.

"Move!" Evir commanded his men, motioning for them to exit the chamber through the one the kieresta had been blocking. Evir kept his sword raised and fended off the wild swipes from one of the knights until his men were out of the chamber, then followed them into the corridor.

"How long will it last?" Evir asked Vekk-oth as he trotted past to take the lead.

"A minute, Inquisitor. Less maybe with so many."

More echoes of shouting bounced off the stone walls of the tunnels. The sounds were too mixed and distorted to be able to tell what was said. They passed tunnels branching toward other areas of the residences. Evir had spent more than enough time over the past two days looking at the map of I'fa to know exactly where he was going. He took the first tunnel to the left, then his second right to a short spiral passage that took him down another level.

They passed one of the residence's commons, an open area where many of the residents took their breakfast and dinner meals together. As in other Kuldrith settlements, the commons also served as the center for other community gatherings, including a music and dance hall, a hall of justice for working out low-level disputes between neighbors, and occasionally worship services.

Today it served as a holding area for the purge.

Several kieresta stood guard over I'fa residents sitting on mats, and a vaesh'katir-atan paced in front of them, extolling the vital importance of complete submission to Teraithia's will. Some of the kieresta looked in Evir's direction as his group passed, but none of them moved to stop him. He hoped his luck held long enough to find the other group of the Door's soldiers without running into any further trouble. Their route took them past some branching mine shafts and empty storage areas from the days when I'fa was still an active mine, then he veered into a tunnel with more residence chambers.

His ears picked up the sounds before he saw what was ahead, and his heart sank. The air was tinged with the warm metallic smell of fresh blood. Soon Evir was carefully making his way through the bodies of dead and dying littering the floor of the corridor and inside the residences. Everything he saw disturbed him. Too many of them were ordinary men, women, and children. The brutality of the killings sickened him. One thing in particular caught his attention—some of the bodies had freshly shaved heads and wore gray robes with black sashes. *Dorothi priests.*

It had been more than two years since he had seen a priest traditionally dressed. The clergy of all the gods other than Teraithia had stopped wearing outward signs of their faith as the overlord and the Church made it increasingly dangerous to do so. *Why now? Did they know the purge was coming? If so, why stay and fight a hopeless battle instead of fleeing?*

A few black-and-gold armored bodies scattered among the others told him the Dorothi had taken down some of the kieresta as well. A long, thin knife protruded from deep in the eye socket of one of the knights whose lifeless hand still held a broken onyx statuette of Vai Doroth. Evir had never believed it was necessary or even advisable to destroy the religious symbols of non-Teraithian believers, especially the Dorothi. Justice was a fundamental tenet of Dorothi Faith, which often was expressed in the form of the saying, *give as you receive*. Defiling their religious icons invariably evoked retaliation. Perhaps that's what the kieresta were hoping for if this massacre was any indication.

How many more will end up dead like this today? Evir wondered grimly. His mind's eyes imagined hundreds, maybe thousands of bodies lying just like this in many more corridors and residences throughout Kierden. Frustration edged with sharp anger gripped him, but he clamped down on it.

Evir suddenly stepped back as a thin, dark-gray hand reached toward him. He nearly slipped in a pool of blood on the stone floor but quickly caught his balance. The young girl whimpered unintelligibly, tears running down her cheeks and a deep gash across her torso. Her other hand hugged a blood-soaked doll to her chest, which was probably the only reason she was still alive. She would not survive more than another few minutes. Anger flared in Evir, anger at those who would execute such a brutal act on his people—anger mixed with compassion and a feeling of helplessness due to the urgency of his mission. He did his best to push it all down. He had no time to help the child or feel for her right now. That would have to be for later.

You must stop further bloodshed.

Evir felt the voice inside himself more than heard it. He was not sure of its source, but he was certain this was why he had awoken so abruptly and felt the urgency to be out of his residence. *I'm too late! If I had been quicker, could I have prevented her death?* Evir wondered to himself.

No, you could not have stopped this. But you must hurry before others die.

Evir's heart wrenched as stepped away from the pleading eyes of the girl and past the last body. He quickened his pace, spurred on by a pressure in the pit of his stomach that neared desperation. He turned into the tunnel leading down to the residences where the pool was located. The maps indicated this area was a dead end, which would help capture the Dorothi priests, but it also made Evir feel he might be walking into a trap. The echo of voices ahead pulled his attention forward as he strained to hear what was said. The reverberation was too heavy to make anything out clearly, but he was certain he heard anger.

The tunnel opened abruptly into a small, rough-hewn cavern in rusty-brown stone. He barely spared a glance to note empty iron walkways over his head that disappeared into the darkness. His attention was torn between the grizzly scene of dead bodies scattered around the cavern and the group of over a dozen kieresta standing between him and the Dorothi residences. The fallen warriors were a bloody mix of regent's men, Dorothi priests, and some of the Door's soldiers. Evir desperately wanted to know what had happened here, but there was no time to investigate. Several kieresta suddenly turned, weapons raised, as Evir's group entered the cavern.

"Stay where you are!" one of the knights ordered. Evir and his men complied. From his slightly elevated position, he could see over the heads of the kieresta to the Dorothi residence chambers. He was relieved to see Kt'caris, commander of the Door's soldiers, barring the entrance to one of the chambers. He caught sight of more of the Door's soldiers behind the commander with a few smaller men with shaved heads. Dorothi prisoners—priests, no less. Kt'caris wouldn't be here with captives unless he had completed his mission.

"Who is your commander?" Evir asked the kieresta with a calm belying the mix of apprehension and disgust churning beneath the surface. A woman pushed her way through the heavily armored holy knights, her dark eyes wide with fury. She wore a bright metal breastplate over layered black leather armor, and an elaborate metal helmet only worn by the vaesh'katir. Her blue cope chased in silver overlapping angles told Evir her rank was *amet,* between atan and akai. Evir spoke as the priestess stepped over the lifeless body of a soldier, a kukri protruding from his chest.

"I am Evir Inquisitor of the Obsidian Door. I am—"

"Inquisitor?" the amet cut him off, skeptical and angry. Doubt played on her face for the briefest moment. "No matter," she continued resolutely. "Your soldiers are defying Teraithia's will! Order them to stand aside, or they will be cleansed with the others."

Evir stood little chance of cowing the priestess into submission. The vaesh'katir were some of the most zealous of the Church's clerics. Even in the best of times their methods of dealing with heretics and non-believers were extreme. In the midst of a purge, he dreaded what may come.

"They are following my orders, and I am following the overlord's orders. I will not interfere with your mission, Vaesh'katir-amet—I suggest you do not interfere with mine."

"Behold, my servants are my sword, and I am their shield. Those who defy my sword shall be cut asunder!" Evir vaguely recognized the passage from the Book of Divinity the priestess quoted. He was in no position to argue scripture with her and was certain it would make no difference to her even if he could.

"In matters of faith, I would not question your authority, Amet. However, this is a matter of state, and the overlord's authority demands that I take the rebels into my custody." Evir advanced, intent on brushing past the priestess without another word. Several swords were suddenly leveled at him, bringing him to an abrupt stop. One of the regent's men reached for his own sword, but Evir signaled him to hold.

The amet's voice echoed loudly off the stone walls as she practically screamed, "You dare presume to put the Goddess in a box? To dictate where Her power begins and ends?"

Evir quickly tried to assess his options. There were some things Vekk-oth might be able to do, but the vaesh'katir's training bestowed a heightened ability to cope with many elantic effects. He could order Kt'caris to attack from the rear, but Evir had no idea how many men he still had with him or what they might be dealing with inside the Dorothi residences. *No good options*, Evir thought in frustration. As much as it galled him, he might have no choice but to surrender to the vaesh'katir and take up the matter with Jt'alin Kavartha-akai later.

"Your hesitation marks your lack of faith!" the priestess shouted accusingly. She grabbed the medallion of Teraithia's symbol hanging from a chain around her neck and thrust it forward. "Repent now! Kneel and confess your weakness before our most Holy—" The vaesh'katir stopped mid-sentence, anger, and indignation written on her face.

Suddenly, Evir felt a weight in his mind and chest, pressing him to cooperate with the priestess, to stand together as equals, to comply with her will. He shook off the impulse and focused on the amet. Was the priestess dispositioning? No, she looked as confused as the others.

"I... we..." the priestess began haltingly, her voice strained but drained of anger.

Evir heard stones clacking and hard leather scraping on the stone floor behind him, no doubt from some of the regent's soldiers kneeling as she commanded. *We can help each other*, Evir wanted to say, but he found it difficult to speak.

All eyes were on the vaesh'katir and the inquisitor, as if everything hinged on the outcome of their confrontation. The eyes of the Door's soldiers remained locked on Evir, trembling but awaiting word to stand down or carry on with their mission against the wishes of the Church. Evir felt as if the attention of the very gods were on him in this moment.

Something was out of place. Evir looked beyond the amet and kieresta to where Kt'caris stood looking around with alarm. A bald head atop a lithe form slid past the Door commander toward the Teraithians. With great effort, Evir focused on the Dorothi priest, who appeared older than Javinth, racing forward and weaving through the startled kieresta. Raised swords and armored bodies jolted aside, faster than any of the warriors could respond.

Before the vaesh'katir could pull her eyes away from Evir, the slight form of a man gracefully slid between two of the kieresta and stood calmly behind the still-confused vaesh'katir, placing his hand firmly upon her shoulder. He looked unthreatening except for the serpentine way he had slid through the soldiers guarding her. His face showed only a determined resignation.

Evir was torn between a furious urge to save him and a calm, penetrating desire to remain still.

"Give as you receive," the man uttered the Dorothi maxim, almost as a prayer.

The vaesh'katir tried to shake the priest's grip loose, but he held like the jaws of a vice eel. She screamed in fury, "How dare you defile me with your touch, you filth!" Her efforts looked like a child struggling in the firm grip of a parent. "Kill him!" she commanded. Without hesitation, swords from the nearest kieresta lashed out.

The vaesh'katir screamed as a sword cut across the Dorothi's arm, and blood ran from identical wounds on both their arms, though Evir was sure no blade had come anywhere near the priestess. Suddenly her back arched and she screamed in agony as another blade cut the Dorothi priest from behind, his jaw clenched against the pain, his eyes locked on the priestess before him. Evir's mind struggled to understand what was happening. He saw the killing blow cutting through the air, aimed perfectly at the Dorothi priest's neck. Blood sprayed into the air as two heads fell to the floor.

The kieresta recoiled from the lifeless bodies as they slumped to the ground as though they were coiled vipers.

Evir did not fully understand what had just happened, but he knew enough to recognize this was his chance to end the standoff. "He laid a curse on her. Stand back before it corrupts us all!"

The kieresta took a few more steps away from the blood flowing from the headless corpses to mix with the blood already covering the stone floor of the cavern.

"Vekk-oth, can you neutralize it?" Evir asked loudly enough for everyone to hear him. He hoped to the gods the elantir would play along with the ruse in time to make it believable, but it was the best he could do at the moment.

"I don't know, Inquisitor, but perhaps I can contain it." The jar of hive crickets grew brighter as Vekk-oth drew on their life force. He opened the jar and instructed the soldiers holding it to lay it down. The crickets crawled out and the elantir made a sweeping gesture toward the two headless bodies. The crickets swarmed through the blood and covered the bodies.

Vekk-oth spread out his hands and the crickets began emitting a high-pitched noise that sounded to Evir like a thousand tiny screams. He watched with fascination and disgust as the crickets fused and hardened into a single shell in the shape of the corpses beneath. The glow faded, leaving the chamber in the pale light of the cheap purplish lumens attached to the walls.

Evir walked past the bodies, making a show of cautiously skirting around them. The kieresta didn't try to stop him as he approached the entrance to the chamber where Kt'caris had stood the whole time, watching. No doubt it was him the vaesh'katir had been arguing with when Evir arrived. The commander towered over the Dorothi prisoners, and even over the other Obsidian Door's soldiers. His imposing, muscular physique and lighter gray skin pebbled with freckles gave him the look of being chiseled from speckled granite. He saluted formally, hands out to his sides, palms forward and his chin raised. Evir returned the salute with his right hand held forward, fingers close together and palm down, his left hand reaching over the top to wrap around the knife-edge of his other hand, both at the level of Kt'caris' throat. Evir hoped the formality and respect from his subordinate would help make the kieresta more likely to listen to him when Evir told them to leave.

"You have four guards to post around those bodies?" Evir asked Kt'caris. It was the simplest way Evir could assess the condition of Kt'caris's forces without divulging too much in front of the kieresta. He also hoped the commander had registered that he should refer to Evir by his true title. No sense in raising more uncertainty with the warrior-priests.

"Of course, Inquisitor." Evir was relieved. Whatever else had happened here, Kt'caris was in control of the residences with at least four soldiers to spare.

"Excellent. Ensure no one goes near those bodies." Kt'caris turned to his soldiers inside the residence to give the orders and Evir turned his attention to the kieresta, some of whom seemed to be discussing what they should do in hushed tones. He was not completely out of danger yet, but the Dorothi priest's attack on the amet, as unfortunate as her death was, may have given him the opening he needed to come through this day with victory.

"What was the vaesh'katir-amet's name?" Evir asked solemnly.

"Addat-qu," one of the kieresta answered.

"We all regret her loss. I will ensure her body is returned to the temple once my men can do so safely. The rest of you should report to your commander." He paused for a moment before adding, "Unless you would like to carry her body yourself. I defer to you in the matter."

The kieresta glanced at each other and shifted in discomfort. For a moment, no one spoke, and Evir feared they would refuse to do as he had suggested. They glanced at Evir and apprehensively at Kt'caris behind him, then back to each other. Finally, the one who had told Evir the priestess' name gave the orders, and the remaining kieresta departed, glancing down at the cricket-encrusted bodies as they went. Evir let out a silent sigh of relief and waited while Kt'caris's men surrounded the bodies, and the kieresta left the chamber the way Evir had arrived.

Evir returned to Kt'caris. There was no need for the Door's soldiers to stand at attention on an operation, but Kt'caris came close.

"Tell me where things stand." Evir had several questions, but he allowed the commander to decide where to start.

"The fighting has finished, Inquisitor. We faced greater resistance than expected. Several of the priests nearly broke our lines. They were... I've faced Dorothi before. These were a different class of fighter, Inquisitor. They've been captured now, but it was not without losses." Evir noticed several of the stone tiles on Kt'caris' armor were fractured, and a few were shattered entirely, the cords lacing the tiles together beginning to slacken. It took a heavy blow to break one of the elanticly reinforced tiles, let alone shatter one.

The commander shook his head, looking down at Evir. While the inquisitor was slightly taller than the average Kuldrith, Kt'caris was easily a head taller than Evir. Many of the Door's commanders and elite warriors underwent an augmentation process similar to what the kieresta went through as part of joining their order. What they lacked in size compared to the Teraithian knights, they made up for with augmented speed and unique training. Not all survived the ordeal, but those who did were physically superior in nearly every way, though the transformation was not without its toll.

"What kind of losses?" Evir had other questions, but he wanted to know the cost of the operation. Not only did it send the right message to the soldiers under his command, it also kept Evir focused on what mattered—

they were fighting these battles to save people. If they ever lost sight of the cost, they lost sight of their purpose.

"Eleven of our soldiers have fallen, Inquisitor." A hint of incredulity flickered in both his voice and his eyes. "Several others wounded, some seriously. They should survive, except maybe Ska'evet. Perhaps Vekk-oth can help her survive long enough to get to her to the temple—if they will even offer healing after today."

Evir nodded, acknowledging the challenges today's events would pose for life in Kierden.

"The Dorothi summoned a demon. I've never seen anything like it," Kt'caris said with a hint of awe. "In truth, I hardly saw it all; it was blinding like the sun. Burned everything it touched. If it had lasted longer our losses would have been much worse."

Evir glanced around the cavern floor to assess the dead and noted several crushed hive crickets on the floor as his eyes searched for his men. Eleven Obsidian soldiers was a heavy toll. Some of his operations had been conducted without losing even one. He had suffered losses before as well, but today was the worst since his days in the army many years ago fighting the Eastgatians. He was grateful he was not fighting on the surface anymore.

"How many others?" Evir asked.

"Perhaps twenty-six or twenty-eight? I haven't counted, though it's not pretty." There were not that many bodies in the cavern and none of them appeared scorched. Evir concluded there must have been much more fighting inside the residences. "The demon wasn't the worst though. Akraharr's shade walked among us when Artencu Vice-regent's soldiers attacked. It was difficult to distinguish the regent's soldiers on our side from those fighting against us. But..." Kt'caris shook his head and shifted on his feet, showing an unusual discomfort.

"The Dorothi fought like I've never seen. At times they moved among us like we were standing still. Several of them might have even been able to best me in one-on-one combat, Inquisitor." Kt'caris was not given to false modesty or exaggeration, which made his statement even more surprising. "The confusion of fighting Artencu's troops was difficult enough, but the Dorothis were... worse. Many of the regent's soldiers broke ranks and lost cohesion. I thought we were lost, but something changed and the Dorothi master called out for them to surrender." He hesitated. "It was fortunate he did; victory was far from certain at that point. I guess our numbers were enough to overcome them in the end."

Kt'caris didn't sound convinced, but Evir had more pressing questions, so he put the matter of how exactly they had won aside for the moment. "And the vaesh'katir?"

"We knew the purge was coming, but with so many prisoners, we decided to secure the area and hold our position until you arrived. The priestess demanded we surrender and turn the Dorothi prisoners over to her. She was not pleased when I refused." Evir managed a slight smile at the obvious understatement. "I don't know how long we would have lasted against the kieresta if they had attacked. I'm just glad you showed up when you did, Inquisitor."

"Where did that Dorothi priest who killed the vaesh'katir come from? Was that your idea?"

"I don't know how he did it, but he got loose and danced through our hands when we tried to grab him. We were distracted and..." The warrior seemed at a loss for words but plowed on with his explanation. "Slippery bastard. But I wasn't about to run after him into the middle of all those kieresta."

Evir put a reassuring hand on the towering commander's shoulder. "You did very well, Kt'caris. Now, unless there is anything else I need to know, show me to the prisoners," Evir stated, motioning for the others to follow him and Kt'caris into the residence.

A short corridor led to the main chamber of the residence. The entrance curtains had been torn aside and left in a mass on the floor, faintly scorched on one side. The room was much larger than Evir expected, almost like a commons. This was different from what was shown on the maps he had studied. Stone benches cut into the side walls were the only decor in the room, plain and utilitarian. Typical of the Dorothi spartan lifestyle. The room was dimly glowing with the warmer white light of newer lumens set into the ceiling.

"Vekk-oth," Evir said as he turned to the elantir, "Ska'evet Enforcer is badly wounded. See if there's anything you can do to help her." Kt'caris ordered someone to lead the elantir to their fellow soldier.

Evir's attention moved around the room, sliding past several more bodies, many of them lifeless, their blood darkening the reddish-brown stone. The stench of burned flesh was strong. Kt'caris pointed to an area on the floor where the stone appeared misshapen, an odd feature in a room where everything else was smooth.

"It melted where the demon stood," Kt'caris said, shaking his head incredulously. Evir wasn't sure whether he wished he had been here to see it, but it was the least of his concerns. He turned his attention to the living.

A mix of Obsidian soldiers and regent's troops were guarding many prisoners on their knees facing one of the walls, hands bound behind their backs. Among the prisoners were soldiers that Evir assumed were the vice-regent's followers, as well as a few Dorothi priests and several ordinary men and women. Evir frowned when he saw the bodies of four Dorothi priests with their hands tied behind them, no longer upright or moving, near many dead civilians.

"You need to know," Kt'caris began carefully, "the regent's soldiers put some of the prisoners to death before we could intervene."

Evir's reply had an edge of steel to it. "What happened?"

"They lined up those they had taken prisoner, even the slaves who surrendered without a fight." Slaves, as rare as they were among the Dorothi, were sometimes a font of information and a valuable resource in any case, so killing them was never warranted except in the most exigent circumstances. "Morev and I intervened when we realized what they were doing. Things got... heated. They cut down over half of them before we could put a stop to it."

Evir held back a curse. He had wanted to keep the loss of life to a minimum. He knew there was always the risk of casualties with this kind of operation. Information was often paid for in blood, but killing the sources of information was a grievous offense in Evir's world. Needless bloodshed was disgusting. "Do you think they were acting under other orders or were their tempers just running hot?"

"They claimed they were following orders. 'Protocol,' they said. I didn't have time to press it further, and my blade made it clear my orders were different. They didn't test my resolve."

"There's nothing to do about it now. We will question them afterward." Evir kept his voice flat, impassive, not letting the anger taint his words. It was more difficult than usual, possibly because the stakes were so high. Sometimes he envied the Dorothi's degree of self-discipline. There were stones that showed more emotion than a priest of Vai Doroth who did not want to reveal anything.

"There are more this way," Kt'caris motioned to a passage on the left leading downward. Evir noticed more hive crickets in the corridor. He was anxious to retrieve the Katharis Pool, but he needed to get the situation under control first and foremost. They emerged into a round chamber lit by two yellowish-white lumens suspended from a chain at the apex of the slightly domed ceiling. More bodies were strewn about. Many had limbs bent at sickening angles and sharp instruments plunged into vulnerable gaps in their heavy armor. Three were Evir's men. Only one was a Dorothi priest.

Four prisoners were on their knees along the left side of the chamber, their hands bound behind them. Evir immediately recognized Artencu Viceregent, though his disheveled appearance was a stark contrast to his usual immaculate presentation. A fresh welt ran along one cheek matching his mood, dark and angry.

The others all had freshly shaved heads and wore the black sash of Dorothi priests. They had no sign of rank, but their age marked them as senior clerics, which Evir guessed was close to his, except for the priestess, who was at least ten years his elder. Another Dorothi priest had crumpled to the floor in front of a captain of the regent's soldiers, an Eastgatian judging from his brown skin and wavy hair, obviously a requited who had not only earned his freedom but some authority in the regent's service as well. The man stood threateningly over the fallen Dorothi. The priest slowly started to rise, but his knee gave way in the attempt. Blood ran from his nose and mouth.

"Where is it?" the regent's captain snarled, his armored fist suddenly smashing down to deliver a vicious blow. The priest crumpled again to the floor. "Tell us where it is, or Teraithia help me I'll—"

"Step away, captain," Evir ordered calmly, doing his best to keep his anger out of his voice. Sometimes those freed from shackles could be the most zealous of persecutors. However, it was never a good idea to undermine your troops in the middle of an operation. He would decide later how to deal with the abuses from the regent's soldiers.

"And who are you?" the captain asked belligerently.

"Evir Inquisitor," he announced, as much to put the captain in his place as to let the Dorothi know whom they faced. The captain looked frustrated and appeared more than willing to take it out on the prisoners, but stepped back as Evir had commanded.

The crumpled priest, with agonizingly slow movements, pushed himself up on all fours, spitting out blood onto the floor. With a sharp intake of breath echoing through the chamber, he placed one of his feet on the floor and slowly tried his best to stand without putting much weight on his other leg. Blood ran freely from a new cut from his temple to the middle of his cheek, but the priest appeared not to notice. Pain flickered across his face for only a moment as he straightened, still keeping the weight off his right leg. He stood erect. His breathing was labored, and blood ran down his face and neck, dripping from his jaw and adding to a prior bloodstain on his gray tunic. He stared straight ahead, and his focus seemed to be somewhere beyond the chamber.

All other eyes were on Evir as he strode calmly, almost leisurely, into the chamber. There was nothing leisurely in his focus, though, as his gaze swept over the room. His first impression was that it appeared to be a library of sorts. Shelves freshly carved into the stone walls, higher than Kt'caris' head, were filled with scrolls, bound sheaves of copper and kanthis, and stacks of clay writing tablets and slate. Two tile-covered tables stood in the middle of the room surrounded by several chairs, some of which were knocked over. The holy symbol of Vai Doroth, two intertwining squares circumscribed within a circle, was inlaid in gold into the center of each tabletop.

This was no residence, but a Vaisoht, a Dorothi temple.

Evir quietly moved to the shelves and glanced through the contents, lifting a few of the sheaves of copper to see what lay underneath: something about purifying water, a theological treatise on the journeyings of the soul after death, a bit of poetry he didn't recognize. The inquisitor moved slowly from shelf to shelf, letting his silence build tension. Artencu Vice-regent began to protest but was silenced by a raised finger from Evir and the fact that Kt'caris took a menacing step toward the subdued politician.

When at last Evir approached the prisoners, the Dorothi were still as stones. They practiced meditating for many tenth-tides without interruption, and their self-mastery showed in their stoic demeanor. Artencu, on the other hand, looked like a cornered animal. Evir inspected him as if he was a new attraction at the Hall of Curiosities in Stierve. The bruises and scrapes on his face would deepen and turn black soon, but they were superficial. Evir turned to Kt'caris. "Have your men take him out with the others and ready him for transport to the pits for questioning. Leave his face exposed."

"No, you can't—," protested the vice-regent as Kt'caris roughly took hold of the politician and hauled him to his feet. "Inquisitor, you have no idea what's really going on."

"Gag his mouth though."

"As you wish, Inquisitor." Kt'caris sounded as if he would have executed him on the spot, had Evir ordered it. The commander handed Artencu to one of his men who unceremoniously ushered the still-protesting vice-regent from the chamber.

Evir considered each of the other prisoners as he walked past them to where the injured priest stood. Truth be told, they were all injured to one degree or another, but it was clear the one struggling to remain standing was in the worst shape. The man kept his gaze fixed intently on some distant point, and Evir had no illusion that the man's spirit was broken. That might come in time, but Evir had his doubts.

The man had a strong physique, though it was nothing like the augmented bodies of the kieresta or Kt'caris. His dark skin was slightly warmer in tone than Evir's ashen-gray. His hairless scalp had a sheen that made Evir wonder if he was naturally bald, or if he used some alchemical method other than shaving to remove his hair. Up close, Evir saw the man had suffered multiple cuts, at least four of them. None of them looked fatal on their own, but he was losing blood and his leg was developing a noticeable tremor. The inquisitor was not certain he would remain standing for long.

Evir turned calmly to the regent's captain who had struck the prisoner. "Your survival is conditioned on his," he said with a steely tone, letting some of his anger seep into his words. "See that he is properly bandaged, immediately."

The captain seemed about to protest, then clamped his mouth shut before finally answering. "Yes, Inquisitor," he said, then hurried out of the chamber.

Evir turned to Kt'caris. "Send for Vekk-oth, once he's done with Ska'evet." Ve'rivve, another of the Door's elantir, was already in the chamber, but she had no skill in healing. She could end up doing more harm than good if she tried. It was better to get Vekk-oth.

"And get this man a chair," he ordered to no one in particular. A soldier moved to retrieve one of the chairs around the tables for the priest.

Evir looked at the three clerics kneeling on the ground. He wondered which, if any of them, was the grand master. Had he successfully captured all the Dorothi leaders, as he had hoped? His information about their hierarchy had always proved frustratingly unreliable. He considered where to start the questioning, but one of them spoke first.

"Thank you."

"You would be better served begging for mercy," Evir chastised the priest. "Your defiance may have caused the death of hundreds, perhaps thousands. The only reason you're still alive is because you might be of some use to me. Otherwise, the Teraithians would have you right now."

"You aren't Teraithian?" the elderly priestess asked, slyly twisting the meaning of Evir's words. Having already been forced to defy the Church today, and frustrated over their interference with his operation, her words hit a nerve.

"I protect the empire against all her enemies. You had best prove that does not include you."

Evir turned back to the injured priest, who had refused to sit in the chair offered to him. "What was the captain asking you about?" The priest drew a deeper breath, then slowly let it out, but remained obstinately silent.

"Some artifact," the soldier who had retrieved the chair said. "We were supposed to be looking for a big basin of some kind, but it's nowhere to be found." Evir looked over at Kt'caris, who shook his head. "Artencu Vice... he seemed about to tell us something, but this one hit him to shut him up," the soldier said, motioning to the injured priest, who showed no reaction to the soldier's report. Evir caught a slight smirk on the face of one of the kneeling Dorothi priests.

He approached the man and squatted so he was almost at face-level with him. "It will go better for you if you cooperate. One way or another, you will tell me everything I want to know; but I assure you, telling me now is your best option." Evir didn't say it as a threat, merely as a statement of fact. The Obsidian Door used different methods than the vaesh'katir, but it still would not be gentle.

No one spoke. Not that Evir had expected them to. He turned to Kt'caris. "Take them out and ready them for transport with the others. Only take Artencu and the Dorothi. Tie up the vice-regent's soldiers and leave them here for now. We need to move as quickly as possible to get past the purge. Keep all our troops on alert until we reach the Door. And take everything in this room."

Evir watched as some of the Door's soldiers began carefully taking down the documents for transport back to their chambers in the Regent's Hall. Evir decided he had done all he needed to do in this chamber and was turning to head out when Ve'rivve motioned him aside.

"Intendent... oh, apologies!" she caught herself. "Inquisitor, there's a passageway hidden behind those shelves," she said in a low voice. Evir looked where she pointed. He didn't see any indication there was anything other than solid rock, but the elantir had an uncanny stone sense, even for a stone-shaper, which she had been before joining the Obsidian Door.

"Can you find a way in?" he asked, then chuckled as she raised an eyebrow as if it was a ridiculous question.

She approached the shelves and removed their contents, handing the items to the soldiers. Once cleared, Ve'rivve put her hands on the stone and bowed her head in concentration. Evir waited patiently, occasionally glancing around the room to watch the activity of his soldiers preparing to leave. Evir realized there was more than they could carry, and he didn't want to take the time to sort through it with the purge still happening. He hated leaving it here for any remaining Dorothi to recover it, or, more likely, for the Teraithians to come and destroy it.

Evir recalled the old priestess's question, 'Are you not a Teraithian?' He could not put his finger on why it bothered him so much, but of all the tide's chaotic events, that one troubled him the most. The image of the little girl lying on the tunnel floor sprang to his mind to shatter his assertion. Evir gritted his teeth against the emotions rising with the memory. Vekk-oth entered the chamber and came toward him.

"How is Ska'evet?" Evir asked.

"I believe she'll live. Other than that, time will tell." Evir didn't know exactly what the elantir meant, and this was not the time or place to get into it. Whatever it was, it was not good.

"I need that man stabilized for transport to the Door as well," Evir said, pointing to the sole remaining Dorothi priest, who still refused to sit in the chair.

"I need you first," Ve'rivve said to Vekk-oth, then quickly added to Evir, "if that's all right, Inquisitor?"

"Whatever you need," Evir said supportively, though he gritted his teeth with impatience.

"There's something... holding this stone together. I've shunted the elan away from the seam, but for some reason, there always seems to be more. It makes no sense."

"What do you want me to do?" Vekk-oth asked.

"Feel the seam?" Ve'rivve asked.

Vekk-oth closed his eyes for a few moments. "I can feel where the extra elan is. Mostly volkh and ka, but... a line of chi, too. I assume that is the seam?"

"Exactly. Now, try to pull the elan away. The chi specifically." They both went silent again. Evir had no idea what the elantir were doing but was starting to get impatient. Perhaps the Dorothi had somehow sealed the passageway like how the Teraithian temple vaults were sealed. If so, it could take some time to get in—time Evir didn't have.

"Don't worry about the ka," Ve'rivve scolded. "Focus on the chi only. I'm going to try something."

Vekk-oth's eyes narrowed as his fellow elantir concentrated and began to work in a manner invisible to Evir. "Watch it. You're drifting into kosek. And don't internalize it, there's too much."

"I can't put it into the stone like you can," Vekk-oth said with a hint of frustration in his voice.

"Put it in the corpses."

"Ugh, no."

"Don't get squeamish on me, Vekk. Just do it." Evir was about to tell them to stop, but his curiosity got the better of him. "And I need you to do it in one sharp pull. All the chi; otherwise I can't get the dam in place. Open the shunt, but don't pull until I touch the yldrath."

Evir stepped back and noticed the injured Dorothi priest watching them, the first sign he was concerned about anything happening. Evir wondered whether that was a good thing. Before he could give it any thought, his heart began pounding and his stomach lurched into his throat. He tensed and reflexively assumed a defensive posture, his hand on his sword hilt, knuckles turning an ashen-gray. Suddenly, his consciousness registered what was happening.

The corpses on the ground twitched grotesquely; not the movements of intelligent beings, but in erratic spasms. An eyelid fluttered open and closed and the dead man's face contorted into horrific, inhuman expressions. Some of the movements made blood spurt from the wounds that had proven fatal. It turned Evir's stomach and he had to look away. The others in the room appeared disturbed by the sight as well. Only the two elantir had their attention focused elsewhere.

"There!" Ve'rivve said triumphantly, and a section of the wall slid back slightly. Vekk-oth panted as if he had been through some strenuous exertion and bent over, hands on his knees. The twitching bodies subsided and then went still.

The Dorothi priest shook his head in open disbelief. "That shouldn't have been possible without—" His lips clamped closed, and he defiantly resumed his distant stare.

Ve'rivve pushed on the section of shelving and it slid easily inward with a slight sound of scraping stone. Light from the chamber spilled into a dark tunnel that seemed to curve sharply so Evir could not see more than a few feet. He looked on the walls for lumens but saw none. Evir and Ve'rivve reached into their pockets. Most Kuldrith carried lumens with them everywhere they went in case they ever found themselves in darkness. They were small, like a marble, but emitted enough light for the two to make their way through the curving tunnel.

They didn't have to walk far before they came to another chamber, much smaller than the one they had just come from. Shelves were carved into the stone walls, and a small stone dais and cushions were set in the middle. No lumens were set into the ceiling, but instead, a large golden symbol of Vai

Doroth hung directly above the seat behind a plain desk, supported only by thin chains that appeared far too delicate to support its weight. Evir could not imagine feeling comfortable sitting in the chair with the symbol precariously hanging just above his head.

No sign of the Katharis Pool, and no way out. Frustration made Evir want to lash out, but he kept his emotions in check. "I don't suppose there are any other hidden passages?" he asked jokingly.

"Not that I can tell, Inquisitor." It was strange that Ve'rivve used Evir's title again. She rarely did that, even when she should.

"Is everything all right?"

"Something is... off. I don't know what." She didn't look at Evir, but slowly surveyed the room as if trying to find what it was.

He didn't sense anything himself but proceeded cautiously as he looked through the items on the desk. He was anxious to return to the Door's offices in the Regent's Hall, but there could be critical information here. His pulse quickened at the sight of sheaves of copper and slate tablets on the desk. One of them might have been a message from the mole inside the Obsidian Door. He leafed through them quickly, but unfortunately, none of them were blank. The messages inscribed on the Door's copper sheets using the Synoptic Stones automatically vanished within a tide after being created. These appeared to be correspondence with others about various matters, mostly religious in nature. Evir was shocked when his eye caught one word on the copper pages—or rather a name.

Raen Qil.

He quickly scanned the surrounding lines on the page, but they didn't make sense. He scanned further, trying to find the beginning of the thread. Raen Qil was reportedly the leader of a mysterious rebel group called the Qilerate, but Evir had never been able to find hard evidence it was a real person or that the group actually existed. Many acts of sabotage, vandalism, and other mayhem had been done in the name of Raen Qil and the Qilerate, but investigations had always run into dead ends. Often, it was just criminals trying to misdirect attention from themselves, or disaffected youth who liked the idea of being part of a shadow rebellion. However, this might finally be something real, something useful for a change.

Suddenly, the inner voice came to him again. *Take it with you and go. Now!*

Not when I'm this close, Evir protested. His reaction surprised him as much as seeing the name itself. There didn't appear to be any reason to believe this was different from similar evidence he had seen before that always turned out to be a smoke screen or false lead. His intuition was telling him otherwise.

It will wait. The voice seemed far more patient than Evir felt. *Go now.*

Evir picked up the stack of copper sheets and headed out through the narrow tunnel. "Can you reseal the door?" Evir asked Ve'rivve. "Just like we found it?"

"Yes, but—"

"Do it." They emerged back into the larger library chamber. "Carry what you can but put everything else from this room inside that chamber. Now!" Evir barked the order, and his soldiers moved with urgency. Vekk-oth had somehow managed to get the Dorothi priest into the chair and had a hand resting on his arm. The blood on his temple had stopped flowing at least. There was not enough time for more. Kt'caris was just coming back down the corridor from the large chamber above.

"Get everyone moving. We're leaving."

CHAPTER XXXVI
SHIRALLA

'Hear your sentence.' Shiralla could still hear the words echoing in her mind; still see the anger and revulsion in Prince Andric's eyes as he glared with contempt at Warden Commander Sammet. 'You will be branded from head to foot with the symbols of all the gods except Teraithia.'

It was a barbaric sentence. It had left her shaken and disgusted, and yet it seemed so— No! It didn't matter how fitting it might feel. It tasted too much of revenge rather than pure justice. The prince should have taken the moral high ground.

'I hope you don't survive the ordeal,' he had continued hotly, righteous indignation burning in his eyes as he stared down a defiant Sammet atop the dais of the accused. 'But if you do, you will live out the remainder of your miserable life as a witness that your goddess will never rule this world!'

It was a terrible pronouncement. Shiralla tried to focus on the positive. Order had been restored in Tarsapta, and the people there felt vindicated and protected. The message had been sent in no uncertain terms that such horrific zealotry as Sammet displayed would be met with swift and unwavering judgment from the crown.

She forced herself to turn her already over-taxed attention to the task immediately before her. She had spent another restless night thinking through the countless details of the mission ahead, and now she was making her way under the early morning sun toward the large white pavilion that served as the Sharinist temple in the Remalian camp to another meeting with Consul Rellat. There was a time when she had liked meetings and appointments and enjoyed observing policies being created, strategies being debated, and decisions being made that shaped the future of people's lives. However, she now found them nothing but unwelcome interruptions to her busy schedule, interfering with her ability to accomplish the things on her endless task list.

As she approached the pavilion, she noted that its beautiful golden pennants snapped proudly in a breeze that didn't exist. The stagnant morning air would not have stirred a down feather. This was undoubtedly the latest flourish added by the consul. Over the past several weeks, the various faiths had fallen into a competition to show who had the grandest accommodations for their adherents. The churches' pavilions and tents had grown larger and more extravagant one after another, adding elaborate embroidery, artwork, and other flairs. Most recently they even added elantic effects.

The other day she had heard that the Yerinites had a harp that played music by itself under the influence of Yerin. Well, almost by itself. It turned out the harp was elanticly bound to another harp secretly being played in a separate tent by one of their clerics. It had been an embarrassing little scandal for a few days. Shiralla considered it all petty and a waste of resources, but Consul Rellat was not about to allow the Sharinist pavilion to be outdone. At least people weren't killing each other over it; not yet anyway.

She passed the guards posted at the entrance to the pavilion and walked down the center aisle past rows of empty wooden benches to the rear where an area had been sectioned off and tent walls erected to serve as the consul's private office. One of the knight defenders announced her arrival as soon as he saw her approach. She sat in one of the large, cushioned chairs outside his office for guests waiting their turn to meet with the consul. There was only silence from behind the fabric walls of his office, but she was used to that by now. Certain top officials had been designated to receive the anti-eavesdropping services of the elantir, including Rellat.

She didn't have to wait long before Ambassador Staltard emerged from the consul's office. At seventy-two, he was the oldest and longest-serving ambassador in Remalia. She knew he was supposed to have been traveling south with the first embassy to Calavia as the lead diplomat, but ill health had caused Rellat to assign Ambassador Jeaven in Staltard's place. It had to be disappointing for Staltard.

Shiralla could relate. She had been disappointed when Rellat informed her that her mission would now only be to the Vanassi. As a loyal subject of the kingdom, she was pleased they had reestablished communications with Teris. They could now dispatch diplomats to Calavia much faster. Nevertheless, it was a setback for her career. She had been thrilled at the prospect of possibly being the one to negotiate with the Navarchos Conclave to hire their mercenary army. Still, the Vanassi mission was vital and the most significant assignment she had ever been tasked with. Sharin Dara willing, she would do her best to get the resources they desperately needed.

Shiralla stood and curtsied politely to Staltard. "Good morning, Ambassador."

"What he sees in you, young lady, I will never understand. Do try not to embarrass us." Without another word, he strode away. His words stung slightly, but she already knew the elderly ambassador disapproved of her rapid rise through the ranks of the priesthood. At least there was some consolation in the implication of his words, that the consul hadn't changed his mind about sending her with Prince Andric.

Rellat's assistant invited her to enter the consul's office. She entered and curtsied deeply in front of the dark red mahogany desk behind which the consul sat. It was ridiculous that he brought it with him in the midst of a war, but it was a luxury the consul had insisted upon. A beautiful tapestry hung behind him, depicting streams of golden glory emanating from Sharin Dara standing above the world, kings and emperors kneeling in worship before the Queen of All Peoples.

"You may sit," he said without looking up from a sheaf of papers he was reading. As she took her seat, he continued. "Staltard thinks I'm a fool for allowing you to lead the second envoy."

"But I'm not leading it. Prince Andric is the senior official."

Rellat snorted as he turned over a page and kept reading and speaking simultaneously. How he was able to do that was a mystery to Shiralla. "In title, perhaps, but we all know you're the lead diplomat. To be fair, it is probably a position that should be filled by an ambassador, even if you aren't going to Calavia anymore." He looked at her over the rims of his reading glasses. "He said he's willing to have you come along as his assistant, but I told him the soldier's empty bellies wouldn't appreciate waiting until next year for this to be resolved."

Shiralla better understood now the ambassador's comment a few moments earlier. There was a mischievous twinkle in Rellat's eye, then he returned his attention to the papers. "I commend you again for your creative recommendation on the friendship offering for the Vanassi. I know it took some persuading, but you did an excellent job."

"Thank you, Consul." It had been decided to keep Prince Andric's delegation relatively small and stage a larger contingent of troops at Tarsapta for deployment to the Vanassi if those were the terms agreed upon. That had still left the question of what to take as an opening gift to their hopefully new friends and allies. Shiralla had convinced Prince Stephir to have his artisans craft an ancestral menhir. Such monoliths were rare and highly prized artifacts among many tribes in the Kushaani empire, including the Vanassi. Because they were considered valuable and sacred, they were often taken by unscrupulous tribes as spoils of war. Empress Arrdiwat had a collection of dozens of menhir from all over the Kushaani Empire, including some from the Vanassi.

The one being crafted by the Remalians was supposed to take a full two weeks to complete, with craftsman and elantir working day and night. But Prince Andric had insisted that he intended to depart by the summer solstice, cutting down their timeline to just thirteen days. Shiralla had worried that cutting several days off their schedule risked ruining the menhir and wished they could have called on some of the artisans in Teris who were true masters. She was relieved to receive a report that they had been successful in the initial tempering stage when the risk of it being ruined was greatest. She had checked their progress the previous night and was convinced it would be sufficiently impressive to the Vanassi. Her concern now was that it might make the tribe more likely targets of aggressive neighbors who would seek to come and destroy or steal the Remalians' gift. Yet she also saw how that could work in their favor to help convince the Vanassi to allow the Remalians to send more troops to help protect them.

"Have you settled on whom you will take with you?" His gaze remained on the papers, but his words were focused on the intercessor.

She started with the one who had been the easy choice. "Lady di Greven, for one." She was pleased to see Rellat nod quickly in agreement. Di Greven was an able traveling companion and had an uncanny ability to lighten the mood in any situation with her easy smile and brilliant charm. The fact that she could hold her own in battle was a given, and far less of a concern given the security she would enjoy being in the prince's company. "I am confident she will be invaluable, especially with a small contingent such as this one." She realized she was speaking formally as if she were back at exams testing for rank advancement. She did that when she was anxious.

"And the second?"

She had been struggling with this question, but she didn't want Rellat to see that, especially if he was being pressured to choose a more senior cleric instead of her. "I haven't decided yet. I have had more pressing things to take care of in preparation for leaving, one of which I was hoping—"

"Shiralla, who will be the second?" he asked, finally looking up from the papers.

She didn't like it when he used her given name. It made her feel like a child. Why was he pressing this? Did it really matter to him, or was he just testing her? She was tempted to try and deflect again but sensed Rellat would not tolerate that. She decided simple honesty was her best option at this point. "I have had a difficult time deciding who should be the second."

The consul nodded slowly. If she didn't know better, she would have sworn he was hiding some disappointment, but perhaps it was her imagination. "Go on," he prompted, putting the papers down and giving her his full attention for the first time since she entered.

"I have been leaning toward Lady Bucklan. She has years of experience dealing with the Kushaani. But having only women representing Our Lady feels unbalanced. Perhaps having a man's perspective available to me might prove an advantage in negotiations."

Rellat squinted and shook his head vigorously. "You don't need a man's perspective, or a woman's for that matter," Rellat said dismissively. "What you need is to learn to listen to Sharin Dara's voice better. You rely too much on your own talents, considerable as they may be. It's your greatest strength and your greatest weakness."

"Sir Americk would be a good choice as well." Why was she vacillating? She was so rarely indecisive. Americk was an excellent knight. The fact that he was rather dashing, the picture of what a knight should be, didn't hurt either. "He has much more experience than I do serving with the nobility, which could help in dealing with the prince."

"Were you aware that Lord Nophet stepped down as archpaladin last night?"

"Really?" she asked in shock. "Why?"

"That is what I want you to tell me."

Why did Rellat think she would have any idea? Or was he trying to make a point? She tried to think it through. There had been the incident in the war council when he had lost his temper with Sir Mar. That was a breach of etiquette, but certainly not enough to warrant quitting the position he had held for years. Had Prince Stephir pressured him? She was not aware of any tensions between the two. A power play by a rival within the Divinarim perhaps? Nothing else made sense.

"Try to look at it from the perspective of the Goddess. What is going on?"

"Consul, I know people see me as a know-it-all, but I assure you I'm not omniscient." It was an attempt at humor, but Rellat apparently didn't find it funny.

"Neither is Sharin Dara. She sees more than we ever will, to be sure, yet she can only see what light can illuminate, can only hear what ear can perceive."

"Then how does she hear the secret prayers of our heart?" She was not trying to be impertinent, but neither was she willing to accept unchallenged a doctrinal pronouncement that flew in the face of reason.

"Faith is a vibration, as are light, and sound, and elan. I don't know by what faculty the gods perceive the vibrations of faith, interact with them, draw strength from them, but my experience tells me that they absolutely do. So what does Our Lady perceive is happening with Nophet?"

Her thoughts drifted again to Sir Mar. As far as she was aware, the mission to Tarsapta was the only other time the two men had interacted. She searched her memories of the journey. There had been a moment of tension on the road when she was asking Nophet about the archseraph's Writ of Divinity to the Teraithians. "Wait! The Writ of Divinity. Is that what this is about?"

"Go on."

"Perhaps Lord Nophet feels he failed to live up to the mandates of the writ by siding with the prince against Sammet. Maybe he feels unworthy to continue serving—"

"You are thinking from your perspective again. See it from Her's."

Shiralla was frustrated with this conversation, but she was not sure if it was more with Rellat or herself. How was she supposed to see from a goddess's perspective?

You have not even tried, her inner voice gently reproved her.

She breathed in slowly, deeply, through her nose, taking a few extra seconds to calm her nerves. She released the breath, carefully keeping her face a mask of serenity that she didn't feel. Most men seemed to feel women were overly emotional, and any display of emotion was interpreted as cracking under pressure. If a man had an outburst, at most it was considered bad manners and was often seen as a sign of strength. The double standard was galling. But it was reality, and Shiralla had worked hard to ensure she never played into the stereotype, despite it being unfair.

How does the Goddess see this situation? One of Sharin Dara's most fundamental teachings was that everyone wanted something. Every human behavior was an attempt to satisfy some desire, some need. If one understood what a person desired, one understood their behavior. Of course, it was always more complicated than it seemed because there were many simultaneous desires and needs, often conflicting with each other.

Rellat said Nophet had stepped down as archpaladin. Assuming that was true, what did he desire that could explain his behavior? *'Do not question my faith,'* Nophet had said to her on the road to Tarsapta. *'Teraithia's holy knights have faithfully served and protected this royal bloodline for generations,'* he had shouted at Sir Mar. Whatever else he was, he was a man of faith. It was a holy calling to him to defend the royal family. What could make him give that up?

Only a higher calling. But what was a higher calling than his life-long task of defending the royal family? *What does Sharin Dara see that I cannot?* Shiralla opened herself to Sharin Dara's light, inviting it into her mind and heart to illuminate her. A calm sense of joy filled her breast, a feeling of connectedness with the world around her. Sharin Dara's divine presence helped to focus her thoughts and intuition. The words of the archseraph's Writ of Divinity came to her mind: *'... make every effort to bring more souls to the embrace of Our Holy Lady, Teraithia, Goddess of All.'* Did he intend to become an evangelist? No, that didn't seem likely. As the archpaladin, Nophet had access to the highest nobles in the kingdom. Where could he have a greater influence than where he was? Of course, it was well known that Crown Prince Stephir was a devout follower of the Holy Couple. And Prince Andric—it struck her in a flash.

"He wants to accompany Prince Andric. He can't do that if he is archpaladin."

"Excellent. And why does he want to accompany our young prince?"

"You think Nophet wants to try and convert him? That will never happen. You didn't see how Andric despised the warden commander and her revolting crimes committed in the name of Teraithia."

"Open your eyes, Shiralla!" Rellat exclaimed in apparent exasperation, but she knew him well enough to know his outburst was entirely intentional. Every word he spoke, every voice inflection he used, was calculated for its desired effect. He seemed intent on jolting her out of her normal thought pattern. "The temptation toward authoritarianism is rising everywhere in the world, regardless of religious affiliation, political alignment, or economic station. You must learn to see the true threat."

All right! What does the Goddess see? She recalled Andric's pronouncement in Tarsapta. *'Your goddess will never rule this world!'* She tried to see Andric through Sharin Dara's eyes. She started to list his qualities, then realized she was still doing it. *How do I choose not to think? I can't do that. Why would Sharin Dara even want that?*

"Consul, forgive me, but—"

Rellat got up from his seat, walked around to her side of the desk, and stood behind her. He put his hands gently on her shoulders. She cringed inwardly but sat stone still. *What is he doing?*

"Shiralla," his voice was gentle, sweet almost. "You need to relax your mind... relax your body..." He started to massage her shoulders.

This was not right. She wanted to pull away, to flee the tent, but she was rooted to the chair. If she ran, Rellat might pull her from the prince's mission. This was the most important assignment she had ever received. If she offended Rellat, it might all be over.

"Relax," he coaxed.

How do I get out of this? she thought desperately. "Consul—"

"Shhhh." The massaging continued. He bent closer and whispered, "What does Our Lady want?"

Just answer him, then it will be over, she urged herself. Her heart pounded. Shiralla felt the familiar sensation of Rellat pressing at the edge of her consciousness, inviting her to link her mind to his in communion. They had done it many times before, and it was almost instinctive to accede to the connection, but now her mind recoiled from it. She feared he would be offended by her rejection, but she could not bring herself to participate in the divine benefaction this time. She felt panic rising in her chest.

Sharin Dara, help me!

Suddenly she felt disconnected from her body. Her perception shifted, expanded. Not like attunement—this was something different. She understood that her body was not actually herself. It was just a body. It could have been someone else's body, it just happened to be hers. She was safe, regardless of what happened to it. Rellat's voice sounded far away, as if she was hearing him through a tunnel. Her mind was sharp, crystal clear. She saw the beads of sweat dripping down the outside of the brass pitcher resting on the side table. A fly buzzed along the tent wall, trying to find a way out. She wanted to laugh. That had been her just a moment ago.

Rellat caressed her hair.

She imagined Lord Nophet, kneeling in his tent, asking his goddess for her divine help. *What does Teraithia want of him?* The goddess wanted what all the gods desired—faithful followers. Her mind's eye saw his connections to others arc out like beams of light, touching the royal family, the other Divinarim, the archseraph in Teris, a mother and father he barely remembered. And each beam of light that touched a person branched off to more connections, and more, until she could see a web of light connecting the whole world. It was too much. She could not follow them all, and her mind snapped back to Rellat as he released her shoulders and returned to his seat behind the desk. He interlaced his fingers and leaned forward, looking at her intently.

"Why did you allow that to happen?" he asked her carefully.

She blinked once, and then a second time. Was he honestly blaming her for his actions? She should be angry, or perhaps scornfully amused at how ridiculous it was, but she was still safe, and she merely felt curious. What made Rellat do it? What motivated his actions? Her first thought was to the obvious, but that wasn't right. She knew he had looked at her with desire before, but this was something different. More calculated.

"I didn't." *Didn't I? I did not follow my instinct to run. Why did I stay?*

"You did not stop me."

She had no answer.

"I can see that you're upset. Forgive me," there was no remorse in his careful words, "but you needed to see that anyone can be moved in any direction under the right circumstances. Even toward something they find *revolting*, as you put it. You think Nophet is safe because the prince hates what Sammet did in Tarsapta. Nophet doesn't have to convert him, he only has to tilt him toward seeking power over others. Do you understand now?"

Shiralla instinctively nodded, but her mind was elsewhere.

Rellat's face hardened and his eyes narrowed. "We cannot allow that to happen. Andric may be Prince Regent someday. Even if not, he'll likely wield significant power in the kingdom. He has finally seen the evil of Teraithianism, and he must not lose sight of that under the influence of a charismatic father figure."

She thought of Sir Mar. She did not understand why he had chosen to become a Sharinic knight, let alone risen to the Order of the Third Wave. He was too abrasive at times and too nonchalant at others. He also seemed to have little respect for authority. *So why does Sharin Dara want him to go with you?*

"I will take Sir Mar." She didn't know why that choice was right, but it was clear who she should take.

"It is, of course, your decision, but do you think that is the wisest choice? I would advise against taking him simply because you think he'll be a thorn in Nophet's side. This is much—"

"It isn't that. I don't particularly want him to go. I could list a dozen reasons not to take him, but that is who I feel it should be." Even though she didn't fully understand the reasons, she felt comfortable with her decision and confident in knowing Sharan Dara was behind her choice. At the same time, however, she felt exhausted. Strange that she should be worn out from the simple act of deciding.

"Very well. I will have di Greven and Mar informed of their assignment," Rellat said, leaning back in his chair once again. "Do you need any assistance with your other travel arrangements?"

"No, thank you."

"Do let me know if you change your mind about anything." Rellat picked up the papers from his desk and Shiralla knew the appointment was over. She curtsied and then left the pavilion. She could still feel the weight of his hands on her shoulder, on her hair, and she tried to shake the feeling of revulsion from her mind. The task ahead weighed on her like a heavy blanket. While the thought of accompanying and guiding Prince Andric and negotiating an alliance with the Vanassi had initially excited her, the details of the under-taking and the cost of failure now felt daunting. She found herself more worried about failure than excited about success.

She just needed to lay down and rest for a few minutes. The thought of going back to her hot tent sounded miserable, but there was nowhere else she could get to without a hike, and that was currently beyond her strength. She trudged past the tents of other Sharinic knights, clerics, and servants, all arrayed in rows as neat as the landscape would allow. Everyone seemed busy with their daily tasks, but conversations were kept to a minimum. A somber mood had settled upon the camp since the defeat at Balinth's Fortress. Unless something changed, Prince Stephir had more challenges ahead than just feeding his men.

She reached her tent in short order and pulled back the flap. It was already hot inside, so she tied the tent flap back to allow a little air to flow through. Glancing back at the consul's tent, she was surprised to find it only a short distance away. It seemed like she had walked further than that. Was she just distracted? Her mind must be as tired as her body felt.

She removed her kemrelac and hung it on a small wooden rack but left her dress on as she lay down on her cot. She tried to go back through the meeting with Rellat in her mind. So much had happened. Had she truly felt Sharin Dara's inspiration, or was it all in her imagination? She remembered feeling Rellat's hands on her hair, and she felt sick to her stomach. She wondered if bringing Sir Mar was the best decision. She remembered feeling certain, feeling a calm reassurance, but doubts were creeping back in. A tear slipped from the corner of her eye and landed on her pillow. She could think more about it when she was feeling rested, when her mind was clearer, when her stomach wasn't feeling as if it was full of sour milk.

For now, she needed sleep.

She curled into a ball on her bedroll and clutched the linen blanket meant to keep the chill of the night air at bay. Exhausted as she was, it would be another hour before her troubled heart and mind allowed her to drift into a restless sleep.

CHAPTER XXXVII
ANDRIC

Lieutenant Garreth stepped into Andric's tent followed by his ever-present shadow, Master Lonset. He stood erect and announced, "My lord, Captain Major Minanthsolum has arrived."

Andric had decided Lonset was not well suited for the trip to the Vanassi and instead selected the young lieutenant as his assistant for the journey. Lonset had been doing his best to train Garreth in the duties and protocols of attending to a member of the royal family, but Andric was going to miss having Lonset. Gods willing, they would be done and back within a month. "Good, send him in."

Andric was happy to see Captain Major Min again, but he was strangely nervous about this meeting. He knew the Sa'ari should consider the new assignment Andric was about to inform him of a privilege, but part of Andric worried he would be disappointed. He considered standing to receive Min but thought better of it and instead settled back in his seat. He was in charge and wanted to impress that fact on the Sa'ari. Standing might send a mixed message.

"Captain Major," Andric said pleasantly as Min walked in and saluted sharply, fingertips at the sword hilt hanging at his hip. Andric noticed the last time they had met the man had chosen to adopt the soldiers' salute instead of the scouts'. "It's good to see you again. Please, come have a seat."

Min thanked the prince as he took a seat opposite the small table where Andric had laid out maps, rosters, ledgers, and other documents he forced himself to review when he was not meeting with one person or another.

Lonset whispered something to Garreth, who quickly served his two superiors cups of chilled wine, then they both left the tent.

"How was your journey here?" Andric asked.

"Uneventful, thankfully, Your Highness."

"Thanks in no small part to your excellent work providing security on our western flank."

The captain major gave a reserved smile. "I'm happy to have been of service."

"There's no need for modesty with me. You have given great service, and I have a new opportunity for you. But a question first. How have you enjoyed having a combat command? Do you like it better than being a scout?"

Min did not respond immediately, and Andric wondered if he was trying to decide, or was choosing his words carefully. "I am honored to have been entrusted with such a prestigious command. I understand if you feel I am better suited elsewhere. I will serve in any capacity in which I can be useful." He sounded sincere, which Andric liked about Min. The captain major and Barak had that in common.

"I know you've only been in your current assignment for a short time, but I am leading a diplomatic mission to the Vanassi, and I want you to be my second in command. It's a smaller force than you've had under you these last few weeks, but I assure you this isn't a demotion."

Min shook his head, and Andric worried his fears about Min being disappointed were proving true, then Min chuckled. "Prince Andric, I am deeply honored. But may I ask, why me? Surely you have hundreds of men to choose from who are more qualified than I am."

"Nonsense. You've proved yourself loyal to Remalia, and perfectly capable in various situations, regardless of the circumstances. And I think we will work well together." Andric had other reasons, but he was keeping those to himself. "So, what do you say?"

"When do we leave?"

Andric took Min's answer as an acceptance. He wished he knew how Min felt about it, whether he felt he had no choice, or was accepting out of duty, or because he really did feel it was an honor to be serving with Andric, and if so, if it was just because Andric was a prince. He would probably never know for sure, but maybe time would give him a better sense of the truth.

"We are just waiting for the craftsmen to finish our gift to the Vanassi, which is supposed to be any day now."

"What will your offering be?"

"Some large ancestor crystal-thing. Figuring out how to transport it has been the real problem. They decided it's too big to take in one piece, so some elantir are coming with us to help with the final assembly once we get there."

"And how many others are coming with us?"

"I was hoping you could help me settle on that." Andric moved some papers and pulled out a map of Kushaan. He traced his finger along the route he had discussed at length with the intercessor and one of the scouts assigned to the area. "This is the route we believe is best to take considering both speed and security."

"We should consider going south to this point here," Min said, pointing to a section of the map. "The bridge across the Parabati River up here is in poor condition. It will add a day to the journey but is much safer."

They spoke for several minutes about the route and logistics until Garreth and Lonset stepped into Andric's tent. "Pardon the interruption, my lord. Master Ve'Aurben is here to see you." Andric let out a heavy sigh. Barak hadn't been happy when Andric told him he wanted him to come with him on the mission to the Vanassi. They had never really argued that Andric could recall, and not just because Andric was the prince. It just wasn't in Barak's nature to lose his temper, but this had come about as close to it as anything Andric had seen. Andric feared he might have to resort to outright commanding Barak to go. They hadn't spoken since that conversation a couple of days ago. Andric hoped Barak had come to tell him he had changed his mind.

"Send him in." Garreth held the tent flap open and Barak entered. Andric could see from his face that he was not happy to be there. "Come on Barak, you look like someone killed your cat. It won't be as bad as—" Andric cut himself short as an elantir entered a moment after Barak.

"Andric, I'm not here about that." Barak's tone was grave, and Andric was instantly afraid it was news of his father. "Captain Major Minanthsolum, it's good to see you again." Quarian stood and bowed slightly.

"You as well Master Ve'Aurben."

"Andric, may we talk privately?" The fact that Barak was not keeping any pretense of formality was not a good sign.

"Captain Major, I have taken the liberty of having quarters prepared for you. This is my assistant, Lieutenant Garreth," he said gesturing to his assistant. "He can assist you with getting any supplies or provisions you need. We will resume our discussions as soon as possible, but I may be tied up for a while, so if we don't talk sooner, you will certainly join us for dinner tonight."

"Thank you, Your Highness." Min saluted, then gave a traditional Sa'ari bow before following Gareth out.

"Do you need anything else, my lord?" Master Lonset asked.

"Just ensure no one disturbs us. Thank you."

"Of course, my lord." Lonset bowed, then left the tent as well.

"My father?"

"Yes, but not what you think. Can we sit?" Andric sat back down in his cushioned armchair as Barak sat across from him in a small chair that Andric had ordered to be made for his diminutive friend. The elantir stood by the door.

"Ok, so what is it, Barak?"

Barak looked at the elantir, who nodded. Andric felt the elantir drawing elan from their surroundings and recognized the now-familiar flows to create the ward protecting their conversation. Andric could even duplicate the elant himself, though he could only do the simple version where sound was blocked in both directions. Turning back to Andric, Barak started. "We have found one of the traitors."

"Excellent! Who is it?"

"Let me explain first. We don't yet know if this is one of the elantir who was interfering with our communications. This one is keeping your father alive, or at least appears to be one of the elantir involved. We don't know if there are more, but we suspect so."

"What? Keeping him alive?" Andric was sure he had heard wrong. That didn't make any sense. Why would a traitor be keeping the king alive?

"You know that we haven't been able to figure out exactly how the disease works but have been convinced it was elantic in nature. Even though we've been able to keep the disease from killing him, or so we thought, we never really understood how we were able to do so. We now know that it wasn't us at all. She has been adding additional flows of elan to the healing elants, similar to what was being done with the Bonded. We suspect it doesn't have to be continually maintained, which made it difficult to detect."

"It's a woman?" Barak nodded. For some reason, it seemed more monstrous being a woman. "Who else knows about this? Has she been arrested yet?"

"So far, only Calinda, Corporal Stantow there," Barak gestured toward the elantir by the door, "and I." It took Andric a moment to figure out who Calinda was, and he was surprised when he realized Barak was calling Commander Alscan by her first name. "And now you know. Calinda is informing Stephir right now. I wanted to talk to you separately first in case you had any matters you wished to discuss privately, but we should meet with them soon to discuss our next steps."

"What's her name?"

Barak hesitated. "Andric, we've been friends long enough for me to know that if you know who it is, and you see her, you will not be able to keep it off your face... or worse."

A dozen angry retorts sprang to mind, but Andric held his tongue. He was pretty sure he could prove Barak wrong. He regularly beat Stephir playing Beggar's Bluff or Calavian Gambit, but he knew this was no game. With his father's life at stake, Andric was not going to force the issue. "So nothing has been done yet." Andric let his annoyance spill into his voice, though he was certain he could have kept it out if necessary.

"If she suspects we are aware of her, she'll likely stop whatever she is doing to keep your father alive. We need time to try and figure out how she is doing it. If we can do that, maybe we can even figure out how to cure him."

It was bad enough they had unknown traitors in their ranks, but it galled Andric to leave a known traitor free in their camp, to work who knows what other kind of harm. But Barak's logic was difficult to argue with. "Let's go see what Stephir has to say about this."

"Good. Stephir is in his tent." Barak said as they both stood. "Thank you, Corporal; you can return to your duties." The elantir bowed and preceded them out of the tent.

Andric was amused at Barak's easy assumption of authority with the elantir. He might have guessed it was by virtue of his position as advisor to the prince, but Andric suspected that Barak was earning his own prestige within the elantir corps. Andric felt a twinge of possessive jealousy. Barak was supposed to be here at his invitation, not getting cozy with the elantir.

Two Divinarim fell in behind them as they walked the short distance to Stephir's tent. Andric usually thought it was silly that the guards followed him when Stephir's tent was only twenty paces away. But knowing traitors were in their midst, his imagination was beginning to put assassins around every corner, behind every set of eyes. He was glad to have someone close by whose sole purpose was to watch in every direction for such threats.

Andric's temper simmered as they walked. Somewhere out there, a traitor was walking free in the camp, laying their hands on his father's head. *Not 'their' hands, 'her' hands.* She had a name and a face. Barak just didn't trust him enough to tell him. The thought made Andric lengthen his stride, and his diminutive friend struggled to keep up.

The four guards at Stephir's tent snapped to attention and saluted as Andric approached. Andric saw the young elantir off to the side, whose job was to cool the tent, and wondered if he could be one of the traitors. Shaking his head he ducked into Stephir's tent. Commander Alscan stood and saluted as Andric entered.

"You've heard everything?" Andric asked his brother, a firm tone meant to say he wanted a resolution to this matter. Stephir nodded as Andric and Barak took the remaining two chairs. Barak sat on the edge of the seat to avoid having to scoot further into the chair and leave his feet dangling. "So, do you agree that we're just going to leave this traitor out there?" He wanted to ask if Stephir knew her name but left it alone.

"For the time being, I don't see that we have much of a choice. She's the only thing keeping father alive. Don't worry. The commander assures me she'll be kept under constant watch."

"I want to stay until she is dealt with." Andric's desire for revenge was a hot stone in his chest.

"What good will that do, Andric?" Stephir asked, impatience edging into his voice. "It could be weeks before any action is taken. Weeks we can't afford to delay."

"Then you go, and I'll stay here," Andric said hotly, his simmering frustration boiling over and pushing him to useless arguing. "If the mission is so critical, you stand the best chance of being successful. I think I can handle sitting here doing nothing as well as you can!"

"You're an ass," Stephir said with a steely calmness, a harsher blow than if he had yelled the words.

Andric stared venomously at Stephir, then got up and stalked toward the door. "Do whatever you want," Andric said with his back to his brother. "You always do."

Andric brushed brusquely past the guards, his long, quick strides propelling him away from Stephir's pavilion. He headed for his tent, then thought better of it. Pent up inside his quarters was the last place he wanted to be right now. He was not sure where he should go instead, so he headed in the opposite direction from the elantir quarters. That was the one place in the camp, besides near Stephir, he was sure he did not want to be. He could hear the Divinarim jogging to catch up to him. He wanted to shout at them to leave him alone, but it would make him look ridiculous, so he just let them jog along behind him. Better to let them look ridiculous.

"Prince Andric!" Barak's voice was just shy of a shout.

"Not now, Barak," Andric said, not bothering to look behind him at his friend running to catch up.

Barak didn't answer, but he didn't stop running either. He caught up to Andric and jogged alongside him. "I just wanted..." Barak said between heavy breaths, "to let Your Highness…" his short legs pumping, "know that I'll be…" more panting, "out for a ride…"

Without pausing or looking back, Barak kept right on running. Andric wanted to laugh, despite his anger. Barak was not much of a runner, that was for sure. Andric wanted to be angry, but his temper cooled in spite of himself. Barak disappeared behind some tents, but Andric headed toward the horses, knowing he would find his friend there. He slowed his pace to make it easier for the Divinarim to keep up.

Barak was still panting, sweat streaming down his face, when Andric walked up next to him. "Mind if I join you?" Andric asked. He had meant to sound casual, but his mood twisted his intonation to monotonous and dry.

"It would be my pleasure, my lord," Barak managed to get out in a single breath, then returned to panting. Andric shook his head and smiled wryly.

"So where are we headed Master Ve'Aurben?"

"The healers' pavilion… may be in order after… that monumental exertion." Now Andric laughed outright. Across the fenced riding circle he could see Kobo and Steed being saddled. A ride would be good. He hadn't been out of the main camp in several days.

"Your Highness," said one of the guards who was sweating heavily, his polished steel armor probably baking him in the heat.

"Yes, retrieve your mounts. We'll wait," Andric answered the unasked question. The other knight saluted and walked off quickly. The Divinarim mounts were kept at another horse line. Barak retrieved the water skin slung from the saddle horn and drank greedily, spilling water on himself and choking. "Easy. I would prefer not to have to spend my last day in camp at the healers' pavilion."

Barak smiled through his coughing. Andric spent some time talking to Kobo. He could not be sure, but he believed Kobo missed his brother. Horses were lucky; they didn't have to deal with obnoxious siblings. Andric's guard soon returned leading a second horse for the remaining knight, and they all mounted.

"Where to?" Barak asked.

"This is your ride; I'm just tagging along." Barak seemed content to wander aimlessly through the camp a bit. The smells and sounds of battle preparation filled the air: the twang of bowstrings at the archers' range; the ring of steel on steel or thudding against wood dummies at the practice yards; fires and ringing of hammer on iron near the smithies. They all blended into a familiar cacophony. Andric was content to merely follow as his mind focused on everything that had happened in the last hour. Eventually, he decided he wanted to escape the camp altogether, so he wordlessly took the lead and headed east toward the forest. It was an hour's ride each way, but there should be enough time to get back before dinner.

Beyond the camp, they entered the area where the construction of siege equipment was underway. Everywhere were piles of logs brought over from the forest. Most of it was green wood, which didn't make for the best construction, but they had little choice. Remalia had some of the best engineers in the world; if anyone could make the most of what was available, they could.

They passed a near-steady stream of carts either going to camp with logs or returning empty to the forest, ready for the next load. It was mid-afternoon when Andric started seeing signs of the wood harvesting along the forest's edge. Every few moments one of the tall silver silkwood trees along the foothills would topple. Soon Andric could see hundreds of Kushaani prisoners of war working at the tree line, chopping trees, clearing branches, and loading the logs onto carts. They started passing wide swaths of stumps before they were even close enough to hear the work.

"Not exactly the forest excursion I had in mind," Andric said as much to himself as any of his companions. He thought about turning off the path, but the field of stumps and trampled underbrush would be dangerous for the horses and would only slow him down. Instead, he kicked Kobo into a slow gallop. The powerful warhorse strained at the reins to go faster, but Andric held him in check. He didn't want him tiring too much. Besides, Steed wouldn't have been able to keep up at any greater speed.

Soon enough Andric reined in a lathered Kobo as they entered the work area. Andric and the others dismounted. He wiped a hand across his sweating brow, but his hands were so damp he could not tell if he had succeeded in making his face any drier. He had been trained from a young age not to wipe his face on his sleeves, but right now he didn't care if it was a breach of etiquette. His fine linen jacket sleeve came away darkened with sweat and dirt. They walked the horses to a watering trough for the mules and let them drink. Pulling out their water skins, everyone drank deeply. The water was warm and unsatisfying, but it cleared his throat, so he drank his fill.

A sweating sergeant rode up and gave a perfunctory salute. Andric could forgive the man considering he had been working all day out in the heat.

"Good day, my lords. May I be of service?"

"We are just here to refresh ourselves for a moment before riding into the woods."

"Of course, my lord. Then I shall leave you to your refreshment. Please signal me or my men if we can be of any assistance."

"Thank you, sergeant." The man saluted again, a bit more sharply this time, before riding away. Maybe he recognized the prince as they spoke, or at least realized it was someone more important than he first guessed. After the horses had their fill, the men remounted and moved ahead into the woods. There was no clear path, so they had to pick their way slowly through the underbrush.

It was cooler in the shade of the forest, but the heat and humidity were still stifling. The trees were sparse in this part of the foothills, unlike the denser jungles to the south and west. Soon they had passed enough of the trees to muffle the sound of the work behind them, and a peaceful silence began to settle over Andric. The soft, rhythmic thumping of the horses' hooves on the leaf-carpeted forest floor added to the soothing effect. He hadn't realized how pervasive the noise of camp was until now, and it impressed him what a welcome difference a moment of quiet could be.

Andric heard the trickle of a nearby small brook and wandered in that direction until he found it, running clear and cool in the dappled forest light. Andric urged Kobo to wade into the shallow water and reigned him to a stop. He sat with his eyes closed, trying not to wonder what the others were thinking of him at this moment.

"Your Highness," Barak's quiet voice cut through silence.

"I know, we should go soon," Andric said, regretful but resigned.

"Actually, I'm happy to stay as long as you like. I wanted to speak to you about your mission."

Andric sighed heavily. "You don't have to go, Barak. I shouldn't have pushed so much."

"You may want to stop assuming what I'm going to say. You're not scoring very well today."

Andric could hear the amusement in his friend's voice and looked to confirm there was a smile to match it. "By all means then," Andric answered pleasantly. The slight breeze on his face and a bit of peace had done wonders for the prince's demeanor.

"May we ride apart a bit further for a private discussion?"

Andric looked at the Divinarim, then at Barak. He knew both men. There was no reason not to trust them. They were the most loyal soldiers in Remalia; but then, he might have said the same of the elantir who turned out to be traitors. "Very well. You will wait here," Andric said to the Divinarim, then spurred Kobo out of the brook and picked his way carefully further into the woods. He glanced occasionally to gauge the distance from the guards. He was tempted to sneak away, but that was a child's game best left in the past. When they had gone a fair distance he dismounted, and Barak followed suit. "I'm all ears."

"I owe you an apology for my words yesterday. I came with you as your friend and advisor, but I have been thinking more of myself." Barak's naked sincerity sometimes made Andric feel uncomfortable. He wanted to lighten the moment with a joke, but he worried it would be unfair to his friend, so he remained silent. "I still don't really understand why you want me to come, but if it's important to you, I will do my best to be there for you."

"There are plenty of reasons I could give you," Andric answered, "but I guess mostly it's that you help me to be my best self."

Barak dropped his eyes to the ground and Andric could see his jaw muscles working. He clenched his teeth sometimes when he was trying to control his emotions. Barak rubbed his eyes and cleared his throat. "I'm truly sorry about your father. I wish we had been able to figure out how to help him. Even if we are back in a month as planned, with what we know now about the one keeping him alive... he may not be here when we get back."

"I know."

"Don't tell anyone you're saying goodbye, but you should do that before we leave."

Andric nodded and thought of his father lying on his deathbed, but that just led his thoughts back to the traitor. "I hope Stephir keeps her alive until we get back. I want to execute her myself."

"I can't say what they'll do, but you know as well as I do that arresting and holding elantir is dangerous. The nearest place designed to hold them would be Luresh, but given what we know about their capabilities, even that may be inadequate. This is a complicated matter. When the circumstances are right, it will likely be over quickly."

"Can you at least tell me how many there are?" Andric asked.

"We can't be certain, but there are at least four that we are aware of."

"How did the Kushaani turn so many?" Andric struggled to keep his voice from rising to a shout.

"I don't think it was the Kushaani."

"Who then, the Kuldrith? But how?"

"*How* is the one question to which we have too few answers."

"How about, '*What's for dinner?*' Can you answer that one?"

Barak leveled a look at Andric that said he should be taking this more seriously, but simply said, "You're a prince of Remalia. I'm sure the answer to that is, *'Whatever Your Highness wishes.'*"

"Not without pissing off my brother. He ordered Lord Macen's rations cut in half for three days for cheating on the food quotas. He's becoming a tyrant."

"He's doing his best to keep everyone alive in difficult circumstances, and he needs your full support."

"He just uses me however suits him."

"That's unfair, and you know it." Barak's voice was gentle, but his words felt harsh.

Andric didn't want to fight with Barak again, so he remounted and turned toward the Divinarim. "Let's get back to camp. If we're lucky there will be something left for dinner."

The last two days had been a flurry of activity, but now Andric sat on the edge of a chair, leaning over and looking down at his father, holding his frail hand, a web of thin blue veins showing through the yellowish opaque skin. He had left this to the last possible moment. The troops were assembled and waiting. He could not explain it, but it had taken a supreme effort to make himself attend to his father. If everyone hadn't kept asking him about it, he may have left without making the visit at all. Now that he was here, he was baffled by his previous reluctance.

He could not help wondering where the traitor was at this moment. He felt somewhat guilty for how he felt toward the treacherous elantir, but part of him was grateful for her efforts in keeping his father alive. At least he knew she was not in the room with him now. He had asked to be left alone to say his goodbyes.

He was acutely aware this might be the last time he ever saw his father, but he felt strangely detached—as if he was watching himself from across the room. He wondered what he should say. A thousand thoughts ran through his head, but he could not pin one down long enough to say anything. He sat, staring vacantly at a face he scarcely recognized—barely a shadow of the man he once knew as his father. Could he ever be restored to full health? Somehow Andric doubted it. He wondered how long he should stay here so others would think he had bid a proper farewell. Had it been long enough, or should he wait a bit longer? He decided longer would be interpreted as he cared more, so he stayed.

Time seemed to slow nearly to a stop, measured in heartbeat after distant heartbeat. He patted his father's hand, held weakly in his own, and looked toward the top of the tent, letting out a sigh. Why couldn't he look at his father? Why did he feel the compulsion to avert his eyes, to look everywhere but to the man who lay dying before him?

It's time to go, he thought. But now that he was ready to leave, he could not get out of the chair. He did not particularly want to stay; he just could not seem to make himself move. He forced his eyes to wander down to where his father lay, but he kept his vision unfocused for some reason, as if he were staring past the bed toward the floor beneath. A pain grew in his chest. He could not breathe. *Can't breathe... breathe... breathe.* He felt as though he was about to be swallowed in emptiness.

A tear welled in his eye, and he wondered how long it might stay there. He willed it to fall, but it hung on the edge, stinging ever so slightly. He had nearly given up when at last it fell, tickling as it rolled down his cheek. Should he wipe it away, or leave it for others to see that he had cried? He wanted to wipe it away, but he could not move his hand.

Again his lungs would not release his breath. His heart beat fiercely in his chest. *Just get up,* he told himself. *They're all waiting for you.* At last, he forced himself slowly to his feet. He wiped the tear away, then bent and kissed his father's forehead. *Goodbye,* he thought, then turned and walked out into the blinding morning light.

CHAPTER XXXVIII
EVIR

There it is, thought Evir. *That is what made him vice-regent.*

Artencu stared at him from the other side of the open interrogation pit, trying to appear calm and in control, as if he was in a position to bend the situation to his will. The vice-regent stood straight, leaning slightly forward, arms folded. His good looks and natural charisma gave him a certain presence greater than one would expect from his small stature. If not for the distinctively ashen skin and broad face characteristic of the Kuldrith, he could almost pass for a surfacer.

The intense red light from the lumens mounted into the stone walls of the pit added a heaviness to the confined area, matching Evir's mood. He hadn't spoken about it to anyone, but he had hardly slept in the tides since the raid, haunted by the blood and screams and, above all, by the question of what he could have done to prevent it. The purge was the worst massacre he had ever seen, and he had witnessed his fair share. His people and their armies were sometimes brutal and efficient. However, he had a job to do, and there was no room for his personal grief at the moment.

Normally prisoners were kept in cells and only brought to the pits for questioning, but Evir had left Artencu down here since his capture. He had instructed the interrogators to cause minimal physical harm and pain to the vice-regent. Not out of respect for his station—his crimes had stripped him of any consideration in that sense. Evir simply didn't believe it would be the most effective approach. A few days of sleep deprivation, physical discomfort, isolation, hunger, and hearing the screams of other prisoners were enough to prime the man for Evir's questioning. Artencu was aching to talk. He had let the vice-regent ramble a bit to get the words flowing. Now Evir just needed to push him in the right direction.

"But even if you had been successful at seizing power, what then?" Evir asked, sounding genuinely interested. "You had to know the empire would come down on you like an angler spider on a signalfish."

"Not if we collapsed the tunnels into Kierden first."

Evir raised an eyebrow as if it was a good point. "But Kierden can't sustain itself. We would starve in less than a month."

Artencu smirked. He probably meant to look knowing, but it only made him look petulant. "I guess the Obsidian Door doesn't know everything."

"If we knew everything," Evir said in a darker tone than he intended, "I wouldn't need you alive." He could see the weight of the words was not lost on the vice-regent. The smirk faded from his face as he glanced nervously at the guards standing around the pit's edge several feet above their heads. The echo of a distant piercing scream punctuated the momentary silence. Evir wondered if it bothered Artencu as much as it did himself.

The questioners had been doing their work nearly without pause since Evir first returned from I'fa with his prisoners. He detested their methods, but it was a necessary evil in his profession and had no doubt saved countless lives. However, it was in no small part the reason he hadn't been back to the prison until now, to personally question the vice-regent.

"What was your plan then? How would you feed eighteen thousand people, cut off from the supplies the empire constantly delivers here?"

Artencu looked at the floor, almost certainly trying to decide how much to reveal. Evir knew that one way or another, he would eventually reveal everything. Evir let the heavy silence hang between them. With some prisoners, that would just make them close up tighter than a poked rock worm; but for Artencu, speaking was like water to a fish—he would suffocate without it.

"Did you know that in my younger years I was assigned to a mission sent to Calavia?" Artencu asked.

Evir did know that, but he played ignorant. "Something with your father?" Artencu's father had served the Mavin Tar, the Kuldrith supreme counsel, officially as a foreign envoy, although Evir also knew he had secretly served as a spy for the previous overlord. Evir wondered if Artencu was aware of that fact. Kuldrith children were rarely close with their parents, though he was old enough to have been raised in the days when the empire's policies allowed children to remain with their parents long enough to form strong memories of them before being given to the state for their training and education.

"Yes, he was sent to determine what the Navarchos Conclave could offer to aid in the fight against Eastgate. That mission was a complete failure. Do you know why?" It was a rhetorical question, so Evir remained silent. "Because," Artencu went on, growing more emphatic, "the Calavians understood something that the Kuldrith never have—that there is far more power and prosperity to be found in cooperation than subjugation. They didn't want anything to do with our fight with Eastgate. We have been at war for hundreds of years, and look at us—we scrape out a meager existence in holes in the ground with dreams of dominion while those on the surface grow fat on the prosperity of peace. We should stop our endless striving with the sword and triumph through truce and trade!"

At any other time, Artencu's over-alliteration would be laughable; but in the wake of so much tragedy caused by the vice-regent's treasonous actions, the trite political rhetoric was jarring and offensive. *Don't get pulled in*, Evir coaxed himself away from his growing anger. *Go back to the question.* "So you planned to buy your food?" A stone fell into place in Evir's mind. "Is that why you stole the coin from the temple vaults?" Artencu didn't respond, but Evir could see that his guess hit close to the mark. "But if you collapsed all the tunnels, who would you trade with?"

"There are options."

Evir was curious about that, but it was not his main concern, so he tried a different thread. He would come back to it later. "Like the Qilerate?"

"What? No! I don't know anything about them." Artencu said emphatically.

Evir understood why he would want to distance himself from the notorious rebel group, or new religious faction, or ghost story, or whatever they were. Everyone knew *of* them, but nobody seemed to know anything *about* them. "But you referenced them several times in the communications with the Dorothi we found in their I'fa compound." *Several times* was an exaggeration. Artencu had only mentioned them twice, and the Dorothi only a few more times in other documents.

"That was actually their vaisoht. Did you know that?"

"We suspected," Evir said, although he had been nearly certain for weeks. But there was no point in laying out all his stones. Sometimes it was best to give a prisoner room to feel they were being helpful.

"Pathetic by our Teraithian standards, but they seemed content with it."

He appeared deep in thought, so Evir waited. "I don't know anything about Raen Qil, except for rumors and such. You have to believe me."

"'Would you invite Raen Qil here?'" Evir quoted from one of Artencu's letters to the Dorothi grand master. "'What does Raen Qil offer?'" he quoted from another. "Sound familiar? That doesn't make me inclined to believe you."

"Those were rhetorical questions," Artencu explained defensively. "I could just as well have been asking if Vai Doroth himself was going to join our cause. The Qilerate are a myth. Pakoran Grand Master claimed to be in communication with them, but I assumed he was just trying to make himself seem like a stronger ally by claiming connections to the group. Not that it mattered anyway. He said the Qilerate advised against our plan, urging us to wait."

"Maybe you should have listened."

"Look what waiting cost us," Artencu said bitterly, then barked a brief laugh. "Maybe that was Raen Qil's plan—to make the Dorothi wait until the Church could wipe them out." Then, with a look of mock realization, he added, "Maybe Arku is Raen Qil! Yes, that would explain a lot."

"Arku Overlord," Evir corrected him but ignored the sarcastic accusation. "You will refer to him with the respect of the position he has earned." Evir needed to ensure Artencu was kept in line, that he remembered his predicament. Sometimes correcting minor infractions in the face of a more grievous one could be more effective.

"Earned?" Artencu asked acidly. "He hasn't *earned* anything. He stands on the necks of our people, keeping us bent down, licking the dust!"

Evir was in no mood to argue politics with the politician. He went back to safer ground. "How did the Dorothi communicate with Raen Qil?" Artencu shook his head, and Evir could only guess his intent. "You don't know, or you won't tell me?"

"There's nothing to tell!" the vice-regent exclaimed, throwing his hands up in exasperation. "Why are you wasting your time with this? Unless..." Artencu looked at Evir intently. "You must believe they're real if you're asking this many questions." The smirk slid back onto Artencu's face. "But you're truly in the dark on this."

The truth of Artencu's words galled Evir, but he shrugged it away and lied. "I actually agree with you. I don't think they exist. It's probably just a name people throw around when it suits their purposes. But my job is finding threads and seeing where they lead. That's why I've known for months about your connection to the Dorothi and that you were planning this little rebellion."

Artencu did an admirable job keeping his expression flat, but Evir could read the signs of stress clearly: his left thumb rubbing his index finger, the vein in his neck pulsing harder, the tightening at the corner of his bottom lip, the slight repositioning of his feet. Evir had struck a nerve. It was time to press.

He lightly tapped a finger on his thigh three times. One of the *guards* at the lip of the pit was Vekk-oth, who had been watching Evir for just such a signal. Now the elantir would work to manipulate Artencu's heartbeats, making them irregular; no easy feat, even for an elantir such as Vekk-oth. Not enough to harm him; that would be too obvious and distract the subject from talking. Evir just wanted him to feel uncomfortable, anxious.

"So far you've given me no reason to believe you can be of any use to me. I am inclined to let the questioners have you. Or perhaps the vaesh'katir." The vice-regent undoubtedly knew something of what that questioning would entail, and it was enough to disturb his calm façade.

"I swear by Teraithia's all-seeing eye, I don't know anything about Raen Qil or the Qilerate! What else do you want to know?" It was disappointing, but Evir believed him. He decided the best he could hope for was to glean everything the vice-regent knew about his co-conspirators.

"How many followers of Vai Doroth are in Kierden?"

"All of them, to hear the grand master speak of matters." Evir was not sure what to make of that answer, but he let Artencu continue. "The Dorothi, those that are left anyway, the ones Arku has—Arku *Overlord*," Artencu corrected himself, "has not put to death, have been migrating here over the past few years. They have come from every corner of the empire, building their strength here in Kierden. Why else do you think I accepted them as allies?"

Evir shrugged. "Because they're handy in a fight?" It was usually ill-advised to make a joke during an interrogation, but the vice-regent was cooperating, and being too heavy-handed with his type could shut him down. It was better to keep him unbalanced by constantly mixing tones, switching between casual conversation, flattery, indulgence, and the occasional veiled threat. And by now Vekk-oth should be working his elant.

"Why Kierden?" Evir had discovered over a year ago that Kierden was the destination for many Dorothi fleeing the empire's crackdown on dissenting groups in other cities. However, if they had truly been assembling for a decade, then perhaps there was something happening beyond his under-standing.

"Your guess is as good as mine. You can never really be sure of everything the Dorothi are thinking. I always assumed it was because Kierden was as far from Stierve as they could get. They hoped to find peace, but the Church and the empire kept after them, which made them desperate. That's when they came to me."

"Came to you? Are you trying to tell me the rebellion was their idea?" There was that agitated reaction again. Evir could not put his finger on what was bothering Artencu. Another wailing cry echoed to them.

"They came to me because they knew I was the one person who was not out for their blood." He said it as an accusation, and it struck a nerve in Evir. Anger, grief, and regret rose suddenly in Evir's heart as the image of the dying girl in the tunnel reaching for him flashed through his mind. He struggled to focus on Artencu's words.

"But my initial efforts had nothing to do with fighting for inde-pendence."

There it is, thought Evir. Artencu didn't want to be labeled as a rebel. He preferred to think of himself as a liberator, perhaps even as a savior if Evir's guess was correct. *Would he ever be able to see that he was the cause of the conflict, that without his actions there may have been peace?*

"I tried to convince Morizhin and Jt'alin to make Kierden a haven for everyone, that we would prosper better living together in peace than in constant conflict, especially amongst our own people."

"So you wanted to make Kierden a sanctuary for criminals?"

"What is their crime? To worship a lesser god? That makes them fools, not criminals."

Artencu's contempt made Evir reconsider his evaluation of the vice-regent's motives. Definitely not the savior of a downtrodden people. *What then?* "You don't sound like you care for their cause. Why risk everything for them?"

"It wasn't just for them. I wanted a better life for everyone. I wanted a life not bled dry by an empire that has a never-ending thirst for blood. They try to convince us that Teraithia has declared it our divine destiny to conquer the world, but all I see is sacrifice and poverty and misery and death."

And it's your fault! Evir wanted to scream at him, to grind it into his face with his fist. Evir was almost shaking, and he had to take a deep breath to calm down before he could trust himself to speak. When he finally did, his words smoldered with his suppressed anger. "Now you question the Queen of Heaven? You're on loose stones, Vice-Regent."

Artencu rubbed his chest and shot a glance up at the guards at the edge of the pit, then turned his troubled gaze to Evir. Did he know Vekk-oth was manipulating his heartbeat? Or maybe he was just worried a vaesh'katir was up there, watching. "I didn't take you for a zealot, Inquisitor."

Evir was relieved Artencu had misinterpreted Evir's reaction. Better that he believe Evir a zealot than the truth that— Evir's mind veered sharply away from trying to identify whatever the truth was.

"Am I the only one who sees this religious fervor as a problem for the empire?" Artencu almost asked the question as if thinking out loud.

"You think religion is to blame for your difficulties?"

"Everywhere you turn, the world is in turmoil. And what is at the heart of the conflict? The gods, or at least those who claim to be acting on their behalf. I wonder if we wouldn't be better off if the gods just left us to our own devices."

"How do you know things wouldn't be worse if they did?"

"How could things be worse?"

Evir heard a clicking noise from above that caught his attention. He looked up and saw Javinth standing at the edge. He gave a subtle hand signal that meant, *I need to speak with you.* Interrupting an interrogation was unusual unless the questioner gave the sign asking to be interrupted. Javinth wouldn't do so now unless he deemed it very important. Evir signaled for the small iron platform to be lowered down.

Evir turned one last time to the vice-regent. "You're wrong, Artencu," Evir said, his expression taking a hard edge. "Things could always be worse."

Without further word, he stepped onto the metal platform and was winched into the air. As the platform was maneuvered over the ledge, Evir discreetly signaled for Vekk-oth to desist his work on Artencu, then walked with Javinth out of the pit chamber into the large corridor connecting to other pit chambers and holding cell areas. The prison was filled to bursting over the past few tides: the commanders of the regent's soldiers who had sided with Artencu, the regent's soldiers who had murdered the Dorothi after capturing them, and more Dorothi than he knew what to do with.

Evir motioned for his assistant to lead the way. When they were out of earshot of Artencu's pit, Evir asked with a hint of anxiety, "What is it?"

"It's Pakoran Grand Master." Javinth seemed hesitant.

Evir was suddenly worried something had happened to the Dorothi leader. "Have the questioners pushed too far? He isn't dead, is he?"

Javinth shook his head. "No, nothing like that. He wants to speak with you."

"Really?" That was the last thing Evir had expected. Artencu talking had been a foregone conclusion, but Evir imagined Vai Doroth himself was more likely to speak to Evir than the grand master. The reports Evir had received indicated nothing the questioners had tried had elicited a single word from the priest. "Did he use my name or title?"

"Just Evir."

"Did he break, or do you expect him to try something?"

"I think Creation itself is likely to break before that one does. And I always expect a trap, Inquisitor. That's why you keep me around." Evir tried to force a smile onto his face, but it was fleeting. "He's in a holding cell now. Would you like him moved to an interrogation pit?"

"No, I'll speak to him there."

"I will remain with you if you wish," Javinth offered sincerely. Evir took a measure of comfort in having the steady support of his second in command, but he felt this was something he should handle alone.

"That won't be necessary." They entered a long, straight tunnel of rough-hewn stone with several iron doors lined with more of the red lumens illuminating the passage. Evir did his best to block out the crying and pained whispers locked behind each one. Guards were posted along the corridor, and Evir hated the thought of having their duties right now.

"Is everything all right?" Javinth asked.

Evir took a deep breath and thought of all the things weighing on him, thoughts he knew he would never share with anyone. "Ask me that after we see what Pakoran has to say." They reached the end of the corridor and Evir nodded to the guard on the right, who unlatched and swung the door open. Darkness greeted him from within.

Evir took a red lumen from where it was mounted at the side of the door and entered the cell, setting it in the iron bracket just inside the doorway. The cell door sounded ominous as it clanged shut against the frame with a heavy resonance that echoed in the bare chamber. The Dorothi grand master knelt with his hands and feet bound by chains behind him, and the iron collar around his neck was chained to the stone wall. It had to be very uncomfortable, and Evir felt a twinge of regret, but it was a necessary precaution. Artencu had remained unbound and unhurt, yet even restrained like this, the grand master was more of a danger to the inquisitor than the vice-regent ever could have been.

His eyes were closed and his breathing was steady. If it was not for being in an upright position, Evir might have suspected he was asleep or even unconscious. Blood caked over a dozen wounds strategically inflicted over his half-naked body to cause maximum pain without immediately threatening the man's life. Clearly, the questioners had been persistent.

As Evir contemplated how to begin, a thought came clearly to his mind— *give as you receive.* Why would he think of that Dorothi tenet of faith now? Surely the Dorothi priest had plenty of reason for revenge. Was his mind cautioning him to be careful? It didn't feel that way. Instead, he felt a surge of empathy for the man.

Show some compassion. Make him more comfortable.

All the reasons that was ill-advised rushed into Evir's mind to fight against the impulse. But cutting through it all was the simple truth that Evir was sick of all the suffering, and maybe this one small act could bring some relief to himself as well. Evir tapped on the door. The latch was lifted and the door swung open. Javinth stood looking at him expectantly, his expression laced with a hint of concern. His friend was not going to understand, but that didn't stop Evir. To one of the guards he ordered, "Bring me some water and a blanket." Then to the other one, "Remove his bindings so he can sit."

"Inquisitor?" Javinth asked cautiously.

"It's all right. Just do as requested, please." There was no room for discussion. The three men entered the cell and Javinth kept his hand on his weapon, tension written on his face, as Evir and the guard unchained the Dorothi's hands and feet. Bloody stumps were left from where a few fingers had been severed from his hand. Anger burned beneath his skin, but his mind found no target to direct it toward, so he pushed it down. The man moved stiffly and drew a few ragged breaths as they helped him into a seated position and leaned him against the cell wall. His skin was cold and clammy, and Evir felt small muscle tremors in his body, no doubt a combination of shock and exposure.

"Bind his hands," Javinth ordered the guard, but Evir waived him off. "Inquisitor..." The pleading in Javinth's voice was clear, but Evir kept his expression calm and said nothing. The other guard returned with a blanket and Evir took it without a word and wrapped it gently around the priest. The man's puzzlement nearly matched Javinth's as Evir gave the prisoner a drink of the water, then another.

"Wait outside," Evir gently instructed the three men.

The two guards stepped out quickly, but Javinth hesitated. Evir donned a smile that came easier this time and nodded for his friend to leave. Javinth's jaw clenched as his eyes hardened, heaving a heavy sigh, but he did as instructed. The door clanged shut again, but this time Evir felt less alone. He looked at the priest's injured hands again to determine whether he was at risk of too much blood loss. The bleeding had mostly stopped, cauterized by some kind of burn or hot instrument. Probably the work of an elantir.

"Thank you for coming," Pakoran said quietly with a raspy voice. "I had begun to wonder if they had given you the message at all." He blinked only briefly, his eyes struggling to adjust to the red glow from the lumen as he looked up at the inquisitor. Red light was less of a strain on the eyes after being in darkness, but it still required time.

"It would have been easier on us both if you had cooperated from the beginning."

"I'm sorry to have inconvenienced you," the high priest said with no hint of sarcasm, though Evir was certain it was intended. "Your men seemed to enjoy their work. Who am I to deprive another of their purpose?" Pakoran's eyes held Evir's in an intense, probing gaze, then suddenly closed them and bowed his head.

"If the pain is too much, I can have something brought that will numb it," Evir offered.

"You sound more like a Sykorian than a Teraithian," the priest replied without opening his eyes. Evir could not tell if it was a joke or an insult. Perhaps both. The priest winced, then let out a sigh and looked at Evir with a piercing gaze. "Forgive me, Evir." The apology sounded profoundly sincere, and it took Evir off guard. "I have spent a lifetime working to master myself, yet I must confess that sitting face to face with the architect of our persecution is revealing how much more tunnel I have to travel, and my time is running out."

Evir bristled at the accusation he had persecuted the Dorothi. "I am not your tormentor. I was trying to prevent anything like the purge from happening." Evir's anger ran ahead of his control, and his voice growled his frustration. "I didn't want the massacre of your people! It was your crimes that brought this down on your head, despite everything I tried to do to stop it!"

Pakoran replied with a peace that tamped down the flames burning in Evir's chest. "You've hunted us for years, driven us from our homes, destroyed our temples, told us we are not allowed to exist."

"Those were not my choices. I only did what was required to uphold the law and protect our people."

"Now you sound almost Dorothi," Pakoran said, sounding mildly amused. The priest contemplated Evir, and his expression softened slightly.

"And if I didn't know better, your compassion toward me would suggest you might be a Servari. Perhaps you simply do not yet know who you are."

The conversation had focused far more on Evir than he was comfortable with. It was time to change the subject. "Why did you ask to speak with me?" Evir asked.

The priest took a deep breath and let it out slowly. He shook his head once, then spoke with resignation in his voice. "Because it is Vai Doroth's will." Yet another cleric claiming to know the intentions of their god.

Evir usually ignored such claims, but this time it might offer an insight into the priest's mind, which could prove useful. "He told you that?" It came out far more condescending than Evir should've allowed.

If the grand master was offended, he gave no sign of it. Instead, Evir felt the high priest's presence deepen, as though he was becoming his own locus of gravity. A corner of his mind searched for an explanation, even as Evir found himself hungry to hear what the priest was going to say. *Is this what enlightenment feels like?* he wondered.

"The gods speak to us all from time to time, though most of us lack the ears to hear it."

"So why does Vai Doroth want you to speak to me?"

"Our Divine Master does not always make his reasons known to me, though believe me, I asked. He simply commands me to aid you."

Evir was immediately suspicious, though his instinct was tempered by the feeling that he should listen to the man. Talking could mean a lot of things and included a lot of room for various intentions. But a Dorothi offering to help someone he considered an enemy? That simply did not happen in Evir's experience. He decided to test what exactly the Dorothi intended. "Excellent! Let's start with the Katharis Pool. Where is it?"

The grand master bowed his head and remained silent for some time before answering. "I don't know. I entrusted it to some fellow servants and instructed them to take it far away from Kierden and make sure no one would ever find it."

Such a claim was too implausible for Evir to accept at face value. "Why would you do that? Why go to all the trouble to steal it, only to send it away forever? You must have some way to find out where it is."

"Artencu thought if we could determine how to use it, the Pool would help protect us once we cut ourselves off from the empire." Evir noted the high priest didn't use the vice-regent's title either and wondered if it was a form of personal resistance or something else. "But when it was clear our cause was lost, I ensured at least it could not be used to harm anyone else."

"What do you mean, 'when it was clear our cause was lost?'" Evir asked, trying to keep his tone casual to mask his keen interest.

"Our only desire was to be left to follow the path of our life in peace. Arku and the Mavin Tar seek the literal fulfillment of Teraithia's promise to make the world bend to her will."

"Arku Overlord," Evir reflexively corrected the informality of referring to the overlord by only his given name, although coming from Pakoran, it sounded somehow much more personal. Still, it was not appropriate.

"Kierden was to be our last hope," the priest continued, ignoring the correction as if he hadn't heard it. "Some suggested we leave the empire altogether, to go find a home on the surface. But that was not Vai Doroth's will."

"Why not? He would rather you remain here and become criminals, to be hunted and killed? Does he not value your lives?"

"The Divine Master values our lives enough to teach us the profound truth that *how* one lives is much more important than *how long* one lives."

Tell that to the children cut down in the purge, Evir thought bitterly.

"And so, we came to Kierden to set up our last refuge. We believed that if we migrated here slowly, over the span of years, it wouldn't attract too much attention from Stierve, and wouldn't turn the people of Kierden against us. But we were wrong." Pakoran straightened himself to sit a bit taller, drawing another deep breath and letting it out slowly as if to calm himself before continuing. "It seemed to be working for a time, and our numbers here grew. But you came for us in other cities before we could finish the migration. And here in Kierden, Jt'alin and others grew wary of our growing numbers, and the persecutions began here as well. That's when we turned to Artencu. He was motivated by his greed and ambition, a true Teraithian, but Vai Doroth can turn even the basest of people to his divine purposes.

"We agreed to his plan and prepared to cut ourselves off from the rest of the empire. That is when Raen Qil first contacted me." Evir knew he had failed to keep the eagerness from his face when Pakoran raised an eyebrow at Evir's reaction. "You would hunt Raen Qil and his people as you did us." It was a statement, not a question. The priest fixed Evir with a hard look, then abruptly closed his eyes again.

Evir waited for several moments, but when the prisoner gave no sign of resuming, Evir feared the man had decided his cooperation was at an end. *No! I have too many questions!* Evir thought desperately. *How do I keep him talking?* he wondered.

He considered his options carefully, fearing it might already be too late. He could threaten to turn the priest and the other prisoners over to the vaesh'katir. Jt'alin Kavartha-akai had already sent several demands that all Dorothi be turned over to her custody, but so far Evir had refused. He feared she might send the kieresta to take them by force at any time, and Evir knew, with their numbers witnessed during the purge, there was no chance of stopping them if they committed to the action. But Evir doubted that any kind of threat would work with the grand master. Perhaps the opposite would work.

"Pakoran, is there anything you need or want? Anything I can do for you?"

"What I want is the satisfaction of withholding from you what you want. But that is my own weakness, and Vai Doroth chastises me for it. We have little time, and I *will* pass this test. Ask me what you will."

Evir was not sure why the priest thought they had little time, but Evir was not going to waste this chance trying to find out. "Who are the Qilerate? Are they Dorothi, like you?"

The grand master's jaw clenched tightly, but he breathed deeply as if resigned to his course of action and responded. "No, nothing like us. They are no Dorothi. They never would have been able to remain silent this long had they been Dorothi. I believe the time will soon come when their words will burst forth like a voice from the stones."

Evir vaguely recognized the phrase as a reference to some sacred text. "Why are you quoting Teraithian scripture?"

A smile spread on Pakoran's parched lips. "The Ultideic Prophecy isn't Teraithian, or at least not exclusively Teraithian. Every faith believes the prophecy, though we certainly have different opinions about how it will be fulfilled."

Evir didn't want to get sidetracked with some obscure theological tangent. "So why did Raen Qil reach out to you? What did he want?"

"To warn us that staying in Kierden would mean our end. They offered us their assistance to flee Kierden. But as I said, that was not Vai Doroth's will for us, so we remained."

Warn them? How did they know we were this close? Evir was finally getting close to the heart of the matter. If there was someone to warn them, they must have had knowledge on the inside, knowledge from someone deep within the Door. No other contact could have known how close they were, how much they knew. That was deeply troubling. He would need to approach this carefully. "Where were they going to help you go? Another city in the empire? Did they want you to join them?"

Pakoran shook his head sadly. "You have no balance, Evir. All you see are dangers, and lies, and schemes, and troubles. You fail to see there is good, and beauty, and kindness. The Qilerate did not want anything from us. They simply offered us aid in our time of need."

"They sound like Servari."

"True, that would be consistent with Yonvaar and Kerail's doctrine. But not everyone who serves others is a Servari. I am aiding you now; does that make me Servari?"

Evir wanted to point out that aiding enemies of the state was a crime as well, but it wouldn't help matters at all, so he kept the thought to himself. "Where can I find Raen Qil?" It was inartful to ask so bluntly, but he saw no point in dancing around it any longer.

"You will not find him; he will find you. When he does, the world will seem in chaos. He will extend his hand. Vai Doroth offers you this counsel: trust yourself."

Trust myself? More useless platitudes. "Was it Raen Qil who gave you the information about the Pool?"

"No, that was initially Artencu, though it eventually made its way to us through other veins as well. He didn't prove as reliable an ally as I had hoped. I warned him to curb his tendency for words to pour out of him like Ettin's Veil."

"Artencu told you?" Evir was surprised. He had assumed the mole would leak the information to the Dorothi the same way he had. "When did he tell you?"

"Weeks ago. He knew of the danger the Pool presented to us, which vault it was in, even the wards that protected it."

Evir felt grim satisfaction and a sinking feeling at having his suspicions confirmed; the information had been leaked to Artencu before Evir put it out on the streets in Kierden. He knew there was nothing more Pakoran could help with on that problem, so he returned to the Qilerate. "What can you tell me about the Qilerate organization? Who are their leaders? How many followers do they have? What are their objectives?" Evir didn't usually like showing how little he knew about his target, but it was worth it if the priest could give him any useful intelligence.

"I cannot answer that for you. We don't have the time."

"Pakoran Grand Master," Evir used the honorific in hopes of conveying the sense that Evir was not the enemy, "I will give you all the time I have to determine—"

"Your place in the history of our people will continue to grow, whereas mine has come to an end. You will find the answers you seek soon enough, though they will not bring the peace you think." He bowed his head, his shoulders relaxed, and he carefully let out a measured breath.

Evir worried at the finality of his tone. "Grand Master, if you would just give me—"

The metal latch was removed and the heavy iron door swung open. Javinth was well trained at showing only what he wanted others to see, which made the mix of anxiousness and apology strange to see. He even saluted formally, hands out to his sides, palms forward and his chin raised. "Inquisitor, there is an urgent matter that requires your attention."

Evir hesitated, then slowly returned the salute informally, dropping his chin in a slight nod. Javinth wouldn't interrupt unless it was urgent. But Evir felt he was so close to getting information that could break open the investigation that had been stymied for far too long. He could not waste this kind of opportunity.

"Thank you, Javinth. I will attend to it when I have finished."

"Jt'alin Kavartha-akai is at the entrance, Inquisitor. We have very little time."

Evir cringed. Javinth knew better than to disclose such items in front of prisoners unless he had to, and Evir hadn't given his assistant much choice.

"Please excuse me, Grand Master," Evir said politely, doing his best to sound casual. "We will continue our conversation at a later tide."

Pakoran closed his eyes. "I have walked the path laid before me to its conclusion, and I remain in balance. We will never meet again, Evir. I wish you gods' speed on your journey. You will not have to wait long for your answers."

Evir considered the priest for a moment, then exited the cell. The guards began to enter the cell with weapons at the ready, but Evir stopped them. Although it was strictly contrary to the Dorothi faith, the priest's words made Evir concerned he might try to take his own life.

"Bind him comfortably, but do not take your eyes off him. He is not to be questioned further by anyone except me. And see that he's given water and a meal," Evir instructed the guards. He could see their discomfort and remembered what a threat the Dorothi still was. "And double the guard." Then he and Javinth hurried along the passage.

"The kavartha-akai is in the Regent's Hall, demanding the release of all the Dorothi prisoners, especially Pakoran," Javinth muttered grimly, bringing a frown to Evir's face. "She's not happy, and she brought with her forty-one kieresta."

Evir could not help but chuckle while he shook his head grimly. "She certainly has a flair for the dramatic, doesn't she?" The symbolism of the number was not lost on Evir. Most Kuldrith had a passing familiarity with the stories of K'varen and her Peacekeepers.

"I think she's aiming for more than symbolism this time," Javinth said with an ominous tone. "I stalled her as much as I could, but she had some specific information about our prisoners; probably the vaesh'katir are getting it from some of the regent's soldiers."

"Speaking of Morizhin Regent, where is he?"

"Hiding in his chambers. I can't say I blame him, though. He has to stay here and live with the kavartha-akai long after we're gone."

Evir nodded but said nothing. His thoughts returned to reviewing his conversation with Pakoran Grand Master. Why did the man think he would encounter the Qilerate soon? Were they interested in speaking with him or hunting him down? Did he need to be on his guard? He could not help but wonder if the Door's traitor was a member of the shadowy group. If so, was he no longer safe even behind the Door?

Approaching the front entrance to Regent's Hall, the corridors were packed with the regent's soldiers lined up behind a number of the Door's soldiers, weapons at the ready, blocking Jt'alin and her warriors from proceeding further into the Hall. The tension in the air was palpable, written in a language Evir was fluent in: the set of shoulders, the tightness of muscles gripping weapons, the fleeting glances. Jt'alin had no jurisdiction here, but that was not holding her back. Ever since the purge, she had grown bolder in her demands, certain her actions were justified by her righteous faith. The situation was primed for more bloodshed, which was the last thing Evir wanted.

"Evir Intendant!" The high priestess's voice rang out in the chamber as he made his way through the ranks of his soldiers. Her silvery hair was pulled back in a severe knot, accentuating the cheekbones and clenched muscles in her jaw. The usual white of her skirt had been soiled at the hem with the ubiquitous dust and soot of Kierden. Her chest was covered with a cuirass of intricately carved stone tiles, threaded together in the traditional lamellar style of the kieresta, ebony stone trimmed with gold, an odd contrast to the delicate cut of her skirt. She carried an ess'at and v'kar, matching her warrior-priests. "Or is it actually Inquisitor? Regardless, you have resisted Our Lady's will long enough. She will be denied no longer!"

The ranks of kieresta standing behind Jt'alin extended back out onto the causeway in the central cavern. Their armor platelets had been dulled to give off less reflection, a sign they had come prepared to fight. The imposing warriors appeared even larger than the Door's soldiers and dwarfed the regent's men.

"Akai, we are not ignoring your requests. We are acting on—"

"Jt'alin Kavartha-akai, Inquisitor! I speak for the Queen of Heaven here and I will not be treated with anything but the utmost reverence."

So, the informality is completely gone, Evir thought. That was hardly a surprise. His nerves were running high, but he was well-practiced at appearing at ease. "No offense intended, Kavartha-akai, but as I was saying, we are acting under the authority of Arku Overloud in this matter. We will release the prisoners to you when we have completed our duty."

"No! You will release them now, Inquisitor. Your orders come only from mortal authorities; mine come directly from Her." Jt'alin's hard expression and fiery eyes bored into the inquisitor. The air around her seemed to vibrate with power, as if the entire cavern were closing in around the inquisitor. Evir had been trained to recognize when he was being dispositioned and to withstand the promptings, but he was certain it should have felt more powerful than it did; more akin to what happened outside the Dorothi temple in I'fa while facing the vaesh'katir-amet, a primal urge to cower in fear and bow to the high priestess's power. Instead, he shook off the urge with far less difficulty than it should have required.

Out of the corner of his eye, he could see some of his soldiers trembling, a sign of the struggle between their religious devotion and their duty to withstand the demands of the akai at this moment. The regent's men lining the walls in their usual guard positions were bowing their heads and a few even sank to their knees under the power of her dispositioning.

Evir contemplated the akai, no longer with defiance but with curiosity. "We will not, Kavartha-akai. We have not yet fulfilled our mission."

Jt'alin's eyes widened, but whether in shock or outrage, it was difficult to tell. Perhaps it was both. Anger twisted her face and the air in the chamber seemed to shudder. "We invited you into the heart of Her home, we have stayed our righteous hand, we have exercised all patience." Her voice rose to a crescendo, and her face darkened with rage. Even Kt'caris began to shake, though he remained firmly staring forward.

We will get through this, Evir willed toward the commander as indignation rose in the inquisitor. Jt'alin dared to come here and try to exercise her power over him, over his people. Evir found it suddenly difficult to keep the anger from his face as he became acutely aware he was standing before the person who had given the order to start the purge. Anger and the oppressive dispositioning made for a dangerous combination. Was she deliberately trying to provoke him into a confrontation?

The priestess continued shouting, but the words rolled off Evir's troubled thoughts. He saw in his mind the bodies of hundreds of slain Kuldrith, Teraithian, and Dorothi alike. He saw the vaesh'katir-amet and Dorothi priest's heads severed from their bodies. He saw the young girl dying in the corridor of I'fa, reaching for him to save her. *There was nothing you could do to save her.* No, that was the akai's fault. She had given the order. It had all been her fault. *Not all, but enough.*

He could see the subtle shift Kt'caris took on his weapon, readying it for impending use. He could see the high priestess's weight shifting forward, almost on the balls of her feet. He could see one of the kieresta sizing up the Door's soldiers, analyzing which was the greatest threat.

Jt'alin stood before him, hand on her weapon, her face red and sweat beaded on her brow. She had finished her demands and seemed to be awaiting Evir's answer. Glancing behind him he could see several of the regent's men on their knees, cowering in fear or staring in awe. He locked eyes with one of the warriors still on her feet, a look of calm determination on her face. It struck Evir as remarkable that she and Evir alone seemed to withstand the priestess's dispositioning. Did she need to die today? Did any of them?

Evir let out a resigned sigh. He was not about to let this turn into a blood-bath, though Jt'alin didn't seem to share his priorities. He leveled his eyes at the priestess. "There is no need to disposition my soldiers, Jt'alin. The prisoners will be turned over to you forthwith." He was not sure why he felt the need to drop her title. It was petty and did not go unnoticed.

"Kavartha-akai. Show respect to her priesthood, if you value your life," the vaesh'katir-akai standing just behind Jt'alin demanded, sounding more petulant than indignant.

Evir ignored the threat and continued. "It troubles me deeply to see the Church so out of step with the Mavin Tar and Arku Overlord's orders. I assure you, this matter will be reviewed by the highest authorities when I return to Stierve."

"This has nothing to do with the empire. This is a matter of defending the Faith against heretics. Take care that you stay on the right side of that ledger, Evir."

"Evir Inquisitor, if you please," Evir replied smoothly. "As I said, the Dorothi will be turned over immediately. Your trip here was unnecessary, but an impressive display nonetheless."

Jt'alin's eyes narrowed as she looked at Evir from across the chamber. The inquisitor had never noticed how much she looked like a bloodmole when she was flushed. "All of them," she sneered, her lip curling up at the corner. "Even their grand master, Pakoran."

Her knowledge of the prisoners was disappointing, but it was to be expected when he had to rely on the regent's men for support. Evir desperately wanted to continue his conversation with Pakoran. He was so close to a breakthrough in uncovering something about the Qilerate, but the finality of the grand master's words and the peace on his face convinced Evir that his interrogation of the man was concluded. Still, it rankled Evir to turn him over knowing what they would do to him and his people.

"As you wish. Now, you are welcome to wait out here or return to your temple, or I would be happy to have someone give you a tour of our facilities if you would prefer, but I am afraid I must be getting back to my duties of rooting out enemies of the empire."

The priestess' lips formed a thin line. She gathered herself up and squared her shoulders to the inquisitor. "We will not leave until we have them all in our custody."

"Captain," Evir said to the captain of the regent's soldiers as he kept his eyes fixed on Jt'alin, "send your men to the prison and fetch every Dorothi prisoner and bring them to the kavartha-akai. And get K'varen's Peacekeepers some palestalks and water for refreshment. Since they want to play the part, let's give them the full experience." Her face flushed at the insult, but Evir turned away before she could speak. He motioned with a nod for Javinth to follow him as he turned and strode from the chamber.

"Your actions here will be recorded, Evir Inquisitor," Jt'alin called out menacingly. "They will not be forgotten!"

Without looking back, he replied, "I am counting on it, Kavartha-akai."

CHAPTER XXXIX

EVIR

Evir tried again to read the words inscribed on the copper sheet they had taken from the Dorothi temple, but his mind veered off track, insisting instead on replaying moments of the tense confrontation with Jt'alin, the strange discussion with Pakoran, the strained exchange with Dae'yen last night. Frustrated, he gave up and tossed the metal sheet back onto the documents resting on his desk. A corner of the thin metal leaf bent as it jammed against a slate tablet. A prick of guilt penetrated the frustration. It somehow felt disrespectful to Pakoran.

But why should he care about that? The man had led a group of rebels who had been a thorn in Evir's side for years. *What is their crime? To worship a lesser god? That makes them fools, not criminals.* Artencu's words rang truer than he cared to admit. Without thinking, he was on his feet, moving before he knew where he was going. He started toward the chamber where Javinth and Kiavi were working, but that was just force of habit and not where he really wanted to go.

He found himself descending through the tunnels toward the now mostly empty prison. Evir gritted his teeth against the swelling frustration rising in his chest like a bubble of hot magma; frustration that he no longer had custody of the grand master, could not ask him about Raen Qil and the Qilerate, or just talk to him about anything; frustration at Jt'alin for stepping outside the boundaries of her authority, for instigating the purge, for the suffering her orders had caused, and were continuing to cause at this very moment in the plaza in front of the temple as her questioners tortured the Dorothi priests.

Is she any different from you? You saw what your questioners did to Pakoran and the others.

I only do what must be done. I don't relish it as she does. The memory of a small hand reaching for him in the tunnel came unbidden. *I would never have let that happen!*

He arrived at the lip of the pit still holding Artencu and stepped onto the metal platform. The clanking of metal gears and the heavy chain as the guards lowered him down echoed loudly in the silence, waking the vice-regent. *What am I doing?* Evir wondered. Going into an interrogation unprepared was never advisable. Artencu sat up and leaned against the wall, one arm draped casually over his bent knee.

"On your feet!" Evir barked, angry at the disrespect from the traitor. *Easy,* Evir coaxed himself toward calm. *Only show emotions that serve your purpose.* Artencu scowled at Evir but obeyed, climbing wearily to his feet.

"We didn't get to finish our conversation the other tide. I'm hoping this time you give me some reason not to hand you over to the vaesh'katir as the kavartha-akai has demanded." It was not exactly a lie. Jt'alin had demanded all the prisoners, but Evir had only given her the Dorothi. She seemed satisfied—at least for now.

"I told you everything. What more do you want?"

Artencu hadn't even come close to telling Evir everything he wanted to know. He quickly considered whether it would be more effective to go straight to the important matters while Artencu was still half-asleep or prime him with little things as he had before. He opted for the first approach. He could always pivot if the prisoner resisted. "You said you had other people to trade with after you collapsed the tunnels and cut us off from the empire. What was your plan?"

"Some miners found a cave system that runs nearly to the surface. I have contacts in Kirresaar who would be delighted to trade with us."

"We have had conflicts with the Kirrelassi nearly as long as the Eastgatians. I imagine they would just as soon kill you as trade with you."

"That kind of imagination has kept us at war for countless centuries, kept us hiding in holes while..." Artencu stopped, perhaps realizing he was repeating himself from their last conversation.

Evir wondered how many times he had repeated those words to others, and to himself. "And what did you plan to do with everyone who did not go along with your plan? Morizhin Regent? Jt'alin Kavartha-akai? Me?"

"You probably think we would have put everyone who opposed us to the sword. That's the way you people always think. There is never enough blood to satisfy you—but you're wrong. You would have been given the choice to join us or leave before we collapsed the tunnels."

"With enough supplies for thousands of people to make the journey to Galeh M'veri? Of course not. That isn't a choice—that would be a death sentence for most."

"You assume thousands would choose to leave. I think it would have been a mere handful who could not accept that they could no longer keep their boots on the necks of the people."

"I hope you're wrong. The vaesh'katir are questioning prisoners in the temple plaza as we speak, and they don't appear to be making much distinction between rebels and heretics. If there are as many rebels as you say, there may not be much of Kierden left when they're finished." Evir feared too much of his frustration and bitterness came through.

Artencu's breathing quickened and his face tightened, though it didn't look nearly as much like fear as Evir had hoped. "As I said, never enough blood to satisfy." Artencu's words dripped acid. He dropped his eyes to the stone floor of the pit.

Too much. Ease him back. "How did you know the purge was starting? You mustered your troops and reached the I'fa residences even sooner than we did."

Artencu remained silent.

"Pakoran corroborated your statement that they were the ones who reached out to you first. Perhaps the whole rebellion was their idea in the first place. He said you were a true Teraithian. Maybe there is some way I can keep you out of the Church's hands."

Artencu raised his eyes. His interest was piqued. Maybe he was daring to hope.

"Unfortunately, you gave the Dorothi the information about the Katharis Pool. That's probably the most damning tidbit Pakoran revealed. If he tells the questioners that..." Evir let the implications fill the silent space between them. "But maybe if you give up the source who told you in the first place..." Still silence. "I'm sure the kavartha-akai would much rather find the traitor within her own ranks. Who told you about the Pool?"

"I don't know who it was, but it had to be someone high up," Artencu sneered. "They were able to slip the information right under your nose. Maybe it's you who should be put to the questioning, for incompetence."

Good. Belligerence would keep him talking. He hoped overstating his own competence would make Artencu want to prove him wrong. "I assure you, I did not become an inquisitor because of incompetence. Nothing *slips* past my attention."

Artencu laughed bitterly. "The information came in a sealed message through your offices."

The mole sent the information to Artencu? No wonder they had missed it. Evir decided to try pretending he was worried, covering it up with denial. Artencu was shrewd, so it had to be subtle. "So pathetic, trying to cast mud at me while you're sinking."

"Oh, it's more than mud, I assure you."

"Your word isn't even worth the clay it would be written on."

"Copper. I have it written on the Door's own copper." Evir tightened the corner of his mouth and made his eye twitch. Artencu sneered again, feeding on Evir's feigned anxiety like a starving cave tick on a juicy xanath. "Maybe I should give it to your superiors to prove how pathetic you are, Inquisitor!"

Evir laughed. "You're a fool, Artencu. Any sealed message on a Door foil would have disappeared weeks ago. Even if you weren't a lying *izenta*, you still have nothing but your word." Artencu looked down again, only half-hiding the grin he could not keep off his face. *He has something. It's time for threats.* Evir put a dark expression on his face with a sneer of his own. Without taking his eyes off Artencu, Evir spoke to the guards. "Bring me the questioners."

The vice-regent's eyes went wide. "No! You can't!"

"I'm done playing with you, Artencu. Give me what you have, or my questioners will wrest it from your mind."

"If I give it to you, promise that you will keep me out of the Church's hands. I want a civil trial."

Evir reached behind him and slowly drew his knife from its sheath hidden in the small of his back as he spoke, his voice barely above a whisper. "Give me what I want, or you will be begging me to turn you over to the vaesh'katir." Evir took a step toward Artencu.

"Ok! Fine," the man said, throwing up his hands as if to shield himself. Evir took another step. "Just stop! It's... it's hidden in the desk in my office," he said, sounding defeated.

"We went through every inch of your desk and found nothing. We know how to look for hidden compartments." Evir expected Artencu to gloat over Evir having missed something, but there was no resistance.

"It's not a compartment... not exactly. It's inside the desktop itself, hidden between the layers of kanthis stalk."

"If you are lying to me, I will not be alone for our next conversation." Evir turned and stepped onto the metal platform and was hoisted into the air. As his head rose above the pit's edge, he saw Javinth casually leaning against the wall, his arms and legs crossed. Evir slid the dagger into its sheath as he walked past his friend. They left the pit chamber in silence until they were out of earshot.

"Did you actually use that knife for a change?" Javinth asked.

"No need. He sang a lovely tune all on his own."

"So, his office?"

Evir nodded. "After we get Kiavi."

They chatted about minor official matters for the benefit of anyone who might overhear them as they ascended to the Door's main chambers. Kiavi was in her usual place, and the elantir quickly joined them when Evir wordlessly signaled for her to follow. She was undoubtedly itching to ask a dozen questions but kept them to herself as they made their way through the Regent's Hall to the vice-regent's office. Two Door soldiers moved aside to let the three pass.

"Admit no one," Evir ordered as he pushed the heavy curtain aside and entered. The entrance was not usually covered, but the scene had drawn too many curious eyes following the purge, so Evir had ordered the curtain to be hung. He was especially glad it was in place now.

He had been here enough times, both before and after the purge, to know every inch of the space. He motioned for Kiavi to raise a sound ward as he made his way to Artencu's desk. He remembered the desk being overturned while the office was being searched, but it had been put back in its proper place. He sat down in the vice-regent's chair and ran his hand along the edge of the desk, feeling for anywhere the thin metal sheet might be inserted between the layers of kanthis stalk lacquered together to make the desktop.

Nothing. But he was almost certain Artencu had been telling the truth. The man had no reason to lie about something like this. It was too easy for Evir to verify and return with the questioners. *Enough time to take his own life if someone has given him the means.* He hoped that was not what this was about. "Kiavi, I need you to search the desktop for a copper sheet."

"Can't do both," she said, her words clipped while she concentrated on her elant. Evir wished he could use more elantir in their efforts to hunt down the traitor, but it might attract more attention than he wanted. Secrecy was more important than convenience at the moment.

"I understand. Artencu said he kept the message containing the information about the Pool."

Kiavi's eyes widened slightly as she realized the implications. She nodded and moved to the desk. Closing her eyes, she laid her hands on the desktop. "There is something," she said under her breath, indicating the spot directly in front of Evir. She knelt next to him and ran her hand along the edge, just as he had done. She stopped, then slid her hand back and pushed her thumbnail into the edge.

A thin piece of the desk material, several inches wide, pivoted slightly. She smiled and pulled it out. A delicate, silver braided cord was attached to the back of the desk piece, and she pulled on that as well. Evir let out a sigh of satisfaction as a copper sheet slid out from the thin slot in the desk. He was surprised to see writing on it. It should have faded by now if it was a Door message. His eyes were scanning the words even before Kiavi had fully removed it. *Katharis Pool... temple vault... Dorothi.* It certainly seemed authentic.

He held out his hand waiting for Kiavi to give him the sheet, but she shook her head and handed the edge piece to him instead. He looked at her, concerned, but inserted the piece of the desk back in place while Kiavi lifted her blouse and put the metal sheet flat against her stomach before tucking her shirt back into her trousers. The three nodded and Evir began commenting about Artencu's endless deceptions and lies as they left his chamber. It was unlikely any of the guards were reporting directly to Stierve, but he could not be too careful.

Once back in their chambers behind the Door, Kiavi raised a sound ward and bound it in place. Like the temple vaults with wards to keep intruders out, the walls of this chamber were designed to hold a sound ward longer than natural stone could. Even when not protected by an elantic ward, the stone walls and ceiling had been shaped by the Door's stoneshapers into a bizarre textured pattern that was very effective at keeping voices from carrying beyond the chamber.

Kiavi pulled the copper sheet out from under her shirt and handed it to Evir. "Artencu must have had an elantir harden this somehow to keep the message from fading and stiff enough to slide into that slot in the desk. I was worried the copper might be too brittle and crack if you tried to roll it back up." Evir appreciated Kiavi's quick mind in addition to her considerable elantic talents. "And the hardening ruined the signature of the elantir who inscribed it."

"Can you still match it to its copy?" Javinth asked.

"Let's hope so," Kiavi said as she went to the chamber's vault and retrieved the stack of copper plates containing copies of all the messages transmitted through the Synoptic Stones over the past several weeks—copies that never should have existed in the first place, and which Evir would be relieved to finally destroy now that they had what they had been looking for.

Javinth moved closer to Evir and they both read the message. It had all the details Evir provided in his report to Qin'acht Overseer and Malithir Lord Overseer, the true ones and the exaggerated ones. Evir finished first and handed the sheet to Javinth to finish reading on his own while Evir turned his thoughts to the next section of the path they were now on.

First, he had to find the elantir who sent the message and hope they were directly linked to one of his superiors. That would make the most sense, given the nature of the message. This was not the kind of thing the traitor could afford to risk sending through open channels. If the trail led him to one of the overseers, he could go to the lord overseer. Kiavi could manage that as well as he could, better maybe, and it would be much less complicated to send her. However, if the lord overseer turned out to be the traitor, the matter would have to be taken to Arku Overlord, and Evir was the only one with a connection who could get him a private audience with the overlord.

Evir leaving Kierden without anyone knowing was the most difficult part of their plan. In the end, they settled on Kiavi's suggestion to mask Evir's identity and change Javinth's appearance and voice to become Evir's doppelganger. Evir worried the process might be too much for his older friend, but Javinth was the only one with enough knowledge of Evir's duties, habits, mannerisms, speech patterns, and the rest to have any chance at successfully portraying Evir for the several weeks it might take the inquisitor to travel to Stierve and unearth the mole.

Evir didn't relish any of what lay ahead, but his greatest apprehension was telling Dae'yen. There was only so much he was able, or at least willing, to tell her. The more she knew the more risk there was for them all. He just hoped he could convince her to go along with the plan.

"This is the one," Kiavi announced, holding up a blank copper sheet.

"And it has enough traces of the elan for us to track down the elantir who sent it?" Evir asked, both hoping and dreading an affirmative answer

It took Kiavi a moment, but she finally nodded. "Enough. I can make it work." It was the final stone falling into place for the first phase of their plan. They had gone as far as they could on their own. The next steps required bringing Vekk-oth into their confidence to help with the disguises.

"Any reservations about moving forward?" Evir asked as he looked at each of them in turn.

"And miss the opportunity to make you look good for a change?" Javinth joked. Kiavi shook her head, though Evir guessed it was both an answer to his question and her usual disapproval of Javinth's humor.

"Go get Vekk," he told Kiavi. They had discussed possible cover stories to tell Vekk-oth instead of the truth, but deception on a matter of this magnitude was too risky. Evir didn't know the elantir as well as he would like, but he had seen nothing in the past several months to suggest he could not be trusted.

"Does Dae'yen know what's coming?" Javinth asked.

"You'd better get used to calling her Dae, my friend. At least for a little while."

"All right," Javinth rolled his eyes. "Does *Dae* know what you're asking of her?"

"No. Do you want to take a practice run at being me and break the news to her?"

"I would rather bathe in hive cricket queen juice."

Evir laughed. He was going to miss his friend's wry humor while he was away. "Speaking of hive cricket queens, we should discuss how to deal with Jt'alin while I'm away."

"As little as possible and every bit as delicately as I did the others, I assure you." Then Javinth's expression turned serious. Lowering his voice, he continued. "I know you've always had your own approach to worshipping Teraithia, and I would never presume to judge you on such matters. But lately, your veneer of devotion has seemed particularly thin. You can't afford to give others any reason to doubt your piety."

Evir appreciated his friend's cautioning advice. He knew Javinth was right, but he was unsure how much his conscience would let him maintain the charade anymore. "Then maybe it's for the best that you will be me for a while."

Kiavi returned with Vekk-oth, cutting the conversation short. This would be a good rehearsal for the conversation he would have with Dae later this tide. He just hoped he did not regret either one. Kiavi put up the ward and Evir invited them both to sit. At least Vekk-oth now knew he was an inquisitor. The extra authority should help, or at least he hoped so.

"Vekk-oth, we have become aware of a security leak. So far only Kiavi, Javinth, and I are aware of the problem, but the next phase of our plan requires your help. However, this is a very delicate matter and it is imperative that it remains between the four of us for now. No one else can know of this or it will put all our lives in danger. Before I tell you more, I need you to decide whether you're willing to take that risk, and if you are, I must have your oath that you will not speak a word of this to anyone else."

Vekk-oth regarded Evir in silence before asking, "Why me?"

"Two reasons. You have certain skills we need, but more importantly, I believe I can trust you with our lives." The second part was more of a hope than a belief, but he needed to cement their rapport as firmly as possible, and telling someone you trust them enough to place your life in their hands could help accomplish that. The elantir's silence stretched on much longer this time. Evir could appreciate the difficulty of making such a decision with so little information.

"Is this some kind of plot against Jt'alin Kavartha-akai?"

Evir was somewhat taken aback by the question. "No. Why would you think it was?"

"She is the only one who could pose a serious threat to our lives. And it's clear that a fire fissure has opened between you two since the purge." Vekk-oth's statement was more proof that Javinth's observations about Evir's veneer of devotion were accurate. He needed to be more careful.

"It's true that recent events have strained my relationship with the kavartha-akai. I will have to work on repairing that," he said as a bit of instruction for Javinth, "but I assure you the two have nothing to do with each other."

Vekk-oth finally nodded. "Then I agree. I will help you, and I give you my oath, under Teraithia's all-seeing eye, to tell no one." Evir thanked him and proceeded to recount the relevant details to this point. It took surprisingly little time to get through it all. It felt like he had been dealing with this for ages.

"Fire and ash," Vekk swore under his breath when Evir finished. "What do you need me to do?"

"I need to return to Stierve in secret to track down the mole. I want you to change my appearance so I'm not recognized and help Javinth become me while I'm gone."

"Stand next to each other," Vekk instructed. The two men complied and the elantir scrutinized them, looking back and forth from one to the other, walking around to look at them from different angles. "Inquisitor, say a phrase and Intendant, you repeat it in your natural voice, but try to match the tempo and inflections." Again they did as Vekk instructed. He had them repeat the exercise, walk around the room, and sit and stand together. "The height difference is the biggest problem," Vekk finally said. "It will take a month, maybe more, to fix that."

"We don't have that much time," Kiavi said. "There is barely enough elantic signature in the sheet as it is. I have sealed it to slow the fading, but it's a three-week journey to Stierve. Evir must leave as soon as possible if he is to have any chance of finding the mole."

"If we had a full fist of bodyshapers, maybe we could do it in a week, assuming he could survive the strain."

"It doesn't have to be perfect," Evir interjected. "Our operations here in Kierden are essentially complete. Javinth can spend most of his time sitting at my desk or in my residence. Focus on his face and voice, and work on the height a little every tide."

"It's not that simple. It will require constantly adjusting the fit of his clothes, or your clothes rather," Vekk corrected himself, nodding toward Javinth. "And he walks differently than you do. Age, fitness, habits, the pain of the process, all of it will show to a careful observer. He would need to train for days, watching you, with me coaching him. And his speech patterns—"

"I know Vekk," Evir interrupted. "None of this is ideal, but we have no choice. And don't forget that you have to change me too."

"You don't need to look like anyone in particular, just not yourself, correct?" Vekk asked.

"True."

"Perhaps I can just disguise you," Vekk said almost hesitantly. "There is a method of changing the appearance that does not involve altering the body. It subtly plays with light to make the eyes see something different from what is actually there."

Evir vaguely remembered hearing about such a trick used by Sa'ari spies from Dakraelath, but he was unaware of the Kuldrith being able to duplicate the feat. "You know how to do that?"

"I have been working on it for years. I have made some progress, but it's far from perfect."

"Could you do that for Javinth?" Evir was interested in any option that could spare his friend the pain and danger ahead.

"I'm afraid that would be far too risky," Vekk replied. "Such elants will fool the eyes at a glance, but for anyone familiar with you or under prolonged interaction, it would become evident something is amiss. Someone would figure it out sooner or later."

Evir was disappointed, but probably not as much as Javinth was. He cast a sympathetic look at his friend. "You're still sure you want to do this?"

"You just better hope Dae doesn't decide she prefers this version of Evir better," Javinth replied, gesturing to himself. "She may refuse to take you back." Evir cringed at Javinth's use of her familiar name. Perhaps it was fortunate he wouldn't be around to hear her mentioned so casually.

"I'll take that as a yes. I'll get your transfer processed as cover for your disappearance. You leave immediately."

"Where am I going?"

"Ivalderi, to follow up on a lead about the Qilerate we got from Pakoran Grand Master. You'll love it there. The snow won't be gone for another month, and you haven't seen the skies in several years, have you?" Evir's smile was playful and pained at the same time.

"Ivalderi? What did I do to get sent to the armpit of the empire?"

Evir chuckled. "I'll leave that to everyone's imagination. I'm sure half the guesses will be right. Pack your things and arrange for them to be transported to Ivalderi. Take what few things you need to my quarters. In the meantime, I'll go take care of things with Dae." Turning his attention to Vekk-oth he continued. "I'm going to fall ill in the next tide, and you're going to come to my residence to treat me. Kiavi, I need that tracking device."

"I'll have it to you within a tide."

"May Teraithia guard our steps," Evir said. All three saluted with hands out to their sides, palms toward Evir, their chins raised. Evir saluted in return but did not give the usual salute of a superior, instead giving them the informal salute of equals, his fist over his heart. Surprise was written on their faces, but they changed their salutes to match his, then they all left the chamber.

Evir left the two Obsidian guards outside the entrance of his residence, one of whom was Kiavi in disguise. He had brought her to raise a sound ward as a precaution while he talked to Dae. He called out for his wife as he walked toward their bedchamber. Haisi came into the corridor from the kitchen to greet him, hands out to her sides, palms toward Evir, and bowed low, eyes toward the ground. In return, Evir held out his open hand, palm up. Dae had instructed their slaves and servants to only offer their salutation once each day and always in front of guests.

With that formality out of the way, Haisi straightened and informed Evir that Dae hadn't yet returned from her work. Evir was disappointed. He was home earlier than expected, but Dae should have been here by now. He instructed Haisi to bring him some food, then informed the guards to watch for Dae. No sense in

Kiavi maintaining an elant for no reason. He walked to his bedchamber and reclined on the cushioned divan. He removed his boots and propped a cushion under his head, thoughts spinning with too much information from the day.

Dae shook him. "My love, wake up."

Evir sat up and looked at his wife, confused. "Haisi said you weren't home yet," he said sleepily. Dae affectionately ran her fingers through his short-cropped, steel-gray hair.

"That was a tenth-tide ago. I'm glad to see you were finally able to get some sleep. You told me not to expect you for dinner and there are guards at the entrance. Is everything all right?" Dae asked, concern etched in the corners of her beautiful, obsidian-black eyes. Her silky black hair was still tied up, emphasizing the pronounced cheekbones beneath her smooth, slate-gray skin. Her dark lips seemed almost a blackish purple in the dim light.

Evir wanted to kiss her but was caught by a sudden yawn. He rubbed his eyes wearily. "Everything's fine. It's just... some things have come up that we need to discuss."

"All right," she said with a mix of curiosity and apprehension, her eyebrow raised, "but can we talk over dinner? I'm starving."

"Of course. I need to go clean up. Can you please send Haisi and Takir out for a while?" Dae nodded, her brow furrowed, but she left to deal with the slaves while Evir headed to the washroom. The water in the stone bowl had probably been hot when he fell asleep but now was barely lukewarm. He washed slowly, trying to think through everything Dae might ask and how he would respond, just as he had a hundred times before. He knew he was stalling.

He began drying his hands on the soft, red towel. His imagination turned the towel to blood, covering his hands. *Fitting*, he told himself bitterly as he thought of the Dorothi priests, stripped and chained to posts in the temple plaza, scourges in the hands of the vaesh'katir; the dead bodies in the corridors of I'fa, and Otpon, and Gai'da, and Gu-Tir; a child's hand clutching a blood-soaked doll to her chest.

He realized his fingers were trembling from his grip on the towel. He forced his fingers to uncurl and took several deep breaths before he trusted himself to join Dae. By the time he sat at the table, the simple meal was laid out and she was already eating. He sat down heavily and served himself a bowl of braised xanath stew and tore off a piece of tavva bread. "I haven't asked you in a while how your research is going. Anything interesting?" he asked between bites. His voice sounded distant.

Dae flashed a patient smile. "I have let you avoid talking about what's happening for several tides, but now you're going to tell me what this is all about."

Leave it to Dae to drive straight to the point. Evir was not sure where to begin, even if he had wanted to. He stared at the unfinished bread lying on the table between them, trying to organize his mind; to find solid ground to start from. Everywhere his thoughts turned felt unsteady, dangerous. The memory of the child reaching for him returned and he shook his head to force the image away.

"What were you just thinking about?"

Evir said nothing, trying to think of anything else to say, but his mind would not let go of the memory. It was difficult to breathe... *Why her?...* difficult to breathe... *Why her?...* breathe...

"It's ok, you can tell me," Dae whispered as she reached across the table and gently rested her delicate hand on his arm.

His vision suddenly blurred as tears welled at the edge of his eyelashes. "There was a priest..." Evir lied, then tried clearing his throat to stop his voice from quavering. *Why her?* "He was the leader of the Dorothi here in Kierden. An older man. He spoke to me..." *Breathe.* "Didn't have to, but he chose to talk."

Why would he lie to Dae? He sensed the truth, buried deep in his chest—he could not bring himself to tell her the details of that horrible scene, the sights and sounds in the tunnels during the purge. And he dreaded telling her he was leaving. Some part of him found it easier, safer, to talk about Pakoran. He tried to picture the grand master, sitting peacefully in his cell in the Door's prison. But behind the blood and bruises, the cuts and missing fingers, he saw the body of the young girl, her tiny hand reaching for him as her light faded from the world.

"And what did he say to you, my love?" Her voice was gentle and patient, a warm blanket in the darkness of his thoughts. He could feel the tears starting to seep into his lashes, threatening to fall.

"I'm not sure. Just that I had a part to play in the story of our people, that Vai Doroth told him to talk with me. He gave me some of what I needed, though there was nothing he could hope to gain for it." *Why did they have to start the purge just then? Why couldn't they have waited just one more day?* So many would have been saved if only he had acted faster. Why could he not share this with Dae? Why couldn't he shake the image of that little girl on the streets? *Why her?*

"Perhaps following the dictates of his god was its own reward. A last act of devotion before an end he knew was near."

"Yes, he knew it was the end. He spoke with such calm, such certainty."

"You sound as if you admire him."

"I do. I wish..." There were so many things to complete that statement. Dae squeezed his arm.

"Wish what?"

"I wish I could have saved him." It felt like a fist was squeezing his heart. "I should've saved them all." A tear, trembling on the edge of his lashes, finally fell to the table below, a dark blot on the dried kanthis matt under his bowl.

"What could you have done?" The earnest compassion in her voice hardened into anger as she continued. "Was the akai not threatening to take them by force? Could you have stopped her and her zealots? It could be you out there, right now," she jabbed her finger toward the central cavern. Contempt radiated from her as she shook her head in disgust, her loose hair cascading around her face. She sat back roughly in her chair, folding her arms to keep her hands under control. "You did everything you could."

"And it wasn't enough."

"Was it your command that sent the Church's butchers into the residences? Did you raise your sword against innocent children?" Anger was edging into Dae's voice. Evir knew she had no love for the Church, but she was wandering into dangerous ground—for both of them. Her words too closely echoed his own troubled feelings. Javinth's words came to his mind. *'You can't afford to give others any reason to doubt your piety.'*

"Have a care," he softly admonished her.

She lowered her voice, but her words took on a harder edge. "I do care, and so do you, which is more than I can say for them." Evir didn't like seeing Dae get like this. Thankfully it didn't happen often, but when it did, it could feel like an earthquake, threatening to loose a shower of rocks down upon their heads.

"They aren't all like that. Akriel will perhaps be able to change them from within," he said, trying to change the subject.

"Yes, please remind me of the fact that our son is being turned into one of *them*."

Evir and Dae were rare among high-ranking Kuldrith for choosing to raise and educate a child into his adolescent years. Most of their peers, even those few who chose the commitment of marriage, gave their children to the empire to be raised as soon as they were eligible. The more gifted the child, the younger they reached eligibility. Akriel had been eligible at four. Most parents would have been thrilled at the honor of having their child accepted into an academy so young. Evir and Dae were not like most parents.

They had sired two children before bringing Akriel into the world. It had been painful when they turned their first daughter over to the Ministry of Education, but they were both early in their careers with great ambitions, and raising a child longer than necessary would have been too much of a hindrance to their advancement. When their second child came of age, Dae tried to persuade Evir that they should continue to raise him themselves. Evir had been tempted, but not only was it becoming rarer and more difficult for parents to raise their children beyond the age of qualification, many saw it as a sign of disloyalty to the empire and to Teraithia herself. In the end, Evir had pushed her to give up their son to the Ministry. It had ripped Dae's heart out, and he was not sure she had ever truly forgiven him for it.

For a few years, they could not bring themselves to have another child, but eventually Dae had prevailed upon Evir to sire a third. As Akriel grew, he became their greatest joy. It was apparent the boy had a bright mind, a fierce drive, and a hunger for excellence. Dae had hoped that raising him herself would guide him to follow in her footsteps and become a scholar. Despite the frequent pressure to give him up, they kept him until, at age fourteen, he had chosen to enter the priesthood against Dae's vehement protests. There were not many things he could have done to upset her more. It had left a deep rift between them, with Evir remaining in the middle to try to keep the connection with their son alive. That was five years ago, but Dae had not gotten over it, and her pain seeped out occasionally. Like now.

Evir knew it wouldn't help, but he had to say it. "I received a report that he's doing very well in his studies."

"Of course he is. Such a waste." She almost said it to herself, the regret evident in her voice. Her icy eyes once again became distant. Heavy silence hung between them. When Dae spoke again, it was clear her thoughts had gone to a dark place. "It won't be long before he'll be leading the purges for them or conducting the public interrogation of the Church's enemies."

Anger flared in Evir, and he was shocked at the sudden urge to lash out. He had never struck Dae in his life and was not about to do so now, but the anger was like the crack of a whip, sharp and painful. *She wasn't there. She didn't see the bodies. She didn't hear the cries of the dying, the pleas for...* Years of disciplined control dropped like a ton of stone on his emotions, burying them beyond feeling. His hand was shaking, but he was in no danger of doing something he would regret. *She didn't know. How could she?*

"I have to leave Kierden for a while," he said flatly. A part of him felt vindictive telling her like this. Another part of him felt guilty for it.

"What? Why?"

"I wish I could tell you. The guards out in the corridor will be here for several days. One of them is an elantir, putting up a sound ward as we speak. But Dae, you can't breathe a word of this to anyone after tonight."

"You're scaring me. Are we in danger?"

"There is no immediate threat here in Kierden. At least, not yet. But that's why I have to leave; I have to stop it before it's too late."

"How long will you be gone?"

"A month or two, at the least."

"A month or two?" Dae cried out in distress. Evir was glad he had brought Kiavi.

"I know, capturing the Dorothi and stopping the rebellion was supposed to mean we could return home to Stierve. But I need everyone to believe I am still here in Kierden."

"And how are you going to manage that?"

"We are going to disguise Javinth to take my place while I'm gone."

"Evir, you can't ask this of me."

"Dae, please. I have been over this a thousand times and looked at every possible alternative. If there were any other way, I would gladly take it."

"Why does it have to be you? Why does it always have to be you?"

"I wish it was someone else. But right now, this falls on me. And I can't do it without you."

Dae stared at him, fear and helplessness written on her face. He stood and walked to the other side of the table, enfolding her head in a gentle embrace he did not feel. "Everything will be all right," he assured her as he stroked her silky black hair. "We'll be together again before you know it." He wished the promise didn't feel like a lie.

Too many wishes and lies, he thought darkly. He feared he was relying on them too much these days. If he did not find solid footing soon, it might be his first and last broken promise to Dae.

CHAPTER XL
SHIRALLA

After nearly three weeks of riding game trails and small paths along the foothills of the Velspars, the charm of the natural beauty surrounding Shiralla had long since worn off. Losing two soldiers and a horse to venomous snake bites and one of the scouts to a terrible fever caused by an insect bite hadn't helped. As beautiful as Baon might be, Shiralla was constantly reminded that what was pleasing to the senses was often a trap for the unwary.

They were supposedly past the worst of the rainy season in this territory, but they had still been drenched a few times. In the oppressive humidity, even when it was not raining there was not a dry moment to be found. She hated riding wet, but at least the rain gave a moment's respite from the constant buzzing of insects and chirping of tree frogs, monkeys, and birds otherwise creating a constant background din that left her head hurting most days. She had already used her entire supply of amberbark tea and was now, out of desperation, chewing on some calamai leaves she had gotten from Physician Puarrol, the royal physician accompanying the delegation. They were terribly bitter but effective. She had to be careful, though; calamai leaves were said to be highly addictive. Perhaps that explained why they were a staple at many Sykorian temples.

The dense canopy high overhead left the forest floor in persistent shade dappled by occasional streamlets of sunlight. She was grateful when the prince called a halt for the day. Everyone had settled into a routine by now and quickly got to work on their respective tasks: setting up camp, starting fires, and cooking dinner, including any wild game the scouts had managed to bring down throughout the day.

Shiralla appreciated their evenings much more now that the elantir had learned how to create an elant that repelled the insects in a small area where they could camp. They had learned the trick from an elderly elantir in a small Kushaani village they had stayed in a few nights ago. She wished they could make it work while they were on the move, but it only worked in a fixed place. Still, she was sleeping better now without insects buzzing all around them, crawling into everything.

Their dinner consisted of some roasted birds and stewed vegetables. It was more plentiful than the rations they had back in the main camp with the army, and it was better quality than most meals she had eaten on the road before. She was sure they had Prince Andric to thank for that. Traveling with royalty had its perks. But she would gladly have traded the luxury of her meals for more attention from the prince.

Things had started well enough when they discussed their objectives and negotiating strategy in broad terms. But when Shiralla had started to delve into the nuances of Vanassi history and culture, etiquette, the legal differences of pacts versus treaties, and other important topics, the prince had proved far less attentive than she would have liked. And now they were little more than a week from Sunapra, the Vanassi capital, and Shiralla was feeling more anxious than ever about the prince's preparedness for this important mission. For the past several days he had rebuffed her efforts to engage with him on these or any other subjects, and she was getting desperate to find a way to get back into his good graces so they could at least work together in a unified way when they reached the Vanassi.

She had decided to broach the subject with the prince's advisor and friend, Master Ve'Aurben, but it had been difficult to find an opportunity to speak with him apart from the prince. Even now that supper was finished and things were settling down for the evening, Shiralla noted they were still together near one of the fires, along with Captain Major Minanthsolum and Knight Commander Nophet. As the second highest ranking person in the delegation, she had every right to be with them, but she was keenly aware of the difference her presence seemed to make whenever she joined them during their halts. The laughing and banter stopped, and the discussions invariably turned to official matters. They were respectful to her, but she was clearly not one of them.

Loneliness gnawed at her stomach, but she did her best to ignore it. *I will not give in to self-pity*, she thought firmly in an effort to steel herself against those feelings that had haunted her most of her life. *I just need to work.* That was always her answer. Work harder. Bring Sharin Dara's will to life and make the world a better place for everyone. Then she would be happy.

"Lady di Greven," Shiralla said with a practiced voice balancing pleasantness, entreaty, and command few managed as well as clerics of Sharin Dara, "could I trouble you to assist me with some training?"

"Of course, Intercessor. What would you like to work on?" the knight asked, looking up from polishing a piece of armor, green eyes bright, her hair the color of honey playfully reflecting the flickering light of the fire.

"Communion," she said without a thought. Shiralla was surprised by her answer. She had meant to say *dispositioning*. That was the benefaction she usually chose to practice. She believed the ability to influence another's emotions and desires was by far the most useful power the gods shared with mortals, and she worked hard at enhancing her skill in this area.

"As you wish," di Greven answered with only a hint of surprise before Shiralla could correct herself. She could have changed her answer if she wanted to, but it had been a long time since she had practiced communion, so she decided to go ahead with it. By now she could easily manage a basic link with di Greven and Mar well enough for words to be exchanged between them, but there were more advanced degrees of skill she had never taken the time to learn to do well.

Sharing images was much more difficult than words, particularly if there was any motion of the images involved. And maintaining a link with one other mind was challenging enough, but each additional mind added to the link was exponentially more complicated. Then there was the matter of speaking one thing verbally while simultaneously having a second conversation through communion. Useful to be sure, but potentially more harmful than helpful if not done effectively.

"Sir Mar, would you please be ready as a third?"

The dark-skinned holy knight, his brown eyes never looking up from the piece of honeywood he was carving, answered with a simple, "Mmhmm." Sometimes she wondered how he had managed to become a knight of the Third Wave. He had no refinement, no common courtesies. *Don't be so hard on him,* her inner voice reproved her. *You have no comprehension of what he has gone through to be where he is.* Shiralla sighed and tried to clear her thoughts of Sir Mar altogether. She needed her heart, mind, and soul to be resonant with Sharin Dara's divinesence. Recriminations toward herself or others were out of harmony with her goddess.

The two women had settled into comfortable positions sitting cross-legged and facing each other on Shiralla's ground blanket. The priestess placed her palms together in front of her chest, fingers pointed toward the heavens, then opened her hands leaving just the heels of her palms touching as she prepared to speak a prayer of supplication. Lady di Greven followed suit. Sir Mar should have, but the whittling continued. She wanted to reprove him for his lack of piety but held her tongue. *Don't judge him*, she coaxed herself as she closed her eyes and raised her face toward the night sky. She sensed the divine power as if it were a lover separated from her by a diaphanous veil, waiting for her to open the way so it could reach through and embrace her. She could have invited it in at any moment, but an invocation helped her focus on the source and purpose of that power.

"Holy Lady, Bringer of Peace and Goodness, we sanctify your name." Shiralla's voice was soft and reverent.

"Sanctify us," both holy knights responded in unison.

"Your glory is from everlasting to everlasting."

"Fill us with light," they answered again.

"Your mercy is extended over all the world."

"Grant us strength."

"Make us thine." She had said the words a thousand times, and her mind was already jumping ahead to the exercise she would do with di Greven and Mar.

"Make us thine," the holy knights repeated as they finished the simple invocation.

The divinessence of her goddess enfolded her, expanded within her heart and mind, ready to be directed as she willed. She focused the power into a thin shaft like a ray of sunshine that streaked from her mind to di Greven's. Years ago, as a young initiate, this would have been a frustratingly difficult exercise, but by now she already knew the feel of di Greven's mind, and having di Greven sitting directly in front of her made it a simple, almost instantaneous task. Just as quickly, di Greven accepted the link and their minds were joined.

"Our Lady's grace," Shiralla sent the thought. The practiced words gave Sharin Dara's clerics an easy place to start, as it could sometimes be difficult to formulate exactly which words to send.

"Peace be upon you," di Greven replied.

"I will try to send you an image." Shiralla felt the knight's agreement more than heard any words. That was already a sign of their more advanced skill with communion, as feelings were a difficult thing to share clearly, and was more akin to dispositioning. The two benefactions could be combined, but it

was quite complex to manage both at the same time, and few clerics could do it well. Consul Rellat was one.

Her consciousness quickly shied away from thoughts of the consul. That was dangerous ground, especially during communion. Instead, Shiralla turned to thoughts of Prince Andric and the trouble she was having with him. She had already voiced some of those concerns to Lady di Greven, but she felt she would be better served at the moment focusing on a positive image of him. She imagined him sitting atop his black destrier, on a grass-covered hill, sunlight glinting off his polished armor.

Once she had the image clearly in her mind, she allowed it into the link and sent it to her companion. The images in her mind and di Greven's mind were superimposed and wavered slightly where the two images did not quite match. Shiralla focused on various details in an effort to clarify the image in di Greven's mind and minimize the distortions. Soon the images converged well enough, and Shiralla was pleased.

"He is quite handsome, isn't he?"

"Please focus on the exercise," Shiralla admonished the golden-haired knight as she erased the image and started over, this time choosing Master Ve'Aurben as her subject. She pictured the Cannessi scholar as she had seen him many evenings, sitting by the fire reading a book. Again, once she had the image clearly defined in her mind, she sent it through the link. The images converged, and Shiralla began focusing to clarify the image.

"Another handsome one," di Greven thought, a sense of happy approval coming through the link.

"Seriously?" Shiralla thought with amused disbelief at Emerly's reaction. *"You find him attractive?"*

"In a bookish sort of way."

"It doesn't bother you that he is two-thirds your size?"

"That doesn't affect his face. I'm not saying I would marry him, but I might let him warm me on a cold night if he ever looked up from a book long enough to notice me."

"I'm going to try and add Mar to the link," Shiralla said, changing the subject. She spent a moment to ensure the image was stable in di Greven's mind and slowly tried to open a second space in her own mind. The image wavered and she had to refocus the image before trying again. She finally managed to create enough of a space to reach out with a second conduit, seeking connection with Sir Mar. The man's mind was so still and quiet that it was sometimes difficult to find him. Her searching was slower than usual because she was carefully trying to maintain the image of Ve'Aurben in di

Greven's mind, and searching quickly took too much of her focus away. Within a few moments, she found him and touched his mind with the invitation to join in communion. He accepted the link and their minds connected.

"Our Lady's grace," Shiralla sent the thought. The words were routine and could be said without losing clarity of the image she was maintaining with di Greven.

"Peace be upon you."

"I will..." her words halted as the image wavered. She refocused the image and tried again. *"I will add you to the other link."* The words felt echoey, but she ignored it. It was the best she could manage for now. Slowly she brought the link with Mar into the conduit with di Greven's mind. A third image of Master Ve'Aurben was overlaid on the image she had been maintaining with di Greven. The images distorted and she struggled to bring them into focus.

Mar's words came firmly into her mind. *"You are straining too hard for control. Surrender to Our Lady's guidance."* She had heard this many times, but it was so counterintuitive. How did one gain control by surrendering control to another? How would she even go about doing that? Was she supposed to turn her mind off? She took a deep breath and tried to create yet another channel of communion, one that would link her with the goddess.

"No, you're still trying to control. Just open yourself—let her in."

How does he even know that? she wondered momentarily. He shouldn't have been able to know her inner workings unless she willed him to. Was he just guessing based on some sense he had of her emotions? Perhaps she would ask him later. The thoughts distracted her, and the images distorted into a hazy mess. She started to concentrate again on the images.

"Intercessor, let them go."

"I don't accept failure."

"That's what keeps you from succeeding."

Shiralla sighed in frustration but felt she should heed Sir Mar's advice. The thought crossed her mind that he might be dispositioning her, but she dismissed it. There was no chance Mar could disposition her without her knowing it. She let the images of Master Ve'Aurben disappear and instead tried to empty her heart, mind, and soul. Emptiness was even more difficult than focusing on the images.

"Relax," Mar coaxed with a gentle insistence. The word struck a nerve. It was too close to what Consul Rellat had said to her that night before she left. Abruptly the memory of him touching her, caressing her hair, came rushing unbidden into her mind before she could stop it. A mix of anger and shame flared in her.

"What was that?" Lady di Greven asked, her green eyes narrowed, her words laced with concern. Shiralla immediately severed the connections with the holy knights. Communion was over. But somehow Mar's words still came through.

"Shiralla, I am sorry that happened to you. He should never have done that." Deep empathy came through the connection. She felt understood and safe. It was like a key unlocking a door holding back a wave of emotions. Tears sprang to her eyes. She felt awkward and dreaded the next words she was certain would come from Mar telling her to be strong, or that everything would be all right. But all she felt was a consistent feeling of support. When she realized there was no judgment, only comfort, and that Mar was the source of such a tender mercy, the tears flowed freely. She had certainly judged him unfairly.

Sharin Dara, I am an unworthy servant.

You are learning, her inner voice said. The voice had been there most of her life, but now she sensed an immensity behind the voice. *It is time to grow beyond yourself, to become a source of beneficence in the world.*

How? I can't even... The list of her shortcomings seemed too endless to pick just one to name.

Small and simple acts can make a world of difference. Shiralla was aware the link with Mar was still open. Was he somehow aware of her thoughts? It didn't matter. She was just grateful for him.

"Thank you, Lathon," she sent the thought to him with all the depth of gratitude she could muster. The connection between them intensified, deepened, swelled. She was aware of how much her appreciation meant to him. It seemed out of proportion to the situation, but it was real.

The divinessence, familiar and comfortable, was suddenly swallowed up and disappeared in the presence of the truly divine. Sharin Dara's radiant glory filled every corner of her being, and her heart swelled in exultation as Sharin Dara's approbation descended upon her. The benefaction of communion was a mere shadow of this pure connection with her goddess. Thoughts and images coursed through her mind, through her entire body, faster than she could grasp, but she let it wash through her. She felt an overwhelming sense of beneficence toward Lathon and Emerly. Then it expanded to include Andric and Barak, Vikkin, Quarian, and on through their retinue. And the villagers of Mittat, and Appana, and the great city of Kushaan, and the Remalian army at the gates of Balinth's Fortress.

It was too much. Her mind was stretched to the point of breaking. A new vision filled her. She was walking among the Vanassi, smiling benevolently upon the crowds flocking to her as Sharin Dara used her as a conduit to bestow benefactions on the people and bathe them in the light of her teachings. Shiralla saw herself journeying throughout the Kushaani lands blessing the people and bringing them to Sharin Dara's will. She wanted more than anything to make this vision a reality. The desire filled her with such an aching that she felt it might consume her.

The image shifted again, and an army rose up to destroy the Sharinists. Shiralla stood before them and Sharin Dara's power coursed through her. A blast of dispositioning shot out like a wave, driving the army to its knees. She opened a conduit to every mind and sent blinding rays of Sharin Dara's glory burning through their senses, and they cried out in anguish. She felt the goddess's righteous indignation against those who would seek to destroy her people.

A thought hovered at the edge of Shiralla's consciousness. *No, this isn't right.*

Sometimes the highest good for the greatest number of people can only be found on the other side of conflict. You will bring the people together in my name, and there will be peace.

The divine presence withdrew, and Shiralla was left alone in the dark jungle, basking in the afterglow of the visitation. She wanted to jump up and carry out the vision she had seen, but as she opened her eyes she felt such a profound exhaustion she could barely move. Emerly was staring at her, concern written on her face. Shiralla wanted to laugh and cry at how misplaced such concern was. She looked at Lathon, who gave a single nod as his only acknowledgment of what had transpired. She smiled and nodded back.

"Would you like to talk about what just happened?" di Greven asked in a way that was not a question.

"I don't think so," Shiralla said quietly, a sense of reverence still enveloping her.

"Well, *I* would like to talk about what just happened."

"Now is not the time," Sir Mar said flatly, leaving no room for argument. Shiralla appreciated his firm manner in a new light. She nodded her thanks and tried to stand but felt as though she was moving through molasses.

"Easy," Lathon held out his hand signaling her to stay seated. "Give yourself a few minutes."

"If I stay down, I fear I won't get up again." She remembered how tired she was after what happened in Rellat's quarters. This was an almost painful exhaustion. "Lady di Greven, if you would please..." She held out her hand, seeking assistance to rise. The knight stood and took her by the hand to help her to her feet. She was unsteady, feeling lightheaded, but it passed quickly. "Thank you." Di Greven kept a strong hand on Shiralla's arm. "I'm all right," the intercessor assured her companion, putting on a smile to emphasize her point. She turned to look for Prince Andric, but the only one still sitting by the fire was Master Ve'Aurben, reading a book. She wondered how much time had passed since she started her practice session.

Shiralla almost laughed at herself. *Practice session* hardly seemed the appropriate term for what she had just experienced. She quickly expressed heartfelt thanks to Sharin Dara for the goddess's condescension. She felt overwhelmed by the implications of what she had seen, but there would be time to consider that later. She needed to act now, even if it was nothing more than addressing the growing tension between the prince and her. Then she could allow herself to sleep. She forced herself into motion and carefully made her way over to Ve'Aurben to ask where the prince was.

"Good evening, Master Ve'Aurben. Do you know where I might find Prince Andric?"

"He left with Captain Major Min to go see some waterfall that apparently is quite beautiful to see in the moonlight on certain nights. They said they would be back before too long." Shiralla was disappointed she didn't get to see the falls for herself, but it was a small loss compared to what she had seen tonight. She considered whether her original plan to enlist Ve'Aurben's help was still the best approach and decided it could not hurt. She noted the book he was reading was one she had lent him. *The Litany of Crinnavar* was an ancient sacred text that was foundational reading for all Sharinic clerics regarding the spiritual philosophy of foreign relations and diplomacy.

"How goes the reading?" she asked.

He looked down at the book and didn't immediately answer. "Thank you for lending it to me. I must confess that it's a pleasure reading something new, even if I don't fully understand it." She tried to gauge where his finger was in the book and guess what he was reading.

"It looks like you might be in the litanies on cultural incongruity."

"Actually, I just finished those and was starting on..." he paused to open the book, flipped back a few pages, then read the section title aloud, "'Fostering Nonaggression in Circumstances of Divergent Interests.' It's very interesting."

Shiralla laughed lightly. "Master Ve'Aurben, you must be one of three people on Baon who finds those litanies interesting to any degree, let alone *very interesting*." She was exaggerating of course. The litanies were written as beautiful, even poetic, supplications to Sharin Dara to help the reader learn Her way of treating with others. "So what do you find difficult about them?"

"I suppose it's mostly the style. They're not as straightforward and logically organized as I am used to reading." The sound in the distance of an echoing roar by some large animal followed by a momentary cacophony of birds and monkeys chattering in response drew her attention from the conversation, but his next words brought her back. "Can I ask you a question?"

"By all means." The fire settled and a few sparks flew into the air before he spoke. She wanted so badly to sit, but she was afraid she might not be able to get back up. Instead, she leaned against a smooth-barked tree.

"You use benefactions to assist in your service as a diplomat. For example, you would use dispositioning to push the Vanassi toward agreeing to help us, correct?"

"We would say that Sharin Dara espouses cooperation among people to bring about the greater good. Benefactions can aid with fostering cooperation."

"And presumably, if the Vanassi or some other group you were negotiating with had their own Sharinic clerics, they would be trying to do the same thing to you."

"I suppose so, although that might be difficult for them to manage without me knowing about it and taking measures to protect against undue influence."

"Exactly! Why does Sharin Dara grant her powers to opposing sides to use against each other? That seems like it would be a contradiction of her doctrine."

"That's a fair question. First, as with any of the gods, the benefactions aren't granted directly by Sharin Dara, they are simply expressions of the power that emanates from her glory. Her clerics access that power by being in tune with her divine nature, but what they do with it is entirely up to them. Second, dispositioning doesn't allow us to control another person, it merely engenders certain emotional, mental, and spiritual conditions within them. If both parties disposition the other toward an increased desire for cooperation, that only enhances Sharin Dara's purposes."

"But you mentioned taking measures against undue influence. That implies that at least sometimes you would consider what another cleric does to not be in your best interest."

"True. I suppose as with any power, it can be abused to some extent, and that is a subjective standard in any case. What one side considers *undue influ-*

ence, the other side may consider only to be a vigorous expression of Sharin Dara's doctrine. But if a cleric strays too far out of alignment with the goddess's divinessence, the power of the benefactions diminishes, and can even be lost altogether, so there is some check on things going too far astray. Still, that leaves a fair amount of room in the middle for people to have a difference of opinion on these matters."

Barak nodded, a slight smile touching his face. "That's a good answer."

"Thank you." She shifted her position against the tree, then asked, "May I ask you a question?"

"Certainly."

"Forgive me if this is too personal, and I understand if you don't want to answer it, but why have you never been ordained?"

The scholar didn't respond immediately, he just stared into the fire. Shiralla worried she had offended him or touched on something too sensitive. She was about to change the subject when he finally spoke.

"For nearly as long as I can remember, I have wanted to be an elantir. I have studied the subject for many years, but no matter how hard I try, I can't touch elan. Viance teaches that the path of holiness is the obtaining of knowledge itself, but if you can't do anything with that knowledge, of what use is it?"

"Did you not put your knowledge to use in discovering the solution to the problem with the Bonded?"

"I provided information that others used to solve the problem. I served no greater function than a book. It does not seem to me that a book should be ordained a priest just because it has many words in it." Shiralla felt the ache in his heart but had no answer for it. While it saddened her, it also gave her an opening to steer the conversation toward the prince.

"Prince Andric obviously values your counsel. I think you may be of more use to him than I am."

"He values you too, but he doesn't like being pushed." Shiralla wanted to object to his characterization of what she had been trying to do. *Listen to what he is saying*, her inner voice coaxed her. Shiralla realized more clearly than ever that her inner voice had a certain quality akin to what she had felt earlier. Perhaps the people who had suggested it was actually the voice of Sharin Dara were right after all.

"I suppose I do push a bit sometimes. Do you have any suggestions?"

Barak looked around surreptitiously and lowered his voice. "Use the benefactions to make things more exciting for him. Make it a contest to see how quickly he can notice when you're trying to disposition him. Put the exercises in a military light. Teach him how to defend against undue influence the way he would defend against a sword."

"That isn't quite how it works, but I take your meaning."

"Tell him it's a contest to see if you can keep the Divinarim from noticing. That will add some mischievous stakes to the game."

"It isn't a game."

"You and I know that, but Andric doesn't need to. Before long, you'll have him an expert on all things Vanassi."

She didn't like the idea of turning their mission and Sharin Dara's powers into some sort of game. And it seemed a bit insulting to the prince. But she also could see the wisdom in the scholar's suggestions. She may have to swallow her pride, but she would probably give it a try. She could feel the last of her strength fading quickly. "Thank you for your kind suggestions, Master Ve'Aurben."

"Please call me Barak."

"Very well. Good night, Barak."

"Good luck."

She bowed with a smile, then made her way back to her tent. Her knees nearly buckled as she ducked to go through the tent opening. She caught herself on the edge of the short cot and slumped onto her bed and was asleep in an instant.

CHAPTER XLI
QUARIAN

Quarian would have been happy to have a few more scouts with them. They had done well steering the prince's delegation through difficult terrain in enemy territory, staying off the common routes, but they were tired. Nearly two weeks of constantly fanning out through the territory to find a safe passage was taking its toll. He wanted to give them a rest as soon as he could, but it was probably not feasible until they reached Sheerbahar in a few days.

There had been unusual Kushaani troop activity to the south recently, including some minor skirmishes between villagers and imperial forces. Intercessor Henden guessed it may have been some disturbance being quelled, but Quarian was not so sure. He knew that happened on occasion, but usually the empire left it up to the local factions to resolve their own disputes. It would be a death sentence for a village to resist the empire's troops, so the reports from the scouts of losses on both sides didn't fit the usual scenarios.

He had convinced the prince for the past few days they should continue to stay in the wilds as much as possible, despite the fact they were running desperately low on supplies. But this morning, Prince Andric had decided it was worth the risk to try to find a small village to procure enough provisions to hopefully last them until they could reach the safety of Vanassi territory.

Most villages didn't show up on any of their maps, and it was easy to completely miss the smaller ones in the dense jungle. They had sent out the scouts to find a suitable option as they continued their journey westward. Several had been found, but they were either too small to have provisions for such a large party, or too close to major roads and waterways to be safe. It was already well past midday, and Quarian was beginning to think they might not find anything today. Apparently the prince had the same concern.

"If we don't find supplies today, we may need to risk pushing further south."

"Let's see what happens," was all Quarian replied. He knew better than to outright argue with the prince. At times Quarian wished he was still a scout, out observing with his own eyes rather than relying on reports from his men. But as a commanding officer, his role was to stay with the prince and coordinate the soldiers' actions. He hoped it didn't come to more than that.

They rode in relative silence until one of the soldiers up ahead called out. "Rider!" Soon one of their scouts approached from the trail ahead. It was Corporal Stenner. She was an excellent scout and Quarian was happy to have her. He had been able to hand-pick each of the scouts, and they were some of the best Quarian had worked with in his years serving in the Remalian army.

"Highness," Stenner said as she reined her horse to a stop and saluted, fingertips to her brow.

"Did you find anything?" the prince asked hopefully.

"There's a large village 'bout an hour southwest o' here, but it's... it was attacked. Probably just a couple days ago, best I could tell. It don't appear no one was left alive."

The prince cursed under his breath.

"Any sign of who might have attacked them?" Quarian asked. Intercessor Henden, Knight Commander Nophet, and Master Ve'Aurben had all moved their mounts forward to hear the report better.

"Sir, I'd say almost certain it was imperials. They... it was bad. They didn't treat the dead the way locals do. No proper burials, just..." the scout shook her head.

"Do you think there are any supplies left there that we could get?" Andric jumped to what he was most concerned about.

"Maybe, Yer Highness." Stenner seemed uneasy, but she didn't elaborate.

"What's your threat assessment?" Quarian's focus was different from the prince's. "Any sign of enemy troops in the area?"

"Not that I could tell. I left Teek to scout the area some more. He'll warn us if there's a problem."

"Then let's go," the prince ordered. Corporal Stenner took the lead and headed back the way she had come. Quarian tried to catch the tone of the conversations he could hear happening along the line of riders behind him. Mostly he thought he heard the same sense of anxiety he felt at the prospect of entering a village so recently attacked. He was already organizing the soldiers in his mind to search the village as quickly as possible. They might have to ride a bit longer tonight to put some distance between them and the village before they stopped, but both moons should be out early giving them better light to ride with.

After a while Corporal Stenner took a fork that turned sharply south. They crossed a small stream, and Quarian noticed they were heading slightly downhill. Soon the trees started to thin. "Finally," Prince Andric said almost as a sigh of relief as the trail opened into a narrow valley between steep hills. The trail they had been riding on widened slightly and almost became a small road. He scanned the hilltops for any signs of life. He saw nothing but remained alert, scanning the ridges for any sign of threat. He knew Stenner and the Divinarim were doing the same.

As they made their way further from the dense jungle, Quarian noticed signs of terracing on the hillsides for growing rice and guessed they must be nearing the village. Up ahead he saw another rider on horseback waiting in the road and guessed it was Corporal Arell. Stenner waived and Teek waived back, indicating everything was fine to proceed. Quarian felt himself relax a bit. *In and out quickly*, he told himself, hoping it proved true.

When they got close enough to Teek, Quarian called out, "Corporal, any activity in the area?"

"No sir, all quiet."

"Good," the prince said enthusiastically, "now hopefully we can find some supplies." The Divinarim moved into a tighter defensive formation around the prince as they moved along the road toward the village, watching for signs of trouble. The prince looked cautious but composed.

"You're not going to like what you see," Teek called back over his shoulder, a warning in his voice. Then the corporal pointed off the road into the rice fields. The uniform rows of verdant plants appeared to have been somewhat trampled near the road, and he was surprised to see narrow, misshapen tree stumps sticking out of the rice paddies. A moment later Quarian's stomach clenched as his mind registered that he had been mistaken—the dark shapes were not tree stumps, they were human limbs. And they were spaced too far apart to be attached to bodies.

"Dear gods!" the prince exclaimed in horror. Quarian shared the prince's sentiment but kept it to himself.

"The heads are in the village," Teek said flatly. The buildings came into sight moments later as they rounded the curve of the hill. The houses were crudely made of lashed bamboo and other wood, with heaps of old, grayish-brown palm branches piled on top to make domed roofs. A heavy, sickening stillness lay over the whole village. Quarian wanted to be gone as soon as possible.

He halted and signaled for his men to dismount and gather around. "This village looks big enough to possibly have had a surplus for trading, so we might get lucky and find some supplies. By twos, go house to house. Bring any food to the village center and we'll figure out what we can take. Then we'll get out of here. Move quickly."

"Watch out for the heads," Teek offered as Quarian moved with the prince and his advisors toward the largest building near the center of the village. He noticed Prince Andric gripping the hilt of his sword. He wanted to help put the young man's mind at ease, but there just didn't seem to be anything appropriate to say under the circumstances, so he remained silent.

Despite being the only living souls in the valley, he could not help but look for positions from which they could defend themselves if attacked. *Archers up on the terraces on the hillsides*, he thought. *I need to find flat dry land for the cavalry and knights to do any good.* However, he didn't have much hope there. Every open flat place seemed to be a rice paddy. Fighting in the shin-deep water and mud was a terrible proposition. Probably better to just fight on foot. Better yet to be gone before any fighting was necessary.

As they neared the large central building, one of the Divinarim sucked in a hissing breath between clenched teeth. Piled up on the steps and front porch were about two score severed heads. Ants were swarming on them and had already partially stripped a few of them to the bone. Dark reddish-brown patches in the rutted dirt road told Quarian that the villagers had probably been butchered on the spot.

"Lieutenant Werdalm!" the prince called out for one of the elantir. After calling a second time, the two elantir appeared from between the houses.

"Yes, Your Highness?" Werdalm asked, concern written heavily on her face.

"Get rid of these ants!" The lieutenant looked in disgust at the heads and quickly turned away, but did as she was ordered. She held her hands out, palms toward the ground as Quarian had seen her do for the past several nights when they made camp. It took a few minutes, but soon the ants were scurrying away. Prince Andric ordered some soldiers passing by to move the heads off the porch so he could go inside.

"Your Highness, don't you think we should give them a proper burial?" the intercessor asked.

"We don't have time for that. The Kushaani can bury their own."

"This is about more than just the dead, my lord. This is about who we are. Are we civilized and compassionate, or are we the same as our enemies?" Quarian felt the conviction of her words, felt they were right, even as the thought of the extra time it would cost chewed into his already strained patience.

"Are you dispositioning me?" the prince asked accusingly.

"Do I need to? Surely your heart tells you that this is right."

Quarian could not explain it, but something in the intercessor's demeanor had changed. When they had started this journey, she was like most Sharinic clerics Quarian had known: shrewd, cunning even, usually scheming to direct the flow of events, but always circumspect and diplomatic. Now she seemed to have an air of confidence and authority Quarian found refreshing, but was not so sure Prince Andric felt the same.

"Fine. Captain Major, when the men have finished searching the village, have them bury the heads."

"And the limbs as well," she said to Quarian, making it sound like a simple clarification, although it certainly seemed like an additional order, which she technically didn't have the authority to issue. The prince grimaced, though whether out of disgust at the thought of the gruesome task or frustration with the intercessor, Quarian could not tell.

"Knight Commander, let's see what's in there," the prince said, gesturing to the large building in front of them. Nophet ordered two Divinarim to move some of the heads to make a path for the prince. Quarian called Teek and Stenner over and ordered them to get to higher ground and watch the approaches to the village for any signs of trouble. They mounted and rode away in opposite directions to find paths up the steep, terraced hillsides.

Quarian waited outside while the prince followed the Divinarim into the two-story building. He noticed a livestock pen nearby, empty, the gate left open. He suspected whoever had done this to the village had already cleared out everything worth taking. Scanning the area, he watched his soldiers moving between houses, most of them empty-handed. *We're wasting our time*, he thought with mild frustration, but let it go. It was better to just work quickly and get out as soon as possible.

He decided to look around for the best place to dig a mass grave. He wondered where the torsos of the dead were. Maybe they had been buried nearby, and they could just place the severed heads and limbs back with the bodies. The rice paddies would be soft ground, but being flooded would make them difficult to work in. This valley was no doubt rocky though, so unfortunately it might be their best option.

He skirted around the dark stains on the ground and strode quickly along the winding paths between the houses. Many had small vegetable or herb gardens, but nothing that would suit his purposes. He had almost reached the outskirts of town when he found a small open field of long grass and beautiful yellow flowers. There was a low stone wall that ran in a wide circle around the area. It didn't seem to serve any particular purpose, so he decided it would probably serve his.

He was on his way back to the village center to set the men to work when he heard shouting. He held his sword by the scabbard and dashed the short distance to the village center where the commotion was. A group was gathered around the steps of the building the prince had entered, but Quarian could not make out what the trouble was. It appeared some of the soldiers were kneeling on the ground, working on something.

"Let me through," Quarian ordered, and the men moved aside obediently. Three of the soldiers were on the ground next to one of the heads, digging in the dirt.

"He's alive," Lady di Greven said in answer to his unasked question. "Barely."

"How?"

"Buried up to his neck, then they stacked the other heads all around him."

Quarian shivered despite the heat. He guessed the man was the village chief. They must have buried him, then killed and mutilated the men of his village in front of him. It was a cruel and barbaric punishment, but punishment for what, he wondered?

"Has he said anything?"

"No, we only discovered the head was still attached when the men tried to move it with the others. The elantir confirmed that he's alive, but that's all we know." It was agonizingly slow to dig the man out, and once Quarian had confirmed all the houses had been searched he put the bystanders to work. Some were tasked with packing what few supplies they had scavenged, others he assigned to move the heads out to the field where they would be buried, or to go collect the severed limbs, or to find tools and dig the grave.

They only had a few hours of daylight left, and he knew they would be lucky to be an hour away from the village by the time darkness fell. Once he was satisfied things were moving as well as could be expected, he went back to check on the progress freeing the buried man. He was surprised they had cleared the dirt nearly down to his waist. Physician Puarrol cradled the unconscious man in his arms, while the two soldiers worked to dig out the rest of the dirt. Sir Mar cleaned and applied bandages to some of his wounds, but that was probably going to be of little help. Infection had obviously set in. The man was probably nearly dead from dehydration, let alone who knows what other causes. Quarian wondered if it wouldn't be more merciful to put him out of his misery.

"Is he going to survive?" Quarian asked the remaining bystanders. All he got for an answer were shoulder shrugs and silence.

"I should oversee the preparation of the gravesite," Intercessor Henden said, sounding sick to her stomach, and she turned to go.

"I'll go with you," Quarian offered, feeling too anxious to stand around watching others work. Lady di Greven followed wordlessly as well. The intercessor didn't keep her usual brisk pace, and it grated on Quarian to have to slow down to match hers. "What's entailed in preparing the gravesite?" Quarian asked, hoping the answer required as little time as possible. In his homeland of Qelasaar, the preparations could take many hours depending on which clerics were responsible for it.

"I am not entirely sure what the rites would be for their tribe, but I will do my best based upon what little knowledge I have."

She sounded troubled, but Quarian was not inclined at the moment to probe her reasons for being upset; there were plenty of obvious ones to pick from. He had other concerns on his mind. "I don't mean to be insensitive, but I feel we need to be away from here as quickly as possible. May I ask how long it will take and what we can do to assist in making the preparations?"

"Just two things. If your men could collect stones to put in a ring around the grave and gather flowers to place on top. Red ones preferably; I hope that's right anyway."

"Now that you mention it, the site I picked out may already suit our purposes, or may already be a gravesite."

"What do you mean?"

"You'll see in a moment. It's just ahead, past those trees," he said, pointing along the path. Soon they were close enough to see the soldiers digging with simple farming tools they had found in the village.

The intercessor nodded her head as they approached. "I think you were right, Captain Major. I believe this may be a gravesite, although in the ones I have seen the stones are placed around individual graves, not a whole area like this. And the flowers here are yellow, but that may be their own tradition. Or maybe it's just a coincidence." Then under her breath, she recited quietly, almost like a prayer, "Flowers, for freshness on the soul's path. Stones, for a portal to the afterlife. Grain, for nourishment on their journey."

After that last phrase, Quarian could guess what was in the small sack she had brought with her. The men were making good progress, and he hoped they would be finished and on their way before long. He helped the intercessor and her knight protector gather the yellow flowers the soldiers had discarded as they dug the widening hole. The first soldier leading a horse carrying its grim load of severed limbs wrapped in a blanket arrived and they helped set them to the side. The soldiers digging started hitting rocky soil just a couple of feet down, and their progress slowed to a crawl.

"Maybe this wasn't a grave site after all," the intercessor said. "We haven't found any bones, and they would have cleared most of these stones out over the years."

Quarian held back a frustrated growl. "I wish we had time to dig a proper grave, Intercessor, but we really should be away as quickly as possible. It could take hours to get down another few feet—hours we don't have. As much as I hate to say it, I think this is going to have to be a shallow grave." The intercessor fixed her eyes on the ground but gave no response. Quarian feared she was going to disagree with him and insist they do the job properly.

"I'm sure you won't get any argument from the prince, so I suppose it will have to do." Quarian did his best to keep the relief he felt to himself.

"Is there anything else then?"

Before she could answer a high-pitched whistle echoed through the narrow valley. Quarian could not tell exactly where it came from, but he knew a scout's whistle when he heard it. He scanned the hilltops until he found Corporal Arell waving his arms. Quarian wished he had his spyglass with him, but it was packed with his horse out grazing with the others back in fields on the far side of the village. He signaled back and did his best to understand what Teek was signaling. He was too far away to make out the hand gestures, but it was clear something was approaching from further down the valley. Quarian didn't need more details than that.

"We're done here! Gather the horses and muster at the village center. Now!" Everyone dropped whatever they were doing and ran. Quarian mounted the soldier's horse and galloped the short distance back along the road. As he rushed into the village center only four of the Divinarim could be seen, standing next to a deep hole where the man had been buried alive.

"Your Highness!" Quarian called out as he leaped off the horse before it had even come to a full stop.

"In here," a muffled voice called back from inside the large building. Quarian bounded up the short steps and through the front door. The dimly lit interior was a single spacious room with sleeping mats on one end and sitting cushions gathered around a central fire pit. Several large wooden ancestral totems stood on the other end of the room, and the thick support beams throughout the building were carved to match. The small group had their attention on the man lying on one of the sleeping mats, and Lieutenant Werdalm and Physician Puarrol were kneeling on each side of him, their hands resting on his dirt-stained chest. Knight Commander Nophet looked up as soon as Quarian entered the room.

"We have company approaching the village." All eyes turned immediately on the captain major. "I don't know who or how soon they will get here, but we need to leave immediately." Nophet rushed outside and started issuing orders to the Divinarim.

"We'll have to leave him," the prince said to Werdalm and Puarrol. The elantir nodded and accepted the prince's offered hand to help her to her feet. The priest was slower to respond. "Which direction are they coming from?" the prince asked.

Quarian could not be sure it was a *they*, but it was a safe assumption, and he wasn't about to argue semantics. "Northwest, I believe, but I couldn't be sure. I suggest we go back the way we came. Perhaps we can be gone before they arrive." Quarian was the last one out the door, sparing a brief sympathetic glance toward the man lying unconscious on the bed mat. They may have rescued him from his partial grave only to leave him to fall into the hands of another threat. Outside, soldiers were rushing to gather the horses and prepare to leave.

Quarian heard a pair of riders galloping hard, coming from the direction where they had been burying the bodies. But all the horses were on the other side of the village. He released the sword grip once he saw the two Remalian scouts. Corporal Barnet was in the lead and was already reporting as he and Stenner brought their mounts to a halt just a few strides from the group standing in the road.

"M'lords," both rider and mount were breathing heavily, "Kushaani coming. 'Bout forty riders, mostly soldiers."

"Who are they?" the prince asked, a mix of worry and defiance in his voice.

"Difficult to say, m'lord. I only ran 'cross 'em a few hours ago on my way back ta find you."

"How did you know where to find us?"

"Didn't. I was stayin' ahead of 'em, figurin' I'd see where they went 'fore I came back to report. It wasn't 'til Stenner came an' met me that I had any idea you was here."

"How long before they get here?" Quarian asked.

"They's less than an hour back."

"And there are only about forty you said?" the prince asked for confirmation.

"Yes, m'lord."

"Then we stay and meet them."

"Your Highness," Nophet responded before Quarian could, "Teraithia certainly favors the bold, but there is no glory to be had defeating a worthless enemy. We should let the dust of this place lie."

"I would rather face this threat now, on my terms, than have them follow us and attack in our sleep."

"I can ensure we will not be caught unawares," Quarian insisted.

A look of annoyance flashed in the prince's eyes. "We're staying, so make the preparations," he stated emphatically, then he strode off in the direction of where the horses had been turned loose.

Quarian exchanged a knowing glance with Nophet, then both men set about the task of carrying out the prince's command. "You two, get back up to higher ground," he said to the scouts as he pointed up the steep terraced slopes. "They may already know we are here, and information is more important than secrecy at this point, so signal their progress as best you can."

"Sir," Barnet said, "many of them are Vidyahar warriors."

Quarian gritted his teeth. Elite imperial troops were the last thing he wanted to deal with. He wondered if that piece of information would sway the prince, but he doubted it. "Get moving," he ordered, then hurried off to retrieve his mount.

Soldiers were quickly donning their armor and preparing weapons. He designated several to head up onto the hillsides and take up positions as archers. He wanted to make the approach to the village as dangerous as possible. It might leave them somewhat outnumbered on the ground to start with, but between the Divinarim, the Sharin Darin knights, and three fists of lancers on horseback, he was confident they could hold their line long enough for the archers to thin the enemy's ranks from the higher ground.

"Your Highness, we should form ranks on the west side of the village," Quarian said to Prince Andric, whose squire was buckling on his breastplate.

"There is no need to defend the village," Knight Commander Nophet countered. "Draw them to us here. The village will either funnel them along the road or disperse them and make them easy to pick off."

"No, it will give them cover and make it harder for us to hold them in a formation for our archers to take out from the hillsides."

The prince cast a glance back and forth between the two men, then looked toward the village in the direction the enemy would be approaching from. Finally, he nodded. "I agree with your plan Min. Give the orders."

Quarian issued a few basic orders to those around him and word was passed efficiently among the lancers. He fetched his spyglass from his saddlebag and scanned the hillside for scouts. He quickly spotted Teek, who hadn't moved from his position. Quarian gave a high-pitched whistle that echoed loudly through the valley. In a few moments, Teek turned to look for them, and Quarian waved his arm to get Teek's attention. Teek signaled *enemy* and pointed to where in the valley they were, much closer than Quarian liked.

"They're getting close," the captain major called out loudly to pass the information along to everyone. He was playing catch up getting his armor on, and two of the lancers who were already done helped him with the buckles and adjustments to go faster. Quarian had learned the new armor that came with his promotion was not the normal practice, as he had assumed, but was actually a gift from Prince Stephir. It made him appreciate the elegant armor even more. Polished metal plates were riveted to black brigantine over his torso, shoulders, and upper thighs. It was smart-looking and better than any he had ever owned in his life. Quarian felt almost guilty keeping it when Andric mentioned offhandedly that it was elanticly enhanced. It was armor fit for nobility, and he truly was grateful for it. However, having to rely on help from someone else to get his armor on was irritating.

He was relieved when Intercessor Henden spoke to the prince, diverting his attention as Quarian did his best to finish his preparations quickly. "Prince Andric, if I may."

"Yes?" the prince said, sounding as though the only reason he was hearing her was because he didn't have anything better to do at the moment.

"My lord, I would simply caution that we don't know anything about who approaches. We should seek to treat with them if at all possible to ascertain their intention."

"If the opportunity to hear them presents itself, I will."

"Perhaps if a smaller party of us rode ahead to meet them, we could—"

The prince held up a hand, bringing the priestess to silence. "You saw what they did in the village. These people are savages who don't live by any rules of decency! I will not put our company at greater risk in the vain hope that they will honor the code of civilized discourse. If their intentions are peaceful, they have nothing to fear from us. If not, we will be ready to deal with them from a position of strength."

Quarian was nearly finished. He hoped that would put an end to the discussion, but Sir Mar was already responding with his characteristic bluntness that was unusual for the knights of his order. "Your posture of strength may push us toward a fight that could be avoided by displaying a modicum of restraint, my lord." Quarian winced inwardly. Mar said it with such a casual tone that Quarian could almost believe it was meant as an offhanded comment, not a harsh rebuke. But he knew better.

"I apologize for the delay, Your Highness," Quarian said as he mounted his horse. "I'm ready when you are." He hoped his neutral words would avoid insulting Sir Mar while giving the prince an opening to move forward without an argument. He was relieved when the prince wordlessly spurred his horse forward. They rode at a canter through the village and looked for someplace on the far side to set up their line. He kept an eye on the soldiers moving up the hillsides with their bows. Their progress was slow, and he hoped they would be in place by the time the Kushaani arrived.

The prince made a disgusted noise. "There isn't a decent piece of flat ground anywhere!"

"No, Your Highness," Quarian agreed. "I recommend we divide into three units. Three lancers will stay with you and the Divinarim to hold the road. Eight will move into that rice paddy over there," he said pointing off to the right. "It will cut off any route to get onto your flank. I will take the non-combatants and the remaining lancers on the left, near the base of the hill up there."

The prince made a face that made clear he thought the plan was less than ideal. He looked around the area, no doubt hoping to think of a better option. Finally, he shook his head. "Fine. Give the orders."

Quarian gave brief instructions, then everyone rushed toward their assigned positions. Intercessor Henden did not seem pleased at being separated from the prince, but she didn't argue. When they got to the top of the small rise overlooking the road, Quarian ordered the pack horses to be secured to a small copse of trees while he and his fist of lancers lined up along the rise facing the road.

"Intercessor and Master Ve'Aurben, please remain by those trees over there." He knew he didn't need to tell the elantir they were included in the order. Their primary responsibility was to preserve the gift to the Vanassi. They would stay with the carts carrying menhir and keeping the horses calm. The royal physician was already moving there as well. Intercessor Henden, on the other hand, was not about to be relegated to the rear so easily.

"Captain Major, I appreciate your concern for our safety," she said, putting his instructions in the most charitable light possible, "but I must be able to see what is happening if I am to perform my duty. So do you prefer that we stand near you or on the other end of the formation?"

Quarian had some thoughts on where he would like to tell her to go, but he didn't have the time or inclination to argue. He quickly weighed his options and decided he preferred to have her near him where he stood a chance of discussing things before she did anything rash. At least having her knight protectors on the line would make them look more imposing to the approaching Kushaani.

"I would be pleased to have you stay with me, Intercessor," he said in his most diplomatic voice. Everyone moved into position, then waited in silence, taking the opportunity to check weapons, adjust armor, drink from water-skins, or offer a prayer to their deity of choice. Quarian took out his spyglass and checked on the scouts and archers on the hillsides. The archers behind him were nearly in place, but those on the other side were still climbing the steep slopes to an optimal height. He moved the spyglass to Teek's position. Based on where the scout was pointing, the Kushaani should be leaving the dense jungle cover any minute.

He ran battle scenarios over in his mind considering the effects of the terrain, being separated into three groups, possible Kushaani formations, and tactics he had seen or at least heard about from other commanders. He didn't get far with those thoughts. The first Kushaani riders came into view, riding two abreast along the rutted dirt road leading to the village. Quarian recognized the distinctive appearance of the elite Vidyahar warriors, their faces and long beards painted in streaks of black and red, and red silk scarfs tied above their elbows and knees. They wore various animal skins, but he knew mail or plates were fastened beneath.

As more riders appeared on the road, he watched carefully for any sign of a threat. They bore various weapons, but all were sheathed. He noted the handles of their traditional long, blackened blades rising over their shoulders from where the swords were strapped to their backs. That was an odd way to carry them. He could imagine they would be difficult, if not impossible, to draw from that position.

He counted twenty Kushaani warriors before other riders started to appear. A single banner-bearer rode a piebald horse, holding forward a pole with a long, narrow banner hanging from it. Although Quarian could not quite make out the details, it was white with black markings. It seemed unusual since the Kushaani always were a bit garish in their use of color. The banner-bearer was followed by four other riders also not bearing any armor or weapons. Quarian was almost certain one of them was a woman. This was clearly not a military unit. Perhaps it was an honor guard of some kind.

The forward riders were nearing the prince's position, and Quarian heard Knight Commander Nophet shout something. He could not quite make out the words, but he was pretty sure it was a warning for them to keep their distance. The Kushaani riders gave no heed to his words and continued riding forward. The Divinarim lowered their halberds and the lancers followed suit.

"The prince can't see the other riders," the priestess said urgently to Quarian, concern written on her face. "We have to warn him before they do something rash!"

"What are you talking about?"

"The colorless banner, bearing no weapons... they're approaching in peace." Quarian was not certain what she was referring to, but her assessment felt right.

"What are you waiting for then? Go!"

"I need you to come with me. The prince has been itching for a fight, but he listens to you."

Quarian was reluctant to leave his men, but he knew the prince found the intercessor wearisome at times and tended to resist her counsel as a result. If Quarian could help avoid an unnecessary battle, it was worth the risk. He quickly put Lieutenant Vinnard in charge, then spurred his horse to ride with the intercessor and her knights back down to the prince. As they approached from behind, the lancers in the rear moved aside to let their commander through.

The Divinarim didn't move aside as readily but finally relented as Intercessor Henden pressed forward unwaveringly. "Your Highness," she called in a quiet voice from behind the prince.

"What are you doing back here?" the prince's voice echoed inside his metal helmet, but Quarian could still hear his annoyance. He didn't want that ire directed toward him, but it would be worse to appear to have been dragged along by the intercessor. The first Kushaani horsemen had come to a halt, their painted faces staring grimly toward the Remalians.

"Prince Andric," Quarian jumped in, "they appear to be some kind of honor guard. There are riders further back wearing no armor or weapons."

"They bear a colorless banner, Your Highness," Henden added, again without explanation. Quarian still didn't understand the significance, but now was not the time for a lesson in politics. The prince motioned them to ride up next to him as he lifted the slotted visor, the sun glinting off the golden stallion silhouettes riveted to it.

"So you don't believe they're a threat?" The prince asked, turning his head toward the captain major.

Quarian cringed inwardly at the obvious slight to the intercessor. "I can't be sure, my lord. But I knew you would want to know so you could make a fully informed decision." Quarian knew that was stretching the truth a bit; the prince didn't always wait to have all the information before making decisions, but that was probably just a matter of gaining more experience and maturity. He hoped stating it as if it were truth would help train the young prince without insulting him.

Motion from the line of Vidyahar caught their attention. The Kushaani warriors all suddenly had javelins in their hands. The prince swore, and Quarian silently berated himself for having made the wrong call as he drew his sword, his heart pounding.

"Prepare to charge!" Prince Andric called out to his men as he quickly dropped the visor with a clank of steel.

"Wait!" Intercessor Henden pleaded. "Look." The Vidyahar were spreading their line, but something was off. They weren't forming attack ranks, they were moving to the sides of the road and then turning to face the center. A command was barked and they raised their javelins as the unarmed riders proceeded toward the Remalians.

"Hold!" the prince commanded. The banner-bearer, followed by the four others, rode a short distance past the first Vidyahar and stopped. A high whistle sounded sharply, and the painted warriors rested their javelins on their laps.

"Thank the gods!" Prince Andric said as he fully removed his helmet this time. He still wore a smaller metal skull cap with chain mail hanging all around it like a veil, covering his neck and shoulders. He set the helmet on his lap, one arm resting leisurely on top. "It looks like you were right after all," he said while keeping his eyes fixed on the Kushaani.

"Yes, it's the Vanassi emissaries," the intercessor replied.

Quarian breathed a sigh of relief. He had no desire to fight a battle when it could be avoided.

"Why are they being escorted by Vidyahar?"

"I don't know, Your Highness. Perhaps we should go and ask them."

"Anything I should know before we ride out there?" the prince asked the priestess.

"Just that we should meet them with four riders as well."

Prince Andric quickly designated the three others. "Nophet, Min, and Henden, you're with me." Then he called for his squire. Quarian felt awkward sitting in the silent valley with everyone watching while Jase dismounted and ran forward. Without a word, Jase took the large helmet from the prince. "Intercessor, you will be at my side. Do you remember their names? Telani or something like that?"

"His name is Bejurn sud-Ta and hers is Jalanti san-Rivva."

"Jalanti, that's right," the prince repeated to himself. "All right, let's go see what they want." He kicked his horse forward into a prance, and Quarian fell in behind next to Nophet. It was a short ride to where the Vanassi delegates waited. They had chosen a place to stop where there was enough room to the sides of the road that four riders could stand abreast. Their banner bearer stood behind the four riders, holding the long strip of white cloth high overhead.

When the prince reined his horse to halt, the knight commander moved to the prince's left side and Quarian edged his mount off the road into the thick ferns and tall grass on the other side of the intercessor. Up close, Quarian could now see that their colorful clothes were delicate silk robes worn over their normal riding clothes. They probably put them on just before approaching the village.

The four Vanassi emissaries offered a formal greeting in unison, raising their hands to their faces and touching fingertips to their eyes, ears, lips, and heart, then extending their open hands toward the Remalians. Quarian had to force himself to look past the beautiful woman to the tall man at her side. The captain major assumed these were the two the prince and intercessor had mentioned moments ago.

"Prince Andric Laconeus," the man began formally, "we give you welcome to Vanashar. Our homeland is open to you and yours."

"Thank you, Bejurn sud-Ta. It's a pleasure to see you again. And you as well, Jalanti san-Rivva. We had not expected to find you here, and thought that we may have been forced to fight the Vidyahar that accompany you, especially after what we found in the village."

A look of concern passed over Bejurn's face that was matched by the others. "What has happened in Tepeti?"

The prince hesitated for only a moment before answering. "The women and children are gone. All the men were killed, save one, who was buried alive and left for dead." The four riders exchanged troubled looks before crossing their arms over their chest and touching their shoulders, then reached their hands to the sky, repeating the gesture two more times. When they finished, Prince Andric asked, "If you did not know, why did you come here?"

"We were journeying back to your lands to bring news of our gift to you and your king. We have done as you asked of us, as you may have heard." Bejurn bowed low in the saddle, his head nearly level with his horse. The other three followed suit. Quarian had no idea what the man was referring to and guessed from the look exchanged between the intercessor and prince that they had no idea either.

Prince Andric returned the bow as best he could, which in full armor amounted to little more than a nod. "And we have brought a gift for you as well, and also a token of our esteem for the Vanassi people, although I must confess, I had hoped to present it to you in Sunapra."

"If that is your desire, perhaps it would be best to journey there together. As you have seen from Tepeti, it is dangerous to be this far south."

"Do you know why Tepeti was attacked?" Intercessor Henden asked.

"It is the same as has been done in other villages. The Kushaani attack us for revenge."

"Revenge for what?" the prince asked.

It was Bejurn's turn to look confused. "You haven't heard then? Empress Arrdiwat the seventh is dead. The Vanassi have killed her, as you requested." Quarian could not believe what he was hearing. Prince Andric had asked the Vanassi to assassinate the empress?

"Even now we are suffering the wrath of the central provinces, though this is just the breeze before a great storm. Your aid has come not a moment too soon."

"You what?" Prince Andric sounded incredulous. "You've killed your empress?"

Bejurn frowned slightly but quickly regained his composure and gave a reassuring smile. "She was never our empress. Panthalu Arrdiwat was a tyrant to the Vanassi and has now paid the price. Even as we speak, the Kushaani and the other provinces are splitting their forces, bringing their men northward to fight us. Now is your chance to strike, to plunge your armies deep into the heart of Kushaan!" The Vanassi ambassador's eyes were wide with eager anticipation, as if he had just delivered the news that would change the tide of the war. Perhaps he had, Quarian mused. Just not the way he thought.

The prince's face was flush, and Quarian could only guess what was going through his thoughts. The Kushaani would turn their armies on the Vanassi with a vengeance. It would give the Remalians some reprieve from the harassing attacks on their borders, but it also meant there would be no hope of receiving the supplies they desperately needed. In fact, unless the Remalians committed a significant part of their armies to attack the Kushaani, the Vanassi stood little hope of surviving.

The intercessor finally stepped in to relieve the awkward silence filling the air between the two groups. "Your sacrifice is truly astounding, Emissary sud-Ta. We have much to discuss. May I suggest that we return to the village for further talks?"

"Wise counsel, Intercessor. We will follow you." Without a word, the prince backed his horse up until he could turn around on the road. The intercessor followed suit and took her place next to the prince again, followed by Nophet and Quarian.

"We're all dead," the prince said under his breath. Quarian winced and hoped the Vanassi hadn't heard him. He might be right, but they needed to present a strong front if they were to have any chance at accomplishing their mission. Quarian had decided long ago he had no use for the gods, but for the briefest moment, he reconsidered.

No. It was in mortals' hands to decide their own fate. He did his best to steel himself for the precarious future unfolding before him. One thing was certain, the prince was going to need him now more than ever. He just hoped the prince realized that before it was too late.

CHAPTER XLII
CALINDA

"Ambersol squad is in position, Commander." Captain Ambersol's voice came to Calinda's ears as if he were right next to her, though she knew her second in command was in another part of the camp. Her hand was placed within the watertight bag at her waist, grasping the tentacle of the bonded fachim, feebly writhing as if still alive. Technically it was, while bound to a shard of red carnelian crystal.

She continued feeding a small portion of her own elan into the elant to keep the six channels open and spoke her reply. "One more still to report in. Wait for my command."

She had instructed the elantir who had the other portions of the bonded fachim to only use their own elan until they commenced the operations to take the traitors into custody. It was usually ill-advised to siphon one's own elan, but in this case, it was better than risking the traitor elantir sensing the trap before it was sprung. And this operation was already risky enough trying to capture so many at once, with gods only knowing what tricks were up their sleeves.

She had been shocked when their investigations had led to six elantir and a priest who were involved in either sabotaging their communications through the Bonded or using the mysterious met'elan to prolong the king's near-death condition. Calinda had heard years ago that the Elantic Order knew a way to trace an individual's portion of an elant back to them, which was useful when multiple elantir were working on a joint project and they needed to check if anyone was underperforming. They were able to detect the traces from the individual's elan in the flows. But as with all the guild's knowledge, they hoarded it more jealously than a redshark with a kill. It had taken her nearly a week to discover which of her elantir had the knowledge and then to finally pry the carefully guarded secret out of them.

It turned out the tracing technique was more difficult than she would have guessed, and it took at least two elantir to do it. In this case, it was further complicated by the fact that the traitors used elantic modalities most Remalian elantir considered forbidden and had no experience with. But this was war and they had traitors among them, so she had bribed and threatened and cajoled until she had tracked her quarry. She just never imagined there would be so many. And she could still not be certain she had found them all, but Prince Stephir had decided they could no longer risk having so many enemies loose in the camp.

She directed her thoughts through the communion link with the priest at her side, Father Daemmer. She had a difficult time trusting anyone inside her head, but Daemmer had been handpicked by Stephir to assist her, and the less that could be spoken aloud, the better. She had learned the technique quickly enough, but the undercurrent of dissonance reverberating through her was a distraction she did her best to ignore.

"Is the dispositioning in place?" she asked. Father Daemmer and Intercessor Pendergrand were tasked with dispositioning the target into a submissive state, as were the priests in the other squads.

She heard, or rather felt, the affirmation come through before his words formed. *"Yes, but we are going slow, as instructed. It has probably not reached its peak yet."*

She glanced at the others in her squad, packed into the commander's office within the elantir command post. Four of Commander Chamdon's finest soldiers stood at the ready, two with crossbows and two more to put Captain Hovald in irons. They had the steeled look of men who had seen death enough times to wait calmly to face it again. Sergeant Pauld did not look nearly as calm. None of the elantir were as battle-hardened since they were always relegated to a support role, and Pauld was no exception. But Calinda knew she could trust her, and she had proved reasonably adept at elantic fettering, so between the two of them they would hopefully be able to subdue Hovald quickly.

"Eskett squad in position now, Commander," Captain Eskett's voice came through the elantic conduit. Finally, they were ready. It was a complicated matter to arrest seven at once. They had arranged for most of them to be in separate areas of the camp on one pretense or another to avoid the traitors sounding the alarm or helping each other. They had considered many other options, everything from drugging them to killing them in their sleep; but in the end, this was the course that had been chosen. Now it was time to put their plan into action. She just needed to give Eskett's priests time to put the dispositioning in place.

"Commander, Achio is leaving. What should we do?" Lieutenant Sandrow sounded panicked. It was not ideal, but they were out of time.

"Execute now." It was a simple command, spoken and sent through the fachim. Calinda didn't need it to be any more elaborate. *Let's get this distasteful business over with.* She dropped the link through the fachim and pulled the drawstring on the bag closed. For now, the squads were on their own. She took a moment to establish an elantic connection with Pauld. It would be far less noticeable to Hovald if they were already linked than if she reached out while in his presence.

Once the link was in place Calinda nodded for her team to move. She led the way out of her office with Pauld on her heels, followed by the soldiers, and the priests bringing up the rear. She only had to move a few feet down the main corridor formed by the high fabric walls to the room where Hovald was working. Her heart was pounding. She paused to take one more deep breath, then stepped into the room. All three elantir in the room looked up expectantly.

She directed her attention to Corporal Jeks. "Corporal, do you have an update on my requisition order for the additional ore samples?"

"I'm so sorry," Jeks gushed his apology. The other elantir went back to their duties. "I don't remember it coming in, but let me look again, Commander." The corporal seemed excessively eager to please her. It was no doubt the effects of the dispositioning. Not quite submissiveness, but she understood dispositioning affected people differently. Calinda hoped it was closer to the mark with Hovald as she focused all her attention on the captain behind the small desk just a few feet away.

She drew elan through her link with Pauld and carefully but quickly began the elant to fetter Hovald's ability to draw on the elan around him. She felt Pauld adding to the flows, but the corporal pushed too hard and her elan surged. Hovald's head snapped up and his eyes fixed on hers. She could feel him reaching for elan.

"Commander?" Jeks asked as he and Sergeant Lassot looked around, questioning looks on their faces. She threw caution to the wind and tried to get the fetter in place around Hovald.

"Take him now!" she shouted, hoping to surprise Hovald and gain a few extra moments. The rest of her squad surged into the room. Pauld quickly stepped behind Calinda and put a hand on her shoulder, strengthening their link as the soldiers rushed toward the captain. He was on his feet in an instant, hands on the desk.

The traitorous elantir attacked with what elan he was able to muster. Two thin whips of energy lashed out at the nearest pair of soldiers as they closed the distance, leaving a trace of faint green afterglow on Calinda's vision. She had never seen anything like it. It was an amazing use of a limited amount of elan, but flows were running through it that Calinda now recognized—modalities forbidden in Remalia.

The soldiers cried out in agony and fell to the floor, writhing in pain. Calinda desperately wanted to order the other two soldiers to fire their crossbows and end it now before he could get a second attack in, but she knew taking the traitors alive was of vital importance. "Help me fetter him!" she commanded Jeks and Lassot. She felt Lassot carefully add his elan to the flows, but Jeks simply opened himself up for her to use his elan. It was a mistake and Hovald was too fast, ripping the elan from Jeks before he could correct it. Jeks collapsed like a rag doll, papers scattering as his limp body hit his desk before toppling to the ground.

Calinda knew the fetter was not yet strong enough to completely cut off Hovald from reaching for more elan, but she hoped it was enough to stop him from doing more harm for the moment. She enveloped Hovald in the elant, wrapping the flows around him like an invisible shroud. She felt his flows of elan disappear, but a sudden sharp thrust pierced through the fetter before she could cinch it tight. He must have pulled all the elan inside himself to prevent being cut off from it. But that much elan should have killed him.

Another tendril of elantic energy lashed out, just missing Calinda as it streaked past her head. Pauld cried out and reeled from the attack. The hold on the commander's shoulder weakened for a moment, then the sergeant gripped harder. A dangerous amount of elan suddenly surged through her link with Pauld. Calinda spared a glance at the sergeant and saw a fiery determination in her eyes, though the commander could see blood oozing between Pauld's fingers pressed over a wound on her face.

A palpable aura of cooperation and compliance filled the room. Intercessor Pendergrand held his hand out toward the traitor, a calm, almost serene look on his face. Hovald put both hands on his desk to brace himself, shaking his head to clear the effects of the dispositioning now focused on him. Calinda didn't waste a moment. She sealed the bands of the fetter together, then collapsed it tight against Hovald. He struggled to break through again, but she had him now. The traitor dropped to one knee, seemingly unable or unwilling to carry on.

"Take him!" she barked at the soldiers, a bit sharper than she had intended. The two with manacles ran forward and seized the traitor. As they put him in irons, she spoke to Pauld and Lassot. "You two must keep the fetter tight. Pauld is the primary, do you understand?" Both elantir nodded.

"What's going on Commander?" Lassot asked. Calinda could appreciate how confusing this must all be, but she had more pressing concerns than to explain. She knelt next to Jaks as she answered.

"All you need to know right now is that there are traitors in our ranks, and Hovald is one of them. You will keep that fetter in place at all costs." She put a hand on the corporal's forehead and extended her elan to feel for signs of life. His life force was there, barely, fluttering on the edge of disappearing. She was no healer, but she trickled a small amount of her elan into the young man.

A piercing scream sounded from somewhere outside the command post, followed by a resounding boom. Calinda cursed under her breath as she stood and ran from the room and out of the tent into the brilliant morning daylight. She used her elan to instantly adjust her eyesight; a trick she had learned long ago when she served aboard ships in the Calavian merchant fleet.

"Which one?" The thought came through the communion link from Father Daemmer. The only other traitor close enough was Corporal Askko in the research pavilion. Without a word, she ran in that direction, fear mounting in her chest. She rushed through the tent's opening into a scene of chaos. Captain Tefreyne stood at the far side of the tent, panting from exertion. Father Daemmer knelt next to two elantir lying motionless amidst a scattering of books and other materials. A gaping hole was torn in the pavilion roof above them, the cloudless blue sky bright overhead.

In the center of the tent was a lone elantir, face down amidst a pool of blood. *Askko.* A rush of anger swept over her at the thought of the corporal's betrayal. The same questions she had asked herself a thousand times flooded her thoughts again. *How could she do this? How could I have been so blind?* Flashes of memories of the hours they had spent together studying, training, eating, laughing. She had tried to be a mentor to Askko. *How could she betray me like this?*

She forced her attention back to the present as she looked down at the bodies of a half dozen elantir and soldiers lying around her, some moaning, others still as stone. Blood was splattered in a circular pattern away from the traitor. One of the soldiers was helping a priestess to stand, her hair and clothes in disarray, blood running from her nose as she fumbled blindly for his arm. Calinda felt the contents of her stomach rising into her throat. *No, not now!*

Another thunderous boom sounded in the distance. Everyone ducked instinctively. "Go," Tefreyne coughed, struggling to stay on his feet. "This one is no longer a threat."

"Help them," was all she said to Father Daemmer, and felt the communion link with the priest close as she ran out of the pavilion to find where the next threat was. Crowds of soldiers were gathering around the elantir area of the camp, many with weapons in hand and concern written on their faces, but watching from a safe distance. She hoped they did not consider her a threat and do something rash. She scanned the camp in the direction where the other squads should be but saw nothing. She untied the bag at her hip and reached her hand inside the sea water, carefully gripping the bonded fachim tentacle.

She channeled elan from around her and opened the links. "Anyone, report in." She waited a moment, but no reply came. Frustrating, but it was what she had expected. No doubt they all had their hands full. She needed to get to a higher position. A wagon stood nearby loaded with crates. She ran to it and climbed into the back and up onto the crates. It was enough to give her a view of most of the camp. It only took a moment to find another gap in the churning sea of soldiers where they kept their distance in a ring around the blacksmiths' area. That was where Simrick was supposed to be captured.

Calinda jumped down and ran toward the area, ordering soldiers out of her way as she pushed through the swarm of bodies. She broke into the clearing and was dismayed at the destruction. Tents were collapsed or half blown apart; metal scraps and tools were scattered everywhere amidst the bodies and blood. Calinda thought she recognized a blackened and smoldering body as Corporal Stantow, one of the elantir assigned to the squad responsible for capturing Sergeant Simrick. Brother Batson lay beside him, seemingly unmarred by the flames, but just as still as the others. The grass all around them was limp and blackened; not from fire, but from having so much elan siphoned from it.

"Shoot them!" someone yelled from the other side of a tent wall that was still standing. She heard the snap of crossbow strings firing and bolts clattering to the ground. She reached for elan as she moved forward, but there was almost nothing. The area felt empty and lifeless except for the bright points of the humans still fighting just out of sight. She reached further out until she found the edge where elan was beginning to seep back into the leached ground from the surrounding area. It was difficult to pull elan at that distance, and she didn't have any time to spare. She would have to make do.

She rounded the corner and saw Sergeant Simrick standing defiantly in the midst of the wreckage, sweat soaking his black curly hair from the heat and the strain of battle. She was surprised to see Captain Freidlan by his side, her clothing torn at the shoulder and blood running from a wound. She was supposed to be on the outskirts of the camp where the siege equipment was being constructed. *How did she end up here?*

There was no time to dwell on that question. A young soldier was bent impossibly backward, looking like he was about to fall but kept on his feet by a coil of elan around his throat. His face was purple from the force holding him in place, his eyes wide with terror and his hands clawing wildly at the invisible chord choking the life out of him.

Calinda lashed out with her own elant and severed the line. The soldier fell to the ground, coughing and gasping for air.

Simrick snapped his head in her direction, eyes narrowing defiantly. "Alscan," he said to his companion. Freidlan tore her eyes away from the six remaining elantir, soldiers, and priestess they were keeping at bay to spare a glance over her shoulder in Calinda's direction. The commander could sense that Simrick and Freidlan were linked, which gave them the advantage.

Lieutenant Whitsol, the only other elantir in the area who was on her side, was too far away to easily form a link with her. She needed to buy time to figure out how to capture the traitors. She considered commanding the dozens of soldiers standing at the periphery to attack, but that would undoubtedly cost many lives, including the traitors', whom she still hoped to take alive. They might not know that though.

"It's over Simrick, Freidlan! You're surrounded. The entire army stands by to end your treachery! Surrender now, or at my command your lives are forfeit."

"I am tempted to surrender, if only in the hopes of living long enough to see Remalia's utter devastation. Alas, yours will have to do." Simrick took a lunging step toward her, hands spread as if to shove her, even though he was thirty feet away.

Calinda hardened her elan into a shield and braced for the impact she was sure was coming. Instead, waves of elan enveloped her, vibrating with a restrained intensity she had never experienced before. She feared Simrick was going to try and fetter her, but suddenly the waves of elan burst into searing heat.

Before she even had time to think, her years of training on the merchant ships in Calavia dealing with the threat of fire took over. She released her shield and pushed her elan into the air around her, mixing it with the heat. She squeezed her eyes shut, then released her elant. An icy chill washed over her as the heat was transmuted into a blinding flash of light. Several voices around her cried out in surprise and pain.

Wisps of smoke rose from her smoldering clothes and her skin was raw and painful from the burn Simrick's elant had caused. Tears leaked from the corners of her eyes that were now squeezed against the pain instead of the light. *No time to wait. Move!* Others in the vicinity were still blinking away the effects of being temporarily blinded. She only had moments before the traitors would recover.

Calinda wanted desperately to fetter them, but there was not nearly enough elan in the area, and she feared drawing more from herself. Linking with Whitsol was her best option. She gritted her teeth in frustration at the precious moments she would lose getting close enough. The lieutenant was down on one knee with her hands pressed to her eyes. Calinda hoped the woman had enough elan left to spare to be useful.

She forced her feet to move a few halting steps forward, then stopped short when she heard footsteps running toward her. She could not afford to waste a moment, but she needed to deal with the new arrivals, whether enemy or ally. Against her better judgment, she drew a small amount of her elan and readied herself.

Calinda was relieved to see Father Daemmer followed by two of her elan-tir. She immediately felt the pressure from the priest in her mind requesting to link in communion. She let him in and felt his concern and support before his words formed. *"How badly are you hurt? What can we do?"*

"I'll live," she answered, then said aloud, "We need to bind—" Her words were cut short as Sergeant Chaemons threw up a shield just in time to take the brunt of another attack from Simrick. Several tendrils of elantic energy cracked loudly as they struck and the shield collapsed.

"They're too strong. We need to link!" she commanded her elantir as she spun to face the two traitors. Chaemons put a hand on her shoulder and Calinda opened the link. Elan flowed into her like a refreshing drink of water. She realized how thirsty she actually was, but pushed the thought away and began preparing the fetter. She did not believe she could manage two fetters at once and focused on Simrick first.

She heard the heavy beat of horse hooves approaching fast, but could not spare any attention for them. She pushed her flow of elan forward, positioning it to envelop Simrick. Calinda could feel the traitor reaching out around him for more elan, but she knew the area was depleted and once the fetter was in place, he would be completely cut off. She felt lightheaded as she pushed more of her own elan into the fetter. It had to be strong enough to cut him off.

With an audible shriek, two of the approaching horses shuddered and collapsed to the ground, their riders scrambling to avoid being crushed beneath the falling animals. She felt a surge of elan flowing into Simrick and realized too late that Freidlan had ripped the elan from the horses and was channeling it to her accomplice. In a cry of desperation, the commander clamped the fetter tightly into place, but Simrick drove a wedge into the seam before she could seal it. She felt her elant fall to shreds under the pressure from Simrick's counterattack.

How can they hold so much power?

Suddenly, a rending sound that Calinda felt almost as much as heard shook the area and a slash of light like the noonday sun opened in the air beside Simrick. The rift widened into a bright hole, radiant light pouring out in such magnitude as Calinda had never seen. Simrick and Freidlan threw their arms up to shield their faces and fell back, stumbling away from the rift as quickly as they could.

The trampled grass and collapsed tents nearest the rift began to smolder as if being burned by the light, though Calinda could detect no heat. She worked quickly to rebuild the fetter, but her attention wavered as a horrible roaring filled the air. A bestial, clawed hand from inside the rift gripped the side of the hole and tore it even wider.

"Dear gods, someone is summoning!" Father Daemmer said through their communal link. She shared the fear pouring through the connection with the priest.

From the radiant opening crawled an enormous creature, filling Calinda with both dread and awe. The daemon resembled a massive, fiery cat, taller than a horse at the front shoulders by half again, with heavily muscled front legs that looked more like an ape's arms ending in bestial hands tipped with heavy, gleaming silvery claws. Its hind legs were just as muscular, though much shorter, giving the beast a hunched look as if it were about to pounce at any moment.

Flames sprouted wherever it touched the ground. It swung its enormous head from side to side, eyes burning with intensity as it surveyed the area. A ferocious snarl revealed a gaping mouth full of ebony teeth, like jagged daggers. Its hide was as radiant as the rift behind it and seemed to be wreathed in fire and light, as best Calinda could tell through her squinted eyes. It was beautiful and horrible at the same time.

"Who's insane enough to summon that thing?" She looked around and saw Seraph Vestin, the presiding high priestess of Teraithia in the camp, standing near Lieutenant Whitsol, her arms outstretched toward the daemon, fingers curled with strain into claws of her own.

"Of course it's a Teraithian," Father Daemmer's words were infused with an intense contempt that was so foreign to his usual calm demeanor.

His intensity was mirrored by the fury in Seraph Vestin's voice as she screamed her command to the summoned creature, "Kill them!"

The daemon looked down on the retreating traitors and lunged. It reached surprisingly far with its massive front arms, grasping toward Sergeant Simrick. Desperately he threw up a shield of his own and was driven backward as the gloriously terrible creature slammed against the invisible barrier. Burning radiance surged all around the daemon as its metallic claws bit deep into flaming earth and its muscles rippled with the effort of straining against the force keeping it from reaching its prey.

Captain Freidlan cried out in agony as a crossbow bolt sank deep into her shoulder and spun her around before she fell to the ground. Her link with Simrick evaporated in an instant. The daemon stumbled forward as the shield suddenly crumpled. With unbelievable speed, it got its feet under it and spun on Simrick. The traitor turned to flee, but the creature was too fast. It lunged the last few feet and its teeth sliced deep into Simrick with a crunch of bones and searing flesh.

Calinda reflexively looked away from the horrible sight, but her eyes were drawn back as Seraph Vestin screamed again, her fury now tinged with panic, "No! Not them. Her!" Calinda saw no trace of Simrick, and the daemon was charging at the soldiers who stood near the priestess. It appeared to be headed for the one reloading his crossbow until the soldier at his side fired a bolt that bit into the creature's muscular chest, bursting into flame from its contact with the divine beast. The enormous head swung with lightning speed, its jaws snapping shut around the soldier, cutting short the man's terrified scream.

Calinda's link with Father Daemmer disappeared, and his voice boomed, augmented by the Holy Couple's divine power, as he called out to Seraph Vestin, "Banish that abomination before it does more harm!" A palpable aura of righteous indignation radiated from the priest. The daemon threw back its head and let out a piercing roar. The priestess looked at Daemmer, hesitation playing on her face. Finally, she nodded, and a new portal opened next to the creature. It sniffed toward the portal and took a few halting steps toward it while it continued to look side to side, perhaps looking for some other threat or prey.

Calinda sensed an intense flow of elan suddenly open between Captain Freidlan and the portal. The elan seemed to be appearing out of nowhere. Calinda concluded that she must be pulling elan directly from Teraithia's realm on the other side of the portal. The commander had never heard of such a feat and was fascinated by the idea, but she shoved the thought aside. "We have to fetter her!"

Calinda felt elan flowing through the link with the elantir behind her, but it was weak. They were all exhausted. It would never be enough to fetter Freidlan. The traitor was frantically weaving a complex pattern of elan around her, eyes darting about in panic. This was not being directed outward, but inward. It was a pattern Calinda hadn't seen before, although she could feel that it relied heavily on kosek, one of the forbidden modalities.

More troublesome by far, though, was how much elan was building in the elant. If Freidlan managed to strike, Calinda knew she wouldn't be able to defend against it. She needed more elan, now! The summoned creature was partially into the rift. At any moment it would be completely through and the portal would close. If the traitor could draw elan through the conduit, maybe she could too.

In desperation, she reached through to Teraithia's realm. Her senses reeled from an overwhelming intensity. It was not sound or light or heat exactly but seemed somehow to be all of those and more, combined into a single energy impossible for her mind to comprehend. She blindly opened a channel for elan to flow. A crushing pressure of life force flooded through the link. She tried to hold it at bay, to manage it outside of herself, but it was too much. Her veins burned with the intensity as it rushed into her, threatening to incinerate her out of existence.

Calinda slammed shut her link to the realm on the other side of the portal. The flows disappeared and she crumpled to her knees, gasping for breath. She barely felt connected to her body, but somehow managed to raise her head in time to see the rift close behind the celestial creature as it disappeared back to the world that was its home. She wanted nothing more than to lie down and lose consciousness, but there was one more task to finish. She shifted her attention to Freidlan.

Calinda could hardly believe the amount of elan seething around the traitor. Even if she could muster enough strength to create a fetter, it would never hold against so much power. Whatever elant Freidlan was constructing was rapidly intensifying like a tightly harnessed storm. She focused her elan like a surgeon's blade and tried to cut into the flows of the elant. A jolt of searing energy shot back through the flow of her own elant. She winced from the shock but shook it off.

She looked at the others surrounding Freidlan, hoping to see if they had a better idea than she did. A shift in the looks on their faces told her something was wrong. Her eyes darted back to the traitor, afraid of what danger was coming next. Instead she was sickened by what she saw.

Freidlan was bent backward, suspended in the air, her toes barely touching the ground. Her back was arched impossibly far, perhaps broken. Calinda wondered if she was even alive. Had the traitor's elant killed her? The need to finish this drove the commander forward. Her steps felt heavier than her weariness should account for. She realized she was gripped by fear before her mind understood the reason, and she recoiled from the sight before her. Freidlan's eyes were pools of blood-red, darkening to a blackness that was spreading across her face. Her fingers and hands were disfigured and twitching as black tendrils crawled under her skin up her arms.

She had to do something to stop this. The flows of elan seemed chaotic, mutating and twisting in and out of any structure she might hope to recognize. Still, there was something her mind was trying to show her. She could feel it, frustratingly just out of reach. Freidlan's back arched further and the sound of bones snapping made Calinda sick. The traitor groaned in pain.

How is she still alive? Suddenly Calinda knew where she had seen this elant before. These were the same flows they had discovered woven into the king's body, keeping him unnaturally alive. Only these were the polar opposite, turning the traitor's own elan against her, consuming her. Or it was almost that. The elan was still there, bound within the seething elant, building on itself. The harmonics were amplifying with an astounding intensity. Her eyes went wide as she guessed what was happening.

"Everyone fall back!" Sergeant Chaemons and two other elantir moved toward her, but she shouted for them to run. In desperation, she reached out for any source of elan that could provide more power. Without thinking she linked with the nearby soldiers' mounts and ripped the elan from them as hard as she could. She heard their cries at the edge of her consciousness but slammed the door on her heart screaming out in protest at what she had just done. The tear that fell from her lashes was the only sign betraying her emotions.

Calinda threw up her shield but realized it would only protect her and those behind her if an attack was directed at her. That was not good enough.

Captain Freidlan was as still as a corpse and didn't appear to be in control of the elant roiling around her body. Calinda extended her shield around the traitor, encasing her like a cocoon. She feared her elant was not strong enough to contain so much power. Perhaps she could shunt the excess elan into the ground if only there was enough time. She worked frantically to add the links from the shell down to the ground. Delicate tendrils snaked out in all directions like the roots of a sapling, delving into the earth.

A wave of death and cold erupted from Freidlan's blackening body. The shield held for a moment as a torrent of elan flowed through the conduits into the thirsty ground, then disintegrated under so much power. Her elant shattered and a soundless shockwave blasted through the area, sending anything that was not anchored to the ground hurtling through the air.

A painless and empty blackness overtook Calinda before her body hit the ground.

CHAPTER XLIII
SHIRALLA

Step. Step. Step. The steady rhythm of hoof beats on the heavily rutted dirt road was a deceptively calm counterpoint to the undercurrent of anxiety running through the group. Shiralla was grateful the Remalians now rode in the company of the Vanassi toward Sunapra, but that was little comfort given the much larger Kushaani force doggedly tailing them for the past two days, never more than a day behind. Shiralla feared every village they passed would become a repeat of the horrors at Tepeti, but the Vanassi sent riders ahead to warn their people to hide in the jungle until the threat passed.

Of course, it galled Prince Andric to run when all he wanted was to turn and fight. Shiralla desperately wanted to protect the villagers and found herself more willing than usual to consider fighting to shield them from the horrors coming behind them. Their scouts reported the Kushaani forces barely slowed enough to set fire to the simple village dwellings before resuming their relentless pursuit of the Remalian and Vanassi delegations. She took some comfort in knowing that at least the people were safe for now, though it saddened her when she caught glimpses of smoke through the occasional breaks in the dense jungle canopy. Their homes had been destroyed, but the people survived.

Bejurn assured the prince that if the Kushaani pursued them deeper into Vanashar, Vanassi forces could be marshaled to help even the odds in fighting their enemy. And so they pushed themselves northward along the road, mile after mile blurring together in a sweltering haze of green and brown and buzzing. The road generally followed the Meer River but rarely got close enough to see it. Shiralla had learned that the Meer flooded its banks during the rainy season, so the road had to be far enough away to avoid being washed away every year. The villages, with homes built on stilts to keep them above the highest water level, were closer to the river, often completely hidden from view of the road, making the journey even more monotonous.

It was late afternoon when Shiralla noticed a Vanassi scout riding quickly toward the ranking members of the delegation in the center of the long column of mounted warriors. The scout maneuvered his horse to cut in front of her so he could ride just behind Bejurn and Prince Andric to give his report. She was grateful to be riding close enough to hear the report first-hand.

"Uncali," the scout used the Vanassi honorific to address Bejurn, "the Sheerbahari refuse to leave, and the vedic begs that you come and speak to him."

Shiralla could not see Bejurn's face, but she sensed in the silence of his delayed response he was not pleased.

"And he gave no reason?"

"No, Uncali."

After a further pause, Bejurn finally sighed. "Then I suppose I had better go and speak with him. Gather a small escort. We will speak with the vedic, then rejoin Prince Andric as soon as we can."

"Emissary," the prince interjected, "if the people refuse to leave, they will be killed or taken captive. I can't allow more lives to be lost on our account." Shiralla had been in communion with the prince a few times in the last couple of days and had pieced together that he felt uniquely responsible for the terrible situation they found themselves in because of his careless words back in Nanjab. It was eating at him, and 'running away,' as he put it, was making it worse by the day.

"I believe I can convince them to leave," Bejurn said, though Shiralla heard doubt in his voice.

"I hope you're right," the prince replied, "but if not, we must make our stand against the Kushaani here."

"It is only a small force compared to what is to come. Even if we save Sheerbahar today, it won't be long before the Kushaani arrive with even greater numbers. Please, Prince Andric, we should stay the course as we have discussed."

"My men and I are coming with you," Andric said firmly, his voice making clear that his mind was made up.

"Vedic Pujar will be grateful we are coming to his aid," Bejurn said diplomatically, "but it will make it more difficult to persuade him to leave."

"Then perhaps he'll have some men that can help us fight."

Bejurn bowed his head slightly, then said over his shoulder to the scout, "Go and tell Hitesh we are going to Sheerbahar."

"Yes, Uncali." Shiralla watched as the rider made his way forward along the column and disappeared around a bend in the road. A heavy silence hung between the riders. Sometimes silence could be a powerful tool, sometimes it was a festering wound that needed to be lanced.

She turned to Jalanti who rode next to her. "Tell me of Sheerbahar. Have you been there before?"

"I have only been there once before, on our first journey to find you in Nanjab. It's an important village for this region because it holds one of the provincial granaries. They also have a large market where other villages come to trade goods and news." Jalanti lowered her voice a bit and said in a confessional tone, "And they're known for making beautiful head scarfs! I received one as a gift when we were here."

"I remember you wearing it in Nanjab," Shiralla offered with a complimentary tone. Jalanti looked down demurely, which she did often, as was customary for the women of this region. The intercessor liked Jalanti well enough, but she was a simple young woman and not one for deep conversation. Not that their circumstances were conducive to much of that anyway. Besides, her role as part of the Vanassi delegation seemed little more than capturing the attention of the Remalian men, which she did well enough. Especially Prince Andric. *Perhaps if I were more beautiful, I could get his attention more.* She immediately chided herself for thinking that way. She didn't need such a crutch. But some part of her felt that was a lie.

"Perhaps we can find one for you, something to match your beautiful red hair."

Shiralla was much more hopeful of finding food than a head scarf as her stomach complained about how much time had passed since her last meal. Now that they traveled with the Vanassi they didn't have to worry about starving, but rations were still tighter than she would have liked. She could already tell that her clothes were looser fitting. Much more of this and she would need to visit a seamstress before her clothes started hanging on her like a sack.

Their idle talk soon drifted back into a silence that remained unbroken until they reached Sheerbahar. The usual dim light of the dense jungle was beginning to deepen as the sun slipped lower in the sky when the trees abruptly yielded to wide-open rice paddies flanking the road like a patchwork quilt, reflecting the blue and gold of the afternoon sky. A slight breeze blew across the road, delightfully refreshing after the oppressive stillness among the trees. Not a soul was out in the fields. She guessed word of the impending Kushaani threat had drawn everyone back to the village.

Sheerbahar was much larger than Shiralla expected. Well over a hundred wood and thatch dwellings and other buildings spread out along the wide backdrop of the Meer River. On the north end of the village, stone and plaster houses covered a hillside, above the level where the flooding of the Meer would put them at risk. At the top of the hill, stacked-stone steps led up to an elaborate limestone building, the largest by far in the area. Statues adorned the side overlooking the village. On the far end, the building rose in a tall cone shape, the outside covered in smooth, white plaster.

"Is that the granary?" Shiralla asked Jalanti, pointing to the building.

"Yes. It also serves as the village shrine to the gods and to the ancestors."

Shiralla's training as a Sharinic priestess and diplomat had taught her to be tolerant of most cultural differences. Among most tribes in the Kushaan Empire, that included their tendency to worship the gods collectively rather than being devoted to one deity in particular. It was a strange notion to Shiralla's way of thinking, but nothing that had ever particularly bothered her. Her vision from Sharin Dara had made clear, though, that the time for such primitive ambiguity was at an end. It was time for all the waters of the world to be poured into a single vessel. She felt an echo of Sharin Dara's divinessence stir within her and began to consider how she might fulfill the mission her goddess had placed upon her shoulders.

Up ahead the column of soldiers turned off the main road and headed toward the village. The rider in front of Bejurn raised the same white banner the Vanassi delegation carried when they approached the village of Tepeti. She had gambled that it was a sign of peace for the Vanassi as it was for the Kushaani. Fortunately, her gamble had paid off. She meant to ask Bejurn or Jalanti about it, but it had slipped her mind until now, and she didn't want hers to be the lone voice to break the somber silence. The front riders were just reaching the outermost buildings when she finally turned onto the road to the village. The sun sparkled on the surface of the Meer as the breeze rippled across the swirling currents of the river.

The Vanassi soldiers began stopping and formed a row on each side of the road, facing inward, javelins drawn but resting on their laps, the same as they did at Tepeti. As she passed between them, she could see a large group of the village men gathered on the road where it entered the village. Many of them were dressed in a similar fashion to the Vidyahar warriors, with red cloths tied above their elbows and below their knees, and several carried javelins or spears and tall wicker shields.

"Vedic Pujar," Bejurn called out in a loud voice, "the gods grace us to meet again, though I wish it were under a clearer sky."

A tall, wiry man, wearing a wooden mask carved in the likeness of a large cat and painted black with white spots, stepped forward from the group of men and hit the ground twice with the end of his spear before speaking. "The ancestors have brought you to fight with us. They've answered our prayers. We thank you." The man removed his mask and dropped to one knee, his head bowed. The men of the village followed suit.

Shiralla looked past the kneeling men into the village and saw the worried faces of women and children peeking out of windows and doorways to watch the unfolding scene. She yearned to find a way to avert the impending danger racing toward them. Divinessence grew inside her, a light that both made her feel whole and inspired her to become more. *Which benefaction should I use? What course of action should I guide them to?* Too many possibilities swirled through her mind, her thoughts lurching from one path to the next.

"Vedic, the army that comes behind us is fire that turns the earth to ash." Bejurn's voice was filled with urgency. "The ancestors would have you live to fight another day. Take refuge among the trees until it passes."

The vedic stood, and the men again followed his lead. "I warned the elders that killing Arrdiwat would anger the ancestors and the gods. Now we must appease them with our blood. But I swear we will take more of theirs than they take of ours before it's over!" He hit the ground twice more with his spear. The exceptionally large metal head, which was almost certainly more ceremonial than practical, vibrated from the force of the gesture.

Guide them in my path, the voice inside Shiralla instructed, urging her to act.

Tell me what I should do, she begged, desperate to not make a mistake.

No outcome is certain. The power to act is given to you.

"Take your people to Sunapra," Bejurn urged the vedic. "We will find a place for you there until the conflict has passed."

Whatever decision the group standing here in the middle of the road came to, Shiralla would do what she could to ensure it was done under the influence of Sharin Dara's guiding light. Dispositioning was better suited than other benefactions to simultaneously affect multiple subjects, although it became less potent and precise without the cleric focusing it on a particular person. She extended her will to radiate dispositioning through the divinessence. The vedic stood stubbornly silent, unmoving.

"It will take time for our new allies to push their army into Kushaan and draw the enemy soldiers away," Bejurn explained. It still bothered Shiralla that Andric would not agree to be more forthcoming about the Remalians' predicament, but it was a precarious situation that could go badly whichever course they chose, so she had agreed to defer to the prince on the matter. "There could be many waves of attacks before then. We must think of the long road to our freedom, not just a single battle."

Shiralla sent delicate tendrils of the benefaction reaching out toward Bejurn and Pujar. It was critical to keep the dispositioning subtle so the subjects would not feel she was interfering with their discussion. She could feel with surprising clarity the complex currents of emotions and motives churning inside them: pride, frustration, dignity, fear, the desire to prevail, the desire to be seen by others to prevail, the desire to protect their people.

"We have endured many threats," the vedic growled.

Shiralla felt the current of an old anger rising in Pujar. She could not begin to guess what memory the anger was tied to, but she needed to direct his thoughts away from it. She shared his desire to protect his people, so dispositioning him to accentuate that inclination was a natural place to start. She scanned the villagers, looking for a face or set of eyes to connect with, but she struggled to focus on any one individual. They blurred together as her mind pulled back. *Is someone trying to disposition me*, she wondered but knew that was not the problem.

The memory of communion several days earlier with Sir Mar came unbidden into her thoughts. *'You are straining too hard for control. Surrender to Our Lady's guidance.'* She balked at the thought. Her control wavered and she struggled to regain her focus. *'That's what keeps you from succeeding.'* Mar's words stung as they came to her with a reproving force.

"And I pray you survive this one as well, brother," Bejurn said.

Shiralla felt the sincerity of his words, though there was an undertone of something else, sadness maybe. *Are they actually brothers?* No, he meant the term to convey connection, not relation.

They are all connected.

Her perception shifted and the world blurred. It was as if she was looking through someone else's eyes while still seeing through her own, like trying to hold a flood of images in her mind during communion.

Let go.

She took a deep breath and slowly relinquished her straining grasp as she gradually released the air from her lungs. Her mind's eye saw a thousand strands of connection like a web of light running between the villagers: parents who loved their children, lovers who longed for one another, warriors who had fought together and saved each other's lives, friends who fished the river together, planted in the fields together, played games in the woods together. Shiralla saw that the strands of connection were not simply links between individuals, they were the connective tissue of a single body.

They are one.

An image of herself dispositioning the whole village came into her mind, but she knew that was impossible. She wished she had the devotion of someone like High Consul Penrossart, whom Shiralla had witnessed marshaling enough of Sharin Dara's presence to disposition a whole congregation of worshippers at the temple in Teris. *Maybe I can't, but perhaps with Lathon and Emerly...*

Shiralla had participated in the benefaction of unification before, but only as a constituent, never as the principal. She had never imagined needing a stronger divine presence than she could muster on her own, so hadn't devoted herself to practicing this particular benefaction. However, she had been in communion with the two holy knights often enough that she hoped she could manage unification between the three of them. They rode just behind her and she reached out to their minds to request communion. They acceded and the links formed. She wanted to skip the usual formalities, but unification required bringing the constituents' minds, hearts, and souls into harmony to allow their combined devotion to convoke a greater focus of their goddess's divinesness.

"Our Lady's grace."

"Peace be upon you," both knights responded. Shiralla detected curiosity from Lady di Greven and approbation from Sir Mar.

"I need us to perform unification."

"Now? Out here on the road?" di Greven asked, not as a challenge, but in surprise.

And perhaps a hint of skepticism, Shiralla acknowledged in the corner of her mind where she had pushed her own uncertainty. She hoped she was successful in keeping her doubt out of the communal link. Those thoughts would not make the task any easier. *"Yes. This is important and I need your help."* She felt both knights' agreement. There was no time to waste. Anger was growing between Bejurn and Pujar, but Shiralla did her best to block them out. *"Holy Lady, Bringer of peace and goodness, we sanctify your name."*

Shiralla shared the familiar words through the communal link, imbuing them with reverence.

"*Sanctify us,*" the holy knights responded in practiced unison.

"*Your glory is from everlasting to everlasting.*"

"*Fill us with light,*" they answered.

She could feel them open themselves to attune with Sharin Dara's divinessence. Shiralla entwined her will with theirs, and theirs with the divine power present all around them. Their combined devotion became a wellspring of light running between them, through them, straining to escape the confines of her will and radiate to the Sheerbahari. She felt divine glory infusing the divinessence more intensely, deepening her bond with the people. She struggled to breathe as she exerted herself to manifest her intentions through the glorious divinessence. She had never felt so much power before. *Could it really be this easy,* she wondered in amazement.

"*Your mercy is extended over all the world.*" She infused the words into the divinessence. A wave of dispositioning erupted from her. Silence fell over the world, or perhaps the sound was swallowed up in the rushing sensation of the divinessence resonating through the area.

"*Grant us strength,*" the words intoned in her mind, but she could no longer tell if they were the knights' or hers.

"*Make us thine.*" She pushed the invocation for unity into the dispositioning. *We are all one,* she thought. She felt the reality of it resonating in their hearts and minds. The conviction of that truth flowed through the strands of connection between the people, many of whom now looked at her with wonder. *How do they know the dispositioning is coming from me?*

"*Make us thine,*" the words echoed back from holy knights but seemed to give voice to the flames of devotion springing up in those caught in the torrent of dispositioning. Some of the men dropped to their knees and bowed their heads to the ground while others looked around, confused or afraid.

Prince Andric turned his mount toward her, concern bordering on anger written on his face. "What are you doing?"

If only she could make him understand. Her voice reverberated with Sharin Dara's power. "The contention and strife rolling over the world is a plague. It can end." The longing for unity flowed from her toward the prince. "It *must* end."

Knight Commander Nophet interposed himself between Shiralla and Prince Andric. "You will desist immediately, Intercessor!"

Shiralla was incensed at Nophet's interference yet again. He had been a thorn in her side the entire journey. She felt the hard steel of another dispositioning fill the prince. It was one of the ways the knights of the Order of Divine Flame protected the royals from benefactions that might unduly influence them. But even one as strong as Nophet could only partially lessen the dispositioning surging from Shiralla.

"Stand aside Knight Commander. Your services are not needed here." Her voice was far calmer than she felt. Sir Mar edged his horse closer to Shiralla. She was grateful for his protection but was certain it was not needed. A part of her considered what she could do to Nophet with so much of Sharin Dara's power at her disposal. *No, that isn't right.* Her words were tinged with guilt at her weakness. The unification waivered and her connection to the divinessence began to ebb. She strained to hold on to it.

"It is a crime to disposition the royal family," Nophet said, lowering his halberd between them. The subtle threat was not lost on Shiralla.

"It is enough," Sir Mar sent through the shared link, gentle yet firm. *"Let it go."*

Unification broke and she felt dizzy with the sudden absence of her connection to the divine. Only a shimmer of Sharin Dara's spirit now remained within her. "I—" she stopped, unsure what to say. Her instinct was to apologize, but felt that would be a betrayal of her divine mission. She could feel many eyes upon her, but she looked directly at Prince Andric. "I meant no offense, my lord. Forgive me."

The prince's eyes smoldered with indignation. Without a word, he turned away and said to Bejurn and Pujar, "I apologize for the interruption. I believe we were discussing—"

One of the older men from the back of the group pushed his way forward, past the vedic, and walked between Andric and Bejurn toward Shiralla with a look of solemn meekness on his face as he kept his gaze fixed on her. He carefully reached out and took her hand in his and pressed his forehead to the back of her hand. His skin was dry and leathery, but the gesture was so gentle she hardly noticed. "You must stay, yes?" the man asked with a pleading, raspy voice.

She should have looked to Bejurn and the prince for guidance, but instead replied, "Yes, of course."

The man took her horse by the reins and led her back through the crowd toward Sheerbahar. The vedic's anger seemed to turn to confusion as his mouth worked to formulate something to say but appeared to be at a loss for words. Some of the village men backed away to clear a path while others reached from their places on the ground to touch her boot or the hem of her riding skirt as she passed. Several men walked alongside her or behind her, forming a silent escort. She felt a pang of anxiety being surrounded by armed strangers without her knight protectors at her side, but it quickly passed as she remembered the feeling of unity with the villagers. *We are one.*

Many of the women and children had already left the safety of their simple homes and were crowding onto the main road. The brightly colored fabrics and simple earth tones of their clothing swirled in front of her. As she neared, some of them began to fall to their knees and pressed their heads to the earth the way the men had done. *Oh no*, she thought with alarm, *they mustn't mistake me as the object of their worship.*

She dismounted and approached one of the women. "Please stand up," she said with a caring voice as she gently grasped the woman's arm and pulled her to her feet, then moved to the next young girl. "I am but a servant, like you." She gestured to those still kneeling on the ground to stand. She raised her voice to reach those farther away. "It is Sharin Dara that your hearts respond to, not me. She alone is worthy of your adoration."

Despite the press of the gathering crowd, she felt someone step close behind her. She looked over her shoulder and saw Lady di Greven standing there, her hand resting on the hilt of the arming sword buckled around her waist, bright green eyes scanning for any sign of threat. She smiled to express her appreciation for the knight's service and to say there was no need for worry. Then her attention was drawn back to the people as someone was putting a necklace of flowers around her neck, then another.

The crowd gradually moved further into the village until they reached what appeared to be the village square. Empty booths and tables indicated that at other times this functioned as the village market. Tall palms and flowering trees provided pleasant shade from the late afternoon sun dropping lower in the eastern sky. She could not tell if the simple wood buildings around the square were homes or storehouses, but they were decorated with brightly painted flowers, birds, and other animals around the doorframes and windows.

The people near her suddenly took a few steps back as someone approached her from behind. She turned and saw Vedic Pujar approaching, surrounded by the warriors of the village. The Vanassi and Remalians had dismounted and led their horses to follow behind the Sheerbahari. The vedic stopped a few paces away and struck the ground twice with the end of his spear. "You come and seek to bewitch my people?" It was more an accusation than a question.

Shiralla sensed the currents of troubled waters around her. "Vedic Pujar, we are only here to help you protect your people."

"And this requires twisting their minds, turning them against the ancestors?" He seemed to be speaking as much to his people as to her. Andric and Bejurn were making their way around the knot of villagers. Adding them to the conversation was only going to complicate matters. She considered trying to disposition the vedic again, but the risk seemed too great.

She needed to de-escalate the situation quickly. "Please forgive my manners. We haven't been properly introduced." It was a jarring transition, but that was a calculated tactic. "I am Shiralla Henden of the Kingdom of Remalia, an intercessor for Sharin Dara and emissary of King Jevorak Laconeus and his son, Prince Andric Laconeus." She curtsied with an appropriate flourish, then stood up straight. "And may I have the honor of knowing your name, Vedic?"

The vedic looked disconcerted for a moment, then he quickly drew himself up and responded in a loud voice. "I am the Vedic Movitra Hashbahanni Bucharpta Pujar, son of Vedic Bucharpta Attowali Daodaddu Pujar, of the Sheerbahari Vanassi people."

"Vedic Pujar, it is a deep honor. With humility and gratitude, we ask for shelter under your roof." She placed her hands together in front of her heart and bowed as she finished, following the Kushaani custom this time rather than the Remalian one. Lady di Greven followed suit. She could not be sure if the traditional greeting she had learned during her time in southern Kushaan would be applicable here, but she hoped it conveyed her intent well enough.

The vedic stood unmoving, perhaps using his silence to assert his dominance. Shiralla was unfazed and simply waited for him to speak. An older woman with a beautiful mix of lustrous white and black hair, partially covered with a purple head scarf fringed in orange, stepped out of the crowd next to the vedic. She wrapped her hand around his upper arm in a way that looked both intimate and supportive, but Shiralla saw her squeeze his arm with strong fingers.

"I see you're familiar with the old ways," the vedic said noncommittally, but Shiralla guessed the decision had already been made.

"I am always trying to learn more of your beautiful culture." The woman's hand squeezed enough to make depressions on the vedic's arm.

"Then my roof is your roof, my board your board, my fire your fire. May you find shelter from the sun and rain all your days." He brought his hands together up to his mouth and kissed his fingertips as he finished, returning her bow stiffly. "This is my heartfire, Naharyttah," the vedic said, introducing the woman at his side.

"Please, you will just call me Ryttah," she said, releasing the vedic's arm and coming to take Shiralla gently by the arm with a warm smile. She had the bearing of a proud woman, and Shiralla was happy to be walking at her side through the crowd of villagers that now kept an arm's distance from the two women as they walked through the square toward the hill with the stone houses and temple.

"You've made quite an impression on our village. This will be all anyone talks about for weeks to come."

"I wish that were true, but I fear it will be swallowed up in the violence that follows on our heels."

Ryttah nodded. "War has come many times over the years. It's as much a fact of life as the flooding of the Meer during the rains. But this is different. I have never felt anything like what you did." She leaned her head a bit closer to Shiralla, and whispered with a hint of awe, "How did you do it?"

It was a question Shiralla had never been asked before. Of course, she had never witnessed anything quite like it herself and was uncertain how to respond. "Sharin Dara has tasked me with sharing her light with your people. The power is hers—I am just a vessel." The smell of something delicious cooking drifted from a nearby house and Shiralla's stomach growled with hunger.

"An empty vessel, apparently. We'll fix that soon enough," Ryttah said pleasantly, patting Shiralla's arm in a motherly way as they climbed the rough stone road up the hill from the village square toward the temple. Ryttah chatted amiably as they walked, asking Shiralla about her home and her family until they reached their destination.

The vedic's residence was one of the last before reaching the crest of the hill. A low stone wall, no more than knee high, separated the road from a beautiful garden with flowering bushes and vines crawling up arched lattice-work frames covering a stone pathway leading to the two-story house. The dark wood framing the doorways, windows, and along the eaves was a stark contrast to the white plaster-covered walls. Ryttah led Shiralla along the garden path around the outside of the house to a tree-shaded terrace veranda that offered a breathtaking panoramic view of the river cutting a path through the jungle to the west, the village below them to the south, and the rice paddies and more vast jungle to the east, backlit by the setting sun.

Her heart dropped at the sight of smoke rising in the distance from the dense jungle further south. She wanted to address the urgency of getting the people to safety, but no doubt that would dominate the conversation in the hours ahead. For now, she allowed herself to be seated on one of the wide ground cushions designed for relaxed reclining, though Shiralla sat upright to remain as dignified as possible. Ryttah gave orders to two women who came through one of the arched doors to bring everything her guests might need to be comfortable and refresh themselves.

Lady di Greven stepped to the side to stand guard in as unobtrusive a manner as possible while the vedic ushered Prince Andric, Master Ve'Aurben, Emissary sud-Ta, and Jalanti to seats of their own. She noticed Bejurn managed to subtly steer Jalanti to sit next to the prince. It seemed an obvious ploy, though she doubted Andric minded at all. Knight Commander Nophet declined to sit and instead took a guard position on the other side of the group. He seemed to glower at the intercessor when she looked at him. Things were going to be more complicated with him after what happened today, and she worried her actions would make it easier for him to pull the prince toward Teraithia. *One problem at a time*, she told herself.

The four Vanassi and Barak seemed at ease reclining on the cushions, but Shiralla and Prince Andric remained sitting upright. It was not Remalian custom to be so informal, especially in mixed social company.

Ryttah looked at them, concern on her face. "Is something wrong, or something you need?"

"No, Mistress Pujar," Andric said politely. "You have a beautiful view here. This reminds me of the view from my family's summer estate. Although I must admit, the scenery is somewhat tainted by the certain threat of the approaching enemy forces."

The young woman who was handing simple glazed earthenware cups of wine to the guests looked at the prince with concern, then quickly averted her eyes as she handed a cup to Shiralla.

"How many spears do you think approach?" the vedic asked.

"Our scouts estimate approximately three hundred seventy soldiers," Andric stated matter-of-factly. "Between Emissary sud-Ta and I, we have about seventy soldiers with us. How many fighters do you have here in the village?"

"We have forty prime spears, though we can double that number if needed."

"That still leaves us outnumbered more than two to one," Bejurn said. "Movitra, surely you can see the wisdom in avoiding this fight until we can muster superior forces."

"I can see the wisdom in getting you cleaned up for supper," Ryttah interjected with a smile. Two young women placed a carved wooden bowl with a towel in it next to each guest and poured steaming hot water from copper kettles over the towels. The vedic seemed to be the only one who could handle the steaming towel immediately and started wiping his leathery face, neck, and hands. The others had to let their towels cool a bit before they could do the same. Shiralla found it delightfully refreshing to have the closest thing to a hot bath she had experienced in several days. Cleaning with cold water was effective enough, but nothing about it was pleasant. She was dismayed to see the amount of dirt that appeared on her white towel. She envied Jalanti's beautiful darker skin that hid the grime of the road so well.

When they finished, the bowls were cleared away and trays of fresh fruits and cheeses with warm flatbread were placed on the ground near the feet of the guests. The vedic and Ryttah moved their cushions near the trays and laid forward. Bejurn and Jalanti followed suit, so Shiralla did likewise. Andric was the last to maneuver himself into position, clearly no more comfortable with it than Shiralla was. It was strange to eat lying down, and she had a hard time finding a position that felt even close to natural. Fortunately, the food was delicious, although one of the cheeses had a sour taste that made her question whether it was even safe to eat.

"We could be much more effective fighting the Kushaani if we could find dry, flat ground," Andric said, not following Bejurn's lead in pushing for the villagers to flee into the jungle. "Is there anywhere nearby like that?"

"Perhaps that would be best for your men, but for us that would be very bad. The trees are our allies—they protect us. We should depart when the moon rises and run swiftly to Pradan-ur. There we can ambush the invaders more easily."

"Do you know this Pradan-ur?" Prince Andric asked Bejurn.

"Yes," Bejurn said flatly. Shiralla guessed he was not pleased the prince was considering the vedic's plan, no doubt making it harder, if not impossible, to convince Movitra to lead his people away from the impending conflict.

"Well, an ambush could work. What is the layout of Pradan-ur? Is there an elevated place or concealed location where we could position archers to attack from their flanks? And what about an envelopment? We could block them on one end and you could sweep in from the rear."

"Maybe you could have your priestess control their minds and we could avoid any fighting at all." Shiralla could not tell if the vedic meant it sarcastically or was actually suggesting it, but either way was bad.

Before she could answer, Master Ve'Aurben responded. "I had considered that myself, but dispositioning does not, at least in theory, work that way. You see, the dispositioner does not impose their will on the subject, particularly when it's contrary to the intent or will of the subject. It's more akin to fanning an ember that is already afire than controlling the flame itself. For that, you would need met'elan. Now, if one could combine the two, perhaps—"

"Master Ve'Aurben," Prince Andric cut him off. "Thank you for your insight, but I believe we will have to explore that idea at a later time."

"Our ancestors will come to Pradan-ur to aid us in our fight," the vedic continued. Shiralla knew that most tribes in Kushaan revered their ancestors almost as much as the gods themselves. Some even had superstitions about ancestors coming back to punish or reward deeds done by the living, but those seemed to just be stories parents told to make their children behave.

"You mean another tribe or village?" Andric asked, sounding as if he was trying not to be offensive.

"No, I mean the spirits of our ancestors who have passed to the other side. The veil between our world and the next is thin there, and their spirits can reach through to aid us."

"You don't believe the spirits go to the realm of their god?" Andric asked, sounding dubious.

"Wherever they are, they continue to watch and care for us, as we do for them. They will be there to help us, you will see."

The prince turned the conversation back to battle strategies, which Shiralla had no particular interest in. Instead, her mind wandered back to the scene on the road when she had so much power at her disposal. Would she ever have that again? She imagined standing in the midst of the two forces tomorrow, dispositioning them into a truce. The scene played itself over and over, both sides falling to their knees and bowing before her. The ground shook with Sharin Dara's power.

With a sudden start she awoke, embarrassed that she had drifted off. She glanced around furtively to see if anyone had noticed, but something was wrong. Someone nearby was shouting and everyone was climbing to their feet. Lady di Greven stepped forward to offer Shiralla a hand up.

"What is it?" Shiralla asked, trying to stifle a yawn. It had grown darker and torches in wrought iron stands around the veranda were burning brightly. She noticed with chagrin that different food was on the trays and concluded she must have been asleep longer than she realized. The vedic was running through the garden out to the road with the others following on his heels.

"Some kind of trouble at the temple it seems," Lady di Greven answered. "We should go as well." Together they hurried back along the dark garden path out to the road. Several people stood looking up the hill toward the temple where a crowd carrying torches and lamps had gathered. She could see Movitra and Ryttah were already hurrying up the hill as well.

Sir Mar stood in the road, surprisingly in his full armor. "Things may have gotten a bit out of hand," he said in what was almost certainly an understatement if she knew him at all. He easily kept pace with her as she rushed after the vedic, worried something terrible was about to transpire—if it was not already too late. "You appear to have inspired a rapid change of devotion in some of the villagers, which has not been well received by others. They may be trying to work out their differences up at the temple."

The road ended at the wide stone steps that climbed the last several feet to the hilltop. Sir Mar took the lead and pushed his way through the crowd to open a path for her. Several people were shouting, and she was sure one of the voices was Vedic Pujar.

"Enough of this!" and "Stop!" were met with other angry shouts of "She alone!" and "Her will must be done!"

She looked around in alarm at the chaos in front of her as she finally arrived at the center of the conflict. Some of the villagers were smashing the temple's statues while others were pulling on a rope tied around a statue of Yonvaar, trying to topple it like the others already lying on the ground. Another group of villagers stood with their backs against Sharin Dara's statue, crude weapons in hand, looking like cornered animals ready to fight for their lives against another group that appeared ready to attack at any moment.

Without thinking she rushed forward to place herself between the two groups. "Stop! What are you doing?" she cried out. Some of the villagers redirected their ire toward her, while others dropped to their knees and bowed to the ground at her approach. An older woman swiped a hand at Shiralla's face, but Sir Mar grabbed the woman's arm and firmly restrained her with a gauntleted hand until she stepped back, rubbing her arm. A fierce anger burned in her eyes.

One of the men holding the rope released it and bowed. "We are following your commands, priestess."

"My commands?" she asked, shocked and confused by his words. "What do you mean? I never said anything of the sort."

"But you clearly taught us that she alone is worthy of adoration," the man said, gesturing emphatically toward Sharin Dara's statue behind a wall of armed villagers. "Did you not?"

Shiralla's heart sank at hearing her words twisted in such a way. "I only meant—"

"The blasphemy of worshipping the false gods must be brought to an end!"

Sharin Dara, guide me, Shiralla prayed fervently. Ardent devotion was admirable, desirable even, but she could not help but recall Warden Commander Sammet's zealotry in Tarsapta. Revulsion welled up inside her at the thought that this could go the same way if not quelled. "You cannot worship Sharin Dara by doing actions contrary to her will. You do this in her name, but these actions are more in keeping with the teachings of Teraithia or Akraharr. Sharin Dara teaches collective beneficence and harmony. You cannot achieve that through conflict and destruction." She thought she saw doubt begin to show on some of the faces illuminated by the flickering light of the torches and lanterns.

"Blood has been spilled for a thousand generations because of the other gods," the man countered. "If Sharin Dara was the only one, we would have peace. The others must be brought down!" He grabbed the rope and began pulling on the statue again. Shiralla felt a draw on her elan and instantly resisted. She assumed it was Prince Andric but had no idea what he intended to do. Suddenly the rope snapped, and the villagers stumbled backward.

The prince spoke, his voice amplified and echoing loudly the way she had heard some clerics do when attuned to divinessence, though if he was, it must be to one of the gods other than Sharin Dara. "The people must decide for themselves whom to worship. The choice cannot be made for them." The commotion stopped and all eyes fixed on Andric. "Do not contend with one another. You will have fighting enough tomorrow. But you will fight to protect your families and your homes and your freedom, not with each other."

She waited to hear more, but the prince remained silent as he looked slowly from one face to another. When he finally spoke again, his voice was his own. "Return now to your homes and prepare for tomorrow."

Slowly people began to move. Movitra and Ryttah quietly directed the people to disperse. As the villagers made their way down the hill, Shiralla looked with dismay at the damage done to the shrine's statues. She wished she could set things right, but she was not even sure she knew what that meant anymore. She also wanted to ask the prince what had just happened to him, but she knew to leave well enough alone for now. There was nothing left to do tonight but try to get some sleep. She turned to leave, but the prince stopped her.

"Intercessor, you will stay." She faced the prince, steeling herself for what was going to be an unpleasant discussion. "I would speak with you alone."

She looked at Sir Mar who stood silently nearby, moonlight glinting off his polished armor. She took comfort in having him nearby but didn't want to provoke the prince's ire further. "Thank you for your service, Sir Mar. That will be all for tonight." He saluted curtly, but somehow his brusqueness gave her comfort this time.

They waited for the holy knight to make his way down the steps before the prince spoke. "What am I to do with you?" He sounded angry but kept his voice controlled. "We're on a diplomatic mission, and you're riling up the locals against one another. What were you thinking?"

"That was certainly not my intention, my lord." She could feel herself putting on formality like armor and tried to resist the instinct. It would be better if she could remain personal. "I was trying to inspire unity."

"By telling them that Sharin Dara is the only god they should worship? Sammet already tried that in Tarsapta, and you saw how that turned out." The prince's strained words were a slap in the face.

"That isn't what I meant. I just didn't want them to misplace their devotion toward Sharin Dara onto me."

"Well, you could not have chosen your words more poorly from the looks of things," he said, gesturing to the destruction around them.

"I should think you would understand better than anyone what it's like to have destruction come from your words being taken the wrong way, Your Highness." The prince stiffened and she instantly regretted her words. It was a petty attack, unworthy of a representative of Sharin Dara and servant to the crown.

She swallowed her pride and anger and forced herself to apologize. "Forgive me, my lord. That was out of line." He looked away, his jaw muscles working as he clenched his teeth, his anger palpable. She sighed, fearing she had already done irreparable harm to their relationship.

She took a desperate gamble, hoping to salvage some shred of connection. "Andric," she said gently, taking the prince by both arms and stepping softly into the line of his gaze. She looked earnestly into the eyes. "I know you think the Kushaani attack is your fault, but it's not. I know you feel you're alone, but you're not."

"Maybe I would be better off if I was." He was trying to be hurtful.

She released his arms but remained close. "If that is what you wish, I will remain here when you continue on to Sunapra."

"What I wish is that just one damn thing would go right!"

"You've gotten us this far," she rested her hand on his arm, "and I have every confidence that you will lead us where the gods intend for us to be."

"I fear the gods' intentions may be to cause the world to burn."

"If that were true, they could have done it a long time ago. I think perhaps instead they want us to help them stop that from happening."

"Then I suppose we should stop setting so many fires."

"Easier said than done for The Firebrand," she said with a teasing smile. Andric laughed, and the anger seemed to ease. She dared hope things would be better.

"I'll do my best if you will," he said lightly.

"Deal." She turned back toward the village and took Andric by the arm, letting him escort her from the hilltop. Smoke from burning villages to the south drifted through the moonlit sky.

"Now if only we can get the Kushaani to agree," he said grimly.

"I'm sure you will show them the light," she replied, patting his arm with more assurance than she felt.

CHAPTER XLIV
ANDRIC

Pools of torchlight around the village square held the deep darkness of the early morning hour at bay. Fenthal, the larger of the two moons, had already disappeared, and Silmal was only a quarter full, offering little light to the world. Despite getting only a few hours of fitful rest, Andric was wide awake, his blood pumping hard in his veins in anticipation of fighting his first real battle. The Vanassi warriors chatted quietly amongst themselves while waiting for the Remalians to finish their preparations. Andric was eager to be on the move, not the least because he would be free of having to deal with Intercessor Henden, at least for a few hours.

They had ended the disastrous events last night on a positive note, but this morning she returned to clamoring for more negotiations—for a chance to make amends. "If Your Highness would please reconsider. You felt how much power Sharin Dara has put at my disposal. Let me put it to use in trying to avoid more bloodshed. I am certain she will guide us in finding another path."

Andric wanted to just command her to stay behind in Sheerbahar, but he decided to give blunt logic a try as a last resort. He pulled the priestess aside and spoke in a hushed but stern voice, the way he had seen his father do with more than one noble that needed cowing. "Intercessor, it's possible that those of us who confront the Kushaani won't survive the day. If that's the case, I need you to continue to Sunapra and do your best to complete the mission. Remalia can't afford to lose both of us out there today." He knew it was unlikely he would fall in the battle, with all the protection of the Divinarim around him, but it was an undeniable possibility nagging at the back of his mind. It was hard to tell in the flickering torchlight, but she looked like she was preparing a rebuttal. He feared he would have to resort to commanding her to stay after all.

At last, she bowed her head, acquiescing. "As you wish. Is there anything else you would have me do, Your Highness?"

"Take care of Barak. He won't..." Andric stopped, not wanting to think about what would become of Barak if things went badly today. The priestess put a hand on his arm. She had done the same last night, up the hill at the temple. Her touch was a welcome comfort. Was it something about her, or just the touch of any woman in this moment? He thought about Jalanti and wished it were her standing with him instead.

"Sharin Dara's blessings be upon you, my lord," she said gently, then curtsied before retreating into the darkness. She truly was regal in her demeanor and in the way she carried herself in these circumstances, a fitting advisor even if she could be overbearing at times. Though they may disagree on the manner in which they accomplished things, he was reassured by her presence.

Andric returned to check Jase's progress in preparing Kobo for battle. He passed Knight Commander Nophet who stood stoically watching the prince's movements, keeping an eye out for any threat. It was still difficult not thinking of him as the archpaladin, especially when armored, as he was now, in his distinct red-gold plate and winged helm. Andric was grateful for Nophet's faithful service, especially going into battle before the day was over. There was no other Divinar he would rather have at his side.

He had even enjoyed their occasional theological discussions in the long hours on the journey here. He wished more Teraithians viewed their religion the way Nophet did, as a path to gaining greater influence through personal excellence. It was the part of the goddess's doctrine Andric had always been attracted to, but it was only one part. So many of her teachings justified pursuing any means to obtain more power. As tempting as that path might be, it always seemed to lead to far more harm than good as far as Andric could tell.

"He's ready, my lord," Jase said confidently, giving Kobo's shoulder an affectionate pat. "I wish I could be there to see you tear through those Kushaani." Andric knew what Jase really wanted was to fight the Kushaani himself; it was a sentiment Andric understood well. He had debated whether to let Jase come with him. His squire's combat training was improving, but he was not ready, especially with the odds they faced today.

"I know, but I need you here when I get back," Andric said, hoping he didn't have to have another argument about someone staying behind. Gratefully, Barak had put up no such resistance.

Captain Major Min appeared next to him without a sound. "The men are ready, my lord." Sa'ari warriors had a reputation for being stealthy, and Andric wondered whether it was an innate ability, some special Sa'ari training, or his years as a scout that made Min so quiet when he moved. Andric motioned for the captain major to follow him to where the vedic was talking with a few of his men.

"Vedic Pujar, we are ready to move out." The vedic had dressed in the accoutrements of a traditional Kushaani warrior. His hair, what little there was, had been slicked back and his face was painted in streaks of red and black the width of two fingers. More paint was streaked on his neck and arms where his bare skin was exposed. Under his arm he carried a leather helmet covered with the orange and black striped skin of some animal Andric had never seen before and encircled with a tight iron band. The same striped skin covered much of his armor as well, though it was scarred in places as if it had been torn long ago and repaired on several occasions. He also wore bands of red silk tied to his elbows and knees, which should have meant he was part of the Vidyahar, the elite warriors of Kushaan and favored guards of the emperors. He even carried the heavy, straight blade of the Vidyahar across his back, fastened with a wide leather belt tooled with images of plants and animals. Given the current political situation, it seemed a strange thing for any of the Vanassi to be wearing. However, if the Vedic truly had been a Vidyahar warrior at some point, which Andric could not quite imagine, it would have been long ago.

The Vedic looked doubtful at the assembled Remalians. "Do you not want any war paint? Anything to become the warrior?"

Andric felt confused but did his best to keep it from his face. He could not help but raise an eyebrow at the offer of face paint, though. The thought of something so primitive on the riders of Remalia was almost laughable. "No, thank you."

"I don't understand. Will you do nothing to put off yourself and get ready for something so barbaric as battle?"

Andric glanced around. His men stood at the ready, fully armored and armed, waiting for the order to mount up. He didn't see anything lacking. "I assure you; we are more than ready."

The Vedic seemed somewhat disappointed, almost saddened. "But what will you do when you return? Will you merely take off your armor and assume the warrior inside you will go with it? My apologies," Movitra seemed to abruptly remember his manners, "I don't know your customs as I should."

Andric was surprised to find himself wishing Shiralla was here to help him. It was clear there was something he was missing. "We remove the armor and set our weapons down when they aren't needed, but we are always warriors." He thought about the assassination attempt back in Teris. "You never know when you will have to fight for your life. A warrior must be ready to fight at any moment."

Movitra looked saddened at the prince's answer. "I see. That... that must make you great warriors." His words did not sound like a compliment.

Andric's curiosity was piqued. He was eager to be on the move, but he felt this was something worth understanding. "Does the face paint somehow mean more to the Vanassi? I assumed it was just a tradition of your people." He hoped he was not being offensive by asking.

Vedic Pujar looked at the ground and adjusted the black leather sword strap to a more comfortable position. "It is tradition, but it's more than that," he began hesitantly but his pace quickened as he continued, his eyes fixed intently on the prince. "When we go to war, we see things, do things, that we would never do here," he said, gesturing to the village. "We paint ourselves to become something we are not—something savage, ready for killing without mercy.

"Before we return home, we wash ourselves of all this, wash away the warrior we had to become to protect our lands and our families. We leave the warrior and his terrible deeds out there," Movitra said, gesturing toward the jungle, "and only return home once we are ourselves again."

Andric had always found the Kushaani idea of war paint and garish battlefield attire somewhat primitive and uncivilized, but now he saw it in a different light. He was not about to take the vedic up on the offer to paint himself, but he could appreciate their tradition. "Thank you, Vedic. I am honored that you shared your custom with me. It is time to have our warriors do what they must to protect your lands."

"I am grateful to have enlightened you on our ways. I hope to meet you afterward across the table of my house again." Movitra bowed, then gave a high-pitched whistle. The Sheerbahari warriors hit the butts of their spears on the ground twice, then formed two long columns on the road behind the mounted Vanassi warriors accompanying Bejurn. Andric was not pleased to be riding nearly in the rear, but he had relented in the end. These were not his lands; he was a guest here, and he would carry himself with dignity even if they didn't treat him with the honor one of his station deserved.

Min gave the signal for the Remalians to mount, and the sound of shifting metal and leather filled the quiet darkness. Jase helped Andric climb into the saddle, then wished him gods' speed before moving away. Kobo pawed the ground, no doubt as anxious as Andric to finally be moving. He enjoyed riding his palfrey, Sunfire, but it was nothing compared to the power of having his charger beneath him. The prince patted Kobo's neck. "Soon enough, boy."

As if on cue, the men ahead of him started walking. They carried their long spears over their shoulders, angled back toward Andric. He gave them plenty of space before spurring Kobo forward, Min on one side, Nophet on the other. The village square quickly narrowed to the dirt road out of the village, leaving room for only two abreast. Nophet and another Divinar moved ahead, while Min rode at his side.

A few village elders stood with flickering torches at the side of the road, blessing the soldiers as they passed. Andric felt the light touch of Yerin's divinessence from a man who looked like he had no teeth, his wrinkled lips practically disappearing inside his sunken mouth. From an elderly woman on the other side of the road, Sharin Dara's divinessence infused with a feeling of reassurance brushed across his consciousness. Shiralla had informed him of this tradition, and he had instructed Nophet not to intervene. Andric was certain he was in no danger from the mild dispositioning the elders offered as the gods' blessings upon the departing warriors.

They passed the dark rice paddies and turned south, back along the road toward the Kushaani force that had pursued them for the past few days. In a few hours, they would split their force, with the Sheerbahari fighters going to set an ambush at the place they called Pradan-ur. Apparently many battles had been fought there, and the Vanassi had some kind of tradition about the spirits of their ancestors coming to help fight the invaders. Andric was not sure what to believe, but anything that helped them was fine with him, even if was just superstition.

The difficult part was luring the Kushaani there. The plan was for the Remalians and some of the Sunapran riders to engage the Kushaani and then retreat, hopefully drawing the invaders into pursuing them into the awaiting ambush. The accounts he had heard from Stephir, Min, and others about their skirmishes with the Kushaani made it seem like this was a common tactic, which made him wonder why they wouldn't see through the ruse this time. *Because they won't want to*, had been Bejurn's answer, and the vedic concurred. That seemed like a thin hope to pin their strategy on, but in the end, he had been left with little choice but to agree.

He didn't like the idea of being bait or of running away, even if it was strategic. He was certain they could easily win the battle if they could just find a decent piece of dry, flat ground in this accursed country. Kobo hadn't been able to run full out since they entered Kushaan, and he had been getting restless. Today, both of them were finally going to put their years of training to the test. At least as far as the fighting was concerned. It was bad enough that he was technically under a foreign command, but he especially chaffed at the idea of taking orders from a rice farmer. He had found out that little tidbit last night from Min. The commander of the Vanassi troops, and the one Andric had agreed to accept direction from during the battle, turned out to be a common rice farmer in Sheerbahar. He hoped to the gods Stephir never found out.

The noises in the jungle around them grew louder as pre-dawn light illuminated the sky overhead. It was the same as so many previous mornings, and Andric couldn't help but feel there should be some warning in the weather, some unusual chill or a morning fog, some sense of foreboding to let the world know there was to be an impending battle. People would die this day, perhaps a lot of people—perhaps even a prince. Shouldn't there be a sign?

In front of him, Nophet held up a hand to signal a halt. They stood quietly on the road, not moving. Andric's senses were alert, trying to listen for any sound of an attack or other sign of danger. "Why did we stop?" Andric asked Min. "I thought we weren't splitting for another couple of hours."

"I can't say, Your Highness. I'm sure we'll find out soon enough." Min didn't sound particularly troubled, and Andric admired the Sa'ari's calm demeanor. It conveyed an unconscious confidence that spoke more loudly than all the arrogant posturing in the world. He wondered if others felt he conveyed the same confidence. He certainly hoped so.

The column started moving again without explanation. "Maybe General Long Grain had to water the trees," Andric joked under his breath to Min as they spurred their mounts forward.

"I found out he was actually a rather renowned general among the Peljathi. He was captured by the Vanassi many years ago and was settled in Sheerbahar after his period of requital was over."

"They have a famous general working the fields as a rice farmer? How humiliating. I suppose if the Vanassi beat him they don't consider him much of a general anymore."

"On the contrary. They hold him in rather high regard. They spoke of how well he defended his people before finally being captured. That's why they put him in command today."

"Well, I hope history doesn't repeat itself. Being made a rice farmer might be fine with him, but I don't think it would quite suit me."

Andric meant it in jest, but Min didn't laugh or even smile. He kept his eyes on the road ahead as he replied casually. "Winning or losing isn't always the best metric by which to judge a commander's worth. Sometimes the greatest feats are managing to keep your losses to a minimum." It didn't sound like a rebuke to Andric, more like a perspective born of personal experience.

Andric wanted to probe further, but he saw the Vanassi commander on his horse waiting on the side of the road as they approached. Min's story would have to wait. "Prince Andric, may I join you?" Min drew back to make room for Commander Navindra to ride next to the prince.

Andric hoped the man hadn't heard his earlier comments. No sense in needlessly antagonizing him. "What is it, Commander?"

"Our scouts report the Kushaani pushed into the night and are closer than we anticipated. Now we must run to reach the road to Pradan-ur first. I would ask that you ride ahead and slow them as best you can to give us more time. You will need to stop and fight a few skirmishes. This will mean more losses, but it still gives us the greatest chance of victory in the end."

"Is there anywhere to set up an initial, smaller ambush? Archers and a small group of lancers?" Andric asked, trying to think of the best way to slow them down while minimizing losses, an uncomfortable echo of Min's words just moments before.

"We don't want to make them cautious by using that tactic too soon. We need them chasing you as far into Pradan-ur as possible before we spring our trap."

"Min, any thoughts?" Andric asked over his shoulder.

"Your idea wasn't a bad one, Your Highness. I suggest fists of six riders each wait on the road with bows. After they fire, they'll retreat past the next fists waiting on the road, who will shoot when the Kushaani catch up, then rotate to the rear. Space them a quarter mile apart. It will only make the horses sprint a short distance at a time."

Commander Navindra nodded his approval. "Don't space your fists too regularly. Always make the Kushaani wonder how far they must come to find you," the commander advised. It was a good idea, and Andric wished he had thought of it. "Also, I will leave our scouts with you to watch your flanks in the forest. The Kushaani will become wary of using the road and will try to attack you from the sides. Let them take the forest paths. It will be slower, which is the most important thing for now. Always be sure to keep them behind you, or you will end up in trouble quickly." Any reservations Andric had about following a rice farmer were gone. "Any questions?"

"No, I understand our task." It seemed simple enough. Andric heard his father's voice saying the words he had said a hundred times. *War never goes as planned.*

"Then I wish you gods' speed. You should hurry. We will meet you in Pradan-ur."

Commander Navindra kicked his horse into a quicker pace and rode ahead while Captain Major Min took his place at Andric's side again. "We should tell the men now," Min advised. "Give them the time on the ride there to prepare for what's ahead."

Andric called a halt and gathered the men on the road. All the Sheerbahari warriors were already taking off at a measured run followed by the mounted Vanassi. A handful of the Vanassi scouts joined the Remalians to receive their instructions. Andric was surprised to see Sir Mar among them. His duty was to protect Intercessor Henden. It was always good to have another sword, but if for some reason Mar did not survive the day, would the priestess blame Andric? Or perhaps this was her idea in the first place—a way to keep tabs on the prince. That thought irked him, but he let it go.

It only took a few minutes to organize them into fists and ensure everyone was clear on their orders. The scouts informed him their ride should take less than two hours. They quickly remounted and set off at a quick but sustainable pace. They didn't want their horses winded before their plan was even put into motion.

In short order, they caught up to the Vanassi soldiers, who moved to one side of the road with spears raised and cheered as the Remalians sped by. They passed a village with no signs of life. He was certain it was one they had warned to flee before the Kushaani arrived. It was some small comfort that their plan today might save this village. He tried to imagine where he would be if the Sheerbahari had chosen to flee instead of fighting. Probably close to Sunapra by now. For a moment he wished he was there instead of here, but quickly shoved the thought aside. He had been waiting for months for the chance to fight. Now that it was here, he was not going to let a slight case of nerves ruin it for him.

As the minutes ticked by, he occupied himself with imagining the victory he almost felt certain would be his today. Scouts pointed out where the road veered east toward Pradan-ur as they rode further south. They passed another small, empty village. He hoped that attacking the Kushaani would cause them to spare this one in pursuing him instead. That thought took him back to again envisioning himself putting the enemy to the sword. He was contemplating another battle scenario when he saw scouts ahead on the road just before a sharp bend in a hillside, signaling Andric to halt. They would have picked a spot far enough away from the Kushaani to not be in immediate danger, but he couldn't help looking around for any sign of a threat.

"Report," Min called out when they were close enough to speak without shouting.

"They burned Rahgpurrah, less than a league away, but no villagers were there. They will be here soon." The scout's Vanassi accent was thick, but Andric was getting used to it and he could understand with little difficulty. "Some Peljathi warriors have joined the Kushaani."

Andric bit back a curse. "How many?"

"We could not be sure. Maybe fifty... maybe a hundred."

"We have scouts in the forest?" Min asked.

"Four on each side. They will not get past without you knowing."

"Well, the road should keep most of them funneled. It will have to do," Andric replied. "I'll stay with the first fist."

"My lord," Nophet said, the objection already in his voice. "May I suggest you would be most effective in ensuring the correct positioning of the other fists along the road? In a game of cat and mouse, it is better to be the cat."

Andric knew a commander's priority was to command, not necessarily to fight, but appearing cowardly was anathema to the prince. "Min and the scouts can figure that out. I have to stay here to ensure our strategy is sound, or make adjustments as needed." He knew Nophet wouldn't leave him without protection though. "You and one other will stay with me. Have the others wait with the next two fists." Nophet gave the orders as Andric turned to Quarian. "Ride back along the road and put the fists wherever you think best."

"Good luck, Your Highness," Min said before turning to go. Andric found it strange the man never invoked the gods. Yet another enigma about his first officer he would have to dig into later. He was also surprised to see Sir Mar staying where he was. Andric knew practically nothing about the man except he was a member of the elite Order of the Third Wave and he had fought Kuldrith near Eastgate, so he had to be at least a halfway decent fighter. "Sir Mar, are you joining us?"

"Unless Your Highness objects."

"The more the merrier." Andric noticed Nophet seemed to look at the man askance. Perhaps some professional rivalry? The prince dismissed the thought and turned his attention to preparing for the attack.

The only weapon Andric usually rode with was his arming sword, but today he also carried his lance and shield. They wouldn't be useful in hit-and-run skirmishes on the road, but he hoped to put them to good use once the trap was sprung at Pradan-ur. He had considered taking a bow from one of his soldiers but decided instead to try one of the elants he had been practicing with the elantir back at the Remalian camp before setting out on this mission. The soldiers in his fist were busy preparing their bows and working out their positions on the road to shoot and flee quickly without running into each other. He didn't want to interrupt, but he needed to inform them what he intended. He wished he had practiced this on the journey, but he had not anticipated needing it.

"You all should expect to see flashes of light in front of the first ranks of Kushaani," Andric announced. "Ignore them." He received a couple of side glances but couldn't tell if there was judgment or just curiosity behind them. He put it out of his mind and instead focused on opening his elantic center. His thoughts were racing, laced with anxiety about the strategy, how the soldiers would perform, what tricks the Kushaani would try to employ, and who would die.

With some difficulty, he managed to quiet the whirlwind enough to open a void in his center and fill it with a small flow of his elan. It was not enough to perform the elant he intended, but drawing from himself was an easier place to start. As he became more centered, he slowly extended his awareness outward. There was Nophet, always at his side. And Divinar Pratzic. He could feel them, bright points of intense elan, but could not draw on their life force. As Divinar, they were somehow protected from elantic influences, including siphoning their elan.

He reached out to the dense, wild forest on either side of the road, teaming with life. It would be easy to draw what he needed from the plants, animals, and insects closest to him, but not without doing irreparable harm to them or even killing them. Instead, he sent out small channels like thin roots snaking throughout the area, connecting to countless points of life.

The elan came as a trickle at first, but he kept it outside himself, pooling it in the air around him before it became too much to safely hold within his body. The discomfort of the chaotic vibrations as the elan writhed through all the modalities was almost like an itch he could not scratch. He willed the elan into two streams and sent them flowing toward the bend in the road and began attuning them to the modalities he needed. Usually, elants requiring multiple modalities were performed by a group of elantir, each one responsible for a single modality. Attuning to more than one modality was like trying to sing more than one note at the same time. Andric was used to practicing alone and could usually manage two modalities well enough.

He modulated one of the streams to thet, which would produce the light. The other he coaxed into yldrath, which would cause the light to spread out like a flash. He closed his eyes for better concentration, struggling to keep the two flows separate but synchronized until the moment he was ready for them to merge. The yldrath flow started to waiver, slipping toward vis.

Bowstrings snapped. Without thinking Andric tied the two flows together, twisting them just so. He opened his eyes in time to see the front ranks of Kushaani warriors throw up their woven wicker shields. There was no large flash of light as Andric had intended, but instead, a thousand tiny sparks burst among the Kushaani ranks. Screams of pain and fear erupted from the men who ducked and swatted at their faces.

Andric was perplexed, but there was no time to wait and watch. The Remalians turned their horses and raced back along the road. The jungle flew past as the horses sprinted the short distance to where the next fist of soldiers waited on the road. They had left the center of the road open so the retreating riders could pass easily. Andric was tempted to stop and wait with the second fist, wanting to try his elant again and figure out what had gone wrong. However, if the Kushaani were chasing after them, there likely wasn't enough time. It was better to stick with the plan.

They slowed a bit and Nophet turned to the prince. "I suppose the time spent with the elantir was not entirely a waste after all." Andric could not tell if the knight commander was teasing or complimenting him. It was hard to imagine either one. Andric played it safe and simply nodded.

The road rose before sloping down into a wash between two hills where the next fist waited. It was difficult to see them because of the angle of the slope, which made it an excellent place for an attack. Andric reined Kobo to a halt. The others came to a halt as well. "I think I should wait here and try that again."

Some of the soldiers laughed and Andric was chagrined. "Aye, Your Highness," one of the men said enthusiastically. "That'll slow 'em down more than our bolts will." Others nodded their agreement, smiling. Chagrin turned to confusion. A soldier from the third fist asked what had happened. "The Firebrand here gave them a face full of embers, like a swarm of flaming firebees." The other men nodded. Andric was unsure what he had done, but he was not about to admit it was an accident or prove it by failing to repeat the elant.

The Vanassi scout spoke, though Andric couldn't tell if he was angry or scared. "Prince, we did not know you were an elan master. Did the vedic instruct you about wielding elan on the sacred grounds?"

Andric felt embarrassed at being called an elan master in front of his men. He wondered if this was how Barak felt being given the title *master*, but he was more confused by the scout's words. "No, I have no idea what you are speaking about."

"Forgive me for speaking plainly, but it is forbidden to touch elan in Pradan-ur."

"Why?" Andric asked, more surprised than upset by the strange revelation.

"The larran. It is dangerous."

Andric didn't understand, but now was not the time to explore their superstitions. He had no intention of performing met'elan during battle.

"Thank you for informing me. I will refrain."

The scout nodded, apparently satisfied. "I believe you should wait at the road to Pradan-ur. Seeing you go that way gives the best chance they will follow." Andric agreed and wished his men gods' graces before continuing up the road.

They passed two more ambush points before reaching the road to Pradan-ur where Min waited with another fist. "How do things look, Your Highness?" the captain major asked.

"As well as could be expected, I suppose. We'll just have to wait and see what comes up the road. I'm staying here with you." Andric sent the rest of the soldiers ahead, then took a position in the middle of the east road where the Kushaani would be sure to see him. After complimenting Min on the excellent selection of ambush points, they settled into silent waiting. Andric set his mind to trying to figure out what had happened with his elant. He wished Barak were here to help him. No doubt he would have a half dozen theories already.

The anxiety and boredom of waiting for the next attack soon pushed him from merely thinking the problem through to trying to recreate the elant. The scout's warning came to mind, but they weren't in Pradan-ur yet. He opened his center and reached out to draw elan into a pool, each step as he had done before. Two streams, modulated to thet and yldrath, flowed toward the junction in the road, held in check by his will. He remembered the yldrath stream had started to waiver, slipping toward vis. That must be part of the answer. Vis and thet could be combined in a certain ratio to make a spark, but he had pulled the modulation back toward yldrath. Perhaps he had somehow managed to channel all three modalities together at the last moment.

Andric was disappointed. He knew it was possible, but it required a level of mastery well beyond his own to manage three flows. Perhaps if he tried to change it at the last moment. He tried to create the third modality but started to lose the flow of elan from the forest. There were just too many variables to maintain while experimenting in the middle of a skirmish. He decided it was best to settle for the elant he had intended the first time.

The next fist of riders should have arrived by now. One of the soldiers broke the silence, pointing above the treetops. "Smoke."

Andric's heart sank. Apparently catching him was not urgent enough to keep them from burning the abandoned village. Anger stirred in him, causing his grasp on the elan to waiver momentarily. He closed his eyes and imagined the elan cascading over him like a waterfall, washing away everything else. Once again centered, he waited patiently until finally the next fist came riding up the road. All six were present. No losses so far. The third fist came just minutes later. That was not a good sign. It meant the Kushaani hadn't slowed down as they had hoped.

"Report," Captain Major Min called out to the lead rider as they approached.

"They rushed us. No hesitation. We fired, but they just took the casualties and tried to catch us. Hit us with javelins, but no injuries," the soldier said, knocking on his armor.

Min turned his horse to face Andric. "My lord, I think we need to adjust our strategy. The Sheerbahari are less than an hour ahead. If the Kushaani keep coming at this pace, we'll barely have time to get the ambush in place."

"What do you have in mind? There's nowhere to form a full charge."

"A three-pronged attack. Two fists on the main road and ours here. One fist from each side fires bows. Hopefully, shooting from two angles will surprise them. Then the second fist charges with lances to clear a path through their forward ranks to reach us and all three fists retreat." It was a risky plan, but he didn't have a better idea. Perhaps because half his mind was focused on holding the elan in place. He nodded and Min gave the orders.

The waiting seemed interminable. Andric wished he could silence the sounds of the jungle around them so he would have some chance of hearing the Kushaani before they arrived. Finally, he heard hoofbeats pounding on the dirt road as the last fist came riding hard. Min was waiting at the cross-roads to give them their new orders then quickly rejoined Andric's fist. Once again, they sat in strained silence, listening for the sounds of approaching soldiers.

Andric felt the sudden bright elantic presence of someone enter the area where he was drawing elan from the forest south of the road. "In the forest," he said pointing, alerting his fist. Heads and bows shifted, scanning the area for a threat.

"Carroi," a voice called out from the shadows of the trees. Everyone relaxed when they heard the watchword identifying the Vanassi scouts patrolling the forest. Andric still thought it was strange they used the name of a fish, but it worked as well as any other he supposed.

"Come out," Min replied. A man wearing little clothing and painted in black and reddish-brown stripes quickly stepped into the road. He was small, maybe only half a head taller than Barak, but he moved with an easy agility that seemed incongruous with the anxious look on his weathered face.

"They coming through the trees. Many of them, spread out," he said, swinging his arm in an arc behind him. "The ones on the road move slower to give them time. We can't wait here. Must move or they encircle us for sure."

More than a few curses escaped his soldiers' lips as Min spurred his horse back to the road to order the retreat and the rest of them began stowing bows and turning their mounts. Andric felt both relief and emptiness as he released the elan he had been holding and moved into the lead position. Min and his men were turning onto the east road when cries erupted. He turned in time to see javelins flying past his men. One sank deep into a horse's flank as the mount shrieked in pain and stumbled, nearly knocking over another rider.

"Go!" Nophet shouted. Andric wanted to ride back and help ensure his soldiers' safety, but Nophet slapped Kobo's hind quarter and the horse jumped forward. Andric growled his frustration but knew fleeing was necessary. They might all die if he didn't move. He spurred Kobo into a dead run. A thunder of hooves filled the air as they raced up the small dirt road.

He tried glancing behind him, but his plate armor and helm made it nearly impossible while Kobo was galloping. His heart pounded harder in his chest than the heavy hoofbeats of the horses. *Just stay—*

A loud clang rang off his armor on his right side. He had been hit by something! He was certain he hadn't been hurt, but he knew he was in danger. A familiar invitation to join in communion pressed at his mind. He opened himself to the link.

"Your Highness!" Nophet's thoughts were strong and clear, though brought with them an internal sense of discord that had never been present before Tarsapta. *"Are you hurt?"*

"No. *What was—*" A sudden sharp bend in the narrow road nearly unseated him as his mount turned hard to the left. A lesser horse would have had to slow, but Kobo had been bred and trained for battle maneuvers, though it would do Andric little good if his riding skills failed to match. The link with Nophet evaporated as Andric strained to stay in the saddle. Embarrassment burned on his face beneath his helm. He righted himself and dropped his weight onto his heels. With the weight of his armor, he wouldn't be able to maintain that position for long, but it helped realign him with Kobo's movements.

Shouts and a clash of metal rang out close behind him. Fear gripped him and he kicked Kobo to run faster. *Too fast. You need the Kushaani to follow you*, a part of his mind told him. *That won't do us any good if I'm dead*, he argued back. If he was being honest, fear more than rationality drove him to debate the point longer than he should have. The communion invitation came again and he accepted.

"We should slow down, Your Highness. We have outpaced them, and we don't want to leave them behind. We need them on our heels." The dissonance that accompanied communion with the Divinarim was worsening, or maybe his ability to ignore it was weakening. Andric knew it was connected to his inability (or unwillingness) to sense Teraithia's divinessence. He had more sympathy for Stephir who had to live with this all the time.

"There might be more ahead of us, trying to cut us off."

"I don't think they could have moved this far east through the jungle, at least not with any numbers that could hope to stop us."

It was a risk either way, but Andric knew the horses could not sustain this pace much longer so he decided to follow Nophet's advice. The prince gently reigned Kobo back to a more moderate pace. *"How will we know when they are close enough?"*

After a moment with no reply, Andric felt the link with Nophet expand. *"Divinar Shapper,"* Nophet sent through the additional connection, *"how close are they?"* Andric could not manage links with more than one person at a time, but Nophet was a master at it and could manage several.

"Just a few minutes I believe," Shapper answered. *"They hardly slowed after taking down the others."*

"How many did we lose?" Andric asked, a mix of fear and anger tasting bitter in the back of his throat at the thought of leaving his men behind in the hands of the Kushaani. He pictured their heads piled on the ground, their armored limbs planted in a rice paddy beside the road.

"Only two I think," Shapper replied.

It could have been worse. He just needed to get the rest of them safely to Pradan-ur. *"I need Min."* Andric pushed the words into the connection with Nophet, then felt the link expand again to include more Divinarim.

"Who has eyes on the captain major?" Nophet relayed the prince's request through the shared link.

"Thurlton does," someone answered. *"I'll send him up."*

Andric heard someone behind him shout something, but with his helmet on and the horse hooves pounding on the dirt road, he could not make out what was said. Within moments the Sa'ari was at his side. "How much further?" Andric asked.

"Less than a league, I believe," Min answered.

"How many more fists ahead?

"Four."

"Should we stick to the plan or just ride?"

"I think... *"They're behind us! We need to move!"*... the valley. If—"

"Ride!" Andric shouted, cutting off Min as he kicked Kobo back into a gallop.

"They're coming ou—"

Andric lost connection with the Divinar commander. He could not tell whether Nophet closed the link or if something else had happened, but he was certain of one thing—they weren't stopping again until they reached the valley.

CHAPTER XLV
ANDRIC

Andric felt a hint of relief when he finally saw the last fist waiting on the road. They had to be close to Pradan-ur. He slowed just long enough to issue the same command he had given to the previous three fists. "Change of plans. Fall in and stay with us!" He resisted the urge to push Kobo into a gallop again. They needed the horses in fighting condition, not exhausted from a needless sprint to the valley. They hadn't ridden far when the Vanassi scout pointed toward the skyline.

"Look there, Prince." A massive outcropping of stone stood out from a rocky cliff high above the treetops, silhouetted against the bright blue sky. He thought it looked vaguely like the head of a giant bird. "The larran keep watch." Andric was unsure what the scout meant, but he was more interested in keeping ahead of the Kushaani troops at his heels, so he simply nodded.

Soon the road was winding its way between towering natural columns of gray rock streaked through with reddish-brown, making them appear as though they were covered in rivulets of dried blood. Vines, small trees, and other foliage clung to the rocky monoliths, clothing them in garments of green and brown where they rose above the increasingly dense jungle. Andric was surprised the road was still clear even though there was no sign that any surrounding vegetation had been cut back or otherwise kept at bay by any human intervention.

"Pradan-ur is just beyond the Sentinels," the scout said, pointing ahead toward a close group of stone pillars through a rare break in the thick canopy.

They appeared to be a short distance away, yet somehow it felt as if he would never reach the landmarks. Andric was not sure if it was the oppressive closeness of the sweltering jungle or the pressure of a bloodthirsty enemy at his back, but he had a growing sense he did not belong here. Try as he might, he could not shake the feeling. *You're a prince of Remalia. Act like one!* he adjured himself. The blurred sounds of insects buzzing, birds chirping, and horse hooves pounding on the packed dirt road were broken by sudden shouting in the distance behind him.

"Your Highness, they appear to be rushing to catch us," Knight Commander Nophet said from just behind him, his voice urgent but controlled. "I suggest we—" Andric was already pushing Kobo into a run before Nophet could finish his words. The prince scanned the path for any sign of danger, more from rocks and roots than any enemy, though he kept an eye out for both.

The road began to climb a wide slope in the terrain and soon Kobo was panting hard. In frustration, Andric slowed their pace again but was relieved as they passed into the shadows cast by the Sentinels towering overhead. It was perhaps his imagination, but the world seemed quieter here. No, that was not quite right. The usual jungle sounds surrounded him as always, but somehow they no longer felt apart from him, outside of him. He almost thought he could sense their meaning.

Kobo hesitated as if reluctant to continue, then stopped abruptly, his ears turning as if he too was listening. For a moment Andric worried the Kushaani might somehow have flanked them in the jungle, but that seemed impossible. He urged Kobo forward at a canter and kept scanning the jungle on either side of the road for any sign of an attack. He saw nothing but monkeys and birds in the trees, though they appeared to watch the riders with unusual interest rather than scattering as they usually did. He was surprised to see a wild boar in the underbrush, watching the road as well.

Andric gave a short whistle to the Vanassi scout and pointed at the animals. "What are they doing?" he asked.

"The larran keep watch," was all the explanation the scout offered.

They reached the crest of the rise between two stone columns, then the path began to descend, even as the surrounding land remained level. The steep path sloped down toward the wide, flat valley floor below while the earth on each side became walls and then cliffs rising overhead. He feared the Kushaani would take positions above them where they could fire from an elevated position, possibly pinning Andric's forces and the Vanassi in what appeared to be an enclosed, bowl-shaped valley ringed by steep cliffs and sentinel stones with no visible alternate exit route. Andric suppressed a curse.

Nophet's communion request pressed on Andric's consciousness, and he accepted the link with the Divinar commander. *"On your guard, Your Highness. Something is... off."* An unmistakable undercurrent of uncertainty flowed through the link from the knight commander, which was far more unsettling than his cautionary words. Andric felt it too but could not identify what it was as they rode away from the cliffs into the basin.

Dense trees grew along the edges of the valley. Andric guessed that was where the Vanassi were waiting to spring their final ambush. The path disappeared beneath the wild grass that covered the valley floor. Mist hovered over a small, emerald-green lake a short distance away on the left. Andric felt a twinge of guilt for the ugliness about to taint the beauty of this place. He tried to glance behind to ensure the Kushaani were on their heels, but his helm cut off his peripheral vision. His rising frustration evaporated as a jolt of panic shot through him at the sight of motion along the rim of the valley, then morphed into bewilderment as he realized it was not the Kushaani but a host of animals gathering along the clifftops surrounding Pradan-ur.

"Why are the animals watching us?"

"I don't know, my lord, but the Kushaani are nearly within bow shot."

They were already halfway across the valley, so it was now or never to stage the final run from the enemy to lure them in as far as possible. Once more he spurred Kobo into a gallop, but he could tell his mount was already tired from the day's exertions and was running slower than usual. *Just a bit further, boy,* he thought encouragingly. He was startled to feel a loving determination flow back to him from the horse through the communal link that was open with Nophet. Was it just his imagination?

"Did you feel that?" he asked Nophet.

"I don't... You must focus on the task at hand, Your Highness," Nophet admonished. The plan was for the Remalians to ride into the dense trees on the far end of the valley and wait for the Kushaani to follow. However, Andric knew that would squander his chance at a mounted charge through their ranks. The prince pushed forward until they had nearly reached the tree line, then called out a command for his soldiers to turn and form ranks. The Vanassi scouts continued into the trees as planned, but the lancers and holy knights executed their well-practiced maneuvers beautifully and in moments faced the enemy in two lines, their horses panting.

He called out to Captain Major Min a few positions down the forward rank. "Don't aim for the middle, we'll get swallowed. Cut through their flanks." Min hesitated, then nodded his acknowledgment. Thin wisps of mist began to rise from the ground they had just ridden across and hung above the grass the way it did over the lake. He didn't have time to give it much thought as the Kushaani abruptly stopped and launched a volley of arrows toward them. A few clanked off their armor and thudded against raised shields but most fell short of the Remalian lines. The Kushaani continued marching forward to get within range for another attack. Andric was not about to wait for that to happen. Without hesitation, the prince shouted his command. "Forward!"

"Prince, no!" someone called out from behind, but he ignored them as he raced forward. Finally, he was leading the cavalry charge he had imagined so many times! It didn't matter that there were a hundred times fewer soldiers behind him or a thousand times fewer enemies ahead. Today was going to be his first glorious battle. He wished Stephir could see him.

Something was wrong. Movement in the grass caused the horses to falter. Suddenly, chaos swept along the charging lines as the Remalian mounts began rearing and stamping the ground wildly amid fearful shrieks. The tall grass writhed like thousands of thin snakes anchored to the earth. The effect was disturbing to Andric, and he understood why the horses were in a panic. Was this something caused by Pradan-ur, or perhaps the Kushaani? *It couldn't possibly be them! It would take so much elan to do this.* Then he remembered the scout's warning about the prohibition against channeling elan in the valley. *I guess they forgot to inform the Kushaani!*

Andric fought to get Kobo under control as another volley of arrows flew through the air. The Remalians raised their shields to cover their mounts more than themselves, trusting their armor for protection. The arrows fell, one deflecting off Andric's shield. Another rider off to his right was not so fortunate and was thrown when his horse reared and fell, an arrow protruding from its hind quarter.

"My lord," Captain Major Min called out over the noise of the horses' screams, "we can't stay here in the open! We have to move."

The horses were never going to cross the field with the grass writhing as it was. If this was a Kushaani elant, perhaps he could counteract it enough to resume the charge. The question was whether he could do anything useful before the Kushaani arrows took them down. If he didn't act fast, they would be forced to stick with the original plan and retreat into the trees. He was not about to give up his chance at glory so easily.

"Give me a moment!"

"*Your Highness,*" Nophet urged through their link.

"I just need a minute!" Andric replied then abruptly severed the link. Nophet commanded the Divinarim and Andric's lancers to form a protective ring around the prince, while Min and his lancers tried to maneuver their horses into a tight fist that might afford better protection.

The Kushaani were already preparing to loose another volley when war cries from the trees a short distance away pulled everyone's attention in that direction. A glance was enough to confirm it was not some new threat. Dozens of Vanassi Vidyahar rushed through the writhing grass toward the Kushaani left flank. *They're buying me time!* Andric thought with relief. He didn't have a moment to lose.

He closed his eyes and opened his center. The familiar discomfort of touching his elan ran along his nerves, but he had long ago grown accustomed to it, and it hardly registered in his awareness as he focused his attention on what to do next. Time seemed to slow, and it was as if he were viewing the events around him from afar—or perhaps through the lens of distant memory. He was vaguely aware of elan outside himself moving wildly and guessed the Kushaani may have infused the grass with elan modulated to yldrath, the modality most associated with movement. Perhaps if he pushed the grass's elan out of synchronicity he could dampen the movements.

As if from a distance he heard the muted sound of iron arrowheads clanking against armor and shields. He felt Nophet's invitation to link but ignored it. The knight commander resorted to speaking aloud. "We will fall if we do not move, my lord." He didn't shout, but his words hit Andric with the weight of his divine mantle. Even if he was no longer archpaladin, he was still one of Teraithia's greatest champions, and her celestial favor rested on him. "The way behind us is clear."

I can do this! Andric thought to himself, trying to ignore the frustration at being second-guessed and the pressure of knowing he was running out of time. He forced himself to face the reality that he didn't possess the skill to discern the pattern of the Kushaani elant and devise a way to counteract it. Perhaps with enough time, and probably needing Barak's help, but those were two things he didn't have. His only chance was to kill the grass by siphoning off enough of its elan.

He had never intentionally killed anything using met'elan before, other than the occasional spider or buzzing fly in his chambers in the palace back in Teris. He had accidentally extinguished a ring of hedges in the royal garden last year when he first experimented with combining elan and divinessence. He later found out he had been lucky he didn't end his own life that day. Andric had no intention of taking that risk today.

Instead, he extended his awareness down to the earth where the grass sprouted and sent a thin wave spreading along the ground, opening a channel to draw life force as it went. Andric's breath caught in his throat as a torrent of elan rushed in to fill his void, threatening to overwhelm him, to consume him from the inside out. It vibrated ecstatically, wild living energy with a thrumming undercurrent reverberating through his whole body. He had never felt so much power in his life! No wonder the grass writhed. How could it not?

The usual itching from elan's vibrations became the agony of a thousand needles pricking his skin, his muscles, his organs, his mind. With this much elan perhaps he could smother the Kushaani elant. He pushed past the intense discomfort and tried to separate a thread of elan, modulating it to yldrath. It seemed to anticipate where he willed it to go, racing into the familiar pattern, but just as quickly strained to leap into other modalities. Trying to control the roiling energy was like embracing a whirlwind. He had to cut off the flow and shunt the elan away or he would be consumed.

Andric tried to close his center, but the flow was too powerful, rushing through him, swirling, darting away, then back again. He was caught in a tidal wave of elan, and he couldn't breathe. *Nophet, I need your help!* his inner voice cried out, but the link was not there. He tried to channel Teraithia's divinessence in the hopes of somehow communing with his knight protector; but even in his distress, he could feel his disdain for the goddess whose teachings had inspired the atrocities at Tarsapta and elsewhere throughout his kingdom. He would never be in tune with her divinessence again.

With alarm, he realized the rush of elan was not slowing. It overflowed from his void and poured into his body. He screamed in pain as the wild elan danced with his own elan, pulling it out of the natural rhythms of his life force. His heartbeat was erratic, stopping then suddenly racing, pounding furiously against his ribs. He tried to push the elan back into the grass, the ground, the air, anywhere it might go, but there was already so much elan there—like a sponge full of water.

He felt lightheaded and feared he would lose consciousness. He needed to keep his composure if he was going to survive. Self-mastery was the essence of Vai Doroth, and he clung to that idea like a drowning man clinging to a capsized boat in a storm-tossed sea. With desperation, he recited the words of the great Dorothi mantra: *Surrender is mastery, mastery is oneness, oneness is freedom, freedom is the power to surrender.*

Andric stopped fighting the whirlwind and sank deeper into it, surrendering to it. Beneath the pain and elation coursing through his body, he sensed Vai Doroth's divinessence. He reached for it, but it slipped beyond his grasp. Panic pressed in on his consciousness. His blood pounded in his ears—felt like it was going to burst out of his veins. He reached again but realized he was too desperate. Try as he might, attuning to Vai Doroth's will in these conditions was beyond his abilities.

On the edge of his awareness, impossibly far away, pain pushed a tear onto eyelashes, then trickled slowly down a cheek. He was sure it was his own face, but it seemed too far removed to be himself. *Holy Couple, save me!*

Somehow their dual divinessence was there, encircling him. The disorientation of attunement bent his mind painfully. He was connected to Yonvaar and Kerail, but he was somehow connected to Vai Doroth's divinessence as well. Strange, he had never attuned to more than one at the same time before. *Am I dying?* he wondered. His mind searched for the echo of a memory that wouldn't come to him, though the thought of dying seemed to have found a piece of tranquility in the midst of the chaos engulfing him.

No, not chaos—not entirely. He sensed some kind of connection, an order concealed behind the effervescent maelstrom. He struggled to distinguish one divinessence from the other from the elan. A part of him that was somehow outside himself embraced the energies, joined with them, coaxed them into the connection beyond.

The elan was no longer just itself, it was also divinessence, it was him, and they were all something more. A will infused the elan and he felt a different attunement begin to reverberate through them all. *Be divinessence.*

A shock of relief hit him as the elan disappeared into the connectedness, leaving his body an empty shell. His mind barely had time to register the reprieve when a deluge of divinessence erupted from the void. His senses were overwhelmed as he saw through every set of eyes, heard through every ear, felt the heartbeat of every living thing in Pradan-ur. He could no longer tell where his own body was as the world pitched and swayed.

Somewhere he sensed a disorienting island of stability pulling him away from the expansive connectedness. He tried to resist, longing to sink deeper into the connection, but instead drifted inexorably toward the island. Then he was in himself again, solid and unmoving, like stepping onto land after being in a rocking ship.

His stomach lurched. His arms felt like lead as he reached up and tried to pull off his helm. He was too slow, but it made no difference. The sound of the prince dry-heaving the non-existent contents of his stomach was the only thing that broke the silence in the valley.

Nophet had a firm grip on Andric's pauldron but otherwise didn't move.

Some of the knights and soldiers surrounding him were slumped in their saddles, their weapons and shields fallen to the ground, while others were as motionless as Nophet. Andric panicked as he realized his own lance and shield were no longer in his hands but were lying on the ground as well. He looked past his immediate soldiers toward Min's group. It took a moment for his eyes to focus at that distance, but as his vision cleared it appeared they were in the same condition.

No one moved. No one made a sound. Even the wind seemed to hold its breath.

He turned his gaze to the enemy ranks, fearing they may be preparing another attack on the now defenseless Remalians. Instead, he saw that many of the Kushaani and Vanassi had fallen to their knees or stood dazed, weapons sagging in slack grips or lying on the ground while their owners looked around slowly in half-conscious confusion. Even the animals along the edge of the cliffs overlooking the valley appeared unmoving.

"What... what did you do?" someone near him asked. He turned and saw Sir Mar looking back at him, his squinting dark eyes barely visible inside his helm. Andric had no answer for the man but was grateful he was not the only person left alive. He was about to ask Mar if he knew what happened when motion along the ground pulled his attention back down to the earth.

His heart sank at the thought of his failure to clear a path for the cavalry charge. But it was not the now-still grass that had caught his eye. The filaments of mist hovering in the placid air stirred as if caught in a breeze that touched nothing else in the valley. Wherever the thin vapor coalesced, forms began to appear. Indiscernible at first, the shimmering air quickly took form, though Andric could hardly believe his eyes.

Translucent warriors wielding pale weapons and shields began to appear, some running in various directions while others seemed to be fighting some pitched, invisible battle. Perhaps they were some new kind of Kushaani illusion meant to distract him. The apparitions made no sound, but the silence was suddenly shattered as a cacophony of primitive screeches and howls from the animals surrounding Pradan-ur echoed through the valley.

"The larran have come!" someone cried out triumphantly from across the field as chaos broke loose. Several Vanassi repeated the shout or simply cheered while others scrambled for weapons dropped just moments before. The Kushaani looked around wild-eyed in the midst of animal screams still echoing from the cliffs, otherworldly figures swarming around them, and the Vanassi preparing to resume their assault. He could hear their commanders desperately issuing orders for them to retrieve their dropped weapons and prepare for battle.

Andric tried to shout the command for his men to form ranks, but coughed hoarsely, his throat bone-dry. He drew his arming sword and waived it weakly toward the Kushaani. Nophet had released his grip on the prince and gave the orders Andric was unable to. "Form Ranks! Lances in front, swords in the rear!"

Andric was grateful for the help but refused to be in the rear rank. "Give me a lance," he croaked hoarsely as he sheathed his sword and fumbled with his helm. Divinarim and lancers quickly maneuvered around him into their positions while a lance and shield were passed to the prince. He almost dropped the shield trying to slip his gauntleted hand through the straps, but finally, he was set and nodded to Nophet.

"Forward, trot!" The knight commander called out. *Why didn't he order a full charge?* Andric wondered with frustration. *We need to attack before they fully regroup!* As Kobo began to move, Andric could feel his gait was off. The horses must have been affected like the rest of them and were still recovering. He realized with shame that if he had been giving the commands their line might have become strung out. He needed to do better.

Both rider and steed were deeply fatigued, and it took several strides before they found a smooth rhythm together, just in time for Nophet to call out, "Forward, gallop!" Andric urged Kobo into the running pace of the formation. The space between the two forces was quickly disappearing. Through the narrow eye slits of his visor he saw Kushaani knocking arrows and desperately wanted to close the gap before more of them followed suit. Out of nowhere three of the misty warriors suddenly ran across his path, then were gone again before he rode them down.

"By twos, charge!" Nophet called out. Andric didn't have time to consider why Nophet had called for such a complicated maneuver. It took all his concentration to ensure he steered Kobo through the steps to reform their ranks from a broad line into a spear-like formation.

The enemy line bristled like a porcupine with scores of spears leveled at the charging Remalians. Fortunately, traveling through the jungle had prevented the Kushaani from carrying the long pikes that could be so devastating to cavalry. Andric wished he had a full lance, but the dense forests had also limited the Remalians to the more modest demi-lances.

At the last moment, Nophet yelled, "Right oblique!"

Andric could see the Kushaani spearmen brace as the Remalian knights bore down on them. He suddenly veered to the right just out of the reach of the spears, cutting into their ranks at a sharp angle toward the end of their line. Spears thudded into his shield, and one hit the cuisse on his left thigh, but they were impotent to penetrate his armor. He felt invincible as rode through the midst of the enemy, sensing the jolt of each soldier Kobo smashed into as they attempted in vain to get out of the warhorse's path.

A soldier threw a poorly aimed javelin at Andric and the weapon sailed harmlessly past his head. He drove his lance forward with a hard thrust. He aimed for the man's chest, but the tip glanced up off the hardened breastplate and went clean through the man's neck, spraying blood into the air. The sudden weight on the lance was too much and ripped it out of Andric's hand, unbalancing him. An enemy spear managed to find its way through the opening in his defenses and landed a hard blow on his shoulder, threatening to unseat him. He clamped his legs under the horns of his saddle and managed to keep himself atop Kobo.

Andric grabbed the hilt of the arming sword on his hip and ripped it from its scabbard as he rebalanced himself, quickly scanning for enemies. He was grateful to see Knight Commander Nophet ahead and Divinar Geon on his right, keeping the Kushaani at bay. In mere moments they were through the enemy ranks.

"Left-about wheel! Two ranks!" Nophet called, ordering them to regroup for another attack, hopefully before the enemy could reform their ranks. Andric desperately wanted to take over the command, but his mouth and throat stung from being so dry. He knew there was no possibility he could call commands until they stopped and he got something to drink.

As Andric maneuvered into position, a swirl of mist circled next to him and a tall, translucent figure appeared, wearing a dark mask like the one Vedic Pujar had worn the day before. Andric wanted to reach out and touch the apparition, to see if it was tangible, but there was no time. Min and his lancers were pushing through on the far end of the enemy ranks while the Vanassi filled the air with hurled javelins.

"As skirmishers, charge!"

The Remalian horses lurched forward again. Kushaani archers fired at will. No more than two score spears were raised against the onslaught of the overpowering cavalry. In seconds the loose ranks fractured, and Andric found himself in the midst of the enemy. He swiped his sword downward, cleaving deeply into a soldier's shoulder with surprising ease. He jerked the sword free as the man screamed and dropped his blade.

A warrior with red chords woven through the braids of his glossy black hair, marking him as a Kushaani captain, drove a spear toward Andric. He blocked it with his shield and turned Kobo to bring the man within reach of his sword. The captain was quick and followed the circling horse to stay behind him, out of range of the prince's blade. Andric lost sight of him and felt something strike him in the back. He signaled Kobo to do a reverse double kick. A brief cry of alarm was cut off by the sound of crunching armor and bone. Kobo completed the turn and Andric saw the captain's body lying in a heap among other bodies, blood soaking into the trampled earth. He checked side to side for his next target.

It should have felt different. Thrilling, or sickening, or even frightening. But Andric felt nothing except the need to kill the Kushaani. Was something wrong with him?

He had long since lost the sound of Nophet's shouted commands over the din of battle, but he knew what needed to be done. One of the Divinarim was dragged off his horse and the Kushaani swarmed around to drive their spears into the defenseless holy knight. Andric kicked Kobo into a run and sliced his blade down across the back of a screaming warrior, then spun to attack another. The anger of the loss of his father, and perhaps even his home-land, fueled every swing.

Somehow, a wounded Kushaani warrior managed to grab Andric's saddle as the prince struck down a soldier on the other side. Alarm quickly gave way to annoyance as Andric realized the man had dropped his weapon and clung with both hands, bleeding profusely from a wound on the side of his neck. The blood was running down the side of his horse's barding in pulsating splashes. He wouldn't last another minute. Andric kicked him off, feeling nothing but anger. The prince should have felt pity or revulsion, he was sure of it, but nothing else came.

His jaw was clenched. His muscles felt like aching cords of steel.

He realized with a flash of dread he was straying toward the far flank of the enemy. He needed to find his group before he became surrounded and ended up being swarmed like the Divinar. The field was chaos and he worried he wouldn't be able to tell Vanassi from Kushaani, though they had assured him it would not be a problem. To Andric, they all looked savage and foreign and barbaric.

Andric snarled as he rode another Kushaani archer down, Kobo barely missing a step. He brought his sword savagely down on another soldier, and a second, then a third who was part of a larger group of Kushaani engaging some of the Vanassi warriors who were indeed somehow distinguishable. Death swarmed around him in the form of savage foot soldiers, painted in all the wrong colors.

Keep riding. Keep swinging your sword. Stop and you die.

Two Vanassi warriors bearing the markings of the Vidyahar roared as they pushed back five Kushaani soldiers. Several bodies surrounded them, bloody, still dying. How strangely peaceful the Vanassi had seemed only hours before. Now, they were anything but. The savagery of the Vidyahar, the sheer might and ferocity, was almost breathtaking as they brutally wielded their long, blackened swords, nearly a forearm's length longer than Andric's blade, and with devastating power. A Kushaani sword was raised to block one of the blackened swords, but the slender southern blade shattered as the two came together. The Vidyahari blade plunged downward, cleaving through skull and flesh.

The screams of the dying mixed oddly with the roars of anger and fear of those still alive, making a ghastly, hellish kind of music Andric wouldn't soon forget. But there was no time to dwell on it. He looked around for the next enemy, only to realize he had reached the far side of the battle near Captain Major Min who was on foot and shouting commands to his men and some of the Vanassi troops. Sir Mar was beside him, also scanning for threats, his sword coated in blood.

The Sharinist knight radiated his goddess's divinessence. Or almost her divinessence. Something was off. A fleeting thought flew through Andric's mind. *Is there something wrong with me now?* he wondered but didn't have time to dwell on it.

More enemies ran than fought. The Remalians were winning. It almost seemed hard to believe. Despite the greater than expected numbers of the Kushaani, he was winning, and convincingly.

Nophet's link entered Andric's thoughts. *"My lord, what is your command?"*

"None of them leave this valley alive."

Nophet's strong voice rang out orders, piercing the din of battle. Andric was already spurring Kobo to pursue the fleeing Kushaani. He heard Min call to him, but there was only one thought in Andric as he bore down on the enemy covered in too much blood for it to be all their own and still be on their feet.

Some dropped their weapons in an effort to run faster, but there was no chance they could outrun the mounted Remalians. At the last moment, the Kushaani soldiers turned and threw their hands in the air, offering surrender or pleading for mercy or something of the sort. Andric didn't hear their words—or didn't care to. Death cut their pleas short.

He signaled for his riders to wheel around and scanned the field for any others trying to escape. There were none he could see. Kobo and the other horses panted heavily, ready for further commands from their riders, but it was clear none needed to be given.

The battle was over.

He returned to the center of Pradan-ur where black-and-red-painted Vanassi warriors walked among the fallen, separating their own from the Kushaani, and ending the suffering of any who were beyond saving. Min and his lancers were doing the same for the Remalians. The captain major pulled off his helmet at the prince's approach and tucked it under an arm.

"Prince Andric," Min said as he saluted, fingertips at the sword hilt in its scabbard on his hip as Andric dismounted. "The victory is ours, m'lord," his second said flatly. Andric didn't know what kind of greeting he expected at the end of a victory, but certainly something more than this.

"It is indeed," Andric tried to say with a forced smile, but his hoarse voice croaked. He retrieved his waterskin from behind his saddle and drank carefully, allowing the water to dampen his dry mouth and throat before swallowing.

"Your Highness fought with skill and valor," Nophet added warmly, his expression not quite a smile, but was laced with pride. "It is an honor to accompany you on this mission. Your father would have been proud of you today."

Andric didn't doubt that in the least. This was the war Jevorak had wanted for his sons. Somehow that seemed to bring the reality of what he had done into focus. His anger finally abated. But in its absence, nothing else came to take its place. He felt empty.

And sick.

He looked about him at the field, at the bodies and blood and worse. Much worse. So many bodies. So many dying and bleeding. Most of them were Kushaani, which should have brought Andric some comfort, but all he could feel was the horror of the carnage around him. He averted his eyes and looked down at himself. His armor from his thighs down to his boots was stained with blood. Disgust and sickness rose within him. He concentrated on his breathing. *Keep it down*, he told himself.

It was no use. For the second time that day, Andric leaned to the side and retched. His traitorous stomach heaved a second time and a third, producing nothing. Shame burned on Andric's face. It took him a couple of moments while his stomach threatened more revolt before he was able to recover.

Andric glanced at Min and Nophet, who had thankfully been silent while the prince showed his lack of battle hardening. The captain major had turned and was surveying the battlefield while the knight commander curtly ordered the Divinarim to surround the prince. They took their horses a few paces outward, and Nophet spoke in a low voice, "Just concentrate on the victory, Your Highness, not on your surroundings. The victory; the next step; and the next."

Andric nodded weakly. He was not yet ready to speak. He heard someone else nearby also emptying their stomach into the carnage. Glancing around, he saw it was a young Sheerbahari fighter, probably near Andric's age. It somehow made him feel a bit better, less... weak. At least he was not alone.

Captain Major Min spoke with a lowered voice. "The Vanassi fought well. These are not your run-of-the-mill Kushaani soldiers."

Nophet absently nodded as if conceding a point. "They indeed fought like lions. We will do well with them on our side. We could forge further into Kushaan while Prince Stephir breaks through Balinth's Fortress and secures Remalia from the invaders." Andric noticed the knight commander was still loath to name the Kuldrith. Not that Andric blamed him. He also caught Nophet's suggestion about continuing the campaign into Kushaan despite Stephir's emphatic rejection of the idea.

He was spared having to reply as Commander Navindra and Emissary sud-Ta left a group of Vidyahar warriors and came to speak with the Remalians. Bejurn stood out because he was the only Vanassi not wearing any armor or paint and carried no weapon. Notably, he had no blood on him either. The same could not be said of the commander. Both men gave the Vanassi greeting of respect as they raised their hands and touched their finger-tips to their eyes, then their ears, lips, hearts, and finally extended their open hands toward the three Remalians.

"We are honored you fought with us this day, Prince Andric Laconeus of Remalia, Son of Jevorak," Bejurn said. "Without you and your mighty commanders, the battle might have ended differently."

"The glory belongs to us all," Andric said with as much conviction as he could muster. He caught Commander Navindra observing him with an inscrutable expression that made Andric uneasy. Was the man judging him for having a weak stomach, or perhaps some other unknown offense? He suddenly remembered the prohibition on channeling elan in this valley and wondered if that's what the commander was upset about.

"Gather your men. It is time to depart Pradan-ur," Commander Navindra said flatly.

"What about the bodies?" Andric asked. He knew the Kushaani usually left the dead after a battle, but it somehow seemed inappropriate in this place. And he certainly was not going to leave his fallen men without burying them.

"Our own will remain here. We only want our ancestors to come for the next battle. The others we will carry to the Sentinels as a sacrifice for the larran," Navindra answered as if speaking to a child. Andric looked up to the cliff tops and saw that the animals were no longer there.

"We don't leave our dead to be eaten by wild animals. May we bury them here, or should we take them to be buried beyond the Sentinels?"

The rice farmer general turned away without another word, striding back to rejoin the other Vanassi. Bejurn answered diplomatically, "It would be an honor for them and for us if you were to leave them here, but you may take them with you if you wish." With that, Bejurn too walked away.

"They don't seem very appreciative that we saved their hides today," Andric said, annoyed at their apparent lack of respect.

"They're not used to fighting with others who don't observe their honored traditions. That can be a bitter tincture to swallow." In Min's characteristic fashion, he said the words without accusation or reproval, but Andric still felt guilty. "I assume you will want to take our fallen with us, m'lord?"

Andric considered the matter for a moment. Perhaps he should leave them here to appease the Vanassi. Intercessor Henden would undoubtedly tell him it was the diplomatic thing to do. But he thought about how he would feel being left behind to bloat in the sweltering sun and be eaten by wild animals, and he knew what the answer had to be. "Yes, bring them with us."

Min nodded and turned to carry out Andric's wishes. Nophet patted his shoulder, then also walked away to start issuing orders for the Divinarim to prepare to depart. Andric took another draft of water and watched as Sheerbahari soldiers tended to several Kushaani captives, roping them together and ensuring an armed escort was provided for them. Then they brought water for them to drink. There was no abuse or anger, and the captives didn't appear upset or dejected at having been defeated or the certain prospect of becoming slaves. These were an unusual people, to be sure.

He saw a group of his men leading their horses to the small lake across the field. Kobo needed to be watered as well. "You were magnificent today," he said affectionately, patting the horse's neck as he led him around the carnage toward the lake. The sun was past its zenith, and it would be well past dark before they arrived back at Sheerbahar.

Conversations hushed as the prince approached the water. "You all did an excellent job today," he complimented his soldiers and royal guards. "I will see that each of you receives a commendation for this." He received simple replies of thanks in return, but nothing more. Something was off, but there were too many possible causes, so he kept his curiosity to himself. Things would return to normal once they left this place.

The Vanassi and Kushaani had already made one trip carrying bodies out of the valley and returned for the rest by the time the horses had drunk their fill and grazed on some of the grass, which appeared to rejuvenate them considerably. Andric gave the order for his men to mount up and fall in behind the others as they solemnly made their way out of Pradan-ur, many with bodies slung across their shoulders.

This was not the victory procession he had imagined after his first battle, but it seemed fitting for the two Divinarim and eight lancers whose bodies lay across their saddles. Four other lancers had silk bandages dressing various wounds, including one who was missing his left hand. The poor man looked like he was barely staying in the saddle. He would be lucky to survive long enough to complete the journey to Sunapra where he could be properly healed. Even then, he would never fight again. He had lost nearly half of his soldiers. Heavy losses, but not as bad as they could have been. *'War never goes according to plan,'* his father had often said.

His mind replayed the day's events during the somber climb out of the valley and through the Sentinels. Too many things seemed beyond his comprehension. He wished Barak was here to discuss them. Of course, Barak likely would have been too excited by the new topics and filled the quiet air with his pontificating. Andric almost laughed at the thought.

They halted before passing the last of the towering columns, and those carrying Kushaani bodies walked into the jungle, then returned empty-handed. Andric half expected to see animals watching the road again, but none came to observe their departure. He was not sure when the regular noises of the jungle returned, but before long the monotonous sounds nearly lulled him to sleep more than once. He thought he saw spectral warriors shadowing them through the trees, only to disappear as he was startled awake again.

Darkness fell and their journey was illuminated by the warm light of a full Fenthal high overhead. Andric could not tell how far they had come or how much further they had to go but was surprised when they veered onto a small path before reaching Sheerbahar. Within moments, the jungle gave way to a clearing beside the wide Meer River, moonlight glistening across its rippling surface. Quietly, almost reverently, the Vanassi warriors removed their armor and weapons, stowing them in a sack or carefully setting them to the side.

It was a strange sight to the prince when they all silently began to pad down to the riverbank and proceeded to wade into the water. It was difficult to tell in the moonlight, but Andric thought he could see the paint and blood begin to melt away in the swirling current of the river. Quiet words were exchanged between the men in the water, one or two at first, then eventually spreading to everyone. Relieved conversations broke out. The talk turned to laughter as warriors became men again. It seemed to Andric as if the water washed away all the horror and regrets of the Vanassi soldiers, and he envied them. He didn't share their customs or beliefs, nor did he completely understand them; but this one, on this day, seemed to resonate with the prince.

Without thinking, perhaps because he feared if he stopped to consider his actions he would be stopped by self-doubt, Andric dismounted and waded into the river, his blood-smeared armor disappearing beneath the dark surface step by step. The cool water brought him fully awake. He crouched down and scooped up a handful of water, splashing it on his face. It felt good. Clean.

He waded into the water to his waist and felt the cleansing water wash away the blood and grime and dust. His boot slipped on a rock on the riverbed, and he almost went down, but a few of the Vanassi steadied him. Andric got his footing under him and nodded his thanks. He heard the unmistakable clanking of armor that told him others were dismounting. He glanced back to see the Remalian soldiers slowly make their way down to the water's edge—hesitant at first, but willing to join their prince in the impromptu ritual.

Some soldiers removed their armor first, one piece at a time, but many waded in and took the opportunity to clean it all. Captain Major Min looked curiously at the prince, then gave him an appraising nod as if Andric had done something surprisingly right. Andric hadn't anticipated the feeling of pride that swelled up in his breast, but it came nonetheless. As Min dismounted and entered the water Andric was even more surprised as Nophet followed suit, followed by the rest of the Divinarim and finally Sir Mar.

After the Vanassi and Remalians had finished in the river and put themselves in order, the Kushaani captives were allowed to enter the river and wash themselves as well. Whether it was a sign of respect or merely a practical measure, not wanting filthy slaves, Andric could only guess. Commander Navindra was nowhere to be seen, blending in with the rest of the men, once again just another rice farmer. No one seemed interested in giving orders. No one had to. Together they made their way to the main road and headed north toward Sheerbahar. Toward their homes.

But it was not home for Andric. His home felt a world away. A homesickness he hadn't felt since leaving Teris washed over him, hanging heavy on his heart. He longed to be finished with this mission so he could rejoin Stephir and ensure their home was safe, just as he had done today for Sheerbahar.

If it was not already too late.

The fire in his stomach that had abated after the battle was rekindled, and a grim determination settled on him as he rode through the night in silence.

CHAPTER XLVI
STEPHIR

Anger, grief, and fear tore at Stephir like ravening wolves trapped inside his chest, clawing to get out as he walked behind the funeral bier that bore his father's emaciated body encased in brilliant armor that seemed made for someone else. The king had lain in repose for two days after his passing to allow the army to come and pay their last respects. He had intended to keep his father with him until he could return to Teris and lay the king to rest in the royal catacombs beneath the Mount of the God. However, the growing number of subjects from the surrounding areas who also wished to come and pay their respects threatened to turn their already desperate food situation into a full-blown crisis. So last night he had decided to send Jevorak's body to Luresh until Teris could be secured.

The Divinarim bearing the king lifted the bier into the grand coach that had carried him the many miles from Nanjab. The priests waiting inside began securing the bier in place for the journey. Stephir offered another pleading supplication to the Holy Couple that his father's soul would be allowed into their divine realm. It was hard to say which deity his father's life had been most in harmony with, so the destination of his spirit was anything but certain from Stephir's perspective.

Jevorak was by no means a strict adherent of the Holy Couple's teachings. He had embodied the role of fierce protector of the kingdom and had been a just, sincere, and honest man, all of which aligned with Yonvaar's nature. But compassion, loving fatherhood, caring for the poor, sexual intimacy strictly maintained within the bounds of marriage—Stephir feared the scales would not be weighted nearly enough toward the Holy Couple in those aspects. He hated the idea of his family not being together in the eternities.

Those dark thoughts had occupied his mind too much over the last couple of days. He had told himself he wouldn't dwell on those today, but he could feel them creeping in despite his best efforts. He needed to move.

Stephir nodded to Archpaladin Merrek, the new commander of the Order of the Divine Flame, who firmly closed the glossy lacquered door. It felt like a door closing on a future he had dreamed of, but now would never be. A contingent of Divinarim and a company of Messian cavalry escorted the king's carriage as it rolled slowly through the camp toward the Spice Road. Stephir's gaze lingered for a few moments longer, the golden morning sunlight glinting off its polished surface, before turning away. He walked in silence toward the war council pavilion. He had been avoiding it ever since his father passed, but some matters could easily become crises if ignored any longer.

Frey and Father Daemmer, who had been at his side more than anyone else over the past few days, accompanied him while the others he had summoned to his war council waited on his arrival in the pavilion. He wished he could be out riding through the camp, inspecting, giving orders, anything to keep the wolves inside quiet. But today's conversations needed to be done in private, so he did his best to steel himself for the struggle of the hours ahead. He ducked through the tent opening and the few council members present stood and bowed as he strode to his seat on the small wooden dais. At least he would get to enjoy the cool air instead of the sweltering heat of the high summer days. The summer solstice was already three weeks past, but it would still be another month before the weather would begin to noticeably cool. As much as he looked forward to relief from the summer heat, it also meant the year would be progressing toward winter, and he desperately hoped to have the Kuldrith (if that was what they really were) defeated long before the first snows fell in Teris.

He took his seat and nodded to Captain Major Ambersol, Commander Alscan's second-in-command and the recently promoted acting head of the elantir corps while Calinda was incapacitated, to raise the ward to protect their conversation. Ambersol gave the signal to the elantir standing near the tent wall, the only person other than Ambersol, Frey, Consul Rellat, Father Daemmer, and High General Kuymon that had been allowed inside the council pavilion. Even the Divinarim had been commanded to stand guard outside. Archpaladin Merrek had objected, although not as strenuously as Nophet might have; perhaps Merrek understood the precarious grounds his order was on with the new king. As a concession, Stephir had given Merrek the option to stand guard himself. He had somewhat hoped the Divinar commander would decline, but the man took the guard position standing behind Stephir's seat on the dais. Ambersol bowed his head to indicate the elant was in place.

"First, allow me to thank you all for your unwavering support during these difficult days." Stephir did not try to hide the weariness in his voice. It would be inappropriate to appear too unaffected by the loss of his father. Tomorrow he would don the visage of the stalwart monarch. "You are the pillars on which stand this kingdom and our hopes for a brighter tomorrow. You have my eternal gratitude." He placed his hand over his heart and bowed his head to those gathered. They all returned the gesture.

"Your Majesty," Father Daemmer began, but Stephir cut him off.

"Forgive me for interrupting Father, but you raise the first point I wish to address." This was going to be the most difficult of the topics he planned to discuss today. He had spent much of the last few days considering it and felt mostly settled on his decision. But faced now with sharing his previously undisclosed thoughts with his closest advisors, he felt trepidation.

"Upon my father's death, all the rights, authorities, and duties of the crown passed to me by operation of law. However, under these dire circumstances, I do not yet feel it is appropriate to take on the title. I will remain crown prince until Balinth's Fortress is back under my control."

"Your Maje—Your Highness," Consul Rellat began diplomatically, but Frey cut in, his words carrying no such measured tone.

"Why would you do that? It won't accomplish anything except point Duke Garamond's tiny compass needle at your throne."

"I agree with Marquis de'Venneshen," Rellat said without any hint of annoyance at being cut off or at Frey's vulgarity. "Delay in assuming the crown and its titles can only serve to strengthen any who might wish to take advantage of these 'dire circumstances,' as you said."

"And what kind of king would I be if I took up the crown when the kingdom is invaded, and I can't even return to defend my people? I will not begin my reign as an outcast king. Retaking Balinth's will prove to my people and our Holy Parents that I am worthy to be Remalia's king."

"You are the most worthy heir to the throne I have seen in my lifetime," High General Kuymon said quietly. "I mean no disrespect to your father, whom I loved as my own blood, but he is the one who put the kingdom in this predicament, not you. Whether we retake Balinth's tomorrow or in a hundred years, you are our king now. The army doesn't need the distraction of wondering why no one wears the crown."

"Then we turn this into a grand mission for all of them. 'Retake Balinth's Fortress so Prince Stephir can put on the crown.' They will help make me king and share more fully in the glory of our victory." Stephir tried to sound enthusiastic. If he could not convey his vision to his closest advisors, the message would never be delivered to his soldiers with the conviction he was hoping to inspire.

"I suppose there is some merit to that strategy," Rellat said, seemingly unconvinced but at least wanting to appear cooperative. "We could trumpet the message long and loud that you will take the formal step of coronation in Balinth's Fortress as a show of power and divine approval. Make it the center-piece of our purpose. It would leave little room for dissenters to spin it as a sign of weakness, at least in the short term. But Your Highness," the consul said with concern, "if we do not succeed in retaking the fortress relatively soon this could lead to very unfavorable outcomes. I'm not sure it's worth the risk."

"Then we had better ensure we can retake it soon. On that subject, Captain Major Ambersol," he said, turning to the elantir commander, "how are your efforts progressing on developing the elants we discussed? And before he answers, let me remind all of you that this subject must remain a secret held in the strictest confidence within this group." They all knew there could still be spies within their camp. It had been the subject of whispered questions and wary glances ever since the known spies were captured or killed four days ago. "We can't risk our strategy getting into the hands of the Kuldrith."

"We wouldn't have this problem if we intensified the interrogation of the prisoners," Frey said with thinly veiled frustration. He was not the only one who disagreed with Stephir's orders on this point, but no one else would state it so bluntly.

"You don't know that. Even if they gave us additional names, there would still be no way of knowing if we found them all. We would be no better off than we are now, and we would have stooped to the same level of barbaric practices we came here to stop. What good does it do us if we gain a bit of information but lose our souls in the process?"

"And if your lofty ideals mean your kingdom is lost and your people slaughtered? How do you think your soul will stand charged then?" Stephir felt anger rising in him. He could not afford Frey undercutting his orders when they convened the full war council. In private was one thing, but this public criticism had to stop.

"This is the last time I'm going to say this—I will not condone the torture of prisoners. End of discussion. Captain Major, the elants?"

"We are making progress, Your Highness. I have some groups working on controlling water and others trying to manage thermal cycling, but it is slow. Not very effective yet as a surprise attack. Other groups are working on various techniques as well to hide our true focus."

"Have you been able to duplicate the holes the Kuldrith managed to make in the walls above Balinth's and at Teris?" Kuymon asked.

"We can, of course, manipulate stone in several ways—seal joints in masonry, harden surfaces against weathering, strengthen delicate sculptures, and so on, but we can't figure out how they do it so quickly. As best we can tell they made hundreds of the fist-sized holes in mere minutes, all while they were descending." The bewilderment in Ambersol's voice made it sound like what he was describing shouldn't be possible.

"Might it have something to do with the additional elantic modalities the Kuldrith use? Like what the spies did to block our communications or the disease that was loosed at Nanjab?" Stephir asked, frustrated by the lack of progress Ambersol was reporting.

"Your Highness, with all due respect, those modalities are forbidden. I'm as reluctant to transgress those boundaries as you are to sanction torture."

"Oh, for the love of Akraharr's mother!" Frey cursed.

"I, of all people, appreciate your concerns, Captain Major," Stephir responded before Frey's language got any worse. "But those boundaries kept us in the dark for weeks while the enemy attacked Teris and captured Balinth's. It was only thanks to Commander Alscan's willingness to step across those lines that we have any notion of what we're facing. If we can't even look at what the Kuldrith are capable of, we stand little chance of winning. And what good will those boundaries do us then?" Stephir realized the double standard even as he spoke the words. He avoided looking at Frey who might take the opportunity to call him out for it. He would have to grapple with it later.

"Even if I am personally willing," Ambersol said with little inflection, "we will have open rebellion in the elantir ranks if I give that order."

"I'm giving it. Let them hate me, but we can no longer afford to remain in the dark. Father Daemmer, can you work with the other presiding clerics to craft messages regarding this change being condoned by the gods?"

"Your Highness, that is no simple request. We don't just change doctrine to fit whatever is expedient at the moment. And with the current... lack of cooperation between the faiths, getting them to agree on a common doctrinal position that changes centuries-old beliefs on an obscure theological issue will be no mean feat. But I would be happy to convene a clerical conference to discuss the matter."

"Do it today. And I want to attend."

"As you wish, my lord. But having you in attendance may have a chilling effect on an open discussion of the issues, or at the very least complicate the matter with extraneous topics certain others may have an interest in discussing with Your Highness. If haste is your priority, might I advise against it?"

"Father, it seems Consul Rellat is starting to rub off on you. You're sounding more like a Sharinist every day." Stephir meant it as a joke, but no one laughed. "Fine, but I need an advocate in that meeting, so if you have any reservations about what I'm asking, we had better work those out."

"Perhaps the captain major and I can discuss things first, and I will report back to Your Highness with an update before commencing the conference of clerics."

"Captain Major?" Stephir asked the elantir, trying to convey with his tone that he would brook no dissent. He detested strong-arming his advisors, but time was of the essence. Stephir didn't know Ambersol well, but Calinda had been willing to trust him completely, and that had to be enough for Stephir.

The usually stoic man's jaw muscles worked as he considered his response. "I will... do my best, Your Highness." It was not as strong a commitment as Stephir would have liked, but it would have to suffice for now.

"Excellent. High General, how is the new siege equipment coming?"

"Master Caldren's new battering ram designs are... unusual to be sure. I had to make the smiths start over because they just couldn't accept that they would be effective, but they're on track now. The modified towers with Caldren's rams should work well, assuming the rest goes according to plan. However, the trebuchets are another matter. The canyon is so narrow that we must get them into the kill zone to be in the right position. It will be so slow getting them there and... well, we can all imagine how that is likely to turn out. The engineers have tried a number of designs to make them lighter so we can move them faster, but nothing they've tried can also deliver the force we need."

"So the main issue is the vulnerability of the men while getting the trebuchets into place and operating them?" Stephir asked, seeking confirmation that he understood the problem.

"Yes, plus the trebuchets themselves will be within bowshot. Flaming bolts and other projectiles could burn them down in no time."

"Can we have elantir suppressing the fires?" Stephir asked.

"With our numbers reduced after dealing with the traitors, every remaining elantir who can manage enough elan is needed for attacking the walls," Ambersol replied. "Maybe we could try to train some apprentices to do their best to help with the fires, but I wouldn't count on that."

"Can we build a trebuchet inside a siege tower?" asked Father Daemmer. Kuymon scoffed, not even deigning to respond.

"No, that could work," Frey said as he sat forward in his seat, looking earnestly at Stephir. "You can fully protect the front and sides, and the back just needs a narrow slot for the arm and sling to swing freely. It would look the same as any other siege tower from the outside."

"But it would weigh twice as much. We would hardly be able to move it through the canyon." The high general knew his business when it came to traditional warfare, but innovation was not his forte. Stephir made his directions clear.

"We must have them, or the plan is doomed before it starts. I want the engineers and any spare elantir working on it. Make the frame and fortifications as light as possible. The elantir will reinforce the materials enough to survive a few hours. That should be enough."

"Even if this is possible, I don't know if we will have enough time to implement everything," Kuymon said flatly.

"You mean our supplies." The dwindling foodstuffs were an ever-present hourglass haunting his every step, and the sands were running out. The wolves inside raked at his chest. "Where do we stand?"

Kuymon slowly shook his head before answering. "The strict rationing is taking a toll on the men. We have sent as many troops to forage and secure supplies from the borderlands as we can, but desertions are increasing. It's hurting morale, and we can't afford much more if we expect to have an army to fight the Kuldrith after we retake Balinth's. Unless we receive supplies from the Vanassi or retake the fortress soon, we will not be able to stay here much longer. We may have no choice but to attack Curritan just to find enough food to stay alive."

"How soon?"

"Unless something changes, we will have to leave for Curritan in the next twelve days or we won't have enough food to keep us alive long enough to march there, let alone fight the battles to capture their stores."

Stephir wished he knew how Andric's mission was faring. Two scouts assigned to his brother's delegation had returned yesterday to bring word that the Vanassi had assassinated Empress Arrdiwat, and the Kushaani were moving against them in retaliation. The timing could not have been worse. He wondered what in Yonvaar's name had motivated them to do it in the first place. At least it seemed to have pulled many of the Kushaani forces away, reducing the attacks along his borders.

With any luck, Andric should have reached Sunapra by now. His stomach clenched at the thought of everything that could still go wrong. And worse, that he might never know. If Andric's mission failed and they didn't get food soon... Stephir could not bear the thought of having to turn away from Remalia and the path back to Ilyanara and his children.

"I pray it doesn't come to that. Now let's get to work."

The wolves seemed to recede into the background, but he could sense their deep growls, waiting to pounce again. They could have him later. For now, his kingdom needed him, and he knew what had to be done. He prayed Yonvaar and Kerail would make him equal to the task.

CHAPTER XLVII
EVIR

The purplish-white lumens affixed to the tunnel walls were the first sign they had finally reached the outskirts of Stierve. For weeks they had journeyed with only the lights they carried to hold back the darkness. It was sufficient for safely navigating the miles of monotonous tunnels that had brought them to the empire's capital, but it shrunk the world to a tiny pool of unchanging light. It felt as if he had walked in place for days, never progressing. It was useful to be reminded that far too many of his people felt this way about their lives, day in and day out. Too long in such conditions could drive a person mad. It was a mixed blessing that Evir had plenty to occupy his thoughts as he had trudged along, mile after mile, next to the wagons.

He had traveled with the plodding caravan under the cover of being a simple guard. His duties primarily consisted of ensuring the slaves working as wagon hands were kept in line. Although it was rare for slaves to get too out of hand, they had gone the entire journey without a single incident. Perhaps that was due to the contingent of twenty soldiers assigned at the last minute to travel with the ore shipment to Stierve. The soldiers were sent as reinforcements to fight in Remalia. Evir hated guarding the slaves and wished his cover had been as one of the soldiers, but even if there had been enough time to work out the details, he would have received more scrutiny than would be wise. For the good of the mission, his cover served him well.

Although there were hundreds of tunnel networks branching around Stierve, all the roads from other cities and strongholds throughout the empire funneled into two major arteries into the capital city, one on each side of the Grand Chasm. And, of course, the Path of Reckoning, the road between Stierve and the surface, down which the Kuldrith had originally traveled when driven underground five hundred years ago after the War to End All Oaths. That road had been sealed off generations ago, and while the Kuldrith still had unending conflict with their neighbors, there had been no real threat to Stierve itself in centuries.

His attention finally focused on his surroundings as they approached the checkpoint of the city's orderguard. Most shipments from other cities would never have been allowed through the Grand Chasm, but metal shipments from Kierden were to be delivered to the army's storehouses, which had a dedicated network of tunnels unreachable any other way. Evir had been in and out of Stierve many times, and he waited for the guards to quickly finish their perfunctory inspection of the stacks of ingots in the wagons and the more cursory inspection of the wagoners before waving them through.

"Remove the tarps and stand against the walls!" the guard captain barked his order to the chief wagoner. Anxiety leaped into Evir's stomach. Was this something to do with him? The chief hopped down from his seat and began issuing orders for the wagon hands and guards to do as instructed. Evir watched as the wagon hands untied the ropes and removed the protective oilcloth covering the cargo, then moved against the walls with the others. The black-stone armored orderguards spread out among the wagons, climbing onto the piles of ingots and even inspecting the undercarriages, doing a more thorough investigation than Evir had seen before.

Satisfied with the wagons, the guards turned their attention to the slaves and guards. They rooted through satchels, made some turn out their pockets, and patted down a few others. He could see no pattern in their inspection.

Random searches. They're not looking for me.

He breathed a bit easier, though things could still go sideways. Vekk-oth's disguise had seemed to hold through his journey, but he was not safe yet. A stray touch to his face would disrupt the illusion of Vekk's elant, and patting down his chest would reveal the attunement rod from Kiavi, and possibly the note sewn into a hidden pocket inside his jerkin.

A guard with rotten breath stepped close to Evir and ran his hands along the inquisitor's waist. The wagon guards, including Evir, carried a simple baton that hung from their belt, but most carried an extra blade as well. When the inspector reached the small of Evir's back, his hands stopped then unsheathed the knife Evir had hidden there. The guard brought it into the light and turned it over, inspecting it intently.

"Strange blade," he said, more with a tone of curiosity than anger.

The guard next to him stopped what he was doing and looked down at it also. "Looks foreign."

"You've got a good eye. Battle of Feldare," Evir lied easily. It was believable enough, being a moderately well-known victory over Eastgatian forces a couple of decades ago, but not so common as to be obvious. Plus, it was not far from the truth, though Evir was sworn to secrecy about his operation. The best lies strayed only slightly from the truth. "Took it from a dead Muir Hadim."

Both guards nodded appreciatively, and the one inspecting him gave the blade back to Evir before continuing down the line. Soon the inspection was over, and they were securing the tarps and straps back in place before proceeding through the checkpoint along the final stretch of tunnel toward Stierve. Evir was not sure what to make of the increased security. Perhaps word of the purge in Kierden had reached them and they were on the lookout for Dorothi. Or maybe they were looking for the Katharis Pool. Maybe it had nothing to do with the affairs in Kierden at all. He hoped it was an isolated issue and not indicative of deeper troubles in Stierve.

The echoing sounds of the city reached him in the tunnel before he could see the Grand Chasm. Despite his fatigue from the long journey, Evir felt his pulse quicken as the cacophony of the bustling city washed over him. It swallowed the too-familiar clopping steps of the large volthox and rumbling of the wagon wheels that had dominated the silence since leaving Kierden. It was the sound more than the sight of thousands of people moving within the confines of the Grand Chasm that told him he was home.

He lifted his gaze as he approached the end of the tunnel opening onto the staggering expanse of the Grand Chasm. Here there was no constant background noise of industrial hammering and smelting he had lived with for the past seven months. Here was the song of the vibrant heart of the empire's government, commerce, learning, and spirituality. Off to his right, at the center of it all, were the twin seats of power, two identical pyramids of flecked granite like a giant stalactite and stalagmite, one built up from the cavern floor, the other built down from the ceiling.

The lower pyramid was the grand temple of Teraithia, Uruth'atar in the old tongue, the Footstool of the Goddess, the most magnificent of all the temples in the empire. The upper pyramid was Tir-hakkiv, the Throne of the Overlord, that housed the key agencies of power in the Kuldrith Empire: the overlord and his generals; the Mavin Tar, the ruling high council, and their respective bureaus; and the Obsidian Door. Where the tips of the two pyramids met, an enormous crystal connected them, radiating brilliant golden light into the chasm.

A pair of bridges nearly a hundred feet above the chasm floor spanned the gap between the walls of the chasm and the temple on each side, leading to entrances reserved exclusively for high-ranking clerics. A matching set of bridges several hundred feet higher up on the wall soared through the air to entrances into the Throne of the Overlord for use by the mavin tar and other powerful government officials. Evir had passed them many times as he climbed to the public entrance located in the stone ceiling above the Grand Chasm. Perhaps one day he might become an overseer and finally earn the privilege of using the bridges himself.

Other enormous lumens hovering in the air formed globes of light helping to keep the darkness at bay. Thousands of smaller lumens attached to the walls and ceiling glittered like stars in the surface's night sky. Elevated balconies and walkways lined with meticulous rows of lumens, steady and brilliant white, climbed the chasm walls, connecting hundreds of tunnels leading off into the vast networks of residences, storehouses, commons, farms, and other work areas branching away from the central chasm like the roots of a great tree. Evir was still convinced he had never seen a more breathtaking sight in his entire life.

The wagon train turned to the left, away from the pyramids, and followed the Bloodline, one of the two main roads that skirted the base of the soaring chasm walls. The road passed under a massive arched passageway that supported the coliseum's seating high overhead. The din filling the chasm now was nothing compared to the roar that reverberated off the walls during the games and other spectacles. Kierden had its own version of tournaments, of course, but they were nothing compared to the grand competitions held in the coliseum. He was not here to enjoy the games, though. That would have to wait until his task was completed.

They passed from beneath the coliseum's archways and followed the curve of the wall driving them toward the opposing wall of the narrowing chasm. The vast cavern ran nearly a mile in roughly a crescent shape, with the temple and throne pyramids occupying the center point. On the far end of the chasm was Teraithia's Breath, a towering waterfall that was a remnant of the river that had carved the Grand Chasm in the eons before the Kuldrith came to live here. The falls fed the River Vangene, its gurgling and rushing dark water ran the length of the chasm, beneath the temple, and through the middle of the coliseum and Emporium before disappearing beneath the chasm wall. It was more a stream than a river, though it was deceptively deep and turbulent in places where it filled the original fault of the chasm. The water pouring over Teraithia's Breath ebbed and flowed with the artificial tide controlled elanticly by the dam at the vast aquifer in the distance upstream. It was from the changing of those simulated tides that the Kuldrith took their measure of time. Evir could not help but smile at the memory of the sight from the walkways behind the falls near his old residence in the Veilwatch district. In between the tidal flows of the falls, the view of the Grand Chasm and the distant temple radiance was breathtaking.

At this end of the chasm was the Emporium, the sprawling market where the people could come and legitimately trade for extra goods. With essential food, clothing, and shelter provided by the empire, the Emporium was mostly frequented by the upper tiers of society who had the means to acquire more exotic items such as furniture, food delicacies, finer clothing, art, books, jewelry, and other trinkets beyond the means of many commoners. The orderguard was a constant presence, patrolling the avenues between the beautiful buildings and stalls in sufficient numbers to deter would-be thieves.

It was nearly time for Evir to slip away from the caravan before they reached the military district at the end of the chasm, just past the Emporium. The Crux was a plaza where the Cardinal Line, the other major roadway that ran along the base of the other chasm wall, joined the Bloodline. That was his opportunity. He stayed at his post at the rear of the wagons, keeping up the pretense of scanning the crowd for any sign of danger. In reality, he was keeping an eye out for anyone who might recognize him. He knew it was unlikely, especially with the disguise Vekk had worked on his face, but Evir was not about to let a chance encounter jeopardize all their work.

The caravan entered the plaza and the soldiers spread out to form a protective ring around the wagons, keeping the crowd at a distance as they passed. Evir checked the other guards to ensure they were all looking elsewhere, then let himself fall behind enough to slip between two of the soldiers. He quickly removed his helmet, turned away, and disappeared into the crowd. *Head up*, he reminded himself. He kept his eyes forward and focused on his destination, not avoiding eye contact, but never lingering on anyone as he walked. The constant tingling on his face caused by Vekk's elants drawing their power from Evir's elan was his only assurance the disguise still held. All it would take was for one person to recognize him, one old acquaintance, one member of the Door to spy a familiar face that shouldn't be present, and his cover and chance at catching the traitor unaware would be finished.

Evir brushed his hand over the folds of his heavy tunic, feeling for the attunement probe Kiavi had given him. He resisted the urge to reach in and take hold of the pronged instrument and begin searching the crowd for the elantir the probe was attuned to—the one who would hopefully indicate who the traitor was. Using the probe would drain small amounts of his elan, and Kiavi had warned him about the risk of falling into vitalic lethargy if he used it for too long at a time, especially with Vekk's elants already drawing on his elan. He had to be strategic in his approach. His first priority was establishing a base of operation, which meant he needed to find Daopek.

Daopek was not exactly a friend. Evir had plenty of those, though none who could provide what he needed at the moment—an out-of-the-way place to work from, a network of eyes and ears outside the Door, and fierce loyalty to Evir. In his younger years, Daopek had been an Obsidian Door operative, but he had long since passed the age where he could meet the Door's stringent requirements for service. Now he spent his waning years collecting food tokens at his local dining hall. Evir had saved his life years ago, and the man had sworn to help the inquisitor if he ever needed it. Evir never expected he would have occasion to take Daopek up on the offer, but that day had finally come.

He found a waste bin in a dark corner and quietly deposited his helmet and baton. Carrying those might attract attention, and leave an impression in their memories; that was the last thing he wanted. He made his way up the zig-zagging paths along the chasm wall until he reached the tunnel opening he was looking for, roughly midway between the floor and ceiling. The residences nearest the top and bottom of the chasm were the most desirable, requiring less climbing to reach key destinations. Evir spared a moment to look out over the balcony into the wide expanse of the Grand Chasm, relishing the sight of being home, then turned into the tunnel.

Daopek lived in the Warrens, officially called Labor's Rest, though no one called it that anymore. It was mid-tide, so there weren't nearly as many people in the tunnel as there would be after the tide turned. The faded, purplish-white lumens here in the Warrens weren't half as bright as the brilliant white ones in the Grand Chasm, which suited Evir's desire to remain unnoticed. Not that most people here were likely to pay him much mind anyway. Life in the Warrens was not exactly conducive to socializing. While no one was allowed to live in squalor, the Warrens came as close as one would find in Stierve, especially the deep Warrens, where conditions were even worse than most slaves lived in.

The Ministry of Habitation ensured every worker had a place to call home, but the residences here were little more than holes in the earth, small chambers excavated in the stone. The newer excavations were either vast hives of individual rooms that held little more than a bedroll and a change of clothes, or larger chambers where ten to twenty people occupied the same space. Some of the older residences in the Warrens (the ones nearest the Grand Chasm dated back centuries) had originally been designed to accommodate families; but as society changed and families remaining together became less common, Labor's Rest devolved into the Warrens and the Ministry of Housing designated other districts for families. Having babies had become a way out, at least until children were old enough to qualify for an academy, apprenticeship, or other training program. Then children were given over to the state, and parents were sent back to the Warrens or one of the other similar residential quarters.

Daopek had lived with his family in the same residence since before Evir was born, an aspect of life in generations past Evir admired and wished had not been lost to the supposed advancements of modern life. Although Daopek's wife and children were gone, he was well enough respected to be allowed to keep his residence despite it having much more space than one person needed. It also made it perfect for Evir's purposes—out of the way, but still in a relatively safe section of the Warrens. The orderguard kept enough of a presence here to discourage most theft, assault, and other mayhem that seemed to plague the Deep Warrens, but not nearly so many as patrolled the Templeward or Lightsreach districts where the elite resided, so there was less chance of guards noticing his comings and goings.

Evir navigated around a handcart filled with freshly baked bread being pulled by a couple of porters. He didn't want to appear hurried, but he had had more than his fill of plodding along behind wagons on the journey from Kierden. A short distance along the tunnel a crowd was lined up outside a dining hall, presumably waiting to receive their rations. It was strange that they would be here mid-tide. He wondered if there had been food shortages recently or if something else was prompting the line. Their faces had a weary, resigned look rather than the anxiety of a crisis or anger caused by oppression. He listened carefully as he walked past, trying to pick up clues about the situation, but heard nothing out of the ordinary.

Someone ahead was speaking loudly, and Evir's already taught nerves tensed for conflict. As he rounded a bend in the tunnel, he was startled to see an oteya'satir accompanied by a pair of kieresta who towered over the Warren's inhabitants. The oteya'satir-atan strolled with a casual authority as she extolled the virtues of obedience to Teraithia's word and shared sacrifice for the good of the empire. Evir resisted the urge to put his hand to his face as he walked by, not wanting to disturb Vekk's illusion. Instead, Evir gave the salutation to someone of much higher social standing, his hands held out wide to the side, palms toward the priestess and bowed, eyes lowered. She barely returned the salute with her hand held out, palm up, glancing at him just long enough to confirm he was beneath her further attention.

Evir continued with only a glance over his shoulder to confirm he was not being followed. He veered to the left onto a sloping path that took him down through a small natural cavern that had been mostly left in its natural state. The small stalactites and other formations here weren't particularly interesting compared to many others throughout Stierve, but colored lumens had been carefully placed to make it a rare oasis of beauty in the otherwise mundane Warrens. A couple leaned against the wall, kissing passionately, one of the women with her hand under her partner's shirt, fondling her. With virtually no private areas in the Warrens, people took their pleasures wherever they could find them. This cavern seemed as nice a place for it as any other, and better than most.

The tunnel leveled out as he made his way deeper into the Warrens. Daopek's residence was still a fair distance away, and Evir had to keep telling himself this was still his best option, though he could think of a dozen others that were more appealing. He had to push his way through a bottleneck of bodies who crowded against one side of the tunnel to get around a pair of orderguards holding tightly to a leashed *ouranak*, a long, sleek reptile nearly knee-high and the length of an adult human, a creature usually reserved for crowd control, not simple guard duty.

The orderguards kept watch over a trio of people in chains, two Kuldrith and a Cannessi. The three criminals on slave duty were hard at work scrubbing graffiti off the walls of a spring-fed grotto where the residents could collect water and bathe in a small pool, though the smell down here indicated it was rarely used for that purpose. The grotto walls had been defaced with a stylized word 'Qil' painted on them in several places. He had seen similar markings in other cities and knew it was short for Raen-Qil or Qilerate. He doubted it was anything more than simple vandalism by a few disgruntled workers, though after what he had learned from Grand Master Pakoran and the not-so-subtle changes he was seeing here in the Warrens, he wondered if it was a sign of something deeper. He forced himself to store the thought away for later. He could not afford to get distracted with larger social currents right now.

He passed another dining hall, this one with a longer and more unruly line of residents along the side of the tunnel. He was surprised and more than a little concerned to see children in the line as well. If any of the adults standing near them were their parents, it was not obvious. Another pair of kieresta walked the corridor, an aura of authority surrounding them like a pool of light, momentarily quieting the crowd as they passed. Evir could not help but think back to the last time the Church sent its swords into the residences and the bloodshed that ensued. At least for the moment, he didn't detect any signs of strain or threat. Still, it was yet another troubling sign things had changed while he was away.

There were no signs and few landmarks to indicate he was going the right way. He got turned around at one point and had to backtrack to find the correct path. He was grateful to leave the crowds behind as he continued through the Warrens. Something about that thought troubled him. A realization broke the surface of the troubled waters he had been ignoring in the back of his mind. There were too many people here.

The workers who lived in the Warrens rotated between working and returning to their residences every tide so that roughly half the population was working at any given time. There was always more traffic around the tide-turnings, but things quickly settled once the changeover was completed. But now the Warrens felt like they were in the midst of a changeover, or at least in the areas where the crowds were gathered. He felt more urgency to get to Daopek's residence and get some answers.

A shout rang out in the tunnel, cutting through his thoughts. "Leave me alone!" A young man appeared at the entrance of a nearby residence, disheveled and trying desperately to escape, but unseen hands yanked him back inside. A few others walking along the tunnel ahead of Evir glanced in the direction of the attack before hurrying away.

This isn't your fight, Evir told himself, even as his steps slowed.

The young man was on the ground, pinned by a larger man straddling him. The boy struggled to keep his arms free to protect his head from the short, driving kicks of a rough-looking woman who stood above him. "Someone help!" the youth cried out.

He's not calling to you. Evir took a step closer. He felt for the baton on his hip, then remembered he had discarded it. That was unfortunate. Instead, he slid his hand behind his back and grasped the hilt of his blade.

The man on top landed a brutal punch to the side of the young man's face. A bloody hand reached up in a feeble attempt to hold him back. *The mission comes first!* The little girl in I'fa had reached out with a bloody hand, but she had been too far gone for Evir to do anything. This was different.

"I swear, I don't have anything!"

"Shuddup! Give it over," the woman barked, driving another kick into his ribs, "or you're dead." A short dagger was suddenly in her hand as she squatted next to him, pushing the knife into his field of view.

Evir could hold back no longer. "Get away from him." His voice was softer than he intended. He realized he was still trying to avoid drawing unwanted attention to himself. *Too late for that.*

The woman snapped her head toward Evir. Her face tightened into a threatening, contemptuous scowl. "This don't concern you, old man. This Yerinite cur is ours!"

Old man? Evir continued forward, not yet drawing his blade. As he stepped to the threshold of the residence he heard the slight crunch of sand under his boot, a precaution sometimes taken in poor areas to indicate approaching visitors. He didn't want to have to fight in the tight quarters and hoped he could draw them out into the corridor. "Yerinite? You don't look like vaesh'katir. Why do you care?"

"Walk away. Now!" the woman growled through gritted teeth, pointing the dagger at Evir. The large thug pulled the young man's arm aside and swung another bruising punch into his face. Evir made a show of slowly drawing his blade from its sheath and bringing it around in front of him. The woman stood straight and took a balanced stance, the dagger held in tight next to her body. She obviously had some training, probably during military service.

Her companion stopped his assault on the young man and looked up. "Get 'im outta here or gut 'im. I don't care, just hurry up!"

Evir took a few steps back into the corridor and held his blade out toward the woman the way one might expect from a former soldier who was once trained but long out of practice. She advanced on him, swaying slightly like a ratsnake. He held his position at a distance to force her to stop on the sand. She feinted a quick stab at him. He obliged with an over-reacting swipe at her dagger that was already back close to her chest, leaving himself open.

She jabbed at him again, and Evir swiped hard, again leaving himself open and adding a look of worry on his face. He heard the grinding of her boot on the sand as she pivoted her foot just before lunging. She knew what she was doing, and her blade came close, but Evir leaped aside and exaggerated a flailing defense, drawing his own blade across her outstretched arm before she could pull it back. She sucked in a hissing breath and slapped her free hand over the wound. It was a superficial cut, but enough to start putting her body into shock.

"Leave now, before this gets any worse," Evir offered sincerely.

"Varch!" The woman's voice was filled with anger and pain as she called to her companion.

The man cursed. "Stay down!" he barked at the young man lying on his back, then stood and drew a karambit, a claw-like knife used by lower-class criminals for dirty, in-close fighting. He stepped into the tunnel and circled to Evir's left. As Evir tracked him, he saw two young people back down the tunnel watching the confrontation.

"Get the orderguard!" he shouted at them. For a moment they looked like they weren't going to move, then one pulled the other and they turned and ran. Varch suddenly stepped forward and swung the blade in a tight arc toward Evir's face, then back again. Evir leaned his head away but didn't retreat, instead kicking his assailant hard in the shin and raking the edge of his boot down the shin bone before finally stepping away. Varch roared a curse as he gingerly lifted his injured leg. It would only slow him for a moment, but Evir hoped it would make his attacks more cautious.

The woman slid along the tunnel wall, undoubtedly hoping to flank Evir. He was not about to let himself be trapped between the two. That was a death sentence. He darted into her path, slashing with his knife to slow her down. She ducked and tried to rush past him, slashing low with her dagger. A risky move against even a competent opponent, but a deadly mistake against someone with Evir's training.

He shot forward like a viper, driving her head into the tunnel wall with his hip while controlling her blade arm with his knife. It was an unnecessary precaution. She dropped to the floor like a sack of millet. He hoped she was only unconscious.

"Yza!" Varch screamed her name and rushed at Evir, his face contorted with rage. His posture indicated he was more intent on grappling Evir than slicing him. The inquisitor tried to step to the side, but Yza was slumped against his leg and he stumbled. Without thinking he dropped his shoulder into a roll.

Stupid! he scolded himself before he hit the ground. Varch kicked him mid-roll and Evir went careening off to the side. *Get to your feet!* he thought as he tumbled wildly, but his back slammed against the tunnel wall, nearly driving the air from his lungs. Varch bore down on him, the karambit poised to slash at anything he could reach. Evir kicked low and hard.

Varch turned his shin away, and Evir drove his heel against the side of the man's knee. Bones crunched and Varch crumpled to the ground, screaming and holding his knee as he rocked back and forth in agony. Evir rolled out of arm's reach and climbed to his feet as a flurry of footsteps came rushing along the corridor toward them.

"On your knees!" someone shouted. He looked up as he rose to his feet and saw two kieresta-atan, blades bared and v'kar at the ready. Evir's heart sank. *Ash and open flame!* he swore. What were they doing here? Where was the orderguard? He shouldn't have intervened. *And let them beat the young man—or worse?*

"He's the one who told us to get you," one of the youths behind the kieresta offered helpfully.

"Put your weapon on the ground and step back." The command left no room for question, but there was less threat behind it. Evir carefully bent and placed the knife on the stone floor, his other hand open to show compliance with the approaching knights. He backed to the far side of the tunnel.

"He's got a blade, atan," Evir warned as they neared Varch. "So does the woman, but I think she's unconscious."

"Toss your blade aside, and get on your knees," the holy knight barked at Varch. The clang of steel striking stone rang out as the man let his karambit fall to the ground. The atan kicked the blade to the side and aimed his sword tip at the thug.

"He might have a hard time gettin' on his knees," Evir offered by way of explanation for Varch's failure to follow the atan's orders, adopting the slang of the Warrens. "Might be I kicked him when he tried to get me."

"He broke my leg!" Varch finally spoke through gritted teeth.

"Why did they attack you?" the smaller of the two kieresta asked Evir. He didn't want to put their attention on the young man who had been the original target of the attack, but avoiding the truth was likely to raise more questions than he was willing to answer.

"They was hurting the young'un in those quarters there," he said, pointing. "I just tried to stop 'em. I'm still shakin'," he lied. Evir knew they were likely to search him at some point and wanted to give them a reason to keep their distance. He coughed, trying to sound ill, though careful not to overdo it.

The second atan walked over and knelt next to the still form of Yza on the floor, reaching to check for a pulse on her neck. Looking up, he glanced at his companion. "This one's gone." The senior kieresta turned his attention back to Evir. "Your doing?"

Evir didn't have to exaggerate much to push his sadness into an expression of horror. "I didn't mean to kill her, I swear! She had a knife and..."

"You took on both of them? Why?"

"He's pro'ly a Yerinite, like th'other one," Varch growled. "We was just tryin'a bring 'im to the Church."

"Really?" The kieresta raised an eyebrow. "How did you know he was an apostate?"

"We found this on him," Varch said, reaching into his jacket, but stiffening as the warrior moved the tip of his sword closer to the thug's throat. He cautiously withdrew a small figurine from his coat and extended it toward the waiting kieresta. Evir had no way of knowing the truth of the man's claims and guessed it most likely didn't matter to the atan one way or another at this point. Evir made a show of looking on with curiosity, then coughed again.

The kieresta sheathed his sword and snatched the figurine from Varch, turning it over in his hand as he examined it. The knight's face remained flat, but the slight shake of his head and the stiffening of his back and shoulders told him the kieresta was not pleased with what he saw. Evir was certainly no expert on Yerinite practices, but his understanding was that they had no fixed symbol of their Faith. Instead, it was up to the individual to choose an expression of the ideal of their beliefs. This would make them difficult to identify, though he had never needed to do so.

"Is it legitimate?" the kneeling knight asked as he rose to his feet.

"Hard to tell. Staeris Vaesh'katir-amet will have to decide." Varch groaned a curse under his breath, but quickly clamped his mouth shut. Evir heard the crunch of sand as the larger warrior stepped to the entrance of the young man's residence.

"Step out here," the atan ordered into the small room. Evir was relieved to see the young man was able to walk as he tentatively stepped past the towering knight into the passageway. His face was already swelling, and bruises were starting to show, but he would be all right. Evir was less certain whether that would remain true after being turned over to the vaesh'katir. The kieresta-atan directed the young man to stand against the wall and searched him for any contraband.

"Is this yours?" the other one asked, holding up the small stone figurine. Evir could now see it was an intricately carved stone figure of a woman. To his surprise, the young man nodded. It would have been so simple to lie, and they would have no way of knowing. "Where did you get it?"

"I made it," the youth replied simply.

"So you're a master stoneshaper?" the knight scoffed.

"No, atan. I'm a street paver. I just like to make things."

"See, a Yerinite!" Varch exclaimed, as if the young man's words proved his claim. Evir shook his head. Perhaps in some abstract theological sense, the act of creating the figurine could be interpreted as in line with Yerin's teachings, but that was by no means proof that the boy was an apostate.

"Do you worship Yerin?" the atan asked, sounding skeptical. The other knight stepped into the residence and began ransacking the place.

"No," the boy said but cast a worried glance toward his residence. It might have been just concern over his belongings, or it might be fear of incriminating evidence being discovered. In a moment the knight was done and stepped back into the tunnel. Evir coughed, a bit harder this time, and spat on the tunnel floor.

"A few more of these and some tools," he said, holding up another stone figurine. "Some drawings on the walls too."

The smaller atan sighed. "Search him, too," he muttered, motioning toward Evir.

The inquisitor's stomach clenched. The last thing he had wanted was increased scrutiny. They were no vaesh'katir, but all clerics received some training in rooting out deception and apostasy during their schooling. Evir coughed, then tightened his lips and made small coughing noises as though trying to hold more back.

The kieresta crossed the tunnel toward Evir with a look of disgust on his face. He turned his shield over and held it between them. "Everything out of your pockets and place it on the v'kar." Evir quickly complied, stifling the occasional cough. Everything the inquisitor carried was intended to make him appear exactly who he was pretending to be. Everything except the attunement rod and his note for Daopek. Those would likely get him taken to the vaesh'katir for questioning. Evir patted himself down and found one more item he had intentionally missed and placed it on the blade-edged shield, then let his hands fall to his side, indicating it was everything. The kieresta glanced over the items, then shrugged toward the other one. "Nothing unusual."

Evir coughed and spat.

With a look of disgust that matched his companion, the smaller knight nodded and slid Evir's knife over with his toe before turning his attention back to Varch and the young man. Evir began to place his belongings back in his pockets, inwardly breathing a sigh of relief. He slowly knelt and retrieved his knife, looking it over critically before sliding his sheath from his back to his hip and sheathing the blade.

"Will they be turned over to the orderguard?" Evir asked, trying to sound only mildly curious.

"The vaesh'katir will have to decide what to do with him," the atan said pointing at the young man. *Has this all been for nothing?* Evir wondered grimly. "This one will be questioned, too," the knight continued with a nod of his head down toward Varch, "but I expect he'll be fed to Teraithia's Burning Heart like the other violent criminals and unrepentant apostates." Evir had no idea what the knight was referring to, and he couldn't ask without raising suspicion, but Varch appeared terrified by the threat.

"No, I didn't do nothin'!" the thug howled in protest. "He killed Ysa!" he yelled, pointing an accusing finger at Evir.

"Seems to me she got what she deserved. I might let him have another go at you if you don't get on your feet now!" the other knight ordered, kicking Varch to make him move.

"I can't. Leg's broke, like I said."

The kieresta called to two men in the nearby crowd of onlookers to come and help the injured Varch up. They obeyed quickly, running forward and doing their best to aid the large man to stand. Varch grunted in pain, and it was clear he would be unable to walk on his own. The larger knight pressed the two helpers into assisting Varch as he directed them back along the tunnel toward the Grand Chasm. The other atan retrieved Varch's and Ysa's blades.

"You too, let's go," he said to the young man. The kieresta-atan gave a final nod to Evir who simply nodded back and watched them leave. He took one more glance at Ysa's body before turning and heading in the opposite direction. A few people in the crowd patted him on the shoulder as he passed and offered their congratulations on a job well done. *Far too much attention,* Evir lamented.

Soon he was past the crowd, and before long he arrived at what he hoped was Daopek's residence. Evir listened for a moment in the corridor but heard no sounds inside. He was not surprised the man was not in his quarters. Glancing both ways along the tunnel to ensure no one was looking, he quickly stepped inside.

He took a moment to let his eyes adjust to the dim light coming through the open entrance from the lumens in the corridor outside. A coarse and worn xanath wool rug covered most of the floor in the main room that was not much wider than twice what Evir could reach. A low, crude table made of kanthis stalk sat against one wall with woven reed mats on the floor on each end. The only ornamentation in the place was a simple painting of Teraithia hanging on the stone wall above the table. He quickly checked the only other room in the place, a bedchamber large enough to sleep three or four people, though there was only a single bed mat. A modest residence, but more than many others in the Warrens enjoyed. He moved his knife to the small of his back again and sat on one of the straw mats with his back against the wall to wait for Daopek.

His mind swirled with a hundred questions. So many subtle changes had come to Stierve; the increased checkpoint security, the sheer number of people, the lines at the dining halls, the Church's presence in the Warrens, the stray children, open attacks with no orderguard responding. He tried to puzzle through what it could all mean, but he just had too little information to go on. He hoped Daopek could provide a few answers for him.

He guessed it was nearly two tenth-tides later when he finally heard someone saying goodbye just outside the residence. The light dimmed for a moment and a stooped figure was silhouetted in the entrance as he came inside. Evir waited for the man to enter further before he called softly to him, altering his voice to keep himself from being recognized.

"Daopek, is that you?"

The figure yelped and recoiled. "Who's there?" the old man's voice asked.

"I was sent by Evir Inquisitor to find Daopek Scribe First Class of the Obsidian Door."

"Well, you found him, though you just nearly sent me to Teraithia's bosom. So who are you?"

Evir could tell it was Daopek, but he continued to follow the script he had carefully planned for this moment to avoid as many difficulties as possible. "I have a message from the inquisitor for you."

"How is Evir these days? Still in Kierden last I heard."

Evir handed the old man the folded message he had carried with him for weeks. Daopek opened the message and pulled out his small lumen. He looked it over, but his head was moving too fast to be reading it. "Well, that's very nice, but my eyesight has finally caught up with the rest of me. Can you read it to me?"

Evir took the note back and pretended to read it, though he had every word memorized. "I hope this message finds you well. Do you remember Orvat-athun? I ask that you aid my courier as you would myself and regard his word as my own. I will come see you when I return to Stierve."

Daopek remained silent for a few moments before finally responding. "Someone's into some trouble. Is it you or Evir?"

"Neither. At least not yet, and with your help, we'd like to keep it that way."

Daopek's mouth drew into a subtle smile that Evir readily recognized. "Oh, I'll help you, no question about that. It would just be nice to know what we're dealing with so I can plan accordingly."

"Why don't you have a seat and I'll explain," Evir suggested. The inquisitor felt some of the tension leave him as the older man moved to the other side of the table and slowly lowered himself to the floor with a bit of effort. He pulled a small cushion out from under the table and propped it behind him as he leaned against the wall. Evir had considered telling Daopek the truth, but it was safer for them both if Evir kept up the pretense of being someone else for the time being.

"I am Ska'atrien. Evir Inquisitor fears the rebellion he was sent to Kierden to stop may be more widespread than originally believed. He found evidence of a possible Qilerate plot that implicates some very powerful people here in Stierve. Raen-Qil may even have spies within the Door." Daopek whistled at the implications of that, though the truth was actually much worse. "He sent me to begin the investigation in secret until he is officially ordered to return."

"And what do you need from me?" The man sounded excited at the prospect of being connected to some action again.

"The inquisitor said you could provide a safe place to stay while I conduct my operation. And perhaps some information."

"Of course, anything you need is yours."

"Thank you. I need your discretion above anything else. No one can know I'm here."

The old man feigned an exaggerated injured look. "Of course, of course. I'm no apprentice scratchpad. I still hold secrets you would never imagine," he said, tapping his head.

"Good to know. Then what I could really use right now is information about Stierve. This isn't the same place I remember from when I was here last."

The two men talked for several tenth-tides. Everything Daopek told Evir confirmed his fears, and worse. It seemed Stierve was a hotbed of lava flowing beneath a crust of relative calm, and Evir was about to go traipsing across it, poking holes in it.

He hoped he did not get burned.

CHAPTER XLVIII
BARAK

Barak knew that the riding order of the Remalians and Vanassi for entering Sunapra had been carefully planned to balance every consideration: observing Vanassi customs, honoring the Remalian delegation, ensuring security for the prince, even placing shorter riders on the west side of the road to minimize the shadows cast on the other riders in the brilliant morning light. Still, it didn't make him any happier about being stuck riding next to the persistently uncommunicative Divinar Staneff. He had tried to engage the man in conversation, but too many monosyllabic replies to Barak's questions made it unbearable to continue. There had been a brief reprieve when Jalanti had pointed out to Shiralla some of the features and history of Sunapra's surrounding lands, but Shiralla hadn't asked nearly enough questions for Barak's liking. It was too awkward to ask many questions from behind them, so he had finally sunk back into a dispirited silence.

What Barak really wanted was to be riding next to Andric. His friend was clearly troubled by something, though what it was, Barak could only guess. The prince had craved fighting in a battle for as long as Barak had known him, and he should have returned elated after winning his first decisive victory. Instead, he had hardly spoken a word in the three days since the battle at Pradan-ur.

At first, Barak thought that Andric was taking the deaths of his soldiers particularly badly, but that seemed to only partially account for his friend's uncharacteristic silence. Barak had tried to get a better account from others of what had transpired, but all he received were vague descriptions and calculated compliments for the prince's heroic actions, all frustratingly intended to appease the prince's advisor. He knew better than to hope his friend would open up to him riding in the midst of the other delegation members, so he had no choice but to bide his time until he found a moment alone with Andric.

In the meantime, Barak did his best to occupy his hungry mind with taking in their surroundings as they neared Sunapra. Moss, vines, and even huge trees with snaking roots covered the crumbling ruins of ancient temples, monuments, and statues along the red-clay road; echoes of the once-great Vanassi kingdom of centuries past, now largely swallowed by the relentless jungle. His ever-present curiosity was tinged with sadness at the sense of loss for the bygone splendor. He wished he could have seen it in its prime. Of course, he wished that about every ancient civilization he read about. At least now he was seeing the remnants of this one first-hand instead of relying only on his imagination to bring words on a page to life.

At last, the dense forest gave way to manicured vegetation, with evenly spaced trees and beautiful flowering bushes. After days on the road in the heavy jungle, he was grateful for the change of scenery, but without the shade of the trees for protection, the sun was free to beat down on them mercilessly. The hard-packed red-clay road eventually reached a long stone bridge that crossed a wide, slow-moving river, the late morning sunlight sparkling off its surface. Barak could not swim and generally stayed clear of the water, but he might make an exception today if it meant even a moment's reprieve from the sweltering summer heat.

As they moved out onto the bridge, Barak had an unobstructed view of the impossibly steep, rocky hillocks surrounding the sprawling city and the soaring Velspar mountains beyond. The larger hills had been carved into countless terraces to hold the ubiquitous rice paddies with which he had become so familiar traveling through Vanashar. Out on the river, fishermen stood in a handful of shallow flat-bottomed boats surrounded by several large birds that dove into the water. He wondered if the birds were trying to steal the fishermen's catches, then watched with amazement as the birds swam to the boats to deposit the fish they had caught, only to return to the water to do it again.

"How do they keep them from swallowing?" Barak asked, mystified. His mind raced through too many possibilities, never staying with one long enough to fully think it through. Talking out loud helped him focus on one thought at a time. "Do they feed them bad fish to condition them?" Barak hypothesized. "Although that would probably lead them to stop fishing altogether."

"I beg your pardon?" Staneff asked.

"The birds," Barak said pointing enthusiastically. "They don't swallow the fish." The Divinar glanced out at the river, then turned his attention back to the road ahead. Barak watched the fishing birds for as long as he could, trying to peer between the people they passed on the bridge, hardly paying any attention to the farmers leading ox-pulled wagons and other travelers who quickly moved out of the way of the heavily armed company of Vidyahar, Divinarim and Messian lancers.

Once over the bridge, they approached a tall archway formed between the legs of a towering elephant statue which stood in the middle of a blackened stone wall capped with elaborate masonry stretching off in either direction as far as he could see. The wall was nothing compared to the massive fortifications surrounding Teris, but it was fitting for Sunapra. Steeply domed temple roofs dotted the skyline above the city wall, their once red-clay bricks, light-brown limestone tiles, and gray granite blocks were all now blackened with age and weathering.

Barak enjoyed a moment's respite from the brutal sun as they passed through the shade beneath the enormous statue. On the other side of the elephant gateway, Sunapra spread in every direction, an incongruous amalgam of numerous prosaic structures crowded between the majestic, if somewhat deteriorated, ancient city of their ancestors. The broad main avenue, lined with tall palm trees and stylized statues of lions, elephants, and other creatures Barak didn't recognize, cut a straight course through the middle of Sunapra toward the largest building he had seen since passing through Balinth's Fortress. Ahead he heard Jalanti tell Shiralla that they would be meeting the Vanassi elders at the palace.

"Who lives in the palace?" Shiralla asked.

"No one lives there anymore. It is a building that belongs to all the people now."

"It's called the Sunburst Palace, is that right?"

"Yes, that is one of its names. It is also called the Palace of the Gods, Jahamartra's Palace, and some call it the Stormborn Palace."

"How did it get that name?" Shiralla inquired. Barak was grateful the priestess was finally asking some decent questions.

"There is a prophecy among our people that one day a great storm will cover the whole world. One born in the midst of that storm will rise up to restore the Vanassi kingdom and establish an era of peace for a thousand

thousand years, and will make the palace their home," Jalanti replied, then leaned closer to Shiralla and continued in a low voice Barak had to strain to hear. "Some people whisper that we are seeing the prophecy begin to be fulfilled."

"I hope they're right," Shiralla said warmly.

They crossed another gently arcing bridge. Barak noted that shallow boats and rafts loaded with sacks, barrels, crates, and even live animals, moved along the busy river channels. He was fascinated by the idea of having a water transportation system running throughout the city and the benefits and challenges such a system would entail. Then he noticed something that took his mind in another direction entirely. He looked around for evidence that it was not his imagination or just an anomaly. It didn't take long to confirm it was true.

Many of the inhabitants of the city were Cannessi. Knowing the Vanassi practice of holding slaves, he could not help but wonder if these were perhaps being held against their wills. But everything he observed indicated they were simply regular members of Vanassi society: shopkeepers, merchants, gardeners, fishmongers. He urged Steed forward, bypassing Lady di Greven, to ride next to Jalanti, ignoring Shiralla's earlier admonition to remain in their assigned positions.

"Master Ve'Aurben, is everything all right?" Jalanti asked with concern. More than a week in her company had done nothing to mute the impact of her stunning beauty, but at the moment he was much more interested in the information she could provide.

"Yes, thank you. I couldn't help but notice that many of the Sunaprans appear to be of Cannessi descent."

"Yes," she acknowledged with a questioning look on her face.

"Well..." Barak wanted to know everything about them but could not think of where to begin. The first question to finally tumble out was, "How did they get here?"

"I... I don't know what you mean," she said with an apologetic tone. "They have always been here. Is everything all right?" she asked again.

"Master Ve'Aurben," Intercessor Henden spoke up from the other side of Jalanti, "is this really something that needs to be addressed now? Maybe later we can find a historian to answer your questions."

Barak knew when an attempt was being made to silence him. Usually, he ignored such efforts, but this was different. Ahead, he could see the last section of road before arriving at the palace was being kept clear by Vanassi warriors blocking anyone from entering the central avenue from side streets.

His questions would have to wait. He slowed to let the column pass until he could move into his assigned spot again.

Lady di Greven gave him a warm smile and a slight wink as she rode past. She seemed to have been doing things like that since Sheerbahar. Barak could not decide if she was teasing him, being playful, or expressing a serious interest in him, though he was nearly certain it could not be the latter. *Could it?* a small corner of his mind wondered. *Don't be ridiculous*, he chided himself. *As if she could ever be seriously interested in you.* That stung too deeply, and suddenly poignant memories of Calinda kissing him came unbidden. *Only in your dreams*, his inner voice said with mocking laughter.

Barak's mind quickly turned back to the problem of the fishing birds. *Maybe they feed the birds too much food before they fish so they don't want to swallow. But again, that would probably simply stop them from fishing at all.*

As they approached the final bridge before reaching the palace, ornately painted boats lined the canal and carried drummers who beat large, deep drums with mallets, slowly at first but picking up speed as the delegation crossed the stone bridge and entered the broad plaza where dozens of onlookers stood in the shaded colonnades along the edges. The horses' iron-shod hooves clacked loudly on the smooth paving stones, a sound he only then realized he had not heard in several weeks—one that reminded him of home.

The Vidyahar soldiers leading the group widened their lines and finally reined their mounts to a halt facing inward, their javelins raised the same way Barak had seen them do at Tapeti and Sheerbahar. Several children in colorful, knee-length silk tops and baggy tan breeches carrying wicker trays full of flower petals came forward and began strewing the beautiful petals on the ground as the delegation members continued toward the wide stone steps where the Council of Elders waited to greet them.

Despite being Andric's friend for a few years, Barak had never found himself included in much ceremony. Now that he was caught in the middle of it, he didn't care for it in the least. All he could think of was not making a fool of himself or his friend. The Remalians followed Emissary sud-Ta's lead as he dismounted and bowed to the gathered elders. Andric's bow was not nearly as deep as the rest of them. As the last of the riders climbed from the saddle, the drums behind them stopped and Bejurn's rich tenor voice filled the echoing silence.

"Elders, it is with deep gratitude and heartfelt honor that I introduce to you His Royal Highness, Prince Andric Laconeus, son of the great Jevorak and Serenne Laconeus, Sovereigns of Remalia."

"I am Elder Gottara," one of the elders greeted them. There was no discernible mark of rank or higher status that distinguished the stern-looking woman from the rest. "Be welcome in our homes, Prince Andric Laconeus. And your companions as well." In unison the elders gave the Vanassi greeting Barak had now become familiar with, raising their hands to their faces and touching fingertips to their eyes, ears, lips, and heart, and finally extending their open hands toward the Remalians. As Barak ran his gaze over each of the elders, he was astounded to see that two of them were Cannessi, and one looked more Remalian than Vanassi.

The children who had set their baskets aside approached Andric, Shiralla, and Barak and tied bracelets of woven thread and flower petals around each of their wrists and gestured for them to bend down so they could tie them around their necks as well. The petals felt cool against his skin, but the girl tying his string made it a little tighter than he cared for. Any tighter and he would have to remove it before eating, which he hoped...

"Bands!" Barak exclaimed with sudden glee. "It's brilliant!" Andric and Shiralla looked at him with confusion and concern. "That's how they keep the birds from swallowing," Barak continued, certain he had discovered the correct answer. "They tie a string around the bird's neck to prevent it from swallowing the fish." Shiralla was blushing crimson while Andric did his best to conceal a smirk. "Forgive my outburst, Elders," Barak offered a sincere apology as he bowed low again.

"There is nothing to forgive, child," another elder said, a soft-spoken man with gentle brown eyes and deeply wrinkled, leathery brown skin. "We are delighted you've found genuine appreciation for a part of our culture. It's the highest compliment one could give."

"We would be happy to arrange for you to go out with the fishing boats during your stay so you can see the cormorants first-hand if that would please you Master Ve'Aurben," Elder Gottara said flatly. Barak was surprised she already knew his name without an introduction and wondered if she was annoyed with his interruption or if she was just always this way.

"That is a gracious offer, Elder" Andric interjected. "However, I fear the matters we have come to discuss will afford us little time to experience the many wonders Sunapra has to offer, as we might otherwise desire." Barak was impressed with Andric's response. His words were measured and polite but conveyed the sense of urgency Barak knew his friend felt deeply.

"Then perhaps it would be best to get you situated and refreshed," another elderly woman replied, "then we can sit down together and hear one another's stories."

"Yes," Elder Gottara agreed and looked to other council members who were also nodding their agreement.

"Elders," Bejurn spoke up quickly, "two of Prince Andric's soldiers are very sick, and he is anxious for them to receive healing care," he said, gesturing toward the rear of the Remalian riders where a covered wagon held the two men who had taken a turn for the worse since being wounded at the battle of Pradan-ur.

"Yes, arrangements have been made to care for them at the Calendula Sanctuary. Elder Dama will escort them." One of the Cannessi elders descended the steps and made her way to the wagon. Barak nearly asked if he could accompany them so he could talk to Elder Dama, but knew Andric expected him to remain with the delegation, though for the life of him, he had no idea what good that would do. Barak had been of no use to Andric the entire journey. If anything, he had slowed them down, which was the last thing they needed.

The matter of the injured Remalians having been addressed, Elder Gottara continued. "It is generally our custom to invite our guests to stay in our homes, but it was felt that you and your companions might prefer to remain together, so you're invited to reside in the Sunburst Palace during your stay." The elder's words and expression gave Barak the impression she had not agreed with the decision. "However, if you prefer, we could always find more traditional accommodations." Barak glanced at Bejurn and Jalanti to see if he could discern how they felt about this development. Maybe it had even been their idea in the first place. Bejurn's stoic face and Jalanti's downcast eyes revealed nothing.

"The Council is most considerate," Andric answered. "We would be honored to accept your offer to stay in the palace."

"Very well then," Elder Gottara said. With a subtle gesturing toward the Remalians, the plaza became a flurry of activity as dozens of Vanassi servants hurried forward to take care of every need. A light, fruity wine was served in brass cups etched with elaborate designs, and damp cloths were offered with which to wipe the sweat and dirt of their travels from their faces and hands. Servants unloaded bags and packages from the horses while others tended to the animals themselves. Captain Major Minanthsolum was busy giving orders to the lancers while Andric and Shiralla were introduced to the rest of the council members.

The second of the two Cannessi elders approached Barak after his moment with the prince and intercessor. "Master Ve'Aurben, it's a pleasure to meet you," the gray-haired man said with a reserved smile and slight bow, his hands held behind his back. "I am Elder Shanyasar. Welcome to Sunapra."

"Thank you, Elder. I am grateful to have finally arrived."

"Yes, we heard of the troubles you faced on the journey here." Everyone climbed the steps toward the palace, so Barak and the elder followed along. "I'm certain we will hear all about it later. The priestess said you have some questions that I may be able to answer for you in the meantime."

Barak was touched Shiralla would think of him with everything else that was happening. He made a mental note to thank her later. "As a matter of fact, I was curious about a few things that you might be able to shed some light on."

"I will be happy to try."

"First of all, if you don't mind me asking, how is it that the Vanassi allowed a Cannessi to become an elder?"

Elder Shanyasar smiled knowingly. "I understand your question, but your question does not understand me. I am not Cannessi. I am Vanassi. My identity does not come from my blood but from my heart. I was born and raised in Vanashar, as were my parents, and their parents, and their parents' parents."

"But you are of Cannessi descent, every bit as much as I am."

"Are you Cannessi or Remalian?"

"I suppose it depends on who you ask. Most Remalians would say I am Cannessi, living in Remalia."

"And what do you say?"

Barak was tempted to give the easy answer, the diplomatic answer, but the truth was he had struggled with that question most of his life. "I confess I do not have a clear answer to your question."

"Then perhaps you have not found your heart's home yet."

"How did so many Cannessi come to be in Sunapra?" Barak asked, turning the conversation away from himself as they entered the ancient palace. There were no doors, just open corridors and rooms, which Barak felt might explain why no one wanted to live there. He tried to convince himself he wasn't any more exposed than he had been for the past several weeks on the open road.

"There's not much I can tell you, I'm afraid. Five generations ago, there was turmoil among the Cannessi living in the mountain stronghold of Elginfir. Infighting over who should rule I believe, though I do not know more than that. A number of the Cannessi were unhappy with the unrest and chose to leave. Some chose to start a new community in the mountains, which is now the village of Yylghar, but most came to live here among the Vanassi, who welcomed them with open arms." After a pause, he added, "Perhaps you are following the same path."

Is he inviting me to stay in Sunapra? Barak wondered. The question stirred up a whirlwind of emotions and thoughts. The delegation would certainly benefit from Barak staying behind, but the idea had an undertone of betraying Andric and their friendship.

They passed through vacant areas of the palace and finally arrived at the wing where the Remalians would be staying. The rooms had been swept clean and strewn with crushed reeds, and the air was filled with the fragrance of numerous flower bouquets lining the walls. The servants carrying their supplies and baggage deposited them in their assigned rooms. Barak found it curious they didn't need to be told which items belonged in which room and wondered if someone was orchestrating their activities through communion or if there was a more mundane explanation.

What of my research? He doubted the Vanassi had anything close to the resources available to him in Teris. *If I ever see Teris again.* That thought reminded him of the Kuldrith invaders threatening his home. But Sunapra was no safer, with the Kushaani imperial forces marching toward Vanashar at this very moment. He sighed. It seemed all options led toward conflict.

He followed the others as they were introduced to their quarters. He was excited to learn a bath was available. He hadn't had a real bath in weeks and was eager to do a thorough job of washing away the evidence of their travels. The elaborate mosaics covering the floor, walls, and large pool of clear water occupying the center of the chamber were still beautiful despite missing many of their tiles and the grayish-brown stone beneath showing through. Servants in loose linen robes stood around the pool's edge holding white towels and trays of cleaning supplies. His heart suddenly sank. As tantalizing as the water was, he hadn't been in Kushaan long enough to be ready to adopt their custom of communal bathing. He doubted he would ever be comfortable with it. He would just have to wait until the others were done to take his turn —after asking the servants to wait outside, of course.

Would I even enjoy living in Sunapra? They had so many strange and uncomfortable customs, and yet there were so many exciting and new things to learn.

"I will leave you to refresh yourself," Elder Shanyasar said.

Barak had been so lost in his thoughts he hadn't realized the elderly Cannessi was still with him. *Vanassi*, Barak corrected himself. "I'm sorry, Elder. You've given me a lot to think about."

"No apologies necessary. We can speak more at the banquet, or whenever you wish." Elder Shanyasar bowed and joined the other departing elders.

Much to think about indeed. Barak shook his head and went to his room to get himself situated. He hoped Andric had not heard his conversation with Shanyasar. No sense in raising questions prematurely. Fortunately, his friend didn't appear to be anywhere in the immediate vicinity. *Being unimportant occasionally has its benefits.* That thought brought his loneliness uncomfortably close to the surface.

You could always join Emerly for a bath, his inner voice teased him.

Shut up, he replied glumly.

CHAPTER XLIX
QUARIAN

"That's the place, sir," Corporal Stenner said quietly, pointing ahead as they made their way along the dark, narrow alley toward the building where some of Quarian's men had apparently been causing a bit of a scene. From the outside, it looked like any of the other two- and three-story buildings flanking the alley. Worn-out orange silk lamps cast dim light on crumbling plaster-covered walls revealing dark timber and lime-stone blocks beneath. According to Stenner, this was a Sykorian temple.

As if I needed more proof the gods cause nothing but grief.

Quarian generally tried not to judge his soldiers for how they chose to spend their free time and coin, but he had no tolerance for disorderly conduct, especially while guests in a foreign city, and on a diplomatic mission no less. He just hoped he could take care of it quietly before anything had to be elevated to the attention of the prince. The young lord had enough on his mind trying to negotiate with the Vanassi elders. Already three days in Sunapra and they had little to show for their efforts. At least, that was the impression Quarian had from Andric's complaining each night upon returning to the Remalians' quarters in the palace ruins.

He stopped for a moment at the wooden front door to listen for any sounds of trouble. He could hear boisterous laughter and someone calling for another drink, but otherwise, there was nothing out of the ordinary. "Wait out here and alert me if anything looks concerning," he instructed Stenner, then lifted the door latch and stepped inside.

A fat Vanassi man with a double chin and shaved head leaning against a post near the door cast a quick glance at Quarian as he entered. The man had no shirt under an embroidered brown vest that was nearly the color of his skin, mustard-colored breeches, and a wide black sash tied around his waist. Quarian nodded to the man, then they both turned their attention to the large common room.

Through the pungent, smokey haze he could see men and women lounging on wide cushions and colorful silk pillows next to low, round tables covered with pitchers, wine bottles, mugs, cups, and strange-looking metal and colored-glass smoking implements. Exotic flowers in an array of colors added a sense of mysterious beauty to dimly lit the room. Servers carefully navigated their way between the tables, draped in sheer material that left little to the imagination. It appeared the native Sunaprans generally preferred to keep to the shadows along the walls, which made it easy to locate the Remalians who occupied two tables in the center of the room.

"Don't run away just yet!" Lanceman Carram said loudly as he wrapped a firm arm around a young woman next to him who appeared to be trying to depart. Her blouse slipped from her shoulder, threatening to expose her to his laughing and leering companions.

Quarian's anger surged, but his more immediate concern was the large man next to him who appeared to tense up and ready himself to move into the room. "They're leaving," Quarian said placatingly. The man nodded and relaxed back against the column as the captain major strode toward his soldiers.

"Akraharr's balls," one of them groaned. Teek. Putting on a jovial disposition, the scout called out, "Captain Major, have you come to join us?"

"Let her go, Carram. Now." The lancer released the girl, who adjusted her clothes with a strained smile as she stood and moved to the other side of the room. Quarian could feel all eyes in the place focused on him. His voice was steel but quiet. "Everyone up. It's time to go."

"But we're just having a bit of fun, Min," one of the younger lancers drawled. Teek sucked a hissing breath in between his teeth, presumably at his companion's disrespect to their commander.

A woman in her middle years approached the group as a few of his men struggled to their feet. She was dressed head to toe in crimson finery. A gossamer veil hanging over her face did nothing to hide the seductive smile behind it. He guessed she was the presiding priestess of the temple. "Uncali," she said in an unctuous, sultry voice. "I am sure the lads meant no harm. They just need a firm hand to teach them some manners." She ran her long, painted fingernails through Lanceman Prennick's hair as she passed, but kept her eyes focused on Quarian. He felt a pleasant heat growing in his chest, then spreading up his neck and onto his face.

He could not say she was exactly beautiful, but his attraction to her was undeniable. The world seemed to tilt ever so slightly. Instinctively he shifted the heel of his foot and bent his knees to give himself better balance. *Firm hand? Yes, they do need a firm hand. Perhaps I could stay a little.* His thoughts were muddled. Quarian wasn't sure if divinessence was at play or if this was something to do with whatever incense they were burning, but he tried to shake off the tenacious feeling.

"Why don't you come sit with me?" She ran her nails up his sleeve and gently wrapped her fingers around his arm. He wanted to follow her, wanted to feel her touch.

"I'm... I'm sorry," he heard himself saying as if from a distance. "We have to go. Everyone outside." He noticed that Lieutenant Garreth, the prince's attendant, was passed out on a pillow. "Get him on his feet." Two of the men hoisted Garreth up and slung his arms over their shoulders, then began fumbling their way toward the door. Quarian pushed a small purse of coins into the priestess's hand. "For your troubles."

"Come back soon, my love," she cooed behind him. His head was swimming as he scanned the room to ensure he was the last one out and that no one was following them. The air outside didn't smell as sweet but was somehow more refreshing. The heat slowly faded from his face and chest, and with it the nagging desire to go back inside. He made a quick headcount, then got them moving toward the palace. As Garreth came to, they had to stop for him to empty his stomach at the side of the alley. Teek looked like he was preparing to relieve himself onto a wall, but Quarian's anger finally got the better of him.

"You hold that until you're back in quarters!"

"But the Vanassi—"

"Keep moving!" Quarian shoved Teek along the alley, still fumbling with the ties on his breeches. No one spoke another word the rest of the way to the palace. His head had fully cleared by the time they were climbing the steps, but his ire hadn't abated. Discipline was better meted out once everyone had a chance to regain their composure. He ensured they all made it back to their rooms safely, then gave orders not to leave until he came for them in the morning. He repeated his instructions to the soldiers who had remained at the palace and charged them with making sure the others followed his orders as well.

When he was finally satisfied things were settled for the time being, he headed off to find his favorite spot, a quiet garden in a courtyard of an empty wing of the sprawling palace. He was tempted to retrieve a lamp, but he knew the way well enough by now, and walking in the dark helped him feel alone. His booted footsteps echoed quietly in the stone corridors, making him feel more isolated. He was surprised, and a little disappointed, to see a light ahead as he approached the garden. He was even more surprised to find Master Ve'Aurben there.

"Captain Major Minanthsolum, I thought you might eventually show up here," the young scholar greeted him pleasantly.

"Please, Quarian for tonight if you don't mind. I've had enough of being Captain Major for one day."

"Very well, Quarian. Is everything all right?"

"I believe so. Just a small issue with some of the men. But what can I do for you, Master Ve'Aurben?"

"First of all, it seems only fair that you call me Barak." Quarian smiled politely and nodded as he leaned against one of the tall, natural standing stones in the garden near the bench Barak was seated on, a white silk lantern next to him. "Second, I have gathered from whispers and hints among the soldiers that something unusual happened at Pradan-ur, but so far, I haven't been able to discuss it with Prince Andric. I was hoping you could shed some further light on what happened."

Quarian was fairly certain he knew what Barak was referring to, but he was not entirely comfortable talking about it. Mostly because he had no reasonable explanation for what he had seen. Perhaps saying as much was the best place to start.

"I wish I knew what happened. We were mounting our first charge against the Kushaani when the grass began to move as if it was alive, like a thousand snakes. It spooked the horses. They stamped and reared but refused to move in any direction. The Kushaani were firing arrows at us, but the prince ordered us to hold. Then the Vanassi attacked their flank. The Kushaani turned to face them and then..." Quarian tried to find the words to describe what happened next, but none seemed to fit. "It was like all the world was in my head, or my mind was everywhere in the world at once." Quarian shook his head in frustration. Neither of those was quite right. "It was... too much. I couldn't think; couldn't move. None of us could. It was almost like we were dead, or were... pushed into somewhere else."

"You mean traversification?" Barak asked. Quarian had no idea what that meant and didn't particularly want a lesson on some obscure theological concept, but the Cannessi was too quick with a clarification. "When someone's spirit leaves their body temporarily. They retain—"

"Maybe," Quarian cut him off. "I really couldn't say. But then it went away. The grass wasn't moving anymore, and the battle resumed."

"Some of the men seem to think Andric was responsible for what happened. What do you think?"

"I don't know for sure. On the road, before we reached Pradan-ur, the prince used met'elan to throw fire in the faces of Kushaani. It seemed to make quite an impression on the men. Maybe they just assumed that if he did one, he did the other."

Barak sat quietly for a few moments staring at the ground. Quarian took the opportunity to look up at the stars in the night sky above them. Part of him wished he could just be a scout again. But he had a feeling those days were forever behind him.

"Could it maybe have been some kind of hallucination, or dispositioning?"

"Your guess is as good as mine. Probably better," Quarian chuckled.

"And did you see the warrior-apparitions?"

"I don't know what they were, but yes, something like that. They were not..." Again Quarian struggled to find the right words. "They didn't seem real, or at least not aware we were even there. They were more like echoes or memories of past battles."

"The Sheerbahari claim they are their ancestors come to aid them in battle."

"I couldn't say. Honestly, when they seemed to pose no threat, I focused on fighting the Kushaani."

"Well, if you recall any other details, I would appreciate it if you would let me know." Barak stood up and bowed, a habit he seemed to have picked up from the Vanassi. "Just maybe not around the prince for the time being," he added as an afterthought.

He appeared to be about to leave, and Quarian decided to try and garner the scholar's support on a matter he had been preparing to broach with the prince. "May I ask you a question?"

"Only if it's a good one."

"How much do you want to return to Remalia?"

"Why do you ask?" Barak replied.

Quarian was not sure, but the prince's advisor seemed bothered by the question—suspicious perhaps, or maybe just cautious. "I believe I have found a way to get us through the mountains and back to Remalia."

"Really? Have you told Andric?"

"Not yet. I have been putting the pieces together over the last couple of days. I planned to raise it with him tonight when he finishes with the elders."

"I'm sure he'll be very interested in what you have to say."

"And what about you? If the choice were yours, what would you choose?"

"That's hard to say. What are the risks of crossing the mountains compared to remaining here or trying to make the journey back through Vanashar and Kesh to Balinth's Fortress? And what are the benefits of each choice? Even if we could make it through to Remalia, what then? There seems little we could do to help Prince Stephir retake the fortress or to help with the siege on Teris without his army. I suppose Andric might be useful in raising more troops if that isn't already being done.

"On the other hand, I'm not sure what use staying here in Sunapra would serve. If the Vanassi are somehow able to stave off the empire's attacks, and assuming Andric is successful in negotiating the terms of a treaty with the Vanassi, then perhaps remaining could help ensure the alliance survives its infancy. But Andric's heart is almost certainly set on rejoining Stephir as soon as possible."

Quarian noted that even when asked what he would choose, he placed himself in Prince Andric's shoes as he thought the question through. The captain major recalled similar conversations and realized Barak always did that. Maybe that was why the prince chose him as his advisor. He never seemed to have a personal agenda, only considering what was in the prince's interest. But he was no bootlicker either. He spoke his mind freely. It was a rare combination.

"So you think the prince will choose to try to return to Balinth's Fortress?"

"Oh, I don't have any idea what he'll choose. You asked me what I would choose, and those are the considerations I would weigh. But I am sure he'll appreciate you bringing him another option. He hates feeling that he has no choice but to take one path, which is often how he feels."

"Well then, I hope my suggestion helps in some measure."

"I'm headed to find him now. Would you like to join me?"

Quarian was tempted to remain and enjoy at least a moment of the solitude he had come here seeking, but it might be better if the prince saw the two of them arriving together. Perhaps some of the prince's goodwill toward Barak might rub off on Quarian. He pushed himself away from the standing stone and set his pace to match his diminutive companion. They made small talk for the few minutes it took to return to the area of the palace the Remalians occupied. He checked in with the soldiers on watch duty to make sure the others he had brought back were following orders, then continued to the prince's quarters.

"Ah, Barak and Min," Prince Andric said with sarcastic joviality and a bit of a slur in his speech, evidence he had been drinking more than usual, "regale us with the tales of your day! We need something to lift our spirits."

Knight Commander Nophet, Intercessor Henden, and her two knight protectors were also present. Quarian could not tell why, but a palpable tension filled the room—definitely not the circumstances he had hoped for to present his plan to the prince. The two new arrivals took their seats with the others on the plush rugs and cushions that had been placed in the royal sitting room. Silk lamps hung from brass hooks protruding from the intricately carved stone walls. It reminded Quarian of the Sykorian temple. The captain major shifted uncomfortably.

"I visited Gerson and Hassted at the Calendula Sanctuary as you requested," Barak responded. "Gerson is recovering well under the healers' care. They said he can join us here in another couple of days."

That appeared to be all Barak wanted to say. Quarian knew what his silence meant, but the prince wouldn't leave it be. "And Hassted?"

"They're doing all they can, but the infection has spread beyond his arm. They can suppress the fever with met'elan, but as soon as they leave him on his own, it comes back."

"Then they need to have someone with him at all times."

"He is being kept as comfortable as they can make him, Andric. Perhaps you would like to visit him tomorrow."

"Well, it couldn't be any more of a waste of my time than—"

"I'm glad Gerson is on the mend," Lady di Greven chimed in, cutting the prince off. He didn't appear to take any offense and instead took another long draft from his wine cup.

"Send for Lieutenant Werdalm," Barak called out to the Divinarim standing guard outside the room.

"Why? Is something wrong?" Andric asked, concern leaping to his face.

"No. I also stopped by the menhir today to check on their progress in assembling it. Werdalm and Elles weren't there, so I just wanted to ask how things were coming along. The spot the elders selected is beautiful. I think it will be well received by the Sunaprans, but I had expected it to be complete by now."

Werdalm entered the room and curtsied elegantly. Quarian had gathered from her mannerisms and the rare words he had heard her speak over the last few weeks that she was a worshipper of Sharin Dara. Besides Nophet, the elantir was the only other member of the delegation near Quarian's age.

"My lords and lady summoned me?"

"Yes, Lieutenant. How's the work progressing on assembling the menhir?" Barak asked.

"We had some... unexpected setbacks at first, your grace. The surfaces of the shards that we prepared before departing Balinth's Fortress warped unexpectedly during the journey. To do the bonding properly requires us to rework the shards. But the elantic sources volunteered by the Vanassi have helped speed up our work. With the extra elan, I expect we will finish in seven to ten days."

"Elantic sources?" Andric asked. Quarian didn't have any idea what they were talking about, but the prince did not sound happy.

"Yes, m'lord. The Vanassi have brought their requitals for us to—"

"You mean slaves," Andric cut her off, a flash of anger in his voice. "You are drawing elan from their slaves!"

"Andric," Barak said with a mollifying voice, but the prince lashed out.

"Am I the only one with any sense of decency left? We came to Kushaan to stop slavery, not take advantage of it ourselves. I will not have the gift that represents our friendship forged with lifeforce stripped from those who have no say in the matter. If the Vanassi want to help, they can volunteer themselves. Do I make myself clear?"

"Yes, Your Highness," Lieutenant Werdalm answered, her voice barely audible and she began to quiver.

"Then you're dismissed," the prince said flatly.

"Lieutenant," Barak called quickly as Werdalm curtsied again and was turning to leave, "do you know the elant for clairaudient blocking?"

"No," her voice quavered, "but Elles does. Shall I send him?"

"Yes, thank you."

"What is that for? Do you think—" the prince started, but Barak interrupted.

"How was dinner? I'm sorry I missed it," the scholar said, holding a finger to his lips and shaking his head slightly, indicating the prince should hold his tongue for the moment.

"It was delicious," Intercessor Henden answered quickly, "but some dishes were far too spicy for my palate. I couldn't taste anything for several minutes after eating the lamb and purple peppers. That was so painful." The idle chatter continued for a few minutes until Corporal Elles appeared at the door. The heavy-set man gave the unusual salute of the elantir corps. Quarian decided it was time he learned its meaning. He could ask Barak about it later.

"Corporal, we need to have a private conversation, if you please," Barak said politely, as if it was nothing out of the ordinary, although it was the first time Quarian had seen it done the entire journey. He knew Nophet and Henden often used communion to have private conversations with the prince, and he wouldn't be surprised if Master Ve'Aurben did as well. He wondered what was different now.

"Of course, Master Ve'Aurben." Elles moved to the side of the room and closed his eyes. After a moment the sounds of the outside world were suddenly cut off and the room was left in unnatural silence. It was disquieting to Quarian to not hear anything beyond his immediate surroundings.

"All right, Barak, what's this about?" the prince asked, sounding more curious than anything.

"You have something you want to get off your chest, and it seems best that we keep it amongst ourselves."

"I don't know—"

"You've started to say something harsh or critical of the Vanassi at least three times since I came in. So what is it? Did something happen during the negotiations today?"

"No, nothing happened." The prince seemed too agitated to stay seated. He climbed unsteadily to his feet, spilling wine on the rug in the process. "That's the whole damn problem. Nothing's happening. Three days of this and nothing to show for it!"

"Your Highness," the intercessor began cautiously, "I know the talks can seem frustratingly slow, but this is how negotiations often work. And if I may say so, the elders have been listening to our demands with a great deal of patience."

"Patience? I don't want them to be patient. I want them to hurry up so we can finish, and I can get back to my brother."

Quarian found the opening he had been waiting for. "I don't think that's going to be possible anytime soon, Your Highness."

"What are you talking about?" Andric asked, dread and doubt both playing in his voice.

"I managed to keep a contact or two among the Vanassi scouts." Quarian left out the detail about bribing them. "They inform me that Kesh has sided with them against the Kushaani."

"But that's a good thing. It will help keep the route open back to Vastan."

"In the long run, maybe. But it also means the empire is now attacking

Kesh as well. This is spiraling into civil war." Quarian let that sink in for a moment before delivering the next blow. "And the two main bridges across the Hathani River have been destroyed."

"That's insane! They will take forever to rebuild. Who did it?"

"My contacts didn't know whether it was the Peljathi or Kushaani or maybe even the Vanassi themselves."

"But that means we can't get supplies back to the army."

"There's a small ferry crossing further north we might try, but if the fighting on either side of the river forces us too far north, we risk running into the Mahyrastah Gorge. I have never seen it myself, but I have heard of people being lost there and never making it out. Assuming we were able to get through, it could easily add a week or two to our journey. From the eastern end, we would head for Hirstani, then Tarsapta, where Remalian forces should be waiting." The others in the room all glanced at each other at the mention of Tarsapta. Quarian had heard about the trial of the provincial warden there, and the prince's brutal sentence.

"This is all the more reason we need to move quickly," Andric growled. "If we wait too long, we could be cut off. I refuse to be stuck here while Stephir and our soldiers starve to death."

"And if we push too hard, we risk leaving empty-handed," the Sharinic priestess cautioned with a measured tone, "which will surely end in the same place."

"I'm afraid the window for making that choice is quickly closing," Quarian continued. "The Kushaani are being slowed by the combined Vanassi and Keshi forces, but it also is funneling them in this direction. They're expected to reach Sheerbahar the day after tomorrow."

"That means they could reach Sunapra in five or six days!" The prince exclaimed, stating the obvious.

"Your Highness," Knight Commander Nophet spoke for the first time, "while the thought of failing our mission pains us all, we must consider your safety. Though it is a long journey, perhaps we should make our way through the Tan'nikin Province and Kolrathi Wilds to the Western Marches."

"The Kolrathi pose as much of a danger as the Kushaani do," Sir Mar said flatly, finally adding his voice. "Maybe more so; I have heard they take no prisoners. And for all we know, the Kuldrith are attacking the Western Marches as well."

Barak's earlier counsel came to mind. *He hates feeling that he has no choice but to take one certain path.*

"There is another option, my lord." *Careful,* Quarian cautioned himself.

Don't appear overly eager. "I came across a couple of Vanassi guides who would be willing to lead us through the Velspars to Holbrooke."

"But I thought the mountains were impassable except through the Worrin Gap," Intercessor Henden said, sounding skeptical.

"Nothing is impassable, just sometimes very difficult. Especially for an army. But there's an old trade route to the ruins of Elginfir, and these guides know the way."

"Elginfir?" Prince Andric squinted his eyes in concentration. No doubt the alcohol was making that more difficult. "I remember something about that. It was a Cannessi stronghold, wasn't it Barak?"

"Yes. In fact, the ancestors of many of the Cannessi here in Sunapra were from Elginfir."

"Is there anything you don't know something about?" the prince asked with a smirk.

"If I find something I'll let you know."

"How long of a journey are we talking about?" Nophet asked.

"Approximately three weeks. Fortunately, we are in the middle of summer, which is the best time to cross, with the least chance of being caught in a blizzard or avalanche. Runoff from snowmelt is also at its lowest, making any stream crossings a bit easier."

Nophet nodded his approval. Quarian knew he was painting this path in the best possible light. There were dangers also, of course, but he feared disclosing them would dissuade the prince from choosing this option. Quarian had given all their choices a great deal of thought and felt this was the best. He just hoped the prince agreed.

"It can't be an easy route. Do you think we can all make it?" Prince Andric asked.

"Traveling through the mountains always comes with its dangers, Your Highness; but yes, I think we should all be able to make it. The route is passable with horses the entire way."

"I think it's an excellent option," Prince Andric said enthusiastically. "Well done Min. How long would it take to make the arrangements?"

"We can be ready in two days. Procuring the food will be the biggest challenge. And it will take most of the reserve coin we brought with us. The Council of Elders might start clamping down on the food supplies at any time, and they're not likely to be willing to provision us if we're not heading back to Prince Stephir. We should start first thing in the morning." The voice in the back of Quarian's mind nagged him to tell the rest. He had expected more opposition from the prince, more objections to anything except finding a route back to Balinth's Fortress. If anything, the prince seemed unusually eager.

"Do it," Andric said decisively.

"Your Highness," Henden said, her voice edging on pleading, "if the elders suspect us of preparing to abandon our mission, the negotiations will collapse entirely."

"Then this is your chance to show us what you can do. I am turning the negotiations entirely over to you, Intercessor. I will continue to attend the sessions so as not to draw unwanted attention, but I'm done trying to twist myself into knots for them. Min, make the preparations quietly. My preference is still to return to Balinth's, so try to find us a way there. But this way we have a backup plan." Andric smiled and heaved a sigh of relief that sounded final.

Quarian wanted to leave it at that. *I can always bring up the other bit of information later*, he thought, but he knew he was not being entirely honest and could not be at ease without giving Andric the full picture. "Your Highness, there is one other thing you should know. The guides took a fair bit of persuading before agreeing to lead the trek. There is some superstition about the mountains being cursed. They say no one who has attempted the journey in the past few years has returned."

"Did they say why?"

Quarian hesitated, not wanting to say it. After Pradan-ur, the prince might believe the superstitions, but the cat was already out of the bag. "They believe it's the larran."

"What is the larran?" Barak asked.

Quarian remained silent, hoping Andric would answer, and was surprised when Nophet replied. "It is the name the Vanassi give to the spirits of their ancestors who they believe return from the afterlife to help them fight battles at Pradan-ur."

The prince nodded, his eyes fixed on the floor as he slowly paced around the room. Their breathing was the only sound disturbing the heavy, unnatural silence. Quarian feared he was losing the young prince and looked at Master Ve'Aurben for any clue as to what to do, but the scholar just watched his friend until the prince finally spoke. "We don't have to decide tonight, but I want to move forward with the preparations. Barak, help Min with whatever he needs." The prince spoke to the intercessor while he refilled his cup. "Shiralla, you have two days. We all have a busy day tomorrow. Get some rest." With that, the prince turned and left the room followed by Nophet and the other Divinarim.

"Is there anything you need from me tonight?" Barak asked Quarian.

"Not that I can think of. Let's discuss it in the morning." Barak agreed as he got to his feet, wishing them all a good night before leaving. The sounds of the world suddenly returned as Corporal Elles ended his elant and followed Barak out. The Sharinists bid Quarian a good night as well before leaving him alone in the room.

He poured himself a glass of wine and drained it quickly, his head spinning with everything that had happened, and everything he had to do. He climbed wearily to his feet and headed off to bed, hoping against hope he was able to find some rest. He suspected it might be the last chance for a good night's sleep for a long time.

CHAPTER L

Evir

He had only been back in Stierve twenty tides, but the vibrant bustle of the city was already wearing thin. Or perhaps it was just the frustration of his fruitless investigation; or a bit of the vitalic lethargy setting in. Fourteen dead ends. He had tracked down nearly all the elantir connected directly to Qin'acht and not one of them activated Kiavi's attunement probe.

He might have had more luck if he just stood near the public entrance to the upper pyramid where all the Obsidian Door's elantir would have to pass on their way to or from the Door's chambers. He could have used the probe on everyone who walked by, but he might not survive long enough to make his case to anyone who could save him if he was discovered. Instead, he had to carefully track each elantir to a location where he could be close enough for the probe to work, but still have a chance of escaping once it did. He had crisscrossed Stierve too many times to count by now, had seen neighborhoods he hadn't even known existed, had made up excuses for business in the Emporium, had found covers for going into Lightsreach and Veilwatch, and all of it amounted to little more than a numb exhaustion.

Kiavi had warned him that using the probe would be draining, but the more he used it the faster he got fatigued and the longer it took to recover. Now he felt he was carrying a weight around Stierve all the time even though he had slept nearly a tide since he last used it. Perhaps if he was an elantir he would be more conditioned for such efforts. His dogged determination to pursue his objective pushed him to continue despite his exhaustion, but he also knew the importance of working within his limits. He was going to burn out, perhaps literally, if he didn't give himself some time to rejuvenate. So while he had come to Stierve with no intention of participating in any recreation, he had permitted himself some today.

Of course, this was no ordinary day of games at the coliseum. Today, the graduating cohort of Teraithian initiates, including Evir's son, Akriel, were having their final martial skills examination in the form of a tournament in front of all Stierve. This was nothing compared to the grand tournament held each year on Retribution Day in which the greatest kieresta and other warriors would compete, but today was far more meaningful for Evir.

He had seen very little of Akriel over the past five years, but he had kept track of the boy's progress. He was at or near the top of his cohort in every discipline, and Evir could hardly be prouder. The initiates' placement in each exam helped determine which of the four branches of priesthood they would be called to serve in. Those who excelled in the tournament today were likely to be chosen as kieresta, but it was good for the people to see that every cleric, from the governing kavartha order to the oteya'satir who conducted worship service, had training in serving Teraithia with the blade if need be.

In previous years when Evir had watched the initiates' martial trials, the coliseum had been only partially filled. This year, not a single seat was empty, and many spectators were left crowding along the concourse railings. Scores of kieresta and orderguards were posted throughout the coliseum to encourage civil behavior. Evir had arrived early enough to easily find an empty seat. He had chosen a spot as close to the coliseum floor as he could manage so he could try to see Akriel, but out on the fringe of the seating so there was little chance of being near anyone who might recognize him. Not that he particularly worried about that anymore. Vekk-oth's elant had proven effective several times when he had found himself close to someone he knew, and they never gave him a second look.

The rushing River Vangene ran through the middle of the coliseum but was hidden beneath wide platforms made from thousands of reedwood poles lashed together. Today, black canvas sheets were stretched tight over the platforms, and the overlapping angles of Teraithia's holy symbol had been painted in gold to mark the bounds of three combat areas. Elants had been placed on those golden borders so that if the combatants stepped across the lines anywhere other than the side angles where they entered, they would experience a painful though harmless shock—a harsh reminder that allowing oneself to be driven by the enemy was not in harmony with Teraithia's will.

He glanced across the coliseum to where fourteen platforms, one for each of the thirteen mavin tar and one for the atan-akai, the presiding high priestess of Teraithia, stood apart from the stone bench seating for the rest of the spectators. Each platform had a single, high-backed chair, though additional folding, backless seats with armrests were available for the mavin tars' guests. The overlord, though technically a mavin tar himself, had a grand seat upon the Overlord's Dais, a large platform flanked by towering marble statues.

The seats of the overlord and most of the mavin tar stood empty, though that was to be expected. The examination of initiates—exciting enough in the lives of Stierve's commoners—could hardly be expected to merit the attention of the overlord and ruling counsel, especially with the war in Remalia and unrest growing throughout the empire. It was remarkable Vetat Atan-akai and five of the mavin tar had chosen to come at all. Perhaps they hoped their presence would inspire in the people a greater sense of unity and duty. The only effect it had on Evir was to keep his gaze returning to scan the guests on the mavin tar platforms, thinking he might catch sight of Malithir Lord Overseer or Qin'acht Overseer. Not that it would make any difference in his investigation, but he felt it would somehow reassure him he was still on the right course.

A single, deep note from a score of horns reverberated throughout the Grand Chasm, sustained and building on itself. Drums joined in, beating out a slow rhythm: *boom, boom, ba-doom.* Thousands of spectators rose to their feet in anticipation of the arrival of the initiates who were making their way in procession from the temple to the coliseum. He kept his eyes fixed on the arched entrance, more eager to see Akriel than he had expected.

An enormous red banner hung above the archway bearing the symbol of the Kuldrith Empire—a golden sun inscribed within Teraithia's holy symbol, the sun's rays radiating toward the edges of the banner. Even with his growing antipathy toward the Church, Evir was still deeply moved to see the ancient symbol of his people displayed with such splendor. He yearned for Arku Overlord's success in fulfilling his promise to raise the Kuldrith out of obscurity and at long last fulfill their divine destiny to unite the world under a single banner. If only there was some path to that glorious future not littered with the corpses of the innocent. The memory of a small hand reaching for him from the tunnel floor in I'fa took his breath away as his chest clenched.

Cheers went up at the sight of the first initiates walking through the archway into the coliseum. Evir felt strangely detached from what was happening around him. The soon-to-be priests and priestesses marched tall and proud in their black stone-scale armor, carrying their helmets in one hand and their v'kar in the other, doing their best to seem the stoic warriors many of them aspired to be; but even at a distance, Evir could see the anxiety written on their youthful faces. The testing had to be stressful enough, never mind having to perform in front of thousands of spectators.

The initiates were ordered according to their height, tallest in the front. Akriel had an average build, so Evir was forced to wait patiently as nearly a hundred initiates passed through the archway before Evir finally caught sight of his son. A warmth coursed through his chest, his fatherly pride assuaging the pity he felt for those around him, most of whom would never know the joy of watching their child come of age. With a faint, dull ache he wondered what had become of his older two children. Were they perhaps sitting here in the coliseum, watching a brother they knew nothing about?

Those thoughts led him to Dae'yen. He felt guilty realizing he was grateful she wasn't here. She would have hated everything about this day, and her dark mood would have tainted what enjoyment Evir was able to find in Akriel's achievement.

Eventually, all of the nearly three hundred and fifty initiates were in the stadium and lined up facing Vetat Atan-akai to receive her benediction at the commencement of the exam. It was still hard for Evir to imagine how the cohorts in recent years had grown to such large numbers. For as long as Evir could remember, it would have been unusual for a cohort of initiates to number more than one hundred, but in the last few years, their numbers had grown to three and four times that size. What the Church intended to do with them all was anyone's guess, but he hoped it was not more of what had happened in Kierden.

All eyes in the coliseum lifted toward the chasm ceiling, shrouded in darkness but for the thousands of twinkling lumens affixed there. Vetat's powerful voice echoed through the silent coliseum as she pronounced her blessing on the assembled initiates. As she prayed for Teraithia's power to be poured out in abundance on the initiates, the background of pristine light always shining in the Chasm began to grow brighter. Gasps of awe and delight rippled around the spectators in the coliseum as the illumination intensified. Evir could not see the source from his vantage point, but he quickly guessed it was coming from the crystal joining the two pyramids, though he had never seen this before. It was an unusual display of power.

"Strengthen our swords and shields that we may be instruments in thy hands to bring about the fulfillment of thy great promises, that the world shall be subdued beneath the feet of the Kul-a'durith, thy chosen people!" Evir thought it was peculiar the atan-akai would use such an archaic name for the Kuldrith, but he shared her sentiments entirely. "All hail Teraithia, Queen of Heaven and Baon!" Vetat fished exultantly.

The roar of fifteen thousand spectators shouting the invocation in reply reverberated off the walls of the Grand Chasm. Evir joined with the others out of reflex, but it felt dishonest in a way he had never experienced before. He had told countless lies as an agent of the Obsidian Door, but this was somehow different. Saying those words was a betrayal of something deeply sacred—more sacred than the Church, more than Teraithia herself.

Those were dangerous thoughts. He did his best to push them aside as he turned his attention back to Akriel. The initiates began assembling around the three testing areas as several kieresta stepped up onto the wide platforms to judge the matches. It took Evir a few minutes to locate Akriel among the milling initiates. He looked calm, but Evir thought he recognized the anxiety masked behind his relaxed exterior. Akriel turned to one of the other initiates and seemed to make some sort of joke, evoking a nervous-looking laugh from his companion who gave him a playful shove.

Akriel's steel-gray hair, shoulder-length like all the acolytes, was pulled back to fit into the open-faced helmet he carried in his right hand. His face had many of the same sharp angles as Evir, but his complexion was smooth and ashen like his mother's. And while he had inherited Evir's athletic build, his average height came from Dae. Evir was anxious to see how Akriel dealt with opponents who had a size advantage. It would take skill and cunning more than brute strength, traits Akriel had displayed an aptitude for in his younger years. Evir could not help but think how much better served the empire would be if his son had chosen to follow in his footsteps and join the Obsidian Door rather than go into the priesthood, but Akriel had always been determined to follow his own path.

The first few matches were always between some of the best fighters. Evir guessed it was to help set the appropriate tone for the other initiates and to make the best showing for the spectators. The initiates' prowess with the ess'at and v'kar unmistakably marked them as top candidates for the kieresta order. The crowd cheered enthusiastically with each blow that landed. Slaves weren't permitted to enter the coliseum, and every capable Kuldrith was required to serve three years of military service, except for those who entered the priesthood. So nearly everyone watching the trials today had enough training to truly appreciate the skill on display.

Soon the lower-ranking initiates were also fighting their bouts, and the excitement in the coliseum waned. Nearly a tenth-tide had passed before Akriel was finally called to the dais for his first match. Evir felt a thrill rush through him, but as much as he wanted to, he could not afford to call attention to himself by cheering before the match had even started, let alone call out Akriel's name. That would be enough for some to guess at a familial connection, which at a minimum would mark him out as an oddity, and possibly be tantamount to announcing himself to the whole city if anyone connected the stones.

Since Stierve was the only place in the empire where initiates were trained, many of them had no family at all watching from the seats. And even for those who did, most had entered the seminary by the age of ten, so few families would even recognize each other. However, Evir and Dae'yen had kept Akriel at home until he was fourteen, overseeing his training and education before he finally insisted on entering the seminary. It appeared to have served their son well, but it also made it all too easy for anyone who knew Evir to connect him to Akriel, so Evir watched in anxious silence as the two initiates donned their helmets and climbed onto the platform.

Akriel's first opponent was much larger, but Evir could tell for all his size the young man was soft. They took their positions on opposite sides of the large gold holy symbol, then saluted and took a ready stance. At the command from the kieresta-amet standing at the head of the match area, the initiates stepped inside the overlapping gold angles and carefully closed the distance between them, weapons and shields at the ready. Akriel started cautiously, taking the other initiate's clanging blows on his v'kar while only responding with the most basic of counterstrikes.

His opponent decided to press his advantage, launching a flurry of not-so-precise attacks. Akriel retreated under the barrage, getting closer and closer to the gold line marking the bounds. The other initiate tried to bash Akriel with his v'kar, but the distance was just enough to make the initiate overreach. His son suddenly pivoted and smashed his own v'kar into his opponent, who was too off-balance to stop himself from stumbling out of bounds while Akriel sliced a killing blow across the back of his opponent's neck. The young man cried out in pain as the elants were triggered, but the cheers from the crowd quickly drowned him out.

All four kieresta judging the match stepped forward and called the bout in Akriel's favor. It was an excellent win, even though it was now clear to Evir the other initiate was no match for his son's superior skill. Evir's heart swelled with fatherly pride. The young men descended from the dais and Akriel was greeted with smiles and enthusiastic pats on the back as he rejoined his peers. The loser's reception was much less warm.

It was almost two more tenth-tides before Akriel's next match. His opponent was an attractive young woman nearly as tall as he was. They went through the usual ritual to start the match and soon they were trading skillful blows. This time there was no subterfuge on Akriel's part, just skill against skill. The first rounds of elimination were already pushing the more skilled fighters into matches together, and these two seemed to be evenly matched. The fighting continued for several minutes, each trying to gain the advantage. Fatigue was beginning to affect Akriel's opponent, slowing her responses and taking the edge off her agility. He saw her shield sagging ever so slightly. Akriel must have seen it too because he brought his sword down hard, not aiming to hit her but instead striking the edge of her v'kar, driving it down. He immediately thrust toward her exposed chest. She tried to raise the shield, but all she managed to do was force the blunt tip of his sword into her face.

The crowd gasped as the initiate fell to the ground, holding her gauntleted hands to her injured face. Akriel moved in, sword poised for the killing blow, but the amet barked a command, bringing him to an abrupt halt. The corner judges entered through the safety of the side angles and knelt next to the young woman. One held a blue cloth to her face as they helped her to her feet and walked her out of the combat area. The amet declared the match for Akriel to the cheering and applause of the spectators and other initiates.

The horns suddenly blared again, drowning out the cheers of the crowd and the clash of combatants alike. From the confused and curious expressions on the faces of the spectators, initiates and even the clerics around the coliseum, Evir was not the only one who had no idea what was happening as he rose. He looked around for any clue that would shed light on the unexpected interruption. Across the coliseum, several Than'katar, the overlord's honor guard, filed in and surrounded his dais. Cheering broke out among the crowd closest to the seat of power. Arku Overlord must have deigned to attend the final portion of the initiates' exams. The excitement spread as Arku ascended the steps, his wavy, charcoal hair held back by a silver circlet, and his white tunic and breeches trimmed in black made a striking contrast to the black clothes worn by the other mavin tar. Only Vetat Atan-akai was likewise adorned in white, her priestly vestments trimmed in gold.

The overlord stopped in front of his gilded chair and faced his assembled people. He placed his hands together in a cupping shape and slowly swung them from one end of the coliseum to the other in the gesture of accepting their lives into his hands. All present returned the appropriate gesture, hands held out wide to the side, palms toward the overlord and bowed low, eyes toward the ground. Evir felt his heart and mind pulled toward the overlord, wanting to please him. He had never felt this way toward any of the previous overlords. Respect, certainly—even admiration occasionally. But Arku inspired such great hope in Evir that he felt he would do anything to help the overlord realize his vision for the Kuldrith people.

At least, that had always been the case before. Today, for some reason, his desire felt more tepid, which worried the inquisitor. *Is it the fatigue?* he wondered to himself, though that didn't seem quite right. Perhaps having to hunt a mole among the Door's leadership was throwing him off. As he rose from the bow, he hoped finishing his mission would quickly set his sense of the world aright. Evir wondered if Arku would speak, but the overlord simply waved everyone back to their seats and gestured for the testing to continue.

Only twenty-four initiates remained. The penultimate match would be a three-versus-three fight, then the three initiates on the winning team would fight each other in the final match. Evir tried to imagine what it must feel like to test in front of Arku Overlord. Intimidating probably didn't begin to describe it. Evir's stomach clenched when Akriel's name was announced for the third match and assigned to the center platform. His anxiety deepened as the largest of the initiates ascended the dais ahead of his son. Evir recalled the young man from previous matches, and while his technique was not as refined as some others, he more than made up for it with overwhelming force.

The two combatants went to their respective corners, saluted, and took a fighting stance, or at least the larger one did. Akriel remained in a natural stance, staring at his opponent. Evir was too far away to see the details of his son's expression to tell if something was wrong. The kieresta-amet gave the command to commence the match, but Akriel remained still as the other initiate stepped into the ring and quickly moved to the center, shield raised and sword held over his shoulder. It was a mistake to give the other initiate the advantage of the center position in the confined area, leaving himself less room to maneuver.

Evir had never seen this before. He was not sure what the rules were for testing, but if they were the same as other tournaments, a count would begin and if the opponent failed to enter the combat area by the end of the count, the match would be forfeited. Initiates and spectators alike shouted encouragement and insults at the unmoving Akriel.

The amet looked at him and began counting. "One... two... three..."

Akriel snarled and threw his shield aside, pointing his sword at his opponent as he stepped one foot into the ring.

"KNEEL!"

Akriel's shout was barely audible above the jeers and cheering, over the ringing of steel on steel from the other bouts, and yet Evir felt the shockwave of dispositioning sweeping over the crowd. Awe and obedience, the same feelings he had felt just moments before toward Arku Overlord, stirred in him again.

Several heads around Evir bowed in reverence, while Akriel's opponent began to bend the knee. Akriel took a swift, lunging step forward, lashing out with his blade. He struck a vicious blow to the side of the other initiate's head, knocking him momentarily to one knee.

Realizing what Akriel had done, the larger youth surged to his feet with a roar, swinging his sword ferociously, but Akriel had already pulled back and circled out of harm's way. The amet called a halt to the match, but the other initiate refused to stop, rushing Akriel like an enraged volthox.

Akriel tried to deflect the charging attacker, but there was too much force. The other initiate grabbed hold of Akriel with his shield hand and pulled him into his thick-armed embrace. Both men tumbled across the gold line of the match bounds in a tangle of stone, metal, and bodies. The kieresta judging the match ran to the pair and dragged them apart. Akriel stood and calmly smoothed the stone tiles of his armor, while the other initiate struggled futilely against the restraining hands of the full-fledged warrior priests.

"Was that even legal?" a woman nearby finally voiced the question they all had in their minds. No one seemed to have an answer. Once order was restored down on the dais, the initiates retrieved their v'kar and swords and returned to their respective corners to await the ruling from the match judge. The coliseum was abuzz with chatter about the highly unusual match, wondering who this initiate was and what this meant for future contests. Whatever the outcome, Akriel had unwittingly called more attention to Evir than Evir himself ever could. Word of this was bound to reach Evir (or Javinth pretending to be Evir) and Dae'yen back in Kierden.

Finally, the match judge returned to the head of the combat area and indicated the bout had been decided in Akriel's favor. The coliseum erupted in a loud mix of cheering and the shouts of those decrying the decision. Evir could not tell which was more prevalent. He saw Arku Overlord nodding, though it was impossible to know if it was a sign of his approval or meant something else entirely. The other acolyte turned in disgust and strode to the edge of the dais, not even bothering to take the stairs, but instead he jumped down into the midst of the other initiates. Akriel casually walked down the steps, his head held high and his face an unreadable mask. Evir had taught him that.

There were fewer congratulatory pats this time as the other initiates gave him a wider berth than before. The discussions around Evir continued even as the next round of matches got underway.

"It's supposed to be a test of combat skills, not benefactions. That had to be cheating."

"They called the match for the initiate. Obviously, the kieresta-akai considered it a fair move."

"Have you ever seen anyone try it before?"

"No, but others will certainly try again."

"Good! It just means the Church will be that much stronger."

"That one's going to be selected for the kavartha order for certain."

"Why? Because he cheated? That doesn't automatically make him kavartha. Vaesh'katir, maybe."

Evir's heart swelled with fatherly pride knowing his son's victory, unorthodox as it was, would be the topic of discussion throughout Stierve for some time. He was not sure Dae would feel the same. A part of her would no doubt have been proud of his accomplishment, but she almost certainly would be disappointed with the manner in which he won. Evir longed to see the two of them patch up their differences. Having the two people he loved most at odds with each other was a dull ache in his heart.

Akriel's name was soon again called, and the coliseum fell into a muted buzz as the two initiates climbed the steps to the platform. They moved to their respective corners and saluted, stepping into guard positions. Nothing like the last match. The amet gave the command for the match to begin and the two stepped across the gold lines of the corner angles. Akriel's opponent quickly scored a point with a swipe of his v'kar followed by a quick sword strike to the top of Akriel's head. The initiate's technique was quite good. Akriel managed to score a few hits by the end of the match, but he simply could not keep his opponent's sword tip from finding its mark more often. It was a well-fought match, but in the end, it was clear the other initiate had won. It was probably better for Akriel anyway. Another win, especially with any kind of irregularity, would have been too much for some of his son's peers to tolerate without some retribution back at the seminary dormitories.

He wanted so badly to talk to Akriel, but even if Evir had been here under normal circumstances that would have been impossible. He would simply have to wait for another day. Evir rose from his seat and made his way down the line of spectators, confident they weren't paying any attention to him. Leaving this close to the end of the trials was unusual, but a handful of others around the coliseum were doing the same. It was his best chance to get out ahead of the crowds.

As he made his way onto the Cardinal Line he was tempted to resume his search, but he decided it was enough for today to have seen his son, to witness him successful and doing well. Instead, he headed back toward Daopek's residence in the Warrens. Somehow the burden of his task seemed a little lighter as he left the cheers of the crowd in the Grand Chasm behind.

CHAPTER LI
SHIRALLA

"Don't try to lay the blame for your civil war at my feet! No reasonable person would believe I was asking you to go out and assassinate the empress," Andric practically shouted. Shiralla looked at her hands folded in her lap, a subtle sign to the Vanassi that she didn't approve of the prince's manners. Despite his assurance last night that he would turn the negotiations over to her, he seemed to be doing everything possible to kill the negotiations short of walking out. She tried to open communion with him again, but he still refused to let her in.

"So you think we are unreasonable," Elder Gottara said icily. Even the smile that seemed permanently etched on Elder Mubali's leathery face disappeared.

"See, there you go, taking my words out of context again."

"Your words were literally, 'You could start with killing Empress Arrdiwat. That would certainly do the trick.'" Bejurn said, reciting the prince's rash words at their first meeting nearly two months ago in Nanjab.

"You asked for a sign, and it has been given," Gottara continued, "because we believed we could count on the Remalians to hold to their word and defeat the Kushaani."

"I never said our intention was to defeat the Kushaani, only to end the slave trade. You kicked the hornets' nest, hoping to leave us no choice but to fight them to the bitter end and win your independence for you," Andric countered.

Elder Mubali spread his arms wide in a look of utter innocence, marred only by the annoying, placating smile creeping back onto his lips. "We made a dangerous choice, hoping by a great blood sacrifice to seal a lasting alliance with the great Kingdom of Remalia."

Shiralla knew the prince would not respond well to the elder's statement and tried to head it off. "Perhaps we should—" Shiralla interjected, but Andric wouldn't be silenced.

"Blood sacrifice? Do you think we would ever accept such an abomination as a gift of friendship? I came here to figure out how our peoples could work together to establish peace, not drown the world in blood."

Sharin Dara, help me. This is spiraling out of control. She knew she needed to de-escalate both sides quickly, but how?

"No, you came to beg for food before your army starves to death. But your plan is to abandon the fight with Kushaan as soon as you can return to Remalia, is it not?"

Peace. The word resonated in her bosom. It was what they all wanted, what they needed. *Sharin Dara's peace.* She opened herself to the goddess's divinessence. She only needed to feel it for a moment, to remind herself what it was so she could lead them there. She had touched that source so often in the last few days that it came with ease, lighting upon her heart with the gentlest of touches. She sensed the countless souls surrounding her, in this room, in the palace, out into Sunapra and the countryside beyond. She sensed their interconnectedness, though she could not see the threads of light linking them through the expanse as Sharin Dara had shown her before. She recalled the day she arrived in Sheerbahar and marshaled so much power. Why then and not now? It would be so much more useful now.

"To expel an invading force, yes. Or would you have us lose our home fighting for yours?"

"And is your request of us any different?" Gottara's words dripped with acid.

Shiralla remembered her vision of walking among the Vanassi, protecting them, bringing them to the light. *Small and simple acts can make a world of difference.*

"At least I—"

"I love you," Shiralla said quietly. The room froze in awkward silence. She looked around at those seated at the ancient stone-slab table. She had no idea what she was saying, but the words flowed from her heart, pounding in her chest, not with anxiety or embarrassment, but with ardent affection. She was not a diplomat in this moment, she was a priestess. "Each of you is wise and good and noble. I admire you and am grateful for you."

She let those words and the feelings of her soul hang in the air. They violated every lesson she had been taught about diplomatic negotiations: *'Do not make it about you,' 'Do not show your heart,'* and *'Use emotion sparingly, strategically.'* All eyes in the room were fixed on the floor, on the table, anywhere but on each other. "I suggest we take some time apart to reflect on our true purpose here so we can come back tomorrow ready to see things in a fresh light," Shiralla said gently.

Andric was the first to stand. He turned and stalked out of the room without a word, escorted by Knight Commander Nophet and Divinar Jessol. Elder Mubali followed suit, the smile back on his face and bowing his head to Shiralla before departing with Elder Yylghar on his heels, leaving only Elder Gottara and Shiralla seated at the table. "You may have moved the others, but your dispositioning didn't work on me," Gottara said with stony pride.

"I didn't disposition anyone," Shiralla said matter-of-factly, but gently. "I simply did what everyone else was doing—speaking what I felt was true."

The elderly woman considered the priestess for a moment, though what she was thinking was impossible to tell. "Then I thank you for sharing your truth," the elder said with no warmth in her voice as she rose to her feet. "I hope you have more than honeyed words when we resume our talks." With that, the elder left the room.

Shiralla let out a sigh.

"If that somehow ends up working, they're going to have to add a new chapter to *The Litany of Crinnavar*," Lady di Greven said lightheartedly as the knight moved from her place against the wall behind Shiralla and took Prince Andric's seat next to the priestess, removing her gauntlets and setting them on the table. "Or perhaps you've secretly converted to worship of the Holy Couple and didn't tell anyone," she teased with a smile.

"It was very brave," Sir Mar said, walking in the other direction. Shiralla thought he was leaving the room, but he circled to the other side of the long table where the elders had been sitting.

"It doesn't matter. We are no closer to an agreement than the day we arrived. Further, maybe."

"Well, if His Highness had kept his word about allowing you to handle the negotiations..." Emerly left the rest unspoken.

Shiralla had thought the same many times throughout the day, but she was no longer sure. "It isn't just Andric," she replied. "Something is off with the elders as well, but I can't figure out what it is."

"Perhaps it has something to do with the army marching toward their city and killing their people," Lathon said flatly.

"Then why waste their time talking with us at all? Reason dictates they should have either agreed to terms quickly or ended the talks days ago."

"You're falling prey to the same trap again, reasoning from your own perspective. See it through their eyes," Sir Mar offered.

She felt the old frustrations start to creep up. Consul Rellat had said the same thing to her. Thinking back to their conversation made her skin crawl. She quickly turned her thoughts to the Vanassi. It was clear Elder Gottara was the key to breaking the deadlock, but how was Shiralla supposed to figure out what made the woman tick? Maybe if she had more time.

"I am considering staying with the Vanassi." She knew the thought was coming out of the blue for the knights, but she had been giving it a great deal of consideration for several days.

"What good will that do? The prince is leaving in a day or two, and without him, you can't obtain a binding treaty," Emerly said. "Besides, the Kushaani are coming, and the Vanassi are preparing to leave Sunapra and head west. Even if you were to reach terms on an agreement, they would be in no position to provide the aid we need."

"I know. I would not be staying in my capacity as intercessor, so you would be free to leave with the prince."

"What are you talking about?" Emerly asked, confusion and concern playing on her face.

How can I tell them? she wondered. She guessed Mar already had some idea since they had somehow been in communion when she had her... vision. But they had never spoken of it. "I..." she began, then stopped and tried again. "Sharin Dara has other work for me to do. She wants this people to know her better—to be blessed by her teachings. And I believe she wants me to help do that."

"We don't evangelize," Emerly said flatly, sounding more like Mar for a change. "We attract and persuade people to her path by showing the benefits of her doctrine in practice."

These were fundamental tenets of Sharinism, at least as espoused by the Remalian branch of the Faith. The Celendrian church had less compunction about actively recruiting adherents. "Perhaps it's time for things to change."

"That is not for us to decide."

"If not us, then who?" Shiralla countered.

"High Consul Penrossart is the only one authorized to alter our divine mandate."

"Or Sharin Dara herself."

"Are you claiming to speak for Sharin Dara now?"

Shiralla did not know how to answer. To say yes was to speak blasphemy against the Faith, and to say no was to speak blasphemy against the vision Sharin Dara had shown her. "Lathon," Shiralla said to Sir Mar. It felt odd using his given name, but she hoped to remind him of their shared experience. "You know why I should stay."

"I know," Lathon replied quietly.

"Then will you stay with me?"

Lathon's hard eyes bore into her. "Consul Rellat also told you of Nophet's designs on Andric. That must not be allowed to happen. We can do nothing to protect him if we stay here."

"How do you even know about that? And do you really think one prince is more important than saving tens of thousands of souls?"

"What are you two talking about?" Emerly said with frustration that sounded so foreign from the indomitably sanguine knight.

"There is a much bigger picture to consider," Lathon answered, though Shiralla was not sure which question he was responding to. "I fear we are nearing the time of the gloaming of the gods, and that Andric will play a role in tipping the scales to determine which god remains. They may not ultimately tip in Sharin Dara's favor, but for the sake of the world, Teraithia must be prevented at all costs from prevailing—even if it means defying a divine calling."

"How can you say that?" di Greven asked in disbelief. "Our holy commissions as knights and priestess have boundaries set by the Church," Emerly said emphatically, driving her finger onto the stone table to emphasize her point. "Do you think you will be aligned with Sharin Dara's will if you transgress those bounds? You won't. You will be apostates."

"My path lies with the prince," Lathon said, seeming to completely ignore his fellow knight.

"And how can I turn my back on Sharin Dara's will?" Shiralla asked, tears beginning to well in her eyes as she tried to focus on Sir Mar's hard-set face.

The knight's jaw muscle worked beneath his dark skin. When he spoke, his voice was thick with emotion. "There are some things more important than the will of a god. Even a god you love with all your heart." Sir Mar rose and left the room.

"He's wrong, Shiralla," Emerly said, resting a gentle hand on the priestess's arm. "The bounds Sharin Dara sets are the greatest expression of her love for us, for they mark the path that leads forever into her light. And our obedience is the purest expression of our love for her." Tears fell from Shiralla's lashes. Emerly patted her arm, then rose and left her alone.

Sharin Dara, please give me a sign of which path I should take. She repeated those words again and again, but no answer came. *Lathon and Emerly will not stay with me. I cannot bear it if you leave me alone, too.* She wiped more tears from her cheeks.

Eventually, her thoughts wandered to the negotiations with the Vanassi. Today had gone so horribly wrong. She was certain there was no hope of salvaging the talks and wondered what she could have done differently. Her dreams of becoming an ambassador were over after this humiliating failure, assuming she ever saw Remalia again.

She imagined herself speaking with Elder Gottara in a peaceful garden, with no care in the world. She wondered what the woman would be like. Would she laugh? Shiralla almost giggled out loud at the thought of the woman's stern face crackling as she attempted a smile.

You should visit her.

That was the last thing Shiralla wanted to do. It was nearing dinner time, and though the thought of food was unappealing, the others would be gathering. At least she wouldn't be alone. She pushed herself to her feet and slowly walked from the negotiating chamber. *How would I even find her house?* she wondered. She tried to picture the kind of house the woman would live in. Did she have a family or live alone?

Shiralla passed by the corridor leading to the Remalians' quarters and wandered aimlessly until she found steps that took her outside to a wide porch with crumbling statues and broken paving stones overlooking a quarter of the city she hadn't seen before. She found the elaborate domed roofs of the temples and towers rising out of the sea of gray- and red-tiled roofed houses quite beautiful. Perhaps one of them could become a temple to Sharin Dara.

"Tucali," a young man's voice called out behind her, "are you lost?"

She turned and saw one of the Vanassi servants. "Do you know where Elder Gottara's home is? I need to find her." Shiralla was surprised at her words.

"Yes, tucali. But supper will be served shortly. Would you like me to show you after you've eaten?"

"No, I need to see her now, please."

The young man bowed respectfully. "If you will follow me, lady." He led her back through the palace, stopping only briefly to inform another servant where they were going. She tried to take in the sights of the canals, shops, gardens, and unique buildings they passed as they wound their way through Sunapra's maze of streets, but her mind kept racing ahead to where they were headed. What was she going to say? Was the elder even home? Would she be willing to talk to Shiralla?

At last, they arrived at a high, white plaster wall enclosing a garden filled with palm trees and flowering bushes. There was no gate, so her guide led her inside and along a cobblestone path to a small house like many others she had seen, though admittedly few with their own private gardens. Before she had time to reconsider, the young man knocked on the painted red door and stepped to the side.

Shiralla heard footsteps approaching, and a moment later the door swung open to reveal an elderly woman dressed in a loose, rose-colored blouse and purple skirt with gold-thread embroidery along the edge, her beautiful white hair pulled back into a large bun on the back of her head. She raised her eyebrow and considered Shiralla for a moment. "You must be Intercessor Henden," she said. Her voice was smooth and pleasant, almost musical.

"I am. I'm looking for Elder Gottara. Is she here?"

"Come in," she said, gesturing for Shiralla to enter. The young man waited outside as the woman closed the door behind Shiralla. The house was not particularly large to begin with, but several baskets and crates stood stacked around the room, making it feel crowded. The red silk wallcovering on one wall had dark, unfaded spots in the shapes of items that had been recently removed. A basket half filled with cloth-wrapped items sat on a low table in the center of the main room. Everything told Shiralla the house was being prepared for departure.

"Chantani," the woman called out, "you have a visitor."

From deeper within the house, she heard a familiar voice respond. "A moment, please." The sound of water sloshing came from the same direction, and a moment later Elder Gottara entered the room, her sleeves rolled up and her hands still glistening with water from whatever she had been doing. Shiralla thought she detected a hint of concern behind the elder's otherwise even expression.

"Intercessor, is everything all right?"

"Forgive my intrusion, Elder. Yes, everything is fine, thank you. I was hoping to speak with you, but I can see this isn't a good time. It can wait until tomorrow."

"Now is fine. Be welcome in our home. This is my love, Pruusha," the elder said, indicating the woman who had answered the door.

"It's a pleasure to meet you, Intercessor," Pruusha said warmly, though she sounded tired. "Chantani has told me much about you."

Shiralla curtsied deeply. "It's a pleasure to meet you as well."

"Would you care to stay for dinner?" Chantani asked. "It will be ready soon. I'm afraid it will not be as extravagant as what you would have at the palace, but we would be honored for you to join us."

Shiralla didn't want to impose, but she feared it would be more offensive to decline. Besides, she did not want to go back to the palace right now and had nowhere else to go. "You are most gracious, Elder. I would love to stay, if you are sure it isn't too much of an imposition."

"What an odd thing to say," Elder Gottara said with a slight smile. "As if I could now say, 'On second thought, it *is* too much of an imposition. You are no longer welcome.'"

"Chantani," Pruusha said with a gentle mix of reproving and warning. "Intercessor, I would offer you a seat in here, but I'm afraid things are a bit chaotic. Why don't I put some chairs on the balcony?" The woman moved efficiently to take some chairs through double doors on the far end of the room that opened onto a balcony overlooking the garden.

"I need to finish cooking," the elder said. "Would you like to help me in the kitchen, or wait outside?"

"I'm afraid I could only make the meal worse if I tried to help, but I'd be happy to keep you company."

Chantani raised an eyebrow, but Shiralla could not guess what it meant. She had seen that expression dozens of times over the last several days. "Come along then."

Shiralla followed the elder back the way she had come to a cooking area also being packed for leaving. "How soon will you leave?"

"As soon as we have no other choice."

Shiralla knew that day was fast approaching. And she understood the pain of having your home threatened. Even now, Teris was under siege. True, it was more likely to fend off being conquered than Sunapra was, but the weeks of anxiety for the safety of her home made her deeply empathetic to the Sunaprans' plight. Before she could find the words to express her feelings, the conversation turned to the practical matters of finishing the cooking and serving up three plates of spiced chicken, rice, flatbread, and thick cream sauce. It felt good to be busy with mundane tasks where lives were not hanging in the balance.

They carried the plates out to the small balcony with a beautiful view of the garden that extended beyond the house for some distance with a canal running through it. They took their seats and ate the simple meal as the two women answered Shiralla's questions about their lives in Sunapra, about how they met and fell in love, about Pruusha's work as a singer and music teacher, about Chantani's career as a silk merchant before turning the business over to their son and daughter when she was selected to the Council of Elders.

The sky overhead was burnt umber as the sun set somewhere in the east when Pruusha stood up and collected their plates. "I'll bring some tea, then leave you two to talk."

Shiralla could hardly believe how different Elder Gottara was in her home from the way she was during their negotiations. She was loath to disrupt the pleasant evening by discussing official matters, but there would never be a better time. "Will we have privacy out here?" Shiralla asked.

"As long as we don't raise our voices," Chantani said wryly. "You can't see them from here, but there are gates blocking the canal so no one accidentally comes through our garden. What is it that raises the concern for privacy?"

"Do you see any reason to continue our negotiations? Forgive my bluntness, but it appears we are all but out of time. We could waste what little remains maintaining our usual posturing, but I prefer to see if openness gets us anywhere different."

"It's a shame we waited until now to resort to what perhaps should have been our posture from the beginning." Pruusha brought out a tray with tea, kissed Chantani on the forehead, then went back inside, closing the double doors behind her. "But to answer your question, there is always time to work things out until there isn't."

"Then here is the truth of our position. King Jevorak is dying, perhaps dead already. Only a miracle could save him. For all intents and purposes, Crown Prince Stephir rules the kingdom already, and he will be king at any time. He wants to form an alliance with the Vanassi, not simply to secure the supplies he desperately needs right now, but because he is a good man who worships the Holy Couple and believes in their teachings to love and care for others, especially those in need of help. He will be an excellent ally to your people and will commit whatever troops Prince Andric agrees to. But his first priority will be to secure his kingdom from the invaders, which means he may not commit them in time to be of any use to you."

Chantani looked deeply into Shiralla's eyes for much longer than Shiralla was comfortable with. She wanted to turn away, but she had committed to openness, so she let herself be weighed or judged or whatever the Vanassi elder was doing. At last, the woman turned her gaze back to her garden and silently drank her tea. As the silence stretched on, Shiralla feared she had been too honest, painting too bleak of a picture and killing any hope of an alliance. She was glad Andric and the others weren't here to witness her failure.

"We have survived attacks by the Kushaani for hundreds of years, and they survived attacks by my people for hundreds of years before that. The difference of a week, a month, or a year is only a ripple on the surface of the river. We will send your crown prince the food your people need."

"Thank you," Shiralla managed to spit out through sheer habit, despite being stunned by the elder's unexpected promise. "But how? My understanding is that the imperial forces have made the route east impossible."

"While we have been negotiating with you, we have also negotiated a treaty with the Keshi. They are now our allies against the Kushaani. They are prepared to send the supplies you need and can deliver them in a few days' time."

Shiralla was again taken aback by the superlative news, but her instincts told her the deal was not yet sealed. "And how can we show our deep appreciation?" she asked.

"Commit to send your troops when you can. We will be patient. In the meantime, a token of your commitment is all I ask." It was Shiralla's turn to weigh Elder Gottara with her gaze. What could the woman possibly have in mind? "Leave a fist of your soldiers with us when you depart."

Shiralla's heart sank. If she had asked anything else, it might have been possible. But Shiralla knew the prince's mind regarding leaving anyone behind. "What if I stayed instead?" Shiralla offered hopefully. It would solve both of her problems. "I could help with—"

"Intercessor... Shiralla, with all due respect, though I would be glad to have you stay among our people, the tokens of our alliance, at least for now, are food for soldiers. You are not soldiers. And if we are being completely honest, I think Prince Andric would not consider it a great sacrifice to agree for you to stay. His soldiers, on the other hand... that would seal our pact with a genuine sacrifice from the prince."

The truth of the elder's words was a knife in Shiralla's gut. Her mind raced down a dozen paths, looking for any alternative, but nothing compared with the horrible elegance of Chantani's proposal. She dreaded the thought of taking this to Andric. He would feel she went behind his back, despite his words turning the mission over to her. Worse, he would hate her for forcing him to choose between saving the army and saving his men. She hated herself for putting him in this position, but she saw no other way. Let him hate her then if that is what it took to save the army—to save Remalia.

"I will take your generous proposal to Prince Andric. Thank you for your hospitality and your assistance," Shiralla said, rising from her seat. Elder Gottara stood up and escorted her back inside.

"You've proven yourself a very capable representative of your people,

Shiralla. I had my doubts when they sent such a young one to us, but their confidence in you was well placed."

The gracious praise nearly took Shiralla's breath away. She said a brief goodbye to Pruusha then left their house. Outside, she found the servant waiting and followed him back along the dark garden path beneath a twilight sky. Her steps were heavy, weighed down by the dread of the conversation she now faced with Andric.

It was dark as she crossed the plaza in front of the palace. Iron braziers filled with burning wood lit a path to the steps where she saw Emerly standing motionless, firelight reflecting off her armor, presumably waiting for her. Shiralla thanked and dismissed her guide as she climbed the steps toward her knight protector.

"Today might not have been the best day to go for a jaunt through the city by yourself, Intercessor."

"Well, that remains to be seen, but you may be right. Do you know where Prince Andric is? Not too inebriated yet, I hope."

"Oh, I don't like the sound of this." The two women made their way to the Remalians' quarters. The prince was where she expected to find him, in the sitting room with Barak and Quarian, a cup in his hand. What she hadn't expected was to find Jalanti sitting with him as well. She could not help noticing how close the two were to each other.

"Intercessor Henden, we missed you at dinner. Come have a drink with us."

Shiralla was dismayed at the obvious signs of Andric's intoxication. "Your Highness is kind to offer, but I have an important matter that I was hoping to discuss with you in private, if I may impose on you for a few moments of your time."

"I'm sure whatever it is can wait until tomorrow. Tonight, we're celebrating because Jalanti is coming with us—wait, I have a great idea," he said excitedly, resting a heavy hand on Jalanti's leg. The gesture grated on Shiralla's nerves, and she studied the young woman's reaction to try to discern how she felt about it. No sense interfering if she welcomed the prince's attention. Shiralla thought she detected a hint of uneasiness there, but was unsure if she was simply projecting her own feelings onto Jalanti. "We could appoint you to my retinue as a permanent envoy of the Vanassi people. Would you like that?" he said with a smile.

"Prince Andric," Shiralla interjected, "there are channels by which these things are properly handled. I would be happy to assist with shepherding the matter through the process once we return to Remalia." She hoped this was only the alcohol talking and that Andric would let it go by morning. Perhaps he was not in the best condition for discussing Elder Gottara's proposal, either. *That is just your fear talking*, she told herself.

"Well, either way," he continued, turning his attention back to Jalanti, "you will love Remalia. Especially Teris! We—"

"Your Highness," Barak interrupted this time. "I think perhaps we should hear what Intercessor Henden has to say."

"Oh, fine. But sit down and have a drink first, then we'll hear what's so important that it can't wait until morning. You too Lady di Greven. Min, pour the ladies a drink."

"Thank you, Your Highness, but I'm afraid we will have to decline for now. Perhaps you and I could take a walk, my lord."

"I should go," Jalanti said, moving as if to get up.

"No, you're one of us now. There's no need to leave," Andric said, his tone half-command and half-pleading. Jalanti cast her eyes to the floor and sank back down. "Go on, Shiralla."

Shiralla knew this topic should be discussed in private, but perhaps having the others here would moderate the prince's reaction, or at least they could help mollify him once he heard what she had to say. Jalanti was the real concern. Shiralla was certain she would report every detail of their discussion to the council, or at least to Bejurn. Did it matter, though? If Andric did not agree tonight, they would simply be in the same place they were when the talks ended that afternoon. She drew in a deep breath.

"As you wish. I had dinner with Elder Gottara tonight." Andric smirked and seemed to want to make a snide remark, but she pushed ahead. "She agreed to send the supplies to Prince Stephir."

"Really?" Andric asked, as pleasantly shocked as Shiralla had been. "That's excellent news," he said, a smile broadening on his face. "But how are they going to get past the Kushaani?"

"They have formed an alliance with the Keshi tribes, who will deliver the supplies. Food will arrive in the Curritan Province in less than a week, and at Balinth's Fortress within two."

The prince let out a triumphant shout. "Thank the gods!"

"Congratulations, Intercessor," Captain Major Minanthsolum said, toasting her with his drink. Jalanti simply smiled, a look of relief on her face.

Only Master Ve'Aurben did not appear ready to celebrate. "On what terms?" he asked calmly. His question was like water dousing a fire, ruining the timing she had been hoping to manage for maximum effect.

"Prince Andric is to commit Remalia to send troops to fight the Kushaani as soon as we have dealt with the Kuldrith."

"Done!" Andric said, still sounding pleased. "I'll lead the army myself!" Shiralla saw Knight Commander Nophet give a slight nod of approval from his position behind the prince. She realized he was always near the prince, even when other Divinarim were standing guard. Perhaps Sir Mar and Consul Rellat were right to be concerned about the Teraithian knight's influence over Andric. She listened as Andric boasted of his future exploits, delaying as long as possible the moment she knew was coming.

"There's something else," Barak said. Her heart skipped a beat as dread gripped her. She was impressed with the Viancian scholar's discerning mind and wanted to throttle him for not keeping it to himself.

"Yes, there is." She took a deep breath to calm her nerves, but they refused to comply. "As a token of Remalia's commitment to send troops in the future, they have asked that we leave a fist of our soldiers here in Sunapra."

The bright sunshine of Andric's approbation disappeared in an instant, his face darkening with anger. "Absolutely not!"

"Your Highness, it is but five soldiers. They will be—"

"There are already fifteen, soon to be sixteen, Remalian bodies we are leaving behind in this land. I will not lose even one more!"

"Do you prefer to lose thousands to starvation?"

"You want to make me a slave trader of my own people," he retorted accusingly. "Their freedom for a price!" It was an unfair comparison. They wouldn't be staying as slaves, but it was useless to argue semantics with him now. Silence served her best. "How would you like it if I left *you* behind?"

"I already offered to stay in their place, but Elder Goleta said it must be soldiers," she said quietly. Her words seemed to have a sobering effect on the prince, who climbed to his feet and started pacing.

"Andric," Barak said, "I don't like it either. But if it means obtaining food for the army..."

"I know!" Andric barked at his friend. "But how do I even choose who to leave here?"

Shiralla's heart fluttered in her chest. The prince was talking about how to choose. Was the argument over already?

"Explain the situation to the men and ask for volunteers," Quarian advised. "They might surprise you."

"And if not?"

"Then you make the hard decision that is required of you."

"That's easy for you to say. You're not the one who has to make it!"

"I have had to make decisions knowing it would cost men their lives," Min said somberly. "It is one of the most difficult things we ever have to do. But you are strong enough for this moment."

The prince continued pacing, stopping occasionally to look up at the ceiling or stand with eyes closed before resuming his pacing. He finally shook his head. "Fine," he said, sounding defeated and angry. "Tell them they'll have their trophies!" Then, looking at Jalanti, he added, "And I guess I'll have mine."

Jalanti's face hardened with a defiance Shiralla hadn't seen in the usually docile woman. She rose to her feet with far more practiced grace than any of the Remalians. "I am not your trophy, Prince Andric. Goodnight," she said with a stiff bow and left the room.

"Jalanti, wait! I..." Andric called after her, but she didn't stop. The prince cursed and hurled his cup against the wall, a splatter of wine arcing across the room as it flew. The metallic clamor of the cup hitting the wall and clattering to the floor sent a shiver running down Shiralla's spine despite the heat. The intercessor held her breath.

"Andric—" Barak started, but the prince cut him off.

"Min, how soon can you have us ready to leave?"

"Everything will be ready by tomorrow afternoon, and we can leave first thing the following morning."

"Fine. Make sure it happens. Intercessor, do whatever has to be done tomorrow to seal this deal." Shiralla exhaled a sigh and bowed with no further words, a pained smile finally touching her lips.

"Now everyone get out!"

CHAPTER LII
ANDRIC

Andric stood facing the gathered soldiers on a shaded porch next to one of the open courtyards on the palace grounds. He felt like he had been trampled by wild slattars. His stomach roiled and his head was pounding, though how much of each was from too much drinking last night or the difficult task before him, he couldn't tell. He was grateful to have Min and Barak standing nearby to take over in case he needed to excuse himself.

"I wanted to share with you that our mission has finally proven successful. Intercessor Henden is with the Vanassi as we speak, working out the last details for them to send the needed supplies to the army at Balinth's Fortress." Smiles and back-slapping broke out among most of the soldiers, though a few looked like Andric felt. He had heard they had spent a few nights out that would make Frey jealous.

"We knew The Firebrand wouldn't fail, m'lord!" one man called out enthusiastically.

Andric had stopped hating the name quite so much until this moment. He felt he was about to betray everything his soldiers thought they meant by it. "I couldn't have done it without you. I thank you all. I'm afraid it's not all good news, though. You know about the empire's retaliation against Vanashar. It is quickly escalating into a civil war and Remalia has agreed to provide troops in aid of our new allies once we have exterminated the vermin that invaded Remalia. But there is one very difficult detail left to work out." He paused, dreading what he was about to say. "They have demanded that we leave a fist here when we depart."

"For how long?" one lancer asked.

"I cannot say for certain. But you have my word," Andric rushed to add, seeing his own concerns reflected in their faces, "we will find a way to get you home as soon as we can."

"Will we be prisoners?"

"Or slaves?" another asked.

"No, I would never leave you here as slaves. You will have the choice to serve as warriors in the Vanassi army alongside the Vidyahar, or to fill another occupation."

"So who's stayin'?" one of the scouts asked; Corporal Teek, if he remembered the man's name correctly.

"I hate the thought of leaving any of you behind." Andric could feel the pressure of what he was about to ask weighing on his heart. "Unfortunately, there does not appear to be any other choice. Intercessor Henden even tried to volunteer to stay instead, but they wouldn't accept. This is the sacri—," Andric's voice broke with sudden emotion, "—sacrifice that is required to save our brothers and sisters in arms from starvation." His heart ached at having to say the words. He stared at the ground, his lungs burning with the effort to breathe. He remembered Quarian's words from last night. '*You are strong enough for this moment.*'

I'm not, he told himself, even as he spoke. "You should know that Captain Major Minanthsolum already offered to stay. And while I am deeply grateful for his willingness, and acknowledge that his life isn't any more or less valuable than anyone else's, the truth is that I need him too much to permit that. It's more than you should ever be asked, but I am asking. Is anyone else willing to remain here?"

No one moved. Andric understood. How could anyone volunteer to give up their country, their family, their home, their—

"Teraithia's teats," Teek swore, "I'll stay." Someone whispered a disparaging remark Andric could not quite make out, but it was something to the effect of, '*Of course a scout wants to stay.*'

It angered Andric; however, reproving anyone at this moment was ungracious and counterproductive. "Thank you, Corporal," Andric said, grateful at least one person was willing to make such a sacrifice. Of course, he could not afford to leave one of the scouts behind. He hoped there were enough other volunteers to get his five without having to reject Teek's willing offer.

One lancer stood up, tall and proud. "I will stay, Your Highness."

"Thank you," Andric replied. He waited as one moment stretched into another before two more raised their hands. They looked at each other and nodded, an unspoken acknowledgment between comrades.

"I will do as you command, my lord," Lanceman Tamon said resolutely. He was the oldest of the lancers in the delegation, older even than Andric's father, and the one all the others looked up to. Andric didn't want to lose him. Besides, Tamon had family, grandchildren, waiting for him in Teris. It felt worse making him stay, but he could not afford to play favorites.

That made five including Teek, but Andric was hoping for at least one more volunteer. He could see the relief on the others' faces mixed with confusion as to why he was still waiting. As the silence stretched into awkwardness, Andric decided to end everyone's misery.

"Again, on behalf of the king and all Remalia, I thank you for your profound sacrifice. The five of you remain here so I may speak with you further. The rest of you are dismissed to finish your preparations for our departure in the morning." The remaining soldiers rose and somberly left the courtyard, offering a simple hand on a shoulder or pat on the back as they passed the five who remained.

"Captain Major, Master Ve'Aurben, a moment please." Andric walked to the other side of the courtyard, out of earshot of the others. He rubbed his temples to ease the pain in his head, squeezing his eyes closed. "Well, that could have gone better."

"You did well with a difficult task," Min said encouragingly.

"But we are going to need all our scouts. I wasn't expecting one to volunteer."

"Why not?" Min asked.

Andric felt a pang of guilt as he realized his statement was perhaps rooted in the same prejudice against the scouts as the disparaging remark about Teek volunteering. He uncomfortably skirted the question. "We need to pick a fifth. Any suggestions?"

Thankfully, Barak answered immediately. "Lieutenant Werdalm."

Andric was surprised Barak would suggest that the elantir stay. "Why her?"

"The menhir is not yet finished, and that is still our proffered token of friendship. The few Vanassi who have been allowed to see it have been very impressed. It would be a shame not to finish it. Also, it gives you the excuse to keep your scout for a reason other than he is a scout."

Min shrugged and slowly nodded. "It's a good suggestion."

Andric considered it for a moment. Something felt off. He thought of the ways an elantir would be useful on the trip back, but he knew that was not entirely the cause of his discomfort. He considered Corporal Elles as an alternative. He was a decent elantir, though not nearly as skilled as Werdalm at completing the menhir. But Andric still preferred the thought of leaving him instead of her. *Why should I leave the stronger elantir?* Before the question fully formed in his mind, he knew it was not the real reason.

It was because Werdalm was a woman. It shouldn't have mattered; she was a soldier, and her duty was the same as any other. In truth, it simply made Andric feel like even more of a monster to abandon a woman to such a fate, but he could see no way around the soundness of Barak's reasoning.

He took a deep breath, trying to calm the churning of his stomach. With a resigned sigh, he made the horrible decision. "Fine. Min, run and catch her. Fill her in and bring her back." The captain major hurried away, and Andric asked Barak the scout's name, just to be sure. "It's Corporal Teek, right?"

"Teek is his first name, but everyone still calls him that. It's Corporal Arell." Andric nodded and called the scout over. He didn't want to tell him in front of the others.

"Yes, m'lord?" Arell asked as he approached.

"Corporal, I can't tell you how much I appreciate that you were the first to volunteer. That took tremendous courage. But I have decided I need Lieutenant Werdalm to remain in Sunapra, which means I have one volunteer too many. You will come with us after all." He studied the scout's reaction and was surprised when he thought he detected disappointment, or something like it. Min knew him better. Maybe Andric would ask him later. "Head back with the others and finish packing to leave."

Teek saluted, his fingertips over the corner of his eye, then walked away. As Andric returned to the remaining four, Quarian arrived with Werdalm in tow, looking shaken. Guilt surged again, but Andric forced it down. He needed a strong drink. *Just a little longer*, he thought.

"There aren't words sufficient for this situation. I'm sorry to ask this sacrifice of you. I hope to have you rejoin us when we return with troops to defeat the Kushaani. In the meantime, know that our constant prayers are with you. If there is anyone you would like to send a message to, let Captain Major Min know, and I will ensure they are delivered. Do you have any questions?"

"How soon do you expect to return, my lord?" Tamon asked.

"As soon as possible," Andric said but realized how hollow it sounded. "But let me be frank with you, it might not be until this time next year. The king will likely want to hold on to all our troops until we have expelled the invaders. I don't know when that will be, but if it takes until winter, we will have difficulty mustering the troops and supplies for the campaign back until the following spring."

"And what am I to do once the menhir is completed?" Werdalm asked, her voice quavering.

"I can't say for sure. You're a strong elantir, and the Vanassi will have a lot to learn from you. Perhaps you can learn something of their methods to help strengthen our army when you come back."

"I also have some ideas we can discuss later, Lieutenant," Barak offered. Andric waited for any other questions, but none were forthcoming.

"I know it will be difficult, but you are Remalians. We are proud and strong, and you will make it through this. Take care of one another and may the gods watch over you." Andric saluted them sharply, arm across his waist, fingertips at his sword hilt. They stoically returned his salute. Min led them away to make their final preparations, leaving Andric and Barak alone on the porch. Andric sat on a hard stone bench and rested his head in his hands.

"I agree with Quarian; you did very well."

"Since when are you two on a first-name basis?" Andric asked. He didn't really care; he just wanted the topic to be anything but himself.

"You know me, formalities are never my cup of tea."

"Speaking of tea, I could use some amberbark tea. My head is killing me."

"I'll let Physician Puarrol know."

"Or a drink."

"We leave early tomorrow. You're better off staying out of the cups today." Barak was probably right, but just one drink would help calm his nerves. He didn't want to talk and figured if he stayed quiet, Barak would fill the silence.

When his friend said nothing, he opened one eye and glanced at him. "What is it?" Andric asked.

"What really happened at Pradan-ur? I've heard from a few others what they experienced, but you keep avoiding the subject, which tells me there is something more than you've let on. You haven't been the same since."

"Can we talk about this later? I feel like I slept in a pool of daxtant bile." Andric laughed at a memory that suddenly came to mind. "Do you remember when we were leaving Teris, and you told that young lieutenant he had the soul of a daxtant, and he scolded you for speaking blasphemy?"

Barak laughed. "I would still like to see one someday. But not as much as I would like you to tell me about Pradan-ur."

Andric growled in exaggerated frustration. "It's all a confused jumble in my head. And it isn't just the drink. I promise, when we have time to sit down without a thousand pressures vying for my attention, I will do my best to give you all the details."

Thankfully, Barak didn't push him as they sat in silence. "There may not be another time," Barak finally said. "Elder Shanyasar has invited me to stay in Sunapra."

Andric could tell by his tone Barak was seriously considering it. Anger rose up in an instant. "No. The Vanassi aren't getting any more of my people."

"Andric, this isn't about them. If I stay, it will be of my own choosing, because I want to."

"Why, for the love of the gods, would you want to stay here?" Andric's headache was the only thing keeping him from shouting.

"What difference have I made this entire trip? None. I am irrelevant in the negotiations, certainly no help in military matters, and heaven knows I'm no elantir. I can't even do my job as your friend because you won't tell me what's happening with you. The real question is why I am here in the first place?"

"Because I need you," Andric replied quietly.

"For what? You're surrounded by some of the most capable people in the kingdom. You don't really need me. And what is waiting for me back in Remalia? Books and the occasional visit from a royal friend are great, but they only go so far. At least here the Cannessi are treated as equal members of society, not second-class citizens or an oddity of the prince's charity."

"Barak, when this is all over, if you want to come back here, I will have a battalion of lancers escort you, with half the books in Teris if you like. But for now, stick with me a while longer. Please." Andric hadn't meant to sound quite so desperate.

A young Vanassi girl, no older than ten or eleven, came running across the courtyard. After bowing, she announced with a chirping voice, "Lady Henden asks you to come now, Prince."

"Thank you. Tell the intercessor I'll be there shortly." The girl bowed again and hurried off to deliver the message. "There is no way I am meeting with the Vanassi without something for my headache first. Come on, let's go find Puarrol."

The two got up and headed for the Remalians' quarters, followed by two Divinarim. Andric had grown to appreciate the Sunburst Palace during their stay. Despite it essentially being a ruin, the Sunaprans had made it very comfortable. Everything except the shared bath, of course. That was something he would never get used to, though he had imagined more than once sharing the bath with Jalanti. He felt another prick of guilt when he remembered his comment last night about her being a trophy. He hoped she was with Shiralla and the Vanassi elders so he could apologize before they left in the morning.

As they neared their quarters, he saw Min coming toward them. "M'lord, I was just coming to find you."

"Do you know where Puarrol is?" Andric asked, not wanting to wait any longer than necessary to see the physician.

"No, Your Highness. But I received some news you need to hear immediately." Those words were never good.

Andric stopped short so they could talk away from the soldiers. "Let's have it then."

"My contacts have informed me that the Kushaani have taken Sheerbahar and are marching on Sunapra." Andric bit back a curse. "The roads east are heavily patrolled. There's no chance we can make it back to Balinth's Fortress right now. Our only chance is to stay with the Vanassi and head west, or take the mountain passes to Remalia."

Andric felt like the walls were closing in on him. Why couldn't one single thing go as he wished? Still, he had been preparing himself for this eventuality. Returning to Remalia through the Velspars didn't sound appealing, but was by no means the worst path forward. "It looks like we are fortunate you found us an alternate route out of here. Can we leave any sooner than tomorrow morning?"

"Possibly, but I wouldn't recommend it. Rain clouds are gathering. The storm will probably hit this afternoon, then blow itself out by tonight. Better to stick to our original plan."

"Fine, but either way, we are leaving first thing in the morning."

"Of course, m'lord."

"Now let's go find Puarrol before my head explodes."

Andric knew Elder Gottara and the other Vanassi elders were assembled and awaiting him to join them for the closing ceremony to seal their new alliance. They had arrived early and just in time to avoid being caught in the afternoon storm Quarian predicted, which was now a torrent outside the palace. The howling wind echoed along the stone corridors but was impotent to reach him in his chambers.

Lieutenant Garreth helped straighten the Laconeus-blue surcoat of

Andric's formal uniform as the prince latched the gold fasteners over his white blouse. With black trousers and black knee-high boots, he imagined he looked sufficiently regal to participate in the sealing ceremony with the Vanassi elders. They had offered him traditional Vanassi clothes of vibrant silks and elaborate embroidery, but Andric had declined. Garreth handed him his sword, and Andric fastened the black leather belt around his waist.

"May we come in?" Intercessor Henden called from the corridor outside his room.

He hated that the palace had no doors, but their stay here was nearly over. He only had to endure it one more night. "Of course," Andric answered politely.

Shiralla and Sir Mar stepped into the room and gave a slight bow. He was not sure if the intercessor had planned from the outset to match his attire, which she did, wearing a sapphire-blue dress with black and gold trim. She must have been saving it for just this occasion because he was certain he would have remembered her wearing something so elegant and beautiful before. She also wore the kemrelac of the clergy of Sharin Dara, a half-cape of blue on the outside for those who served in the diplomatic services, and white inside. "Any final questions before we join the elders?"

Shiralla had already explained that the sealing ceremony entailed sharing a common vision through communion. Nophet had scoffed at the idea. Managing a link with nine minds was difficult enough when all the participants worshipped the same deity, but the dissonance created when they were aligned with different divinessences would make such a feat all but impossible. Shiralla agreed and explained that the participants would need to inhale a drug to suppress their natural consonance and allow them to experience the shared link. Andric had assured her it was unnecessary in his case, but she cautioned him that declining to participate would give offense—not a great way to begin their new alliance.

Andric noted the aura of Sharin Dara's divinessence radiating from Sir Mar, as he did every time he was in the knight's presence ever since Pradan-ur. It was like being near Archseraph Charin or Patriarch and Matriarch Mielka. Except they were enlightened. He might have guessed Mar was enlightened too if the idea wasn't so absurd. Andric wondered if it might interfere with the ceremony. The last thing Andric wanted was to give unintended offense to the Vanassi this close to the conclusion of his mission, especially after how difficult it had been achieving this new alliance.

"I think it would be best if we weren't attuned during the ceremony," Andric said diplomatically.

"I assure you, my lord, you have nothing to worry about from us," Shiralla replied.

Andric looked at Mar, waiting for him to end his attunement, but nothing changed. "Sir Mar?"

"Yes, Your Highness?"

It grated on him that Mar was going to make him spell it out. How was this man in the Order of the Third Wave? "I would be more comfortable if you stopped now, rather than waiting until the last minute." Andric thought he detected a slight shift in the knight's expression before he answered, though the prince could not deduce the meaning behind it.

"I am not attuned, Your Highness."

Now the man was lying to him? It was outrageous! He ignored the voice warning him to tread carefully, to not reveal too much. "Lieutenant, wait outside and keep everyone out." Gareth quickly retreated from the room. "I can feel it all the time," Andric said as soon as Gareth was out of sight, his voice hard-edged despite doing his best to keep from yelling. "You must be attuned, unless you expect me to believe you're enlightened."

Andric felt Shiralla attune. He turned on her. "Now you too?"

"You can feel me attune?" she asked, sounding genuinely surprised. Andric didn't know how to answer, so remained silent. After a moment she said patiently, "I'm not sure what you are sensing, Your Highness, but Sir Mar is not attuned."

"I can feel both of you," Andric said, exasperation edging into his voice. He checked again to assure himself he wasn't losing his mind. The connection in both of them was unmistakable, though now that he was comparing them simultaneously, the divinessence in Mar felt... different somehow, in a way Andric could not quite grasp. *Is there something wrong with me?* he wondered, his question laced with anxiety.

"How long have you had these feelings?" the knight asked calmly. Andric finally heeded the voice inside, urging him to safer ground.

"We don't have time for this. Let's go." Andric turned abruptly and his scabbard clanged against Sir Mar's cuisse.

"Perhaps it would be best to leave the sword behind, my lord," the intercessor said from behind as she and Mar followed. He unbuckled it as he walked and handed it to Gareth without a word when he reached the corridor. Knight Commander Nophet was waiting with the lieutenant, concern written on his face.

"Is everything all right, Your Highness?"

"It's fine. Where's Barak?" he asked Gareth.

"He has already gone to meet the Vanassi elders," the lieutenant informed him.

"Let's get this over with," Andric mumbled. He started toward the chamber in which they had conducted the negotiations over the past several days, but Shiralla directed him to a different area of the palace and up a flight of stairs to a second floor he had not realized even existed. A flash of lightning added brilliant illumination to the candle-lit corridor, followed by a crack of thunder that shook the palace.

At the end of a short corridor, Andric passed beneath a heavy stone archway into a dimly lit room with a domed brick ceiling. The walls were lined with stone statues of creatures that looked more like daemons than actual terrestrial beasts. A large stone altar stood in the middle of the room, draped with a white linen cloth. A tall glass and metal instrument with a long, thin hose coiled next to it rested on top of the altar. Several wide embroidered pillows were arranged in a circle in front of the altar.

Six Vanassi elders turned and bowed as the Remalians entered the chamber. They wore vibrant silk robes of various colors, embroidered with gold thread, and both men and women were bedecked in elaborate gold jewelry. Barak, dressed as he always was in plain Viancian vestments of a long cream-colored linen shirt and light brown pants, looked more like a servant than part of a royal delegation. Andric almost wished he would wear the priestly sash, even if wasn't ordained, so he looked at least somewhat official.

Andric was disappointed that Jalanti was not in attendance. He knew he had offended her, but she was a diplomat and had been present for much of the negotiations. It seemed wrong she was not here now that they had reached the end. He hoped she would be at the dinner following the ceremony.

"Welcome, honored guests," one elder greeted them with a heavy accent. He was an ancient man with a deeply wrinkled face, shaved head, huge ears, and a wispy white beard coming off the end of his chin. Andric guessed from the description Shiralla had given that this was also the chief priest at the holiest shrine in Sunapra. "Come sit with us and make yourselves comfortable."

Andric moved next to one of the pillows and Shiralla stood next to him while Sir Mar and Knight Commander Nophet remained outside the circle behind their respective charges. He was dismayed when Elder Gottara instructed Shiralla to move over to make room for her to stand next to the prince. Barak was similarly moved around a few places until he was nearly opposite Andric. When everyone was situated, the elder that greeted them sat cross-legged on his cushion, and everyone followed suit.

"We give thanks to the gods for bringing us together as new friends and new allies. You are welcome in our homes as you are in our hearts. May we always sit together under the shade tree of peace and harmony."

Shiralla had prepared Andric with words for this moment. "We give thanks to the gods for the day your shadow graced our doorstep." Andric wasn't sure he meant it, but he swallowed his pride and continued. "You are welcome in our homes as you are in our hearts. May we always be found singing the song of kinship and affection." Andric gritted his teeth as he leaned over to exchange kisses on each cheek, first with Elder Gottara, then with the elder on his other side.

Next, Elder Gottara rose and stepped to the altar and spoke the phrase Andric had rehearsed with Shiralla earlier, trying to commit it to memory. "To seal our friendship and bind ourselves and the generations that come after, we invoke the gods to sanctify the vision of our shared future." The elder put the metallic end of the thin hose in her mouth and took a deep breath, then exhaled a cloud of thick white smoke. Andric was next and came forward to take the hose from Elder Gottara, who still had wisps of white smoke coming from her nose.

The prince repeated the words with a little whispered assistance from Elder Gottara. He put the metal tip in his mouth and took a shallow breath. The smoke tasted sweet and pungent and slightly burned the back of his throat. He coughed and a small puff of white smoke shot from his mouth and nose to merge with the much larger cloud exhaled by Gottara.

"Breathe deeper," she prompted him, but he instead handed the tube to the next elder and returned to his place sitting next to Elder Gottara. She reached out and took Andric by the hand. He loathed holding hands with the woman who had been such a thorn in his side during the negotiations. *If you can ask your soldiers to remain behind for the good of Remalia, you can certainly hold this woman's hand for a few minutes,* he scolded himself. Soon everyone in the hazy room was holding hands, except the two knights keeping watch.

The elderly priest began humming a single note. A deep, gravelly note Andric almost had a hard time hearing. The tone was picked up by the other elders, all of whom had their eyes closed. Barak and Shiralla closed their eyes, and he thought he heard them humming as well, though it was hard to tell with the other voices in the echoey chamber. Andric felt a reluctance he did not entirely understand but decided the sooner he joined, the sooner he would be done. He closed his eyes and began humming. Try as he might, the note was too deep for his voice, and he was forced to sing the note in a higher register.

As the note continued to drone on, Andric felt his mind begin to wander. He thought about Jalanti again, which led him to think about leaving tomorrow, which led him to the storm outside, which led to muddy trails through the mountains, to Remalia. A gentle pressure to link in communion intruded at the edge of his mind. He felt Yerin's divinessence at the base of the proffered communion. While he appreciated and enjoyed the beauty and creativity Yerin espoused and inspired in the world, Andric had spent little time pursuing connection with the god's divine essence.

He accepted the link, and suddenly his thoughts were suffused with light and color and flavor and scent and tone and warmth, all blended into a single sensation gently enveloping him. Other consciousnesses were present in the sensory confluence that slowly supplanted all other awareness. He recognized something in the swirling aura that was Barak. This was the first time he had ever been in communion with his friend. He wanted to say something teasing, but the prince knew everyone else would hear his words, so he refrained.

However, something about Barak drew his attention. The Cannessi's mind seemed to stand apart from the others, who were slowly merging. But it wasn't only that. There was something beyond Barak, outside the connection. Though it seemed far away, Andric could feel the muted vibrations of Viance's divinessence. Curiosity pushed Andric to reach through the link and coax that divinessence through Barak's consciousness into the shared connection. Inquisitiveness and the joy of discovery found a place amid the swirling sensations and joy of creation infusing the shared consciousness from Yerin's divinessence. The constant vibration at the base of the communion suddenly had a counterpoint. Not quite dissonant, but not quite harmonized either.

Another consciousness touched his, inviting him to let go of himself and become one with the other. It felt vaguely familiar, though he was sure it was foreign to him. No, that was not entirely true. Something about it was Shiralla, or a part of her that had not yet disappeared into the commingled state of communion. He touched it, connected with it, and followed it through her to Sharin Dara's divinessence hovering in the distance, beyond the edges of the link. He invited it to come and join the dance of shared existence. A more profound sense of cooperation and unity permeated the conjoined awareness. He was losing track of what was himself and what was other. The divinessences of the three gods ran through the communal link like shimmering streams of light through water, illuminating yet remaining separate, apart. He felt like they should coalesce somehow, yet the key to unlocking that door remained just beyond his grasp. He suddenly remembered the Nine Ecclesiastics and wondered if this was how they had managed to harmonize the divinessences.

He felt a will through the communal link urging him to let those threads subside, but he disregarded it, instead seeking threads to other gods. Somewhere there was a filament leading to Vai Doroth's divinessence. He tried to follow the delicate connection, but it evaporated as soon as he turned his attention to it. Another connection to a divinessence slid past his consciousness. Without thinking, he latched onto it before it was gone. He followed it through the mind and heart it was connected to. He knew this divinessence— Teraithia's. He nearly let go, but the curiosity inherent in Yerin's and Viance's divinessence urged him to remain present so as to comprehend.

He relaxed into his openness and turned toward the goddess's divine light. Fortitude, preeminence, the will to hold sway, glory—these and other qualities resonated throughout her divinessence, hovering beyond the edges of the coalescing unity. Why should it not have a place among the others? He shepherded the divinessence through the host consciousness into the communal connection. Reverberations of discordant vibrations radiated through the senses of those connected in communion, intensifying, until suddenly the link snapped like stings on a lute stretched too tightly. Andric winced in anticipation of pain that never came, instead only feeling the jolt of sudden disconnection. He felt isolated, like an island of existence floating in a void, hopelessly separated from the other islands surrounding him in the room.

"Gods, what was that?" Elder Gottara asked, dropping Andric's hand. She sounded shaken.

"How... how did...?" the elderly priest asked, staring at Andric with confusion and fear. "That should not be possible."

The prince looked at Shiralla and Barak to see if they were okay. Barak locked his hands in his lap as he did sometimes when lost in thought. Shiralla brought her interlaced fingers to her lips, her eyes still closed. Knight Commander Nophet stepped forward and put a hand on Andric's shoulder. The prince felt an invitation to join in communion but ignored it. He didn't want anyone else in his head right now.

"M'lord, is everything all right?" the Divinarim commander asked in a whisper that sounded like a shout in the silent room.

No, everything is definitely not all right! Andric's inner voice screamed, torn between the desire to be alone and the urge to confide in someone. The memory of Archseraph Charin's words in Teris sprang to mind.

'If you need to discuss this with someone while you are in Kushaan, consider confiding in Archpaladin Nophet. He has my complete confidence and can do more to keep you safe than anyone.'

Perhaps later, he thought, trying to ignore the guilt of considering sharing this with Nophet when he had refused to discuss it with Barak.

"I'm fine. Check on the intercessor," Andric commanded, then rose and walked over to his friend, ignoring the questioning looks of the elders. "Barak, are you okay?" Barak simply nodded his affirmation, his gaze fixed on the stone floor. Sir Mar stared curiously at Andric while Nophet bent and inquired about the intercessor's condition. Memories of Pradan-ur flashed through his mind. Andric quickly glanced around the room, fearing someone might be hurt or worse, but the elders seemed to be unharmed.

He heard the Cannessi elder whisper to the old priest next to him, "Could he be the Stormborn?" The priest waved his companion to be silent but kept his eyes fixed on Andric as he and the others climbed to their feet. The prince knew he had to say something to break the tension building in the room.

"My apologies for that little mishap. It was certainly not my intention to disrupt the ceremony. I believe dinner is waiting for us. Should we proceed that way now?"

Low murmuring broke out among the elders as they slowly made their way out of the chamber. Andric was half-tempted to skip dinner. At best it was going to be an evening of politely avoided conversations or veiled probes, and at worst an endless litany of questions to which he did not have answers.

Shiralla walked out without looking at him. Was she angry, embarrassed, or just shaken? Perhaps all three. He was sure he would hear about it later. Barak looked up at him, a grimly serious look on his face.

"I know we don't have time to discuss it now, but I'm guessing whatever just happened was similar to what happened at Pradan-ur."

"It wasn't. Not exactly. I just..." Andric could feel himself getting defensive. Who were any of them to judge him? They had no right.

"I don't know how you did that, but it's dangerous, Andric. Probably worse than when you were first trying to mix elan and divinessence. We'll talk about it later." Barak turned and walked out.

Andric hoped there was wine, or something stronger, at dinner. He needed it.

Andric's foggy brain slowly registered that someone was shaking him. "What?" he groaned, pulling the covers over his head, trying to go back to sleep.

"My lord, everyone is preparing to leave," his squire said. Why was Jase waking him?

"Where's Garreth?" Andric asked groggily, shielding his eyes from the lantern light Jase held next to his bed. He looked out the window of his room to guess the time, but it was still pitch dark outside. "What time is it?"

"About an hour before dawn. I couldn't find Lieutenant Garreth. The captain major is looking for him. But you should be up and getting ready."

Andric's head was pounding, and it felt like a desert in his mouth. "I need a drink."

"Your Highness needs a cold bath," a stern voice said from somewhere across the room. Nophet. Andric swung his feet onto the floor. The rug was high quality, smooth but densely woven; nothing like the plush Celendrian rug he had in his room in the palace back in Teris.

"Physician Puarrol made you a cup of amberbark tea," Jase said, holding a brightly painted ceramic cup toward the prince.

Andric was getting tired of the tea, but he was grateful for it nevertheless. He grimaced as he took a sip. "It's cold," he complained.

"Forgive me, my lord," his cousin replied without a hint of apology in his voice. "It was hot when I first woke you." Andric opened his center and channeled a thin stream of his elan into the tea, modulating it to vis and exciting the vibrations to create some heat. After a few moments, he could feel warmth from the cup and sipped carefully at the now-hot tea as Jase laid out Andric's clothes for the day.

At Jase's urging, Andric finally got to his feet and let himself be ushered toward the bath chamber. More lanterns in the otherwise dark chamber showed two servants standing ready with towels, soaps, perfumes, and other bathing supplies. He was too hungover to worry about shyness in front of the servants this morning. He stripped off his clothes and walked into the large pool of steaming hot water. The Vanassi didn't have many luxuries he would miss, but this was definitely one. He already had plans to convert one of the adjoining chambers back home into a bathroom. Hopefully, his father wouldn't object.

The reality that his father would never object to anything again struck him like a punch to his chest. Tears sprang to his eyes before he could push the grief back down. He filled his cupped hands with water and brought them to his face, rubbing the tears away. When he was sure he had himself under control, he stepped out of the pool, quickly grabbing a towel to cover himself. Once Andric had his trousers on, he called Jace in to help him finish getting ready. He was nearly finished when Min was announced from the hallway. Andric told him to come in.

"My lord, we need to move quickly. I just received word that a large Kushaani force is only a half-day's march south of the city."

How did they move so quickly? he wondered. *Or did someone deliver bad information?* Either way, there was no time to waste on pointless questions. "Did you find Garreth?"

"No. It appears he may have snuck out last night and hasn't returned."

"Snuck out? Where? The city is half-empty already."

Min hesitated before answering reluctantly. "He has been frequenting Sykorian temples since we arrived. I gave orders that no one was to leave the palace yesterday, but he may have gone looking for Sykoria's blessing."

"We have to find him," Andric said as they entered his room. Jase hurried to pack the prince's remaining belongings and then handed bundles to servants.

"I already sent a few scouts to search, and assigned soldiers to pack his belongings and ready his horse. But we can't afford to delay leaving. If we can't find him—"

"I'm not leaving anyone behind," Andric said emphatically. He realized he hadn't seen Barak this morning and suddenly remembered their conversation yesterday. "Where is Master Ve'Aurben?"

"I believe he's out with the mounts preparing to leave," Min answered.

Andric sighed in relief and finished buckling his sword around his waist, adjusting it for comfort while riding. "All right, let's go."

"My lord, you should eat something," Nophet said. "You had a lot to drink last night. It will help sustain you for the long day ahead."

"I'll eat in the saddle once we're out of the city." Andric lengthened his stride to hurry toward the front plaza, but Min directed him another way through a series of dark corridors toward the rear of the palace, explaining that they were leaving another way. They finally arrived in an overgrown garden where Vanassi servants stood holding lanterns illuminating crumbling walls and collapsed statues that were no longer recognizable. The area was filled with soldiers and more servants securing the last few packages to horses.

Andric heard faint clanging noises echoing in the distance. "What is that?"

"Alarms to warn the people to get out of the city," Min answered.

He bid good morning to Shiralla and her knights as he made his way toward Kobo. He kept looking around but saw no sign of Barak, or Garreth, or Jalanti. Barak would be easy to miss among this many people, but if Jalanti were here, she would have been easy to spot. If anyone here knew her whereabouts, it would be the intercessor. "Have you seen Jalanti this morning?" he asked Shiralla.

"No, Your Highness. I haven't seen her since she left your company two nights ago."

Andric bit back a curse. His personal assistant, his envoy from the Vanassi, and his advisor—all missing. He was beginning to suspect that five of his soldiers had not been enough to satisfy the Vanassi after all. Anger rose in his chest as he continued to look around more urgently.

"Where's Master Ve'Aurben?" he asked in a voice loud enough for everyone in the garden to hear him. Every reply was that no one knew. Andric stepped on a mounting block Jase was dragging closer to Kobo and climbed into the saddle, hoping the elevated position would give him a better vantage point from which to spot Barak. The others in the company took it as the signal to mount as well. He saw Steed standing nearby, saddled and prepared to depart, but still no sign of his friend.

A couple of scouts ran in from the darkness beyond the garden and approached Quarian. "No sign of the lieutenant, Captain Major," one of the scouts said, panting heavily. "But the city's crazy right now. The streets are filling up with people rushin' ta get out. If we don't hurry, we're gonna have ta fight our way out."

"Your Highness, give the word," Lord Nophet urged the prince. "Your safety is paramount. The others knew they were expected to be here when we departed."

"I'm not leaving without Barak," Andric said with every ounce of finality he could convey. He felt guilty about not including Gareth in that assertion and disappointed about Jalanti not coming, but leaving without Barak was not an option he was willing to consider.

"Did anyone see Master Ve'Aurben this morning?" Nophet called out in a voice that cut through every conversation. A few of the soldiers had seen him earlier in the palace, but again confirmed they had no idea where he was at the moment.

"Organize a search party to comb the palace grounds," Andric said as he started dismounting.

"I'm here," Barak announced calmly, appearing out of the darkness from the same direction the scouts had come. Andric noticed he was carrying a leather scroll case. He casually walked to Steed and packed it into a saddlebag before mounting without another word.

"Are you ready to go then, Master Ve'Aurben?" Andric asked, putting as much of his annoyance into his voice as possible.

"Is anyone ever truly ready for anything?" Barak replied philosophically.

The prince glanced around one last time, hoping beyond hope to see Jalanti rushing in, her hair trailing behind her, and dressed for riding. All he saw were expectant eyes upon him, waiting for his command. He choked down a silent curse. "Let's go," Andric said to Quarian.

He half-hoped the scout was right that they had to fight their way out of the city. Someone should have to pay for what this trip had cost him. He supposed he would have to settle for the Kuldrith.

CHAPTER LIII
EVIR

Eight more dead ends. Evir had exhausted his list of elantir connected to Qin'acht Overseer, as well as the overseer herself, and was now working his way through the elantir in Malithir Lord Overseer's service. He trudged along the illuminated tunnel leading up to the next tier of residences in Fallswatch as he passed a weary group of workers, smiths from the look of them, heading off to start their shift at the forges. The apartments in Fallswatch were nothing like the grand residences in the Templeward or Lightsreach districts, but they were far better than the Warrens. Located at the far end of the Grand Chasm next to Teraithia's Breath, it offered some stunning views of the falls.

Evir could not help but think of the residence, merely a few levels below, where he and Dae had lived and raised Akriel for several years. They had enjoyed countless walks along the balconies behind the falls, watching the glittering lights from the Grand Chasm filtering through the cascading water when the tide was full and the falls were at their heaviest. His steps slowed as a sense of melancholy gripped him, wishing Dae was here with him. He had become more susceptible to these moods lately. He guessed it was a combination of the vitalic lethargy and operating in isolation for so long with only Daopek to talk to. He shook his head to rid himself of the unwelcome feelings and forced himself to resume his pace. He could not afford to be distracted right now.

Twenty-two elantir and still not a single one affected the probe in the least. Only six more to go. Could it be that Kiavi had somehow misconfigured the elants? Or did the traitor have the elantir reassigned or killed? It was possible. Those kinds of questions and the doubts they evoked were unhelpful but were becoming his constant companions. It was time to start facing the reality he may not find what he was looking for. *What then?* he wondered, not for the first time.

He continued onward and upward, away from the walkways along the face of the chasm wall, and headed into the residences. The older apartments, those closest to the chasm, were more spacious and unique, and much more desirable. Perhaps after his mission was complete and he and Dae were allowed to officially return to Stierve, they would be assigned one of those as their residence.

His mind was now wandering into fantasies. He activated the probe. He was not yet close to his next target's residence, but at least probing gave him something to focus on instead of every other thought that seemed to find purchase in his weary mind. He took a deep breath and reached inside his emerald-green tunic, wrapping his fingers around the forked tungsten bar hanging next to his skin. Such a gesture was unnecessary to activate the probe, but it had become a habit, a way to help alleviate the feeling of weight that settled over him whenever he activated it. He opened himself to let his elan flow into the probe. It may have been his imagination, but the runes on the device seemed to raise ever so slightly beneath his grasp. He could feel the drain on his elan as he walked, like a water-soaked cloak hanging heavy about him.

It was still strange to see kieresta patrolling the passageway, a duty that had always been the exclusive purview of the orderguard. But at least the sight of them no longer set his nerves on edge. A group of young children and their caregivers trailed behind the two knights, some of the children imitating their powerful strides to the amusement of the others. Seeing them reminded him of a young Akriel, already fascinated by the temple, the statues, and the priests. Looking back, his son's path seemed already set at such an early age. And where had it led? It had been almost a week since the combat exams and still he heard occasional mentions of the controversial match. Would his son end up as one of these kieresta, relegated to patrolling the residences to keep order and piety front-of-mind for every child who saw him?

Evir turned into a side passage leading to the branch of apartments where his target resided. Ahead in the corridor, a group was leaving the dining commons, the younger ones laughing boisterously. Evir navigated to the other side of the corridor to avoid—

Shocking cold.

Kiavi said he would feel a chill, but it was as if a ewer of icy water had been dumped inside his shirt. A woman stopped dead in her tracks at the back of the group. Selvruen. She was looking directly at Evir. And the inquisitor was looking back. Evir realized the man next to her was Gheanel, the elantir he was looking for, but he clearly had no idea what was happening.

She was the one.

His heart sank as the truth solidified in his mind—Malithir Lord Overseer had to be the traitor. Selvruen's expression shifted from shock to rage, her lips mumbling a curse. She raised her hands to cover her eyes.

Ash! Evir swore as he spun and bolted in the opposite direction.

A brilliant light flashed in the corridor behind him. Cries of alarm and pain rang out from those who took the full brunt of the elant. Turning had saved him from being completely blinded, but a bright green afterimage was burned into his vision, blurring the path ahead. He barreled forward, his hand sliding along the smooth tunnel wall, his heart racing as fast as his feet. Distance was his best defense against the elantir. Why did he have to let his guard down at the very moment—

A concussive blast knocked him off balance and he stumbled sideways, slamming into the wall. He winced as pain lanced through his shoulder. Worse was the ringing in his ears. Blinded and deafened, his situation was getting more desperate by the moment. He knew the effects would wear off quickly, but he could not afford to wait. He had to keep moving or they would catch him.

He tried to push himself off the wall, but the sleeve of his tunic was caught on something. He tried to shake free but it was stuck against the smooth wall. With frustration, he realized one of the elantir must be binding the fabric to the stone. He quickly drew his knife from its sheath at the small of his back and cut through the material. He wrenched himself away from the wall and felt more than heard the fabric rip down his sleeve. A second cut freed him and he stumbled forward, shoving his way past the stunned people in his way.

There was an audible *ting* beneath his tunic, like the sound of metal hitting glass, and he felt the probe shudder as a small shockwave battered his chest, driving the air from his lungs. He gasped for breath, instinct taking over to keep placing one foot in front of the other. He should've been better prepared, more focused! He knew a counterattack was a possibility.

A part of his mind realized the probe was no longer cold. Had he broken it? There was no time to dwell on it now. Selvruen and Gheanel were undoubtedly on his heels.

Something else was off. His face felt numb. No, not numb. He no longer felt the tingle of Vekk-oth's elants drawing on his elan. His disguise was gone. *Ash and flame!*

Thankfully, his vision was finally starting to clear. He sheathed his knife and broke into a dead run. He needed to gain enough distance to hide or get somewhere with enough people to lose them in the crowds. Either way, that meant heading back to the Grand Chasm.

Evir rounded the corner into the main tunnel and was disappointed to see everyone either crouching against the walls or running away from the corridor he had just exited. This much open space would make it much easier for the elantir to attack him again. He hadn't gone ten paces when his stomach lurched in fear at the sight of a pair of kieresta ahead, running toward him; the ones the children had been emulating. Were the children nearby? Evir hoped they were somewhere safe. He almost turned and ran the other way but knew that would be too suspicious. Another idea crossed his mind, and he ran straight toward them.

"Dorothi!" Evir shouted, making his voice sound panicked. "Two Dorothi elantir," he said, pointing back the way he had come. "They said it's revenge for the Purge in Kierden. They're killing everyone!" He kept glancing over his shoulder, his eyes wide as he approached. "We have to get out of here!"

The kieresta drew their swords and raised their v'kar toward the tunnel. Not wanting to give them a good look at his face, he kept his gaze flitting about as if in a panic. One of the holy warriors directed him to move against the wall.

"Wait there," she commanded, then proceeded cautiously with her companion. Another blinding light flashed in the tunnel. Luckily, it was several feet away and Evir was looking in the other direction to his escape route. Some of those crouching against the wall cried out and bolted in terror.

"Burn that!" Evir cursed, as much for effect as from frustration, and turned to flee with the others. He was glad to have civilians around him. He didn't want them hurt, but it would make the elantir hesitant to throw any more elants at him. As he wove his way through the others running toward the Grand Chasm, he glanced over his shoulder and caught sight of the two elantir as they suddenly burst into the corridor, looking each way along the tunnel.

"Stop that man!" Selvruen shouted. "He's a thief. Stop him!"

"Hold right there!" he heard the kieresta bark her command, though whether at the elantir or Evir, he could not be certain.

Evir wanted to look back, but he kept his face fixed ahead. He could not afford to be recognized, or Dae, Akriel, Javinth, and the others who had helped him would all be in danger. Malithir would see to it. He continued racing with the others, hoping for larger crowds he could disappear into once he reached the chasm. Fleeing with the few other bystanders, he rounded the last turn of the tunnel and sprinted out onto the walkway anchored to the stone wall. The rushing water of the nearby falls at high tide and the vast open space of the chasm muted the cacophony of panicked footsteps and shouting.

Evir's heart sank. There was no one ahead of them, nothing but an open walkway for the next several hundred paces. He thought frantically. He had been on the other side of this kind of chase and knew what worked and what did not. Racing along on these walkways usually ended in capture. He could try to disappear behind the waterfall, but there would be fewer people to protect him, and the water gave the elantir more options. He had heard of one escape that worked effectively before, but the thought of trying it himself left a knot in the pit of his stomach. He already knew he had no better choice, though.

Evir slowed his pace and let the last of the group move a few paces ahead of him. As he approached the next beam supporting the walkway, he dropped to his stomach and reached under the protective guardrail, quickly wrapping his arm around the metal beam below where it connected to the walkway. He slid his leg over the ledge and suddenly felt himself cemented to the floor. He looked back toward the tunnel, worried the elantir were bonding his clothes to the floor.

No one.

He tried to move again and realized it was fear, not met'elan, preventing him from sliding the rest of his body over the edge. *They'll be here any second. Move or die!* his mind screamed.

Without another thought, he threw himself off the walkway into the air. The weight of his body yanked against his grip. Sharp pain lanced through his shoulder, the same one that had crashed into the tunnel wall just a few minutes ago. Worse, he felt his hold slipping. In a panic, he scrambled with his other hand for another hold, but all he could do was grab his wrist, locking his arm in place.

Evir dangled in the shadows beneath the walkway, clutching the support beam with all he had.

He glanced down to assess his route to the next walkway. His stomach lurched. There was only air between him and the chasm floor hundreds of feet below. He had thought his weight would slide him down the angled support beam back toward the wall and put the other walkway below him, but his arm held him in place for the moment. He grimaced against the pain and fear, not sure how much longer he could hold on.

Shouts and footsteps echoed on the walkway above him.

Keep moving!

With a surge of desperate willpower, Evir unclasped his hand and reached for the metal beam, hoping he could hook a leg over it and slide toward the wall. But as soon as he let go, his other arm began to slip. He changed his mind and tried to grab his wrist again, but all he managed to do was overlap his fingers. He could feel himself trembling, his grip barely holding as he began sliding toward the wall. He knew he only had a few seconds before his hands gave out. His eyes squeezed shut as he strained to put every ounce of strength into holding on. Small imperfections in the metal sliced his fingers and palms as he slid faster.

He opened his eyes just before hitting the wall. He turned himself enough to take the brunt of the impact on his side. Pain shot through his chest as a rib cracked, but it was lost in the panic of his hands losing their grip on the beam.

Evir was falling.

His hand, arm, and side scraped against the stone of the wall. His eyes shot to the walkway below. Several people were there... landing on someone might save him... it might kill them... this was going to hurt.

He clawed desperately at a lumen mounted to the wall as he entered its pool of white light, but it was too much for his injured body to hold on. His desperate attempt slowed his fall but made his feet swing sideways, leaving him flailing wildly as he slammed into the walkway at an angle.

Blinding pain shot through his body everywhere. At least he was alive, thank the gods!

Evir tried to get up, but his knee and hip felt as if they were on fire. His right arm was almost useless, his hands were bleeding, and he could barely breathe. He wanted to simply lay where he was, but he would not let all of this be for nothing. He stifled a groan as he rolled to the side and used the guard rail to pull himself to his feet. He kept his weight off his right leg as he surveyed the situation around him. Several people nearby stared in confusion and concern at the man who had suddenly plummeted out of the darkness above them.

His physical condition and lack of disguise made getting to the chasm floor without being caught or recognized nearly impossible. His old residence was only two levels below him now, so there was a greater risk someone in this area would recognize him. He needed to get off the walkways immediately.

He limped forward and pushed past the nearest pair of bystanders, making his way toward a nearby tunnel opening leading back into Fallswatch.

"Stop!" a shout rang out from the walkway above. "In the name of Teraithia, stop that man!" Evir feared he had been spotted. His first instinct was to keep his head down, but everyone around him was looking toward the commotion above. He would only be more conspicuous if he didn't do the same. He lifted his gaze, pretending to be curious like the others.

No one was peering over the railing. He kept his feet moving, one limping step at a time, nudging past others with their upturned faces. The sounds of booted steps running along the upper walkway carried from above, followed by another shout for someone to halt further away. The people near Evir shrugged and pressed on. He carefully let out a breath he didn't realize he had been holding.

He entered the tunnel and walked along slowly, hugging the wall, masking his limp as best he could. He was tempted to glance back, but the less he showed his face, the better. Soon he began passing the entrances to residences, but there were too many people walking nearby to assess if any of them were empty without being noticed. For now, he simply kept walking.

His plan had been to return to Daopek's residence, retrieve his few belongings, then make his way to Tel-Kyron Mavin Tar's residence and hope the man was willing to help. But he was no longer safe moving through the city, and it was quickly going to get worse. Within a tenth-tide, the Door's network was going to be on the lookout for someone matching his description, or Evir himself if Selvruen had recognized him. His best chance was to head straight to Tel-Kyron's residence.

The Lightsreach district, where many of the highest-ranking members of the empire resided, was a challenge to enter without an invitation, to be sure, but he had already made arrangements. Of course, he hadn't counted on being injured, losing his disguise, and being the target of a manhunt. It complicated things.

He chuckled grimly at such an understatement. *You nearly died back there and aren't clear of the stones yet!* One wrong step and Malithir Lord Overseer's treason would likely remain hidden forever, with no justice served. Worse, Dae and the others would pay the price along with Evir.

As he limped on, his adrenaline and fear transformed into a smoldering anger. One way or another, the end was near. He swore it would end with the lord overseer paying for what he had done.

CHAPTER LIV
EVIR

Evir was disappointed, but not surprised, to hear the echoes of voices as he finally approached the small cavern with bathing pools for residents in the remote corner of the Auricite District. It had taken Evir nearly a full tenth-tide to make his way here through several smaller tunnels and service corridors, backtracking and finding waypoints to ensure he was not being followed or recognized. At least awareness of the situation with Selvruen didn't appear to have made its way here yet. It was only a matter of time though, so he needed to move quickly. He still took a moment to survey the area from the safety of the tunnel.

Nothing appeared out of the ordinary. A few young children played in the shallow pools under the watchful gaze of parents who chatted amiably nearby. Some bathers were all business, washing themselves efficiently and climbing out of the pools, while others relaxed in the steaming water. An elderly woman sat on her partner's lap, the gentle rocking motion of their coupling causing small waves to splash over the glittering rock edge of the pool.

Evir entered the cavern and skirted along the periphery, careful to keep his torn sleeve near the wall to avoid attracting attention or leaving that detail in anyone's memory. He gingerly made his way around a few larger stalagmites until he was out of view, then ducked behind a stalactite curtain. He grimaced in agony as he knelt and reached into the dark, warm water.

He was so thirsty, and his mouth was pasty and bitter. The thought of drinking the steaming water that may or may not be connected to the bathing pools was nearly enough to make him retch, but he was desperate and was going to need his voice soon. He quickly scooped a few handfuls of water and drank. *Seems okay,* Evir thought, trying to ignore his disgust and convince himself he hadn't made a mistake.

He reached back into the water and felt along the ledge until his hand found the rope tied to a small rock outcropping. He quietly began pulling on the rope until he had hauled up the waterproof sack tied to the other end. Inside was an orderguard uniform. He had planned to change here, but too many eyes had seen him. Coming out fully dressed as a guard would probably raise a few eyebrows and would certainly be a detail someone would remember if questioned about seeing anything unusual. At a minimum, he needed to change his shirt. He untied the sack and pulled out the red linen tunic.

He clenched his teeth against the sharp pain in his shoulder and side as he carefully removed his shirt. He glanced at the forked probe hanging on his chest. The metal looked discolored and burned, nearly black. *There's no time to worry about it now.* He quickly looked himself over to make sure there were no other wounds he wasn't already aware of. The scrapes and bruises were about what he expected, so he carefully donned the new tunic and refastened his belt and knife, then headed back out through the cavern. He was grateful no one seemed to pay him any attention.

Carrying the sack filled with clothing and gear should not have been as difficult as it was proving to be. He needed to find somewhere to change. He passed several residences he guessed were likely empty, but he didn't stop until he finally saw one with a thin layer of undisturbed dust in the entrance. With a quick glance in each direction to confirm no one was in his immediate vicinity, he stepped inside. The apartment had a small common room with a few cushions on the floor and a second, smaller sleeping chamber. It was the smallest residence Evir had seen in Auricite, looking more like it belonged in the Warrens.

Light filled the room as he took out his lumen and limped his way to the back room. He set about the painful ordeal of changing the rest of his clothes, doing his best to stifle his moans and grunts. The worst part was trying to get the lamellar cuirass on and fasten the side buckles. More than once, the pain nearly made him give up, but he knew he stood no chance of getting into Lightsreach unless the disguise was complete.

Finally, he picked up a small velveteen pouch with a hard object inside and carefully tied the strings to his belt, then tucked the pouch into his waistband. Deciding he was well enough put together, he quickly packed his belongings into the sack. He hated to leave behind his things, especially his knife, but carrying it would seem too out of place. He set the sack in a corner, put his lumen in a belt pouch, and exited the apartment. With any luck, he would be at Tel-Kyron's residence within the tenth-tide and could send one of the mavin tar's slaves to come fetch his belongings.

He navigated through the tunnels to the slaves' entrance at the back end of the Lightsreach district. Ten orderguards were stationed here at all times, double the number of any other entrance, but they would be less likely to raise questions about him seeking entrance to the district. A handful of slaves waited patiently as guardsmen inspected their bundles and checked the brands on the back of their necks to confirm they belonged to the esteemed residents of the district.

"Have any of you seen a woman come this way in the last tenth-tide," Evir called out as he approached the checkpoint, doing his best to hide his limp and infuse his voice with commanding confidence, "wearing black trousers and a burgundy overlap tunic?" The guardsmen presented the salute of subordinates to a superior, hands out with palms toward Evir, chins raised. Evir gritted his teeth as he raised his right arm as high as he could manage while making a knife hand, his left hand reaching over to cover it, wrapping around his little finger, then quickly dropping it. He hoped it looked impatient rather than injured.

"No, Inspector," a few answered while others shook their heads, looking at each other to confirm their answers matched.

Evir shook his head and tightened his face into a look of frustration. "We had a disturbance over at Fallswatch. Dorothi elantir causing trouble, but one of them managed to escape." The easiest lies hewed closest to the truth. "You'll be briefed on it later. For now, I need to get to the other checkpoints."

He slowly walked forward, pretending to look around the small chamber as if reassuring himself everything was in order. He shook his head in feigned disappointment and pointed to a loose strap on one of the guardsman's pauldrons. "If you see her, she is to be detained," he said curtly as he proceeded through the checkpoint. He listened to the murmuring behind him for any hint his ruse had failed, but the voices sounded more curious than anything else.

Soon, the tunnel merged into one of the wide main corridors of Lightsreach. Every detail spoke of the privileged status of the ruling members of the empire who resided here. Pure white light from lumens crafted into beautiful shapes and attached to sculpted posts, wall sconces, and chandeliers hanging from the high ceilings reflected off the mirror finish of polished marble paving stones along the tunnel floor. He paid little attention to the magnificent sights he passed along the way: alcoves with statues commemorating historic figures, murals depicting famous battles or other iconic scenes, fountains, and reflecting pools. Instead, his senses were tuned to tracking the movements and other cues from those he passed, mostly slaves and servants by the looks of them, for any signs of a threat.

His heartbeat quickened at the sight of a pair of guardsmen approaching. He prepared to give his rehearsed explanation for his presence, but they simply saluted and continued walking. He realized he was not seeing any kier-esta or vaesh'katir anywhere in Lightsreach. It was a surprising contrast to the rest of Stierve, where he had grown accustomed to not going far without crossing their paths.

The entrances to the grand residences in Lightsreach were few and far between. On the positive side, that meant fewer chances for Evir to be surprised by unexpected variables, but it also gave him fewer options to change course should the need arise. Tel-Kyron Mavin Tar's residence was the only one he had ever had occasion to visit here in the district, and that was only thanks to Dae'yen's friendship with the mavin tar's wife, Zenni. Of all the politicians Evir knew, Tel-Kyron had always seemed the least objection-able to spend time with. He hoped his friendly acquaintance with him, or (more likely) Dae's relationship with Zenni, was enough to get him an audi-ence with the man.

Evir breathed a shallow, painful sigh of relief when he arrived at the tunnel leading to the mavin tar's residence. He drew himself up and turned the corner, fighting through the pain of walking as normally as possible toward the wide entrance covered by sheer fabric curtains. He stopped himself from shaking his head in amazement at the extravagant display of privilege. Since most of the Kuldrith Empire was underground, fabric had always been a constrained resource. Using it to cover the entrance of a resi-dence was unusual in most districts and altogether unheard of in the Warrens. But here in Lightsreach, every grand apartment had yards and yards of the most exotic materials, shimmering silks and plush velvets and others Evir could not begin to name, doing nothing but hanging on display to proclaim to all who approached that power resided behind their supple folds.

Evir could see the outline of the mavin tar's private guards standing behind the translucent curtains as he neared the bronze gong hanging near the entrance. It was merely a formality, but he raised the felt-tipped mallet and gently struck the gong. One side of the curtain lifted and Evir entered the large antechamber. Two large guards stood at ease next to a beautifully sculpted table, genuine wood from the surface by the look of it. One guard kept her hand resting casually on the hilt of the sword hanging from her hip.

A slender attendant rose from her seat to greet Evir as he approached. She wore a loose, overlapping blouse of yellow kanthis linen, a darker pair of wool breeches, and brown leather boots. But he was far more concerned with her face. It had been nearly a year since Evir was last here, but he recognized her immediately. He hoped to the gods she did not recognize him. He stopped and bowed as best his armor and injuries allowed, eyes to the ground and hands outstretched. It was a salute more appropriate for the mavin tar than his servant, but the appearance of a slight miscalculation in protocol fit with his disguise.

The woman returned the same salute far more elegantly than he had done. "Welcome, Inspector. What business may I assist you with today?" It was a polite but efficient greeting. Evir was impressed she was familiar enough with the orderguard structure to use his proper rank and grateful she didn't give any indication she might know who he really was. Had she truly forgotten him, or was she simply being discreet?

"I have a message for Tel-Kyron Mavin Tar, Your Honor. I was instructed to present this," Evir replied as he gingerly reached beneath his cuirass and untied a small pouch from his belt. He made a show of carefully loosening the drawstring and removing a figurine of a golden snake with two heads, one on each end of its body, wrapped around a crystal sphere. Fortunately, Evir had not been carrying it with him in Fallswatch or it almost certainly would have been broken during his escape. Evir extended his hand and offered the item.

The servant donned a thin, practiced smile and motioned for Evir to place the figurine on the wooden table. The woman's eyes carefully tracked Evir as he stepped forward without hesitation and did as he was instructed, then stepped back. The soft scraping of the stone tiles of his armor and distant sounds of voices somewhere in the residence were the only interruptions to the quiet in the chamber as the servant held her hand over the figurine. He was familiar enough with security measures to know the elantir was neutralizing potential threats posed by the figurine.

At last, the woman seemed satisfied and motioned to someone inside the residence unseen by Evir. A young Restani slave, perhaps the same age as Akriel, entered the antechamber and approached the elantir. He carried himself with an air of mild confidence Evir recalled being common among Tel-Kyron's slaves, a trait many other Kuldrith would never have tolerated. The mavin tar's slaves were hardly distinguishable from servants except for not being Kuldrith. While the law forbade them to grow their hair long, he otherwise dressed them as his other servants, with full-length sleeves and pant legs. Evir simply chalked it up to another eccentricity of the powerful.

"Take this to Vyunoth," the elantir instructed. The slave bowed, then carefully picked up the figurine and disappeared back into the residence. "Would you care to have a seat, Inspector?" Evir thought he detected a longer pause before using his title this time. Was it a sign she knew who he was? She might say nothing now, but anyone knowing he was here could prove disastrous.

"No, thank you, Your Honor," he answered politely, despite a chair being the thing he most wanted in the world, second only to a bed. But he knew he would have trouble getting seated, and perhaps more trouble getting up again. *Better to stay on my feet.* The elantir took her seat once again and waited in meticulous silence.

Evir gazed about the antechamber as if this was his first time here. Beautiful sculptures, exotic plants, and other decorations that seemed to come from outside the empire were carefully placed around the area. The centerpiece of the artwork in the room was a large and intricate green soapstone sculpture depicting a great fortress or similar structure in a vast forest. It was a scene inspired by life on the surface, though it didn't match any Kuldrith fortresses he was familiar with. He thought it was a strange choice for a mavin tar's residence. Perhaps he would get a chance to ask Tel-Kyron about it someday.

Another slave brought a tray of assorted drinks for Evir to choose from. He knew it was a breach of manners to ask if he could have both the water and the wine, but it easily fit with the part of the orderguard, and he was desperately thirsty. The slave, of course, readily offered for Evir to help himself to anything he wanted and asked if he should bring more. Evir quickly drained the stone cup of water and said the wine would be sufficient as he lifted the crystal goblet from the tray.

Evir was tempted to quickly drain the wine glass as well, but he could not afford for the alcohol to impair his thinking right now. As time slipped by, he felt a micro-tremor developing in his good leg from having to bear all his wait for so long. He had taken in every detail of the antechamber multiple times over in the prolonged silence and feared perhaps Tel-Kyron would decline to see Evir. He had considered this possibility, but not with a manhunt underway for him. Returning to Daopek's residence now would be incredibly risky, though he didn't see any better options at the moment. Evir realized the emotion sitting like a hot stone in the pit of his stomach was one with which he had not been well acquainted most of his life.

The feeling was dread.

But something else pulled at the corner of his mind. He ignored it and turned his focus back to his predicament, churning through every avenue he could think of, every permutation of the problem, searching for a solution. Perhaps he could find another elantir to disguise him. Tel-Kyron would be the obvious choice, at least to point him in the direction of—

Yes, Tel-Kyron can point you in the right direction. The words did not feel like his own but carried an inexplicable undertone of being safe, of being home. It nearly smothered the dread into nonexistence.

Evir and the elantir turned their gaze in the direction of another set of approaching footsteps. It was a Cannessi slave this time, a man in his middle years if Evir was judging the signs correctly. His people had become a common enough sight in Stierve ever since the Kuldrith had finally opened the portal to reach Remalia. In fact, Tel-Kyron was the brilliant mind behind the elantic research that had finally unlocked the ancient artifact's power, if rumors were true.

"Good tide to you, honored guest," the diminutive man greeted him with the same easy confidence as the other slaves. His eyes, however, conveyed an intense interest in Evir that made the inquisitor uneasy for some reason he could not quite put his finger on. *Just nerves*, he told himself. "The mavin tar will see you now."

Relief washed over the inquisitor like a breath of fresh air after a cave-in.

The slave took the wine glass from Evir and set it on the table as one of the guards stepped forward and asked Evir to surrender the truncheon he carried as an orderguard inspector. Evir gladly handed it over, though he kept it from showing in his demeanor. He felt a slight prickling sensation work its way from the top of his head down his body. He was familiar with elantic security measures and knew the elantir was neutralizing any threat he might be carrying on his body, the same way she had done to the figurine he presented earlier. She stopped at his chest, and he realized whatever Selvruen had done to the probe might raise a concern. It would be very difficult to explain what it was, and worse, would easily connect him to the incident in Fallswatch. The prickling at his chest intensified, then suddenly continued moving down his body. Evir was relieved when the elantir nodded to the Cannessi slave, then again took her seat.

The slave smiled. "If you would please follow me," the small man motioned as he returned the way he had come. Evir strode forward, grateful his guide's steps were short enough to set a pace Evir could reasonably match. The short corridor led to a large, open area that served as the main living area of the residence. The elegantly furnished chamber was a stark contrast to the Warrens Evir had been inhabiting for over a month and the dark, monotonous tunnels from Kierden before that. He was not normally given to jealousy, but at this moment, he felt a twinge of it trying to wrap its seductive grip around his heart.

Plush pillows lined the recessed sitting area in the center of the room, surrounding a large warming stone, a perfect place for conversing with guests, having a relaxed meal, or simply resting. He remembered well reclining there with Dae'yen and their hosts nearly a year ago after receiving his assignment to ferret out the Dorothi in Kierden. He knew the invitation had in truth come from Zenni, who wanted to spend a little more time with her friend before Dae had to leave to the furthest edge of the empire for an extended period. Evir was not concerned about the reason for the opportunity; the meal had been exquisite and the company enjoyable. He hoped the mavin tar felt the same way.

More art hung on the walls and rested on tables and pedestals with motifs consistent with the works in the antechamber, scenes from the world above, and a few of the beauties below the surface. Another table and pair of chairs, highly polished and in excellent condition, were positioned at the side of the room, more for show than for use. Tapestries hung on several walls, absorbing stray sounds and giving the room an intimate, comforting feeling. The room was well lit by several lumens strategically placed to leave virtually no shadows, and the air was clean and subtly scented with a smell Evir was surprised he vividly remembered from his time on the surface so many years ago—fresh flowers—lilies if he remembered correctly.

"I apologize for the long wait," the Cannessi said, pulling Evir from his thoughts. It was taboo for a slave to address anyone from another household directly unless spoken to first or as absolutely necessary. "I hope you weren't too uncomfortable."

The Cannessi led Evir further into the residence, taking a passage off the main living chamber leading to a room Evir knew would be meant for more private meetings. "I'm just grateful your master is willing to see me without a prior appointment."

"He said you must have had quite a journey to bring you here." He paused for a moment, then almost as an afterthought added, "And perhaps ahead of you as well."

Evir was uncomfortable with the degree of openness the slave's words implied existed between the mavin tar and at least this one slave, and perhaps others. He would have to be even more cautious than he had anticipated. "You might say that," Evir replied vaguely, not wanting to divulge any more information than necessary.

The slave didn't request permission to enter but simply led Evir into the room where Tel-Kyron sat in an armchair with his eyes closed and his fingers laced together, his index fingers extended and resting on his dark lips. Evir's figurine sat on top of a book resting on a small table next to the mavin tar. Evir took the opportunity to glance around the room.

There were a surprising number of places to sit: chairs, couches, alcoves with pillow-covered benches. A stone-and-tile desk with a large, upholstered chair stood along the wall at the far side of the room. Evir found it hard to imagine covering a whole chair in cloth. *Such extravagance.* Several shelving units made of stalkwood and reinforced with decorative brass facings lined the walls on either side, filled with a vast assortment of neatly organized instruments, books, decorations, sheaves of thin metal sheets, and other things Evir could only guess at. He was certain he would enjoy perusing their contents for hours.

Tel-Kyron opened his eyes and smiled warmly as he suddenly rose. Evir bowed again, eyes toward the ground, his arms outstretched. The mavin tar cupped his hands and held toward the inquisitor. "Evir, it is so good to see you again." Evir gritted his teeth in frustration at having his name used in front of the slave who still stood next to him. "Forgive me, I didn't hear you come in. I'm afraid I was a bit lost in thought. It happens a lot these days. Come, sit down," the mavin tar gestured to the seat near him.

"Thank you, Tel-Kyron Mavin Tar, but I wouldn't want my armor to damage such a fine chair." Evir also didn't want to show how badly he was injured.

"I think we have a long conversation ahead of us. Perhaps we should get you out of your armor so we can relax and talk properly. You'll stay for dinner, yes?"

Evir had rehearsed this scene many times to prepare for any direction it might turn, but this was not one he had anticipated. It seemed too good to be true and instantly put him on his guard. But he needed the man's help, and at the moment he had no better options for what to do after their conversation. "That is very generous, Mavin Tar. I would be honored."

"Vyunoth, give him a hand if you would, please."

Evir appreciated the peculiar courtesy with which Tel-Kyron treated his slaves—as full members of his household and family, similar to the way Dae'yen treated theirs. Perhaps that was one of the many reasons Zenni and Dae got along so well. He recalled how valuable the slaves in Artencu Vice Regent's household had been to Evir's investigation, how willing they were to share everything they knew. He doubted Tel-Kyron's slaves would be so quick to turn.

The Cannessi helped undo the buckles along the sides of the cuirass. Evir was grateful for the assistance but could not stop himself from wincing a few times at a sharp tug or moving too quickly. Raising his arms was particularly painful. "Is everything all right, Evir? You look like you're hurt." Tel-Kyron leaned forward and placed a steady hand on Evir's arm, a look of concern replacing the welcoming smile.

"Just a little banged up. I will explain everything, but it's a delicate matter, Mavin Tar." Evir wanted to ask him to dismiss the slave, but it would be too impolite. He hoped the hint would be enough. The Cannessi reached up and helped Evir gently slide the cuirass off his shoulders, then went and laid the armor neatly on a nearby bench while Evir and Tel-Kyron moved to their seats. Evir lowered himself as best he could into the chair, holding his breath against the pain.

"Hardly 'a little banged up.' You're a wreck." Turning to his slave, he said, "Go and tell Nyavva to send for Roj'dakt."

"Forgive me, Mavin Tar, but you should hear what I have to say before deciding on a course of action."

Tel-Kyron fixed Evir with his intense, pale-green eyes that stood out in stark contrast to his slate-colored skin and hair that had grayed to the color of unpolished steel. The man was only ten years his senior, but he appeared to have aged significantly in the months since the inquisitor had last seen him. Evir sat patiently, enduring the mavin tar's scrutiny.

"This is not a social call then," Tel-Kyron said wryly.

"I'm afraid not. It... it's complicated."

"I guessed that from you showing up unannounced, disguised as an orderguard inspector, and returning a gift Zenni gave Dae'yen the last time you were in my home before running off to get tangled up in a purge on the outskirts of the empire."

"And you don't yet know the half of it," Evir confessed. Apprehension swirled in his stomach wondering how the mavin tar would react to the difficult circumstances Evir was about to lay at his feet.

"Yes, well, first things first." The mavin tar reclined back in his cushions, his posture relaxed but his eyes still observing Evir with concern. "Zenni will be very displeased with me if I don't inquire about Dae'yen. Is she here in Stierve as well?"

"No, we felt it best that she remain in Kierden until I resolved things here."

"Safer in Kierden with all its turmoil than here in the heart of the empire? What kind of trouble are you in?"

"The worst kind... politics and corruption."

"Ahh. How redundant," Tel-Kyron said with a thin smile. "And whose corruption are we talking about?"

Evir felt he had been rushing toward this precipice for so long, now that he was here, he found it difficult to leap. Once he named Malithir as a traitor to the mavin tar, things would largely be out of his control. *Tel-Kyron can point you in the right direction*, his inner voice coaxed again. "I must warn you, Mavin Tar, that knowing this information might put you and others in grave danger." Evir looked over at the Cannessi, silently pleading for Tel-Kyron to take Evir's meaning and dismiss his slave. "I'm sorry to bring such a matter to you. I assure you, if I knew anyone else who could help me, I wouldn't be here."

"Very well," Tel-Kyron said before closing his eyes for a few moments. Evir could barely feel the currents of elan moving around him. After several moments, the master elantir opened his eyes again. "Speak freely. No one will hear us."

Evir wondered whether the mavin tar had some means of anchoring the warding elant in place or if he could manage the impressive feat of maintaining it while simultaneously holding a conversation—something Evir understood was challenging for even very skilled elantir. His curiosity about it was merely an excuse to stall. He winced as he took an overly deep breath. The pain pushed his mouth into action. "I have reason to believe Malithir Lord Overseer is a traitor to the empire."

Tel-Kyron's face was unreadable as he again held his steady gaze fixed on Evir. He seemed to be weighing more than Evir's words. "I think you had better start from the beginning."

This part of the conversation Evir was well prepared for. He laid out each step leading him to this moment: what caused him to believe there was a mole in the first place; the plan he, Javinth, and Kiavi had devised to confirm there was, in fact, a mole, and the means to identify them; his journey to Stierve and weeks of investigating the elantir; and finally discovering Selvruen was the one he had been searching for and his escape. Tel-Kyron listened intently, nodding or mumbling a subtle interjection occasionally, usually a word of approval at moments when Evir described Kiavi's work. When Evir finished his account, the mavin tar sat back in his chair with his eyes closed, fingers laced together and his index fingers on his lips. Evir could imagine the man had spent countless hours in this position.

"Your logic is sound," Tel-Kyron said slowly, his eyes still closed, "but you're missing a key piece of the puzzle."

Evir nodded. "Why?" It had troubled the inquisitor since he first suspected there was a mole. What could the traitor possibly hope to gain? He had a dozen theories, but none of them truly seemed adequate.

"Too many people focus on the 'what' of things. But knowing the 'why' is the key that unlocks true power."

"I could not agree more. Unfortunately, my line of work often requires me to act with only the 'what'."

"And what action do you propose we take now?"

"*We?* You'll help me then?"

"Let's not get ahead of ourselves," Tel-Kyron said, gesturing for Evir to slow down. "I asked what you propose."

"The only person truly in a position to deal with this is Arku Overlord. I came to ask if you could arrange for me to meet with him without anyone knowing I'm in Stierve."

The mavin tar slowly nodded, but his raised eyebrow and pursed lips told Evir it was not a sign of agreement. "That is no small request these days. We can't even get Arku's attention long enough to have him confirm a new mavin tar." It was strange being in the presence of one of the few people in the empire who could get away with referring to the overlord without the formality of his title and not sounding impertinent.

Evir was aware of Purrev Mavin Tar's passing into Teraithia's embrace while the inquisitor was away in Kierden. She had been a great servant of the people, but Evir had never heard of it taking so long for a vacancy on the council to be filled. "Why the delay?"

"Politics and corruption, I suspect." Both men smirked at the half-jest. "Tell me about the Purge. In her report to the Council, Vetat Atan-akai claimed it was the only option to stop the rebellion and greater bloodshed. Do you agree?"

Evir was not sure what this had to do with the lord overseer's treason, and it felt like dangerous territory. Javinth's words of caution sprang to mind. *'You can't afford to give others any reason to doubt your piety.'* But Evir was in no position to decline to answer the mavin tar's request, nor could he bring himself to lie to the man he was entrusting his life to. "I... cannot say for certain, Mavin Tar," Evir hedged. "It is difficult to guess what might have happened." He hoped his response would be enough for Tel-Kyron to let it pass, but the man simply waited, apparently unsatisfied. Evir took another deep breath and winced at the sharp pain in his side. "I can't help wondering if I could have prevented the whole thing by capturing the Dorothi leaders sooner."

"You would have preferred the Purge did not happen? Why? You've hunted the Dorothi for years. I would think you considered it a great success."

Fear gripped Evir's heart, and he cursed his carelessness. "I assure you, Mavin Tar, my highest aim was to stop the rebellion at all costs, and I am proud of our efforts. But I love the Kuldrith people, and had hoped to avoid their suffering and bloodshed to the extent possible." A mix of horror and fathomless regret flooded into him as the blood-soaked child from I'fa appeared on the rug-covered floor of Tel-Kyron's chamber. He closed his eyes, struggling to resist the urge to squeeze them tighter as he fought to push his churning emotions away. *Not now!* he berated himself as he felt tears building behind his eyelids. He could not afford to show weakness in this moment when he was so close to accomplishing his mission.

"I do not doubt your dedication to our people, Evir. But do you think the Dorothi are the only ones who worship a deity other than Teraithia? What about the Viancians, or Yerinites, or Servari? Will you hunt them next?"

The question struck a nerve with Evir. He knew the law forbade practicing any faith other than Teraithianism. He understood the aim was to foster greater unity, but he could not shake the growing sense that unity would never be achieved by stamping out those who believed differently. Such differences would always persist. He thought of Dae's own fraught relationship with the Church. "My concern is not a person's faith but with those who threaten the empire. I have seen no evidence of any such believers forming resistance groups in open defiance of the will of the Mavin Tar."

"Do you believe the Purge was the will of the council?"

Evir felt he was walking on loose stones. He had no idea where Tel-Kyron was going with this line of questioning, but it set the hairs on the back of his neck on edge. "If it wasn't, then those responsible should be punished."

"Even if that is Teraithia's Church?"

Evir thought of Akriel and his hopes that his son could one day be a voice for tempering the more extreme elements that seemed to be gaining control of the Church. "Not everyone in the Church is responsible for that terrible event. The Obsidian Door could discover who the decision makers were. I have a pretty good idea as to one or two of them right now."

Tel-Kyron gave a derisive laugh. "Trying to untangle that knot would make the matter with Malithir look like child's play by comparison. Unfortunately, this is the treacherous web we would be walking into. If I am going to help you, I need you to see more of the threads so you do not unwittingly, in your earnest desire to fulfill your duty, cross a thread that makes you and me the spider's next meal. Tell me, did you learn anything useful from capturing the Dorothi?"

Evir was grateful to be back on solid ground. "Their high priest confirmed he had received communications from the Qilerate."

"Pakoran Grand Master spoke to you? Of his own free will?" Tel-Kyron sounded incredulous.

"Yes," Evir replied, equally surprised by the mavin tar's questions. "He was fully cooperating with me, answering all my questions. You knew him?"

"Knew of him, yes. Mostly by reputation as one of Vai Doroth's most devoted disciples. Did he say why he spoke to you?"

Evir was again surprised by the mavin tar's first question. The man took seriously his motto about understanding the 'whys.' "He said it was Vai Doroth's will that he answer my questions—some kind of ultimate test of faith."

"Fascinating. So the Qilerate are perhaps real after all. Why did they contact him?"

"They encouraged the Dorothi to flee Kierden and offered to help them do so."

"Do you think Malithir is Qilerate?"

"Perhaps, though it is difficult to imagine why the lord overseer would offer to help them escape at the same time he was encouraging them to launch a rebellion. Or maybe he did what so many others have done—use the name of a phantom to hide his true intentions. It's easier to separate a cave tick from a xanath hide than to sort the truth from lies when it comes to Raen Qil and the Qilerate. My hope is that once the lord overseer is arrested, I can thoroughly investigate and discover where these threads lead."

"I suspect they will lead where they always seem to lead—to dead ends; but followed they must be. I am curious to see if this time will be any different."

"I'll be sure to keep you apprised of any progress on that front, Mavin Tar. But it's a moot question unless the overlord chooses to act against Malithir. Do you think I have any chance of persuading him?"

"It's a difficult proposition to predict what any overlord will do, and Arku more than most. The world is changing more rapidly than in any generation since the Great Reckoning. The overlord believes he is the voice from the stone to fulfill the prophecy in establishing a worldwide Teraithian theocracy."

Evir thought it was a strange coincidence the Dorothi grand master had referenced the same prophecy during their discussion but kept it to himself.

"Something I said struck a chord with you. May I ask what it was?"

So much for keeping it to himself. Evir was usually much better at hiding his reactions. He clearly was not at his best and admonished himself again to be more careful. "Pakoran referenced the same prophecy but seemed to believe it was the Qilerate who would be the voice from the stone."

Tel-Kyron's eyes narrowed, though what the expression meant Evir could not begin to guess. Finally, the mavin tar seemed to reach a decision and nodded, then climbed to his feet. Evir made a move to follow, but the older man waved him back into his seat. Normally Evir would have stood regardless, but too many places on his body protested in pain, so he eased himself back, trying to find a comfortable position. His eyes tracked the master elantir as he made his way toward the Cannessi slave, who had taken a seat and was reading a book—one with paper pages rather than pressed copper. It amazed Evir how generous the mavin tar was with his slaves.

Without any instructions from Tel-Kyron, the slave came and began clearing the table next to the mavin tar's seat, handing the figurine back to Evir. Tel-Kyron stopped where the Cannessi had been sitting and reached forward until his hand almost touched the wall. The inquisitor had been around elantir enough to guess when met'elan was being used. After a few moments, a small portion of the stone wall came loose and swung open, revealing a hidden compartment. Tel-Kyron reached inside with both hands and withdrew a large, ancient-looking tome and carried it carefully, almost reverently, back to his seat. The Cannessi held the book while Tel-Kyron sat and brought the wooden stand in front of him before taking the book back and resting it on the stand.

Confusion and fear suddenly gripped Evir as he recognized the holy symbol of the Servari faith pressed into the leather cover, a gold and silver mobius band twisted into an infinity symbol, representing the gods Yonvaar and Kerail. It was obviously a sacred Servari text, which meant it was outlawed within the Kuldrith empire. Evir was duty-bound to report this to Qin'acht Overseer, though doing so was complicated at the moment. Was Tel-Kyron counting on Evir's desperation to protect him? The pieces of their wandering conversation were suddenly fitting together. The mavin tar made no move to hide the nature of the tome, nor did he give any explanation.

"Why?" Evir finally asked.

A slight smile touched the corners of Tel-Kyron's mouth. "Well, at least you're asking the right question. The most correct answer I can give you is that Pakoran Grand Master is not the only one facing a test of his faith. However, I would guess that response is somewhat less than satisfying, so I will add that it is my hope you will understand what I am risking by agreeing to help you and that we can work together to avoid another purge."

Ash and flame! A mavin tar is Servari. The world felt like shifting stones beneath his feet. The last thing he needed right now was more complication. "You think the Church is going to come after the Servari? Why? My impression is that there are hardly enough of you to threaten them."

"This is not only about numbers and power, at least not the way you would typically think about it." Tel-Kyron opened the tome and silently leafed through several thin copper sheets inscribed with delicate writing. Evir felt a growing sense of unease, though whether because he was witnessing a crime or because he was at a complete loss as to the mavin tar's purpose, he was not sure.

Tel-Kyron nodded, apparently finding what he was looking for. "Forgive the archaic voice, but I think it is worth hearing it as it was written. This is part of a Servari version of the Ultideic Prophecy:

And behold, the inhabitants of the world were divided by the storm beneath the glass, and did contend one with another. And they were the armies of crown and sword, and did fill the expanse of Baon, even unto the ends thereof.

And so great was the contention of the armies that the heavens shook, yea, even until the very thrones of the Nine began to crumble into dust, and were swept away by the storm, until only two thrones remained.

Evir could not, for the life of him, guess what connection Tel-Kyron saw between this obscure prophecy about the war of the gods and the situation with Malithir. He hoped the man was not posing some kind of theological test Evir had to pass before the mavin tar would agree to help him. But if that was what was required, Evir would play along. Tel-Kyron had said the overlord saw himself as a figure in this prophecy, perhaps as some champion for Teraithia. Did Tel-Kyron think Malithir was on the other side? If the lord overseer was Qilerate, perhaps he was.

Listen with your heart, not your mind, his inner voice admonished him. Tel-Kyron scanned ahead, his finger tracing down the copper sheet and onto the next before continuing.

But behold, and lo, the One was laid low, and the two that were One prevailed. And the Nine were no longer, but in One is the Will made manifest.

As Tel-Kyron read the words 'in One is the Will made manifest', Evir felt an unnamable shift deep within. He could not remember hearing those words before, yet they sounded so intimately familiar, as if they were profoundly his own, repeated a thousand times over. He felt a strange mix of elated freedom and utmost calm. A corner of his mind was aware that Tel-Kyron was continuing to read.

And the storm did cease, and the serpent rose no more, and a great peace fell upon all creation, both above the glass and beneath the glass.

And the two that were One remained.

The mavin tar seemed as if he was about to read more but stopped and looked at Evir. "You see, whether people recognize it or not, this is the true struggle playing out in the world right now. Teraithia's doctrine of establishing her dominance at any cost drives the Church and its followers to destroy any who do not follow their goddess. They knew there was no chance they would convert the Dorothi, which is why they resorted to the purge. And they will do so again the moment they believe there is another Faith unwilling to bend to her will."

Evir's mind wanted to solve the puzzle of the mavin tar's purpose for revealing so much of his private beliefs, while his soul longed to bask in the feeling from... what? The prophecy? Tel-Kyron himself? He was not sure, but it felt like home. It made him think of Dae and how much he wanted to be reunited with her, to hold her. He realized Tel-Kyron was waiting for a reply. *What can I possibly say?*

"Mavin Tar—"

"I think we are past the need for titles, at least in private."

"Very well," Evir acceded, at least for the time being. "Matters of the destiny of the world are far beyond my ability to grapple with. I can only assure you that my interests are solely to serve the empire and our people the best way I know how, which at this moment is to deal with Malithir's treachery. I do not wish you or your household any harm." Evir knew there were some, including certain individuals within the Door in the not-too-distant past, who had harshly persecuted the Servari. He wanted to assure Tel-Kyron he had no intention of causing more suffering, but his sense of duty demanded different words. He feared they might ruin any chance of securing the mavin tar's help, and part of his mind demanded that he hold his tongue, but he was powerless to stop himself. "But I will do everything in my power to protect this people from our enemies, whoever they may be."

"And how do you know who is truly an enemy if you cannot see the Kuldrith people, or all people for that matter, in connection with the destiny of the world?"

"I have to trust the overlord and Mavin Tar to make those decisions appropriately. Anything else is chaos and death."

"You trusted Malithir until you decided his actions were at odds with the interests of the people. By what standard did you come to that conclusion?"

"He broke the law."

"So did the Church when it murdered two thousand people. So have I by having this book. The law is neither immutable nor infallible. It is merely an extension of the intentions and values of those who make and execute it. Where those intentions, values, and judgments are flawed, the law will likewise be flawed. If an enemy of the people has the power to make and execute the law, you cannot look to the law as the standard by which to judge if they are an enemy or not. There must be a higher standard."

"The gods?" Evir asked skeptically.

"And how do you know which of the gods is an enemy or not?"

"I suppose your answer is that all of them except the Holy Couple are enemies of the people."

"My answer is that each of us must decide that question for ourselves and then order our lives accordingly. There is no possible appeal to a higher authority than one's best judgment, tempered with the humility to recognize that as we learn and grow, our judgment may need to be amended from time to time."

"You sound like an Akraharrian, recognizing no authority higher than oneself."

"In the singular decision of whom one will choose to follow, I suppose that's true. But that is as far as the similarity goes. Akraharr teaches to follow no authority but oneself. Philosophical complications of that position aside, I believe following that path is a foolish decision, doomed, as you said before, to end only in chaos and death."

"The Dorothi fared no better following Vai Doroth's path."

"True, though not as an inevitable outcome of Vai Doroth's doctrine, but only by coming into conflict with those who follow Teraithia's while they hold more power. And this is the crux of what I want you to see. There is no path a human life can possibly follow that does not adhere to and ultimately advance one or more of the gods' doctrines. We can do so blindly or consciously, but we cannot avoid that fundamental reality. I ask only that you begin doing so consciously. It is too dangerous for both of us if you continue doing so blindly."

The mavin tar had all the leverage in this situation, but if he was using it to manipulate Evir, the inquisitor could not see it. "And you have chosen the path of the Holy Couple."

"I have."

"And do you expect me to follow that path also?"

"Our Divine Parents do not demand that others bend to their will. They simply invite all to see the good and joy to which their teachings lead us and decide for ourselves if we desire it enough to walk their path. The invitation is open to you, but I have no expectations one way or another. I will help you get the audience with Arku Overlord if I can, regardless of what path you choose."

Evir saw no indication the mavin tar was trying to deceive him and believed the man was sincere in offering to help. *Perhaps it's fortunate he is Servari after all.* The inquisitor felt an immense sense of relief, but it was tinged with apprehension for what the rest of the mavin tar's words meant for him. He sensed he had moved from one treacherous path into possibly an even more treacherous one. If anything could be worse than politics and corruption, it was politics and corruption combined with religion.

Tel-Kyron can point you in the right direction.

This time the words reverberated in every corner of his being, though he was even less sure than before what they meant. *One step at a time,* he told himself. "Thank you," Evir said with his deepest sincerity. "I don't know what I would have done without your help."

Tel-Kyron smiled. "Found another way, if I know you at all. But I am happy to be of service if I can. Speaking of which, I believe we have put off attending to your injuries long enough. Vyunoth," he called to his slave, "please tell Nyavva to send for Roj'dakt now. But don't mention anything about our guest or why we need her. She'll just have to trust me." The Cannessi bowed and left the room. "We will talk more of weighty matters later. For now, let's figure out how we are going to keep your presence here a secret while I try to work out the difficult task of sneaking you in for a private audience with Arku."

Not an hour earlier, hearing those words from the mavin tar would have been almost too perfect to dare hope for. Not that he was ungrateful to hear them now. But after everything else he had heard and felt, they seemed so...

mundane. Perhaps with some healing and rest, he would be back to his old self again.

Do you really want to be your old self again?

That question was too uncomfortable, and he turned his focus instead to the safer task of working out the details of his stay with Tel-Kyron. As the mavin tar had said, there would be time for such weighty questions later.

Much, much later, he hoped.

CHAPTER LV
STEPHIR

S tephir felt guilty riding past them. Every time he did, the craftsmen would stop and stare, inquiring whether there was anything they could do for him. Did they not understand that all he wanted of them was to continue their work? He was only interested in inspecting their progress, not impeding it. Sometimes life as royalty was more complicated than it should be. Most of the time, in fact.

"As you can see, m'lord, we are well ahead of our projections. This catapult here should be ready within the next two days. That'll make..." The man continued, but Stephir knew where this was leading. Captain Palipen would point out how hard it was and how well he did, but the job got done. Stephir let him go on, not wanting to seem uninterested. He needed the man. He needed a lot of men these days. But how many would survive the siege... would see their families again? Too few, he mused grimly. Even if they succeeded in breaking through to get back into Remalia, it would be with far too few men, he was sure.

Stephir nodded as if he was listening, and Palipen plowed right on. He had hoped the man would weary of speaking soon, but it appeared that hope was in vain. His empty stomach rumbled loudly. He had only eaten a few bites of the already scant meal that was their lunch. Hardly enough to sustain the men through a hard day's work. But none of the men had complained. He wished the same could be said of the nobles, who could go on as long about their hardships as Palipen could about his work. What made their grumbling particularly insufferable was how so many of them readily agreed to rationing for their troops but refused to adhere to the rationing themselves.

"No," High General Kuymon interjected, looking perturbed at the construction of a pair of battering rams. These particular ones were a key piece of their strategy to retake Balinth's, though that fact was held in the utmost secrecy. "These aren't the specifications Master Caldren gave you. Those tips were to be cast of your best iron and be pointed. These are nothing like—"

"But sir," Palipen interrupted, trying his best to look both patient and put out at the same time. "I can promise you these rams will easily be as effective as any—"

"Reconstruct the tips like Caldren instructed," Kuymon interrupted back with his characteristic stony seriousness, the understated threat in his voice making his next words all the more disturbing, "or I'll use your head as a battering ram and see how well that works."

Palipen looked to Stephir for support.

"You have your orders, Captain."

"As you say, my lord." The man might be pompous at times, and certainly lacking in military discipline, but he was truly a gifted craftsman. As soon as Palipen continued showing them the rest of the siege equipment being assembled, Kuymon nodded his thanks to the prince. The man had been one of his father's closest advisers, and Stephir could see why. Being of common birth had put Kuymon at a disadvantage among other general officers and high officials, nearly all of whom boasted some connection to one or more of Remalia's noble houses. Nobles, regardless of where they came from, always seemed to have one thing in common; they were rarely willing to listen to anyone of lower station. There were occasional exceptions, of course, and Stephir was fortunate to have a few of them with him, though only a few.

Kuymon, however, had quietly managed through the years to earn the respect of most and even somewhat of an equal footing with many of the nobility in the king's court. He had worked his way up through the military ranks during Jevorak's younger years, proving himself a powerful leader, a shrewd tactician, and above all, fiercely loyal to the crown. During the last several years of relative peace, the general had also demonstrated he was a wise and levelheaded counselor, someone his father could turn to for advice without worrying about whether he had his own agenda. Stephir was grateful for the high general's continued loyalty.

The inspection continued, but Stephir knew there was not much more to see. Though they had assembled a decent collection of siege equipment, he had a sinking feeling it would not be enough. And all the siege equipment in the world would do nothing for them if the elantir failed their part of the plan. He wished he felt more confidence, at least enough to instill more of it in the other nobles and officers. Too much grumbling was happening, too many whispers of dissent, even talk of surrender among some. Always around corners, always just out of earshot of the prince. It had to be quelled, but Balinth's had to be his, first.

"Your Highness," one of the Divinarim said as he approached from behind. The prince turned and was surprised to see a middle-aged man in the uniform of an elantir apprentice standing between two of his royal guards. With Stephir's permission, Captain Major Ambersol had been recruiting soldiers into the elantir ranks if anyone demonstrated even a modicum of aptitude. But the few he had found tended to be much greener than this one. "He delivered this message for you," the knight said, handing Stephir a folded piece of paper bearing the seal of the elantir commander.

This was the first time Stephir had seen it since Calinda had fallen unconscious. He hoped it was not a sign something was wrong. He broke the seal and unfolded the paper. His heart sank before he even read the message. At the end of the single line was a symbol Calinda had used when they were making plans to deal with the traitors. It meant she needed to speak with him urgently and in private. He read the sentence to be sure there was not more to the message, then folded the paper as if it was nothing important.

"Tell Captain Major Ambersol I will stop by the Post when I return to camp." The apprentice saluted a footman's salute, arm across his chest before he realized his mistake and bowed instead. He would only be allowed to offer the elantir's salute once he had achieved his first rank. With any luck, the war would be over before then. The man retreated and Stephir did his best to seem interested in completing his inspection of the remaining work of the engineers, carpenters, smiths, and the other craftsmen. He commended their effort and urged them to finish with all haste.

His retinue turned their horses and rode back toward the Spice Road. It was still startling to see how much the forests had been cut down. Between timber taken for building siege equipment, weapons, wagons, fueling fires, and myriad other uses, it would take decades for the region to recover. It was one more tragic cost of war. But he knew a far heavier toll was coming when they attacked Balinth's again. It took nearly an hour to descend the rolling hills to the main camp of the army. He dismounted and dismissed everyone to return to their other activities except Father Daemmer.

"Where are we going, Your Highness?" the Servari priest asked as they walked at a measured pace.

Stephir's only answer was to hand the paper to Daemmer, one of the few besides himself who would understand its significance. After reading the paper, the priest gave it back to Stephir, and they continued in silence. It didn't take long to arrive at the elantir's area of the camp. The area was quiet and orderly, with no hint remaining of the terrible destruction that had occurred only weeks earlier. Elantir guards saluted as he approached. "Captain Major Ambersol is inside?" he asked.

"Yes, Your Highness," the senior guard confirmed as they held the large canvas flaps open for the prince to enter. While Stephir liked the physical characteristics of the unique elantir command post, with its unnaturally high, flat roof, its long, narrow central corridor, and its division into several rooms, nearly every visit here had coincided with receiving bad news. He prayed to Yonvaar and Kerail that this time was different.

The lone Divinarim accompanying the prince inside pulled the curtain open to Ambersol's office. The captain major looked up from documents on his desk, a look of annoyance at the unannounced intrusion. Upon seeing the prince, the elantir commander's expression changed to one of apology before the words even began falling from his lips. "Your Highness, I didn't realize it was you. Please, come in."

Stephir stepped inside, followed by Father Daemmer. He glimpsed an elantir who stopped outside the room before the curtain fell closed. Ambersol held up a finger as the prince and priest took the two open seats in the room. Stephir assumed he was waiting for the silencing wards to be put in place. "Would it be possible to weave permanent elants in place to prevent eavesdropping?" Stephir asked with curiosity. "Tie them to an object, or perhaps the walls of the room, for example?"

"There are some very basic, single-modality elants that can be bound to inanimate matter. To make an object glow or hardening material are two of the oldest examples. However, elants that require modulating the elan into multiple modalities that must be harmonized and balanced require human intelligence to be performed. Without a mind to hold the complex patterns in place, the elan will flow like water back into its natural state. A mind can be bound to an object, such as with the Bonded, which allows elants to be preserved, but short of that I'm not aware of any way to do it." A slight smirk touched Ambersol's face. "It's a goal elantir have been unsuccessfully striving for forever, along with transmuting iron into gold and making women fall in love with us. The Eastgatians are rumored to have been working on such a capability, but to my knowledge, it has never been achieved. Perhaps if Commander Alscan were with us, she—"

"Did something happen to her?" Stephir asked, his earlier concern surging back to the surface.

"No, m'lord. Her condition is unchanged."

"So why did you ask to see me?"

Ambersol's face tightened with anxiety. Whatever it was, it was not good news. "Teris contacted us a few hours ago. The Kuldrith are inside the city."

"Holy Couple, save them!" Father Daemmer cried out. Stephir sat frozen, unable to speak or breathe, but his heart screamed for his wife and children.

"Your Highness?" Father Daemmer said, laying a gentle hand on the prince's arm. He felt an invitation to join in communion with the priest, but Stephir's mind was incapable of opening itself, even to his closest advisor. *Are they dead already?* he wondered.

Like a loving embrace, he felt the Holy Couple's divine presence enfold him, comforting him. He closed his eyes and took a deep breath, allowing the feeling of calm to become his center. He sensed that, somehow, everything would be okay. He paid little mind to the sound of someone entering the room.

"It is forbidden to disposition a royal," the Teraithian holy knight said behind him, a heavy threat in his voice.

Suddenly, his connection to the Holy Couple was hampered by feelings of alarm and suspicion as a countervailing dispositioning from his Divinar protector filled him. Father Daemmer's dispositioning ended abruptly, and the harsh reality of the revelation from Ambersol came crashing in upon him. "It's all right," Stephir said absently. "I'm all right. Please wait outside." After a pause, he heard the familiar soft clang of armor as the knight saluted, then stepped out of the room. Part of him desperately wanted to let Father Daemmer place him within the Holy Couple's comforting embrace again, but his duty demanded he face this with all his faculties alert. "I need to talk to Commander Kalvarne."

"Of course, my lord. Everything is prepared," Ambersol said, gesturing toward the room across the corridor where the Bonded was kept. Stephir rose and straightened his clothes before leaving the captain major's office. He walked past the Divinar and elantir standing in the corridor and entered the chamber where the Bonded Keepers, an elantir and a priest, sat with their hands inside the gold and glass reliquary, resting on the Bonded.

As soon as Stephir stopped, he began shaking with impotent fury. He locked his hands behind his back, trying to bring the trembling under control, but his body refused to obey his will. The curtain closed behind Ambersol as he stepped into the room and ordered the link to be opened. The two Keepers bowed their heads, and a moment later the captain major nodded that they were ready.

"This is Crown Prince Stephir. Is Commander Kalvarne present?"

"No, Your Highness. I am Lieutenant Sperlset. The commander is out at the White Gate. Shall I send someone to fetch him?"

"Just tell me what happened. How did the Kuldrith breach the wall?" The words seemed impossible even as he said them. He may as well have been asking how they broke the world.

"They did not breach the walls, m'lord. We are fairly certain they tunneled under them. Their attack began before dawn in the textiles district. They started pouring into the city from the warehouses."

Stephir's mind tried to imagine how they could have accomplished such a feat without anyone knowing. It should have taken months to tunnel any distance that would have allowed them to do so in secret. Perhaps they had been at it for months. Were there spies in Teris helping the Kuldrith? The possibility made his blood run cold. He remembered the assassination attempt at the palace stables. Perhaps there were more enemies in Teris than any of them had imagined.

"Ilyanara and my son... are they safe?"

"The safest of anyone in Teris, my lord."

Stephir let out a thin sigh of relief. "How much of the city has fallen?"

"They already control five districts west of the Grand Avenue." Nearly a quarter of the city, Stephir thought grimly. "We are trying to hold them back long enough to set up blockades to keep them away from the Mount and the supply depots in the eastern districts."

In the last few weeks, Stephir had imagined countless times the horrors of the Kuldrith burning Teris and doing unspeakable atrocities to his people. He hated to ask, but he had to know. "How badly are they sacking the city?"

"So far, only a handful of buildings have burned, and those appear to have been started by our own people. I even heard one report of the Kuldrith putting out a fire."

Stephir could hardly believe what he was hearing. *The enemy is showing restraint?* If they hadn't come to destroy Teris, then what was their goal? To occupy the city long term? They had to know they could not hold the city forever with an expeditionary force and no hope of reinforcements. Sooner or later, Remalia would take the city back—unless there were more forces attacking other cities. There were too many unknowns.

He forced his mind back to the immediate concern. "Have they made any demands?"

"Nothing new today, Your Highness. They have been demanding our surrender for days, but Princess Ilyanara has refused to treat with them." A moment of pride rose above the anxiety gripping his heart.

"How many forces do we still have?" He was well aware Teris began the siege with nearly eight thousand, but almost half of those were armed citizens, not trained soldiers.

"The losses are mounting quickly. We have lost perhaps a thousand today already. At this rate, I don't know how much longer..."

Stephir knew what Sperlset was leaving unsaid. If the Kuldrith truly had as many forces as had been reported, it was only a matter of time before the Terisians were overwhelmed by sheer numbers—unless they could stop them from coming into the city.

"Have you tried collapsing the tunnels they're using to enter the city?" Stephir asked with a spark of hope.

"Commander Kalvarne had the same thought, m'lord. But the last I heard, we couldn't get past the enemy lines back into the textiles district."

"But we still control the wall?"

"I believe so, Your Highness."

"Then find where the tunnel runs under the wall and collapse it there."

"But Your Highness, that will cause the wall to collapse also. It will open the city to their entire army."

"The city already is open to the entire army if we don't close that tunnel. Send word immediately to Kalvarne that my command is to collapse the tunnel at all costs, even under the wall if he has to."

"Yes, Your Highness."

"And send for my wife. I want to speak with her."

"It shall be done, my lord."

"Close the link," Stephir told the Keepers. There were limitations on how much time an open connection through the Bonded could be maintained before it became exhausted or burned out entirely. He had a feeling those limits were going to be tested today, but there was no sense in wasting precious time keeping a link open for no better reason than to be a security blanket for a worried prince. "Who else knows about this?" Stephir asked Ambersol.

"The four of us in this room."

"We must keep it that way. I need everyone entirely focused on retaking

Balinth's. Morale is bad enough without them thinking there is no point if Teris has fallen."

"But it has not fallen yet, m'lord," Father Daemmer said gently, sounding like he was trying to be encouraging.

"It's only a matter of time, Father. No one breathes a word of this to anyone. Am I clear?" He waited for each of them to acknowledge his command before he looked for a seat and carefully lowered himself. He had conflicting impulses to slump in his seat in despair or to throw the chair across the room in rage, but he refused to give in to either one. His mind raced with a hundred questions and concerns. Years of careful training had instilled in him the discipline to control his thoughts, organize them, deal with each one in turn. But he had no strength for that now. The storm in his mind churned unchecked.

Before long, the need to move drove him to his feet. "I am stepping outside. Inform me as soon as Teris contacts us again." The others bowed as he left the room. Walking along the narrow corridor between white canvas walls, he heard some commotion in the distance. *What's wrong now?* he wondered with a surge of apprehension that seemed barely a drop in the sea of anxiety that filled him.

He hurried outside and headed in the direction of the noise, toward the road, straining to detect any hint as to the nature of the disturbance. No metallic ringing... no horns... no sounds of pain or alarm. It was not an attack. That offered a moment of relief. It sounded like cheering. A fight between soldiers, maybe?

Soon, he was in the midst of a growing crowd all moving in the same direction, his guards keeping a clear space around the prince. Others were asking the same questions he had, so there was no need to reveal his ignorance, but no one had any answers. He wished he was up on a horse so he could get a better view ahead. At last, they neared the road where a company of lancers were using their mounts to push the crowd back. Before he could get close enough to figure out why for himself, the answer and more shouts spread around him.

"It's food. They've brought food!" Confusion replaced worry. Was it really food? Where had it come from? As he made his way through the crowd, he saw a train of wagons pulling off the road behind the lancers, being driven by Kushaani. His confusion deepened.

"Captain," Stephir called to the man leading the knights guarding the wagons, "dare I hope that you truly have brought us food?"

"Yes, Your Majesty." Clearly, word of the king's death had reached the man, but not Stephir's instructions regarding his title. But such a matter could be overlooked for the moment. "Or rather, they have," the captain said, indicating the Kushaani drivers behind him. "They're from Kesh, delivering the food on behalf of the Vanassi and Prince Andric." More cheers erupted around him. He knew he should feel relief, gratitude, and a host of other feelings, but Ambersol's words, 'The Kuldrith are inside the city,' and everything they implied drowned out everything else. He was the crown prince, though, and his duty demanded he keep moving forward.

"Holy Couple be praised," Stephir said loud enough for his soldiers to hear him. "Can you introduce me to our saviors?" The captain walked back to the first wagon where a man in his middle years climbed down from the seat of the oilcloth-covered wagon. He had a pattern of thin scars along each of his cheeks; marks Stephir knew represented enemies killed in battle. Whoever this man was, he was no ordinary wagoner.

"Your Majesty, may I present Vedic Hrotish Avvasata Kuutati of the Sanvara Keshi people," the captain said, carefully pronouncing each name. The vedic put his hands together and touched his thumbs to his forehead, then his mouth, then his chest.

"Vedic, I present his—"

"Crown Prince Stephir Laconeus," Stephir said, interrupting the captain to avoid any confusion for the new arrivals as well as those looking on. "Forgive my interruption, Captain. I have chosen to retain my current title until Balinth's Fortress is again under my control."

"Apologies, m'lord, I—"

"Think nothing of it. Vedic Hrotish, we are indeed grateful for this token of friendship. My brother, Prince Andric, do you have word of him?"

"I bring you greeting from the Council of Elders of the Vanassi. Their hearts' desire is that they one day can sit in the shade of the king's house. They regret that circumstances do not allow them to come at this time." The vedic's words sounded formal and rehearsed, and he didn't seem particularly pleased to be saying them. He also wondered if the man was ever going to answer his question. But above all, he was desperate to get back to Ambersol in the Post and talk with Ilyanara.

"My lord," Consul Rellat called out from behind Stephir. He turned to see the priest approaching, with High General Kuymon and Marchioness Haedep not far behind. Stephir felt he was about to end up stuck here if he didn't extricate himself quickly.

"Vedic Hrotish, may I present Consul Bartan Rellat, priest of Sharin Dara. He is one of my closest advisors. Captain, could you please make the proper introductions? Vedic, forgive my abrupt departure, but I'm afraid your arrival caught me in the middle of something that requires my immediate attention. I invite you to dine with me tonight as my honored guest. Consul Rellat will see to your needs in the meantime."

Rellat and the vedic bowed, and the captain saluted as Stephir turned away. Kuymon and Haedep changed their course to intercept him as he headed back through the crowd toward the Post. He needed to ensure they didn't come with him, but without raising suspicion.

"What's all the ruckus about, m'lord?" Kuymon asked as he approached the prince.

"It appears my brother's mission was a success. Wagons full of food have just arrived." Beaming smiles of relief leaped onto their faces. They had the good fortune of not knowing the news of Teris.

"Rellat is dealing with the Keshi, the ones who brought the food." Kuymon and Haedep both raised eyebrows at that piece of information. "Please get word to Quartermaster General Fenishol about the food. And lift rations for tonight. The men deserve full stomachs for a change. I will see you at dinner."

He did his best not to rush off as they acknowledged his instructions, but all he wanted was to hear Ilyanara's voice, to know she was safe. *She isn't safe*, he reminded himself. *None of them are.* The wolves he had been keeping at bay suddenly lunged, tearing at his insides.

Ambersol stood waiting outside the command post, anxiety written on his face. "Is everything all right, my lord?"

"It's fine. Our food problem has been solved for the moment. My wife?"

"Waiting to speak with you, Your Highness." They went back inside and walked down the corridor to the Bonded room. He recalled Ilyanara's words in their room in the palace at Teris on the last day he had seen her. *'I need to see you strong.'* Stephir took a deep breath and held it before slowly letting it out. He offered a silent prayer to the Holy Couple, pleading for strength, then stepped into the room. Ambersol nodded, indicating the link was open.

"Ilyanara?"

"I'm here, my love. As is High Consul Penrossart. Commander Kalvarne is still out leading the defense of the city."

"I'm sorry I'm not there myself."

"I know you will be here as soon as you can."

"How are Shannyth and Jenden?"

"Thankfully, Jenden is oblivious, but Shannyth asks about everything.

Sometimes she seems to know more than I do. You would be very proud of her."

He tried to determine her emotional state, but it was difficult only hearing her voice through the link. There were a hundred things he wanted to talk about besides the reality of their situation, but he didn't know how much longer the Bonded would last. "I commanded Kalvarne to collapse the tunnel they're using to get into the city, even if it also means collapsing part of the wall."

"We know."

"I fear that will only slow them down, buy you some time. You must reconsider escaping the city."

"Stephir, we have already discussed this. I will not abandon our people."

"But you won't be of any help to anyone once the Kuldrith capture you. At best you'll be imprisoned..." He could not bring himself to say the rest. They all knew.

"I know the risks. I can't explain it, but I know I have to stay." He could imagine the firm set of her eyes and lifted chin when her mind was made up. He was frustrated with her, and proud of her, and loved her more in that moment than ever. He resigned himself to acceptance of her decision.

"Then listen to me carefully. Wait and see if Kalvarne is successful in collapsing the tunnel. If he is, you will be in a much stronger position to negotiate a truce. You need to find out everything you can about why they attacked. The lieutenant I spoke to earlier said they're showing restraint, perhaps even preserving the city, so they must want something. Do they want a ransom? Resources? To make Remalia a vassal state? If there is anything they're willing to accept, we will find a way to reach an accord. But if Kalvarne fails and their numbers inside the city continue to grow, then you must surrender before Teris is destroyed."

There was no response. Stephir feared the link had failed. "Ilyanara?"

"We understand, Your Highness," High Consul Penrossart replied.

"Yes, I understand," Ilyanara agreed, her voice thin.

"My lord, the connection is weakening," Ambersol whispered. "We must end soon." Stephir nodded.

"We will speak again as soon as we can. May the Holy Couple watch over you."

"And you, my love."

Heavy silence filled the room as Stephir walked slowly to one of the cushioned seats along a white canvas wall and sat wearily. He looked at the Bonded and felt envy. No worries, no responsibility—no loss, no heartache—just peaceful rest in a gold and glass bed.

No victory, no triumph, no joy, no love, his inner voice said. *It is practically death without true eternal rest.* A part of him felt willing to strike such a bargain.

Never! another corner of his soul shouted as it rose up inside, swallowing up the other voice. *I will fight for every inch before I fall!* His fist clenched around the hilt of his arming sword. *I will be a king!* He could sit no longer and rose to his feet.

"You better be ready to tear down Balinth's walls," he said icily, fixing Captain Major Ambersol in his gaze, "or we will all die trying."

CHAPTER LVI
VIKKIN

Vikkin rode in silence ahead of the prince. They all rode in silence. Thankfully, even Master Ve'Aurben seemed to finally have run out of things to talk about. The only sound in the barren, dull-gray mountain valley was a cold, thin, whistling wind punctuated by the iron-shod hoofs of their mounts clacking against the stony path. The soaring, snow-capped peaks of the Velspars overhead had been stunningly beautiful for the first several days after leaving Sunapra, but the grandeur of the verdant mountainsides and more moderate temperatures had long been left behind for this cold, rocky, and worst of all treacherous, wasteland.

While they no longer had to worry about pursuit by the Kushaani, the world itself had become their greatest threat. They had already put down three horses due to broken legs and lost another with its rider, one of the scouts, down a deep ravine. Now all he saw everywhere he looked was a towering maze through which they had to find their way along an ancient road that ran beside wide glaciers, crossed muddy mountain streams, hugged sheer cliffs, and sometimes disappeared beneath the occasional rockslide or remains of an avalanche. He was grateful Captain Major Minanthsolum had secured the services of the Vanassi guides. The journey, unpleasant as it was, would have been impossible without their direction.

Despite the inhospitable conditions this deep into the mountains, there were occasional signs the road had once been cared for and frequented by travelers, such as a small section of paving stones still fitted together or a cairn marking which valley to take. But decades of neglect had allowed nature to slowly erase all but the last traces of human presence in this most remote part of the world.

If he hadn't seen it himself, he would never have guessed the last village was only a day behind them. Nearly all the villagers were Cannessi, their heavy accents so thick Vikkin had hardly been able to understand a word they said. Living on herds of miniature mountain goats and what little vegetation they could manage to eke out in the desolate terrain, he almost felt sorry for them. Their life was as far removed from anything he had known as he could imagine.

The Vanassi guides had said it would take almost four more weeks to get through the mountains, as long as the weather held. He was more anxious than ever to complete this unpleasant ordeal, to be back on Remalian soil, and to return the prince to the palace where they both belonged. He longed to resume his former life as head of the Order of the Divine Flame in Teris. It seemed so far away, and some part of him knew things were never going to be the same.

He found himself slipping into one of those rare moments in which he questioned his decision to step down as archpaladin to come on this mission with Prince Andric in the first place. He had no doubts Knight Commander Merrek was capable of fulfilling his duties in his absence and hoped the man was successful in repairing the damage done to the Order's standing by Vikkin's disastrous efforts to lead the crown prince toward the Faith. But Andric's burning animosity toward Teraithia after the unfortunate events in Tarsapta had seemed unquenchable. Nevertheless, Vikkin had remained at the prince's side every waking moment, ever so carefully working to show the prince Teraithia's pure doctrine was not what he saw from Sammet in Tarsapta, but instead how Nophet lived as the true path to order and unity in the world, and glory for those who had the strength to lead others to it.

He thought he had begun to see signs of his efforts paying off. He overheard the prince explaining to Master Ve'Aurben and Intercessor Henden that he had touched Teraithia's divinessence during the final ceremony with the Vanassi, an impossible feat if he was not sufficiently in tune with Her divine will. That he could also touch the other gods' divinessences was still astounding—and still concerning. But Vikkin was beginning to understand it was only a small piece of what was at stake. He had seen firsthand at Pradanur a glimpse of the great potential that slumbered within the boy, and the instrument he might someday be in Teraithia's hands, or—Queen of Heaven forbid—in the hands of one of the lesser gods.

Vikkin was coming to accept, despite believing most of his life that leading the Divinarim was his ultimate divine calling, that perhaps his true destiny was to guide Andric into Teraithia's light. *Or if all else fails, ensure he cannot become the Shadow of the Serpent.* He quickly shoved the dark thought aside. He had no children of his own, but he had watched over Andric's safety the boy's entire life, and with King Jevorak all but gone, Vikkin swore he would watch over the prince like his own son as long as he drew breath.

Glancing at the sky, Vikkin estimated they had less than an hour of daylight left. They would have to stop as soon as they found a suitable location to camp. This section of the trail was carved into a steep slope, the mountain rising sharply on the left and dropping precipitously on their right. Sleeping on the road was fine unless it rained during the night, which Vikkin had learned the hard way could come without warning, turning the road into a small river before finding higher ground. That was how they lost their second horse.

They were approaching a spur in the mountain beyond which a cross valley appeared to widen and flatten somewhat. He guessed that was where the guides were leading them to camp for the night. They had traded for fresh goat meat from the Cannessi villagers, and he was looking forward to dinner for a change. Meals were some of the only breaks in the monotony of the journey, and the dried rations they usually had were certainly nothing to celebrate.

"Lady di Greven," Prince Andric called out to the Sharinic knight riding a few places behind him.

"Yes, Your Highness?"

"Would you be willing to sing us a song to lighten the mood?"

The prince had taken a liking to the lady's singing during their journey, and even more so since leaving Sunapra. Something about her seemed to brighten any situation, especially her laughter, which often sprang from her like a crystal-clear natural spring. But she also had the ability to enhance her gift with dispositioning, particularly when she sang. Vikkin had countered it the first time she had done so with the prince, but Andric had commanded him to let her continue. It grated on the Divinar commander to have the Sharinists gain any more influence over the royals, especially Prince Andric, but there was nothing he could do about it now.

"Of course, my lord," she answered. Vikkin glanced over his shoulder to see her carefully making her way past Master Ve'Aurben and Divinar Staneff on the narrow trail. "Do you have any requests?"

"What was the one you sang yesterday about the huntress and the white stag?"

"The Requiem of Vayal. But that's not exactly a song for *lightening the mood*, my lord," she said, laughing lightheartedly.

"It's beautiful. If you wouldn't mind."

Slowly, the soft notes of her rich alto voice rose faintly above the wind like a melodic whisper. Vikkin was not far ahead of her but found himself straining to hear. The song elicited the image of *Morwyn, the fabled huntress, stalking through an ancient, sun-dappled forest, searching for signs of her prey, a mythical white stag. As she nears a glade, she is surprised to see a man, naked but strong and at ease, ambling through the soft grass and wildflowers. Morwyn remains silent, watching from the shadows of the trees. Her heart beats faster as she drinks in her first glimpse of Vayal.*

Vikkin knew where the song was going and wondered if Emerly ever thought of him that way. She was an amazing woman—beautiful, talented, ambitious, charismatic—everything Vikkin had always wanted in a wife— well, almost everything. *If only she were Teraithian*, he mused, *she would be perfect.* Not a wife then. A lover perhaps, if circumstances permitted.

Morwyn and Vayal's love grows as the huntress returns time and again to the forest, sometimes finding her lover near a brook or atop a steep cliff, and other times searching in vain. No words are ever spoken between them. Their connection is deeper than words, deeper than the roots of the trees of the forest, deeper than the lakes and rivers and mountains, deeper than the world itself.

He could not sense the divinessence Emerly called upon to weave the dispositioning into her song, but he felt its influence extending to the prince and most likely the others, connecting them, knitting their hearts together. Vikkin gritted his teeth in frustration, but still he listened, allowing himself to feel a touch of the longing in the story.

Spring becomes summer becomes autumn, until one day, while searching for Vayal, Morwyn catches a glimpse of white streaking through the falling leaves. Her bow is in her hand as she quietly makes her way through the trees. At the edge of a forest glade, she sees the white stag standing tall and proud, his breath misting in the chill autumn air. He is so beautiful, she almost forgets she is hunting him. She feels his heart beat in time with hers as she nocks the arrow and draws it to her cheek. The arrow flies.

One of the advanced scouts appeared around a sharp bend in the road ahead, sprinting toward them along the rocky path as fast as she could manage, moving her arms in a pattern Vikkin did not recognize but was certain it was nothing good. The fact that she was on foot was not a good sign, either.

"On your guard," Captain Major Minanthsolum called out, quickly dismounting and untying his sword from its place behind his saddle. Lady di Greven's singing abruptly broke off as others followed suit, reaching for their weapons and shields as well.

"What is it?" Prince Andric asked Minanthsolum.

"Enemies."

"Who? How many?"

"I don't know."

"Should we move forward or wait here?"

"Move!" Minanthsolum called over his shoulder as he rushed forward. "Don't run blindly around that corner, but we need to get within bow range." The captain major seemed to be issuing orders to the soldiers as much as answering the prince. Vikkin did not bother to question his judgment. He had grown to respect the man as an excellent soldier and an even better leader.

"My lord, we should wait until we know what we are facing," Vikkin said to the prince. He relished the thought of going with the captain major, but keeping the prince safe was far more important than his appetite for a fight.

"I'm going," Andric said emphatically. Vikkin was both proud of the prince's courage and dismayed at the brashness of his youth. "Jase, stay with the horses," Andric commanded his squire before hurrying after the others. Vikkin wished he had time to change to his plate armor, but the prince was already hurrying after Minanthsolum, leaving him no choice but to follow, wearing only his gambeson.

"We have to stay and guard the intercessor," Lady di Greven said sternly behind him. Vikkin looked back to make sure she was not addressing her comment to him and saw Sir Mar following as well.

"They won't survive without our help," Mar said flatly, not waiting for her reply as he continued along the road.

The arrogance! Vikkin thought, his words suffused with contempt for the Sharinic knight, but there was no time to dwell on it now. He continued after the prince. They only made it a handful of paces before Andric stopped at the front of the horse line, where the two grizzled Vanassi guides sat unmoving in their saddles.

"Any idea what it is?" Andric asked.

One shook his head, wide-eyed and tight-lipped. The other shrugged and spat before answering. "Larran, maybe."

Every time something bad happened, the guides blamed it on one of their primitive superstitions. But after Pradan-ur, Vikkin was not so sure they were wrong this time. He scanned the road ahead for anything they could use as cover. No trees grew this far up in the mountains, and the nearest boulders were strewn along the slope below them, out of reach. He hated being exposed, but at least whatever threat was coming would be in the same predicament.

Andric took off again, trying in vain to catch up to the captain major. Vikkin did his best to both navigate the uneven ground and watch ahead for danger. He looked up just as the scout went down hard but scrambled back to her feet and kept running, now hampered by a slight limp. Minanthsolum was much closer to the scout and called out something Vikkin could not quite understand, but he heard the scout's shouted reply distinctly.

"Kuldrith!"

As if saying the word summoned them into existence, two gray-skinned warriors came rushing around the spur, then pulled up short, seeing the scout was not alone. One of the lancers drew his bow and fired at the enemy. Vikkin could not see where the shot went, but the Kuldrith ducked instinctively, then raised their own bows and shot at the Remalians before turning to flee back the way they had come.

"Don't let them escape!" Minanthsolum shouted. He stopped for only a moment to exchange a few quick words with the panting scout before hurrying on with his soldiers. It soon became clear he was going to do exactly what he had told them not to do—running blindly around the corner. Vikkin understood why, though. They had to do everything possible to stop the Kuldrith before they could alert others. How could they even be here, so far from Balinth's Fortress, so far from Remalia? How many more would they be facing if they failed to stop the fleeing soldiers?

Minanthsolum outpaced his men and was soon out of sight around the bend. Vikkin wished he was up in the lead with him to assess the threat for himself and adjust as needed. *Just another minute or two,* he thought. Divinar Geon stumbled as a loose rock turned under his foot, but Staneff caught him and helped him stay upright. The members of the Order trained to fight in various difficult terrains and situations, but never on loose rocks. He would have to consider adding it to their training when they got back to Teris.

As they began rounding the spur, he could see the road descend gently into a broad, shallow valley with scattered streaks of green and brown scrub vegetation. Jagged, snow-capped peaks still towered on all sides. Shouts ahead drove them on. The road had fewer loose stones on this side of the spur, allowing them to increase their speed. From his vantage point, he could see a few lancers firing their bows at several Kuldrith soldiers spread below them.

The enemy held no formation, instead shifting their positions chaotically. *But they remain in pairs*, Vikkin noted. It made planning an attack against them more difficult, that was certain, but it also meant they would be less effective against the Remalians. *Unless this is a stalling tactic to allow others to escape.* That could spell disaster.

He tried to determine their numbers, but their gray skin and clothing blended into their surroundings, making them difficult to count. His quick assessment put them at half again as many soldiers as the Remalians. A few Kuldrith fired bows, but most carried the short, forward-curved blades Minanthsolum had reported so many weeks ago. They might be well suited for one-on-one fighting but would be virtually useless against a shield formation.

As if reading Vikkin's mind, Minanthsolum and his men slowed and moved into a tight formation, four shields in front and four raised overhead to protect them from enemy arrows. The formation moved around the body of a horse lying in the middle of the road. Probably the one belonging to the scout who had brought them the warning, Vikkin guessed as he ran. But the Remalian scouts traveled in pairs, and he wondered where the second scout and horse were.

One of the lancers cried out in pain and fell to the ground with an arrow through his thigh. Minanthsolum grabbed the man's shield and took his place, raising it overhead to fill the gap in the formation. Vikkin and the others were breathing much harder than they should have, his lungs burning and his heart pounding. It must have been the thin mountain air. He had heard of this effect but had never experienced it firsthand. Overexertion could make you sick. Of course, an enemy sword could be worse, so he kept up the pace.

The Kuldrith archers moved off to the side of the road to take aim at the Remalians' exposed flank. The formation shifted to bring two overhead shields down on each side. As if on cue, three pairs of Kuldrith went rushing forward. *We are almost there. Just hold that formation!* Vikkin thought.

Minanthsolum and the lancers raised their swords, ready to thrust them into the charging Kuldrith. Suddenly, an inky hole of blackness appeared to swallow the area immediately surrounding the lancers. Before Vikkin's mind could comprehend what he was seeing, cries of alarm and confusion mixed with the first dull clangs of metal on metal ringing out from the blackness.

"What is that?" Divinar Jessol asked.

"Met'elan," Andric answered. "Modulated to thet... probably blocking the light. Keep going!" Andric got the words out between panting breaths.

"Which ones are elantir?" Vikkin asked.

Andric stopped short and bowed his head in concentration. "There," he said a moment later, pointing to a pair of Kuldrith standing off to one side of the road. The archers turned their attention to Andric and the Divinarim as they ran toward the elantir. Arrows flew at them, one deflecting harmlessly off Vikkin's shield.

A pair of Kuldrith stood between the Divinarim and the elantir and called for support. Two more pairs came rushing to help their companions. Now Vikkin's group was outnumbered by one. If they had been wearing full armor, he would not have worried; but now, any mistake could be deadly. Vikkin prayed to Teraithia to protect them, attuning instantly to her divinessence in an exultant rush. It took only a moment to adjust his mind to accommodate the second orientation of his goddess's presence.

"I'll take the two in front," he told the prince. "Help Jessol—" The Kuldrith surged forward to attack before he could finish. The Divinarim behind him thrust their halberds at the ones attacking from the side, keeping them at bay, while Vikkin focused on the two in front of him. In unison, they sprang forward, one bearing down with a powerful overhand strike, attempting to reach over his shield while the other circled further along his weak side.

He lunged at the one trying to circle him, bashing him with his shield while simultaneously thrusting at the torso of the other attacker. It was a risky move, leaving himself completely exposed, but Teraithia blessed his blade and it struck true, halting the attacker mid-blow while the other Kuldrith staggered back a few paces. He wanted to press his advantage while the second was off balance, but his sword had sunk deeper than he intended and his blade was pulled down as the man fell to his knees. Vikkin quickly kicked him in the chest as he yanked his blade free. He half expected the blood to be dark gray like the rest of him, but it was as red as any he had seen.

Vikkin had an open path to the elantir, but it would mean leaving the prince and his men still outnumbered. That was no real choice. He stole a glance behind him to ensure the prince was not in immediate danger, then snapped his attention back to the second soldier. The man was in an odd stance, his weight on his forward leg, and had switched one of the knives to a reverse grip. *That will cost you*, Vikkin thought. It shortened his striking range considerably and eliminated nearly all of its power. It would only be useful if he could get very close, and Vikkin was never going to allow that.

He gave a short thrust with his sword, testing the soldier's defenses, but the soldier did not hesitate, rushing forward with an overhand strike. It was a useless attack. Vikkin raised his shield, easily catching the blade at its apex before it could gain any momentum, and thrust his sword forward.

Teraithia's divinessence split his mind in two, one part frozen in time, seeing every detail of the moment, and the other part inching forward, seeing a shimmering image of the soldier sliding away from Vikkin's sword to the opposite side of his shield, still hooking the top with his knife and pulling the shield forward while swinging the other knife in from the opposite side to drive the heavy blade between Vikkin's ribs. He recognized the benefaction of precognition at work, though he had never experienced it like this before. It was more a trick practiced by the Dorothi priests. His mind raced through his options as he felt himself slipping back to the frozen present.

Time started again, and Vikkin spun to his left and shoved his shield hard and fast with both hands. A sharp pain shot through his side as the knife tip penetrated his gambeson and nicked his ribs. He thanked Teraithia it was not worse.

The soldier fell to the ground, rolling away, but managed to land in a crouching position. Strong, fast, and skilled—not the enemy Vikkin had hoped they would be. He did not know if Mar's accusations were true that the Kuldrith were devoted Teraithians, but if so, they were proving themselves worthy disciples. But it might also make them more susceptible to his dispositioning. He willed the goddess's divinessence to radiate from him toward the Kuldrith soldiers. Pushing them toward surrender would be too contrary to their natures, but inspiring awe and obedience should align with their proclivities.

"On your knees before a champion of the Queen of Heaven!" Vikkin infused his command with all the divinessence he could muster. The one who had attacked him slowly dropped from his crouching position onto his knees in a small patch of wildflowers. Out of the corner of his eye, he saw another soldier's hands slump from their defensive position. Suddenly, a halberd lashed out, the tip driving through the soldier's throat. Blood sprayed onto the kneeling soldier as the body of his companion fell to the ground next to him.

A cry of rage brought the man surging to his feet, his eyes fixed on Divinar Staneff, knives poised to attack the holy knight who had just killed his fellow soldier. Vikkin was faster and sliced low, severing the soldier's hamstring. The man stumbled forward, screaming in pain. Staneff brought the axe blade of his halberd down on the soldier's neck, driving him to the ground.

An arrow hissed past Vikkin followed by a grunt behind him. Fearing for the prince, Vikkin turned and saw an arrow protruding from Jessol's back, his halberd sagging to the ground. Vikkin was too far away and watched helplessly as the Divinar weakly tried to raise the shaft of his weapon to block a Kuldrith soldier who leaped forward, delivering a wicked blow to Jessol's neck.

"No!" the prince cried out and cut hard, his sword slicing across the soldier's back. Jessol and the Kuldrith dropped to the ground, the Divinar silently pressing his hand to the wound where his lifeblood gushed out, the Kuldrith thrashing in pain until Andric drove the point of his sword through his chest to finish him. Vikkin rushed forward to protect the prince from the last Kuldrith, but the soldier turned and ran.

No one stood between him and the elantir now, but the sphere of darkness had already disappeared. Min and di Greven stood with Minanthsolum and the lancers in the road, fighting back several Kuldrith. The elantir were still a threat, but commotion on the road behind him drew his attention back to the spur of the mountain. The members of the prince's retinue they had left back around the spur were on their mounts, racing down the road into the valley toward them.

"What are they doing here?" Divinar Geon asked with a hint of frustration. Vikkin felt the same but would have to reprove Geon later about voicing it. That was never appropriate for a Divinar, especially in front of a royal.

"They're being chased!" Prince Andric said as he ran back up the hill, panting heavily. Vikkin wondered how the Kuldrith had gotten past them, but there was no time to dwell on it. He counted twice, but there were only six riders, meaning three were missing. The priest, the elantir, and one of the scouts. It appeared there were only four soldiers on their heels, but that was more than enough to dispatch all the non-combatants in short order if they caught up to them. Part of him wanted to advise the prince to deal with the elantir first, but he would never convince him to change course, so Vikkin simply ran after him.

Lady di Greven was also running back up the road, her sword covered in blood. He admired her dedication to her duty to protect the intercessor. *She never should have listened to Mar when he told her to leave the intercessor in the first place,* he thought acidly. But a part of Vikkin's mind reluctantly acknowledged there was a chance Minanthsolum and the lancers would not have survived if not for the aid of the two Sharinic knights. *Did Min know that would be the case?* he wondered. *And did it excuse leaving his charge?* He set those thoughts aside to be sorted out later.

The Remalian archers turned and began firing at the pursuers. Di Greven stepped off the road to let the riders pass by, ready to face the oncoming attackers, apparently willing to do so alone if need be. She would not survive by herself.

"Staneff, go help her." Kael was one of the fastest runners in the Order. Untethered from his duty to stay at the prince's side, the Divinar sprinted up the hill. Even in his younger days, Vikkin was never that fast. Now his lungs burned with the effort of breathing, but he refused to lag behind the prince.

An arrow sunk into the abdomen of one of the Kuldrith pursuers. The soldier stopped and pressed a hand over the wound. He turned and stumbled off the road, looking around wild-eyed. A second arrow to the chest took him to his knees. The three remaining soldiers were nearly to di Greven, and it looked like Staneff would reach her just in time. The riders stopped in an open section of the road and dismounted, using their horses for cover.

"Are you okay?" Andric shouted in their direction. Ve'Aurben and Henden responded in the affirmative, so the prince continued up the slope, his pace little more than a labored jog. Staneff reached di Greven's side a moment before the enemy did, his halberd lashing out to keep them at a distance. One of the Kuldrith feinted toward Staneff, drawing the knight into a reaching counterattack. Vikkin saw his mistake as a second one sprang forward, a heavy knife falling in a vicious arc toward his exposed arm.

Di Greven reached from impossibly far away with her sword to catch the blow. She had no leverage, and the cut drove her sword down onto Staneff's arm with a dull clang. She spun away from a quick reverse cut as Staneff slammed the butt of his halberd into the Kuldrith's chest, driving him back. It was enough time for Vikkin, Geon, and the prince to reach them. They were out of breath, but the odds were now almost two to one, and the Kuldrith turned to flee.

Staneff lunged forward, hooking the leg of one and pulling him halfway back as the prince stepped in and sliced hard across the soldier's neck. He heard the hissing of arrows flying past him, uncomfortably close, as he charged after another one. Vikkin's strength was nearly spent as the Kuldrith got four, then five lengths ahead running downhill. He was not going to catch her.

Two more arrows hissed through the air toward the soldier. One flew past harmlessly, but the other struck her leg. She stumbled and went down hard. Vikkin saw her arm suddenly snap at an unnatural angle as it struck a moss-covered rock. She cried out in pain and tried to scramble to her feet one-handed as she pressed her broken arm against her chest. Vikkin let his momentum drive his sword through the woman's heart, a gurgling cough the last sound she made.

Looking around quickly for any other enemies nearby, Vikkin realized the battle was over. He stood panting heavily, trying to assess their losses. Mar, Minanthsolum, and five of the lancers were scattered across the area. *Three lancers and Jessol.* Vikkin needed to go see to Jessol's body.

"Puarrol, get over here!" Andric cried out. The prince was on his knees, his attention focused on someone on the ground. Vikkin guessed he was unaware the elantir had not come around the spur with the others. The knight commander was exhausted, but he forced his feet to start running back toward the prince, every step sending a jolt of pain radiating from the cut on his side. *Geon, Staneff, the prince, di Greven... where is Emerly?* Vikkin's heart sank.

Intercessor Henden had not started moving yet. She must not have realized it was her knight protector on the ground. She would learn soon enough. Vikkin arrived at the scene panting. He exchanged a somber glance with Geon and Staneff. A splash of blond hair over the stony, gray ground confirmed it was Emerly. Vikkin took a knee next to Andric. The prince's blood-soaked hands were pressed to the sides of her neck where an arrow protruded.

Vikkin's grief flashed into anger. The arrow was Remalian.

"Puarrol and Elles are missing. You have to do something," Andric pleaded with Vikkin.

"Your Highness, there's nothing I can do." Emerly's eyes fluttered open and she tried to speak but choked on the effort, blood splattering across her cheek. "Perhaps we should call the intercessor to come and ease her pain."

"No! I can't lose anyone else."

Vikkin had never agreed with Jevorak's unfavorable opinion of Andric practicing met'elan. Power was power as far as the knight commander was concerned. Before this journey, it had never seemed more than a plaything to the prince, but things had changed. It seemed to be part of Andric's destiny, and Vikkin intended to help him find it.

"My lord, you are the only elantir we have. Perhaps you should try..." Vikkin left the suggestion hanging.

"I can't. I have no training for this."

"Emerly!" Intercessor Henden cried out from a short distance away. She sprinted up the road and fell to her knees next to the fallen knight. "I'm here,

Emerly." Tears streaked down the priestess's cheeks as she took her friend's hand and squeezed. "Sharin Dara, help her," she whispered.

"Barak, I need your help," the prince called to his friend, still walking toward them. Vikkin noticed the Cannessi scholar studiously avoided looking at di Greven as his short legs hurried the last several paces.

"What is it?"

"How do I heal her?"

"Andric, I—"

"I know! Just... give me some idea. Anything."

Ve'Aurben looked at the wound then closed his eyes, though whether to avoid the sight or help him concentrate, Vikkin could not be sure. The prince closed his eyes as well, and Vikkin guessed he was reaching for elan. di Greven's ragged breathing was the only sound in the shadowed valley, the sun already lost behind the towering peaks. It would be dark soon.

"There isn't enough elan here," Andric growled under his breath.

"Take mine," Vikkin said without hesitation.

"But you're a Divinar. It's impossible."

"There is a way to unlock it." Part of the induction rites of the Order of the Divine Flame used Teraithia's divinessence to seal a Divinar's elan against elantic influence. Vikkin was one of the few who knew the secret of how it was done—and how it could be bypassed. At least, he knew in principle. He hated the thought of revealing that secret in front of non-believers, but it might be the only chance to save Emerly. More importantly, it necessitated Andric channeling Teraithia's divinessence. This might be his best chance to bring the prince toward the goddess's embrace.

"Then do it," Andric demanded.

"Only an elantir can do it."

Andric shook his head and his jaw muscles clenched, but he responded, "Fine. What do I have to do?"

"Channel your elan into me... modulated to kosek."

"Kosek is forbidden," Andric replied but flashed a furtive glance toward Master Ve'Aurben. Vikkin had read reports from the prince's guards regarding the pair's experimentation with unorthodox met'elantic techniques and could guess that included trying the so-called 'forbidden modalities.'

"It is dangerous, as I am sure Your Highness is aware, which is why the Elantic Guild forbids its members from using it. But there is no actual law, mortal or divine, against it."

"I... then what?"

"You should feel something like a barrier. Use your elan as a bridge, then direct Teraithia's divinessence through it into the barrier and disposition it into letting my elan pass back along the bridge to you."

"I can't disposition—"

Emerly coughed again, blood spraying onto Andric's face. Her mouth worked, but no sound emerged. She clutched convulsively at the prince's sleeve and tried in vain to sit up, but Andric held her firmly in place.

"Hurry and do something," the intercessor begged the prince. "Let me commune with you and I can help you with the dispositioning."

"The presence of another god's divinessence will make the unbinding impossible," Vikkin said. The knight commander was not certain whether that was entirely true, but he was not about to allow the Sharinist to taint this moment. "Divinar Staneff can help you."

"Barak, any ideas yet?"

"Yes. I think if—"

"Just hold that thought," the prince interrupted impatiently. "There are already too many things in my head. Wait until I'm ready. Mar, move back. I can't concentrate on Teraithia's divinessence with you this close. Staneff, open the link, but don't say anything until I tell you."

"As you wish, Your Highness," Divinar Staneff said.

The prince closed his eyes again, and Vikkin waited anxiously to feel the connection. It felt like a small victory as the Sharinic knight rose and retreated a few steps. One moment stretched into another, and another, until he finally felt a vibration in his chest at the edge of his awareness. It was almost like a distant, painful itch, but disconnected from any physical location his mind could conceive of itching. He did not remember it feeling like this during the sealing ceremony so many years ago when he took his first vows as a knight of the Order.

He called upon Teraithia's divinessence, fortifying and exacting, in hopes that somehow it would help the prince attune to it more easily. The benefaction of unification might have been useful, but the prince was already balancing too many factors, and time was running out for Emerly. He felt the communal link in the prince and guessed it was Staneff.

Vikkin looked down at the lady knight. He remembered her beautiful singing only a few minutes ago, though it felt like an eon had passed. Even if she survived, she would never sing again. The loss of her voice from the world opened a well of sadness Vikkin had never known.

Finally, the itching of the vibrations subsided and was replaced by a different disquieting feeling of a thousand strands running throughout his body being pulled, like stitches in a garment coming undone. His soul was thrilled at the triumph of leading the prince to Teraithia's divine essence, even as his body reflexively clamped down on his life force. A communal link now pressed at his mind. He accepted the connection and Staneff's thoughts came through.

My lord, the prince says you have to stop resisting so he can draw your elan. Vikkin did his best to relax his body's instinct to cling to the elan. It was like resisting the urge to breathe after holding his breath too long under-water. It took a few attempts, but finally the knot in his chest loosened its grip on the threads and the unraveling sensation resumed.

"What should I do, Barak?" the prince asked.

"You need to close the wounds inside and out, but we also need to get the arrow out. What if you created a seal around the shaft like a sleeve, but kept it separate from the shaft itself so it can slide out after you get the seal in place?"

"Like the door at Selmarine?"

"Yes, actually, that's a good way to think about it."

Vikkin had no idea what they were talking about, but as soon as his mind considered the question, the grip on his elan tightened and the painful vibra-tions returned. He took a deep breath, willing himself to stop resisting. The flow resumed—a trickle at first, then a steady stream. He had thought he was exhausted before, but a profound weariness began to seep into his whole being.

Emerly's eyes opened wide as the prince pulled half of the now-severed arrow from each side of her neck. She clawed weakly at his leg as she tried to gasp for breath. Nophet watched as her skin bunched together where the holes in her flesh were and knitted itself together, leaving ugly, puckered scars. Her mouth worked silently before she got any sound out.

"I—" she rasped. "I'm s— I'm s—" She seemed unable to get more out of her broken throat.

Sir Mar stepped forward and quickly knelt again at her side. "Emerly," his hushed voice carried an unearthly calm, completely at odds with his blood-splattered armor and sword. He laid his weapon aside and took her by the hand. Emerly's eyes widened momentarily at the sight of the dark-skinned knight.

"You're..." The word rattled sickeningly in her throat, but she seemed to have a look of awe in her eyes that sparked a twinge of jealousy in Vikkin's heart.

"Shh. I'm here. Rest easy." Mar glanced at the bloody arrow off to the side —the Remalian arrow. The Eastgatian knight sighed and nodded in understanding, then tenderly stroked Emerly's hair. Somehow, despite their animosity, Vikkin could not hate the man in this moment.

Shiralla shook her head, red locks cascading around her face, hiding the tears that dripped down the end of her nose and fell onto the fading knight. She sniffed and gathered her breath, her voice breaking audibly. "It's okay. You did well. There's no need to..." Her voice failed her.

"I— I f—" she tried weakly. "I f—" Her lips tried to form the words between failed attempts to draw a breath. Slowly, agonizingly, her grip loosened in the intercessor's hand as her empty eyes continued staring at Shiralla.

The world went still.

"I did everything I could," Andric said apologetically, blinking at tears in his eyes. The intercessor buried her face in Emerly's chest and sobbed. Mar placed a comforting hand on her back but said nothing, head bowed.

Vikkin clasped the prince's shoulder reassuringly. "You did your best, my lord. She was simply beyond saving." Andric's head dropped as the knight commander rose to his feet and directed the two Divinarim to remain with the prince. Vikkin didn't remember releasing his attunement, but without the connection to Teraithia's divinessence to sustain him, he felt empty, exhausted. He had no desire to face any more death, but it was his duty to take care of Jessol's body. Pride was the only thing keeping him from succumbing to the desire to let his leaden footsteps pull him with a trudging gait down the slope.

Head up. Walk with purpose. They need to see your strength.

He barely glanced at the Kuldrith bodies as he passed by. There was nothing more about them he cared to know at this moment. It was enough that they were dead and the rest of the Remalians were not. Tomorrow, he would consider what came next.

He took a knee next to Jessol's body and offered a silent prayer to Teraithia for his fallen brother's soul to find its way to her holy realm. Then he slung the body up onto his shoulders and strained to rise to his feet. Finding his balance, he began the slow walk back to the road.

A full Silmal shone brightly as it hung low in the twilight sky behind the snow-capped mountain peaks. It might have seemed beautiful on any other night, but all Vikkin could think about was how lonely this would be as a final resting place, where no one he knew would ever come again. He prayed to Teraithia not to let this be his fate.

Please, just let me see Teris one more time before you call me to your bosom.
He quickly wiped a hand across his cheek before he reached the road.

Head up. Walk with purpose. They need to see your strength.
It was not the last time he would recite those words that night.

CHAPTER LVII
EVIR

It had taken Tel-Kyron several tides to finally secure a meeting with Arku Overlord. Time passed at a whiteslug's pace, but it had proven to be a blessing in disguise. Evir slept more than he could ever remember sleeping in his life, due in part to the healing of his injuries by the mavin tar's friend, Roj'dakt Master Physician, but attributable even more to the deep vitalic lethargy from prolonged use of Kiavi's probe and Vekk-oth's disguise.

His waking hours had been filled with endlessly considering every possible path forward, interrupted by occasional discussions with Tel-Kyron, and sometimes Zenni too. Evir was grateful those conversations had not strayed too far into theological territory again. He did not want to consider such questions at all, but he sensed them slowly churning below the surface, occasionally threatening to rise up and demand his attention. It was only a matter of time before he would have to grapple with them, but for now, his years of discipline allowed him to stave them off and focus on seeing his mission through to completion.

The one notable exception was when Tel-Kyron suggested they be prepared to use the divine benefaction of communion during their audience with the overlord if the need arose. Evir had resisted at first. Keeping the mavin tar's heresy hidden (at least for now) was difficult enough to justify, but actively participating in apostate benefactions meant committing a crime himself. And while he was not aware of any statute that singled out doing so in the presence of the overlord, it didn't take a legal scholar to understand there were no more egregious circumstances under which to violate that law.

But he also knew the overlord and his advisors were devout Teraithians, which should make it impossible for any of them to detect the Holy Couple's divinessence Tel-Kyron would use to perform the benefaction. Having a secret channel open to the mavin tar who could guide him if he got out over a ledge might mean the difference between accomplishing his mission and losing his life. After careful consideration, Evir finally concluded the potential benefits outweighed the downside of letting the mavin tar inside his head and agreed to practice together.

He had always been told communion between those of different faiths was possible but came with difficulties, like the mental discomfort of trying to hold incompatible thoughts in your mind at the same time. However, Evir experienced the opposite. If anything, communion with the mavin tar was clearer than any he had experienced, which worried him. If he was wrong about that, he might also be wrong about the overlord and his attendants not being able to detect their communion. When he raised his concerns with the mavin tar, Tel-Kyron had simply smiled, as if amused, and assured him there was nothing to worry about in that regard. Evir hoped it would not be necessary to test those assertions.

They had also decided a disguise was warranted, but Tel-Kyron didn't have anyone he trusted that could replicate Vekk-oth's technique, so they had called upon Roj'dakt to work her skills to physically alter his appearance: tightening around the eyes, flattening the nose, pulling down the corners of the mouth, loosening of the jowls, wrinkling the forehead. The elantic changes beneath his skin felt entirely different from the illusion of Vekk's elants, slightly painful, but nothing like what Javinth had been through to take on Evir's face. Those changes would be permanent until his friend decided to undergo the process of restoring his face.

Now that the tide had finally arrived in which he was to meet with the overlord, his stomach was in knots. He followed behind Tel-Kyron and the two guards flanking the mavin tar. The guardsmen at the orderguard checkpoint snapped to attention and bowed with arms outstretched as the prestigious resident exited the Lightsreach District into the Grand Chasm. Evir was grateful they were already near the roof of the chasm. His injuries may have been mostly healed, but he was not yet entirely himself and didn't feel like having to climb the ramps leading up above the chasm ceiling to where the public entrance was into Tir-hakkiv, the inverted pyramid hanging like a giant stalactite that housed the government offices.

They crossed a wide balcony leading to a stone bridge with elegantly carved railings spanning the distance from the chasm wall to an arched entrance in the side of the massive structure. He could not see it from here, but he knew an identical bridge spanned the space between the opposite chasm wall and the far side of the pyramid. Similar bridges several hundred feet below them connected walkways along the chasm walls to entrances into Teraithia's great temple. Just as those were restricted to the most powerful clerics in the Teraithian Faith, the bridge entrances up here were restricted to only high-ranking officials. *One day, perhaps*, Evir dared hope.

More guards barred the way onto the bridge but quickly moved aside and saluted, bowing with arms outstretched. Tel-Kyron briefly cupped his right hand, palm up, in a return salute as he passed and made his way out onto the bridge. This was the first time Evir had ever been allowed onto one of the upper bridges, and his head swam with a sense of vertigo as he stole a sideways glance over the railing. The brilliant light emanating from the crystal where the tips of the two pyramids joined was almost blinding, and he had to squint to see the wide expanse opening below them. His stomach clenched at the sudden memory of dangling over the abyss beneath another walkway less than a week ago. Being caught in blinding light and dangling over an abyss were both apt metaphors for what he felt at this moment, walking into Tir-hakkiv to inform the overlord of Malithir Lord Overseer's treason.

On the far side of the bridge, they passed more guards as they walked between two large statues flanking the open corridor leading into the massive structure. The polished white and gray-streaked marble floors and sloping walls were a familiar sight to Evir. His skin almost itched knowing the Obsidian Door's offices were just a few floors below. Pairs of guards were posted at each hallway branching off to other areas of the building. He caught himself scanning every face, looking for anyone familiar, as he had done when he first started hunting the elantir Kiavi's probe was attuned to. He forced himself to stop. That was the behavior of someone who didn't belong here.

They soon reached the grand central staircase, a set of broad double spiral stairs running like a spine down through the center of the pyramid. Despite the stairs being the main artery through the building, they passed few others this early in the tide as they descended, though all of them quickly moved aside and saluted the mavin tar as he passed. It felt odd to continue down past the floor where the offices of the Obsidian Door were located. He had never had occasion to visit any of the lower floors, let alone the lowest level reserved exclusively for the overlord.

The next floor held the Mavin Tar's chambers, followed by offices of the overlord's staff. Finally, the stairs ended in a dimly lit chamber, only slightly wider than the central shaft enclosing the grand staircase itself. There were no orderguards here, only the towering Than'katar, the overlord's elite personal guards. As tall as Evir was, these augmented soldiers dwarfed him, perhaps larger even than the kieresta, though that hardly seemed possible. They held their naked blades at the ready, blackened armor trimmed in gold, accenting their impressive physiques. A man wearing deep green robes, not quite as elaborate as Tel-Kyron's but still indicating his important station, stood watching them from a solitary pool of golden light. He bowed as the mavin tar and his attendants approached.

"Tel-Kyron Mavin Tar," the man said in a brief greeting.

"Sevveth Marshal," Tel-Kyron replied politely, 'it's good to see you again. It has been far too long." Evir had learned enough from his discussions with Tel-Kyron to recognize the mavin tar's greeting was a subtle protest of the fact that in the past several weeks, nearly everyone except the overlord's inner circle, including most of the mavin tar, had been denied audiences with Arku Overlord. By all accounts, the overlord was occupied with the prosecution of the war in Remalia, but his lack of attention to other needs and issues had left the rest of the mavin tar irritated, or worse.

"Yes, the tides seem to flow by in the blink of an eye when so many things vie for the overlord's attention. His Excellency had to set aside several other priorities to make time for your audience. It speaks highly of his esteem for you and your contributions to the empire. So let's not keep him waiting. If you will follow me."

The two household guards who had accompanied the mavin tar this far were directed to wait along the side of the circular chamber while Tel-Kyron and Evir hurried to keep up with the marshal. The corridor followed the curved wall of the stair chamber until they entered another small chamber where more guards and four elantir waited to search visitors before they were allowed to enter the overlord's offices. Evir and Tel-Kyron both squinted as they stood in the bright light of the lumens focused on the center of the chamber, while the edges of the room were cast in dim shadows. Evir could appreciate the security benefits of the contrasting illumination in the room, giving an advantage to those in the shadows.

The familiar prickling of met'elan suddenly began to move over his skin, meticulously probing every inch of his body. The uncomfortable sensation held steady when it reached his face, intensifying. He clenched his teeth against the pain as he felt Roj'dakt's elants collapse and his face began to shift. Tel-Kyron had warned Evir this would happen, so at least he was prepared for it and knew it was nothing to worry about. He rubbed his face with his hands to hasten the muscles' and skin's adjustments back to their natural order. As he opened his eyes, he was taken aback at the sight of several swords leveled at him from every direction.

If the marshal thought it odd to see Evir's transformation or even recognized the inquisitor, he gave no indication. The man simply scrutinized Evir's face until he seemed satisfied. "Thank you, Mavin Tar, for the opportunity to test our security measures on your assistant. It is helpful to ensure we are keeping up with the latest elantic developments. Come, I will announce you to the overlord."

The marshal's words appeared to satisfy the Than'katar, who withdrew their swords and returned to their normal positions, allowing them to proceed. As they entered the curving corridor leading from the inspection chamber, all sound disappeared from the world. He found it disconcerting, walking in absolute silence. The sound barriers used by the Door were thin, like stepping through a veil, with the sound on each side simply unable to pass to the other. The tight curvature of the corridor gave him no fixed point ahead on which to focus, leaving him feeling even more isolated. He wondered if anyone who traversed the soundless corridor ever took the time to admire the beautiful sculptures displayed in well-lit niches or if everyone was too preoccupied with their thoughts to pay any attention. It seemed a shame, but he was as guilty of it as anyone. This was one of the most important moments of his life; he could not afford to be distracted by the artwork, as precious as it may be.

They reached the end of the corridor and Evir estimated they had come full circle to the opposite side of the walls from where the stairs had ended. As expected, the sound returned as he crossed the threshold into the overlord's chambers. He quickly scanned the area, trying to orient himself in the new space to minimize any surprises as much as possible. He was not sure what he had expected, but it certainly was not what he was now seeing.

Other than the curved walls surrounding the central stairwell, there were no walls anywhere in the wide-open area. Instead, the space was interrupted only by the occasional sculpted columns, illuminated by lumens set into the floor at their bases, and the occasional piece of furniture. There was an area with a long, wide table made of rich, brown wood the color of bloodstained soil, with perhaps two dozen chairs surrounding it. Another area had two sprawling couches covered in a plush green fabric with some sort of vine-and-leaf motif embroidered into it. Evir noticed a small spiral staircase near the center wall descending through an opening in the floor and wondered where it led.

The two men were directed to wash their hands and face in a basin of cool water. Tel-Kyron had informed him of the overlord's obsession with cleanliness and that this would be required. It felt refreshing after having to endure the discomfort of the elantic disguise and Evir stopped himself from continuing to rub the water over his face and followed Tel-Kyron's lead. He picked up a folded white towel from the table and quickly dried himself.

As they moved further into the chamber, his surroundings faded away and his entire focus was pulled to the edges of the room where he expected to see exterior walls but instead he saw only the open expanse of the Grand Chasm illuminated by thousands of lumens. He could already feel the vertigo setting in as they crossed the floor toward an unobstructed view of Teraithia's Breath at the far end of the chasm. He had seen this elantic effect a thousand times while crossing the plaza above the ceiling of the Grand Chasm to the public entrance of the hanging government pyramid. The floor of the plaza had the same elantic transparency, making it appear as if one was walking in the air over the chasm and the twin pyramids below. That view had never bothered him before, but now he felt uneasy as they approached the area where Arku overlord stood with his back to them, looking out over Stierve.

"Overlord," the marshal called out, "Tel-Kyron Mavin Tar and his attendant crave admittance to your presence."

The overlord turned and made a disapproving sound through a half-smile. "Sevveth, it's only the four of us. I think we can dispense with the formalities."

Tel-Kyron gave the salute for a close-ranking superior, chin raised and arms outstretched, with his palms toward the overlord. Evir instead bowed low, eyes to the ground, and his arms similarly reaching wide. Arku barely gave the informal salute to a close-ranking subordinate, right hand palm down with his left hand wrapping the knife edge of his right hand, before signaling them to come closer, apparently sincere about dispensing with formalities.

"Tel-Kyron, I have to tell you I was intrigued by your request to meet under such unusual circumstances;" Arku sounded amused as the two men approached, "at such an early hour, with no one else in attendance or even knowing about the meeting, without it being recorded in the registry, and with an unnamed attendant. I must confess, I haven't waited with such anticipation for a meeting in quite some time. That alone has made it worthwhile, but I hope my expectations do not too far outstrip whatever it is you wanted to discuss."

"Unfortunately, I don't think you will be disappointed, Excellency."

Arku laughed with a beautiful baritone timbre. "I didn't think it was possible to be more intrigued, but I am." Arku turned his attention to Evir, who had just stolen another view through the transparent wall. The overlord cast his gaze outward. "The view here is one of my favorite perks of occupying this office." After a moment of taking in the view, he snapped his attention back to the two visitors. "But again, I must admit I am far more interested in hearing what our esteemed mavin tar wants to discuss. Come, let's sit down."

Arku led the way to the nearby set of sprawling couches. Evir was not sure if it was the fact of being in the presence of one of the most powerful men on Baon or some personal charisma of the overlord, but the inquisitor felt a strange pull toward Arku, wanting to follow him wherever he went, wanting to win his approbation. Even being this close, Evir could not see anything remarkably different from what he had expected based on the other times he had seen the overlord, albeit from a distance. His tunic and breeches were a brilliant white, trimmed in black, finely made but free of ornamentation or embellishment. His wavy, charcoal hair was pulled back and held in an etched platinum band inscribed with runes Evir could not make out from where he followed. Crowning his head was a band of polished bdellium ringed with adjoining symbols of their goddess.

"You will join me in taking some refreshment."

"That is gracious, Excellency, but we wouldn't want to impose," Tel-Kyron declined quickly, but the overlord seemed to ignore him.

"Sevveth, three satiils."

The thought of the spicy and slightly alcoholic hot drink hitting his throat was enough to turn Evir's stomach. He had been told many times it was an acquired taste, but it was one he had yet to enjoy. Fetching drinks for the overlord and his guests would have been a task normally left to slaves, but apparently the overlord hadn't allowed any of those to be present, so the task fell to the marshal.

"Let's start with an introduction, Tel-Kyron," Arku said as he slid himself back into a comfortable position on one of the deep green couches while Tel-Kyron and Evir sat on the other, not nearly as relaxed as the overlord. "I'm certain he is no mere attendant."

"Of course. This is Evir Inquisitor of the Obsidian Door."

Arku raised his eyebrows in an expression of mild surprise. "I was under the impression you were still in Kierden."

"For all intents and purposes, I am, Excellency."

"And yet here you are with Tel-Kyron. I wouldn't have guessed an Obsidian Door inquisitor and the Lord Minister of the Elantic Ministry would be friends."

Tel-Kyron had anticipated the overlord would be curious about their connection and had prepared Evir to respond appropriately. "Tel-Kyron Mavin Tar and I have only met a couple of times. It is actually our wives who know each other."

"You're also married," the overlord said with some surprise. "And here I thought Tel-Kyron was one of the last still holding to that quaint tradition. Tell me about this woman who has managed to capture your exclusive attention."

The last thing Evir wanted was to draw unwanted attention to Dae, but he could hardly refuse. "Her name is Dae'yen. She is a master scholar of ancient history in the Ministry of Education."

The overlord's eyes narrowed slightly. "Correct me if I'm wrong, but I believe she is the one who wrote a treatise on the P'vavian War and the subsequent Kul-a'durith diaspora."

Evir was shocked the overlord had heard of Dae. "You are correct, Excellency. Dae'yen will be thrilled to know you are familiar with her work. May I ask how it came to your attention?"

"Before I decided to invade Remalia, I gathered all the information I could on the region, including her thesis. If she is here in Stierve with you, I have some questions I would very much like to discuss with her."

Evir's head was spinning with the realization the means to obtain an audience with the overlord had been with him all along. "She remained in Kierden to help maintain the appearance that I am still there."

"A pity. And I assume Malith doesn't even know you're here." It was not lost on Evir that the overlord used an informal version of the lord overseer's name. Did it signal simply a familiarity borne of years working together or a closer connection?

"I certainly hope not. I've gone to a lot of trouble to ensure that is the case."

The overlord's expression hardened for a moment, then suddenly brightened again. "Before we get to the tantalizing details behind that curious statement, let me start with congratulations on a mission well accomplished in Kierden. A rebellion quashed, heretics brought to justice, and all with very few casualties. Teraithia is truly pleased with your efforts."

The overlord's approval made Evir's heart swell with pride, but the memory of so many bloody bodies in I'fa came rushing to his mind, tamping down the warmth of the moment. Evir did not consider the Purge to include *very few casualties,* but he was not about to contradict the overlord. "Thank you, Excellency. I am pleased to have been of service to the empire."

"And it is some new service that brings you to me this tide."

Evir took a breath and began speaking the words he had rehearsed a hundred times. "While serving in Kierden, it became clear there was a traitor inside the Obsidian Door—someone who was feeding highly sensitive information to the Dorothi. I knew by the timing and nature of the disclosures it must be one of the overseers, or perhaps even the lord overseer himself. I have since determined that it is, in fact, Malithir Lord Overseer."

Arku looked to Tel-Kyron, then back to Evir. "Continue."

Evir began carefully laying out his case one piece at a time, doing his best to strike a balance between concision and clarity. Sevveth brought the cups of steaming satiil and handed them to the men, then retreated. Evir was grateful the task of explaining everything to the overlord gave him an excuse not to drink his. Arku stopped him at times to ensure he understood a particular point but otherwise showed little reaction to Evir's revelation.

"That was a bold plan." Evir thought the overlord sounded impressed, but it might have just been wishful thinking. It was difficult to trust his senses in the Arku's presence. "But to be clear," Arku said almost too casually, pausing to take a drink, "you don't know for certain Malith is the traitor."

"Certainty in this matter would be a gem in an iron mine, Excellency. The lord overseer wouldn't be the head of the Door if he left enough proof for anyone to be certain. But I wouldn't have risked my life to be here unless I was as close to it as reasonably possible under the circumstances."

"Even if Malith is the traitor, you can't be sure it ends with him. There are certainly those who would have benefited from a successful rebellion in Kierden. Perhaps one or more of them is involved."

"That's why I recommend you have Malithir arrested immediately and put to questioning. If there is more to this conspiracy, the Door can find it."

"That would require that you know who you can trust. The Door must be full of those loyal to Malith, not to mention other powerful allies who might try to help him escape or kill him before he can reveal their secrets."

Evir was not sure he was reading the overlord's intention correctly. He seemed to be deflecting the problem back onto Evir's shoulders to deal with. "I'm confident your Excellency has the means to place the lord overseer beyond the reach of the empire's enemies."

"True, but it isn't quite that simple, as Tel-Kyron has no doubt explained."

"Tel-Kyron Mavin Tar has tried to illuminate some of the politics involved, but I suspect we only scratched the surface." Evir felt the sudden pressure in his mind of a request to link in communion. His pulse quickened with the fear of being caught, but the benefits of the mavin tar's guidance might be worth the risk. Before he realized he had decided, he accepted the link.

"He's going to maneuver you into taking all the risk."

"If I were to take Malith into custody without absolute proof of his treason, there are some who would see it, or at least portray it, as a politically motivated action, which would have many complicated ramifications, not the least of which would include making the appointment of Malith's replacement more contentious. It could result in selecting a compromise candidate who is not in the best interest of the empire. Speaking of which, tell me who you would recommend for the position. I'm sure you've given the matter some thought."

Evir had indeed pondered it many times, far more in recent weeks than he cared to admit. "I believe Qin'acht Overseer would be an excellent choice, but obviously I stand to benefit from her promotion, which perhaps limits the usefulness of my recommendation. Kt'Rizzev Overseer would also be a strong candidate."

"I have heard Oshtae-Uru Overseer's name floated in some circles."

Oshtae-Uru oversaw the Door's security forces and had always struck Evir as far too cruel to be entrusted even with her current position, let alone the lord overseer's seat. *"Is she Arku's choice?"* Evir asked through the link.

"I honestly don't know."

"I would, of course, continue to serve to the best of my ability under whomever you and the Mavin Tar appoint." Wisdom dictated he should leave it at that, but he knew he would regret it if he failed to take this opportunity to give his honest opinion and Oshtae-Uru was later appointed lord overseer. "However, I would be remiss, Excellency, if I did not voice my concern with Oshtae-Uru becoming lord overseer. While she certainly excels at ensuring discipline is maintained within the ranks of the Door's security forces, such an approach could easily stifle the flexibility required by the other auxiliaries of the Door to maximize their effectiveness."

"Yes, I've heard that as well. But we don't know how far Malith's rot has spread. It will take a strong hand to ensure every bit of it is rooted out."

"Of course, you're right, Excellency. All I'm suggesting is that perhaps one of the other overseers has the strength and disposition to accomplish both."

Silence hung between them as Arku slowly sipped his satiil again, then finally addressed Tel-Kyron. "I think it's premature to bring this matter before the full council until the inquisitor has had an opportunity to question Malith and find out if anyone else is involved."

"I agree, Excellency. However, under the circumstances, he does not have access to the Door's resources. You are the only one who can provide him with what he needs to deal with Malithir."

"If Malith is guilty, as you claim, his crimes aren't only against the empire. He aided and abetted heretics. When Vetat finds out, she is going to come for Malith and will try him for heresy herself."

"Is he proposing to involve the Church?" he asked Tel-Kyron, desperately hoping he was managing to keep his anxiety out of the link.

"Ask what he recommends."

"How would you recommend I proceed, Overlord? I don't want to give offense to Her Holiness."

"You will obey her command once it is given. What you need is time to question Malith before she gives the command. I can see only one path between those two requirements."

Evir understood the implication immediately and nodded. "The lord overseer will have to disappear quietly."

"This is a dangerous game you're playing," Tel-Kyron warned. Evir could feel the mavin tar's concern through the link. Tel-Kyron continued to speak as Arku replied, and the words became a jumble in Evir's mind.

"This *"Doing* is a *this* matter *in secret* for the *gives* Door to *Arku* deal with *all the* and must *leverage."* be done with the Door's resources. Give me the names of the Door's assets you require, and I will have them at your disposal by the end of the tide."

The end of the tide? Evir thought with alarm. He felt the stones shifting beneath him. Organizing an operation like this within a single tide seemed impossible. It would normally require several tides to gather the necessary intelligence, scout the route, plan for contingencies, then strike at the most opportune moment.

The weight of Arku's gaze shifted to Tel-Kyron, and Evir used the reprieve to take a deep breath and steady himself. "The Elantic Ministry must have a location suitable for questioning someone without fear of detection or interference," the overlord said nonchalantly, as if the issue held no more consequence than what to have for breakfast.

Tel-Kyron laced his fingers together and tapped his extended index fingers on his lips, as Evir had seen him do when he was deep in thought. *"He wants to involve me so he cannot be accused of acting alone."* "Wouldn't it be better to move Malithir to another city? Prokkaya or Vask, maybe?"

The question had been directed to the overlord, but Arku simply looked to Evir and waited for the inquisitor to respond. Evir didn't want to contradict the mavin tar, but he knew it was an unworkable solution. "Ideally, yes, but that would be a complicated operation. When I arranged for the Katharis Pool to be moved to Kierden in secret, it took weeks of planning. Transporting an unwilling, highly skilled, and very valuable prisoner would be much more difficult."

"Apologies. He would have seen through a less truthful answer."

"You're doing fine." Tel-Kyron shrugged, a gesture Evir sensed was meant more for Arku. "I see. I'm afraid solving elantic mysteries is more my strength than clandestine operations. We, of course, have suitable chambers at the academy, but keeping him there in secret for several tides of questioning without drawing suspicion would be very difficult. Perhaps..." Tel-Kyron appeared to be lost in thought again.

The overlord took a drink of his satiil, and Evir no longer had an excuse to avoid following suit. The fear of disappointing the overlord was enough to push him to lift the cup to his lips and sip a small amount of the bitter liquid. *So revolting!* he thought but disciplined his face to keep his expression neutral.

"Not to your liking, eh?" Evir hadn't intended to let his reaction through the link, but he was unused to having someone in his head for this long. Finally, Tel-Kyron nodded and spoke again. "There are a pair of chambers near the coalescence which should suffice."

Evir had no idea what Tel-Kyron was talking about, but the overlord didn't appear pleased at the suggestion. "You know your business better than I do, but I do not want this interfering with the gatestone's operations." Evir knew of the gatestone and guessed that *the coalescence* referred to the source of elan deep below Stierve that powered it. "We must keep the troops moving into Remalia."

"I understand, Excellency. Once Evir gets beyond the guard post, I can arrange it so the inquisitor and his unit can move Malithir into the chambers unseen. The difficulty will be getting through Stierve and past the guards undetected."

"My operatives can get us through Stierve well enough," Evir said, trying to sound more confident than he felt, "but the guards are a different matter."

"Leave that to me," Arku said casually. "Mention the phrase, 'Satiil is the best,' and you will be admitted without question." Had the overlord detected Evir's distaste for the drink and was teasing him? Embarrassment burned in Evir's chest as he thought he detected a smirk and a mischievous glint in the overlord's eye. "Give Sevveth your selected names for the operation and any other details they need to know." Arku abruptly stood, and the two guests rose to their feet as well. "Teraithia bless your efforts, Inquisitor. I look forward to your next report."

"Excellency," Tel-Kyron said, sounding almost apologetic, "clearly you have a great many things on your plate at the moment, but the other mavin tar would hardly forgive me if I did not take the opportunity to ask when we might expect your ratification of a nominee to fill the seat over the Ministry of Transportation?"

Arku's voice took on a hard edge. "I would not be so certain their forgiveness should be your chief concern." Evir felt he might wither under the look leveled by the overlord at Tel-Kyron, but the mavin tar stood serenely waiting for Arku's response. "Let the Council know I am giving it my due attention and expect to respond shortly."

"Thank you, Excellency. I'm certain they will be as pleased to hear that as I am." Tel-Kyron saluted with his hands out to the sides, palms toward the overlord with his chin raised. Evir bowed low, arms outstretched, but the overlord was already walking away. As he straightened, Sevveth Marshal motioned the men to follow him out of the overlord's chambers. Evir longed for any reason to stay a little longer, to find some way to serve Arku more fully, but the thought of having the overlord's ire directed toward him outweighed any desire to remain.

"His presence is sweeter and more intoxicating than satiil, that's for certain," Tel-Kyron pushed the words into his mind. A wave of cleansing clarity surged through the communion link, and the pull toward Arku suddenly dissipated. The mavin tar had warned him of Arku's effect on those in his presence, but Evir hadn't realized until now how much he had been under the overlord's influence. Evir had been trained to withstand dispositioning, but this was different, more subtle yet more irresistible.

"Is it the same for you?" Evir asked.

"Teraithia's enlightenment has little effect on me, but his charisma is its own power."

Evir knew reaching enlightenment was far beyond his grasp during mortality and could never hope to have such influence. He contented himself knowing that by the end of the next tide, at least Malithir was going to feel exactly how much influence Evir could muster.

CHAPTER LVIII
STEPHIR

"Watch out!"

High General Kuymon's barked warning was unnecessary. Stephir's war horse cantered to the side as a stray bolt thudded against his mount's steel barding beside the prince's left knee. Stephir pulled hard on the reins to keep the horse from straying too far from the meager cover they had, but it was not needed. Trenefort was well trained, and the bolt didn't appear to have gotten through to the horse's flesh. Bitter memories of Havvoron screaming and going down with a bolt through his neck the last time Stephir was here came unbidden. He missed his magnificent companion, but Trenefort had been his father's horse, and the rare glossy golden stallion seemed a fitting substitute as they stood in the shadows of the steep canyon walls. It was a king's mount, and he hoped it lived up to that destiny today.

His faith in that prospect was being put to the test as the screams of the dying blended with the wild cacophony of battle cries from those still fighting. Stephir did his best to shove them to the side and focus on the task at hand. Soldiers trying to move toward Balinth's walls were forced to wend their way through a maze of siege towers, catapults, ballistae, and trebuchets choking the narrow canyon. Having so many bunched together substantially reduced their effectiveness, but most of the equipment would have been impotent against Balinth's impregnable walls anyway. Filling up the canyon was the point, at least for the moment. It made the battlefield so chaotic that a couple of trebuchets were even shooting their projectiles against the canyon walls instead of the fortress—or at least, that's how Stephir hoped it would appear to the enemy.

An icy breeze suddenly swept over the prince, unnaturally cold, as if the wind from the heights of the Velspars had been captured and brought down onto the battlefield. His view of Balinth's walls began to be obscured as the biting cold filled the humid canyon air with thickening fog.

A disembodied voice came out of thin air. "Now, High General Kuymon?" The voice belonged to Captain Eskett, an elantir in one of the siege towers several hundred yards further up the canyon. His words were channeled by their auditory, the elantir corporal next to Kuymon with her hand in a bag of seawater on her hip holding a bonded fachim tentacle. Stephir was grateful to have their elantic communications restored.

"Hold until I give the command," Kuymon said impatiently. He was also feeling the strain of the moment. "Not a second sooner."

He could sense the men behind him were feeling the same impatience, but he knew the battle could easily end in a massacre if they rushed their attack. They would advance at Kuymon's carefully planned pace. Stephir trusted the man. So far, the battle was unfolding just as he predicted. Of course, he had predicted that they would suffer far more losses than the enemy and would make almost no progress up to this point, so that was no great feat.

At least there had been no surprises so far. The gates of Balinth's were no longer a trap to spring on them; instead, they were a grim instrument of torture, a slow death for soldiers fighting under the shadow of those looming walls. They needed to draw as many defenders onto Balinth's massive main wall as possible, but his soldiers were paying for that distraction with their lives. For every defender they killed, ten of his men fell before the fortress. It tore at Stephir's gut, but it had to be done. It was just one more item that had to be shoved forcibly to the back of his mind. He would dwell on it later.

'War is a series of grim choices,' his father had told him so many months ago. Stephir thought he had understood it before. He had not.

Another officer called out over the noise. "Their numbers atop the battlements appear to be thinning." Normally, Stephir would take that as a sign they were making progress, but in this case, they had anticipated it might happen if the enemy figured out their real plans.

"There's no time left," Kuymon said in a low growl of frustration. "Redirect the trebuchets and move the siege towers into place!"

The high general's command had already been transmitted where they needed to go. Still, the elantir corporal began confirming the orders with those on the other end of the elantic links. Stephir watched through the swirling fog as the two siege towers with trebuchets inside began turning toward Balinth's walls. At the same time, two other siege towers that had been sitting idle with no path to get to the fortress moved into place against the canyon wall where the trebuchets had been attacking just moments before. Those towers were full of his strongest elantir, and they were the key to their whole strategy.

"Reduce the firing on Balinth's," Stephir ordered. He knew the plan well enough and was not about to make someone else give what was likely to be the most horrific order of the day. "I want as many men climbing her walls as we can manage." Those words were going to cost too many soldiers their lives. There weren't enough spare elantir to have them at every point on the battlefield for communications, so the orders were repeated to a handful of runners who sprinted off to deliver the prince's instructions.

Another blast of chill air hit him, even colder than before. Stephir shuddered involuntarily at the sudden drop in temperature. He could briefly see his breath in the cold air before warmth seeped back in around him. The whistle of a bolt sliced through the air near them, but it clattered harmlessly on the nearby rocks. The defenders were shooting blindly into the fog. Stephir was amazed the elantir had been able to produce such effective cover. For a moment, he dared hope the rest of their plan might succeed, but without being able to see his troops, he felt he was losing control of the battle.

"I need to get closer," Stephir said, more as a frustrated complaint than a serious suggestion, but Kuymon took Stephir's words literally.

"No, Your Highness. We must hold our position until—"

"I know the plan, High General."

Fire suddenly erupted on one of the siege towers with the trebuchets near the east canyon wall. He hated to lose it, but its task was complete. He hoped his men understood there was no need to protect it anymore.

Over the din of the battle, he heard a sound he had never heard before, but one he had been waiting for—a soft but pervasive cracking noise, repeated over and over in rapid succession, coming from the opposite side of the canyon where the two siege towers had moved close to the canyon walls. He could not tell if he was hearing it directly or through the elantic link, but it must have been the elantir doing their work. The soft cracking was followed by the more familiar sound of the battering rams atop the towers smashing into the thick stone of the canyon wall. Then back to the rapid cracking noise again, followed by another thudding strike by the rams.

Stephir tried to imagine what was happening up there. Some of the elantir inside those towers were tasked with forcing water they carried in barrels into cracks that had hopefully been created by the trebuchet attacks. The rest of the elantir were freezing and thawing the water over and over, forcing the cracks to spread, weakening the walls enough for the rams to break through. But it was taking too long. The defenders were going to figure out what they were up to.

With dismay, he noticed the fog starting to dissipate. The elantir who had been producing it were now focused on breaching the canyon wall, allowing the natural summer heat to quickly rush in and dispel the unnatural cold. A renewed frenzy of crossbow bolts flew through the thinning fog, and the screams of his men worsened.

Another siege tower caught fire, this one much closer to Balinth's walls. Stephir hoped it was a sign the enemy still hadn't figured out where the real threat was. Every second that slipped by was agony as he felt the chances of victory evaporating like the fog. He had been a fool to—

A piercing crack split the air as if a heavy pottery jug had shattered, followed by a shower of stone down to the canyon floor. Through the dissipating fog, he could see a dark, gaping hole high up on the canyon wall. The elantir had done it! With no hope of breaching the walls of the fortress, they had chosen instead to break into the tunnels within the canyon walls.

"Forward!" Kuymon shouted. The reserve soldiers behind them rushed forward, shields held over their heads in the hopes of deflecting the falling bolts. One of the soldiers, slowed down by the press of bodies in front of him, looked up at Stephir, wild-eyed. The prince didn't recognize the man in particular but nodded encouragingly.

The soldier nodded back and shouted for all his worth, "For King Stephir!" More heads turned toward Stephir and repeated the cry.

"For King Stephir!"

Stephir's heart caught in his throat. He thrust his sword above his head and shouted back, "For Remalia!"

A hand clapped him on the shoulder. He turned to see Frey had moved to his mount up next to him. "Well, it looks like I'm going to have to go out there after all and make sure those poor fools didn't just embarrass themselves with false shouts of praise. You know... since you're not actually king yet." Frey looked like he was trying to suppress his usual impish smirk.

"Together then?"

"You go out there when there is even a hint of fighting, and I won't be held responsible if your reign ends here today!" Frey sounded like a scolding father, even as a grim smile snuck through.

"Frey, this isn't a game."

His friend's eyes pinched at the corner as his voice dropped to a near whisper. "It's always a game, Stephir." Frey resumed his mirthful tone as he pulled his sandy blond hair back with one hand and placed his helm on his head with the other. "Don't worry. It's a good plan. Just leave the fighting to the rest of us. We can't afford to lose your royal hide to an accident in the heat of battle."

Stephir wasn't sure where Frey's jovial confidence ended and his sarcasm began. With a final clap on Stephir's shoulder, Frey kicked his spurs into his horse and shot forward, ripping out his sword as he rode through the river of armored bodies flowing past them. Stephir longed to follow his friend and fight at his side, but his duty was to be the architect of their victory, not one of its builders.

His heart lifted as the hailstorm of bolts from above suddenly lightened to a drizzle. He could imagine the Kuldrith racing to reposition themselves to confront the Remalians scrambling through the breach in the tunnels behind the canyon walls. The clash of steel on steel drifted back to Stephir, a welcome change from the previous sounds of their futile siege.

So much could still go wrong. What if the imposing Kuldrith were able to bottleneck the Remalians in the tunnels? What if they managed to somehow collapse the tunnels? Their entire plan would be doomed.

An image of Ilyanara and his children facing the brutal Kuldrith in Teris came to his mind. Commander Kalvarne had failed to collapse the tunnel under the outer wall, though he reported the rate of enemies coming into the city had slowed, so perhaps they had managed some small success. Still, the Kuldrith had taken over nearly all of the inner city, leaving the last of Teris's defenders trapped behind the inner wall surrounding the Mount of the Gods. It was only a matter of days before surrender was Ilyanara's only option. Stephir tried to set that aside, tried to focus on the battle, but he couldn't. Each time he shook off the thought, the image of his wife and children in the hands of Kuldrith soldiers returned unbidden. He had to see his family again! He would.

Another resounding crack echoed along the canyon, followed by a shower of stone falling to the canyon floor. He hoped none of his men were under there. They should all be behind the siege tower, but with so many waiting their turn to climb up, he could not tell if any had strayed too close.

"Tell them to stop widening the breach and get more ladders over there!"

Stephir and Kuymon issued the same orders over each other. At least they were aligned on what was needed.

Something drew his attention back to Balinth's walls. Through the last wispy tendrils of fog hanging over the battlefield, Stephir could just make out the shadowy figures of his men doing their best against the impossible task of overtaking those imposing fortifications. The fighting appeared intense on the two ends where the fortress wall abutted the canyon walls. He could not be sure, but the center seemed to have been abandoned by the defenders.

"Look there," he said to the high general, pointing. "Top of the wall near the gate. The men are over the walls!" Kuymon's older eyes weren't as keen as Stephir's, and he raised his spyglass.

"Akraharr's—" the high general began to swear but stopped himself. "Haresh has done it. I can't believe it," Kuymon said with an uncharacteristic half-smile.

The thudding of the rams and cracking stone suddenly stopped. All the sounds of battle seemed distant and muted. Stephir could hear the nervous exhale of his horse, the creaking of the harness and barding of those around him, the hurried footsteps and hushed voices of nervous soldiers as they continued to make their way forward. After what seemed like an eternity of waiting, the crisp sound of distant steel on steel echoed along the canyon. There was still no movement from atop the battlements, but Stephir glanced over at Kuymon hopefully, who nodded back in return.

"They must have made it through."

Stephir could not hold back any longer. "Let's go. I want to see what we've done."

"My lord," the high general said as if he meant to object, but there was no steel in his voice. Instead, he spurred his horse forward to ride at the prince's side. Soldiers moved aside as the Divinarim cleared a path for Stephir and his retinue. Several of the other nobles trailing behind them talked nervously or boasted rashly. Stephir resisted the urge to turn and command them to be silent, to maintain respect for those who sacrificed their lives here. They may have won the battle, but at what cost? How many had fallen?

His stomach turned at the sight of broken and bloody bodies lying beneath the ice-covered rubble that used to be the canyon wall. Strangely, some of the bodies were whitish-blue and unnaturally stiff, as if frozen. "Get some men to clear the stones and reclaim the bodies," he said to no one in particular. Soldiers were still climbing through the jagged hole into the exposed tunnel high above. Shouts to clear a path were repeated as Stephir dismounted and handed the reins to his squire. Divinarim moved quickly ahead of the prince to ensure his path was clear as he climbed the wooden ladders up the platforms inside the siege tower—no easy feat in his heavy armor.

Several elantir on each platform stood at attention in their blue-and-white surcoats over chain and black gambeson, offering the elantir's unique salute as he passed. He wanted to thank each of them for their efforts but now was not the time. He was panting by the time he reached the crowded top platform where the battering ram hung from heavy iron chains affixed to the massive wooden beam. He quickly inspected Master Caldren's new steel cap design to see how it had held up. It was bent and badly dented but still in one piece. More importantly, it had worked.

Stephir walked across the platform that bridged the gap from the tower to the exposed tunnel. He was amazed to see remnants of shattered ice and stone everywhere. Water dripped from the canyon wall where thick white frost was beginning to melt. Stephir could hardly believe the Elantir Corps had managed so much damage, and he spared a thought to consider what more they might do with enough time and the full support of the crown. He hoped Calinda would wake up soon so he could discuss it with her. Captain Major Ambersol was a solid leader and well-organized, but he didn't hold a candle to Commander Alscan's intelligence and ingenuity.

Stephir took a moment to let his eyes adjust to the dim light of the tunnel. He noticed a couple of elantir resting against the stone wall, out of the way, eyes closed. They were almost as pale as the frozen corpses below and had frost covering their clothing and hair. He thought they might be dead, but the faint mist of their breath told him otherwise. Stephir called for soldiers to come and assist them. "Attend to the wounded here. Dress their wounds as best you can. See that they're given something to get them warm again. Hot tea and blankets, or..." Stephir was not sure what they would need, or even if anything could help them. He feared they may have sacrificed too much of their elan and might not survive the day. But at least he could ensure they did not die cold and alone.

Stephir turned to High General Kuymon. "I want everyone to know how much the elantir sacrificed this day. They deserve as much respect as any other soldier."

"It will be so, my lord," Kuymon promised with a curt bow. He lowered his voice so only Stephir could hear. "You make a good king. Your father would be proud."

"I wish he were here with us."

"I am content that he is in the holy realms beyond, and *you* are here with us."

Stephir didn't trust his emotions to let him respond well to the compliment, so he chose instead to keep moving. He continued up the dim tunnel, illuminated only by the daylight coming through the narrow arrow slits that looked down on the canyon outside. Anger stirred in him as he thought about how many of his men had been lost to bolts shot from up here. He pushed ahead, determined to finally see this enemy up close for himself.

He didn't make it far before he was stepping over the bodies of his fallen countrymen. He had to be careful not to slip on the blood spilled on the stone floor. He counted six blue-and-white surcoats before seeing a single dark, gray-skinned body encased in scarred and battered armor the color of soot. He noted the symbol of Teraithia etched into the scales of the soldier's armor and remembered the words of the Sharinist knight who had spoken of their fanatical devotion to the goddess. A Remalian crossbow lay discarded to the side, and two heavy forward-curved long knives lay next to the hulking dead Kuldrith soldier. Were they all this massive, or was this one an anomaly? And why knives? And...

Stephir wished the soldier was still alive. His motivations wavered between a desire to interrogate the man for answers to his myriad questions and the intense desire to kill him himself. There must be some Kuldrith alive somewhere in the fortress. It was time to find them and remedy that.

Soon, the rough excavated stone of the tunnel became the constructed passageway of the fortress. Dead soldiers littered the ground, far more of them Remalian than Kuldrith. He caught himself counting the dead and forced himself to stop. What was important at this moment was that they held Balinth's.

Muted shouts erupted in the distance followed by a thunderous crash, sending a shockwave through the fortress. Stephir's heart sank as he drew his sword. There was no part of his plans that would account for whatever it was.

"My lord," one of the Divinarim said with urgency, "we should—"

Stephir knew they wanted him to withdraw back down the corridor, but he was not going to tolerate any more staying-out-of-harm's-way. "Where's my auditory?" he called out, cutting off the knight. Heads swiveled, looking at those in the prince's vicinity. The request was repeated a couple of times until the corporal came running forward from further back. "What happened out there?" Stephir asked.

"I don't know, my lord," the elantir said in confusion.

"I'm not asking you," he tried to keep the frustration out of his voice. "I want a report from someone outside."

The young woman blushed in embarrassment at her obvious misunderstanding but quickly opened the bag on her hip and began the elant to link with the other auditories outside in the canyon. In a moment, she nodded.

"Can someone tell me what just happened in the fortress?" Stephir asked.

A few voices jumbled together as multiple responses filled the air, but the answer was clear enough. "One of the bridges collapsed. It fell into the courtyard."

Stephir could picture one of the two enclosed bridges that spanned the distance between the half towers built into each side of the canyon falling on his men in the courtyard. The Kuldrith were proving yet again to be a more cunning enemy than he ever would have imagined. At the sound of more shouting, he could not wait any longer. He turned and raced along the passageway toward the courtyard, his guards and other soldiers trailing. He was unsure of the path through the fortress and tried to listen for any clues that might help him discern where the fighting was and what was happening, but the clanging of their armor echoing off Balinth's stone walls drowned out all other sounds.

It felt like an eternity before he finally found a heavy, iron-bound oak door into the courtyard. He braced himself for battle as his knights took positions at the door, then pulled it open and they all rushed into the dust-filled air of the open courtyard. He blinked in the sudden light as he emerged from the fortress into daylight. There was shouting coming from all around him, but he could not see any enemies. Confusion turned to relief as realization dawned on him that the shouting was the victory cries of hundreds of his soldiers.

They had won the day.

He relaxed the white-knuckle grip on his sword hilt and looked up to where the fortress's two bridges should be. The higher bridge was still intact, but only the jagged ends of the lower one remained. Broken stone and ruined sections of the collapsed bridge were scattered around the large courtyard. It was disappointing, but it could be rebuilt.

He moved further into the open, cautious to stay away from the center in case the second bridge collapsed. His eyes scanned the soldiers milling around the courtyard, climbing the stairway up Balinth's wall, and standing atop the battlements, waving their weapons in triumph.

As soldiers began to realize Stephir had joined them, their shouts were quickly replaced with, "Long live King Stephir!", "For House Laconeus!" and "Gods preserve the Stallions of Remalia!"

"Congratulations, my lord!" High General Kuymon said with a genuine smile. "You did it. Balinth's is ours again!"

"No Gul." Stephir corrected him warmly, patting his commander's shoulder. It felt strange but somehow appropriate to use the general's given name in that moment. "*We* did it. You have my eternal gratitude."

"Your Majesty!" a loud and cheerful voice carried over the chaos from the wall above. One very familiar voice. He looked up and saw Frey pushing his way through the celebrating soldiers as he and a few of his men struggled to make their way down the stairs to the courtyard.

"Your Majesty," Frey said again as he stepped in front of Stephir and bowed as eloquently as his armor would allow. "You did say we could call you that once we took Balinth's." Stephir laughed. Only Frey would have some minor annoyance at the forefront of his mind at a moment like this.

"I suppose I will allow it now." It was meant as a jest between friends, but Frey's men repeated the honorific as they dropped to one knee and bowed their heads. Had Frey planned this excessive display as a joke? Stephir wouldn't put it past him. But the gesture began to spread to others around them.

"Your Majesty." The phrase was repeated over and over with solemn respect as more of his soldiers knelt before their king. Love swelled in Stephir's chest, and he wished he could embrace each of his subjects. He regarded them in appreciative silence. Suddenly, he found himself speaking before he had any idea what he intended to say.

"Today, you haven't just won another battle. You haven't just accomplished a feat that has never been seen in a hundred generations while this fortress has stood as a bulwark against the enemies of Remalia. Today, you have opened the way to saving our homes, saving our wives and husbands and children. Today, you have proved to the gods that Remalia will stand forever!" Stephir punctuated his words by thrusting his sword heavenward. His soldiers rose to their feet with renewed victory cries and shouts of jubilation.

Frey stepped closer, a look of serious contemplation on his face. "That was a halfway decent speech. A few nights out with me making toasts in the taverns of Teris and we might make an orator of you yet."

"No toasts for me. It is the men who deserve the toasts. *You* deserve the toasts."

"I do, that's true. And perhaps that 'archmarquis' title we discussed so many weeks ago." Stephir rolled his eyes, a smirk playing on his lips. "But don't sell yourself short, m'lord. Mark my words, the taverns will be buzzing for years to come with tales of today," Frey took a step back and continued with raised voice, performing for the crowd of onlookers, "the day Balinth's Fortress fell to King Stephir, and the mighty Stallions of Remalia returned to claim what is theirs!" More cheered and shouted praises and well wishes to their king.

Frey wistfully spoke as he looked skyward as if remembering a day long since passed, "The battle was glorious. Blood burning. Blades singing through the air." Frey heaved an exaggerated sigh. "You would have loved it."

"I'm sure you're right. Did you see how they took the bridge down?"

"Always the life of the party," Frey said in a mocking tone. "No, I didn't see exactly what happened. We were fighting against a last group of these over-sized wessut droppings up on the wall when I heard—"

"I'm sorry, 'wessut droppings'?"

"You know, the gray skin, bulky muscles—they remind me of wessut scat."

Stephir chuckled. "Why do you know what wessut scat looks like?" Stephir was not sure he wanted to know but was mildly curious.

"Hunting wessut with my grandfather at our chalet near Marbury. I'll take you some time and show you if you like." Then, shaking his head, he said under his breath, "Always the life of the party. Now where was I? Oh yes, fighting the oversized wessut droppings—I heard panicked shouting and noted soldiers scattering down in the courtyard. I managed to look over just in time to see it crash. Nearly jolted me off my feet."

"High General," Stephir said to Kuymon, who stood by giving orders for securing Balinth's. "Try to figure out how they took down the bridge and make sure the second one isn't going to come down on our heads."

"Yes, Your Majesty." It still felt strange receiving the king's honorific, but no longer inappropriate. Perhaps once he was coronated, he would settle into it.

Other nobles and officers began pressing in for a chance to offer their congratulations to the king, and soon Frey stepped away. Stephir knew etiquette, duty, and political expediency demanded he mingle with the nobles and praise his soldiers, but he longed to switch places with Kuymon or Frey or just about anyone else. Out of the corner of his eye, he caught sight of the Kuldrith bodies being thrown from the top of the battlements.

"Were any of them taken alive?" he asked Marchioness Haedep.

"Only a few, lord. Most of them fought to the death. I believe that was the intent of the others as well, but we were able to subdue them."

"Lady Haedep led her soldiers very effectively," Frey praised the marchioness as he maneuvered into Stephir's orbit again.

"Well, they were too powerful for me to fight directly the way Lord de'Venneshen did, who took down the beasts with such... panache." Stephir nearly choked as he drank from the waterskin his squire had handed him.

"Careful, Your Highness," Frey said with a playfully peevish expression, "I would hate for you to meet such an ignoble demise so early in your reign. Here, have some wine!" Frey said, grabbing a cup from a page walking by and offering it to Stephir.

"Where did that wine come from?" Stephir asked, his voice laced with concern.

"The spoils of war, my lord," Duke Frendic called out cheerfully, raising his cup in a toast.

"You mean from Balinth's foodstuffs?"

"Of course! I hope I didn't offend Your Highness by agreeing to let the men have a celebratory drink."

"Fool!" Stephir spat the word out, knocking Frey's proffered cup to the ground. "Stop them now!"

"But Your Majesty..." Frendic said with a plaintive drawl as Stephir's officers and guards began moving through the soldiers, spreading the order.

"Do you want a repeat of Nanjab? The Kuldrith may have poisoned everything. Throw it all out and burn it."

"But our supplies are still stretched thin. Perhaps a more measured approach is in order. The elantir could—"

Stephir cut him off. "The Kuldrith have wreaked havoc in ways that defied our understanding far too many times. I'm not taking any chances." Looking around, he saw the worry and downcast looks on the faces of his soldiers. He had effectively killed the celebratory mood. *Life of the party indeed*, Frey's words stung. He had to repair this. With as much cheer in his voice as he could manage, he called out, "But everyone certainly deserves a celebratory drink for this amazing victory. Send for my best wine. Drinks all around!" The soldiers dutifully cheered, but it did not have the same genuine zeal as it had before.

"Well, that was exciting," Frey said cheerlessly. "I hope you're wrong. I think my sword has a few more of these Kuldrith bastards to dispatch before I'm ready to shuffle off to the great tavern beyond the stars."

"I didn't know you considered yourself a Sykorian," Stephir teased.

"Why not? Perhaps an eternity of peaceful gardening, or meditation, or reading books sounds good to you, but I'll take an eternity of parties if it's an option, thank you very much."

Stephir looked around to make sure his command was being carried out —and probably looking for some other problem in need of fixing if he was being honest.

"If Your Majesty would indulge me, I want to show you something," Frey said sincerely. Stephir gestured for his friend to lead the way. They climbed the stone steps up Balinth's massive walls. Stephir tried to avoid the blood stains as best he could but was not entirely successful. He hoped it was mostly from the Kuldrith.

They reached the top and Stephir kept a careful eye on the bodies strewn across the battlements, angry that so many were Remalian and so few were Kuldrith. Something strange pulled at his attention, but it took him a moment to register what it was. A Remalian woman in Kuldrith armor, blood smeared on her face. *Another traitor*, he thought bitterly. In a fit of pent-up anger, he picked up her body and heaved it over the battlements. He looked down to where it landed, satisfied that she wouldn't be polluting his fortress any longer. After a moment, his gaze wandered to the battlefield in the canyon below them. Soldiers were still carrying out their assigned tasks, helping the wounded, or dismantling siege equipment. It seemed so mundane after what they had accomplished, but he knew it had to be done.

"Very dramatic," Frey said, trying to sound amused and teasing, but Stephir detected a hint of concern in his cousin's voice.

"I probably should have someone investigate how she ended up fighting for the Kuldrith. It might lead us to more traitors."

"Maybe. But look," Frey said simply. Stephir looked at Frey to see where he wanted to direct his attention and saw him looking northward. Stephir turned around and scanned the area for signs of danger or other problems that needed to be addressed. Behind the walls, beyond the buildings of the fortress and the shorter rear wall of Balinth's, Stephir could see the rough canyon extending behind them. The sun was still high in the afternoon sky, glinting off the snow-capped mountains that soared above them, but otherwise, there was nothing out of the ordinary.

"That's the way home," Frey said, motioning for Stephir to direct his gaze outward, not upward. Looking beyond the lower walls of the far side of the fortress, Stephir looked through the pass that parted the Velspars. He could see the paved road that led to Teris, to his family. "Nothing else stands in our way now."

"Nothing but an army of twenty thousand Kuldrith from gods know where." Stephir was tempted to tell Frey about the situation in Teris but thought better of it. Let him and the others have this one day of victory without the pall of such news hanging over them. He would tell them tomorrow.

"Eh. I'll take half, and you and the army can handle the other half."

Stephir chuckled, then fell into silence as they stood enjoying the view. "I wish Andric was here to see this." Stephir glanced around to see if anyone was within earshot before continuing. "I hope he's all right."

"I'm sure he's fine. Probably frolicking with that Vanassi beauty from the delegation Consul Rellat told us about."

"Or maybe her mother." They both had a good laugh at Andric's expense. The respite lasted only a moment before remaining stationary became uncomfortable. He had been standing still for far too long. All he wanted now was to mount his horse and get the army marching again. The urge to move was too much, and he began walking along the wall.

"Well, he shouldn't be the only one having a good time," Frey said, clapping the king on the shoulder with a dull clang of metal. "Let's go get some of your finest wine before Frendic drinks it all."

Stephir dropped his voice to a conspiratorial whisper. "I don't really have any fine wine left. But I do have a very decent brandy we might enjoy later."

"I knew being your friend would pay off sooner or later."

CHAPTER LVIX
EVIR

Evir stood against the smooth stone wall at the junction of a small service tunnel and one of the main corridors in the prestigious Crystal Flowers district. Most residents were still asleep this early in the tide, as he had hoped. Some would arise early to attend the Remembrance Day service held at the temple, but with any luck, he would have Malithir secured in a holding cell before then. He still considered it bitterly ironic the lord overseer's fall for his treasonous actions came on the holiday celebrating their fallen soldiers, heroes who made the ultimate sacrifice to keep the Kuldrith people safe.

He hadn't slept in two tides, but the hot blood pounding in his veins kept the fatigue at bay as he silently waited for the signal that the second unit of the Obsidian Door's operatives was in place near the main entrance to Malithir's residence. He wished Kt'caris was here to lead them, but Gol-vutin was an excellent commander as well, and he was grateful to have her as his second. The first unit stood in the shadows along the wall behind him, waiting for the inquisitor to give the order to put the final phase of their operation into motion.

There had been more than a few surprised looks on their faces a few tenth-tides ago when Evir told them the lord overseer was their target, and their mission was to collapse the shadows on him and move him to an undisclosed location. Arku Overlord had personally commanded them to unquestioningly obey Evir's every word. Nothing short of that would have assured the inquisitor that he could trust the Door's soldiers to remain unwavering as they moved against Malithir. It still made his head spin to think of how much confidence the overlord was placing in him. But he also could not shake loose the sensation he was being played as a stone in a larger game he could not see —a game he feared might lead to him being sacrificed for someone else's advantage. Tel-Kyron Mavin Tar's warning to trust his instincts if he felt anything amiss had not helped allay his unease.

An area next to him on the wall the size of a hand began to faintly glow red. Unit two was in place. It was time.

Evir motioned for the slaves with the food carts for this tide's deliveries to the residences to be released from where they were being held by his soldiers further back in the tunnel. Evir watched each cart roll past him into the main corridor, some heading left and others to the right. The slaves pulling the cart assigned to go to Malithir's residence were actually requited—former slaves that had won their freedom, and these were now serving as Door operatives. Evir waited until they were several paces along the main corridor before finally moving from his position to trail at a distance. He didn't need to look behind him to know his unit was following.

The cart stopped at the auxiliary entrance to the residence and Evir halted as well, his back to the wall. He kept his eyes riveted on his men as one of them retrieved a rough sack of food from the cart and handed it to a pair of hands reaching through the curtains. The second man appeared to fumble the masonry jar in his hands and it fell to the ground, shattering inside the entrance, though no sound of it reached Evir. The man appeared to be apologizing profusely, playing the part of a horrified slave perfectly.

One... two... three... four... Evir counted. *Now!*

Suddenly the two disguised operatives charged inside, daggers in hand, while a third, the elantir hiding in the cart whose task was creating a sound ward, threw off the tarp covering her and leaped to follow them. Evir was already rushing forward, his senses alert for any threat. In moments, he was at the threshold of the residence. The acrid smell of tzevvi vapors wafted into the corridor, but Evir and his soldiers had taken the antidote a tenth-tide ago and were immune to its effects. With v'kar and ess'at at the ready, he dashed inside.

The sounds of choking and fighting suddenly filled the air as he entered the room, moving past the elantic sound barrier. The house slaves cowered on the floor or shrank against a wall, coughing and gagging, tears and mucus running profusely down their faces. Two house guards clad in beautiful serpentine stone lamellar armor fared far worse. They writhed on the floor, blood pooling on the polished marble as it pumped from gaping wounds across their throats.

The operative who had entered first, a Restani man with golden-tinged skin and short-cropped auburn hair, had a hand clasped over a blood stain on his upper arm, a bloody dagger grasped in his other hand. "Are you all right?" Evir asked.

"Yes, Inquisitor," the man replied between panting breaths with a heavy accent, grimacing slightly as he moved his arm to prove it.

"Good. You two keep them here," he said, gesturing with his head toward the coughing slaves, "and have the cart ready for us. Tannik-ulm," he called to his second elantir, who was already standing by the hallway leading further into the residence, "lights." The lumens in the small chamber and hallway suddenly winked out, throwing the room into near darkness. Only thin strips of light filtered in around the edges of the heavy curtains from the corridor outside.

Two soldiers holding v'kar and javelins moved into the hallway, followed by two more with crossbows, then Evir and Tannik-ulm, and the remaining soldiers bringing up the rear. They didn't need to worry about stealth. The other elantir kept the sound barrier around them as they moved. Tannik-ulm extinguished the lumens as they advanced, keeping them always in the shadows.

The curving hallway led past an empty kitchen and a couple of common bed chambers where several house slaves still slept. Suddenly, the front two soldiers crouched until the staccato snap of crossbow strings sent them sprinting forward. The crossbowmen dropped their spent weapons and drew their kukri as they rushed to follow. It took Evir three more paces before he saw the two guards, one with a bolt protruding from the joint of his neck and shoulder inside the neck-guard of his armor, doing his best to shield himself from the lightning-quick thrusts of an obsidian-tipped javelin.

The other guard, a bolt embedded in her v'kar, struck hard with her curved sword against the bladed shield of Evir's soldier. The soldier blocked, then drove the bladed edge down onto her foot, cutting the front half of her foot off. Her scream of agony turned into a gurgling cry, eyes wide with terror as the second soldier's kukri sank deep into her neck.

The first guard parried a javelin thrust toward his face and slid his blade down the shaft. His soldier tried to counter but was too slow. Evir's stomach clenched as he saw the guard's blade slice into the soldier's forward hand. Blood spilled from where his index finger dangled by a piece of armored glove. The move cost the guard his life as another soldier thrust his javelin through the guard's exposed neck, driving him against the wall. The man dropped his weapons and clutched at his throat as he slumped to the floor, leaving a smeared trail of crimson on the polished marble wall to mark his passing.

Evir bent down and took hold of the guard's armor, drawing a small dagger from its sheath strapped to its waist. The man weakly tried to shy away, even as his lifeblood continued to pump through fingers impotent to stanch the flow from the wounds in his neck. Fear and hatred and confusion mixed in the man's eyes as the inquisitor reached under the guard's armor and pulled on his undershirt. Evir thrust his dagger through the material but avoided harming the man further. He would be dead in a few moments, anyway. Evir continued to cut and rip until he had a strip of cloth, then stood up and began quickly binding the wounded hand of his soldier.

"Go back and help ensure no one escapes that way," Evir instructed, then retrieved his sword and shield from Tannik-ulm and signaled his unit to keep moving. The soldiers halted where the hallway ended in a wide chamber disturbingly devoid of anything. No furniture, no artwork. Not even lumens marred the perfect emptiness. Instead, soft white light emanated from behind the polished white marble walls. It was an extravagant waste of space, and Evir wondered if it was intentional or if the lord overseer was simply indifferent to it.

"I don't know how to extinguish the walls, Inquisitor," Tannik-ulm admitted. "Do you want me to try to figure it out?"

Three other hallways joined the large chamber. Evir scanned each one and saw no sign of movement in any of them. He hated being exposed but didn't want to waste more time. "Keep moving," he ordered.

Evir felt a gnawing sense of unease grow as the soldiers led them on a diagonal line across the open room toward the hallway leading to Malithir's bedchamber. His eyes darted between the other corridors, fearing an attack from one of them at any moment. He was grateful to leave the bright and empty space and return his focus to the path ahead through the relatively dimmer hallway where Tannik-ulm had already darkened the lumens.

One of the lead soldiers suddenly stumbled hard against the wall as a thin whip of elantic energy curled around his ankle and yanked his foot. Evir tried to blink away the momentary trail of green afterglow the whip left in his vision. A bolt ricocheted off a v'kar, but a second found its mark and sank into the shoulder of another soldier, dropping him to the floor with a grunt of pain. He rolled aside to leave room for others to get past him. Evir and the rest of his soldiers rushed toward the guards ahead, where the hallway turned a sharp corner.

"Forget the lumens. Shield us!" Evir commanded Tannik as he opened himself to allow the elantir to draw his elan. The pain of a thousand needles pricking his skin meant he was doing a poor job of relaxing his elantic focal points, but it was all he could manage at the moment. If it meant Tannik could protect his soldiers, it was a price he was willing to pay. He ignored the pain and focused on the guards.

A knot of green- and black-armored bodies and weapons swirled violently in the corridor. *Where's their elantir?* That was the biggest threat. He maneuvered around his soldiers to attack the guards from their flank.

A steak of white flashed in the corridor before he could strike. He ducked instinctively, but it was unnecessary. The elantic energy crackled against an invisible shield. Evir glanced up in time to see light arcing back to a guard standing behind the others, momentarily surrounded by a shimmering white aura. Tannik must have added a tracer counter-elant.

Evir was impressed the elantir could manage both by himself, and he was not going to let the opportunity go to waste. He raised his shield and slipped through a gap between one of Malithir's towering guards and the wall. The guard was too fast and aimed a vicious blow from his steel mace at Evir's head. The inquisitor tried to block with his v'kar but knew he was too late. Suddenly, a thin whip of blue light wrapped around the shaft of the mace and yanked it away from its path toward his head. His relief was cut short as the mace's new trajectory brought the weapon down with a sickening crunch against the side of his soldier's exposed face.

Evir wanted to strike back at the mace-wielding guard, but taking down the elantir was still his priority. He suppressed a cry of frustration as he spun to attack the glowing guard. The man had retreated along the short corridor toward the arched entry into what must be Malithir's bedchamber. Evir sprinted forward, shield raised—not to protect himself (his shield would do nothing against met'elan) but to hide the position of his ess'at.

Blinding light flashed in front of him. Evir knew the elantir wouldn't stay in the same place. He tried to listen for the scrape of boots on the stone floor, but all he could hear was the sounds of fighting and disoriented cries behind him. He lunged forward, blindly slicing his blade in a wide arc parallel to the ground, hoping to catch the man wherever he had moved. The tip of his ess'at struck the stone wall with a metallic clang. The elantir must have moved back instead of to the side.

A woman screamed and a man's voice cried out in alarm, "Akraharr's shade!" Neither voice belonged to the lord overseer. Confusion and concern swirled in a corner of his mind. *So much for taking Malithir by stealth*, he thought as he charged forward, his shield braced for impact.

His vision was starting to return around the edges, but a greenish-white afterglow still dominated the center wherever he looked. He caught movement to his left and swung his v'kar into whatever it was. A man grunted as Evir's shield smashed into him. Evir cut low, aiming for his unprotected legs. He felt his blade bite into flesh. The man cried out and crumpled, grabbing at Evir as he fell. He felt a twinge in his side from his mostly healed ribs as he tried to hold the weight. It put him off balance and he stumbled forward, almost falling on top of the man.

Something struck a glancing blow off his shoulder from behind. He feared one of Malithir's guards had come to the attack, but he heard something metallic strike the wall and clatter to the floor. A dagger, probably thrown by someone in the room. In one fluid motion, he sliced the bladed edge of his v'kar across the elantir's throat and brought it around to protect him from any further attack. No one was in his immediate vicinity. He spared a glance back out into the corridor to check on his men. It was difficult to tell with blotchy vision, but it appeared two were down, and the others were finishing off the last house guard.

"Evir Inquisitor," Malithir barked from across the room, "what is the meaning of this?" His voice shook with outrage.

Frustration simmered in Evir, wishing his vision would clear so he could see the lord overseer's face. *A few more seconds*, he told himself.

"Why are you back in Stierve?"

Evir did not answer immediately but pretended to scan the room. In reality, he was trying to observe Malithir in the clear area of his peripheral vision. The lord overseer appeared disheveled, a loose robe hanging askew on his broad shoulders, partially covering his otherwise naked body. A young man with pale skin and a shaved head, obviously a slave, and a middle-aged woman, both naked as well, were still in the lord overseer's bed. Evir could not yet make out their faces, but for the moment, their identities were a secondary concern. The more pressing issue was whether he was going to have to kill them. He needed to give Malithir a plausible cover story to come peacefully. He had considered such a scenario when he started planning for this moment weeks ago in Kierden.

"You aren't safe, Lord Overseer. Please come with me and I will explain everything. But we need to move quickly."

Malithir hesitated. That was a good sign. Evir doubted the lord overseer would believe such a ploy, but he had to know by now resistance was useless. It would be much simpler if the witnesses could later report the lord overseer had come willingly.

"What about me, Malith?" the woman asked, her voice laced with concern and indignation. "Am I in danger too?"

"I don't know," the lord overseer replied, sounding too calm. Evir's eyesight finally cleared enough to make out the woman's face. He felt a sinking feeling in the pit of his stomach. He could not recall her name, but he recognized her as the marshal for Qae'essin Mavin Tar. As the mavin tar's right hand, she was a powerful woman in her own right. "Well, Inquisitor?" Malithir asked Evir impatiently, eyes fixed on his subordinate with a burning hatred. "Is the marshal also in danger?"

"No, Lord Overseer, this only concerns you. Now please, get dressed and let us escort you to a more secure location." By now, the remaining soldiers under Evir's command had entered the bedchamber and stood at the ready.

Malithir looked at them and slowly nodded. "Tannik, I'm so glad to see you're here to protect me as well." To most, it might sound like an innocuous statement, but Evir detected subtle inflections of bitterness and accusation.

"Please, Lord Overseer," Evir put a steel tone in his voice this time, "we really must move quickly."

Malithir didn't answer; he simply crossed the room to an elaborate wooden armoire. "Jannil, come help me get dressed." The young man, a Teugard by the look of him, obediently climbed out of the bed, casually strolled over, and helped dress the lord overseer. Malithir had chosen a set of formal clothing, with layers of cloth that had to be wrapped and draped in an elaborate manner. The inquisitor bit back the urge to demand he choose something simpler, but it would undermine the scene Evir was trying to create for the witnesses.

The woman rose and began dressing as well. "Cali," Malithir called out to her, "I do apologize for the rude awakening. I promise this will not happen again."

"Oh, I don't know," she replied coyly, though to Evir it sounded forced. "It could be fun if this was part of some elaborate game you were playing."

"I assure you, it is, though probably not the kind you have in mind."

"Pity."

"So, Inquisitor," Malithir said without bothering to look at Evir as the naked slave continued to dress him, "at whose behest have you traveled all the way from Kierden in secret to protect me?"

"Everything will be explained once we have ensured your safety, Lord

Overseer." Evir was grateful Malithir didn't ask any further questions. Evir preferred not having to delve into the cover story he had concocted, both of them knowing it was a lie. He and his soldiers waited silently at the entrance to the bedchamber until the lord overseer was finally dressed and turned toward them.

"This way," Evir gestured out of the room.

"No."

"I beg your pardon, Lord Overseer?"

"You have no idea what you've stepped in, Evir, but I'm taking command of this situation," Malithir said, slowly walking a few paces toward the inquisitor. "Soldiers, fall in behind me!" the lord overseer barked his command.

No one moved. Evir let the silence hang in the air for a moment to show Malithir he was in no position to be giving orders.

"What are you—"

"It would be best," Evir cut him off with a calm firmness, "if you remain silent until we reach our destination."

"You little prick! I'll have your stones for this!"

The ruse was gone, and the inquisitor had no patience left for the traitor. He dropped his voice and let some of his weeks of smoldering, pent-up anger bleed into his words. "You're welcome to try, Malithir. You'll need a new pair by the time I'm done with you."

"I answer only to the overlord! Take meeeccccggghh—" It sounded as though his words were lodged in his throat, choking him from inside. Malithir's face contorted in pain and he grabbed the sides of his head.

Evir's eyes darted from one face to another, looking for a hint one of them knew what was happening or who might be doing this to Malith. Everyone appeared as confused as he was. The lord overseer dropped to his knees, still choking.

"Can either of you help him?" Evir hurled the question at his two elantir.

They both shook their heads. "Met'elan can't counteract benefactions," Tannik-ulm replied.

Benefactions? Is someone dispositioning him? This was like no benefaction Evir had ever heard of. The fact he could not detect anything troubled him, but he shoved the vexing thought aside to focus on more pressing questions. Who was doing this, and why?

He quickly ruled out the two who had been with Malithir when he arrived. They had plenty of opportunity before now. It had to be one of Evir's soldiers, but he had no way of identifying which at the moment. Whoever it was, it was very unlikely they were acting on their own. The order had to come from someone outside. Tel-Kyron's warning to trust his instincts if anything seemed amiss sprang to mind again. This definitely qualified, but he could not see what was at play.

Malithir's choking subsided, but he remained on his knees, his head lolling unsteadily, his eyes unfocused. Evir wondered if he was just stunned or permanently disabled. Either way, he needed to keep moving.

"Get him on his feet," he ordered his soldiers. "And bind his hands." He was not going to risk leaving Malithir untied in case the effect ended and he suddenly regained his faculties. As his men crossed the room, he turned his attention to the slave and the marshal. Could he afford to let them live after what they had witnessed? "Sit," he commanded, gesturing toward the bed with his sword. The slave hurried to obey while the marshal's every movement was careful, deliberate.

"Qae'essin Mavin Tar will be expecting me at my duties by her side within the tide," she said, her voice impressively calm under the circumstances. Had he been too hasty in dismissing her as the hidden culprit? He still did not think so. Signs of stress were well hidden but present. "I do hope this won't cause any undue delay."

It was her best available move, highlighting her connection to the powerful figure to give Evir pause before doing anything to harm her. She probably didn't realize how little that factored into the inquisitor's consideration, but it provided him with an excuse to take the time to contemplate his next move. He didn't want to kill them, but it was the most expedient option and the one his soldiers were no doubt expecting. Despite the urgency to keep moving, he forced himself to stop and think the problem through.

As far as Evir could tell, besides himself, only Tel-Kyron and Arku knew about this operation. If Tel-Kyron had wanted to take out Malithir, he wouldn't have gone to the trouble of getting Evir a private audience with the overlord. Dread washed over Evir before the next thought fully crystallized in his head.

Arku was the only logical answer. But why?

The most plausible reason was to keep some secret buried. Evir suppressed the temptation to wonder what the secret might be. He could not afford to indulge his curiosity right now. The more pressing question was whether Arku intended to do the same to Evir. It was impossible to know, but the safest course was to assume so. That would likely mean silencing Dae'yen, Javinth, Kiavi, Vekk-oth, and Selvruen as well.

The thought made his blood run cold. Were plans already in motion?

Probably not yet. It would make more sense for Arku to take care of the loose ends once he had confirmation Evir and Malith were out of the way. His mind raced through a dozen possibilities, searching for any idea of how to prevent that from happening.

"Inquisitor, what are your orders?" one of the soldiers asked.

"We'll leave in a moment." Evir barely managed to say the words without snapping. He wished he could have a moment alone to think. *Alone is the last thing you want to be,* his inner voice told him. He imagined one of his soldiers waiting in the shadows to slide a blade across his throat when no one was watching. He needed to ensure someone was always watching. Arku's words echoed in his memory. *'That would require that you know who you can trust.'*

Evir suddenly felt desperately vulnerable. Part of him wished Javinth and the others were here to cover his back, but he was more grateful they were out of harm's way in Kierden. *At least for the moment,* he thought grimly. If it meant keeping them safe, he could accept dying alone.

You are not alone. You are a servant of the people. You are bound to them, and they to you through your service. You are worthy of their protection.

A profound sense of the truth of those words struck a chord in his heart, and his breath caught in his throat as he fought to control the wellspring of emotion that opened inside him. Gentle tears slid along the edges of his eyelashes. The voice of his years of discipline, of his awareness of others looking to him as inquisitor and operation commander, the voice usually so dominant in his mind, was muted to a near whisper by the surreal calm enveloping him. *What are you doing?* the diminished voice demanded. *You can't afford to show weakness now! Pull yourself together!*

He observed with transcendent curiosity the mundanity of those concerns. Even the danger he perceived with stark clarity lurking at the edge of his awareness no longer seemed nebulous and indiscernible. His mind could barely comprehend the state in which he found himself, but he recognized it as the same sublime sense of connection he felt several tides ago when Tel-Kyron first accepted him into his home.

He was almost certain it was the Holy Couple's divinessence.

Like a swarm of aftershocks following an earthquake, one implication after another shook the bedrock of his reality, each with a thousand fractures branching off beyond his ability to track them, threatening to overwhelm him, to sever him from his sense of himself. Only the unmistakable undercurrent of divine coherence kept him anchored to the concrete reality of this moment, standing in Malithir's bedchamber. Tempted as he was to set his mind to analyzing those implications, the exigencies of completing the mission and surviving the threat required his undivided attention.

He considered returning to Tel-Kyron. Perhaps the mavin tar could both protect him and find a way to reverse the effect on Malithir. He swept the thought aside. If that had been within the master elantir's power, there would have been no need for their current plan. Perhaps if he went to the full council... He rejected the idea before it had even fully formed. Those waters were every bit as treacherous as his current predicament.

The weight of uncomfortable silence and questioning eyes weighed on him, pushing him toward the ledge where there was no choice but to act. He looked at Malithir, the only person not awaiting his decision. The lord overseer stood staring slack-eyed at the ground before him, mouth hanging slightly open. *What kind of benefaction could do this?* The best person to answer that was the last person he wanted to see—Vetat Atan-akai.

Evir felt as if the stones were shifting beneath him.

He should not even be thinking the plan taking shape in his mind. The entire purpose of capturing the lord overseer in secret was to avoid any entanglement with the Church. Besides, the thought of being near Teraithia's mouthpiece on Baon while in the midst of his current predicament felt like a hot stone in his stomach.

However, the high priestess was also the last person Arku wanted involved. And this attack on Malithir did not fit the Church's modus operandi, so he was fairly certain they weren't an immediate threat. Still, bringing this matter to the Church was a huge gamble, not to mention a major breach of Door protocol and a direct violation of the overlord's explicit instructions. But if Arku had a knife waiting for Evir, this might be his best chance to survive and save Dae and the others. It also meant there was no need to kill the witnesses, and somehow the rightness of that outcome made the seismic activity inside suddenly subside.

Evir sheathed his sword. "Let's go," he ordered as he turned and headed toward the corridor.

"Inquisitor, the witnesses?"

"They're not our concern. Move out."

He didn't trust having anyone behind him and waited to ensure he was the last one out of the chamber. He fell in behind the two men guiding a compliant Malithir, who stumbled forward woodenly. Others were stooping to heft the lifeless bodies of their fellow soldiers onto their shoulders. Standard practice for a secret operation was to leave no bodies of your soldiers behind to be identified, but at this point, it didn't matter. Secrecy was a fading echo.

Evir's mind raced ahead, making adjustments to the original plan as they proceeded along the corridor, across the disturbing emptiness of the wide-open chamber, and finally back through the residence toward the slaves' entrance. He was relieved no one else was moving about halls. With any luck, his second unit had eliminated the rest of Malithir's guards, and the other members of the household were still asleep, or at least had the good sense to stay in their beds until he and his soldiers were gone.

The acrid smell of vomit and tzevvi vapors lingered in the air as they entered the last chamber, the slaves still huddling together against one wall, timid and sniffling. The soldiers guarding them looked at him with concern as a shambling Malithir was ushered in.

"Everything's fine," he assured them before they even asked. He saw their hands go to their weapons, no doubt intent on dispatching the last witnesses. "Leave them," he commanded. He could see their confusion, but his changes to their previous plans were just beginning. As his unit began hastily wiping blood off their armor and weapons to avoid attracting unwanted attention as much as possible, Evir continued.

"No one is to disperse," he said, looking around at the faces of his soldiers as he spoke. "Everyone will stay on me, irregular spread, five to ten paces. Allow no one within five paces of the cart, except you two who will steer," he said, pointing to his two requited operatives. He saw heads nodding acknowledgment of his new instructions. "Petaruun, you'll keep a sound ward on Malith, as planned. Tannik, you're next to me. Let's go."

His unit moved quickly out of the residence. He gave a final command to Malithir's slaves. "Spread the word—no one leaves the residence until a new headmaster comes. Do you understand?" Nodding heads was all the acknowledgment he needed before he turned and headed through the heavy curtains.

CHAPTER LX
EVIR

Evir stepped into the spacious corridor of the Crystal Flowers district, alert to any new danger. He caught himself scanning each direction for anyone who might see his men putting Malithir and the bodies of the dead soldiers in the cart, then reminded himself it didn't matter. The secrecy of his mission was over. Now he just hoped to survive the tide.

Some of his soldiers began walking along the wide corridor back the way they had come, while others pulled the tarp over the bodies in the cart. Malithir's eyes were open but still didn't seem to register what was happening. The inquisitor wondered if the clergy at the temple could reverse the lord overseer's condition. Even if they could, it didn't mean they would or that Evir would be allowed to question Malithir. Control over what to do with the traitor was about to slip out of his hands before he had the satisfaction of getting a single answer from the man. At this point, however, he would settle for getting out of this alive.

He followed a short distance behind the cart. Sooner or later, he would have to tell his soldiers to deviate from their course but decided it was best to wait until the last possible moment. He pretended to glance back along the corridor, but he was actually checking everyone's position for any sign of a threat. The soldiers behind him were spread in staggered shadowing escort positions, as he had ordered. Still, he had an itch between his shoulder blades, like some danger was lurking just out of sight, waiting to strike.

He turned his gaze forward again and lowered his voice so only Tannik could hear him. "How are your elan reserves? Do you have enough to shield me?"

"Against what?"

"I don't know exactly. Maybe something like what was done to the lord overseer."

"I can't block a benefaction."

"I know, but perhaps some similar form of elantic attack?"

"A generalized shield is very difficult. I could hold it for maybe a hundred paces."

Evir nodded. "Be ready. I'll tell you when." He had been analyzing the scene in the lord overseer's bedchamber, and his best guess was that the attack had come when Malithir threatened to deviate from their plan. If there was going to be a similar attack on him, Evir guessed it would most likely come when he did the same.

They made their way quickly to the slave tunnels leading out of the district. He was relieved the path ahead appeared to be mostly empty. Things had taken longer at Malithir's residence than he hoped, but there should still be time to reach the temple before the crowds began arriving to attend the Remembrance Day service. For those few others in the tunnels who happened to be in their way, his soldiers made sure they were moved aside against a tunnel wall or into an alcove until the cart passed.

Soon, they turned into the corridor to the South Spiral, one of the wide, ramped tunnels that ran like corkscrews from below the level of the floor of the Grand Chasm to above its ceiling. It took more than a tenth-tide to walk from top to bottom, but fortunately, Crystal Flowers was situated at the midway point. They entered the platform to the Spiral and began their descent. He glanced at the gate barring the opening to the conveyor, a mechanical carriage in the center of the Spiral that transported the elite members of society up and down the many levels of Stierve. He wished he could use it just this once to reach the temple more quickly, but that privilege was above his station.

Pillars spaced evenly along the center of the ramped tunnel divided it into two broad lanes, the descending side taking the outer one. The pillars made for potential ambush points, and Evir stepped closer to the wall to keep as much distance as possible from them. He cringed inwardly as his pauldron scraped against the stone.

Stay focused! he admonished himself.

He wished he could get himself back to the supernal calm and clarity that had enveloped him in the lord overseer's bedchamber under the influence of the Holy Couple's divinessence. Perhaps if he could do so again, it would shield him from the benefaction used to silence Malithir, or at least improve his focus. He tried to open himself to the divinessence the way he opened his elantic center, but nothing came. His mind retraced his steps in the scene back in the residence, straining to remember what had worked before, eager to replicate the experience, but still nothing came. He considered offering a prayer of supplication to Yonvaar and Kerail, but something in him resisted. That blaspheme was a step further than he was willing to go at the moment.

Instead, he focused on the decision points ahead. They had nearly descended to the level with the bridge spanning from the wall of the chasm to the temple. Taking that route would attract the priests' attention more quickly, but the breach of etiquette of using the high-ranking clergy's entrance risked giving offense and creating more obstacles to achieving his objectives. He decided to approach in the open, heading to the front steps of the temple. It might draw more public attention than he cared for, but he saw no better alternative.

Evir had traversed the Spiral enough times to know they were nearing the level of the Chasm floor. The soldiers in the lead should already be exiting the sloped tunnel and following the original route toward the military district at the west end of the Chasm. He called one of the soldiers behind him to come closer. A wave of anxiety washed over him as he realized this was the last moment to either continue with the original plan or change course, but he already knew there was no turning back. "Run ahead and tell Rievaka to follow her orders no matter what she sees me do."

The soldier saluted with his fist over his heart, a salute usually reserved for informal greetings between those of equal rank but was also used by the Door during operations, being more practical than many other salutes and keeping outsiders from identifying the command structure. As the man took off at a run, Evir reminded Tannik to be ready with his shielding elant. It was possible he was just being paranoid, but he was unwilling to take that risk.

The cart left the ramp and moved through the tunnel toward the open plaza surrounding the massive, gray-flecked granite pyramid dominating his field of view. He suppressed a curse at how many people he saw ahead, though he knew it was probably only a fraction of the crowds that would fill the area a tenth-tide from now as the inhabitants of Stierve dutifully made their way to the temple for the Remembrance Day service before exchanging work shifts for the next tide.

Uruth'atar, the Footstool of the Goddess, soared overhead as they left the tunnel and moved into the plaza, drawing his vision momentarily up toward the golden light radiating from Teraithia's Eye. He felt exposed and vulnerable under its unblinking gaze. The cart turned to the left toward his original destination in the military district, pulling his attention back to the demands of his mission. It was time.

"Do it now," he ordered Tannik. He felt the tingling pain of his elan being drawn but ignored it as he called out to the operatives with the cart. "Head for the temple steps." They glanced back at him with questioning looks, doubt written on their faces. He didn't blame them but gave a curt nod to affirm his directions. They immediately adjusted course and cut a diagonal path through the plaza.

Carts rarely left the Bloodline, which still technically hewed to the wall of the Chasm along the edge of the plaza. His breach of protocol immediately drew the attention of others in the area. A pair of kieresta moved to intercept the cart.

Evir quickened his pace to meet them first, pulling out his small slice of obsidian in the shape of a door. "Blessed Remembrance, Kieresta-atan," Evir said flatly, leaving all warmth out of the greeting but holding up his mark of office.

Their eyes narrowed in obvious recognition of his connection with the Door. "And to you. What's your business?" one of the warrior-priests asked, gesturing with his head toward the cart.

"I am Evir, Inquisitor of the Obsidian Door. I am acting under the orders of Arku Overlord in a serious matter that must be addressed immediately with Vetat Atan-akai." It was dangerous to claim his actions were at the direction of the overlord, but it was his best chance of having the matter raised to the atan-akai's attention.

"What's in the cart, Inquisitor?"

"A prisoner, and the bodies of my soldiers whose names are to be recorded in the registry of those remembered this day."

"Who's the prisoner?"

"That is precisely the matter I must bring to the atan-akai."

"You understand we must inspect the cart, Inquisitor."

"Of course." Evir surreptitiously stole a glance around the plaza as he turned and escorted the atan to the cart, scanning the area for any sign of a threat. He gave the subtle gesture for Petaruun to stop the sound warding elant, then carefully pulled back the tarp covering the bloody bodies and weapons. Both kieresta made the sign of Teraithia with overlayed fingers in a brief gesture of benediction over the deceased. Malithir still stared blankly at the lifeless face of the soldier lying next to him. Evir could not tell if the temple guards recognized the lord overseer, but his elaborate clothing certainly indicated his station.

"Come with us," the atan said in a low voice. Evir pulled the tarp over the bodies and followed the two knights who escorted the cart through the plaza, drawing more curious looks from the onlookers, who seemed to be moving in the same direction in greater numbers than before. He felt the draw on his elan suddenly stop and looked at Tannik-ulm, who gave a slight shake of his head. The elantic shield was gone, leaving him feeling even more vulnerable than before.

They rounded the corner of the temple and moved toward the wide granite steps ascending to the colonnaded front entrance jutting out from the center of the west face of the pyramid. One of the kieresta directed Evir to wait with the cart at the foot of one of the tall marble statues of Teraithia flanking the temple steps, this one depicting her as the creator goddess, her right arm outstretched to direct the flow of time, her left hand holding a white sphere representing Baon. He wondered how much she, or any of the gods, actually had a hand in influencing the affairs of the world. He hoped it was very little today.

The kieresta climbed the stairs and disappeared through one of the smaller entrances flanking the enormous main passageway, while the other remained with the inquisitor. Evir considered retrieving Malithir from the cart now, but there were too many eyes in the plaza watching. The wrong set of eyes could spell more trouble than he needed, so he decided to wait as long as possible. There was no sense in tempting the gods more than he already was.

The distant, echoing sound of clerics inside the assembly hall singing the Canticles of Remembrance drifted through the air with hauntingly beautiful harmonies. As Evir scanned the crowd, his eyes were drawn to the colosseum looming on the far side of the plaza. It felt like only a tide or two ago that he was there watching Akriel fighting in front of Arku Overlord, Vetat Atan-akai, and the rest of the empire, proving his worthiness to become... *what? A servant of the people, or their master?* Evir had always considered himself first and foremost a servant of his people and wondered if Akriel saw himself the same way. He suddenly realized his son might be coming to the temple for the Remembrance Day services and resumed searching the faces with a new purpose, though whether he hoped to see his son or not, he couldn't decide.

The numbers filling the plaza continued to increase as a steady stream of

Stierve's residents joined those waiting to be invited up the steps and into the temple for the service. Evir noticed the assembly's attention suddenly drawn toward the temple's entrance, and his head snapped in the same direction. It was still too early for the ceremony to begin. Over two dozen kieresta marched out of the tunnel and down the steps of the temple, fanning out as they descended. These did not carry the ess'at and v'kar like most of their counterparts but bore the two-handed greatswords of the atan-akai's guards, the Divinarim. It didn't take Evir's keen powers of deduction to guess the atan-akai's arrival was imminent. He had hoped to receive a private audience with the high priestess, not a public spectacle.

"Help me get the lord overseer on his feet," Evir said quickly to his soldiers. Now was his best opportunity to do so unnoticed while everyone's eyes were fixed on the temple entrance, waiting for the atan-akai to make her appearance. They positioned themselves to shield the cart's contents from public view as best they could and hauled a still-unresponsive Malithir to his feet. Evir tried to adjust the lord overseer's elaborate cloth wrappings that had become disheveled but stopped as an excited murmur ran through the crowd.

Vetat Atan-akai, arrayed in resplendent white vestments edged in gold, emerged from the gaping entrance. As one, the assembled people bowed low, arms outstretched to the sides, palms facing the high priestess. Evir put pressure on Malithir's shoulder to prompt him to bow, but the lord overseer remained erect, forcing Evir to do the same. He caught himself taking a small measure of satisfaction in that fact and quickly chastised himself for it. He could not afford even an ounce of defiance in the presence of the atan-akai, who had cupped her hands and was slowly sweeping them from one side of the plaza to the other, gesturing her acceptance of their proffered lives.

She ended her salutation facing Evir. It was difficult to tell at this distance, but he felt as though her eyes were resting on him alone. His heart clenched, fearing that she might take offense at his failed courtesy. He bowed his head in a sign of submission, the best he could manage while keeping ahold of Malithir. He was shocked when a pressure on his mind invited him to link in communion. He assumed it was Vetat, though he had never heard of anyone being able to manage the benefaction from so far away without a deep connection between the minds developed through years of dedicated practice.

A cold fear swept over him. He knew communion should not allow the high priestess to read his mind, his doubts and fears, his wavering devotion, but who could guess what powers might be at her disposal? He called upon every ounce of reverence he could muster, then accepted the link.

"Teraithia's blessing upon you this Remembrance Day, Evir, Inquisitor of

the Obsidian Door." The connection carried a faint distortion, metallic and echoey. He carefully steered his mind away from questioning whether it was due to the physical distance between them or his own distance from align-ment with Teraithia's divinessence.

"You honor me, Your Eminence."

"That remains to be seen." The onlookers began to turn their attention toward Evir, no doubt curious about what the atan-akai had her eyes fixed upon. Evir kept his breathing slow and steady, part of the discipline that helped him keep his growing anxiety out of the communion link. *"Who stands at your side? Is it the prisoner I was informed you brought to Uruth'atar this tide?"*

"It is, Your Eminence. Malithir, Lord Overseer of the Obsidian Door, is guilty of treason against the empire and the Church. He conspired with Artencu Vice Regent of Kierden to foment an insurrection, and provided the informa-tion used by the Dorothi rebels to violate the sanctity of Our Lady's holy temple and steal from her vaults an artifact of inestimable value."

"The Katharis Pool. Have you recovered it?"

"Unfortunately, no. I had hoped the lord overseer would be able to provide some insight into its whereabouts, but something has been done to him, some kind of benefaction perhaps. He appears incapable of speaking."

There was no immediate reply, though Evir could still feel the connection in his mind. He thought he detected a hint of caution before her next words came through. *"You are here under Arku Overlord's command?"*

Evir knew he had to tread very carefully here. *"The overlord is aware of my mission to capture the traitor, though the decision to bring Malithir to you was my own."* Evir wished he was closer, speaking with her directly. All his skills at reading people were utterly useless communicating like this, which was not helped by the growing restlessness he sensed in the crowd around him as the curious scene continued to play out, the atan-akai and the strangers with a cart staring silently at each other.

"So you went to Arku first." A hint of displeasure filtered through the link. *"And why have you come to me now?"*

"In a matter of this import, there were a great many considerations, Eminence. In full candor, I had intended to question Malithir in secret before finally bringing him to face your judgment, but his condition required adjust-ments to my plan."

"Perhaps this was Teraithia's way of setting your feet back upon the right-eous path."

"Then I welcome the correction." It was an easy lie.

"Teraithia is not always a tolerant goddess, but your transgressions were minor, and you have returned to the light. Your sins are forgiven. Bring the traitor to me now."

"Stay here," Evir ordered his soldiers, then pushed Malithir toward the steps. As the inquisitor feared, the lord overseer could not even raise his foot to climb the first step. Evir was going to have to drag him. Not exactly the picture of authority he had hoped to convey. He put Malithir's limp arm over his shoulders and was about to wrap his arm around his waist when two kieresta marched forward out of the crowd. Evir felt a wave of relief as he stepped out of the way and let them take hold of Malithir.

"They will follow you. Come stand with me."

Evir did as Vetat commanded. He could hear Malith's booted feet dragging on the marble steps behind him. He kept his pace measured, confident. Murmurs swept through the crowd as he passed between two Divinarim without challenge. He could guess the questions that were no doubt flying past their lips faster than the wind through the Whistling Caverns. He was certain they were very different from the ones whirling through his mind.

He reached the top landing and walked toward the atan-akai, resisting the urge to look out at the crowd again. Was Akriel out there, seeing his father approach Teraithia's mouthpiece on Baon? Imagining his son watching steeled Evir's nerves. He stopped in front of Vetat and this time gave the appropriate salute, bowing low. She held out her cupped hands, then told him to rise and gestured by her side. Without any apparent instructions, the two kieresta-atan deposited the lord overseer on his knees in front of the atan-akai, facing the crowd. As Evir moved to his designated position, Vetat's strong voice rang out over the gathered crowd, and their curious murmurs quickly died down to hear their high priestess as they pressed forward from the edges of the plaza to hear her better.

"My fellow disciples, you have come this tide to the Footstool of the Goddess to remember our great fallen heroes, who sacrificed all to bring about Teraithia's divine purposes in raising up the Kuldrith Empire as a beacon to this beleaguered world—to make us a guiding light, illuminating the path of her righteousness. Even now, our brave soldiers are spilling their blood to pave the way for Teraithia's law to burst forth as a voice from the stones on a new continent. Their names shall be added to the Registry of Remembrance, never to be forgotten!"

A roaring cheer went up from the crowd but quickly quieted again. This was the type of sermon they no doubt had expected to receive in the assembly hall, not out here in the grand plaza.

"This *should* be a day of great celebration. But alas, I am pained to my core by the knowledge of corruption and treason lurking in our midst. Too many stray from Teraithia's bosom, seeking as blind bloodrats after the stench of lesser gods, clawing after their own vain and treacherous desires. I know you see it, defacing our public spaces. I know you hear it, whispered in dark corners. I know you feel it, seducing you away from the divine path of our great destiny. Yes, Teraithia would set her chosen people as a beacon to the world. But a beacon's light must be pure, must burn clear and bright, free of corruption, that we may become the purging fire to cleanse the world and prepare it for the Queen of Heaven to make the whole of Baon her footstool.

"And do not succumb to the lie that it is only the weak-willed, those lesser souls, who stray from the path. In these final days of the struggle of divine wills, even the mighty shall fall if they do not cling with all their strength to the unwavering rod of Teraithia's power. Behold this man, Malithir, Lord Overseer of the Obsidian Door—"

Evir felt he was about to be thrown from a precipice, with no sight of the bottom. His breath caught in his throat; his heart pounded in his chest. All the ways this could go wrong swirled through his mind. *What's going to happen to me?*

"—once one of the mightiest warriors in Our Lady's holy cause, has forsaken his oaths, has betrayed his sacred trust, and turned against her people and her holy Church. His was the voice in the dark, whispering conspiracies of rebellion and insurrection in Kierden, and giving our enemies within the empire the means to violate the sanctity of Teraithia's holy temple. He was the cave viper in our midst that caused Teraithia to unleash her wrath to purge the corruption from our sister city."

Angry murmuring broke out among the assembly. Evir knew the purge was a topic fraught with anxiety, misinformation, and fear. It was a dangerous play to give the people a single scapegoat. Powerful, but only if they accepted it. Otherwise, it might leave them feeling deceived.

"But the will of the goddess cannot be undermined, even by a viper as brilliant and powerful and deadly as the lord overseer. Our Lady has raised up another of her most valiant sons, Evir, Inquisitor of the Obsidian Door, to root out this malignancy in the very heart of the empire. Evir Inquisitor, who has traveled the length and breadth of our lands to hunt down the enemies of the people; who led the effort in Kierden to stop the rebellion before it began; who followed the secret threads of this treason right into the seat of power, hunting his quarry and bringing the traitor at last to face Teraithia's justice before you all!"

Fierce cheering and shouts calling for justice and blood rang out from the crowd. Evir's mind reeled with the implications of his identity being thrust into the open like this. Could he ever work effectively for the Obsidian Door after this? At least he was no longer in immediate danger.

Don't be too sure, his inner voice warned as another thought forced its way to the center of his awareness. Why had the atan-akai believed him so readily, without a single shred of proof? More than that, she had proclaimed Evir a champion of the faithful in front of the whole city. A stone dropped in Evir's stomach as he realized he was caught in an entirely different game than he could have imagined.

It took Vetat several moments to quiet the assembly enough to continue. Her voice rose even more to reach the edges of the swelling crowd.

"The lord overseer will receive justice. But this cannot be, will not be, the end. Teraithia calls each of you to follow the shining example of Evir, a stalwart and indomitable servant of the people. You must root out the corruption wherever you find it: among your neighbors; within your trades; in your homes; even in your own souls. Only when we have purified ourselves will Teraithia truly hold us up as the light bearers to govern the world under her divine dominion!"

So many bodies now filled the grand plaza that the sudden roar of their cheering reverberated off the Chasm walls. Evir felt as though he had been thrown into the treacherous currents of the River Vangene running through the middle of the Grand Chasm below the plaza where the crowd stood cheering. He had no sense of where he was being carried or how he would get out of this. A commotion at the perimeter of the plaza near the Cardinal Line drew his attention.

Evir's heart sank. The hulking Than'katar, the overlord's guards, pushed their way through the crowd, clearing a path toward the steps of the temple. Like a ripple from a rock thrown into a pond, a wave of people dropping to one knee spread from where the overlord walked amid his guards. Evir wished he was anywhere else in the world. To make matters worse, an invitation to restore the communal link pressed upon his mind. He did not want to accept. *As if I have any choice*, Evir thought grimly as he accepted the link.

"Why is Arku here! Is this also part of your plan?"

"No, Your Eminence. The overlord never said anything of this to me. Of course, I was not expected to be here either."

The link was abruptly severed. He should have felt relieved, but it sent a chill down his spine. The Than'katar formed a protective ring at the base of the steps, facing the crowd, leaving Arku to ascend alone. The overlord's pace was regal, commanding, flawless. Only the two templars nearest the center of the steps took a knee as Arku approached, their heads bowed behind their great swords, then rose again when he had passed. Arku kept his eyes fixed on Vetat, never even glancing at the still-kneeling Malithir.

As the overlord reached the top step, Evir offered the highest order salute, as he had to the atan-akai. Arku and Vetat gave the formal salute between those of equal rank, right hands in a fist over their hearts, left hands held low, open palms forward. Evir imagined every punishment about to be pronounced upon him. The desire to do whatever was necessary to be restored to the overlord's good graces washed over him, though it somehow failed to penetrate his heart, like a stone under a waterfall.

Arku was the first to speak. "Blessed Remembrance Day, Vetat Atan-akai."

"Teraithia's choicest blessings upon you, Arku Overlord."

"Rise, Evir Inquisitor," Arku called out gently. "What a pleasant surprise to see you again so soon. And an honored guest of Her Reverence, no less." Evir didn't have the first idea what to say, so he remained silent. The overlord looked back to the high priestess. "That sounded like it was quite the stirring sermon, Reverence." Now that Evir was close enough to see Vetat's reactions, he thought he detected annoyance with Arku's use of *reverence* as an honorific. Evir had not heard it used before, so he had no clue as to what significance it might hold. "I wish I had been here for the whole of it."

"If you care to return for the next tide's service, I'm certain I can manage an even better one."

"I don't doubt it, though you may have to manage without Evir next time. He and I have a few things to discuss."

"His mission is to see justice done to Malithir Lord Overseer, and I intend to ensure he sees it through to its conclusion."

Arku suddenly took a step toward Evir and pulled him into a firm embrace, kissing him heavily on the cheek. Evir nearly recoiled from the unexpected gesture, stopping himself just in time.

"Well played, Evir," the overlord whispered before pulling back, a broad smile spreading across his face. Evir almost felt relief, but something told him to look deeper. There was no true warmth behind that smile. Arku turned toward the crowd and slid his arm around Evir's shoulders, pulling him forward to his side. And leaving the atan-akai behind. The inquisitor felt Arku draw in a slow, deep breath, then raise his beautiful tenor voice to reach the edges of the gathered throng. The volume was astounding, hurting Evir's ears.

"Vetat Atan-akai spoke truly of the valor, fortitude, and loyalty of this man. He has given his life in service to this people, and today it is my profound privilege to bestow upon him the highest honor within my power to give. ATTENTION ALL PRESENT! Under my hand, this tide, I present to you the new lord overseer of the Obsidian Door, Evir, Mavin Tar!"

CHAPTER LXI

ANDRIC

"My lord, I don't see any other option," Min said, his voice low and measured. Small, sparse snowflakes drifted chaotically on eddies of a breeze, stirring Andric's wavy hair at the edges of his face, tickling his windburned skin. It was the middle of summer, for Akraharr's sake! How could it be snowing? It was one more sign the world was conspiring against him. But it was nothing compared to the cruel reality he was forced to face as he stared into the abyss that had once been the narrow stone road cut into the steep mountainside.

Andric knew Min was right, but his mind refused to give up trying to figure out some other option. He just could not bear the thought of abandoning his mounts here in the mountains, especially Kobo. Memories of training the warhorse with Mistress Teer in the royal stableyard flooded his thoughts. This was no way for his noble companion to end his life.

Maybe he could convince one of the Vanassi guides to ride him back to Sunapra and give it to Lanceman Tamon or one of the other soldiers he had left behind. But how would that look, a Vanassi scout returning alone with the prince's horse? Besides, they weren't out of the mountains yet and needed the guides to get them through to Remalia. Maybe he could send one of his scouts instead. There were no good options.

"Your Highness?" Min prodded.

Andric cursed under his breath. "Fine!" His heart ached, knowing he had just sentenced Kobo and the other horses to almost certain death. "We have to give the horses a chance. Get them turned around so they can head back down the road." Min nodded and began issuing orders to unpack the horses and prepare to continue the journey on foot.

Andric made his way to where Kobo stood with a quilted blanket over his back. The prince put his forehead on the bridge of Kobo's nose, the steam of their breath mixing in the frigid mountain air. "You're going to make it. It's only three days back to the Cannessi village. You keep moving."

"My lord," Jase interrupted him, "should I leave your plate or try to carry it?"

Andric wanted to castigate his squire for asking a stupid question but caught himself as he realized it was not an easy answer. They still had to get across the gap in the road and then up over the pass, and the extra weight was going to be punishing to carry. He might have to make the rest of the journey with only the gambeson the guides had procured in Sunapra to protect them as much from the cold as from attacks. It was not as high quality as heavy Remalian gambeson, but it had proved serviceable enough for this leg of the journey.

He glanced around to see what Nophet and others were doing. Food and water were the top priority. Bedrolls and weapons were essential. Everything else seemed a luxury at this point. Still, his armor alone was worth a small fortune, not to mention Kobo's value. *Such a waste.*

"Just do the best you can, Jase. Pack me a bag to carry if you have to." The thought of carrying his own gear like a common soldier galled Andric, but it might mean the difference between life and death until they got through the mountains. He cursed Lieutenant Garreth for disappearing in Sunapra. *I hope the Kushaani got you*, he thought vindictively. Andric's hand slowly slid down the bridge of Kobo's nose and lingered on his muzzle for a moment before the prince pulled himself away.

"How do we get across?" Andric snapped at no one in particular.

"There are already iron anchors for ropes driven into the walls and holes in the rock like at Balinth's Fortress," Min responded, pointing along the rock face leading several spans to where the road resumed. "It seems the Kuldrith have passed this way before."

"I'd rather hang from Akraharr's sack than anything left by those Kuldrith," Teek said as he tied a rope to the first anchor while the other scout tied another rope into a harness around herself. She was going to be the first to traverse the gap. Andric's stomach dropped as he looked into the chasm they would all have to cross. He turned away and busied himself with having Jase help him strap his gear on.

By the time he returned to the ledge where the road ended, half of their party was already across to the other side. Intercessor Henden was inching her way across ropes tied to the anchors. She was visibly shaking, but kept moving as Mar and others encouraged her along. Andric looked around for Barak and saw him crouched against the mountain wall several paces away. A pang of guilt hit the prince as he realized he hadn't checked on his friend.

"Do you have everything you need?" Andric asked as he approached. Barak almost imperceptibly shook his head but otherwise didn't respond. Andric crouched as well and lowered his voice. "You okay?"

Barak looked into the prince's eyes for a long moment before answering. "I can't do it."

"Yes you can. We'll help you get across." Barak shook his head and slowly rocked himself. "I'll carry you on my back if I have to."

"We're going to die."

"Half are already across, and no one has died." Andric stood and offered his hand. Barak stared out into the swirling snow, unmoving. "Well, if you're going to stay, can you make sure Kobo gets back to Sunapra? I was going to have one of the Vanassi do it, but as long as you're..."

Barak scowled up at the prince and took his hand. Andric hauled him to his feet and patted him on the shoulder reassuringly as they walked back to join the others. "We're going next," Andric told Min as they approached. There was no sense in giving Barak more time to fret.

"Who's first?" Teek asked.

"We're going together."

"Um, I'm not sure that's a good idea, Yer Highness. We should keep the weight as light as possible. Plus, yer likely to bounce 'im—"

"Just get us roped," Andric snapped. The gruff scout gave a curt nod, then got to work trying the rope around their chests. The rope was uncomfortably snug, but he had enough padding from the gambeson to keep it from hurting.

"If you fall, keep your arms pinned down at your sides. Don't try to hold on to the rope." Teek instructed. Barak started backing away, but Andric corralled him toward the ledge. He found that helping Barak was calming his own nerves. It took some coaxing, but Barak finally made it onto the thin ledge, which was all that remained of the road. With his short stature, he could not reach the fist-size holes in the rock wall, but he managed to keep one hand stretched up to grasp the anchored rope as he slowly slid the other from one handhold to the next. Andric could feel Barak trembling. He gently urged him forward along the ledge, inch by inch, until finally they reached the other side.

"See, that wasn't so bad," Andric said, slapping Barak's shoulder playfully as the Cannessi moved a safe distance from the gap before collapsing against the mountain wall. The prince began checking faces to ensure everyone was accounted for. It had become an unconscious habit over the past few days. Two were missing: the other scout and one of the Vanassi guides. They were probably having a look ahead, but his anxiety began to build, not knowing for sure.

"Where are Stenner and Praq?" he asked Divinar Staneff.

"Scouting ahead, Your Highness." Andric nodded and walked up the road a bit to have a look for himself. He could not tell if the falling snow was getting heavier or only looked that way across the distance to the mountains on the other side of the gorge and up ahead. Either way, it was not a promising sign. The guides had assured him they would reach the ruins of the ancient Cannessi stronghold of Elginfir within a few hours. If the snow turned into a blizzard, they might have to shelter there until it passed.

It felt like an eon before the rest were across the gap. They made the final adjustments until everyone was ready to continue. Andric cast a last bitter glance back toward where Kobo and the other mounts had disappeared, then snapped his head away and started the climb toward the pass between two peaks. Andric was dismayed at how quickly he found himself panting. The journey on the horses had felt painfully slow, but this was worse. None of them were conditioned for physical exertion in the thin mountain air, and their plodding pace reflected it.

He adjusted the strap over his shoulder, looking for a comfortable position for the weight of the gear Jase had packed for him, but nothing helped much. *One foot in front of the other*, he told himself. Time disappeared as the world became a blur of white except for the dark blue of Knight Commander Nophet's cloak directly ahead of him.

The path began switching back and forth as it climbed toward the pass several hundred feet above them. Andric turned to Barak. "How are you holding up?"

"You should have... left me... with the horses," Barak said between heavy breaths.

"Not much further. You're doing great." Andric took a sip of water and handed his waterskin to Barak. His friend shook his head, but Andric insisted. "You have to drink or you'll get sick." Barak took a swig of the water and then handed the waterskin back with a nod of appreciation.

On and on they climbed. As much as Andric wanted to push harder to get over the pass as soon as possible, he was already worried they were over-taxing the slower members of the delegation. *At least the snow isn't getting any worse.*

The switchbacks stopped and the road resumed a straight course as they climbed the last leg toward the top. Upon reaching the pass, the swirling wind became stronger and found its way through every gap in his clothing, chilling the sweat on his skin. He pulled his fur-lined cloak tighter, trying to keep the wind out as best he could. Ahead, he spotted Stenner and Praq waiting in a nook at the base of a stone outcropping that looked like the remnant of what once might have been part of a huge archway. Andric looked forward to taking a small rest, though he would have preferred to push on and find a spot with more protection from the weather.

"We made it," he said to Barak with a pat on the shoulder.

"Keep your voices down," Min cautioned over his shoulder.

Andric's gloved hand jumped to the hilt of his sword, his senses suddenly alert as the order was repeated back along the line. "What is it?" he asked as he scanned for danger.

"I don't know, but Stenner signaled for us to remain quiet."

Anxiety chilled Andric more than the cold did as they made their way forward, heads swiveling to search the rocky slopes on either side. If there was any immediate threat, Stenner would have let them know, but he still hated being so exposed on the road. Soon, they reached the scout's position and huddled against the rock wall.

"Report," Min ordered.

"The ruins are just beyond the pass, like Praq and Daruv said," the corporal answered, accompanied by head nodding from their Vanassi guides. "But there are Kuldrith down there." Several curses were uttered, including from Andric.

"How many?" Min and Nophet asked together.

"Hard to say for sure. We think there are ten that appear to be rotating guard positions, but they ain't all out in the open at the same time. And there's a statue in the middle of the ruins, biggest I ever seen. We saw two that went into a doorway or tunnel 'tween its legs then came back out, though it was hard to say if they was the same ones or not. Could be there are more inside."

"A statue of what?" Barak asked before anyone else could get their next questions out.

"Couldn't tell for sure. Some kind of person maybe, holding a weapon of some kind, I think." Praq nodded his agreement. "It's real old, and not much detail left to tell what it was supposed to be."

"And the doorway, does it lead into some kind of building?" Andric asked.

"Underground," Daruv answered. "The buildings on the surface was just for tradin' with surfacers and whatnot. The tunnel 'neath the statue leads down into Elginfir."

"Is there any way around that they won't see us?" Min asked.

Corporal Stenner shook her head slowly. "No, sir. Not unless we want to climb over these mountains."

Min turned to Andric. "We should wait until nightfall. Move in smaller groups. It will take longer, but it will give us a better chance of slipping by undetected."

"Not against Kuldrith," Sir Mar said from behind the prince. "Most of them spend most of their lives underground. They see better in the dark than we do."

"What, then? Another fight?" Min asked, his voice conveying the same concerns troubling Andric. None of them wanted to risk another battle, especially the prince. He had lost so many already. Even with ten, the Remalians barely outnumbered them. True, they were some of the most elite warriors in Remalia, but there was also no way to be sure how many more Kuldrith might be in the area. There had been twenty in the group they fought a few days ago. It was hard to believe there would be fewer this time.

"Do we have any choice?" the Sharinic knight asked rhetorically. They all knew he was right. Anger flared in Andric's chest at being forced to put more lives in danger.

"We need to kill them all," Nophet said, his voice cold steel. "We cannot afford to leave any alive to come after us, possibly with greater numbers."

"Agreed," Andric said, trying to match his tone to Nophet's. "But I can't devise a strategy without seeing the battlefield."

"There's only one strategy in this case," Sir Mar countered. "If there are more soldiers than the ones the scout reported, they will be underground. Our only option is to get to that doorway first and cut them off, keep them from warning the others."

Andric knew the knight was right and was ashamed he hadn't thought of it himself. Jase handed Andric some leftover bread from breakfast, a bit of hard cheese, and cured fish. "Ugh, you know I don't like the fish. Do we have any cured mutton or something?"

"I have one quarter that is still sealed. I thought it best to finish our opened supplies before they spoil, but if Your Highness prefers—"

"No, it's fine," Andric said, realizing he must seem the spoiled prince. "You're right. We need to be smart. Thank you."

Jase nodded, then he and the Vanassi guides handed out food to the others. Silence, heavy with dreadful anticipation, enveloped the company more tightly than their cloaks held close against the gusting wind. It hung like a weight around Andric's neck, keeping him rooted to his spot as others began preparing to move.

He forced himself to reach up and accept Nophet's proffered hand. The knight commander hauled the prince to his feet, then Andric turned and offered the same to Barak. Captain Major Min and the two scouts walked among the group, adjusting gear to avoid errant sounds, while those who had them ensured their weapons were ready. When everything was in order, Min and Stenner led them through the pass.

The road wound its way between the steep mountainsides on each side. They passed beneath another archway, this one intact, spanning the space between the rocky cliffs. As they approached a third arch, Min motioned them off the road. They hugged the snowy rock wall as they crept toward the ridgeline. From the shadow of the final archway, they looked down onto the ruins of Elginfir.

Andric's eyes were immediately drawn to the weathered statue rising from the ruins in the middle of the wide bowl. He agreed with Stetter's assessment; whatever the statue had once represented was lost to the ravages of weather and time. The outlines of several buildings were discernible, though most of them had collapsed into piles of rubble. In a few places, it looked as though some of the structures had been partially repaired. Perhaps they were being used as guard posts?

It only took a moment before Min pointed to one such location, but the movement of two gray figures had already drawn Andric's attention to the same spot, confirming his suspicions were correct. The guards walked through the ruins to another partially repaired building and went inside. A few moments passed before they came out again, though Andric thought there was more of a difference in height than before. Maybe they weren't the same ones. It was hard to tell from here, especially through the falling snow, even if it was relatively light.

Min pulled out his spyglass and watched as they went to the next guard post. Inside, wait a few moments, then back out. They watched until the last pair left their post and disappeared into the tunnel beneath the colossal statue. Soon, two more guards came out and walked to one of the guard posts, and the rotation began again.

"They're all different," Min said with a hushed voice. "So at least ten out in the guard posts at a time, with more inside."

"Maybe ten in and ten out," Andric suggested. "Twenty, like the other patrol."

"Could be," Min said noncommittally. "That's the best case. If not..." Min didn't need to finish the thought. Andric knew what it meant if there were more. "At least we have one thing going for us. Do you see it?" Andric thought about it for a moment but had to admit he didn't see anything that would give them an advantage. Min was a teacher by nature, so Andric did not feel belittled by the question as he shook his head. "We've got to make it down the slope and reach the statue before they do. Think about their rotation."

Andric visualized their attack, rushing to reach the tunnel as fast as possible. The Kuldrith would see them in no time. What did their rotation have to do with anything? A pair of guards left one of the posts and walked through part of the ruins to the next. Suddenly, the answer dawned on him. "They're rotating away from us. Only two positions will see us initially if we time it right." Min nodded his head. "But that will only buy us a couple of minutes."

"It's not a lot, I'll grant you," Min agreed. "But it might be enough to tip the scales in our favor."

"Ok, we go when the guards leave the second position, right?" Andric was seeing it now.

"Exactly."

"All together or separate groups?" Andric asked.

Min looked up, and Andric followed his gaze. The gray clouds filling the sky above them were lighter than down in the hazy shadow of the mountains. "We're running out of daylight. There's no time to take a second position. We have to move as soon as the next rotation starts."

Andric nodded, and they spread the word to the rest of the group. Jase handed Andric his shield, the only additional armor his squire had brought. "It looks like your training will finally be put to the test. Do well today, and I'll see that you are knighted when we get home."

"I won't let you down, my lord," Jase said as he tightened his grip on the hilt of Divinar Jessol's sword. Knight Commander Nophet had given it to the squire with a charge to use it in defense of the prince as its previous owner had done.

Andric patted his cousin on the shoulder, then turned to Barak. "If for some reason we get separated, you get to that statue, and I'll find you there. You'll be fine, I promise."

"Is it too late to take you up on that sword training you were always trying to push on me?"

"Not at all. Lesson one," Andric said with feigned seriousness as he drew his sword, "pointy end *toward* your opponent."

"I feel better already."

"We'll have you ready for next year's Charge Days tourney in no time." Andric smiled, hoping to ease Barak's anxiety, but there was no real amusement behind it. Mentioning Charge Days brought back the bitter memory of the Kushaani assassination attempt only a few months ago. He moved his arm to test his wounded shoulder.

The sound of someone vomiting grabbed Andric's attention, worried the noise this close to the ruins might give them away. Shiralla was bent over, one hand pressed against the stone wall to steady herself as she emptied her stomach, though more quietly. Sir Mar rested a comforting hand on her back until the retching stopped.

Min returned to his position by the arch, overlooking the road down to the ruins. There was no indication the guards had heard anything as they continued their rotations. Andric's heart pounded as the tension built, waiting for the right set of guards to walk the route to the next position. As soon as they ducked inside the stacked-stone shelter, Min nodded and rushed forward over the lip of the bowl and down the slope toward the road.

Min held up a fist and everyone froze in place as the next set of guards came out of the shelter. As soon as they turned to continue their route to the next building, Min signaled for the Remalians to resume their hurried descent. Hold... move... hold... move. They were nearly at the base of the bowl when two guards came rushing out of their post, whistling a high-pitched alarm that echoed off the mountain walls.

"Go!" Min shouted as he sped forward.

Andric was torn. *Follow Min or stay with Barak?* His hesitation lasted only a moment. If they didn't get to the statue before the guards, they might not leave Elginfir alive. A pang of guilt gripped him as he rushed after the captain major, who was already pulling away. Other whistles and shouts sounded from various locations around them, driving Andric to sprint as fast as he could.

The road cut a straight course through the ruins. Toppled gray columns and smaller statues, now covered with lichen and a dusting of snow, lined the wide avenue. Divinar Stetter passed Andric and was gaining on Min. Andric wished he could run that fast, but he focused on keeping his sword and knapsack from flying around uncontrollably. Angry shouts nearby told him the

Kuldrith were close. He glanced to the sides to ensure he was not running into an ambush or about to be shot.

The first clash of metal rang out behind him, followed by a scream and another clash. He wanted to turn and look, but Min and Stetter were bounding up a handful of steps leading to the open plaza in front of the towering statue. Two guards entered the area from the other side. They stopped and nocked arrows. Stetter hardly slowed as he took the lead and raised his shield as the arrows flew. The first went high, but a solid thud told him the second hit the shield.

The two men rushed across the open space toward the enemy. The first guard nocked another arrow while the second dropped his bow and drew his sword. Andric bounded up the steps. Two more guards were running through the maze of the ruins and would arrive at the plaza in seconds. Min and Stetter could handle their two guards. Andric headed to block the entrance to the tunnel at the base of the statue.

An arrow flew from the ruins beyond the plaza, but it sailed harmlessly behind him, clattering off the stones to his right. Min's opponent dropped first, the other soldier fighting desperately for his life. Andric looked into the dark tunnel, relieved to not see any enemies yet. He listened intently for any indication of more guards approaching and was relieved to hear nothing.

He scanned the perimeter for more guards. Two stood with bows at the edge of the plaza, aiming toward Andric. He jumped against the tunnel wall, shield raised, but it was unnecessary. The guards turned and fired at Nophet and Geon as the two Divinarim ran toward them, Jase only a few steps behind. Andric started to run out to help them, but something pulled his attention back to the tunnel.

Had he heard something? He could not afford to allow the Kuldrith to surprise them from that direction. The sound of swords and shields clashing in the plaza echoed in the tunnel, making it difficult to hear anything else. Elaborately carved images along the tunnel walls had withstood the weather better than the statue that rose high overhead. Several paces down the sloping stone floor, two heavy stone doors stood ajar.

There didn't seem to be any sound coming from that direction, but something was there, hovering at the edge of his consciousness. He strained his senses to penetrate the darkness. It was not in the tunnel. *What is that?* The question was like a faint buzzing in the corner of his mind. He shook his head and turned his focus back to the situation in front of him. His people were finally reaching the plaza, winded but safe. *Praq, Daruv, Shiralla, Stenner, Barak.*

"Where are Mar and the lancers?" Andric shouted when he realized they weren't together.

"Fighting the guards behind us," Shiralla panted. "He told us to keep going."

A third pair of guards rushed into the courtyard. Min and Stetter leaped forward, but the Kuldrith managed to loose their arrows first. *Their angle is off,* Andric thought with relief. Divinar Geon stumbled forward as both arrows sank into his back. "No!" a scream erupted from Andric.

"We should keep going, Prince," Daruv urged, his voice thick with fear.

"Not yet," Andric snapped. Keeping them together and out of harm's way was the best help he could give right now. The faint vibrations, like an itch in his thoughts, crept back into his awareness. It felt almost familiar, like he should recognize it—or more like he was being recognized. Suddenly, the unmistakable sound of shouts and heavy footsteps rolled out of the tunnel.

"Move over there!" Andric ordered, pointing with his sword to the side of the statue's foot. They all ran. He kept his eyes on the tunnel and took a protective position in front of the others as they crouched behind the giant stone foot. Geon stumbled toward the prince while Nophet's sword struck punishingly against the hopelessly outmatched guard's defenses.

The first Kuldrith soldiers poured out of the tunnel. *Two, five, six, nine... more.* Andric's heart sank. *Too many.* Arrows flew into the Kuldrith, creating an opening for Stetter to grab Geon and move toward the prince while Min protected their flank. Sir Mar charged from the other side of the Kuldrith formation while the four lancers and last scout continued firing arrows. *He's going to get himself killed,* Andric thought with dismay.

Three soldiers converged on Andric. The one in the middle was massive and reminded him of Sir Vanth. *The Bear.* He had only won by dumb luck. This warrior carried a bizarre, unwieldy half-shield and a heavy mace that, unfortunately, looked all too wieldy in the giant's enormous hand. *I'm dead.*

Suddenly Jase was at his side, blood dripping from his blade. Andric was proud of his squire, but now was not the time for praise. The brute roared as he lunged forward, bringing the weapon down toward Jase's head. Jase dodged back, and the mace swung just short of hitting his shoulder.

Andric thrust with his sword, but the other Kuldrith knocked his blade down with her sword. Andric brought his shield around in time to catch her lightning-fast riposte. He thrust again, this time over the top of his shield, toward her face. The knapsack on his back hampered his reach, and she ducked and slid to the left. Her eyes suddenly went wide as Divinar Stetter's halberd tip sank into her chest, driving her back.

Out of the corner of his eye, he thought he caught a flash of white fletching as an arrow hissed past him. Anger burned hot at the memory of Emerly choking on her own blood with a white-fletched arrow through her throat. The Black Bear pulled the mace back, preparing for a powerful swipe. Jase was struggling against the third soldier, and his flank was exposed. He would be crushed.

Without thinking, Andric charged the hulking warrior and smashed into him with his shield. Searing pain shot through Andric's shoulder, and he stumbled to the side. The man staggered back a single step, then rounded on the prince. *He's not a bear; he's a brick wall!*

Andric backed away, shield raised, trying to draw the man away from Jase and toward Stetter, who faced two more soldiers. *Will they ever stop coming?*

The soldier aimed a bruising strike at Andric, but the prince easily deflected it with his shield. Suddenly, the Kuldrith swiped with the edge of his angled shield, taking Andric by surprise. The prince reflexively threw up a block with his sword and caught the edge of the shield. He was confused by the ringing of steel on steel as a blade fixed to the edge of the shield batted his sword aside. The soldier drove the point of his shield toward Andric's exposed face.

The prince pivoted and tried to deflect the strike with his own shield but slipped on a patch of blood and snow and went down hard. Fearing the Kuldrith would drop a crushing blow on him, Andric tried to roll away, but his knapsack stopped him. A heavy-booted foot stomped on his shield arm, pinning him face-down against the freezing earth. Desperately, he tried to yank his arm free, but the straps held him fast.

The soldier raised the mace over his head for a devastating final blow. Andric's eyes caught sight of Barak and saw his own fear reflected in his friend's face. The Kuldrith grunted and Andric braced for the killing blow. Instead, hot, coppery-smelling liquid splashed down on his face. He felt the pressure on his shield lessen and lifted with all his strength. The behemoth fell to the ground, blood pumping from a hole beneath his armpit.

Andric felt a hand grasp him by the arm and haul him to his feet. Sir Mar? How had he gotten here? He had been on the other side of the plaza. Andric was amazed as he looked back and saw a trail of blood and bodies behind the holy knight.

"Are you all right?" Mar asked.

"Yes, thanks to you. I was sure I was dead." The sound of the last fighting pulled Andric's attention in time to see Nophet cut the leg out from under the last soldier standing, then drive his sword into her chest, pinning her against the ground until she stopped moving.

"We're not out of this yet. More will be coming."

"We should leave now, while we have the chance," Min urged.

"They'll be after us any minute," Mar countered.

Jase limped closer and Andric looked around to take stock of their situation as the captain major replied, "We have no idea how many there are. We can't keep this up forever."

Divinar Geon was unmoving, Jase was injured, and one of the lancers was nowhere to be seen. If they stayed, more would die. If the Kuldrith came after them with a larger force, they might all die. They were trapped. If only there was—

"The doors!" Andric exclaimed, not bothering to explain. "Everyone with me," he ordered as he ran toward the tunnel. Muttered curses accompanied the footsteps following behind. He rushed into the tunnel and pointed ahead. "Get those doors closed!"

They hurried down the stone passageway and divided into two groups. Andric grabbed one of the massive doors and started pushing. He put his back against the tunnel wall and heaved while Nophet and Lanceman Chossil pulled. A short, deep grating sound echoed in the tunnel as the door moved a hair's breadth.

"It's not budging," Min grunted from the other door.

"Andric, you'll never get the doors closed this way," Barak said. "Reduce the friction between the stone where the doors are stuck."

"Akraharr's dark hole, Barak. I'm not a stone smith! I don't have any idea how to do that."

"Can you help us push the doors?" Min asked.

"It would take so much elan... more than I have."

"Can you use mine?"

"Have you ever let anyone siphon your elan?" Andric asked, almost certain of the answer.

"No, but—"

"It's almost impossible without training. It won't work."

"Use mine," Nophet interjected.

"It didn't go so well last time," Andric said, his voice thin with the bitterness of that memory. *I can't save us.*

"Do we have any other choice?" the knight commander asked.

"I'm sick of people saying that! Why is it always up to me?"

"We do what is within our power to do," Sir Mar said. "You have been given more power than most in this world, so more often it will be up to you."

It didn't seem fair. He saw the truth but hated it. He simply nodded, not trusting himself to control his temper. He needed to attune himself to Teraithia's divinessence again, and anger was as likely to push him away from the goddess as toward her. Sharin Dara's divinessence still radiated from Mar, but he felt it slip away from the center of his awareness. He closed his eyes and tried to recite his favorite Teraithian verse, but Mar's words kept intruding. *You have been given more power than most in this world... more power than most.*

Yes, he had more power than most. As a prince, as an elantir, as one gifted with rare talents, power was his birthright.

To what end?

Andric thought about what he wanted more than anything else. The answer was simple. *To save my people.*

To what end?

For Teraithia's glory. Even before the words were fully formed in his thoughts, he knew they were a lie. That had been Warden Commander Sammet's answer. It would never be his.

Then you are lost.

And why should I ever listen to you? What do you offer besides death?

Divinessence flooded into Andric in a torrent—exulting, wrathful, glorious. His mind tossed on an endless sea of burning light, threatening to swallow him in the abyss of eternity. A thought that was a voice that was fire filled every corner of the vastness with a roaring whisper. *You have no idea yet what true power is. Take my hand, and I will show you.*

Far away, Andric heard a desperate cry of alarm. *"Kuldrith!"* He tried to open his eyes but could not locate them.

You do not need your eyes to see.

Suddenly, the surrounding scene unfolded in his mind. The floor and walls immediately around Andric were scorched black. Vikkin stared at him in wonder. Fear and awe were written on Kael's face. Shiralla held her hand up, shielding her eyes from the light that shone from him. Reynan had fallen to the ground, her hands and face charred and blistered. He didn't remember knowing Corporal Stenner's given name. Teek said it two nights before they reached Tapeti, trying to convince her to sleep with him. The Kuldrith fell to the earth and a shroud of darkness covered them. A soldier in the last rank trembled, sweat beading on her brow. Praq and Daruv ran toward the tunnel opening. A tear rolled down Barak's cheek.

I will have victory. Reap the tempest.

Lathon stepped into the circle of Andric's burning light and grasped him by the shoulders. A crushing jolt of energy drove the air from Andric's lungs and the world collapsed to a tunnel of darkness.

"Do not touch him!" Nophet commanded.

"Breathe," Sir Mar told Andric, ignoring the Divinar commander. His chest burned and panic gripped him. "Breathe."

Andric feared he would never feel air in his lungs again. Suddenly, his body remembered its first function, and he sucked in a gasping breath. He leaned against the stone door, coughing and gasping. Andric looked past the doors into the darkness, his head swimming. "Where are the Kuldrith?" he rasped.

"Up Akraharr's arse," Teek answered behind him through clenched teeth. Andric turned to where the scout knelt next to an unmoving Reynan, her skin charred and blistered. Nausea gripped his aching stomach.

"What happened to her?"

"What do you mean, 'What happened to her?'" Teek screamed at him. "You killed her, you damn demon!"

Andric looked down and saw a circle of blackened stone around his feet. Nophet stepped toward the scout menacingly.

"Kuldrith!" Divinar Stetter yelled as he ripped his sword from its scabbard. Nophet and Min drew their swords and jumped to positions on either side of the Divinar.

"Everyone out!" Mar barked, half-supporting, half-dragging Andric along the tunnel.

"Wait, I can still close the doors," Andric said weakly. He strained to look over his shoulder for Nophet. Beyond his men, Andric could see the Kuldrith were rushing up the tunnel, nearly to the doors. He opened his center and sent a stream of elan toward the Teraithian knight. *Kosek*, Andric willed into the elan, and it obeyed, dancing, alive. Pain pulsed from his chest throughout his body. No, that was his blood. Or was it both? Or was it outside of him, calling to him, deep beneath his feet? His elan writhed against an unseen force at the edge of Nophet's skin.

He was afraid to reach for Teraithia's divinessence while this close to Sir Mar, but he had no choice. *I will have victory,* he recited and felt it resonate in his core. The goddess's divine essence filled him, though nothing like before. It had to be enough.

The twang of bow strings was immediately followed by clashes of steel on steel. There was no time left. He infused the vibrating thread of elan with

Teraithia's power, willing it to connect the barrier protecting Nophet's life essence. *Open*, he issued the dispositioning command, as Stetter had shown him. The barrier vibrated in harmony with the divinessence flowing through him and bowed before his will.

They reached the mouth of the tunnel. "Stop! Hold them here!" he commanded. Mar scowled but released Andric into Shiralla's arms, then turned to join the others fighting the Kuldrith. Andric pulled on Nophet's elan, but it was like pulling a horse that didn't want to move. The knight would never be able to cooperate while he fought. "I need Nophet... here," he said as he leaned heavily against Shiralla. Pain and exhaustion threatened to overwhelm him. Trying to speak while maintaining his concentration on the met'elan and dispositioning was almost more than he could manage.

"Lord Nophet, the prince needs you!" Shiralla called out.

The knight pulled his sword from his opponent's chest and backed toward the prince. "We can't hold this many!" Nophet shouted.

"You have... to relax," Andric said. His elan wavered as he spoke, and the pain pulsed more intensely. He sank deeper into his center and calmed the void. A trickle of elan flowed back along the channel of Andric's elan. *That's it, just relax.* More elan flowed, too much to hold inside himself. He began to pool their combined elan into a reservoir in front of him.

He opened his eyes to look back down the tunnel toward the doors. It was a mistake to look. A Kuldrith soldier thrust a spear at Divinar Stetter, but Mar's blade lashed out and knocked the spear tip nearly to the ground. Jase used Andric's shield to block two more spears thrust toward the Sharinic knight. The prince felt proud of his—

Suddenly, a Kuldrith war hammer smashed sickeningly into Jace's head. His cousin collapsed, his skull crushed. Mar swung his sword and nearly severed the soldier's arm. *They're dying.*

Rage, guilt, fear, and pain surged through him. He sent the elan coursing down the tunnel, modulating it to *ka* as it arced forward. He anchored one side of the stream to the stone walls and the other end to the doors, then induced the elan into the frequency for repulsion. He thought he felt the space between the walls and doors widen, then stopped. He emptied the reservoir into his elant. The doors moved, but not enough. In desperation, he reached for any elan around him. Shiralla, Barak, the Kuldrith, the stone walls, the earth itself.

He felt a wellspring of elan below him. It was so far away, but if he managed to reach it, there might be enough to make up for the losses over such a distance. He pulled a dangerous amount of elan from himself and sent it snaking down through stone toward the elan. *Almost there.*

His elan touched the source. Exultant, overwhelming elan flooded into him. Too late, he recognized what had been at the edge of his consciousness. *The larran.* Terror seized him. In vain, he tried to cut off the flow. Nophet screamed in agony as his life force was ripped from him, inextricably caught in the torrent coursing through the prince. The knight commander collapsed to the earth.

Elan rushed along the path set by Andric's stream through the tunnel. It strained against the confines of a single modality, slipping toward yldrath. With his last shred of will, he modulated the deluge back to the frequency of ka. Elan surged into his elant.

The doors shattered under the pressure as a shockwave erupted from the tunnel.

The ground heaved and dropped out from under him. He crumpled to the earth in a jumble of arms and legs with Shiralla, but he hardly noticed his body as the flood of elan, free of the constraints of his will, seeped away from him back into the earth, draining him, consuming him. No, not consuming, transforming him. *Into what?* A part of him wondered with detached curiosity.

Into elan itself, something beyond himself impressed the answer upon his understanding.

I can't become elan yet. I have to save my friends. As the singular conviction reverberated through his soul, the divinessence of the Holy Couple began to enfold him—loving, accepting, and peaceful—sealing him in a protective shroud of light, severing the stream of his elan from being siphoned off by the receding torrent.

A second shockwave shook the earth beneath him. He opened his eyes and was face to face with Shiralla. She lay unmoving on his outstretched arm, her eyes closed. He feared she was dead. He brushed a tangle of red locks of hair back from her face and was struck by her beauty. *Please let her be alive,* he begged the Holy Couple.

"*Shiralla?*" He tried to speak her name, but he heard no sound—not his own voice or any other. He shook her gently, fearing the worst. "*Shiralla?*" he tried again, louder, but still his world was filled with absolute silence.

Slowly, her eyelids fluttered open, then alarm registered on her face. Her lips moved, forming words, but there was no sound. Dread gripped his heart. There was no sound anywhere. *I'm deaf,* he thought with an odd detachment.

Shiralla lifted her head and looked toward the tunnel. A shadow fell over Andric. He panicked and flinched away. A firm hand grabbed him and hauled him to his feet. *Sir Mar.*

Time felt disjointed. Had this happened before, or was this the first? Andric looked toward the tunnel, now collapsed, and the colossal statue that lay shattered on the ground. *We would all be dead if it had fallen on us instead. I almost killed us all.*

Divinar Stetter and Min fought a Kuldrith while another turned and ran. An arrow streaked across his vision, hitting the fleeing soldier and sinking deep into his back. The soldier fell to his hands and knees as Stetter drove the point of his sword through the throat of the other one. It felt like a horrible dream, disconnected from reality. There should be screams. There should be agony and pain. There was only silence.

Andric's legs trembled with exhaustion, and he felt as though he might collapse at any moment. The Sharinic knight kept a steady hand on Andric as he helped Shiralla to her feet. Mar stepped in front of Andric, gesturing and speaking, but Andric heard nothing. He tried to say as much and gestured to his ears, though he was uncertain whether he was making any intelligible sound. Andric felt the pressure of an invitation to a communal link. He accepted gratefully. There were two other minds in the link.

"My lord, are you injured... other than your hearing?"

A slight distortion made the words sound like they were being said through a veil of water. He realized he was still attuned to the Holy Couple's divinessence. He tried releasing his attunement but found he had a hard time letting it go. Was he clinging to it for security, or had something else happened? *"I think I'm okay."*

"We must depart immediately," Mar said, his words infused with urgency through the communal link.

"Are any Kuldrith alive?"

"I don't believe so, Your Highness. Not on the surface, at least." Mar turned and said something to Min. It looked like he was shouting. Divinar Stetter took a knee next to Nophet's unmoving body, his head bowed.

Andric looked around for Barak and saw his friend sitting on the ground several paces away, a vague look of horror written on his face but otherwise appearing unharmed. *"Follow me, please,"* Andric said to Shiralla as he stumbled toward Barak. The priestess slung the prince's arm over her shoulders to help steady him. He felt guilty for being so weak, but he wasn't sure he had much choice at the moment. *"Is he all right?"*

Shiralla spoke to Barak as Andric held out his hand. Concern and care suddenly showed in Barak's eyes as he turned to face Andric. A tear rolled down his cheek. Andric felt another mind join the communion.

"I'm so sorry this happened, Andric."

"It's not all bad. At least I won't have to listen to you drone on about your arcane theories any more."

Barak laughed, nodding. He accepted Andric's hand and climbed to his feet.

"The captain major is calling for us, my lord," Shiralla said.

"No more titles." A feeling of acceptance was transmitted through the link. The others were gathering what knapsacks, saddlebags, and weapons they could. *Quarian, Kael, Teek, Lathon, Shiralla, Barak, Praq. Only eight of us left. How could I have failed this badly?* The thought was meant for himself, but Mar replied.

"Eight is better than none. You saved us. Now we need to make sure we stay that way."

"Should we bury them?" Andric asked as he looked around the plaza. He was too numb to take any satisfaction knowing there were far more Kuldrith bodies than Remalians.

"We have no idea when the Kuldrith will find their way to the surface again, but it will be sooner than any of us would like. We must go."

In moments, they were set. Kael took Shiralla's place supporting the prince as they made their way down the mountain, leaving the ruins of Elginfir behind. Andric was chagrined he was now the one slowing the group instead of Barak. He tried not to lean so heavily on the Divinar, but his whole body felt like it was only a moment away from collapsing like the colossal statue back at the ruins.

Remalia lay somewhere ahead, though Andric doubted he would ever see his home again. The gods seemed to take delight in tearing him apart, piece by piece. As he recounted every step of his journey, a whirlwind of emotions rose within him, threatening to drown him. Grief, guilt, exhaustion, hopelessness, fear.

As if in answer to his inner turmoil, the snow turned to sleet, driven by a silent wind whipping around him. He trudged on, but soon it became difficult to even see the road ahead. If the storm got any worse, they would have to find shelter. Maybe they should go back and wait out the storm at Elginfir. Or perhaps in the trees he seemed to remember covering the slopes below them.

Something else stirred deep within the silence, daring him to look and see.

He struggled to put words to it, but the feeling grew louder and louder, driving away every other thought, until it crystallized into a single truth that filled the silence.

There is nowhere to hide from the Storm.

ACKNOWLEDGMENTS

Stacey, without your help, we would have remained adrift in the sea of querying an industry leery of two unknown authors with a *chonky* doorstopper in their hands. With no knowledge of how to bring the pixels on the screen to paper and binding, your arrival helped us bring the wonderful world of Baon to life. We are forever grateful.

Jeff, you helped us take the world we had built on paper, and put it to image in beautiful light and color for all the world to see. You turned our words into pieces of art and wonder. Thank you.

Mom and Dad, you raised us with love and support, showing us that imperfect people can be wonderful, loving, and constant blessings in our lives. Though all but one have passed, you are constantly in our minds and hearts.

To our wives and children, you were infinitely patient with us as we tried to balance our roles as husbands and fathers with our professional careers and with the demands of obsessive writing and worldbuilding, character creation, and plot development. You gave us both inspiration and room to write, even at great sacrifice on your part. Thank you for your patience, support, love, and understanding through the years.

And finally, thanks to you, the reader, for embarking upon this journey with us. We are excited to show you what comes next. We can't wait to introduce you to the rest of the world we have dreamed up and the characters we have come to know and love along the way. Enjoy the ride.

About the Authors

ROBERT WYATT

TODD LARSEN

Bob and Todd met as teens in Alaska and bonded over their mutual love of Dungeons & Dragons, storytelling, and theology. Bob lives in Anchorage with his wife Cindy and their three children, and Todd lives in Idaho with his wife Angela and their five children. To pay for their writing career, Bob works as a safety officer in the oil and gas industry, and Todd works as an attorney in the renewable energy industry.